MARIO VARGAS LLOSA

The War of the End of the World

faber and faber

First published in Spain as *La Guerra del fin del mundo* in 1981
This English translation first published in the USA in 1984
by Farrar, Straus and Giroux, Inc., New York
First published in Great Britain in 1985
by Faber and Faber Limited
Bloomsbury House, 74–77 Great Russell Street,
London WC1B 3DA

This paperback edition first published in 2012

Printed and bound in Great Britain by
CPI Group (UK) Ltd, Croydon, CRO 4YY

A CIP record for this book is
available from the British Library

ISBN 978-0-571-28863-2

8 10 9 7

To Euclides da Cunha
in the other world;
and, in this world,
to Nélida Piñon

The Antichrist was born
To govern Brazil
But the Counselor is come
To deliver us from him.

I

I

The man was tall and so thin he seemed to be always in profile. He was dark-skinned and rawboned, and his eyes burned with perpetual fire. He wore shepherd's sandals and the dark purple tunic draped over his body called to mind the cassocks of those missionaries who every so often visited the villages of the backlands, baptizing hordes of children and marrying men and women who were cohabiting. It was impossible to learn what his age, his background, his life story were, but there was something about his quiet manner, his frugal habits, his imperturbable gravity that attracted people even before he offered counsel.

He would appear all of a sudden, alone in the beginning, invariably on foot, covered with the dust of the road, every so many weeks, every so many months. His tall figure was silhouetted against the light of dusk or dawn as he walked down the one street of the town, in great strides, with a sort of urgency. He would make his way along determinedly, amid nanny goats with tinkling bells, amid dogs and children who stepped aside and stared at him inquisitively, not returning the greetings of the women who already knew him and were nodding to him and hastening to bring him jugs of goat's milk and dishes of manioc and black beans. But he neither ate nor drank until he had gone as far as the church of the town and seen, once more, a hundred times over, that it was dilapidated, its paint faded, its towers unfinished and its walls full of holes and its floors buckling and its altars worm-eaten. A sad look would come over his face, with all the grief of a migrant from the Northeast whose children and animals have been killed by the drought, who has nothing left and must abandon his house, the bones of his dead, and flee, flee somewhere, not knowing where. Sometimes he would weep, and as he did so the black fire in his eyes would flare up in awesome flashes. He would immediately begin to pray. But not the way other men or women pray: he would stretch out face downward on the ground or the stones or the chipped tiles, in front of where the altar was or had been or would be, and would lie there praying, at times in silence, at times aloud, for an hour, two hours, observed with respect and admiration by the townspeople. He recited the Credo, the Our Father, and the Hail Marys that everyone was familiar with, and also other prayers that nobody had heard before but that, as the days, the months, the years went by, people gradually learned by heart. Where is the parish priest? they would hear him ask. Why isn't there a pastor for the flock here? And each time he discovered that there was no priest in the village it made him as sad at heart as the ruin of the Lord's dwelling places.

Only after having asked the Blessed Jesus' pardon for the state in which they had allowed His house to fall did he agree to eat and drink something, barely a sample of what the villagers hastened to offer him even in years of scarcity. He was willing to sleep indoors with a roof over his head, in one or another of the dwellings where the people of the backlands offered him hospitality, but those who gave him lodging rarely saw him take his rest in the hammock or makeshift bed or on the mattress placed at his disposal. He would lie down on the floor, without even a blanket, and, leaning his head with its wild mane of jet-black hair on one arm, would sleep for a few hours. Always so few that he was the last one to retire at night and yet when the cowherds and shepherds who were up earliest left for the fields they would catch sight of him, already at work mending the walls and roof of the church.

He gave his counsel when dusk was falling, when the men had come back from the fields and the women had finished their household tasks and the children were already asleep. He gave it in those stony, treeless, open spots to be found in all the villages of the backlands at the main crossroads, which might have been called public squares if they had had benches, tree-lined walks, gardens, or had kept those that they had once had and that little by little had been destroyed by drought, pestilence, indolence. He gave it at that hour when the sky of the North of Brazil, before becoming completely dark and studded with stars, blazes amid tufted white, gray, or bluish clouds and there is a sort of vast fireworks display overhead, above the vastness of the world. He gave it at that hour when fires are lighted to chase away the insects and prepare the evening meal, when the steamy air grows less stifling and a breeze rises that puts people in better spirits to endure the sickness, the hunger, and the sufferings of life.

He spoke of simple and important things, not looking at any person in particular among those who surrounded him, or rather looking with his incandescent eyes beyond the circle of oldsters, men and women, children, at something or someone only he could see. Things that were understandable because they had been vaguely known since time immemorial, things taken in along with the milk of one's mother's breast. Present, tangible, everyday, inevitable things, such as the end of the world and the Last Judgment, which might well occur before the time it would take for the town to set the chapel with drooping wings upright again. What would happen when the Blessed Jesus looked down upon the sorry state in which they had left His house? What would He say of the behavior of pastors who, instead of helping the poor, emptied their pockets by charging them money for the succor of religion? Could the words of God be sold? Shouldn't they be given freely, with no price tag attached? What excuse would be offered to the Father by priests who fornicated, despite their vows of chastity? Could they invent lies that would be believed by a God who can read a person's thoughts as easily as the tracker on earth reads the trail left by a jaguar? Practical, everyday, familiar things, such as death, which leads to happiness if one comes to it with a pure and joyous soul, as to a fiesta. Were men animals? If they were not, they should pass through that door dressed in their very best, as a sign of reverence for Him whom they were about to meet. He spoke to them of heaven, and of hell as well, the domain of the Dog, paved with burning-hot coals and infested with rattlesnakes, and of how Satan could manifest himself by way of seemingly harmless innovations.

The cowherds and peons of the backlands listened to him in silence, intrigued, terrified, moved, and he was listened to in the same way by the slaves, and the freedmen of the sugarcane plantations on the seacoast and the wives and the mothers and fathers and the children of one and all. Occasionally someone interrupted him – though this occurred rarely, since his gravity, his cavernous voice, or his wisdom intimidated them – in order to dispel a doubt. Was the world about to end? Would it last till 1900? He would answer immediately, with no need to reflect, with quiet assurance, and very often with enigmatic prophecies. In 1900 the sources of light would be extinguished and stars would rain down. But, before that, extraordinary things would happen. A silence ensued after he had spoken, in which the crackling of open fires could be heard, and the buzzing of insects that the flames devoured, as the villagers, holding their breath, strained their memories before the fact in order to be certain to remember the future. In 1896 countless flocks would flee inland from the seacoast and the sea would turn into the backlands and the backlands turn into the sea. In 1897 the desert would be covered with grass, shepherds and flocks would intermingle, and from that date on there would be but a single flock and a single shepherd. In 1898 hats would increase in size and heads grow smaller, and in 1899 the rivers would turn red and a new planet would circle through space.

It was necessary, therefore, to be prepared. The church must be restored, and the cemetery as well, the most important construction after the House of the Lord since it was the antechamber of heaven or hell, and the time that remained must be devoted to what was most essential: the soul. Would men or women leave for the next world in skirts, dresses, felt hats, rope sandals, and all that luxurious attire of wool and silk that the Good Lord Jesus had never known?

His counsel was practical, simple. When the man left, there

was a great deal of talk about him: that he was a saint, that he had worked miracles, that he had seen the burning bush in the desert, like Moses, that a voice had revealed to him the unutterable name of God. And his counsel was widely discussed. Thus, before the Empire had come to an end and after the Republic had begun, the inhabitants of Tucano, Soure, Amparo, and Pombal had heard his words; and from one month to another, from one year to another, the churches of Bom Conselho, of Jeremoabo, of Massacará, and of Inhambupe were gradually springing up from their ruins; and in accordance with his teachings, adobe walls and vaulted niches were constructed in the cemeteries of Monte Santo, Entre Rios, Abadia, and Barracão, and death was celebrated with respectful funeral ceremonies in Itapicuru, Cumbe, Natuba, Mocambo. Month by month, year by year, the nights of Alagoinhas, Uauá, Jacobina, Itabaiana, Campos, Itabaianinha, Geru, Riachão, Lagarto, Simão Dias were peopled with his counsel. In the eyes of everyone, his teachings appeared to be good ones and therefore, first in one and then in another and finally in all the towns of the North, the man who gave such counsel began to be known as the Counselor, despite the fact that his Christian name was Antônio Vicente and his last name Mendes Maciel.

A wooden grille separates the copywriters and the other employees of the *Jornal de Notícias* – whose name is written large, in Gothic characters, above the entrance – from the people who come to its offices to place an advertisement in its pages or bring in a news item. There are no more than four or five reporters on its staff. One of them is checking out information in a filing cabinet built into the wall; two of them are engaged in an animated conversation, having divested themselves of their suit jackets but not their stiff shirt collars and string ties, alongside a calendar that shows the date – Friday, October 2, 1896 – and another one, young and gangling, with the thick glasses of someone suffering from acute nearsightedness, is sitting at a desk writing with a quill pen, paying no attention to what is going on about him. At the far end of the room, behind a glass door, is the office of the editor-in-chief. A man wearing a visor and celluloid cuffs is waiting on a line of customers at the Classified Advertisements counter. A woman has just handed him an ad. The cashier wets his index finger and counts the words – Giffoni Clysters||Cure Gonorrhea, Hemorrhoids, White Flowers and all ailments of the Urinary Tract||Prepared by Madame A. de Carvalho||Number 8, Rua Primero de Março – and tells her the price. The lady pays, pockets the change, and as she leaves the counter, the person waiting behind her moves forward and hands the cashier a piece of paper. He is dressed in a black frock coat and bowler that show signs of wear. Curly red locks cover his ears. He is a full-grown man, on the tall side, solidly built, with broad shoulders. The cashier counts the number of words in the ad, running his finger across the paper. Suddenly he frowns, raises his finger, and brings the text up close to his eyes, as though fearing that he has misread it. Finally he looks in bewilderment at the customer, who stands there as motionless as a statue. The cashier blinks uneasily and then motions to the man to wait. He shuffles across the room with the paper dangling from his hand, taps with his knuckles on the glass door of the office of the editor-in-chief, and goes inside. He reappears a few seconds later, motions to the customer to go inside, and goes back to work.

The man dressed in black crosses the front office of the *Jornal de Notícias*, his heels resounding as though he were shod in horseshoes. As he enters the small office in the rear, full of papers, periodicals, and propaganda of the Progressivist Republican Party – a United Brazil, a Strong Nation – he finds waiting for him a man who looks at him with friendly curiosity, as though he were some sort of rare animal. Dressed in a gray suit and wearing boots, the man is sitting behind the only desk in the room; he is young, dark-haired, with a dynamic air about him.

'I am Epaminondas Gonçalves, the editor and publisher of this paper,' he says. 'Come in.'

The man dressed in black bows slightly and raises his hand to his hat, but he does not take it off or say a word.

'You want us to print this, is that right?' the editor asks, waving the little piece of paper.

The man in black nods. He has a little beard as red as his hair, and piercing bright blue eyes; his broad mouth is firmly set, and his flaring nostrils seem to be breathing in more air than his body requires. 'Provided it doesn't cost more than two milreis,' he murmurs in broken Portuguese. 'That's my entire capital.'

Epaminondas Gonçalves sits there as though not quite certain whether to laugh or fall into a rage. The man simply stands there, looking very serious, observing him. The editor resolves his dilemma by raising the piece of paper to his eyes.

'All lovers of justice are invited to attend a public demonstration of solidarity with the idealists of Canudos and with all rebels the world over, to be held in the Praça da Liberdade on the fourth of October at 6 p.m.,' he reads aloud slowly. 'May I ask who is calling this meeting?'

'For the moment, I am,' the man answers forthwith. 'If the *Jornal de Notícias* wants to lend its support, *wonderful.*' (The last word is spoken in English.)

'Do you know what those people up there in Canudos have done?' Epaminondas Gonçalves murmurs, banging on the desk. 'They're occupying land that doesn't belong to them and living promiscuously, like animals.'

'Two things worthy of admiration,' the man in black asserts, nodding his head in approval. 'That's the reason why I've decided to spend my money on this public announcement.'

The editor sits there in silence for a moment. Before speaking again, he clears his throat. 'May I ask who you are, sir?'

Without braggadocio, without arrogance, with the merest trace of solemnity, the man introduces himself in these words: 'A freedom fighter, sir. Will you publish the announcement?'

'Impossible, sir,' Epaminondas Gonçalves, master of the situation now, replies. 'The authorities in Bahia are merely waiting for an excuse to close down my paper. Though they've paid lip service to the Republic, they're still monarchists. I take it you've realized that we're the only true republican daily in this entire state.'

The man in black gestures disdainfully and mutters between his teeth: 'So I thought.'

'I advise you not to take this announcement to the *Diário da Bahia*,' the editor adds, handing him back the piece of paper. 'It belongs to the Baron de Canabrava, the rightful owner of Canudos. You'll end up in jail.'

Without one word of farewell, the man in black turns round and leaves the office, pocketing the announcement. He crosses the outer office of the paper without looking at anyone, without so much as a nod as he takes his leave, his footfalls resounding, merely casting a glance out of the corner of his eye – a funereal silhouette, fiery-red wavy hair – at the journalists and the customers placing paid advertisements. The young journalist with the thick eyeglasses of someone who is very nearsighted gets up from his desk after he has walked past, and with a sheet of yellow paper in his hand walks over to the office of the editor-in-chief, where Epaminondas Gonçalves is sitting, still watching the stranger's every move as he departs.

'By order of the Governor of the State of Bahia, His Excellency Senhor Luiz Viana, a company of the Ninth Infantry Battalion, under the command of Lieutenant Pires Ferreira, left Salvador today, charged with the mission of wresting control of Canudos from the bandits who have occupied the estate and of capturing their leader, the Sebastianist Antônio Conselheiro,' he reads aloud as he stands in the doorway. 'Page one or inside, sir?'

'Have it set out below the announcements of funerals and Masses,' the editor-in-chief says. He points toward the street, down which the man dressed in black has disappeared. 'Do you know who that fellow is?'

'Galileo Gall,' the nearsighted journalist answers. 'A Scotsman who's been going around asking people in Bahia if he could feel their heads.'

He was born in Pombal, the son of a shoemaker and his mistress, the latter a cripple who, despite her handicap, had brought three boys into the world before him and gave birth after him to a little girl who survived the drought. They named him Antônio, and if there had been such a thing as logic in this world, he should never have gone on living, for when he was still a baby crawling on all fours the catastrophe occurred that devastated the region, killing crops, men, and animals. Because of the drought, almost everyone in Pombal emigrated to the coast, but Tibúrcio da Mota, who in his half century of life had never journeyed more than a league away from that village in which there was not one pair of feet that did not wear shoes made by his hands, announced that he would not leave his house. And he remained faithful to his resolve, staying there in Pombal with no more than a couple dozen other people at most, for even the Lazarist Fathers' mission cleared out entirely.

When, a year later, the émigrés from Pombal began to return, encouraged by the news that the low-lying ground had been flooded once more and cereal crops could again be planted, Tibúrcio da Mota was dead and buried, along with his crippled concubine and their three oldest children. They had eaten everything that was edible, and when all that was gone, everything that was green, and at the end, everything that teeth could chew. The parish priest, Dom Casimiro, who buried them one after the other, asserted that they had not died of hunger but of stupidity, by eating the leather in the cobbler's shop and drinking the waters of the Lagoa do Boi, a breeding ground for mosquitoes and pestilence that even young goats shunned. Dom Casimiro took Antônio and his little sister in, kept them alive on a diet of air and prayers, and, when the houses of the village were full of people once again, sought a home for them.

The little girl was taken in by her godmother, who brought her along with her when she went to work at one of the estates belonging to the Baron de Canabrava. Antônio, then five years old, was adopted by the other shoemaker in Pombal, known as One-Eye – he had lost the other in a street fight – who had learned his trade in Tibúrcio da Mota's cobbler shop and on returning to Pombal had inherited his clientele. He was a bad-tempered man who often drank too much, so that dawn found him lying in a stupor in the street, reeking of raw sugarcane brandy. He did not have a wife, and made Antônio work like a beast of burden, sweeping, cleaning, handing him nails, shears, saddles, boots, and bringing him hides from the tannery. He made him sleep on animal skins, next to the worktable where One-Eye spent all his time when he was not drinking with his pals.

The orphan was emaciated, docile, mere skin and bones, with shy eyes that aroused the compassion of the women of Pombal, who, whenever they could, gave him something to eat or the clothes that their sons had outgrown. One day a group of them – half a dozen women who had known his crippled mother and had stood at her side gossiping at innumerable baptisms, confirmations, wakes, weddings – went to One-Eye's cobbler shop to force him to send Antônio to catechism classes so as to ready him for his First Communion. They threw such a scare into him by telling him that God would hold him responsible if the boy died without having made it that the shoemaker grudgingly agreed to allow him to attend the lessons at the mission, every afternoon, before vespers.

Something out of the ordinary occurred then in the boy's life; shortly thereafter, as a result of the changes that took place in him because of the sermons of the Lazarists, people began to call him the Little Blessed One. He would come out of the sessions where they preached with his eyes no longer fixed on his surroundings and as though purified of dross. One-Eye spread the word about that he often found him kneeling in the darkness at night, weeping for Christ's sufferings, so caught up in them that he was able to bring him back to this world only by cradling him in his arms and rocking him. On other nights he heard him talking in his sleep, in agitation, of Judas's betrayal, of Mary Magdalene's repentance, of the crown of thorns, and one night he heard him make a vow of perpetual chastity, like St. Francis de Sales at the age of eight.

Antônio had found a vocation to which to devote his entire life. He continued to fulfill, most obediently, all the orders given him by One-Eye, but he did so with his eyes half closed and moving his lips in such a way that everyone knew that, even though he was sweeping or hurrying about the shoemaker's shop or holding the shoe sole that One-Eye was nailing, he was really praying. The boy's conduct disturbed and terrified his foster father. In the corner where he slept, the Little Blessed One gradually built an altar, with printed images they gave him at the mission and a cross of *xiquexique* wood that he himself carved and painted. He would light a candle before it to pray on arising in the morning and on going to bed at night, and all his free time was spent before it, on his knees, with his hands joined and a contrite expression, rather than hanging around the ranches, riding unbroken horses bareback, hunting doves, or going to see bulls castrated, the way the other youngsters of Pombal did.

After making his First Communion, he was an altar boy for Dom Casimiro, and when the latter died he continued to serve Mass for the Lazarist Fathers of the mission, even though in order to do so he was obliged to walk a league a day to get there and back. He swung the censer in processions and helped decorate the portable platforms and the altars on the street corners where the Virgin and the Blessed Jesus halted to rest. His religious devotion was as great as his goodness. It was a familiar sight to the inhabitants of Pombal to see him serving as a guide for blind Adolfo, whom he sometimes took out to the pasture grounds for Colonel Ferreira's colts, where he had worked till he got cataracts and which he now sorely missed every day of his life. The Little Blessed One would take him by the arm and lead him across the fields, with a stick in his hand to poke about in the dirt on the lookout for snakes, patiently listening to his stories. And Antônio also collected food and clothing for Simeão the leper, who had been living like a wild animal ever since the villagers had forbidden him to come anywhere near Pombal. Once a week the Little Blessed One took him a bundleful of bits of bread and jerky and different sorts of grain that he had begged for him, and the villagers would spy him in the distance, guiding the old man with long locks and bare feet and covered with nothing but a yellow animal pelt as he made his way along amid the rocky stretches on the hill where his cave was.

The first time he saw the Counselor, the Little Blessed One was fourteen years old and had had a terrible disappointment just a few weeks before. Father Moraes of the Lazarist mission had thrown cold water on his fondest dreams by informing him that he couldn't be a priest because he had been born out of wedlock. He consoled him by explaining to him that a person could still serve God even without receiving Holy Orders, and promised him to take whatever steps he could on his behalf at a Capuchin monastery that might be willing to take him in as a lay brother. The Little Blessed One wept that night with such heartfelt sobs that One-Eye flew into a rage and for the first time in many years beat him badly. Twenty days later, beneath the glaring midday sun, there appeared on the main street of Pombal a lanky, dark-skinned figure, with black hair and gleaming eyes, enveloped in a dark purple tunic; followed by half a dozen people who looked like beggars and yet had happy faces, he strode through the town and headed straight for the old adobe chapel with curved roof tiles which had fallen into such a sorry state of disrepair following Dom Casimiro's death that birds had made their nests amid the statues. The Little Blessed One, like many of the villagers, saw the pilgrim stretch out face down on the ground to pray, and his followers do likewise, and that afternoon he heard him give counsel as to the salvation of the soul, condemn the ungodly, and predict the future.

That night the Little Blessed One did not sleep in the shoemaker's shop but in the public square of Pombal, along with the pilgrims, who had lain on the bare ground around the saint. And the following morning and afternoon, and every day that the saint remained in Pombal, the Little Blessed One worked alongside him and his followers, repairing the legs and backs of the broken-down benches in the chapel, leveling its floor, and erecting a stone wall to enclose the cemetery, which up until then had been a tongue of land creeping out into the town itself. And every night he squatted on his heels before him, listening in rapt absorption to the truths that fell from his lips.

But when, on the Counselor's next-to-last night in Pombal,

Antônio the Little Blessed One asked his permission to accompany him wherever his pilgrimage might take him, the saint's eyes first of all – at once intense and icy – and then his mouth said no. Kneeling before the Counselor, the Little Blessed One wept bitterly. It was very late at night, Pombal was fast asleep, as were the pilgrims in rags and tatters, all huddled up next to each other. The bonfires had gone out but the stars were gleaming brightly overhead and the chirring of cicadas could be heard. The Counselor let him weep, allowed him to kiss the hem of his tunic, and did not change expression when the Little Blessed One begged him again to let him follow him, since his heart told him that by doing so he would be serving the Good Lord Jesus better. The youngster clung to the Counselor's ankles and kissed his callused feet again and again. When he saw that the boy was exhausted, the Counselor took his head in his two hands and forced him to look at him. Bringing his face down close to his, he asked him in a solemn voice if he loved God so much that he would suffer pain so as to offer it to Him in sacrifice. The Little Blessed One nodded yes, several times. The Counselor raised his tunic, and the boy could see, in the first faint light of dawn, that he was removing from around his waist a wire that was lacerating his flesh. 'You wear it now,' he heard him say. The Counselor himself helped the Little Blessed One unfasten his clothes, cinch the wire tightly around his waist, and knot it.

When, seven months later, the Counselor and his followers – a few of the faces had changed, their numbers had grown, among them there was now an enormous, half-naked black, but their poverty and the happiness in their eyes were those of the pilgrims of the past – appeared again in Pombal, enveloped in a cloud of dust, the wire was still around the Little Blessed One's waist, the flesh of which had turned black and blue and then been sawed raw and later on became covered with dark crusts. He had not taken it off even for one day, and since it would gradually become looser and looser just from the movement of his body, every so often he would cinch it up very tightly again. Father Moraes had tried to dissuade him from continuing to wear it, explaining to him that a certain amount of voluntarily endured pain was pleasing in God's sight, but that, past a certain limit, that particular sacrifice could become a morbid pleasure encouraged by the Devil and that he was in danger of going beyond that limit at any moment now.

But Antônio did not obey him. On the day that the Counselor and his followers returned to Pombal, the Little Blessed One was in *caboclo* Umberto Salustiano's general store, and his heart stopped dead in his chest, as did the breath just entering his nostrils, when he saw the Counselor pass by not three feet away from him, surrounded by his apostles and by dozens of townspeople, men and women alike, and head directly to the chapel as he had done the time before. He followed him, joined the noisy, tumultuous throng, and, hidden among the crowd, listened from a discreet distance, feeling his heart racing. And that night he listened to him preach in the firelight in the crowded public square, still not daring to draw closer. All Pombal was there this time to hear him.

It was nearly dawn, after the villagers, who had prayed and sung and brought their sick children to him for him to ask God to cure them and told him of their trials and tribulations and asked what the future held for them, had finally all gone home, and the disciples had stretched out on the ground to sleep, as always, using each other as pillows and covers, when, stepping over the bodies in rags and tatters, the Little Blessed One, in the attitude of utter reverence with which he approached the Communion table, reached the dark silhouette, clad in deep purple, lying with his head with its long thick locks cradled in one arm. The last embers of the bonfires were dying out. The Counselor's eyes opened as he drew close, and the Little Blessed One would always repeat to those listening to his story that he saw immediately in those eyes that the man had been waiting for him. Without uttering a word – he would not have been able to do so – he opened his coarse woolen shirt and showed him the wire knotted tightly around his waist.

After looking at him for a few seconds, without blinking, the

Counselor nodded and a fleeting smile crossed his face. That, as the Little Blessed One was to say hundreds of times in the years to come, was his consecration. The Counselor pointed to a little empty space on the ground at his side that seemed to be reserved for him amid all those bodies huddled up all around him. The boy curled up there, understanding, with no need for words, that the Counselor considered him worthy of leaving with him to travel the paths of this earth and fight against the Devil. The dogs that had stayed out all night, the early risers of Pombal heard the sound of the Little Blessed One weeping for a long time still without suspecting that it was sobs of happiness they were hearing.

His real name was not Galileo Gall, but he really was a freedom fighter, or, as he put it, a revolutionary and a phrenologist. Two death sentences followed him about the world and he had spent five of his forty-six years in jail. He had been born in mid-century, in a town in the south of Scotland where his father practiced medicine and had tried to no avail to found a libertarian club to spread the ideas of Proudhon and Bakunin. As other children grow up listening to fairy stories, he had grown up hearing that property is the origin of all social evils and that the poor will succeed in shattering the chains of exploitation and obscurantism only through the use of violence.

His father was the disciple of a man whom he regarded as one of the most venerable savants of his time: Franz Joseph Gall, anatomist, physicist, and founder of the science of phrenology. Whereas for other followers of Gall's, this science was scarcely more than the belief that intellect, instinct, and feelings are organs located in the cerebral cortex and can be palpated and measured, for Galileo's father this discipline meant the death of religion, the empirical foundation of materialism, the proof that the mind was not what philosophical mumbo jumbo made it out to be, something imponderable and impalpable, but on the contrary a dimension of the body, like the senses, and hence equally capable of being studied and treated clinically. From the moment his son reached the age of reason, the Scotsman impressed upon his mind the following simple precept: revolution will free society of its afflictions, while science will free the individual of his. Galileo had resolved to devote his life to fighting for both these goals.

Since his radical ideas had made life difficult for his father in Scotland, he had settled in the South of France, where he was placed under arrest in 1868 for having helped the workers in the spinning mills of Bordeaux during a strike, and sent to Cayenne. He died there. The following year Galileo went to prison, charged with having helped set fire to a church – priests were the people he hated most, after soldiers and bankers – but in a few months he escaped and began working with a doctor in Paris who had been a friend of his father's. It was at this time that he changed his name to Galileo Gall, since his own name was too well known by the police, and started publishing little political notes and popular-science pieces in a Lyons paper: *L'Etincelle de la révolte.*

One of the things he prided himself on was the fact that he had fought, from March to May of 1871, with the Communards of Paris for the freedom of humanity and had personally witnessed the genocide of thirty thousand men, women, and children at the hands of Thiers's forces. He, too, was condemned to death, but before the execution he managed to escape from the military barracks where he had been imprisoned, dressed in the uniform of a sergeant-jailer whom he had killed. He went to Barcelona and stayed there for several years studying medicine and practicing phrenology with Mariano Cubí, a savant who boasted of being able to detect the most secret traits and inclinations of any man by running his fingertips just once across his head. Galileo Gall had apparently passed his examinations and was about to receive his medical degree when his love of freedom and progress, or his vocation as an adventurer, again impelled him to action and a life on the move. He and a handful of comrades equally addicted to the Idea attacked the Montjuich barracks one night, to unleash the storm that, they thought, would shake the foundations of Spain. But someone had informed on them and the soldiers greeted them with a hail of bullets. He saw his comrades fall fighting, one by one; when he was finally captured, he had several wounds. He was condemned to death, but since Spanish law provides that a wounded man may not be put to death by the garrote, they decided to cure him before they executed him. Friendly and influential persons helped him escape from the hospital, provided him with false papers, and put him aboard a freighter.

He had traveled through many countries, whole continents, ever faithful to the ideas of his childhood. He had palpated yellow, black, red, and white craniums and alternately engaged in political action and scientific pursuits, depending on the circumstances of the moment; throughout this life of adventures, jails, fistfights, clandestine meetings, escapes, setbacks, he scribbled notebooks that corroborated, and enriched with examples, the teachings of his masters: his father, Proudhon, Gall, Bakunin, Spurzheim, Cubí. He had been clapped in prison in Turkey, in Egypt, in the United States for attacking the social order and religion, but thanks to his lucky star and his scorn for danger he never remained behind bars for long.

In 1894 he was the medical officer on a German boat that was shipwrecked off Bahia; what was left of it remained beached forever opposite the Forte de São Pedro. It had been a mere six years since Brazil had abolished slavery and five since it had ceased to be an empire and become a republic. He was fascinated by its mixtures of races and cultures, by its social and political effervescence, by the fact that it was a society in which Europe and Africa and something else he had never encountered before were intimately commingled. He decided to stay. He could not set up in practice as a doctor since he had no medical degree, and therefore he earned his living, as he had before in other places, by giving lessons in various languages and doing odd jobs. Though he wandered all over the country, he always came back to Salvador, where he could be found at the Livraria Catilina, in the shade of the palm trees of the Mirador of the Sorrowful, or in the sailors' taverns in the lower town, explaining to anyone with whom he struck up a conversation that all virtues are compatible if reason rather than faith is the axis of life, that not God but Satan – the first rebel – is the true prince of freedom, and that once the old order was destroyed through revolutionary action, the new society, free and just, would flower spontaneously. Although there were some who listened to him, in general people did not appear to pay much attention to him.

II

At the time of the great drought of 1877, during the months of famine and epidemics that killed half the men and animals in the region, the Counselor was no longer journeying alone; he was accompanied, or, rather, followed (he scarcely appeared to be aware of the human trail tagging along after him) by men and women who had abandoned everything they had to go off with him, some of them because their souls had been touched by his counsel and others out of curiosity or mere inertia. Some of them remained in his company part of the way, and a very few seemed determined to remain at his side forever. Despite the drought, he journeyed on, even though the fields were now strewn with the carcasses of cattle that the vultures pecked at and half-empty towns greeted him.

The fact that it did not rain once all during the year 1877, that the rivers dried up and countless caravans of migrants appeared in the scrublands, carrying their few miserable belongings in canvas-covered carts or on their backs as they wandered about in search of water and food, was perhaps not the most terrible thing about that terrible year. If not, it was perhaps the brigands and the snakes that suddenly appeared everywhere in the backlands of the North. There had always been men who came onto the haciendas to steal cattle, had shootouts with the *capangas* – the hired thugs – of the landowners, and sacked remote villages, outlaws whom flying brigades of police periodically came to the backlands to hunt down. But with the famine the gangs of outlaws multiplied like the biblical loaves and fishes. Voracious and murderous, they fell on towns already decimated by the catastrophe to seize the inhabitants' last remaining food, their household goods and clothing, drilling anyone full of holes who dared to cross them.

But never did they offend the Counselor, by word or by deed. They would meet up with him on the desert trails, amid the cactuses and the stones, beneath a leaden sky, or in the tangled scrub where the underbrush had withered and the tree trunks were beginning to split. The outlaws, ten, twenty *cangaceiros* armed with every sort of weapon capable of cutting, piercing, perforating, tearing out, would catch sight of the gaunt man in the purple tunic whose icy, obsessive eyes swept over them with their usual indifference for the space of a second before he went on doing exactly the same things as always: praying, meditating, walking, giving counsel. The pilgrims would pale on seeing the *cangaço* – the band of outlaws – and huddle together around the Counselor like chicks around the mother hen. The brigands, noting their extreme poverty, would go on their way, but sometimes they would halt on recognizing the saint, whose prophecies had reached their ears. They did not interrupt him if he was praying; they waited till he deigned to note their presence. He would finally speak to them, in that cavernous voice that unfailingly found the shortest path to their hearts. He told them things that they could understand, truths that they could believe in. That this calamity was no doubt the first forewarning of the arrival of the Antichrist and the devastation that would precede the resurrection of the dead and the Last Judgment. That if they wanted to save their souls they should ready themselves for the battles that would be waged when the demons who obeyed the Antichrist – who would be the Dog himself appearing on earth to recruit proselytes – spread out across the backlands like wildfire. Like the cowhands, the peons, the freedmen, and the slaves, the *cangaceiros* pondered his words. And a number of them – Pajeú with the slashed face, the enormous brute Pedrão, and even the most bloodthirsty one of all, Satan João – repented of their evil deeds, were converted to good, and followed him.

And as had happened with the brigands, he gained the respect of the rattlesnakes that as though by a miracle suddenly appeared by the thousands in the fields because of the drought. Long, slithering, writhing, their heads triangular, they abandoned their lairs and they, too, migrated, like the human folk; and in their flight they killed children, calves, goats, and had no fear of entering settlements in broad daylight in search of food. There were so many of them that there were not enough *acauãs* to finish them off, and in those topsy-turvy days it was not a rare sight to see serpents devouring that predatory bird rather than, as in days gone by, the *acauã* taking wing with its snake prey in its mouth. The people of the backlands were obliged to go about night and day armed with clubs and machetes and there were migrants who managed to kill a hundred rattlesnakes in a single day. But the Counselor nonetheless continued to sleep on the ground, wherever night overtook him. One evening, on hearing those accompanying him talking of serpents, he explained to them that this was not the first time that such a thing had happened. When the children of Israel were returning from Egypt to their homeland and were complaining of the hardships of the desert, the Father visited a plague of snakes upon them as punishment. Moses interceded on behalf of the children of Israel, and the Father ordered him to make a bronze serpent, which the children had only to gaze upon to be cured of its bite. Ought they to do the same? No, for miracles are never repeated. But surely the Father would look upon them with favor if they carried about the face of His Son as an amulet. From then on, a woman from Monte Santo, Maria Quadrado, bore in a glass case a piece of cloth with the image of the Good Lord Jesus painted by a boy from Pombal whose piety had earned him the name of the Little Blessed One. This act must have pleased the Father, since none of the pilgrims was bitten by a snake.

The Counselor was spared as well from epidemics which, as a consequence of drought and famine, fed, in the months and years that followed, on the flesh of those who had managed to survive. Women miscarried shortly after becoming pregnant, children's teeth and hair fell out, and adults suddenly began spitting up and defecating blood, swelled up with tumors, or suffered from rashes that made them roll in the gravel like mangy dogs. The gaunt man, thin as a rail, went on his pilgrim's way amid the pestilence and wholesale death, imperturbable, invulnerable, like a veteran ship's pilot, skillfully skirting storms as he makes for a safe port.

What port was the Counselor heading for with this endless journeying? No one asked him, nor did he say, and probably he didn't know. He was accompanied now by dozens of followers who had abandoned everything to devote themselves to the life of the spirit. During the many months of drought the Counselor and his disciples worked unceasingly, burying those dead of starvation, disease, or anguish whom they came across along the sides of the roads, rotting corpses that were food for wild beasts and even humans. They made coffins and dug graves for these brothers and sisters. They were a motley group, a chaotic mixture of races, backgrounds, and occupations. Among them were whites dressed all in leather who had made their living driving the herds of the 'colonels,' the owners of great cattle ranches; full-blooded Indians with reddish skins whose great-great-grandfathers had gone about half naked and eaten the hearts of their enemies; mestizos who had been farm overseers, tinsmiths, blacksmiths, cobblers, or carpenters; and mulattoes and blacks who had been runaways from the sugarcane plantations on the coast and from the rack, the stocks, the floggings with bull pizzles and the brine thrown on the raw lash marks, and other punishments invented for slaves in the sugar factories. And there were the women, both old and young, sound in body or crippled, who were always the first whose hearts were moved during the nightly halt when the Counselor spoke to them of sin, of the wicked deeds of the Dog or of the goodness of the Virgin. They were the ones who mended the dark purple habit, using the thorns of thistles for needles and palm fibers for thread, and the ones who thought up a way to make him a new one when the old one got ripped on the bushes, and the ones who made him new sandals and fought for possession of the old ones, objects that had touched his body to be cherished as precious relics. And each evening after the men had lighted the bonfires, they were the ones who prepared the *angu* of rice or maize flour or sweet manioc boiled in broth and the few mouthfuls of squash that sustained the pilgrims. The Counselor's followers never had to worry about food, for they were frugal and received gifts wherever they went: from the humble, who hastened to bring the Counselor a hen or a sack of maize or cheese freshly made, and also from landowners, who – after the ragged entourage had spent the night in the outbuildings and next morning, on their own initiative and without charging a cent, cleaned and swept the chapel of the hacienda – would send servants to bring them fresh milk, food, and sometimes a young she-goat or a kid.

He had gone all around the backlands so many times, back and forth so many times, up and down so many mountainsides, that everyone knew him. The village priests, too. There weren't many of them, and what few there were seemed lost in the vastness of the backlands, and in any event there were not enough of them to keep the countless churches going, so that they were visited by pastors only on the feast day of the patron saint of the town. The vicars of certain places, such as Tucano and Cumbe, allowed him to address the faithful from the pulpit and got along well with him; others, such as the ones in Entre Rios and in Itapicuru, would not permit him to do so and fought him. In other towns, in order to repay him for what he did for the churches and cemeteries, or because his spiritual influence on the people of the backlands was so great that they did not want to be on bad terms with their parishioners, the vicars grudgingly granted him permission to recite litanies and preach in the church courtyard after Mass.

When did the Counselor and his entourage of penitents learn that in 1888, far off in those cities whose very names had a foreign sound to them – São Paulo, Rio de Janeiro, even Salvador, the state capital – the monarchy had abolished slavery and that the measure had wreaked havoc on the sugar plantations of Bahia, which all of a sudden were left with no labor force? It was months before the news of the decree reached the backlands, the way news always reached these remote parts of the Empire – delayed, distorted, and sometimes no longer true – and the authorities ordered that it be publicly proclaimed in the town squares and nailed to the doors of town halls.

And it is probable that, the year after, the Counselor and his followers again learned, long after the fact, that the nation to which they unwittingly belonged had ceased to be an empire and was now a republic. It never came to their attention that this event did not awaken the slightest enthusiasm among the old authorities or among the former slaveowners (who continued to be owners of sugarcane plantations and herds of cattle or sheep) or among the professional class and the petty government officials, who regarded this change as something like the *coup de grâce* for the already dying hegemony of the ex-capital, the center of Brazil's political and economic life for two hundred years and now the nostalgic poor relation, watching everything that was once theirs – prosperity, power, money, manpower, history – move southward. And even if they had learned of this, they would not have understood, nor would they have cared, for the concerns of the Counselor and his followers were altogether different. Besides, what had changed for them apart from a few names? Wasn't this landscape of parched earth and leaden skies the same one as always? And, despite having suffered several years of drought, wasn't the region continuing to bind up its wounds, to mourn its dead, to try to bring what had been ruined back to life? What had changed in the calamity-ridden North now that there was a president instead of an emperor? Wasn't the tiller of the land still fighting against the barrenness of the soil and the scarcity of water so that his maize, beans, potatoes, and manioc would sprout and his pigs, chickens, and goats stay alive? Weren't the villages still full of idlers, and weren't the roads still dangerous on account of the many bandits? Weren't there armies of beggars everywhere as a reminder of the disasters of 1877? Weren't the itinerant storytellers the same? Despite the Counselor's efforts, weren't the houses of the Blessed Jesus continuing to fall to pieces?

But in fact something *had* changed with the advent of the Republic. To people's misfortune and confusion: Church and State were separated, freedom of worship was established, and cemeteries were secularized, so that it was no longer parishes but towns that would be responsible for them. Whereas the vicars in their bewilderment did not know what to say in the face of these new developments that the Church hierarchy had resigned itself to accepting, the Counselor for his part knew immediately what to say: they were impious acts that to the believer were inadmissible. And when he learned that civil marriage had been instituted – as though a sacrament created by God were not enough – he for his part had the forthrightness to say aloud, at the counsel hour, what the parishioners were whispering: that this scandal was the handiwork of Protestants and Freemasons. As were, no doubt, the other strange, suspect new provisions that the towns of the *sertão* – the backlands – learned of little by little: the statistical map, the census, the metric system. To the bewildered people of the hinterland, the *sertanejos*, who hastened to ask him what all that meant, the Counselor slowly explained: they wanted to know what color people were so as to reestablish slavery and return dark-skinned people to their masters, and their religion so as to be able to identify the Catholics when the persecution began. Without raising his voice, he exhorted them not to answer such questionnaires, and not to allow the meter and the centimeter to replace the yard and the foot.

One morning in 1893, as they entered Natuba, the Counselor and the pilgrims heard a sound like angry wasps buzzing: it was coming from the main square, where the men and women of the town had congregated to read, or to hear the town crier read, the decrees that had just been posted. They were going to collect taxes from them, the Republic wanted to collect taxes from them.

And what were taxes? many townspeople asked. They're like tithes, others explained to them. Just as, before, if an inhabitant's hens had fifty chicks he was obliged to give five to the mission and one bushel of grain out of each ten that he harvested, the edicts decreed that a person was to give to the Republic part of everything inherited or produced. People had to go to the town hall of their community – all municipalities were now autonomous – and declare what they owned and what they earned in order to find out how much they would have to pay. The tax collectors would seize and turn over to the Republic everything that had been hidden or declared at less than its real value.

Animal instinct, common sense, and centuries of experience made the townspeople realize immediately that this would perhaps be worse than the drought, that the tax collectors would be greedier than the vultures and the bandits. Perplexed, frightened, enraged, they nudged each other and communicated to each other their feelings of apprehension and wrath, in voices that mingled and blended into one, producing that belligerent music that was rising heavenward from Natuba as the Counselor and his shabby followers entered the town by way of the road from Cipó. People surrounded the man in the dark purple habit, blocking his way to the Church of Nossa Senhora da Conceição (repaired and painted by him several times in the last few decades), toward which he had been heading with his usual great long strides, in order to tell him the news. Looking past them with a grave expression on his face, he scarcely seemed to have heard them.

And yet, only seconds later, just time enough for a sort of inner explosion to set his eyes afire, he began to walk, to run through the crowd that stepped aside to let him through, toward the billboards where the decrees had been posted. He reached them and without even bothering to read them tore them down, his face distorted by an indignation that seemed to sum up that of all of them. Then he asked, in a vibrant voice, that these iniquities in writing be burned. And when, before the eyes of the dumfounded municipal councillors, the people did so, and moreover began to celebrate, setting off fireworks as on a feast day, and the fire reduced to smoke the decrees and the fear that they had aroused, the Counselor, before going to pray at the Church of Nossa Senhora da Conceição, announced to the people of that remote corner of the world the grave tidings: the Antichrist was abroad in the world; his name was Republic.

'Whistles, that's right, Senhor Commissioner,' Lieutenant Pires Ferreira repeats, surprised once again at what he has experienced and, no doubt, remembered and recounted many times. 'They sounded very loud in the night – or rather, in the early dawn.'

The field hospital is a wooden shack with a palm-frond roof, hastily thrown together to house the wounded soldiers. It is on the outskirts of Juazeiro, whose streets parallel to the broad São Francisco River lined with houses that are either whitewashed or painted in various colors can be seen between the partitions, beneath the dusty tops of the trees that have given the city its name.

'It took us only twelve days from here to Uauá, which is practically at the gates of Canudos – quite a feat,' Lieutenant Pires Ferreira says. 'My men were dead-tired, so I decided to camp there. And in just a few hours the whistles woke us up.'

There are sixteen wounded, lying in hammocks lined up in two rows facing each other: crude bandages, bloodstained heads, arms, and legs, naked and half-naked bodies, trousers and high-buttoned tunics in tatters. A recently arrived doctor in a white smock is inspecting the wounded, followed by a male nurse carrying a medical kit. There is a sharp contrast between the doctor's healthy, urbane appearance and the soldiers' dejected faces and hair matted down with sweat. At the far end of the shack, an anguished voice is asking about confession.

'Didn't you post sentinels? Didn't it occur to you that they might surprise you, Lieutenant?'

'There were four sentinels, Senhor Commissioner,' Pires Ferreira answers, holding up four emphatic fingers. 'They didn't surprise us. When we heard the whistles, every man in the entire company rose to his feet and prepared for combat.' He lowers his voice. 'But what we saw coming toward us was not the enemy but a procession.'

From one corner of the hospital shack the little camp on the shore of the river, where boats loaded with watermelon ply back and forth, can be seen: the rest of the company, lying in the shade of some trees, rifles stacked up in groups of four, field tents. A flock of screeching parrots flies by.

'A *religious* procession, Lieutenant?' an intrusive, high-pitched, nasal voice asks in surprise.

The officer casts a quick glance at the person who has spoken and nods. 'They came from the direction of Canudos,' he explains, still addressing the commissioner. 'There were five hundred, six hundred, perhaps a thousand of them.'

The commissioner throws up his hands and his equally incredulous aide shakes his head. It is quite obvious that they are people from the city. They have arrived in Juazeiro that morning on the train from Salvador and are still dazed and battered from the jolting and jerking, uncomfortable in their jackets with wide sleeves, their baggy trousers and boots that have already gotten dirty, stifling from the heat, of a certainty annoyed at being there, surrounded by wounded flesh, by disease, and at having to investigate a defeat. As they talk with Lieutenant Pires Ferreira they proceed from hammock to hammock and the commissioner, a stern-faced man, leans over every so often to give one of the wounded a clap on the back. He is the only one who is listening to what the lieutenant is saying, but his aide takes notes, as does the other man who has just arrived, the one with the nasal voice who seems to have a head cold, the one who keeps constantly sneezing.

'Five hundred, a thousand?' the commissioner says sarcastically. 'The Baron de Canabrava's deposition came to my office and I am acquainted with it, Lieutenant. Those who invaded Canudos numbered two hundred, including the women and children. The baron ought to know – he's the owner of the estate.'

'There were a thousand of them, thousands,' the wounded man in the nearest hammock murmurs, a light-skinned, kinky-haired mulatto with a bandaged shoulder. 'I swear to it, sir.'

Lieutenant Pires Ferreira shuts him up with such a brusque gesture that his arm brushes against the leg of the wounded man behind him, who bellows in pain. The lieutenant is young, on the short side, with a little clipped mustache like those of the dandies who congregate, back in Salvador, in the pastry shops of the Rua Chile at teatime. But due to fatigue, frustration, nerves, this little French mustache is now set off by dark circles under his eyes, an ashen skin, and a grimace. The lieutenant is unshaven, his hair is badly mussed, his uniform is torn, and his right arm is in a sling. At the far end of the shack, the incoherent voice babbles on about confession and holy oils.

Pires Ferreira turns to the commissioner. 'As a child, I lived on a cattle ranch and learned to size up the number of heads in a herd at a glance,' he murmurs. 'I'm not exaggerating. There were more than five hundred of them, and perhaps a thousand.'

'They were carrying a wooden cross, an enormous one, and a banner of the Divine Holy Spirit,' someone adds from one of the hammocks.

And before the lieutenant can cut them short, others hastily join in, telling how it was: they also had saints' statues, rosaries, they were all blowing those whistles or chanting Kyrie Eleisons and acclaiming St. John the Baptist, the Virgin Mary, the Blessed Lord Jesus, and the Counselor. They have sat up in their hammocks and are having a shouting match till the lieutenant orders them to knock it off.

'And all of a sudden they were right on top of us,' he goes on, amid the silence. 'They looked so peaceful, like a Holy Week procession – how could I have given the order to attack them? And then suddenly they began to shout, Down with this and that, and opened fire on us at point-blank range. We were one against eight, one against ten.'

'To shout, Down with this and that, you say?' the insolent high-pitched voice interrupts him.

'Down with the Republic,' Lieutenant Pires Ferreira says. 'Down with the Antichrist.' He turns to the commissioner again: 'I have nothing to reproach myself for. My men fought bravely. We held out for more than four hours, sir. I did not order a retreat until we had no ammunition left. You're familiar with the problems that we've had with the Mannlichers. Thanks to the troops' disciplined behavior, we were able to get back here in only ten days.'

'The march back took less time than the march out,' the commissioner growls.

'Come over here and have a look at this!' the doctor in the white smock calls to them from one corner.

The group of civilians and the lieutenant walk down the line of hammocks to him. The doctor is wearing an indigo-blue army uniform underneath his smock. He has removed the bandage of a soldier with Indian features who is writhing in pain, and is contemplating the man's belly with intense interest. He points to it as though it were a rare, precious object: at the man's groin is a purulent hole the size of a fist, with coagulated blood at the edges and pulsing flesh in the middle.

'An explosive bullet!' the doctor exclaims enthusiastically, dusting the swollen wound with a fine white powder. 'On penetrating the body, it explodes like shrapnel, destroys the tissue, and produces a gaping wound like this. The only time I've ever come across such a thing is in the British Army Manual. How is it possible that those wretched devils possess such modern weapons? Even the Brazilian Army is not equipped with them.'

'See that, Senhor Commissioner?' Lieutenant Pires Ferreira says triumphantly. 'They were armed to the teeth. They had rifles, carbines, long-barreled muskets, machetes, daggers, clubs. As for us, on the other hand, our Mannlichers jammed and . . .'

But the man who has been babbling in delirium about confession and holy oils is now shouting at the top of his voice and raving about sacred images, the banner of the Divine, the whistles.

He does not appear to be wounded; he is tied to a post, in a uniform with fewer signs of wear and tear than the lieutenant's. As he sees the doctor and the civilians approaching, he implores them with tears in his eyes: 'Confession, sirs! I beg you! I beg you!'

'Is he the medical officer of your company, Dr. Antônio Alves dos Santos?' the doctor in the white smock asks. 'Why have you tied him up like that?'

'He tried to kill himself, sir,' Pires Ferreira stammers. 'He attempted to put a bullet through his head and by some miracle he missed. He's been like that since the encounter at Uauá, and I was at a loss as to how to deal with him. Instead of being a help to us, he turned into one more problem, especially during the retreat.'

'Kindly withdraw if you will, sirs,' the doctor in the white smock says. 'Leave me alone with him, and I'll calm him down.'

As the lieutenant and the civilians obey his wishes, the high-pitched, inquisitive, peremptory voice of the man who has interrupted the explanations several times is again heard: 'How many dead and wounded were there in all, Lieutenant? In your company and among the outlaws?'

'Ten dead and sixteen wounded among my men,' Pires Ferreira replies with an impatient gesture. 'The enemy had at least a hundred casualties. All this is noted in the report that I gave you, sir.'

'I'm not a member of the commission. I'm a reporter from the *Jornal de Notícias*, in Bahia,' the man says.

He does not resemble the government officials or the doctor in the white smock with whom he has come here. Young, nearsighted, with thick eyeglasses. He does not take notes with a pencil but with a goose-quill pen. He is dressed in a pair of trousers coming apart at the seams, an off-white jacket, a cap with a visor, and all of his apparel seems fake, wrong, out of place on his awkward body. He is holding a clipboard with a number of sheets of paper and dips his goose-quill pen in an inkwell, with the cork of a wine bottle for a cap, that is fastened to the sleeve of his jacket. He looks more or less like a scarecrow.

'I have traveled six hundred kilometers merely to ask you these questions, Lieutenant Pires Ferreira,' he says. And he sneezes.

Big João was born near the sea, on a sugarcane plantation in Recôncavo, the owner of which, Sir Adalberto de Gumúcio, was a great lover of horses. He boasted of possessing the most spirited sorrels and the mares with the most finely turned ankles in all of Bahia and of having produced these specimens of first-rate horseflesh without any need of English studs, thanks to astute matings which he himself supervised. He prided himself less (in public) on having achieved the same happy result with the blacks of his slave quarters, so as not to further stir the troubled waters of the quarrels that this had aroused with the Baron de Canabrava and with the Church, but the truth of the matter was that he dealt with his slaves in exactly the same way that he had dealt with his horses. His method was ruled by his eye and by his inspiration. It consisted of selecting the most lively and most shapely young black girls and giving them as concubines to the males that he regarded as the purest because of their harmonious features and even-colored skins. The best couples were given special food and work privileges so as to produce as many offspring as possible. The chaplain, the missionaries, and the hierarchy of Salvador had repeatedly reproved him for throwing blacks together in this fashion, 'making them live together like animals,' but instead of putting an end to such practices, these reprimands resulted only in his engaging in them more discreetly.

Big João was the result of one of these combinations arranged by this great landowner with the inclinations of a perfectionist. In João's case the product born of the mating was undeniably magnificent. The boy had very bright, sparkling eyes and teeth that when he laughed filled his round blue-black face with light. He was plump, vivacious, playful, and his mother – a beautiful woman who gave birth every nine months – suspected that he would have an exceptional future. She was not mistaken. Sir Adalberto de Gumúcio became fond of him when he was still a baby crawling on all fours and took him out of the slave quarters to the manor house – a rectangular building, with a hip roof, Tuscan columns, and balconies with wooden railings that overlooked the cane fields, the neoclassic chapel, the sugar mill, the distillery, and an avenue of royal palms – thinking that he could be a servant boy for his daughters and later on a butler or a coachman. He did not want him to be ruined at an early age, as frequently happened with children sent out into the fields to clear land and harvest sugarcane.

But the one who claimed Big João for herself was Miss Adelinha Isabel de Gumúcio, Master Adalberto's unmarried sister, who lived with him. She was slender and small-boned, with a little turned-up nose that seemed to be continually sniffing the world's bad odors, and she spent her time weaving coifs and shawls, embroidering tablecloths, bedspreads, blouses, or preparing desserts, tasks at which she excelled. But most of the time she did not even taste the cream puffs, the almond tortes, the meringues with chocolate filling, the almond sponge cakes that were the delight of her nieces and nephews, her sister-in-law and her brother. Miss Adelinha took a great liking to Big João from the day she saw him climbing the water tank. Terrified at seeing, some seven feet or so off the ground, a little boy scarcely old enough to toddle, she ordered him to climb down, but João went on up the little ladder. By the time Miss Adelinha called a servant, the little boy had already reached the edge of the tank and fallen into the water. They fished him out, vomiting and wide-eyed with fear. Miss Adelinha undressed him, bundled him up, and held him in her arms till he fell asleep.

Shortly thereafter, Master Adalberto's sister installed João in her bedroom, in one of the cradles that her nieces had slept in. She had it placed right next to her bed, and he slept all night at her side, the way other ladies have their favorite little maidservants and their little lap dogs sleep next to them. From that moment on, João enjoyed special privileges. Miss Adelinha always dressed him in one-piece romper suits, navy blue or bright red or golden yellow, which she made for him herself. He went with her every day to the promontory from which there was a panoramic view of the islands and the late-afternoon sun, setting them on fire, and accompanied her when she made visits and trips to neighboring villages to distribute alms. On Sundays he went to church with her, carrying her prie-dieu. Miss Adelinha taught him how to hold skeins of wool so that she could comb them, to change the spools of the loom, to mix colors for the dye, and to thread needles, as well as how to serve as her kitchen boy. To measure how long things should cook, they recited together the Credos and Our Fathers that the recipe called for. She personally prepared him for his First Communion, took Communion with him, and made him marvelous chocolate to celebrate the occasion.

But, contrary to what should have happened in the case of a child who had grown up amid walls covered with wallpaper, jacaranda furniture upholstered in damask and silks, and sideboards full of crystalware, spending his days engaged in feminine pursuits in the shadow of a delicate-natured woman, Big João did not turn into a gentle, tame creature, as almost always happened to house slaves. From earliest childhood on, he was unusually strong, so that despite the fact that he was the same age as Little João, the cook's son, he appeared to be several years older. At play he was brutal, and Miss Adelinha used to say sadly: 'He's not made for civilized life. He yearns to be out in the open.' Because the boy was constantly on the lookout for the slightest chance to go out for a ramble in the countryside. One time, as they were walking through the cane fields, on seeing him look longingly at the blacks naked to the waist hacking away with machetes amid the green leaves, the senhorita remarked to him: 'You look as though you envied them.' 'Yes, mistress, I envy them,' he replied. A little after that, Master Adalberto had him put on a black armband and sent him to the slave quarters of the plantation to attend his mother's funeral. João did not feel any great emotion, for he had seen very little of her. He was vaguely ill at ease all during the ceremony, sitting underneath a bower of straw, and in the cortege to the cemetery, surrounded by blacks who stared at him without trying to conceal their envy or their scorn for his knickers, his striped blouse, and his shoes that were such a sharp contrast to their coarse cotton shirts and bare feet. He had never been affectionate with his mistress, thereby causing the Gumúcio family to think that perhaps he was one of those churls with no feelings, capable of spitting on the hand that fed them. But not even this portent would ever have led them to suspect that Big João would be capable of doing what he did.

It happened during Miss Adelinha's trip to the Convent of the Incarnation, where she went on retreat every year. Little João drove the coach drawn by two horses and Big João sat next to him on the coach box. The trip took around eight hours; they left the plantation at dawn so as to arrive at the convent by mid-afternoon. But two days later the nuns sent a messenger to ask why Senhorita Adelinha hadn't arrived on the date that had been set. Master Adalberto directed the searches by the police from Bahia and the servants on the plantation who scoured the region for an entire month, questioning any number of people. Every inch of the road between the convent and the plantation was gone over with a fine-tooth comb, yet not the slightest trace of the coach, its occupants, or the horses was found. As in the fantastic stories recounted by the wandering *cantadores*, they seemed to have vanished in thin air.

The truth began to come to light months later, when a magistrate of the Orphans' Court in Salvador discovered the monogram of the Gumúcio family, covered over with paint, on the secondhand coach that he had bought from a dealer in the upper town. The dealer confessed that he had acquired the coach in a village inhabited by *cafuzos* – Negro-Indian half-breeds – knowing that it was stolen, but without the thought ever crossing his mind that the thieves might also be murderers. The Baron de Canabrava offered a very high price for the heads of Big João and Little João, while Gumúcio implored that they be captured alive.

A gang of outlaws that was operating in the backlands turned Little João in to the police for the reward. The cook's son was so dirty and disheveled that he was unrecognizable when they subjected him to torture to make him talk.

He swore that the whole thing had not been planned by him but by the devil that had possessed his companion since childhood. He had been driving the coach, whistling through his teeth, thinking of the sweets awaiting him at the Convent of the Incarnation, when all of a sudden Big João had ordered him to rein in the horses. When Miss Adelinha asked why they were stopping, Little João saw his companion hit her in the face so hard she fainted, grab the reins from him, and spur the horses on to the promontory that their mistress was in the habit of climbing up to in order to contemplate the view of the islands. There, with a determination such that Little João, terror-stricken, had not dared to cross him, Big João had subjected Miss Adelinha to a thousand evil acts. He had stripped her naked and laughed at her as she covered her breasts with one trembling hand and her privates with the other, and had made her run all about, trying to dodge the stones he threw at her as he heaped upon her the most abominable insults that the younger boy had ever heard. Then he suddenly plunged a dagger into her belly and once she was dead vent his fury on her by lopping off her breasts and her head. Then, panting, drenched with sweat, he fell asleep alongside the bloody corpse. Little João was so terrified that his legs buckled beneath him when he tried to run away.

When Big João woke up a while later, he was calm. He gazed indifferently at the carnage all about them. Then he ordered the Kid to help him dig a grave, and they buried the pieces of Miss Adelinha in it. They had waited until it got dark to make their escape and gradually put distance between themselves and the scene of the crime; in the daytime they hid the coach in a cave or a thicket or a ravine and at night galloped on; the one clear idea in their minds was that they ought to head away from the sea. When they managed to sell the coach and the horses, they bought provisions to take with them as they went into the *sertão*, with the hope of joining one or another of the bands of fugitive slaves who, as many stories had it, were everywhere in the scrublands of the interior. They lived on the run, avoiding the towns and getting food to eat by begging or by petty thefts. Only once did João the Kid try to get Big João to talk about what had happened. They were lying underneath a tree, smoking cigars, and in a sudden fit of boldness he asked him point-blank: 'Why did you kill the mistress?' 'Because I've got the Dog in me,' Big João answered immediately. 'Don't talk to me about that any more.' The Kid thought that his companion had told him the truth.

He was growing more and more afraid of this companion of his since childhood, for after the murder of their mistress, Big João became less and less like his former self. He scarcely said a word to him, and, on the other hand, he continually surprised him by talking to himself in a low voice, his eyes bloodshot. One night he heard him call the Devil 'Father' and ask him to come to his aid. 'Haven't I done enough already, Father?' he stammered, his body writhing. 'What more do you want me to do?' The Kid became convinced that Big João had made a pact with the Evil One and feared that, in order to continue accumulating merit, he would sacrifice him as he had their mistress. He decided to beat him to it. He planned everything, but the night that he crawled over to him, all set to plunge his knife into him, he was trembling so violently that Big João opened his eyes before he could do the deed. Big João saw him leaning over him with the blade quivering in his hand. His intention was unmistakable, but Big João didn't turn a hair. 'Kill me, Kid,' he heard him say. He ran off as fast as his legs could carry him, feeling that devils were pursuing him.

The Kid was hanged in the prison in Salvador and Senhorita Adelinha's remains were transferred to the neoclassic chapel of the plantation, but her murderer was not found, despite the fact that the Gumúcio family periodically raised the reward for his capture. And yet, after the Kid had run off, Big João had made no attempt to hide himself. A towering giant, half naked, miserable, eating what fell into the animal traps he set or the fruit he plucked from trees, he roamed the byways like a ghost. He went through the towns in broad daylight, asking for food, and the suffering in his face so moved people that they would usually toss him a few scraps.

One day, at a crossroads on the outskirts of Pombal, he came upon a handful of people who were listening to the words of a gaunt man, enveloped in a deep-purple tunic, whose hair came down to his shoulders and whose eyes looked like burning coals. As it happened, he was speaking at that very moment of the Devil, whom he called Lucifer, the Dog, Can, and Beelzebub, of the catastrophes and crimes that he caused in the world, and of what men who wanted to be saved must do. His voice was persuasive; it reached a person's soul without passing by way of his head, and even to a being as addlebrained as Big João, it seemed like a balm that healed old and terrible wounds. João stood there listening to him, rooted to the spot, not even blinking, moved to his very bones by what he was hearing and by the music of the voice uttering those words. The figure of the saint was blurred at times by the tears that welled up in João's eyes. When the man went on his way, he began to follow him at a distance, like a timid animal.

The two persons who came to know Galileo best in the city of São Salvador da Bahia de Todos os Santos (called simply Bahia or Salvador) were a smuggler and a doctor; they were also the first to explain the country to him, even though neither of them would have shared the opinions of Brazil that the revolutionary expressed in his letters to *L'Etincelle de la révolte* (frequent ones during this period). The first of them, written within a week of his shipwreck, spoke of Bahia: 'a kaleidoscope where a man with some notion of history sees existing side by side the social disgraces that have debased the various eras of humanity.' The letter referred to slavery, which, although abolished, nonetheless still existed de facto, since in order not to die of starvation, many freed blacks had returned to their former masters and begged them to take them in again. The masters hired on – for miserable salaries – only the able-bodied, so that the streets of Bahia, in Gall's words, 'teem with the elderly, the sick, and the wretched, who beg or steal, and with whores who remind one of those of Alexandria and Algiers, the most depraved ports on the planet.'

The second letter, written two months later, concerned 'the infamous alliance of obscurantism and exploitation,' and described the parade each Sunday of wealthy families headed for Mass at the Church of Nossa Senhora da Conceição da Praia, with servants carrying prayer stools, candles, missals, and parasols so that the sun would not damage the ladies' complexions; 'these latter,' Gall wrote, 'like the English civil servants in the colonies, have made whiteness a paradigm, the quintessence of beauty.' But in a later article the phrenologist explained to his comrades in Lyons that, despite their prejudices, the descendants of Portuguese, Indians, and Africans had mingled with each other quite freely in this land and produced a motley mixture of mestizos: mulattoes, *mamelucos*, *cafuzos*, *caboclos*, *curibocas*. And he added: 'Which is to say, that many more challenges for science.' These human types and the Europeans who landed on its shores for one reason or another gave Bahia a variegated and cosmopolitan atmosphere.

It was among these foreigners that Galileo Gall – who at that time spoke only the most halting Portuguese – made his first acquaintances. In the beginning he lived in the Hôtel des Etrangers, in Campo Grande, but once he struck up a friendship with old Jan van Rijsted, the latter gave him a garret above the Livraria Catilina to live in, and got him pupils for private lessons in French and English so that he would have money to eat. Van Rijsted was of Dutch origin, born in Olinda, and had trafficked in cocoa beans, silks, spices, tobacco, alcohol, and arms between Europe, Africa, and America since the age of fourteen (without ever once landing in jail). Because of his associates – dealers, shipowners, sea captains – he was not a rich man; they had stolen a fair share of the goods he trafficked in. Gall was convinced that bandits, be they great criminals or mere petty thieves, were also fighting against the enemy – the state – and undermining the foundations of property, albeit unwittingly. This furthered his friendship with the ex-scoundrel. *Ex* because he had retired from the business of committing misdeeds. He was a bachelor, but he had lived with a girl with Arab eyes, thirty years younger than he, with Egyptian or Moroccan blood, with whom he had fallen in love in Marseilles. He had brought her to Bahia and built her a villa in the upper town, spending a fortune on decorating it so as to make her happy. On his return from one of his voyages, he found that the beauty had flown the coop after having sold every last thing in the villa, making off with the small strongbox in which Van Rijsted kept hidden a bit of gold and a few precious stones. He recounted these details to Gall as they were walking along the docks, contemplating the sea and the sailing vessels, shifting from English to French and Portuguese, in an offhand tone of voice that the revolutionary admired. Jan was now living on an annuity that, according to him, would allow him to eat and drink till his death, provided that it was not too long in coming.

The Dutchman, an uncultured but curious man, listened with deference to Galileo's theories on freedom and the conformations of the cranium as symptomatic of conduct, although he allowed himself to take exception when the Scotsman assured him that the love which couples felt for each other was a defect and a source of unhappiness. Gall's fifth letter to *L'Etincelle de la révolte* was on superstition, that is to say, on the Church of O Senhor de Bonfim, which pilgrims had filled with ex-votos, with legs, hands, arms, heads, breasts, and eyes of wood and crystal, asking for miracles or giving thanks for them. The sixth letter was on the advent of the Republic, which in aristocratic Bahia had meant only the change of a few names. In the next one, he paid homage to four mulattoes – the tailors Lucas Dantas, Luiz Gonzaga das Virgens, João de Deus, and Manoel Faustino – who, a century before, inspired by the French Revolution, had formed a conspiracy to destroy the monarchy and establish an egalitarian society of blacks, half-breeds, and whites. Jan van Rijsted took Galileo to the little public square where the four artisans had been hanged and quartered, and to his surprise saw him leave some flowers there.

Amid the shelves of books of the Livraria Catilina, Galileo Gall made the acquaintance one day of Dr. José Batista de Sá Oliveira, an elderly physician and the author of a book that had interested him: *Comparative Craniometry of the Human Types of Bahia, from the Evolutionist and Medico-Legal Point of View.* The old man, who had been to Italy and met Cesare Lombroso, whose theories fascinated him, was happy to learn that he had at least one reader of this book that he had published at his own expense and that his colleagues considered extremely odd. Surprised at Gall's knowledge of medicine – albeit continually disconcerted and frequently shocked by his opinions – Dr. Oliveira found in the Scotsman an excellent conversational partner, with whom on occasion he spent hours heatedly discussing the physical mechanisms of the criminal personality, biological inheritance, or the university, an institution that Gall railed against, regarding it as responsible for the division between physical and intellectual labor and hence the cause of worse social inequalities than aristocracy and plutocracy. Dr. Oliveira took Gall on as an aide in his medical practice and occasionally entrusted him with a bleeding or a purge.

Although they sought out his company and perhaps respected him, neither Van Rijsted nor Dr. Oliveira had the impression that they really knew this man with the red hair and beard, shabbily dressed in black, who, despite his ideas, appeared to live a tranquil life: sleeping late, giving language lessons at his pupils' homes, tirelessly walking about the city, or spending entire days in his garret reading and writing. Sometimes he disappeared for several weeks without telling them beforehand, and when he reappeared they discovered that he had been off on one of the long trips that took him throughout Brazil, in the most precarious circumstances. He never spoke to them of his past or of his plans, and since he gave them the vaguest of answers when they questioned him regarding them, the two of them resigned themselves to accepting him for what he was or what he appeared to be: an exotic, enigmatic, eccentric loner, whose words and ideas were incendiary but whose behavior was innocuous.

After two years, Galileo Gall spoke Portuguese fluently and had sent off several additional letters to *L'Etincelle de la révolte.* The eighth, on the corporal punishments that he had witnessed being administered to bond servants in the streets and the public squares of the city, and the ninth, on the instruments of torture employed in the days of slavery: the rack, the stocks, the neck chain or *gargalheira,* metal balls attached to the ankles, and *infantes,* rings to crush the thumbs. The tenth, on O Pelourinho, the municipal whipping post where lawbreakers (Gall called them 'brothers') were still flogged with rawhide whips, which were for sale in stores under the marine nickname of *o bacalhau* – codfish.

He spent so many hours, by day and by night, wandering about the labyrinthine streets of Salvador that he might well have been taken for someone in love with the city. But what Galileo Gall was interested in was not the beauties of Bahia; it was, rather, the spectacle that had never ceased to rouse him to rebellion: injustice. Here, unlike Europe, he explained in his letters to Lyons, there were no segregated residential districts. 'The mean huts of the wretched lie side by side with the tiled palaces of the owners of sugar plantations and mills, and ever since the drought of fifteen years ago that drove thousands of refugees here from the highlands, the streets teem with children who look like oldsters and oldsters who look like children, and women who are broomsticks, and among this multitude the scientist can easily identify all manner of physical afflictions, from those that are relatively harmless to those that are terrifyingly severe: bilious fever, beriberi, dropsy, dysentery, smallpox.' 'Any revolutionary whose convictions as to the necessity of a major revolution are wavering' – he wrote in one of his letters – 'ought to take a look at what I am seeing in Salvador: it would put an end to all his doubts.'

III

When, weeks afterward, it became known in Salvador that in a remote town called Natuba the brand-new Republic's tax decrees had been burned, the government decided to send a squad of Bahia State Police to arrest the troublemakers. Thirty police officers, in blue-and-green uniforms and kepis still bearing the insignia of the monarchy that the Republic had not yet had time to change, set out, first by train and then on foot, on the arduous journey to this place that for all of them was no more than a name on a map. The Counselor was not in Natuba. The sweating police officers questioned the municipal councillors and the inhabitants of the town before taking off in search of this rebel whose name, popular name, and legend they would bring back to the coast and spread in the streets of Bahia. Guided by a tracker from the region, their blue-and-green uniforms standing out in the radiant morning light, they disappeared into the wilds on the road to Cumbe.

For another week they followed the Counselor's trail, going up and down a sandy, reddish-colored terrain, with scrub of thorny *mandacarus* and famished flocks of sheep poking about in the withered leaves. Everyone had seen him pass by, the Sunday before he had prayed in this church, preached in that public square, slept alongside those rocks. They finally found him, seven leagues from Tucano, in a settlement called Massetê, a cluster of adobe huts with round roof tiles in the spurs of the Serra de Ovó. It was dusk; they caught sight of women with water jugs on their heads, and heaved a sigh of relief that their search was nearly over. The Counselor was spending the night with Severino Vianna, a farmer who had a maize field a kilometer outside the settlement. The police trotted out there, amid *juazeiro* trees with sharp-edged branches and thickets of *velame* that irritated their skin. When they arrived, in near-darkness, they saw a dwelling made of palings and a swarm of amorphous creatures crowded around someone who was doubtless the man they were looking for. No one fled, no one began yelling and shouting on spying their uniforms, their rifles.

Were there a hundred of them, a hundred fifty, two hundred? There were as many men as women, and the majority of them, to judge from the garments they were wearing, appeared to have come from the poorest of the poor. In the eyes of all of them – so the police officers who returned to Bahia were later to tell their wives, their sweethearts, the whores they slept with, their buddies – was a look of indomitable determination. But in reality they did not have time to observe them or to identify the ringleader, for the moment the sergeant in charge ordered them to hand over the man known as the Counselor, the mob attacked them, an act of utter foolhardiness in view of the fact that the police had rifles while they were armed only with sticks, sickles, stones, knives, and a couple of shotguns. But everything happened so fast that before they knew it the police found themselves surrounded, dispersed, pursued, beaten up, and injured, as they heard themselves being called 'Republicans!' as though the word were an insult. They managed to shoulder their rifles and shoot, but even when men and women in rags fell to the ground, with their chests riddled with bullets or their heads blown off, nothing daunted the mob and soon the police from Bahia found themselves fleeing, dazed and bewildered by this incomprehensible defeat. They were later to say that among their assailants there were not only the fanatics and madmen that they had expected but also hardened criminals such as Pajeú with the slashed face and the bandit whose acts of cruelty had earned him the nickname of Satan João. Three police officers were killed and left unburied, food for the carrion birds of the Serra de Ovó; eight rifles disappeared. Another policeman was drowned in the Masseté. The pilgrims did not pursue them. Instead, they concerned themselves with burying their five dead and caring for the wounded, as others, kneeling at the Counselor's feet, offered their thanks to God. Until far into the night, the sound of weeping and prayers for the dead could be heard amid the graves dug in Severino Vianna's maize field.

When a second squad of Bahia Police, numbering sixty officers, better armed than the first, detrained in Serrinha, they discovered that there had been a subtle change in the attitude of the villagers toward men in uniform. For even though the enmity with which police were received in the towns when they came up into the hills to hunt bandits was nothing new to them, they had never been as certain as they were this time that obstacles would be deliberately put in their way. The provisions in the general stores had always just run out, even when they offered to pay a good price for them, and despite the high fee offered, no tracker in Serrinha would guide them. Nor was anyone able this time to give them the slightest lead as to the whereabouts of the band. And as the police staggered from Olhos D'Agua to Pedra Alta, from Tracupá to Tiririca and from there to Tucano and from there to Caraíba and Pontal and finally back again to Serrinha, being met with nothing but indifferent glances, contrite negatives, a shrug of the shoulders on the part of the cowherds, peasants, craftsmen, and women whom they came across on the road, they felt as though they were trying to lay their hands on a mirage. The band had not passed that way, no one had seen the dark-haired, dark-skinned man in the deep-purple habit and nobody remembered now that decrees had been burned in Natuba, nor had they heard about an armed encounter in Masseté. On returning to the capital of the state, safe and sound but thoroughly demoralized, the police officers reported that the horde of fanatics – fleetingly crystallized, like so many others, around a deeply devout woman or a preacher – had surely broken up and at this point, frightened by their own misdeeds, its members had no doubt scattered in all directions, after having perhaps killed their ringleader. Hadn't that been what had happened so many times in the region?

But they were mistaken. Even though events apparently repeated old patterns of history, this time everything was to be different. The penitents were now more united than ever, and far from having murdered the saint after the victory of Masseté, which they took to be a sign sent to them from on high, they revered him all the more. The morning after the encounter, the Counselor, who had prayed all night long over the graves of the dead rebels, had awakened them. They found him very downcast. He told them that what had happened the evening before was no doubt a prelude to even greater violence and asked them to return to their homes, for if they went on with him they might end up in jail or die like their five brothers who were now in the presence of the Father. No one moved. His eyes swept over the hundred, hundred fifty, two hundred followers in rags and tatters there before him, still in the grip of the emotions of the night before as they listened to him. He not only gazed upon them but appeared to see them. 'Give thanks to the Blessed Jesus,' he said to them gently, 'for it would seem that He has chosen you to set an example.'

They followed him with souls overcome with emotion, not so much because of what he had said to them, but because of the gentleness in his voice, which had always been severe and impersonal. It was hard work for some of them not to be left behind as he walked on with his great strides of a long-shanked wading bird, along the incredible path he chose for them this time, one that was a trail neither for pack animals nor for *cangaceiros*; he led them, rather, straight across a wild desert of cactus, tangled scrub brush, and rough stones. But he never hesitated as to what direction to take them in. During the first night's halt, after offering the usual prayers of thanks and leading them in reciting the Rosary, he spoke to them of war, of countries that were killing each other over booty as hyenas fight over carrion, and in great distress commented that since Brazil was now a republic it, too, would act like other heretical nations. They heard him say that the Can must be rejoicing; they heard him say that the time had come to put down roots and build a Temple, which, when the end of the world came, would be what Noah's Ark had been in the beginning.

And where would they put down roots and build this Temple? They learned the answer after making their way across ravines, river shallows, sierras, scrub forests – days' treks that were born and died with the sun – scaling an entire range of mountains and crossing a river that had very little water in it and was called the Vaza-Barris. Pointing to the cluster of cabins in the distance that had been peons' huts and the broken-down mansion that had been the manor house when the place had been a hacienda, the Counselor said: 'We shall settle there.' Some of them remembered that for years now in his nightly talks he had been prophesying that before the last days the Blessed Jesus' elect would find refuge in a high and privileged land, where no one who was impure would enter. Those who had made the long climb to these heights could be certain of eternal rest. Had they reached, then, the land of salvation?

Happy and tired, they followed along after their guide to Canudos, where the families of the Vilanova brothers, two merchants who had a general store there, and all the other inhabitants of the place, had turned out to watch them coming.

The sun burns the backlands to a cinder, gleams on the greenish-black waters of the Itapicuru, reflects off the houses of Queimadas lining the right edge of the river, at the foot of gullies of reddish clay. Sparse trees cast their shadow over the rocky, rolling terrain stretching southeastward, in the direction of Riacho da Onça. The rider – boots, broad-brimmed hat, black frock coat – escorted by his shadow and that of his mule, heads unhurriedly toward a thicket of lead-colored bushes. Behind him, already far in the distance, the rooftops of Queimadas still glow like fire. To his left, several hundred meters away, a hut at the top of a rise can be seen. His thick locks spilling out from under his hat, his little red beard, and his clothes are full of dust; he is sweating heavily and every so often he wipes his forehead with his hand and runs his tongue over his parched lips. In the first clumps of underbrush in the thicket, he reins the mule in and his blue eyes eagerly search all about. Finally he makes out a man in sandals and a leather hat, drill trousers and a coarse cotton blouse, with a machete at his waist, kneeling a few feet away from him, exploring a trap.

'Rufino?' he asks. 'Rufino the guide from Queimadas?'

The man turns halfway around, slowly, as though he had been aware of his presence for some time, and putting a finger to his lips signals him to be silent: shhh, shhh. At the same time he glances at him and for a second there is surprise in his dark eyes, perhaps because of the newcomer's foreign accent in Portuguese, perhaps because of his funereal garb. Rufino – a young man, with a thin and supple body, an angular, beardless, weather-beaten face – draws his machete out of his belt, turns back to the trap hidden under the leaves, leans over it once again, and tugs on a net: he pulls out of the opening a confusion of croaking black feathers. It is a small vulture that cannot get off the ground because one of its feet is trapped in the net. There is a disappointed expression on the face of the guide, who frees the ugly bird from the net with the tip of the machete and watches it disappear in the blue air, desperately beating its wings.

'One time a jaguar this big leapt out at me,' he murmurs, pointing to the trap. 'He was half blind after being down in that hole for so many hours.'

Galileo Gall nods. Rufino straightens up and takes two steps toward him.

Now that he is free to talk, the stranger seems hesitant. 'I went to your house looking for you,' he says, stalling for time. 'Your wife sent me here.'

The mule is pawing the dirt with its rear hoofs and Rufino grabs its head and opens its mouth. As he examines its teeth with the look of a connoisseur, he appears to be thinking aloud: 'The stationmaster at Jacobina knows my conditions. I'm a man of my word – anybody in Queimadas will tell you that. That's tough work.'

As Galileo Gall doesn't answer, Rufino turns around to look at him. 'Aren't you from the railroad company?' he asks, speaking slowly since he has realized that the stranger is having difficulty understanding him.

Galileo Gall tips his hat back and, pointing with his chin toward the desert hills all around them, murmurs: 'I want to go to Canudos.' He pauses, blinks as though to conceal the excitement in his eyes, and adds: 'I know that you've gone up there many times.'

Rufino has a very serious look on his face. His eyes are scrutinizing him now with a distrust that he does not bother to hide. 'I used to go to Canudos when it was a cattle ranch,' he says warily. 'I haven't been back since the Baron de Canabrava abandoned it.'

'The way there is still the same,' Galileo Gall replies.

They are standing very close together, observing each other, and the silent tension that has arisen seems to communicate itself to the mule, for it suddenly tosses its head and begins to back away.

'Is it the Baron de Canabrava who's sent you?' Rufino asks as he calms down the animal by patting its neck.

Galileo Gall shakes his head and the guide does not pursue the matter. He runs his hand over one of the mule's hind legs, forcing the animal to raise it, and squats down to examine its hoof.

'There are things happening in Canudos,' he murmurs. 'The people who have occupied the baron's hacienda have attacked soldiers from the National Guard, in Uauá. They're said to have killed several of them.'

'Are you afraid they'll kill you, too?' Galileo Gall grunts, with a smile. 'Are *you* a soldier?'

Rufino has finally found what he was looking for in the hoof: a thorn, perhaps, or a little pebble that is lost in his huge rough hands. He tosses it away and lets go of the animal.

'Afraid? Not at all,' he answers mildly, with just the trace of a smile. 'Canudos is a long way from here.'

'I'll pay you a fair price.' Stifling from the heat, Galileo Gall takes a deep breath; he removes his hat and shakes his curly red mane. 'We'll leave inside of a week or ten days at most. One thing is certain: we must be very cautious.'

Rufino the guide looks at him without blinking an eye, without asking a single question.

'Because of what happened in Uauá,' Galileo Gall adds, running his tongue over his lips. 'No one must know that we're going to Canudos.'

Rufino points to the lone hut, made of mud and palings, half dissolved in the light at the top of the rise. 'Come to my house and we'll talk the matter over,' he says.

They start walking, followed by the mule, which Galileo is leading along by the reins. The two men are of nearly the same height, but the outsider is stockier and his stride almost exaggeratedly vigorous, whereas the guide seems to be floating above the ground. It is midday and a few off-white clouds have appeared in the sky.

The tracker's voice fades away in the air as they walk off: 'Who told you about me? And if I'm not prying, why is it you want to go such a long way? What is it you've lost up there in Canudos?'

She appeared at daybreak one rainless morning, at the top of a hill on the road from Quijingue, carrying a wooden cross on her back. She was twenty years old but had suffered so much that she looked ancient. She was a woman with a broad face, bruised feet, a shapeless body, and mouse-colored skin.

Her name was Maria Quadrado and she was making her way from Salvador to Monte Santo, on foot. She had been dragging the cross along on her back for three months and a day now. On the road that went through rocky gorges, scrub forests bristling with cactus, deserts where the wind raised howling dust devils, settlements that consisted of a single muddy street and three palm trees, and pestilential swamps in which cattle immersed themselves to escape the bats, Maria Quadrado had slept in the open, except for the very few times that some backwoodsman or shepherd who looked upon her as a saint offered to share his shelter with her. She had kept herself alive on pieces of raw brown sugar that charitable souls gave her and wild fruit plucked off trees and bushes when, after going without food for so long, her stomach growled. As she left Bahia, determined to make the pilgrimage to the miraculous Calvary of the Serra de Piquaraçá, where two kilometers dug out of the sides of the mountain and dotted with chapels in memory of the Via Crucis of Our Lord led to the Church of the Holy Cross of Monte Santo, which she had vowed to journey to on foot as atonement for her sins, Maria Quadrado's hair was done up in braids with a ribbon tied around them and she was wearing two skirts, a blue blouse, and rope-soled shoes. But along the way she had given her clothes to beggars, and in Palmeira dos Indios her shoes had been stolen from her, so that when she set eyes on Monte Santo that dawn she was barefoot and her only garment was an esparto-cloth sack with holes for her arms. Her head, with its clumsily lopped-off locks of hair and bare skull, called to mind the heads of the lunatics in the asylum in Salvador. She had cut all her hair off herself after being raped for the fourth time.

For she had been raped four times since beginning her journey: by a constable, by a cowboy, by two deer hunters together, and by a goatherd who had given her shelter in his cave. The first three times, as they defiled her she had felt only repugnance for those beasts trembling on top of her as though attacked by Saint Vitus's dance and had endured her trial praying to God that they would not leave her pregnant. But the fourth time she had felt a rush of pity for the youngster lying on top of her, who, after having beaten her to make her submit to him, was now stammering tender words in her ear. To punish herself for this compassion she had cropped her hair off and transformed herself into as grotesque a monster as the ones exhibited by the Gypsy's Circus in the towns of the *sertão.*

On reaching the top of the hill, from which she saw at last the reward for all her effort – the series of gray-and-white stone steps of the Via Sacra, winding between the conical roofs of the chapels up to the Calvary at the top, to which great throngs of people from all over the state of Bahia flocked each Holy Week, and down below, at the foot of the mountain, the little houses of Monte Santo crowded around a public square with two bushy-topped tamarind trees in which there were shadows that moved – Maria Quadrado fell face downward on the ground and kissed the earth. There it was, surrounded by a plain covered with a new growth of vegetation where herds of goats were grazing: the longed-for place whose name had spurred her on to undertake the journey and had helped her to endure fatigue, hunger, cold, heat, repeated rape. Kissing the planks that she herself had nailed together for her cross, the woman thanked God in a confused rush of words for having enabled her to fulfill her vow. And taking up the cross once more, she trotted toward Monte Santo like an animal whose sense of smell tells it that its prey or its lair is close at hand.

She entered the town just as people were waking up, and from door to door, from window to window, she sowed curiosity in her wake. Amused faces, pitying faces poked out to look at her – squat, filthy, ugly, long-suffering – and as she started up the Rua dos Santos Passos, built above the ravine where the town's garbage was burned and the town's pigs were rooting about, the beginning of the Via Sacra, a huge procession followed her. She began to climb the mountain on her knees, surrounded by muleteers who had left off their work, by cobblers and bakers, by a swarm of little kids, by devout women who had torn themselves away from their morning novena. The townspeople, who, as she began the climb, regarded her as simply an odd sort, saw her make her way painfully upward, carrying the cross that must have weighed as much as she did, refusing to let anyone help her, and they saw her halt to pray in each of the twenty-four chapels and kiss with eyes full of love the feet of the statues in all the vaulted niches in the rock face, and they saw her hold up for hour after hour without eating a single mouthful or drinking a single drop of water, and by nightfall they revered her as a true saint. Maria Quadrado reached the mountaintop – a world apart, where it was always cold and orchids grew between the bluish stones – and still had enough remaining strength to thank God for her blessed lot before fainting dead away.

Many inhabitants of Monte Santo, whose proverbial hospitality had not been diminished by the periodic invasion of pilgrims, offered Maria Quadrado lodgings. But she installed herself in a cave, halfway up the Via Sacra, where previously only birds and rodents had slept. It was a small hollow, with a ceiling so low that she was unable to stand upright in it, walls so damp from the dripping water that they were covered with moss, and a powdery sandstone floor that made her sneeze. The townspeople thought that this place would very soon be the end of her. But the force of will that had enabled Maria Quadrado to walk for three months with a heavy cross on her back also enabled her to live in that inhospitable grotto for all the years that she remained in Monte Santo.

Maria Quadrado's cave became a shrine, and along with the Calvary, the place most frequently visited by pilgrims. As the months went by, she began little by little to decorate it. She made different-colored paints from the juice of plants, mineral powders, and the blood of cochineal insects (used by tailors to dye garments). Against a blue background meant to represent the firmament, she painted the objects associated with Christ's Passion: the nails driven into the palms of His hands and His feet; the cross He bore on His back and on which He died; the crown of thorns that pierced His temples; the tunic of His martyrdom; the centurion's lance that penetrated His flesh; the hammer with which the nails were driven in; the lash that whipped Him; the sponge from which He drank the sour wine; the dice with which the impious soldiers played at His feet; and the purse with the pieces of silver that Judas was given as payment for His betrayal. She also painted the star that guided the Three Kings and the shepherds to Bethlehem and a Sacred Heart transpierced by a sword. And she made an altar and a cupboard to store veils for the use of the penitents and give them a place to hang ex-votos. She slept at the foot of the altar on a straw pallet.

Her goodness and devotion made her beloved of the townspeople of Monte Santo, who adopted her as though she had lived there all her life. Soon children began to call her godmother and dogs commenced to allow her to enter houses and yards without barking at her. Her life was devoted to God and serving others. She spent hours at the bedside of the sick, bathing their foreheads with water and praying for them. She helped midwives care for women in childbirth and watched over the little ones of neighbor women obliged to be absent from their homes. She willingly offered to do the most thankless tasks, such as aiding old people too helpless to attend to calls of nature by themselves. Girls of marriageable age asked her advice about their suitors, and boys courting a girl begged her to intercede with their sweetheart's parents if the latter were reluctant to consent to the marriage. She reconciled estranged couples, and women whose husbands tried to beat them because they were lazy or to kill them because they'd committed adultery hastened to take shelter in her cave, knowing that with her as their protectress no man in Monte Santo would dare lay a finger on them. She ate whatever was given her out of charity, so little that the food left in her grotto by the faithful was always more than enough, and each afternoon found her sharing what was left over with the poor. She also divided among them the clothes that had been given her, and in fair weather and foul no one ever saw her wearing anything but the esparto-cloth sack full of holes in which she had arrived.

Her relationship, on the other hand, with the missionaries of the Massacará mission, who came to Monte Santo to celebrate Mass in the Church of the Sacred Heart of Jesus, was not a warm one. They kept warning people against the wrong sort of religiosity, the sort that escaped the control of the Church, pointing out as an example the Pedras Encantadas, in the region of As Flores, in Pernambuco, where the heretic João Ferreira and a group of proselytes had sprinkled the aforementioned stones with the blood of dozens of persons (among them hers), believing that in this way they would break the spell that had been cast upon King Dom Sebastião, a ruler of Portugal who had mysteriously disappeared while on crusade against the Moors, who would bring back to life those who had met their death in the final battle and lead their way to heaven. To the missionaries of Massacará, Maria Quadrado represented a borderline case, verging on heresy. She for her part knelt as the missionaries passed and kissed their hands and asked for their blessing, but she was not known to have ever maintained with these Fathers in bell-shaped habits, with long beards and a manner of speaking often difficult to understand, the sort of intimate and heartfelt ties that united her and the people of Monte Santo.

In their sermons, the missionaries also put the faithful on their guard against wolves who stole into the fold in sheep's clothing so as to devour the entire flock: that is to say, those false prophets that Monte Santo attracted as honey attracts flies. They appeared in its narrow streets dressed in sheepskins like John the Baptist or in tunics that imitated habits, climbed up to the Calvary, and immediately launched into fiery and incomprehensible sermons. They were a great source of entertainment for the entire town, exactly like the itinerant storytellers or Pedrim the Giant, the Bearded Lady, or the Man without Bones of the Gypsy's Circus. But Maria Quadrado never went near the groups of disciples that formed about these outlandish preachers.

For that reason, the townspeople were surprised one day to see Maria Quadrado heading for the cemetery, around which a group of volunteers had begun to build a wall, having been impelled to do so by the exhortations of a dark-skinned, long-haired man dressed in dark purple who, arriving in town that morning with a group of disciples (among whom there was a creature, half human and half animal, that galloped along on all fours), had reproved them for not even taking the trouble to erect a wall around the ground in which their dead had been laid to rest. Was it not fitting and proper that death, which permitted man to see the face of God, should be venerated? Maria Quadrado silently joined the people who were collecting stones and piling them up in a sinuous line enclosing the little crosses scorched by the sun, and began to help. She worked shoulder to shoulder with them till sunset. Then she lingered on in the main square beneath the tamarinds, along with the group that gathered to listen to the dark-skinned man. Although he mentioned God and said that it was important for the salvation of a person's soul that that person destroy his or her own will – a poison that gave everyone the illusion of being a little god who was superior to the other gods round about him – and put in its place the will of the Third Person, the one that built, the one that labored, the Industrious Ant, and things of that sort, he spoke of these things in clear language, every word of which they understood. His talk, while religious and profound, seemed like one of those pleasant after-dinner chats that families had together outside in the street as they enjoyed the evening breeze. Maria Quadrado stayed on in the square, all curled up in a ball, listening to the Counselor, not asking him anything, not taking her eyes off him. When the hour grew late and the townspeople still there in the square offered the stranger a roof over his head for his night's rest, she, too, spoke up – everyone turned round to look at her – and timidly offered him her cave. Without hesitating, the gaunt man followed her up the mountainside.

For as long as the Counselor remained in Monte Santo, giving counsel and working – he cleaned and restored all the chapels on the mountain, built a wall of stones along either side of the Via Sacra – he slept in Maria Quadrado's cave. Afterward people said that he didn't sleep, and that she didn't either, that they spent the night talking of things of the spirit at the foot of the little multicolored altar, while others claimed that he slept on the straw pallet as she watched over his sleep. In any event, the truth was that Maria Quadrado never left his side for a moment, hauling stones with him in the daytime and listening to him with wide-open eyes at night. Nonetheless, the whole town was surprised the morning it discovered that the Counselor had left Monte Santo and that Maria Quadrado had joined his followers and gone off with him.

In a square in the upper town of Bahia there is an old stone building, decorated with black-and-white seashells and surrounded, as prisons are, by thick yellow walls. As some of my readers may already have surmised, it is a fortress of obscurantism: the Monastery of Our Lady of Mercy. A monastery of Capuchins, one of those orders famous for the subjugation of the spirit that they practice and for their missionary zeal. Why do I speak to you of a place which in the eyes of any libertarian symbolizes what is odious? In order to inform you of what I learned when I spent the entire afternoon inside it two days ago.

I did not go there to explore the terrain with a view to bringing to it one of those pedagogically violent messages that in the opinion of many comrades it is indispensable that we deliver to military barracks, convents, and all bastions of exploitation and superstition in general in order to break down the taboos with which these institutions are customarily surrounded in the minds of workers and demonstrate to them that they are vulnerable. (Do you remember the groups in Barcelona who advocated attacking convents so as to restore to the nuns, by impregnating them, their status as women that their sequestration had robbed them of?) I went to this monastery to converse with a certain Brother João Evangelista de Monte Marciano, for as fate would have it, I had chanced to read a curious Account of which he was the author.

A patient of Dr. José Batista de Sá Oliveira, whose book on craniometry I have already spoken to you of, and with whom I collaborate on occasion, he is a relative of the most powerful man in these parts: the Baron de Canabrava. As Dr. Oliveira was purging him for tapeworm, the man to whom I refer, Lélis Piedades, a barrister, recounted how a hacienda belonging to the baron has been occupied for nearly two years now by madmen who have turned it into a no-man's-land. Lélis Piedades is the one entrusted with the responsibility of pleading before the courts for the return of the hacienda to the baron, in the name of the right of ownership, which the aforementioned baron naturally feels it his duty to defend with fervor. The fact that a group of the exploited has appropriated the property of an aristocrat is always pleasing news to the ears of a revolutionary, even when the poor in question are – as the barrister maintained while seated on the basin, pushing hard to expel the tapeworm already done in by chemistry – religious fanatics. But what made me prick up my ears was hearing all of a sudden that they reject civil marriage and practice something which Lélis Piedades calls 'promiscuity,' but which anyone intimately acquainted with the ways of society will recognize as the institution of free love. 'With proof of corruption such as that, the authorities will necessarily be obliged to expel the fanatics from the property.' The pettifogger's proof consisted of the aforementioned Account, which he had obtained through collusion with the Church, to which he also lends his services. Brother João Evangelista de Monte Marciano had been sent to the hacienda by the Archbishop of Bahia, who had received depositions denouncing the heretical practices of its occupiers. The monk went to see what was going on in Canudos and returned very shortly, frightened and incensed by what he had seen.

His Account indicates as much, and there can be no doubt that for the Capuchin the experience was a bitter one. For a liberated mind what his Account suggests between its turgidly ecclesiastical lines is exciting. The instinct for freedom, which a class society stifles by way of those machines to crush what is inborn – families, schools, religion, and the state – guides the footsteps of these men who give every appearance of having rebelled, among other things, against that institution whose aim is to bridle feelings and desires. Their avowed reason being the refusal to obey the law permitting civil marriages, promulgated in Brazil following the fall of the Empire, the people of Canudos have taken to forming unions freely and to dissolving them freely, so long as both the man and the woman agree to do so, and to disregarding the paternity of offspring conceived in their mothers' wombs, since their leader or guide – whom they call the Counselor – has taught them that all children are legitimate by the mere fact of having been born. Is there not something in all of this that sounds familiar to you? Is it not as though certain fundamental ideas of our revolution were being put into practice in Canudos? Free love, free paternity, the disappearance of the infamous line that is drawn between legitimate and illegitimate offspring, the conviction that man inherits neither dignity nor ignominy. Overcoming a natural repugnance, was I right or not to go visit this Capuchin friar?

It was the Baron de Canabrava's petty lawyer himself who arranged for the interview, in the belief that I have been interested for years in the subject of religious superstition (this, as a matter of fact, is true). It took place in the refectory of the monastery, a room whose walls were covered with paintings of saints and martyrs, adjoining a small tiled cloister, with a cistern to which hooded monks in brown habits girdled with white cords came every so often to draw pails of water. The monk forgave all my questions and turned out to be very talkative on discovering that we were able to converse in Italian, his native tongue. A southerner who is still young, short-statured, plump, thick-bearded, he has a very broad forehead that betrays that he is a daydreamer, and the hollows at his temples and the thickness of his neck a nature that is spiteful, petty, and touchy. And, in point of fact, in the course of the conversation I noted that he is filled with hatred against Canudos because of the failure of the mission that took him there and because of the fear that he no doubt experienced there among the 'heretics.' But, once allowances are made for the exaggeration and rancor evident in his testimony, the residuum of truth in it is, as you will see, most impressive.

What I heard from his lips would provide material for many issues of *L'Etincelle de la révolte.* The heart of the matter is that the interview confirmed my suspicions that in Canudos humble and inexperienced people, by the sheer powers of instinct and imagination, are carrying out in practice many of the things that we European revolutionaries know are necessary in order to institute a reign of justice on this earth. Judge for yourselves. Brother João Evangelista spent just one week in Canudos, accompanied by two men of the cloth: another Capuchin from Bahia and the parish priest of a town neighboring Canudos, a certain Dom Joaquim, whom, let me say in passing, Brother João detests (he accuses him of being a toper, of being unchaste, and of arousing people's sympathies for outlaws). Before arriving in Canudos – after an arduous journey of eighteen days – they noted 'signs of insubordination and anarchy,' since no guide was willing to take them there and when they were three leagues away from the hacienda they met up with a patrol of men with long-barreled muskets and machetes who confronted them in a hostile mood and allowed them to pass thanks only to the intervention of Dom Joaquim, whom they knew. In Canudos they encountered a multitude of emaciated, cadaverous creatures, crowded one on top of the other in huts of mud and straw and armed to the teeth 'so as to protect the Counselor, whom the authorities have already tried to kill.' The frightened words of the Capuchin as he recalled his impression on seeing so many weapons are still ringing in my ears. 'They put them down neither to eat nor to pray, for they are proud of being armed with blunderbusses, carbines, pistols, knives, and cartridge belts, as though they were about to wage war.' (I was unable to make him see the light, though I explained to him that they had found it necessary to wage this war ever since they had occupied the baron's land by force.) He assured me that among those men were criminals famous for their outrages, and mentioned one of them in particular, Satan João, 'known far and wide for his cruelty,' who had come to live in Canudos with his band of outlaws and was one of the Counselor's lieutenants. Brother João Evangelista tells of having rebuked the Counselor in these words: 'Why are criminals allowed in Canudos if it is true that you are Christians as you claim?' The answer: 'To make good men of them. If they have robbed or killed, it was because of the poverty they were living in. They feel that they are part of the human family here and are grateful; they will do anything to redeem themselves. If we refused to take them in, they would commit yet more crimes. Our understanding of charity is that practiced by Christ.' These words, comrades, are in complete accordance with the philosophy of freedom. You know full well that the brigand is a rebel in the natural state, an unwitting revolutionary, and you well remember that in the dramatic days of the Commune many brothers who were looked upon as criminals, who had passed through the jails of the bourgeoisie, were in the vanguard of the fight, shoulder to shoulder with the workers, giving proof of their heroism and of their generosity of spirit.

A significant fact: the people of Canudos call themselves *jagunços*, a word that means rebels. Despite his travels as a missionary in the backlands, the monk did not recognize these barefoot women or these men, once so circumspect and humble, as being people with a mission from the Church and God. 'They are irreconcilable enemies of society. They are agitated, all excited. They shout, they interrupt each other in order to utter what strikes the ears of a Christian as the most egregious nonsense, doctrines that subvert law and order, morality, and faith. They maintain, for instance, that anyone who wishes to save his soul must go to Canudos, since the rest of the world has fallen into the hands of the Antichrist.' And do you know what these *jagunços* mean by the Antichrist? The Republic! Yes, comrades, the Republic. They regard it as responsible for every evil that exists, some of which are no doubt abstract, but also for real and concrete ones such as hunger and income taxes. Brother João Evangelista de Monte Marciano could not believe the things he heard. I doubt that he or his order or the Church in general is very enthusiastic about the new regime in Brazil, since, as I wrote you in a previous letter, the Republic, which is aswarm with Freemasons, has meant a weakening of the Church. But that is a far cry from regarding it as the Antichrist! Thinking that he would frighten me or arouse my indignation, the Capuchin went on to say things that were music to my ears: 'They're a politico-religious sect that is up in arms against the constitutional government of the country; they have set themselves up as a state within a state, since they do not accept the laws of the Republic or recognize its authorities or allow its money to circulate there.' His intellectual blindness kept him from understanding that these brothers, with an infallible instinct, have chosen to rebel against the born enemy of freedom: power. And what is the power that oppresses them, that denies them the right to land, to culture, to equality? Isn't it the Republic? And the fact that they are armed to fight against it is proof that they have also hit upon the right method, the sole method the exploited have to break their chains: violence.

But this is not all. Prepare yourselves for something even more surprising. Brother João Evangelista assures me that, along with communal sex, Canudos has instituted the regime of communal property: everything belongs to everyone. The Counselor is said to have convinced the *jagunços* that it is a sin – mark my words well – to consider any movables or semimovables as belonging to any one individual. The dwellings, the crop lands, the domestic animals belong to the community: they are everyone's and no one's. The Counselor has persuaded them that the more possessions a person has, the fewer possibilities he has of being among those who will find favor on Judgment Day. It is as though he were putting our ideas into practice, hiding them behind the façade of religion for a tactical reason, namely the need to take into account the cultural level of his humble followers. Is it not remarkable that in the remote reaches of Brazil a group of insurgents is forming a society in which marriage and money have been done away with, in which collective ownership has replaced private ownership?

This idea was whirling round and round in my brain as Brother João Evangelista de Monte Marciano was telling me that, after preaching for seven days in Canudos, amid an atmosphere of silent hostility, he found himself being called a Freemason and a Protestant for urging the *jagunços* to return to their villages, and that as he pleaded with them to submit to the Republic, their passions became so inflamed that he was obliged to flee for his life from Canudos. 'The Church has lost its authority there on account of a crazy man who spends his time making the whole mob work all day long building a stone temple.' I was unable to share his consternation and instead felt only happiness and sympathy for those men, thanks to whom, it would appear, there is being reborn from its ashes, in the backlands of Brazil, the Idea that the forces of reaction believe they have drowned in the blood of revolutions defeated in Europe. Till my next letter or never.

IV

When Lélis Piedades, the Baron de Canabrava's barrister, officially notified the Tribunal of Salvador that the hacienda of Canudos had been invaded by thugs, the Counselor had been there for three months. The news soon spread throughout the *sertão*: the saint who had wandered the length and breadth of the land for a quarter of a century had put down roots in that place surrounded by stony hills called Canudos, after the pipes made of *canudos* – segments of sugarcane stalk – that the people who lived there used to smoke. The place was known to cowhands, for they often stopped with their cattle for the night on the banks of the Vaza-Barris. In the following weeks and months groups of the curious, of sinners, of the sick, of vagrants, of fugitives from justice, come from the North, the South, the East, and the West, were seen heading for Canudos with the presentiment or the hope that they would there find forgiveness, refuge, health, happiness.

On the morning after he and his followers arrived, the Counselor began to build a Temple, which, he said, would be made all of stone, with two very tall towers, and would be dedicated to the Blessed Jesus. He decided that it would be erected opposite the old Church of Santo Antônio, the chapel of the hacienda. 'Let the rich raise their hands,' he said, preaching by the light of a bonfire in the town going up. 'I raise mine. Because I am a son of God, who has given me an immortal soul that can earn heaven, the only true wealth, for itself. I raise them because the Father has made me poor in this life so that I may be rich in the next. Let the rich raise their hands!' In the shadows full of sparks a forest of upraised arms emerged then from amid the rags and the leather and the threadbare cotton blouses. They prayed before and after he gave his counsel and held processions amid the half-finished dwellings and the shelters made of bits of cloth and planks where they slept, and in the back-country night they could be heard shouting, Long live the Virgin and the Blessed

Jesus and death to the Can and the Antichrist. A man from Mirandela, who made fireworks and set them off at fairs – Antônio the Pyrotechnist – was one of the first pilgrims to arrive, and from that time on, whenever there were processions in Canudos, set pieces were ignited and skyrockets burst overhead.

The Counselor directed the work on the Temple, with the advice and assistance of a master mason who had helped him restore many chapels and build the Church of the Blessed Jesus in Crisópolis from the ground up, and designated the penitents who would go out to quarry stones, sift sand, and haul timber. In the early evening, after a frugal meal – if he was not fasting – consisting of a crust of bread, a piece of fruit, a mouthful of boiled manioc, and a few sips of water, the Counselor welcomed the newcomers, exhorted the others to be hospitable, and after the Credo, the Our Father, and the Ave Marias, his eloquent voice preached austerity, mortification, abstinence to all of them and shared visions with them that resembled the stories recounted by the *cantadores* who wandered over the countryside reciting their traditional tales. The end was near – it could be seen as clearly as Canudos from the heights of A Favela. The Republic would keep on sending hordes with uniforms and rifles to try to capture him, in order to keep him from talking to the needy, but no matter how much blood he might cause to flow, the Dog would not bite Jesus. There would be a flood and then an earthquake. An eclipse would plunge the world into such total darkness that everything would have to be done by touch, as blind people do, while in the distance the battle resounded. Thousands would die of panic. But when the mists dispersed, one bright clear dawn, the men and women would see the army of Dom Sebastião all round them on the hills and slopes of Canudos. The great King would have defeated the Can's bands, would have cleansed the world for the Lord. They would see Dom Sebastião, with his shining armor and his sword; they would see his kindly, adolescent face, he would smile at them from astride his mount with diamond-studded gold trappings, and they would see him ride off, his mission of redemption fulfilled, to return with his army to the bottom of the sea.

The tanners, the sharecroppers, the healers, the peddlers, the laundresses, the midwives, and the beggar women who had reached Canudos after many days and nights of journeying, with their worldly goods in a canvas-covered cart or on the back of a burro, and who were there now, squatting in the dark, listening and wanting to believe, felt their eyes grow damp. They prayed and sang with the same conviction as the Counselor's earliest followers; those who did not know them very soon learned the prayers, the hymns, the truths. Antônio Vilanova, the storekeeper of Canudos, was one of the ones most eager to learn; at night he took long walks along the banks of the river or past the newly sown fields with the Little Blessed One, who patiently explained the commandments and prohibitions of religion, which Antônio then taught to his brother Honório, his wife Antônia, his sister-in-law Assunção, and the children of the two couples.

There was no shortage of food. They had grain, vegetables, meat, and since there was water in the Vaza-Barris they could plant crops. Those who arrived brought provisions with them and other towns often sent them poultry, rabbits, pigs, feed, goats. The Counselor asked Antônio Vilanova to store the food and see to it that it was distributed fairly among the destitute. Without specific directives, but in accordance with the Counselor's teachings, life in Canudos was gradually becoming organized, though not without snags. The Little Blessed One took charge of instructing the pilgrims who arrived and receiving their donations, provided they were not donations of money. If they wanted to donate reis of the Republic, they were obliged to go to Cumbe or Juazeiro, escorted by Abbot João or Pajeú, who knew how to fight and could protect them, to spend them on things for the Temple: shovels, stonecutters, hammers, plumb lines, high-quality timber, statues of saints, and crucifixes. Mother Maria Quadrado placed in a glass case the rings, earrings, brooches, necklaces, combs, old coins, or simple clay or bone ornaments that the pilgrims offered, and this treasure was exhibited in the Church of Santo Antônio each time that Father Joaquim, from Cumbe, or another parish priest from the region, came to say Mass, confess, baptize, and marry people in Canudos. These were always times for celebration. Two fugitives from justice, Big João and Pedrão, the strongest men in Canudos, bossed the gangs that hauled stones for the Temple from nearby quarries. Catarina, Abbot João's wife, and Alexandrinha Correa, a woman from Cumbe who, it was said, had worked miracles, prepared the food for the construction workers. Life was far from being perfect, with no complications. Even though the Counselor preached against gambling, tobacco, and alcohol, there were those who gambled, smoked, and drank cane brandy, and when Canudos began to grow, there were fights over women, thefts, drinking bouts, and even knifings. But these things were much less of a problem here than elsewhere and happened on the periphery of the active, fraternal, fervent, ascetic center constituted by the Counselor and his disciples.

The Counselor had not forbidden the womenfolk to adorn themselves, but he said countless times that any woman who cared a great deal about her body might well neglect to care for her soul, and that, as with Lucifer, a beautiful outward appearance might well hide a filthy and loathsome spirit: the colors of the dresses of young women and old alike gradually became more and more drab; little by little the hemlines reached ankle length, the necklines climbed higher and higher, and they became looser and looser, so that finally they looked like nuns' habits. Along with low necklines, adornments and even ribbons to tie back their hair disappeared; the women now wore it loose or hidden beneath large kerchiefs. On occasion there was trouble involving 'the magdalenes,' those lost women who, despite having come to Canudos at the cost of many sacrifices and having kissed the Counselor's feet begging for forgiveness, were harassed by intolerant women who wanted to make them wear combs of thorns as proof that they had repented.

But, in general, life was peaceful and a spirit of collaboration reigned among the inhabitants. One source of problems was the ban against money of the Republic: anyone caught using it for any transaction had all of it he possessed taken away from him by the Counselor's men, who then forced him to leave Canudos. Trade was carried on with coins bearing the effigy of the Emperor Dom Pedro or of his daughter, Princess Isabel, but since they were scarce the bartering of products and services became the general rule. Raw brown sugar was exchanged for rope sandals, chickens for herb cures, manioc flour for horseshoes, roof tiles for lengths of cloth, hammocks for machetes, and work, in the fields, in dwellings, in animal pens, was repaid with work. No one charged for the time and labor spent for the Blessed Jesus. Besides the Temple, dwellings were constructed that later came to be known as the Health Houses, where lodging, food, and care began to be given to the sick, to old people, and to orphaned children. Maria Quadrado was in charge of this task at first, but once the Sanctuary was built – a little two-room mud hut with a straw roof – so that the Counselor could have just a few hours' respite from the pilgrims who hounded him night and day, and the Mother of Men devoted all her time to him, the Health Houses were run by the Sardelinha sisters, Antônia and Assunção, the wives of the Vilanova brothers. There were quarrels over the tillable plots of land along the Vaza-Barris, which were gradually occupied by the pilgrims who settled in Canudos and which others disputed their right to. Antônio Vilanova, the storekeeper, settled all such questions. By order of the Counselor, it was he who gave out parcels of land for newcomers to build their dwellings on and set aside land for pens for the animals that believers sent or brought as gifts, and he who acted as judge when quarrels over goods and property arose. There were not very many such quarrels, in fact, since people who came to Canudos had not been drawn there by greed or by the idea of material prosperity. The life of the community was devoted to spiritual activities: prayers, funerals, fasts, processions, the building of the Temple of the Blessed Jesus, and above all the evening counsels that often lasted until far into the night. During those everything else in Canudos came to a halt.

*

To publicize the fiesta it has organized, the Progressivist Republican Party has plastered the walls of Queimadas with posters reading A UNITED BRAZIL, A STRONG NATION and with the name of Epaminondas Gonçalves. But in his room in the Our Lady of Grace boarding house, Galileo Gall is not thinking of the political celebration taking place outside with great pomp and ceremony in the stifling heat of midday, but of the contradictory aptitudes that he has discovered in Rufino. 'It's a most unusual combination,' he thinks. Orientation and Concentration are closely akin, naturally, and it would be quite usual to find them in someone who spends his life wandering all over this immense region, guiding travelers, hunters, convoys, serving as a courier, or tracking down lost cattle. But what about Imaginativeness? How to account for the propensity for fantasy, delirium, unreality, typical of artists and impractical people, in an individual in whom everything points to the materialist, to the man with his feet on the ground, to the pragmatist? Nonetheless, that is what his bones indicate: Orientivity and Concentrativity, Imaginativeness. Galileo Gall discovered it almost the very first moment that he was able to palpate the guide. He thinks: 'It's an absurd, incompatible combination. How can a person be at one and the same time the soul of modesty and an exhibitionist, miserly and prodigal?'

He is leaning over a pail washing his face, between partition walls covered with graffiti, newspaper clippings with pictures of an opera performance, and a broken mirror. Coffee-colored cockroaches appear and disappear through the cracks in the floor and there is a little petrified lizard on the ceiling. The only furniture is a broken-down bed with no sheets. The festive atmosphere enters the room through a latticed window: voices amplified by a loudspeaker, clashes of cymbals, drumrolls, and the jabbering of kids flying kites. Someone is alternating attacks on the Bahia Autonomist Party, Governor Luiz Viana, the Baron de Canabrava, and praise for Epaminondas Gonçalves and the Progressivist Republican Party.

Galileo Gall goes on washing himself, indifferent to the hubbub outside. Once he has finished, he dries his face with his shirt and collapses on the bed, face up, with one arm under his head for a pillow. He looks at the cockroaches, the lizard. He thinks: 'Silence against impatience.' He has been in Queimadas for eight days now, and although he is a man who knows how to wait, he has begun to feel a certain anxiety: that is what has led him to ask Rufino to let him palpate his head. It was not easy to talk him into it, for the guide is a mistrustful sort and Gall remembers that he could feel as he palpated him how tense the man was, all ready to leap on him. They have seen each other every day, understand each other without difficulty now, and to pass the time as he is waiting, Galileo has studied his behavior, taking notes on him: 'He reads the sky, the trees, the earth, as though they were a book; he is a man of simple, inflexible ideas, with a strict code of honor and a morality whose source has been his commerce with nature and with men, not book learning, since he does not know how to read, or religion, since he does not appear to be a very firm believer.' All of this coincides with what his fingers have felt, except for the Imaginativeness. In what way does it manifest itself, why has he failed to notice any of its signs in Rufino in these eight days, either while he was making a deal with him to guide him to Canudos, or in Rufino's shack on the outskirts of town, or in the railway station having a cool drink together, or walking from one tannery to another along the banks of the Itapicuru? In Jurema, the guide's wife, on the other hand, this pernicious, anti-scientific inclination – to leave the domain of experience to immerse oneself in phantasmagoria, in daydreaming – is obvious. For despite the fact that she is very reserved in his presence, Galileo has heard Jurema tell the story of the wooden statue of St. Anthony that is on the main altar of the church in Queimadas. 'It was found in a cave, years ago, and taken to the church. The next day it disappeared and turned up again in the grotto. It was tied to the altar so that it wouldn't make its escape, but it managed nonetheless to go back to the cave. And things went on like that, with the statue going back and forth, till a Holy Mission with four Capuchin Fathers and the archbishop came to Queimadas, dedicated the church to St. Anthony, and renamed the town Santo Antônio das Queimadas in honor of the saint. It was only then that the image stayed quietly on the altar, where people today light candles to it.' Galileo Gall remembers that when he asked Rufino if he believed the story that his wife had told, the tracker shrugged and smiled skeptically. Jurema, however, believed it. Galileo would have liked to palpate her head too, but he didn't even try to do so; he is certain that the mere idea of a stranger touching his wife's head must be inconceivable to Rufino. Yes, Rufino is beyond question a suspicious man. It has been hard work getting him to agree to take him to Canudos. He has haggled over the price, raised objections, hesitated, and though he has finally given in, Galileo has noted that he is ill at ease when he talks to him about the Counselor and the *jagunços*.

Without realizing it, his attention has wandered from Rufino to the voice coming from outside: 'Regional autonomy and decentralization are pretexts being used by Governor Viana, the Baron de Canabrava, and their henchmen in order to preserve their privileges and keep Bahia from becoming as modern as the other states of Brazil. Who are the Autonomists? Monarchists lying in ambush who, if it weren't for us, would revive the corrupt Empire and kill the Republic! But Epaminondas Gonçalves's Progressivist Republican Party will keep them from doing so . . .' The man speaking now is not the same one as before, this one is clearer, Galileo understands everything he says, and he even seems to have some idea in mind, whereas his predecessor merely shrieked and howled. Should he go take a look out the window? No, he doesn't move from the bed; he is certain the spectacle is still the same: knots of curious bystanders wandering from one food and drink stand to another, listening to the *cantadores* reciting stories, or gathering round the man on stilts who is telling fortunes, and from time to time deigning to stop for a moment to gawk but not to listen in front of the small platform from which the Progressivist Republican Party is churning out its propaganda, protected by thugs with shotguns. 'They're wise to be so indifferent,' Galileo Gall thinks. What good is it for the people of Queimadas to know that the Baron de Canabrava's Autonomist Party is against the centralist system of the Republican Party and to know that this latter is combatting the decentralism and the federalism advocated by its adversary? Do the rhetorical quarrels of bourgeois political parties have anything to do with the interests of the humble and downtrodden? They are right to enjoy the festivities and pay no attention to what the politicos on the platform are saying. The evening before, Galileo has detected a certain excitement in Queimadas, not because of the festival organized by the Progressivist Republican Party but because people were wondering whether the Baron de Canabrava's Autonomist Party would send thugs to wreck their enemies' spectacle and there would be shooting, as had happened at other times in the past. It is midmorning now, this hasn't happened and no doubt will not happen. Why would they bother to break up a meeting so sadly lacking popular support? The thought occurs to Gall that the fiestas organized by the Autonomists must be exactly like the one taking place outside his window. No, this is not where the real politics of Bahia, of Brazil, is taking place. He thinks: 'It is taking place up there, among those who are not even aware that they are the real politicians of this country.' Will he have to wait much longer? Galileo Gall sits down on the bed. He murmurs: 'Science against impatience.' He opens the small valise lying on the floor, pushes aside clothing, a revolver, removes the little book in which he has taken notes on the tanneries of Queimadas, where he has idled away a few hours in these last eight days, and leafs through what he has written: 'Brick buildings, roofs of round tiles, rough-hewn columns. Scattered about everywhere, bundles of *angico* bark, scored through with the aid of a hammer and a knife. They toss the *angico* into tanks full of river water. After removing the hair from the hides they submerge them in the tanks and leave them to soak for eight days or so, the time required to tan them. The bark of the tree called *angico* gives off tannin, the substance that tans them. They then hang the hides in the shade till they dry, and scrape them with a knife to remove any residue left on them. They treat in this way the hides of cattle, sheep, goats, rabbits, deer, foxes, and jaguars. *Angico* is blood-red, with a strong odor. The tanneries are primitive family enterprises in which the father, the mother, the sons, and close relatives work. Rawhide is the principal wealth of Queimadas.' He puts the little notebook back in the valise. The tanners were friendly, explained to him how they went about their work. Why is it that they are so reluctant to talk about Canudos? Do they mistrust someone whose Portuguese they find it difficult to understand? He knows that Canudos and the Counselor are the main topic of conversation in Queimadas. Despite all his efforts, however, he has not been able to discuss the subject with anyone, not even Rufino and Jurema. In the tanneries, in the railway station, in the Our Lady of Grace boarding house, in the public square of Queimadas, the moment he has brought the subject up he has seen the same wary look in everyone's eyes, the same silence has fallen, or the same evasive answers been offered. 'They're on their guard. They're mistrustful,' he thinks. He thinks: 'They know what they're doing. They're canny.'

He digs about among his clothes and the revolver once again and takes out the only book in the little valise. It is an old, dog-eared copy, whose vellum binding has turned dark, so that the name of Pierre Joseph Proudhon is scarcely legible now, but whose title, *Système des contradictions*, is still clear, as is the name of the city where it was printed: Lyons. Distracted by the hubbub of the fiesta and above all by his treacherous impatience, he does not manage to concentrate his mind for long on his reading. Clenching his teeth, he then forces himself to reflect on objective things. A man who is not interested in general problems or ideas lives cloistered in Particularity, which can be recognized by the curvature of two protruding, almost sharp-pointed little bones behind his ears. Did he feel them on Rufino's head? Does Imaginativeness, perhaps, manifest itself in the strange sense of honor, in what might be called the ethical imagination, of the man who is about to take him to Canudos?

His first memories, which were to become the best ones and the ones that came back most readily as well, were neither of his mother, who abandoned him to run after a sergeant in the National Guard who passed through Custódia at the head of a flying brigade that was chasing *cangaceiros*, nor of his father, whom he never knew, nor of the aunt and uncle who took him in and brought him up – Zé Faustino and Dona Angela – nor of the thirty-some huts and sun-baked streets of Custódia, but of the wandering minstrels. They came to town every so often, to enliven wedding parties, or heading for the roundup-time fiesta at a hacienda or the festival with which a town celebrated its patron saint's day, and for a few slugs of cane brandy and a plate of jerky and *farofa* – manioc flour toasted in olive oil – they told the stories of Olivier, of the Princess Maguelone, of Charlemagne and the Twelve Peers of France. João listened to them open-eyed, his lips moving with the *cantadores'*. Afterward he had splendid dreams resounding with the clashing of lances of the knights doing battle to save Christianity from the pagan hordes.

But the story that came to be the flesh of his flesh was that of Robert the Devil, the son of the Duke of Normandy who, after committing all manner of evil deeds, repented and went about on all fours, barking instead of speaking, and sleeping with the animals, until, having been granted the mercy of the Blessed Jesus, he saved the Emperor from attack by the Moors and married the Queen of Brazil. The youngster insisted that the *cantadores* tell it without omitting a single detail: how, in his days of wickedness, Robert the Devil had plunged his knife with the curved blade into countless throats of damsels and hermits simply for the pleasure of seeing them suffer, and how, in his days as a servant of God, he wandered far and wide in search of his victims' kin, kissing their feet when he found them and begging them to torture him. The townspeople of Custódia thought that João would one day be a backlands minstrel, going from town to town with his guitar on his shoulder, bringing messages and making people happy with his songs and tales.

João helped Zé Faustino in his store, which supplied the whole countryside round about with cloth, grain, things to drink, farm tools, sweets, and trinkets. Zé Faustino traveled about a great deal, taking merchandise to the haciendas or going to the city to buy it, and in his absence Dona Angela minded the store, a hut of kneaded mud with a poultry yard. The woman had made her nephew the object of all the affection that she was unable to give the children she had not had. She had made João promise that he would take her to Salvador someday so that she might throw herself at the feet of the miraculous statue of O Senhor de Bonfim, of whom she had a collection of colored prints pinned above the head of her bed.

As much as drought and epidemics, the inhabitants of Custódia feared two other calamities that impoverished the town: *cangaceiros* and flying brigades of the National Guard. In the beginning the former had been bands gotten together from among their peons and kinfolk by the 'colonels' who owned haciendas, to settle by force the quarrels that broke out among them over property boundaries, water rights, and grazing lands, or over conflicting political ambitions, but as time went by, many of these bands armed with blunderbusses and machetes had freed themselves from the 'colonels' who had organized them and had begun running about loose, living by killing, robbing, and plundering. The flying brigades had come into being in order to combat them. *Cangaceiros* and flying brigades alike ate up the provisions of the townspeople of Custódia, got drunk on their cane brandy, and tried to rape their women. Before he even reached the age of reason, João had learned that the moment the warning shout was given all the bottles, food, and merchandise in the store had to be stowed away immediately in the hiding places that Zé Faustino had readied. The rumor went around that the storekeeper was a *coiteiro* – a man who did business with the bandits and provided them with information and hiding places. He was furious. Hadn't people seen how they robbed his store? Didn't they make off with clothes and tobacco without paying a cent? João heard his uncle complain many times about these stupid stories that the people of Custódia made up about him, out of envy. 'If they keep on, they're going to get me into trouble,' he would mutter. And that was exactly what happened.

One morning a flying brigade of thirty guards arrived in Custódia, under the command of Second Lieutenant Geraldo Macedo, a young Indian half-breed known far and wide for his bloodthirstiness. They were chasing down Antônio Silvino's gang of outlaws. The *cangaceiros* had not passed through Custódia, but the lieutenant stubbornly insisted that they had. He was tall and solidly built, slightly cross-eyed, and forever licking a gold tooth that he had. It was said that he chased down bandits so mercilessly because they had raped a sweetheart of his. As his men searched the huts, the lieutenant personally interrogated everyone in town. As night was falling, he strode into the store, beaming in triumph, and ordered Zé Faustino to take him to Silvino's hideout. Before the storekeeper could answer, he cuffed him so hard he sent him sprawling. 'I know everything, you Christian dog. People have informed on you.' Neither Zé Faustino's protestations of innocence nor Dona Angela's pleas were of any avail. Lieutenant Macedo said that as a warning to *coiteiros* he'd shoot Zé Faustino at dawn if he didn't reveal Silvino's whereabouts. The storekeeper finally appeared to agree to do so. At dawn the next morning they left Custódia, with Zé Faustino leading the way, followed by Macedo's thirty men, who were certain that they were going to take the bandits by surprise. But Zé Faustino managed to shake them after a few hours' march and hurried back to Custódia to get Dona Angela and João and take them off with him, fearing that they would be made the target of reprisals. The lieutenant caught him as he was still packing a few things. He may have intended to kill only him, but he also shot Dona Angela to death when she tried to intervene. He grabbed João by the legs and knocked him out with one blow across the head with the barrel of his pistol. When João came to, he saw that the townspeople of Custódia were there, holding a wake over two coffins, with looks of remorse on their faces. He turned a deaf ear to their words of affection, and as he rubbed his hand over his bleeding face he told them, in a voice that suddenly was that of an adult – he was only twelve years old at the time – that he would come back someday to avenge his aunt and uncle, since those who were mourning them were their real murderers.

The thought of vengeance helped him survive the weeks he spent wandering aimlessly about a desert wasteland bristling with *mandacarus*. He could see black vultures circling overhead, waiting for him to collapse so as to fly down and tear him to bits. It was January, and not a drop of rain had fallen. João gathered dried fruits, sucked the sap of palm trees, and even ate a dead armadillo he found. Finally help was forthcoming from a goatherd who came upon him lying alongside a dry riverbed in a delirium, raving about lances, horses, and O Senhor de Bonfim. He revived him with a big cupful of milk and a few handfuls of raw brown sugar lumps that the youngster sucked. They journeyed on together for several days, heading for the high plateau of Angostura, where the goatherd was taking his flock. But, before they reached it, they were surprised late one afternoon by a party of men who could not be mistaken for anything but outlaws, with leather hats, cartridge belts made of jaguar skin, knapsacks embroidered with beads, blunderbusses slung over their shoulders, and machetes that hung down to their knees. There were six of them, and the leader, a *cafuzo* with kinky hair and a red bandanna around his neck, laughingly asked João, who had fallen to his knees and was begging him to take him with him, why he wanted to be a *cangaceiro*. 'To kill National Guardsmen,' the youngster answered.

For João, a life then began that made a man of him in a very short time – 'an evil man,' the people of the provinces that he traveled the length and breadth of in the next twenty years would add – as a hanger-on at first of parties of men whose clothes he washed, whose meals he prepared, whose buttons he sewed back on, or whose lice he picked, and later on as an accomplice of their villainy, then after that as the best marksman, tracker, knife fighter, coverer of ground, and strategist of the *cangaço*, and finally as lieutenant and then leader of it. Before he was twenty-five, his was the head with the highest price on it in the barracks of Bahia, Pernambuco, O Piauí, and Ceará. His miraculous luck, which saved him from ambushes in which his comrades were killed or captured and which seemed to immunize him against bullets despite his daring, caused the story to go round that he had a pact with the Devil. Be that as it may, it was quite true that, unlike other men in the *cangaço*, who went around loaded down with holy medals, made the sign of the cross whenever they chanced upon a wayside cross or calvary, and at least once a year slipped into some town so that the priest could put their consciences at peace with God, João (who in the beginning had been called João the Kid, then João Faster-than-Lightning, then João the Quiet One, and was now called Satan João) appeared to be scornful of religion and resigned to going to hell to pay for his countless heinous deeds.

An outlaw's life, the nephew of Zé Faustino and Dona Angela might have said, consisted of walking, fighting, and stealing. But above all of walking. How many hundreds of leagues were covered in these years by the strong, muscular, restless legs of this man who could walk for twenty hours at a stretch without tiring? They had walked up and down the *sertão* in all directions, and no one knew better than they the folds in the hills, the tangles in the scrub, the meanders in the rivers, the caves in the mountains. These aimless wanderings across country in Indian file, trying to put distance between *cangaço* and real or imaginary pursuers from the National Guard or to confuse them, were, in João's memory, a single, endless ramble through identical landscapes, disturbed now and again by the whine of bullets and the screams of the wounded, as they headed toward some vague place or obscure event that seemed to be awaiting them.

For a long time he thought that what lay in store for him was returning to Custódia to wreak his vengeance. Years after the death of his aunt and uncle, he stole into the hamlet of his childhood one moonlit night, leading a dozen men. Was this the journey's end they had been heading for all during the long, bloody trek? Drought had driven many families out of Custódia, but there were still a few huts with people living in them, and despite the fact that among the faces of the inhabitants, gummy-eyed with sleep, whom his men drove out into the street there were a number that João did not recognize, he exempted no one from punishment. The womenfolk, even the little girls and the very old ladies, were forced to dance with the *cangaceiros*, who had already drunk up all the alcohol in Custódia, while the townspeople sang and played guitars. Every so often, the women and girls were dragged to the closest hut and raped. Finally, one of the menfolk began to cry, out of helplessness or terror. Satan João thereupon plunged his knife into him and slit him wide open, the way a butcher slaughters a steer. This bloodshed had the effect of an order, and shortly thereafter the *cangaceiros*, crazed with excitement, began to shoot off their blunderbusses, not stopping till they had turned the one street in Custódia into a graveyard. Even more than the wholesale killing, what contributed to the forging of the legend of Satan João was the fact that he humiliated each of the males personally after they were dead, cutting off their testicles and stuffing them into their mouths (this was his usual procedure with police informers). As they were leaving Custódia, he had one of the men in his band scribble on a wall the words: 'My aunt and uncle have collected the debt that was owed them.'

How much truth was there in the stories of atrocities attributed to Satan João? For that many fires, kidnappings, sackings, tortures to have been committed would have required more lives and henchmen than João's thirty years on this earth and the bands under his command, which never numbered as many as twenty men. What contributed to his fame was the fact that, unlike other leaders of *cangaços*, Pajeú for instance, who compensated for the blood they shed by sudden bursts of generosity – sharing booty they had just taken among the poor of the place, forcing a landowner to open his storerooms to the sharecroppers, handing over all of a ransom extorted from a victim to some parish priest so that he might build a chapel, or paying the expenses of the feast in honor of the patron saint of a town – no one had ever heard of João's making such gestures with the intention of winning people's sympathies or the blessings of heaven. Neither of these two things mattered to him.

He was a robust man, taller than the average in the *sertão*, with burnished skin, prominent cheekbones, slanted eyes, a broad forehead, laconic, a fatalist, who had pals and subordinates but no friends. He did have a woman, a girl from Quixeramobim whom he had met because she washed clothes in the house of a hacienda owner who served as *coiteiro* for the band. Her name was Leopoldina, and she was round-faced, with expressive eyes and a firm, ample body. She lived with João during the time he remained in hiding at the hacienda and when he took off again she left with him. But she did not accompany him for long, because João would not allow women in the band. He installed her in Aracati, where he came to see her every so often. He did not marry her, so that when people found out that Leopoldina had run away from Aracati to Jeremoabo with a judge, they thought that the offense to João was not as serious as it would have been if she were his wife. João avenged himself as though she were. He went to Quixeramobim, cut off her ears, branded Leopoldina's two brothers, and carried her thirteen-year-old sister, Mariquinha, off with him. The girl appeared early one morning in the streets of Jeremoabo with her face branded with the initials S and J. She was pregnant and there was a sign around her neck explaining that all the men of the band were, collectively, the baby's father.

Other bandits dreamed of getting together enough reis to buy themselves some land in a remote township where they could live for the rest of their lives under another name. João was never one to put money aside or make plans for the future. When the *cangaço* attacked a general store or a hamlet or obtained a good ransom for somebody it had kidnapped, after setting aside the share of the spoils that he would hand over to the *coiteiros* he'd commissioned to buy him weapons, ammunition, and medicines, João would divide the rest into equal shares for himself and each of his comrades. This largesse, his cleverness at setting up ambushes for the flying brigades or escaping from those that were set up for him, his courage and his ability to impose discipline made his men as faithful as hound dogs to him. They felt safe with him, and fairly treated. Even though he never forced them to face any risk that he himself did not confront, he did not coddle them in the slightest. If they fell asleep on guard duty, lagged behind on a march, or stole from a comrade, he flogged them. If one of them retreated when he had given orders to stand and fight, he marked him with his initials or lopped off one of his ears. He administered all punishments himself, coldly. And he was also the one who castrated traitors.

Though they feared him, his men also seemed to love him, perhaps because João had never left a comrade behind after an armed encounter. The wounded were carried off to some hideout in a hammock litter suspended from a tree trunk even when such an operation exposed the band to danger. João himself took care of them, and, if necessary, had a male nurse brought to the hideout by force to attend to the victim. The dead were also removed from the scene of combat so as to bury them in a spot where their bodies would not be profaned by the Guardsmen or by birds of prey. This and the infallible intuition with which he led his men in combat, breaking them up into separate groups that ran every which way so as to confuse the adversary, while others circled round and fell upon the enemy's rear guard, or the ruses he came up with to break out when the band found itself encircled, enhanced his authority; he never found it difficult to recruit new members for his *cangaço.*

His subordinates were intrigued by this taciturn, withdrawn leader different from themselves. He wore the same sombrero and the same sandals as they, but did not share their fondness for brilliantine and perfume – the very first thing they pounced on in the stores – nor did he wear rings on every finger or cover his chest with medals. His knapsacks had fewer decorations than those of the rawest recruit. His one weakness was wandering *cantadores,* whom he never allowed his men to mistreat. He looked after their needs with great deference, asked them to recite something, and listened to them very gravely, never interrupting them in the middle of a story. Whenever he ran into the Gypsy's Circus he had them give a performance for him and sent them on their way with presents.

Someone once heard Satan João say that he had seen more people die from alcohol, which ruined men's aims and made them knife each other for stupid reasons, than from sickness or drought. As though to prove him right, the day that Captain Geraldo Macedo and his flying brigade surprised him, the entire *cangaço* was drunk. The captain, who had been nicknamed Bandit-Chaser, had come out into the backlands to hunt João down after the latter had attacked a committee from the Bahia Autonomist Party, which had just held a meeting with the Baron de Canabrava on his hacienda in Calumbi. João ambushed the committee, sent its bodyguards running in all directions, and relieved the politicians of valises, horses, clothing, and money. The baron himself sent a message to Captain Macedo offering him a special reward for the *cangaceiro*'s head.

It happened in Rosário, a town of half a hundred dwellings where Satan João's men turned up early one morning in February. A short time before, they had had a bloody encounter with a rival band, Pajeú's *cangaço,* and merely wanted to rest. The townspeople agreed to give them food, and João paid for what they consumed, as well as for all the blunderbusses, shotguns, gunpowder, and bullets that he had been able to lay his hands on. The people of Rosário invited the *cangaceiros* to stay on for the feast they would be having, two days later, to celebrate the marriage of a cowboy and the daughter of a townsman. The chapel had been decorated with flowers and the local men and women were wearing their best clothes that noon when Father Joaquim arrived from Cumbe to officiate at the wedding. The little priest was so terrified at finding *cangaceiros* present that all of them burst out laughing as he stammered and stuttered and stumbled over his words. Before saying Mass, he heard confession from half the town, including several of the bandits. Then he attended the fireworks show and the open-air lunch, under an arbor, and drank toasts to the bride and groom along with the townspeople. But afterward he was so insistent on returning to Cumbe that João suddenly became suspicious. He forbade anyone to budge outside Rosário and he himself explored all the country round about, from the mountain side of the town to the one opposite, a bare plateau. He found no sign of danger. He returned to the wedding celebration, frowning. His men, drunk by now, were dancing and singing amid the townfolk.

Half an hour later, unable to bear the nervous tension, Father Joaquim confessed to him, trembling and sniveling, that Captain Macedo and his flying brigade were at the top of the mountain ridge, awaiting reinforcements so as to launch an attack. The priest had been ordered by Bandit-Chaser to delay João by using any trick he could think of. At that moment the first shots rang out from the direction of the plateau. They were surrounded. Amid all the confusion, João shouted to the *cangaceiros* to hold out as best they could till nightfall. But the bandits had had so much to drink that they couldn't even tell where the shots were coming from. They presented easy targets for the Guardsmen with their Comblains and fell to the ground bellowing, amid a hail of gunfire punctuated by the screams of the women running this way and that, trying to escape the crossfire. When night came, there were only four *cangaceiros* still on their feet, and João, who was fighting with a bullet through his shoulder, fainted. His men wrapped him in a hammock litter and began climbing the mountain. Aided by a sudden torrential rain, they broke through the enemy encirclement. They took shelter in a cave, and four days later they entered Tepidó, where a healer brought João's fever down and stanched his wound. They stayed there for two weeks, till Satan João was able to walk again. The night they left Tepidó they learned that Captain Macedo had decapitated the corpses of their comrades who had been killed in Rosário and carried off the heads in a barrel, salted down like jerky.

They plunged back into their daily round of violence, without thinking too much about their lucky stars or about the unlucky stars of the others. Once more they walked, stole, fought, hid out, their lives continually hanging by a thread. Satan João still had an indefinable feeling in his breast, the certainty that at any moment now something was going to happen that he had been waiting for ever since he could remember.

They came upon the hermitage, half fallen to ruins, along a turnoff of the trail leading to Cansanção. Standing before half a hundred people in rags and tatters, a tall, strikingly thin man, enveloped in a dark purple tunic, was speaking. He did not interrupt his peroration or even cast a glance at the newcomers. João had the dizzying feeling that something was boiling in his brain as he listened to what the saint was saying. He was telling the story of a sinner who, after having committed every evil deed under the sun, repented, lived a dog's life, won God's pardon, and went to heaven. When the man ended his story, he looked at the strangers. Without hesitating, he addressed João, who was standing there with his eyes lowered. 'What is your name?' he asked him. 'Satan João,' the *cangaceiro* murmured. 'You had best call yourself Abbot João, that is to say, an apostle of the Blessed Jesus,' the hoarse voice said.

Three days after having sent off the letter describing his visit to Brother João Evangelista de Monte Marciano to *L'Etincelle de la révolte*, Galileo Gall heard a knock on the door of the garret above the Livraria Catilina. The moment he set eyes on them, he knew the individuals were police underlings. They asked to see his papers, looked through his belongings, questioned him about his activities in Salvador. The following day the order expelling him from the country as an undesirable alien arrived. Old Jan van Rijsted pulled strings and Dr. José Batista de Sá Oliveira wrote to Governor Luiz Viana offering to be responsible for him, but the authorities obdurately notified Gall that he was to leave Brazil on the *Marseillaise* when it sailed for Europe a week later. He would be given, free of charge, a one-way ticket in third class.

Gall told his friends that being driven out of a country – or thrown in jail or killed – is one of the vicissitudes endured by every revolutionary and that he had been living the life of one almost since the day he'd been born. He was certain that the British consul, or the French or the Spanish one, was behind the expulsion order, but, he assured them, none of the police of these three countries would get their hands on him, since he would make himself scarce if the *Marseillaise* made calls in African ports or in Lisbon. He did not appear to be alarmed.

Both Jan van Rijsted and Dr. Oliveira had heard him speak with enthusiasm of his visit to the Monastery of Our Lady of Mercy, but both of them were thunderstruck when he announced to them that since he was being thrown out of Brazil, he intended to make 'a gesture on behalf of the brothers of Canudos' before departing, inviting people to attend a public demonstration of solidarity with them. He would call upon all freedom lovers in Bahia to gather together and explain to them why he had done so: 'In Canudos a revolution is coming into being, by spontaneous germination, and it is the duty of progressive-minded men to support it.' Jan van Rijsted and Dr. Oliveira did their best to dissuade him, telling him again and again that such a step was utter folly, but Gall nonetheless tried to get notice of the meeting published in the one opposition paper. His failure at the office of the *Jornal de Notícias* did not dishearten him. He was pondering the possibility of having leaflets printed that he himself would hand out in the streets, when something happened that made him write: 'At last! I was living too peaceful a life and beginning to become dull-spirited.'

It happened two days before he was due to sail, as dusk was falling. Jan van Rijsted came into the garret, with his late-afternoon pipe in his hand, to tell him that two persons were downstairs asking for him. 'They're *capangas*,' he warned him. Galileo knew that that was what men whom the powerful and the authorities used for underhanded business were called, and as a matter of fact the two of them did have a sinister look about them. But they were not armed and their manner toward him was respectful: there was someone who wanted to see him. Might he ask who? No. He was intrigued, and went along with them. They took him to the Praça da Basílica Cathedral first, through the upper town and after that through the lower one, and then through the outskirts. As they left paved streets behind in the darkness – the Rua Conselheiro Dantas, the Rua Portugal, the Rua das Princesas – and the markets of Santa Barbara and São João and turned into the carriageway that ran along the seafront to Barra, Galileo Gall wondered if the authorities hadn't decided to murder him instead of expelling him from the country. But it was not a trap. At an inn lighted by a little kerosene lamp, the owner and editor-in-chief of the *Jornal de Notícias* was waiting for him.

Epaminondas Gonçalves held out his hand to him and asked him to sit down. He came straight to the point. 'Do you want to stay in Brazil despite the order of expulsion?'

Galileo merely looked at him, without answering.

'Are you genuinely enthusiastic about what's going on up there in Canudos?' Epaminondas Gonçalves asked. They were alone in the room, and outside, the *capangas* could be heard talking together and waves steadily rolling in. The leader of the Progressivist Republican Party was watching him intently, with a very serious expression on his face, and nervously tapping his heels. He was dressed in the gray suit that Galileo had seen him wearing in his office at the *Jornal de Notícias*, but his face did not have the same nonchalant, slyly mocking look on it that it had had that day. He was tense, with a furrowed brow that made his youthful face look older.

'I don't like mysteries,' Gall said. 'You'd best explain to me what this is all about.'

'I'm trying to find out whether you want to go to Canudos to take arms to the rebels.'

Galileo waited for a moment, not saying a word, looking the other man straight in the eye.

'Two days ago you had no sympathy for the rebels,' he slowly commented. 'Occupying other people's land and living in promiscuity struck you as animal behavior.'

'That is the opinion of the Progressivist Republican Party,' Epaminondas Gonçalves agreed. 'And my own as well, naturally.'

'But . . .' Gall said, helping him along, thrusting his head slightly forward.

'But the enemies of our enemies are our friends,' Epaminondas Gonçalves declared, ceasing to tap his heels. 'Bahia is a bulwark of retrograde landowners, whose hearts still lie with the monarchy, despite the fact that we've been a republic for eight years. If it is necessary to aid the bandits and the Sebastianists in the interior in order to put an end to the Baron de Canabrava's dictatorial rule over Bahia, I shall do so. We're falling farther and farther behind and becoming poorer and poorer. These people must be removed from power, at whatever cost, before it's too late. If that business in Canudos continues, Luiz Viana's government will be plunged into crisis and sooner or later the federal forces will step in. And the moment that Rio de Janeiro intervenes, Bahia will cease to be the fief of the Autonomists.'

'And the reign of the Progressivist Republicans will begin,' Gall murmured.

'We don't believe in kings. We're republicans to the very marrow of our bones,' Epaminondas Gonçalves corrected him. 'Well, well, I see you understand me.'

'I understand that part all right,' Galileo said. 'But not the rest of it. If the Progressivist Republican Party wants to arm the *jagunços*, why through me?'

'The Progressivist Republican Party does not wish to aid or to have the slightest contact with people who rebel against the law,' Epaminondas Gonçalves said, pronouncing each syllable slowly and distinctly.

'The Honorable Deputy Epaminondas Gonçalves cannot aid rebels,' the owner and editor-in-chief of the *Jornal de Notícias* said, again lingering over every syllable. 'Nor can anyone connected with him, either closely or remotely. The Honorable Deputy is fighting an uphill battle for republican and democratic ideals in this autocratic enclave of powerful enemies, and cannot take such a risk.' He smiled, and Gall saw that he had a gleaming white, voracious set of teeth. 'Then you entered the picture. The plan I'm proposing would never have occurred to me if it hadn't been for that strange visit of yours the day before yesterday. That was what gave me the idea, what made me think: "If he's mad enough to call a public meeting in support of the rebels, he'll be mad enough to take them rifles."' He stopped smiling and spoke sternly. 'In cases such as this, frankness is the best policy. You're the only person who, if you're discovered or captured, could in no way compromise me and my political friends.'

'Are you warning me that if I were captured I wouldn't be able to count on you for help?'

'This time you've understood my meaning exactly,' Epaminondas Gonçalves said slowly and distinctly. 'If your answer is no, I bid you good night, and forget that you've seen me. If it's yes, let us discuss the fee.'

The Scotsman shifted position on his seat, a little wooden bench that creaked. 'The fee?' he murmured, blinking.

'As I see it, you're performing a service,' Epaminondas Gonçalves said. 'I'll pay you well for it, and promptly, I promise you, the moment you're about to leave the country. But if you prefer to render this service *ad honorem*, out of idealism, that's your business.'

'I'm going to take a stroll outside,' Galileo Gall said, rising to his feet. 'I think better when I'm by myself. I won't be long.'

On stepping outside the inn, he thought at first that it was raining, but it was merely spray from the waves. The *capangas* stepped aside to let him pass, and he smelled the strong, acrid odor of their pipes. There was a moon, and the sea, looking as though it were effervescent, was giving off a pleasant, salty smell that penetrated to his very vitals. Galileo Gall walked, amid the sand and the lonely boulders, to a little fort with a cannon aimed at the horizon. He thought to himself: 'The Republic has as little strength in Bahia as the King of England beyond the Aberfoyle Pass in the days of Rob Roy Macgregor.' Faithful to his habit despite the chaotic pounding of his blood, he tried to view the situation objectively. Was it ethical for a revolutionary to conspire with a petty-bourgeois politician? Yes, if the conspiracy aided the *jagunços*. Could he be of help to the people in Canudos? Without false modesty, one who was a battle-hardened veteran of political struggles and had dedicated his life to revolution could help them when certain decisions had to be made and once the time came when they would be forced to fight. And, finally, the experience would be valuable if he passed it on to the world's revolutionaries. It might well be that he would leave his bones to molder there in Canudos, but wasn't such an end preferable to dying of illness or of old age? He walked back to the inn and, standing on the threshold of the room, said to Epaminondas Gonçalves: 'I'm mad enough to do it.'

'Wonderful!' the politician answered Galileo Gall in English, caught up by his fervor, his eyes gleaming.

V

In his sermons, the Counselor had so often foretold how the forces of the Dog would come to seize him and put the city to the sword that no one in Canudos was surprised when it was learned, from pilgrims come on horseback from Juazeiro, that a company of the Ninth Infantry Battalion from Bahia had arrived in the vicinity, charged with the mission of capturing the saint.

Prophecies were beginning to come true, words becoming facts. The news had a tonic effect, mobilizing old people, young people, men, women. Shotguns and carbines, flintlocks that had to be muzzle-loaded were immediately taken up and bandoleers threaded with the proper ammunition, as at the same time knives and daggers appeared, tucked into waistbands as if by magic, and in people's hands sickles, machetes, pikes, awls, slings and hunting crossbows, clubs, stones.

That night, the night of the beginning of the end of the world, all Canudos gathered round about the Temple of the Good Lord

Jesus – a two-story skeleton, with towers that were growing taller and walls that were being filled in – to listen to the Counselor's words. The fervor of the elect filled the air. The Counselor, on the other hand, appeared to be more withdrawn than ever. Once the pilgrims from Juazeiro told him the news, he did not make the slightest comment and went on supervising the gathering of building stones, the tamping of the ground, and the mixing of sand and pebbles for the Temple with such total concentration that no one dared ask him any questions. Nonetheless, as they prepared for battle, they all felt that that ascetic figure approved of what they were doing. And all of them knew, as they oiled their crossbows, cleaned the bore of their muskets and blunderbusses, and dried their gunpowder, that this night the Father, through the mouth of the Counselor, would tell them what to do.

The saint's voice resounded beneath the stars, in the air without a breath of wind in which his words seemed to linger, an atmosphere so serene that it banished all fear. Before speaking of the war, he spoke of peace, of the life to come, in which sin and pain would disappear. Once the Devil was overthrown, the Kingdom of the Holy Spirit would be established, the last era of the world before Judgment Day. Would Canudos be the capital of this Kingdom? If the Blessed Jesus so willed it. Then the wicked laws of the Republic would be repealed and the priests would return, as in the very earliest days, to be selfless shepherds of their flocks. The backlands would grow verdant from the rain, there would be an abundance of maize and cattle, everyone would have enough to eat, and each family would be able to bury its dead in coffins padded with velvet. But, before that, the Antichrist had to be overthrown. It was necessary to make a cross and a banner with the image of the Divine on it so that the enemy would know what side true religion was on. And it was necessary to go into battle as the Crusaders had when they set out to deliver Jerusalem: singing, praying, acclaiming the Virgin and Our Lord. And as the Crusaders had vanquished their enemy, so too would the crusaders of the Blessed Jesus vanquish the Republic.

No one in Canudos slept that night. Everyone stayed up, some of them praying, others preparing for battle, as diligent hands nailed the cross together and sewed the banner. They were ready before dawn. The cross was three yards tall and two yards wide, and the banner was four bedsheets sewn together, on which the Little Blessed One painted a white dove with outspread wings, and the Lion of Natuba wrote, in his calligraphic hand, an ejaculatory prayer. Save for a handful of people designated by Antônio Vilanova to remain in Canudos so that the building of the Temple would not be interrupted (work on it went on day and night, except for Sundays), everyone else in the settlement left at first light, heading in the direction of Bendengó and Juazeiro, to prove to the chieftains of evil that good still had its defenders on this earth. The Counselor did not see them leave, for he was in the little Church of Santo Antônio praying for them.

They were obliged to march ten leagues to meet the soldiers. They made the march singing, praying, and acclaiming God and the Counselor. They halted to rest only once, after passing Monte Cambaio. Those who felt a call of nature left the crooked lines of marchers, slipped behind a boulder, and then caught up with the rest farther down the road. Traversing the flat, dry stretch of terrain took them a day and a night, without a single soul asking for another halt to rest. They had no battle plan. The rare travelers who met them on the road were amazed to learn that they were marching to war. They looked like a crowd heading for a fiesta; a number of them were dressed in their fanciest clothes. They were carrying weapons and shouted, 'Death to the Devil and to the Republic,' but even at such moments the joyous expression on their faces softened the effect of the hatred in their voices. The cross and the banner headed the procession, carried respectively by the ex-bandit Pedrão and the ex-slave Big João, and behind them came Maria Quadrado and Alexandrinha Correa carrying the glass case with the image of the Good Lord Jesus painted on cloth by the Little Blessed One, and behind that, ghostly apparitions enveloped in a cloud of dust, came the elect. Many accompanied the litanies by blowing on lengths of sugarcane that in bygone days had served as pipes for smoking tobacco; with holes pierced in them, they could also be made into shepherd's pipes.

In the course of the march, imperceptibly, obeying a call of the blood, the column gradually regrouped, so that those who had belonged to the same band of brigands, people from the same hamlet, the same slave quarters, the same district of a town, members of the same family were now grouped together, as if, as the crucial hour drew near, each person felt the need to be as close as possible to what had been the tried and true in other decisive hours. Those who had killed gradually worked their way to the front of the line and now, as they approached the town of Uauá, named that because of the many fireflies that set it aglow at night, Abbot João, Pajeú, Taramela, José Venâncio, the Macambiras, and other rebels and outlaws surrounded the cross and the banner at the head of the procession or army, knowing without having to be told that because of their experience and their sins they were called to set the example when the hour came to attack.

Past midnight, a sharecropper came to meet them to warn them that a hundred and four soldiers were camped in Uauá, having arrived from Juazeiro the evening before. A strange war cry – 'Long live the Counselor! Long live the Blessed Jesus!' – stirred the hearts of the elect; excited and jubilant, they picked up the pace. As dawn broke, they sighted Uauá, a handful of little huts that was the obligatory stopping-off place for the night for cattle drivers going from Monte Santo to Curaçá. The marchers began to recite litanies to St. John the Baptist, the patron saint of the town. The column was soon spotted by the drowsy soldiers posted as sentinels on the banks of a lagoon on the outskirts. After staring for a few seconds, not believing their eyes, they headed for the town on the run. Praying, singing, blowing on their *canudos*, the elect entered Uauá, arousing from their sleep and plunging into a nightmarish reality the hundred-odd soldiers whom it had taken twelve days to get there and who hadn't the least idea where the prayers that had suddenly awakened them were coming from. They were the only living souls in Uauá, since all the inhabitants had fled during the night. But there they all were now, along with the crusaders, circling round the tamarinds in the public square, watching the soldiers' faces as they peered out the doors and windows, registering their surprise, their hesitation as to whether to shoot or run or tumble back into their hammocks and rickety beds to sleep.

A bellowed command, which caused a rooster to break off his cock-a-doodle-doo right in the middle, set off the shooting. The soldiers fired, supporting their muskets on the low partition walls of the huts, and the elect began to fall to the ground, drenched in blood. The column gradually broke up; intrepid groups following after Abbot João, José Venâncio, Pajeú launched an attack on the dwellings, and others ran to shield themselves in dead angles or curl up in a ball among the tamarinds as the rest advanced. The elect also did some shooting: those, that is to say, who had carbines and blunderbusses and those who managed to load their long-barreled muskets and make out a target amid the clouds of black powder. Throughout the hours of struggle and confusion, the cross never tottered, the banner never ceased to wave, in the middle of an island of crusaders which, though riddled with bullets, continued to exist, compact, faithful, rallied round those emblems in which everyone would later see the secret of their victory. For neither Pedrão, nor Big João, nor the Mother of Men, who was carrying the glass case with the face of the Son, died in the fray.

The victory was not soon won. There were many martyrs in these hours of deafening noise. The sound of running feet and shots would be followed by intervals of immobility and silence which, a moment later, would again be shattered. But before midmorning the Counselor's men knew that they had won when they saw some half-dressed figures, who, by order of their leaders or because fear had overcome them before the *jagunços* did, were running off pell-mell across country, abandoning firearms, tunics, leggings, boots, knapsacks. The men from Canudos shot at them knowing that they were out of range, but it did not occur to anyone to pursue them. Shortly thereafter the other soldiers fled, and as they ran for their lives some of them fell amid the nests of *jagunços* that had formed in this corner or that, where they were beaten to death with spades and shovels and done in with knives in less time than it takes to tell. They died hearing themselves called dogs and devils, amid prognostications that their souls would be condemned as their corpses rotted.

The crusaders remained in Uauá for several hours after their victory. Most of them spent these hours sleeping, propped up one against the other, recovering from the exhaustion of the march and the tension of the battle. Some of them, however, urged on by Abbot João, searched the huts for rifles, ammunition, bayonets, and cartridge belts left behind by the soldiers as they fled. Maria Quadrado, Alexandrinha Correa, and Gertrudes, a street vendor from Teresina who had a bullet wound in her arm but continued to bustle about nonetheless, went around placing the dead bodies of *jagunços* in hammock litters so that they could be carried back to Canudos to be buried. The women who were healers, the herb doctors, the midwives, the bonesetters, any number of helpful souls gathered round the wounded, wiping away the blood, bandaging them, or simply offering prayers and incantations to ward off their pain.

Carrying their dead and wounded and following the riverbed of the Vaza-Barris, at a slower pace this time, the elect walked the ten leagues back. They entered Canudos a day and a half later, acclaiming the Counselor, applauded, embraced, and greeted with smiles by those who had stayed behind to work on the Temple. The Counselor, who had neither eaten nor drunk a single thing since they had left, gave his counsel that evening from a scaffolding of the towers of the Temple. He prayed for the dead, offered thanks to the Blessed Jesus and to John the Baptist for the victory that had been won, and spoke of how evil had put down roots here on this earth. Before time began, God filled everything and space did not exist. In order to create the world, the Father had had to withdraw within Himself so as to create a vacuum, and this absence of God gave rise to space, in which there sprang up, in seven days, the stars, light, the waters, plants, animals, and man. But once the earth had been created through the withdrawal of the divine substance, there had also been created the conditions favorable for what was most opposed to the Father, namely sin, to establish its kingdom. Hence the world was born beneath the sway of a divine curse, as the Devil's realm. But the Father took pity on men and sent His Son to reconquer for God this earthly space ruled by the Demon.

The Counselor said that one of the streets of Canudos would be named São João Batista after the patron saint of Uauá.

'Governor Viana is sending another expedition to Canudos,' Epaminondas Gonçalves says. 'Under the command of an officer I know personally, Major Febrônio de Brito. This time it's not just a handful of soldiers, such as the little band that was attacked in Uauá, who are being sent out, but an entire battalion. They will be leaving Bahia at any moment now, and perhaps they have already done so. There isn't much time left.'

'I can leave tomorrow morning,' Galileo Gall answers. 'The guide is waiting. Have you brought the arms?'

Epaminondas offers Gall a cigar, which he refuses, shaking his head. They are sitting in wicker chairs on the ramshackle terrace of the manor of a hacienda somewhere between Queimadas and Jacobina, to which a horseman dressed all in leather, with a biblical name – Caifás – has guided him, taking him round and round the scrubland, as though trying to disorient him. It is dusk; beyond the wooden balustrade are a row of royal palms, a dovecote, several animal pens. The sun, a reddish ball, is setting the horizon on fire.

Epaminondas Gonçalves slowly puffs on his cigar. 'Two dozen French rifles, good ones,' he murmurs, looking at Gall through the cigar smoke. 'And ten thousand cartridges. Caifás will take you to the outskirts of Queimadas in the wagon. If you're not too tired, it would be best to come back here with the arms tonight and then go straight on to Canudos tomorrow.'

Galileo Gall nods in agreement. He is tired, but all he needs is a few hours' sleep to recuperate. There are so many flies on the terrace that he keeps one hand in front of his face to chase them away. Despite his fatigue, he is overjoyed; the wait was beginning to get on his nerves and he was afraid that Gonçalves might have changed his plans. This morning, when the horseman dressed all in leather came without warning to get him at the Our Lady of Grace boarding house and gave the proper password, he was so excited he even forgot to eat breakfast. He has made the journey here without having had a thing to eat or drink, with a scorching sun beating down all day.

'I'm sorry to have made you wait for so many days, but collecting the arms and getting them this far turned out to be a fairly complicated business,' Epaminondas Gonçalves says. 'Did you see the campaigning going on for the municipal elections in any of the towns you passed through?'

'I saw that the Bahia Autonomist Party is spending more money on propaganda than you people are,' Gall says with a yawn.

'It has all it needs. Not only Viana's money, but the government's and the Bahia parliament's as well. And above all, the baron's.'

'The baron's as rich as Croesus, isn't that so?' Gall says, suddenly pricking up his ears. 'An antediluvian character, an archaeological curiosity, there's no doubt about it. I learned a number of things about him in Queimadas. From Rufino, the guide you recommended to me. His wife belonged to the baron. Yes, that's the right word, she belonged to him, like a goat or a calf. He gave her to Rufino as a wife. Rufino himself speaks of the baron as though he, too, had always been property of his. Without resentment, with the gratitude of a faithful dog. Interesting, Senhor Gonçalves. It's still the Middle Ages here.'

'That's what we're fighting against; that's why we want to modernize this country,' Epaminondas says, blowing on the ash of his cigar. 'That's why the Empire fell, and that's what the Republic is for.'

'It's the *jagunços*, rather, who are fighting against the situation,' Galileo Gall mentally corrects him, feeling as though he is about to fall asleep from one moment to the next. Epaminondas Gonçalves rises to his feet. 'What did you tell the guide?' he asks as he paces up and down the terrace. The crickets have started chirping and it is no longer stifling hot.

'The truth,' Gall says, and the owner and editor-in-chief of the *Jornal de Notícias* halts dead in his tracks. 'I was careful not even to mention your name. I spoke only of myself. I told him I want to go to Canudos as a matter of principle. Out of ideological and moral solidarity.'

Epaminondas Gonçalves looks at him in silence and Galileo knows that the man is wondering whether he's saying these things in all seriousness, whether he is really crazy enough or stupid enough to believe them. He thinks: 'I *am* that crazy or that stupid,' as he waves his arms about to chase the flies away.

'Did you also tell him that you'll be bringing them arms?'

'Of course not. He'll find that out once we're on the way there.'

Epaminondas goes back to pacing up and down the terrace again, with his hands behind his back, leaving a wake of smoke behind him. He is wearing a peasant shirt open at the neck, a vest without buttons, riding pants and boots, and looks as though he hasn't shaved. His appearance is not at all the same as in the newspaper office or in the inn at Barra, but Gall nonetheless recognizes the stored-up energy in his movements, the determination and ambition in his expression, and thinks to himself that he doesn't even need to palpate his bones to know what they are like: 'A man hungry for power.' Does this hacienda belong to him? Is this manor house one lent to him for hatching his conspiracies?

'Once you've handed over the arms, don't come by this way to get back to Salvador,' Epaminondas says, leaning on the balustrade with his back turned to him. 'Have the guide take you to Juazeiro. It's the prudent thing to do. There's a train that comes through Juazeiro every other day, and it will get you back in Bahia in twelve hours. I'll see to it that you leave for Europe inconspicuously and with a generous fee for your services.'

'A generous fee . . .' Gall repeats after him, with a huge yawn that comically distorts his face and his words. 'You've always believed that I'm doing this for money.'

Epaminondas exhales a mouthful of smoke that drifts in arabesques across the terrace. In the distance, the sun is beginning to hide itself beneath the horizon and there are patches of shade in the surrounding countryside.

'No, I know quite well that you're doing it as a matter of principle. In any event, I realize that you're not doing it out of love for the Progressivist Republican Party. But we consider that you're doing us a service, and we're in the habit of paying for services rendered, as I've already told you.'

'I can't promise you that I'll go back to Bahia,' Gall interrupts him, stretching. 'Our deal doesn't include that clause.'

The owner and editor-in-chief of the *Jornal de Notícias* looks at him once more. 'We won't discuss it again.' He smiles. 'You may do as you like. In a word, you now know what the best way is to get back to Bahia, and you also know that I can make it easy for you to get out of the country without the authorities stepping in and putting you on a boat. So if you prefer to stay with the insurgents, go ahead. Though I'm certain you'll change your mind when you meet them.'

'I've already met one of them,' Gall murmurs in a slightly mocking tone of voice. 'And by the way, would you mind sending this letter to France off for me from Bahia? It's unsealed, and if you read French, you'll see that there is nothing in it that might compromise you.'

He was born, like his parents, his grandparents, and his brother Honório, in the town of Assaré, in the state of Ceará, where the herds of cattle that were being driven to Jaguaribe and those headed for the Vale do Cariri parted company. The townspeople were all either farmers or cowhands, but from a very early age Antônio gave proof of a calling as a merchant. He began to make business deals in the catechism classes held by Father Matias (who also taught him his letters and numbers). Antônio and Honório Vilanova were very close, and addressed each other, very seriously, as *compadre*, like adults who have been lifelong cronies.

One morning Adelinha Alencar, the daughter of the carpenter of Assaré, woke up with a high fever. The herbs burned by Dona Camuncha to exorcise the evil had no effect, and a few days later Adelinha's body broke out in pustules so ugly they turned the prettiest girl in town into its most repugnant creature. A week later half a dozen townspeople were delirious with fever and covered with pustules. Father Tobias managed to say a Mass asking God to put an end to the dread disease, before he, too, came down with it. Those who were ill began to die almost at once, as the epidemic spread uncontrollably. As the terrified inhabitants prepared to flee the town, they came up against Colonel Miguel Fernandes Vieira, the political boss of the town and the owner of the lands they cultivated and the cattle they took out to graze, who forbade them to leave, so that they would not spread the smallpox throughout the countryside. Colonel Vieira posted *capangas* at the exits of the town with orders to shoot anyone who disobeyed his edict.

Among the few who managed to flee the town were the two Vilanova brothers. Their parents, their sister Luz Maria, a brother-in-law, and three nephews in the family were carried off by the epidemic.

After burying all these kinfolk, Antônio and Honório, strong youngsters, both of them fifteen, with curly hair and blue eyes, made up their minds to escape from the town. But instead of confronting the *capangas* with knives and bullets, as others had, Antônio, faithful to his vocation, persuaded them to look the other way – in exchange for a young bull, a twenty-five-pound sack of refined sugar, and another of raw brown sugar. They left by night, taking with them two girl cousins of theirs – Antônia and Assunção Sardelinha – and the family's worldly goods: two cows, a pack mule, a valise full of clothes, and a little purse containing ten milreis. Antônia and Assunção were double first cousins of the Vilanova boys, and Antônio and Honório took them along out of pity for their helplessness, for the smallpox epidemic had left them orphans. The girls were scarcely more than children and their presence made their escape across country difficult; they did not know how to make their way through scrub forest and found thirst hard to bear. The little expeditionary force nonetheless managed to cross the Serra do Araripe, left Santo Antônio, Ouricuri, Petrolina behind them, and crossed the Rio São Francisco. When they entered Juazeiro and Antônio decided that they would try their luck in that town in the state of Bahia, the two sisters were pregnant: Antônia by Antônio, and Assunção by Honório.

The very next day Antônio began working for money, while Honório, with the help of the Sardelinha girls, built a hut. They had sold on the way the cows they had taken with them from Assaré, but they still had the pack mule left, and Antônio loaded a containerful of brandy on its back and went about the city selling it by the drink. He was to load on the back of that mule, and then on another, and later on others still, the goods that, in the months and years that followed, he peddled, at first from house to house and after that in the outlying settlements, and finally throughout the length and breadth of the backlands, which he came to know like the palm of his hand. He dealt in salted codfish, rice, beans, sugar, pepper, brown sugar, lengths of cloth, alcohol, and whatever else people asked him to supply them with. He became the purveyor to vast haciendas and to poor sharecroppers, and his mule trains became as familiar a sight as the Gypsy's Circus in the villages, the missions, and the camps of the backlands. The general store in Juazeiro, in the Praça da Misericôrdia, was run by Honório and the Sardelinha sisters. Before ten years had gone by, people were saying that the Vilanovas were well on their way to becoming rich.

At this point the disaster that was to ruin the family for the second time overtook them. In good years, the rains began in December; in bad ones, in February or March. That year, by the time May came round, not a single drop of rain had fallen. The volume of water in the São Francisco diminished by two-thirds and barely sufficed to meet the needs of Juazeiro, whose population quadrupled with the influx of migrants from the interior.

That year Antônio Vilanova did not collect a single debt owed him, and all his customers, both the owners of large haciendas and poor people of the region, canceled their orders for goods. Even Calumbi, the Baron de Canabrava's choicest estate, informed him that it would not buy so much as a handful of salt from him. Thinking to profit from bad times, Antônio had buried seed grain in wooden boxes wrapped in canvas in order to sell it when scarcity drove the price sky-high. But the disaster took on proportions that exceeded even his calculations. He soon realized that if he didn't sell the seed he had hoarded immediately, there wouldn't be a single customer for it, for people were spending what little money they had left on Masses, processions, and offerings (and everyone was eager to join the Brotherhood of Penitents, who wore hoods and flagellated themselves) so that God would send rain. He unearthed his boxes then: despite the canvas wrapping, the seeds had rotted. But Antônio never admitted defeat. He, Honório, the Sardelinha sisters, and even the children – one of his own and three of his brother's – cleaned the seed as best they could and the following morning the town crier announced in the main square that through *force majeure* the Vilanova general store was selling its seed on hand at bargain prices. Antônio and Honório armed themselves and posted four servants with clubs in plain sight outside the store to keep buyers from getting out of hand. For the first hour, everything went well. The Sardelinha sisters handed out the seed at the counter while the six men held people back at the door, allowing only ten people at a time to enter the store. But soon it was impossible to control the mob, for people finally climbed over the barrier, tore down the doors and windows, and invaded the place. In a few minutes' time, they had made off with everything inside, including the money in the cashbox. What they were unable to carry off with them they reduced to dust.

The devastation had lasted no more than half an hour, and

although their losses were great, nobody in the family was injured. Honório, Antônio, the Sardelinha sisters, and the children sat in the street watching as the looters withdrew from what had been the best-stocked store in the city. The women had tears in their eyes and the children, sitting scattered about on the ground, looked numbly at the remains of the beds they had slept in, the clothes they had worn, the toys they had played with. Antônio's face was pale. 'We have to start all over again,' Honório murmured. 'Not in this city, though,' his brother answered.

Antônio was not yet thirty. But the ravages of overwork, his exhausting travels, the obsessive way in which he ran his business, made him look older. He had lost a lot of hair, and his broad forehead, his little chin beard, and his mustache gave him the air of an intellectual. He was a strong man, somewhat stoop-shouldered, with a bowlegged walk like a cowhand's. He never showed any interest in anything but business. While Honório went to fiestas and was not unwilling to down a little glass of anisette as he listened to a *cantador* or chatted with friends plying the São Francisco at the helm of boats on which bright-colored figureheads were beginning to appear, Antônio had no social life. When he wasn't off somewhere on his travels, he stayed behind the counter of the store, checking the account books or thinking up new lines of business to go into. He had many customers but few friends, and though he turned up on Sundays at the Church of Our Lady of the Grottoes and occasionally was present at the processions in which the flagellants of the Brotherhood mortified their flesh in order to aid souls in purgatory, he was not thought of as someone possessed of extraordinary religious fervor. He was a serious, serene, stubborn man, well equipped to confront adversity.

This time the Vilanova family's peregrination through a region brought low by hunger and thirst was longer than the one they had undertaken a decade before as they fled from the smallpox epidemic. They soon were left without animals. After an encounter with a band of migrants that the two brothers had to drive off with their rifles, Antônio decided that their five pack mules were too great a temptation for the starving human hordes wandering about the backlands. He therefore sold four of them in Barro Vermelho for a handful of precious stones. They butchered the last remaining one, had themselves a banquet, and salted down the meat left over, which kept them alive for a number of days. One of Honório's sons died of dysentery and they buried him in Borracha, where they had set up a shelter, in which the Sardelinha sisters offered soup made from Spanish plums, rock cavy, and yellow lupine. But they were unable to hold out very long there either, and wandered off again toward Patamuté and Mato Verde, where Honório was stung by a scorpion. When he was better, they continued on south, a harrowing journey of weeks and weeks during which the only things they came upon were ghost towns, deserted haciendas, caravans of skeletons drifting aimlessly, as though hallucinated.

In Pedra Grande, another of Honório and Assunção's sons died of nothing more serious than a head cold. They were in the midst of burying him, wrapped in a blanket, when, enveloped in a cloud of red-colored dust, some twenty men and women entered the village – among them a creature with the face of a man who crawled about on all fours and a half-naked black – most of them nothing but skin and bones, wearing threadbare tunics and sandals that looked as though they had trod all the paths of this world. Their leader was a tall, dark man with hair that fell down to his shoulders and quicksilver eyes. He strode straight over to the Vilanova family, and with a gesture of his hand stopped the brothers, who were already lowering the corpse into the grave. 'Your son?' he asked Honório in a grave voice. The latter nodded. 'You can't bury him like that,' the dark-skinned, dark-haired man said in an authoritative tone of voice. 'He must be properly interred and sent upon his way so that he will be received at heaven's eternal feast of rejoicing.' And before Honório could answer, he turned to those accompanying him: 'Let us give him a decent burial, so that the Father will receive him in exaltation.' The Vilanovas then saw the pilgrims come to life, run to the trees, cut them down, nail them together, fashion a coffin and a cross with a skill that was proof of long practice. The dark man took the child in his arms and laid him in the coffin. As the Vilanovas filled the grave with earth, the man prayed aloud and the others sang hymns of blessing and recited litanies, kneeling round about the cross. Later, as the pilgrims were about to leave after resting beneath the trees, Antônio Vilanova took out a coin and offered it to the saint. 'As a token of our thanks,' he insisted, on seeing that the man was refusing to accept it and contemplating him with a mocking look in his eyes. 'You have nothing to thank me for,' he said finally. 'But you would be unable to pay the Father what you owe him even with a thousand coins such as this one.' He paused, and then added gently: 'You haven't learned to count, my son.'

For a long time after the pilgrims had departed, the Vilanovas remained there, sitting lost in thought around a campfire they had built to drive away the insects. 'Was he a madman, *compadre*?' Honório asked. 'I've seen many a madman on my travels and that man seemed like something more than that,' Antônio answered.

When the rains came again, after two years of drought and disasters, the Vilanovas had settled in Caatinga do Moura, a hamlet near which there was a salt pit that Antônio began to work. All the rest of the family – the Sardelinha sisters and the two children – had survived, but Antônio and Antônia's little boy, after suffering from gummy secretions round his eyes that made him rub them for days on end, had gradually lost his sight and though he could still distinguish light from dark he was unable to make out people's faces or tell what things around him looked like. The salt pit turned out to be a good business. Honório, the women, and the children spent their days drying the salt and preparing sacks of it, which Antônio then went out to sell. He had made himself a cart, and went about armed with a double-barreled shotgun to defend himself in case he was attacked by bandits.

They stayed in Caatinga do Moura about three years. With the return of the rains, the villagers came back to work the land and the cowhands to take care of the decimated herds. For Antônio, all this meant the return of prosperity. In addition to the salt pit, he soon had a store and began to deal in riding animals, which he bought and sold with a good profit margin. When the torrential rains of that December – a decisive moment in his life – turned the little stream that ran through the settlement into a river in flood that carried off the huts of the village and drowned poultry and goats and inundated the salt pit and buried it beneath a sea of mud in a single night, Antônio was at the Nordestina fair, to which he had gone with a load of salt and the intention of buying some mules.

He returned a week later. The floodwaters had begun to recede. Honório, the Sardelinha sisters, and the half-dozen laborers who now worked for them were dejected, but Antônio took this latest catastrophe calmly. He inventoried what had been salvaged, made calculations in a little notebook, and raised their spirits by telling them that he still had many debts to collect and that like a cat he had too many lives to live to feel defeated by one flood.

But he didn't sleep a wink that night. They had been given shelter by a villager who was a friend of his, on the hill where all the people who lived on lower ground had taken refuge. His wife could feel him tossing and turning in the hammock and see by the light of the moon falling on her husband's face that he was consumed with anxiety. The next morning Antônio informed them that they must make ready for a journey, for they were leaving Caatinga do Moura for good. His tone was so peremptory that neither his brother nor the womenfolk dared ask him why. After selling off everything that they were not able to take with them, they took to the road once more, in the cart loaded down with bundles, and plunged yet again into the unknown. One day they heard Antônio say something that bewildered them. 'That was the third warning,' he murmured, with a shadow in the depths of his bright blue eyes. 'We were sent that flood so we'd do something, but I don't know what.' As though embarrassed to ask, Honório said to him: 'A warning from God, *compadre*?' 'Could be from the Devil,' Antônio replied.

They continued to knock about from place to place, a week here, a month there, and every time the family thought that they were about to settle down, Antônio would impulsively decide to leave. This vague search for something or someone disturbed them, but none of them protested against this constant moving about.

Finally, after nearly eight months of wandering up and down the backlands, they ended up settling on a hacienda belonging to the Baron de Canabrava that had been abandoned ever since the drought. The baron had taken all his cattle away and only a few families had stayed on, living here and there in the surrounding countryside, cultivating little plots of land on the banks of the Vaza-Barris and taking their goats up to graze in the Serra de Canabrava, green the year round. In view of its sparse population and the fact that it was surrounded by mountains, Canudos seemed like the worst possible place for a merchant to set up in business. Nonetheless, the moment they had taken over what had once been the steward's house, now in ruins, Antônio acted as though a great weight had been lifted from his shoulders. He immediately began to think up new lines of business that he could go into and set about organizing the family's life with the same high spirits as in days gone by. And a year later, thanks to his perseverance and determination, the Vilanovas' general store was buying up and selling merchandise for ten leagues around. Again, Antônio was constantly out on the road.

But the day that the pilgrims appeared on the hillside of O Cambaio and entered Canudos by its one and only street, singing hymns of praise to the Blessed Jesus at the top of their lungs, he happened to be home. From the veranda of the former steward's quarters, now converted into a combination house and store, he watched as these fervent creatures drew closer and closer. His brother, his wife, his sister-in-law saw him turn pale when the man in dark purple who was heading the procession came over to him. They recognized those burning eyes, that deep voice, that gaunt body. 'Have you learned to count yet?' the saint asked with a smile, holding out his hand to the merchant. Antônio Vilanova fell on his knees to kiss the newcomer's fingers.

In my last letter I told you, comrades, of a popular rebellion in the interior of Brazil, that I learned of through a prejudiced witness (a Capuchin friar). I can now pass on to you more reliable testimony regarding Canudos, that of a man who is himself one of the rebels, sent out to journey all through the backlands, his mission doubtless to make converts to their cause. But I can also tell you something exciting: there has been an armed encounter, and the *jagunços* defeated a hundred soldiers headed for Canudos. Are there not clearer and clearer signs that these rebels are fellow revolutionaries? There is an element of truth in that, but only relatively speaking, to judge from this man, who gives a contradictory impression of these brothers of ours: sharp insights and normal behavior exist in them side by side with unbelievable superstitions.

I am writing to you from a town whose name you no doubt would not recognize, a region where the moral and physical servitude of women is extreme, for they are oppressed by landowner, father, brothers, and husband alike. In these parts, the landowner chooses the wives for his relations and the womenfolk are beaten right on the street by their irascible fathers or their drunken husbands, a matter of complete indifference to those who witness such scenes. Food for thought, comrades: we must make certain that the revolution will not only do away with the exploitation of man by man, but also that of women by men, and will establish, along with the equality of classes, that of the sexes.

I learned that the emissary from Canudos had been brought here by a guide who is also a *tigreiro*, a hunter of jaguars (fine occupations: exploring the world and killing the predators preying on the flocks), thanks to whom I managed to see him. Our meeting took place in a tannery, amid hides drying in the sun and children playing with lizards. My heart began to pound when I laid eyes on the man: short and heavyset, with that pale complexion somewhere between yellow and gray that half-breeds inherit from their Indian forebears, and a scar on his face that told me at a glance that he had been a bandit or a criminal in the past (in any event, a victim, since, as Bakunin explained, society lays the groundwork for crimes and criminals are merely the instruments for carrying them out). His clothes were made of leather – the usual dress of cowherds, I might add, enabling them to ride through thorny brush country. He kept his sombrero on his head and his shotgun at his side all during our interview. His eyes were deep-set and sullen and his manner shifty and evasive, as is often the case here. He did not want the two of us to talk together by ourselves. We had to do so in the presence of the owner of the tannery and his family, who were sitting on the floor eating without looking at us. I told him that I was a revolutionary and had many comrades in the world who applauded what the people in Canudos had done, that is to say, occupying lands belonging to a feudal owner, establishing free love, and vanquishing a company of soldiers. I don't know if he understood me. The people in the interior are not like those in Bahia, who thanks to the African influence are loquacious and outgoing. Here people's faces are expressionless, masks whose function would seem to be to hide their feelings and their thoughts.

I asked him if they were prepared for more attacks, since the bourgeoisie reacts like a wild beast when the sacrosanct right of private ownership of property is violated. He left me dumfounded by murmuring that all land belongs to the Good Lord Jesus, and that the Counselor is building the largest church in the world in Canudos. I tried to explain to him that it was not because they were building churches that the powers that be had sent soldiers to do battle with them, but he answered that it was precisely for that reason, since the Republic is trying to wipe out religion. I then heard, comrades, a strange diatribe against the Republic, delivered with quiet self-assurance, without a trace of passion. The Republic is bent on oppressing the Church and the faithful, doing away with all the religious orders as it has already suppressed the Society of Jesus, and the most notorious proof of its intentions is its having instituted civil marriage, a scandalous act of impiety when the sacrament of marriage created by God already exists.

I can imagine the disappointment of many of my readers, and their suspicions on reading the foregoing, that Canudos, like the Vendée uprising at the time of the French Revolution, is a reactionary movement, inspired by priests. It is not as simple as that, comrades. As you know from my last letter, the Church condemns the Counselor and Canudos, and the *jagunços* have seized the lands of a baron. I asked the man with the scar on his face if the poor of Brazil were better off during the monarchy. He immediately answered yes, since it was the monarchy that had abolished slavery. And he explained to me that the Devil, using Freemasons and Protestants as his tools, overthrew the Emperor Dom Pedro II, in order to restore slavery. Those were his very words: the Counselor has inculcated upon his followers the belief that the republicans are advocates of slavery. (A subtle way of teaching the truth, is it not? For the exploitation of man by money owners, the foundation of the republican system, is no less a slavery than the feudal form.) The emissary was categorical. 'The poor have suffered a great deal but we shall put an end to that: we will not answer the census questions because the purpose of them is to enable the government to identify the freedmen so as to put them in chains again and return them to their masters.' 'In Canudos no one pays the tribute exacted by the Republic because we do not recognize it or acknowledge its right to arrogate to itself functions and powers that belong to God.' What functions and powers, for example? 'Marrying couples and collecting tithes.' I asked what they used for money in Canudos and was informed that they allowed only coins with the effigy of Princess Isabel, that is to say, the coin of the Empire, but as this latter scarcely exists any more, in reality the use of money is gradually disappearing. 'There is no need for it, since in Canudos those who have give to those who do not, and those who are able to work do so for those who are not.'

I told him that doing away with private property and money and establishing communal ownership of all things, in whatever name it be done, even in that of nebulous abstractions, is a daring and courageous act on behalf of the disinherited of this earth, a first step toward redemption for all. I also pointed out that such measures would sooner or later bring down upon them the harshest sort of repression, since the ruling class will never allow such an example to spread: there are more than enough poor in this country to seize all the haciendas. Are the Counselor and his followers aware of the forces that they are arousing? Looking me straight in the eye, without blinking, the man recited a string of absurd phrases to me, of which I give you a sample: soldiers are not the strength but the weakness of the government; when the need arises, the waters of the Vaza-Barris will turn to milk and its gorges to maize cous-cous; and *jagunços* killed in battle will be resurrected so that they will be alive when the army of Dom Sebastião (a Portuguese king who died in Africa in the sixteenth century) appears.

Are these devils, emperors, and religious fetishes the elements of a strategy that the Counselor is using to launch the humble on the path of rebellion, a strategy which, in the realm of facts – unlike that of words – is a most effective one, since it has impelled them to rise up in arms against the economic, social, and military foundation of class society? Are religious, mythical, dynastic symbols the only ones capable of rousing from their inertia masses subjected for centuries to the superstitious tyranny of the Church, and is this the reason why the Counselor makes use of them? Or is all this sheer happenstance? We know, comrades, that there is no such thing as chance in history, that however fortuitous its course may seem, there is always a rationality lying hidden behind even the most puzzling outward appearances. Does the Counselor have any idea of the historical upheaval he is provoking? Is he an intuitive type or a clever one? No hypothesis is to be rejected, and, even less than others, that of a spontaneous, unpremeditated, popular movement. Rationality is engraved within the head of every man, however uncultured he may be, and given certain circumstances, it can guide him, amid the clouds of dogma that veil his eyes or the prejudices that limit his vocabulary, to act in the direction of the march of history. A man who was not one of us, Montesquieu, wrote that fortune or misfortune is simply a certain inborn tendency of our organs. Revolutionary action, too, can be born of this same propensity of the organs that govern us, even before science educates the minds of the poor. Is this what is happening in the backlands of Bahia? The answer can only be come by in Canudos itself. Till my next letter or never.

VI

The victory of Uauá was celebrated in Canudos with two days of festivities. There were skyrockets and fireworks displays prepared by Antônio the Pyrotechnist and the Little Blessed One organized processions that wound in and out amid the labyrinth of huts that had sprung up on the hacienda. The Counselor preached every evening from a scaffolding of the Temple. Worse trials still awaited them in Canudos; they must not allow fear to overcome them, the Blessed Jesus would aid those who had faith. The end of the world continued to be a subject he very often spoke of. The earth, worn out after so many centuries of giving forth plants and animals and sheltering man, would ask the Father if it might rest. God would give His consent, and the acts of destruction would commence. That was what was meant by the words of the Bible: 'I bring not peace, but a sword!'

Hence, while in Bahia the authorities, mercilessly pilloried by the *Jornal de Notícias* and the Progressivist Republican Party for what had happened in Uauá, organized a second expedition with seven times as many troops as the first and equipped it with two Krupp 7.5 caliber cannons and two Nordenfelt machine guns and sent it off by train, under the command of Major

Febrônio de Brito, to Queimadas, with orders to proceed immediately on foot from there to punish the *jagunços*, the latter were readying themselves in Canudos for Judgment Day. A number of the more impatient of them, eager to hasten that day or to give the earth the rest it deserved, went out to sow desolation. In a furious excess of love they set fire to buildings on the mountain plateaus and in the scrub forests that isolated Canudos from the world. To save their lands, many owners of haciendas and peasants presented them with gifts, but they nonetheless burned down a goodly number of farmhouses, animal pens, abandoned dwellings, shepherds' huts, and hideouts of outlaws. It was necessary for Jose Venâncio, Pajeú, Abbot João, Big João, the Macambiras to go out and stop these zealous visionaries eager to bring rest to nature by reducing it to ashes, and for the Little Blessed One, the Mother of Men, the Lion of Natuba to explain to them that they had misunderstood the saint's sermons.

Not even in these days, despite the many new pilgrims who arrived, did Canudos suffer from hunger. Maria Quadrado took a group of women – which the Little Blessed One named the Sacred Choir – off to live with her in the Sanctuary so that they could help her support the Counselor when he was so weak from fasting that his legs gave way, feed him the few crumbs he ate, and serve as his protective armor so that he would not be crushed by the pilgrims who wanted to touch him and hounded him to beg for his intercession with the Blessed Jesus for a blind daughter, an invalid son, or a husband who had passed on. Meanwhile, other *jagunços* took on the responsibility of providing food for the city and defending it. They had once been runaway slaves – Big João, for instance – or *cangaceiros* with a past that included many murders – as was the case with Pajeú or Abbot João – and now they were men of God. But they nonetheless continued to be practical men, alert to earthly concerns, aware of the threat of hunger and war, and as in Uauá, they were the ones who took the situation in hand. As they reined in the hordes of arsonists, they also herded to Canudos the heads of cattle, horses, mules, donkeys, goats that the haciendas round about resigned themselves to donating to the Blessed Jesus, and sent off to the Vilanova brothers' warehouses the flour, the seed grain, the clothing, and most importantly the arms they collected in their raids. In just a few days, Canudos was filled to overflowing with resources. At the same time, solitary envoys wandered about the backlands, like biblical prophets, and went down as far as the coast, urging people to come to Canudos and join the elect to fight against that invention of the Dog: the Republic. They were odd-looking emissaries from heaven, dressed not in tunics but in leather pants and shirts, whose mouths spat out the coarse obscenities of ruffians and whom everybody knew because once upon a time they had shared their misery and a roof overhead with them, till one day, brushed by the wings of the angel, they had gone off to Canudos. They were the same as ever, armed with the same knives, carbines, machetes, and yet they were different now, since all they talked about, with a contagious conviction and pride, was the Counselor, God, or the community that they had come from. People extended them their hospitality, listened to them, and many of them, feeling hope stir for the first time, bundled up all their possessions and took off for Canudos.

Major Febrônio de Brito's forces had already arrived in Queimadas. They numbered five hundred and forty-three soldiers, fourteen officers, and three doctors chosen from among the three infantry battalions of Bahia – the Ninth, Twenty-sixth, and Thirty-third – whom the little town welcomed with a speech by the mayor, a Mass in the Church of Santo Antônio, a meeting with the town council, and a day that was proclaimed a holiday so that the townspeople could take in the parade, complete with drumrolls and bugle fanfares, around the main square. Before the parade began, volunteer messengers had already taken off north to inform Canudos of the number of soldiers and arms in the expeditionary force and the line of march it was planning to follow. The news came as no surprise. What cause for surprise was there if reality confirmed what God had announced to them through the words spoken by the Counselor? The one real piece of news was that the soldiers would come this time by way of

Cariacá, the Serra de Acari, and the Vale de Ipueiras. Abbot João suggested to the others that they dig trenches, bring gunpowder and projectiles, and post men on the slopes of Monte Cambaio, for the Protestants would be obliged to come that way.

For the moment, the Counselor's mind appeared to be more occupied with getting on with the building of the Temple of the Blessed Jesus as quickly as possible than with the war. He still appeared at dawn every day to supervise the construction work, but it kept falling behind because of the building stones; they had to be hauled from quarries located farther and farther away as time went by, and hoisting them up to the towers was hazardous since the ropes sometimes broke and as they fell the huge stones brought scaffoldings and workers crashing down with them. And sometimes the saint would order a wall that had already been built to be torn down and built again somewhere else or would order windows done over because an inspiration had told him that they were not oriented in the direction of love. He could be seen circulating among the people, accompanied by the Lion of Natuba, the Little Blessed One, Maria Quadrado, and the women of the Sacred Choir, who kept constantly clapping their hands to keep the flies from bothering him. Every day three, five, ten families or groups of pilgrims arrived in Canudos with their carts and their tiny herds of goats, and Antônio Vilanova would assign them an empty spot in the labyrinth of dwellings so that they could build one for themselves. Every evening, before giving his counsel, the saint received the newcomers inside the Temple that as yet was without a roof. They were led through the crowd of faithful and ushered into his presence by the Little Blessed One, and even though the Counselor tried to keep them from falling to their knees at his feet to kiss them or touching his tunic by saying to them 'God is other,' they did so nonetheless, whereupon he blessed them, gazing at them with eyes that gave the impression that they were continually fixed on the beyond. At a given moment, he would interrupt the welcoming ceremony by rising to his feet, and everyone would stand aside as he made his way toward the little ladder leading to the scaffolding up above. He preached in a hoarse voice, without moving, on the usual subjects: the superior nature of the spirit, the advantages of being poor and frugal, hatred toward the impious, the need to save Canudos so that it would be a refuge of the just.

The crowd of people listened to him with bated breath, convinced. Religion filled their days now. As they came into being, each narrow winding street was named after a saint, in a procession. In every corner there were niches and statues of the Virgin, of the Christ Child, of the Blessed Jesus, of the Holy Spirit, and each neighborhood, each occupation erected altars to its patron saint. Many of the newcomers took new names, thereby symbolizing that a new life was beginning for them. But sometimes dubious customs were grafted upon Catholic practices, like parasitic plants. Thus, certain mulattoes began to dance as they prayed, and it was said that they believed that by stamping their feet on the ground in a frenzy they were flushing out sins from their bodies with their sweat. The blacks gradually grouped together in the northern section of Canudos, a block of mud and straw huts that later became known as the Mocambo – the Slave Refuge. Indians from Mirandela, who unexpectedly came to live in Canudos, prepared in full view of everyone herb concoctions that gave off a heady odor and sent them into ecstasy. In addition to pilgrims, there arrived, naturally, miracle workers, peddlers, curiosity seekers. In the huts that grew like cysts on each other, there could be found women who read palms, rogues who boasted of being able to speak with the dead, and *cantadores* who, like those in the Gypsy's Circus, earned their daily bread by singing ballads or sticking pins into themselves. Certain healers claimed to be able to cure any sort of sickness with potions of acacia and nightshade, and a number of pious believers, overcome by an excess of contrition, recited their sins at the tops of their voices and asked their listeners to impose penance on them. On settling in Canudos, a group of people from Juazeiro began to practice the rites of the Brotherhood of Penitents in that city: fasting, sexual abstinence, public flagellations. Although the

Counselor encouraged the mortification of the flesh and asceticism – suffering, he would say, strengthens faith – he finally became alarmed and asked the Little Blessed One to examine the pilgrims as they arrived in order to keep superstition, fetishism, or any sort of impiety disguised as devotion from entering with them.

This motley collection of human beings lived side by side in Canudos without violence, amid a fraternal solidarity and a climate of exaltation that the elect had not known before. They felt truly rich because they were poor, sons of God, privileged, just as the man in the mantle full of holes told them each evening. In their love for him, moreover, all differences that might have separated them came to an end: when it was anything to do with the Counselor, these men and women who had numbered in the hundreds and were beginning to number in the thousands became a single, reverent, obedient being, ready to do anything and everything for the one who had been able to reach past their abjection, their hunger, their lice, to fill them with hope and make them proud of their fate. Though the population kept multiplying, life was not chaotic. The men set out from Canudos on missions, the pilgrims brought cattle and supplies in, the animal pens were full, as were the storehouses, and the Vaza-Barris fortunately had enough water in it to irrigate the small farms. As Abbot João, Pajeú, José Venâncio, Big João, Pedrão, and others prepared for war, Honório and Antônio Vilanova managed the city: they received the pilgrims' offerings, distributed plots of land, food, and clothes, and supervised the Health Houses for the sick, the old, and the orphaned. And it was they who heard out the contending parties when there were quarrels over property rights in the community.

Each day there arrived news of the Antichrist. Major Febrônio de Brito's expedition had proceeded from Queimadas to Monte Santo, a place it profaned on the evening of the twenty-ninth of December, its strength lessened by one infantry corporal, who had been fatally bitten by a rattlesnake. The Counselor explained, without ill will, what was happening. Was it not a blasphemy, an abomination, for men with firearms, bound on destruction, to camp in a sanctuary that drew pilgrims from all over the world? But the ungodly must not be allowed to set foot in Canudos, which that night he called Belo Monte. Working himself into a frenzy, he urged them not to bow down to the enemies of religion, whose aims were to send the slaves to the stocks once again, to impoverish people by making them pay taxes, to prevent them from being married and buried by the Church, and to confuse them with such clever hocus-pocus as the metric system, the statistical map, and the census, whose real purpose was to deceive them and lead them into sin. They all stayed up the whole night, with whatever weapons they had within reach of their hands. The Freemasons did not come. They were in Monte Santo, repairing the two Krupp cannons knocked out of alignment as they were being hauled over the rough terrain, and awaiting reinforcements. When they marched off in columns two weeks later, heading up the Cariacá Valley in the direction of Canudos, the entire route that they would be following was teeming with spies, apostates hiding in refuges for goats, in the tangled underbrush of the scrub forest, or in dugouts concealed beneath the carcass of a cow, with the eyeholes in its skull serving as peepholes. Swift messengers brought news to Canudos of the enemy's advance each day and the obstacles that had held them up.

When he learned that the expeditionary force had finally arrived in Mulungu, despite its tremendous difficulties in hauling the cannons and the machine guns, and that, faced with near-starvation, it had been obliged to sacrifice its last head of beef cattle and two dray mules, the Counselor commented that the Father must not be unhappy with Canudos since He was beginning to defeat the soldiers of the Republic before the battle had even begun.

'Do you know the word for what your husband's done?' Galileo Gall says slowly, emphasizing each syllable, his voice breaking in outrage. 'A betrayal. No, two betrayals. Of me, with whom he had an agreement. And of his brothers in Canudos. A betrayal of his class.'

Jurema smiles at him, as though she doesn't understand or isn't listening. She is leaning over the fire, boiling something. She is young, her hair worn loose, framing a face with smooth, lustrous skin. She is wearing a sleeveless tunic, her feet are bare, and her eyes are still heavy with the sleep from which she has been rudely awakened by Gall's arrival a few moments ago. A dim dawn light is filtering into the cabin through the palings. There is an oil lamp, and in one corner a row of chickens sleeping amid casks and jars, odds and ends of furniture, heaps of firewood, crates, and a devotional print of Our Lady of Lapa. A little woolly dog is foraging about at Jurema's feet, and though she kicks him away he comes straight back. Sitting in the hammock, panting from the effort of journeying all night long at the same pace as the ragged guide dressed in leather who has brought him back to Queimadas with the arms, Galileo watches her, still in a rage. Jurema walks over to him with a steaming bowl and hands it to him.

'He said he wasn't going to go off with the railroad men from Jacobina,' Galileo mutters, cupping the bowl in his hands, his eyes seeking hers. 'Why did he change his mind?'

'He wasn't going to go because they didn't want to give him as much money as he was asking them for,' Jurema answers quietly, blowing on the bowl steaming in her hands. 'He changed his mind because they came to tell him they'd pay him what he was asking. He went looking for you yesterday at the Our Lady of Grace boarding house and you'd taken off without leaving word where you were going or whether you'd be back. Rufino couldn't afford to pass up that work.'

Galileo sighs in annoyance. He decides to take a sip from his bowl, burns his palate, makes a wry face. He blows on the bowl and takes another swallow. His forehead is furrowed with fatigue and irritation and there are dark circles under his eyes. Every so often he bites his lower lip. He is panting, sweating.

'How long is that damned trip going to take him?' he growls after a time, sipping from his bowl.

'Three or four days.' Jurema has sat down facing him, on the edge of an old trunk with leather straps. 'He said you could wait for him, and when he got back he'd take you to Canudos.'

'Three or four days!' Gall groans, turning his eyes heavenward in exasperation. 'Three or four centuries, you mean.'

The sound of tinkling sheep bells is heard outside, and the woolly dog barks loudly and leaps against the door, wanting to go out. Galileo gets to his feet, walks over to the palings, and takes a look outside: the canvas-covered wagon is where he has left it, next to the enclosure alongside the cabin in which a few sheep are penned. The animals' eyes are open but they are still drowsy and their bells have stopped tinkling. The dwelling is on the top of a rise and on a sunny day one can see Queimadas; but not on this gray dawn with an overcast sky, when the only thing to be seen is the rolling, rocky stretch of desert below. Galileo walks back to the hammock. Jurema refills his bowl. The woolly dog barks and paws the dirt just inside the door.

'Three or four days,' Gall thinks. Three or four centuries during which a thousand mishaps could happen. Should he look for another guide? Should he take off by himself to Monte Santo and hire someone else to show him the way to Canudos? Anything rather than stay here with the arms: his impatience would make the wait unbearable. Moreover, it was quite possible, as Epaminondas Gonçalves feared, that Major Brito's expeditionary force would arrive in Queimadas before he could get away.

'Weren't you the one responsible for Rufino's going off with the railroad men from Jacobina?' Gall mutters. Jurema is putting the fire out with a stick. 'You've never liked the idea of Rufino's taking me to Canudos.'

'No, I've never liked the idea,' she agrees with such bluntness that for a moment Galileo feels his anger evaporate and nearly bursts out laughing. But she has spoken these words in all seriousness and looks him straight in the eye without blinking. Her face is an elongated oval, with prominent cheek and chin bones beneath her taut skin. Can the bones hidden beneath her hair be as prominent, as sharp, as eloquent, as revealing? 'They killed those soldiers in Uauá,' Jurema adds. 'Everybody says that more soldiers will march on Canudos. I don't want him to be killed or taken prisoner. He feels a need to be on the move all the time. "You have Saint Vitus's dance," his mother tells him.'

'Saint Vitus's dance?' Gall says.

'People who can't stay still,' Jurema explains. 'People who go about dancing.'

The dog begins barking furiously once more. Jurema goes to the door of the cabin, opens it, and pushes him outside with her feet. They hear him barking outside, and once again, the tinkling of sheep bells. With a gloomy expression on his face, Galileo follows Jurema with his eyes as she walks back to the fire and pokes at the embers with a stick. A wisp of smoke drifts away in spirals.

'And besides, Canudos belongs to the baron and he's always helped us,' Jurema says. 'This house, this land, these sheep are ours thanks to him. You're on the side of the *jagunços*, you want to help them. Taking you to Canudos is the same as helping them. Do you think the baron would like it if Rufino helps the thieves who stole his ranch from him?'

'I'm certain he wouldn't like it,' Gall mutters sarcastically.

The sound of the sheep bells reaches their ears again, even louder now, and Gall rises to his feet and reaches the palings of the wall of the cabin in two strides. He takes a look outside: the trees, the clumps of underbrush, the patches of rock are beginning to stand out in the whitish expanse. The wagon is there outside, loaded with bundles wrapped in canvas the same color as the desert, and alongside it the mule, tethered to a stake.

'Do you believe that the Counselor has been sent by the Blessed Jesus?' Jurema says. 'Do you believe the things he prophesies? That the sea will become backlands and the backlands a sea? That the waters of the Vaza-Barris will turn into milk and the ravines into maize cous-cous to feed the poor?'

There is not a trace of mockery in her words or in her eyes as Galileo Gall looks at her, trying to read in the expression on her face what she thinks of all the talk that she has heard second-hand. He is unable to tell: the thought crosses his mind that the long oval of her peaceful, burnished face is as inscrutable as that of a Hindustani or a Chinese. Or that of the emissary from Canudos with whom he talked in the tannery in Itapicuru. Then, too, it was impossible to know, by observing his face, what that taciturn man felt or thought.

'In people who are dying of hunger, instincts are ordinarily stronger than beliefs,' he murmurs after drinking the last drop of liquid in the bowl as he carefully scrutinizes Jurema's reactions. 'They may well believe nonsensical, ingenuous, stupid things. But that doesn't matter. What matters is what they do. They have done away with property, marriage, social hierarchies; they have refused to accept the authority of the Church and of the State, and wiped out an army company. They have fought against authority, money, uniforms, cassocks.'

Jurema's face is a blank; she does not move a muscle. Her dark, slightly slanted eyes gaze at him without a trace of curiosity, sympathy, surprise. She has moist lips that pucker at the corners.

'They have taken up the fight at the point where we abandoned it, though they are not aware that they have done so. They are bringing the Idea back to life,' Gall goes on, wondering what Jurema can be thinking of the words that she is hearing. 'That is why I'm here. That is why I want to help them.'

He is panting for breath, as though he had been shouting at the top of his lungs. The fatigue of the last two days, and on top of it the disappointment that he has felt on discovering that Rufino is not in Queimadas, is beginning to overcome him again, and the thought of sleeping, stretching out, of closing his eyes is so irresistible that he decides to lie down under the cart for a few hours. Or could he perhaps sleep in here – in this hammock, for instance? Will Jurema think it shocking if he asks to do so?

'That man who came from there, the one the saint sent, the one you saw – do you know who he was?' he hears her say. 'It was Pajeú.' And as Gall does not appear to be impressed, she adds in a surprised voice: 'Haven't you heard of Pajeú? The most evil man in all the *sertão*. He lived by stealing and killing. He lopped off the noses and ears of people unlucky enough to run into him on the roads.'

All at once the tinkling of the sheep bells can be heard again outside, along with anxious barks at the door of the cabin and the whinnying of the mule. Gall is remembering the emissary from Canudos, the scar etched into his face, his strange calm, his indifference. Was it a mistake not to have told him about the arms? No, since he couldn't show them to him at the time: he would not have believed it, he would have been even more mistrustful, it would have jeopardized the entire plan. The dog barks frantically outside, and Gall sees Jurema grab the stick that she has put the fire out with and walk quickly over to the door. His mind elsewhere, still thinking about the emissary from Canudos, telling himself that if he had known that the man was an ex-bandit it might have been easier to talk with him, he watches Jurema struggle with the heavy crossbar, lift it, and at that moment something subtle, a noise, an intuition, a sixth sense, chance, tells him what is about to happen. For when Jurema is suddenly thrown backward as the door is violently flung open – with a shove or a kick from outside – and the silhouette of the man armed with a carbine appears in the doorway, Galileo already has his revolver out and is pointing it at the intruder. The roar of the carbine awakens the chickens in the corner, which flutter about in terror as Jurema, who has not been hit by the bullet but falls to the floor nonetheless, lets out a scream. On seeing the woman at his feet, the assailant hesitates, and it takes him a few seconds to find Gall amid the panicked flutter of wings, so that by the time he trains the carbine on him, Galileo has already fired, looking at him with a stupid expression on his face. The intruder drops the carbine and reels back, snorting. Jurema screams again. Galileo finally reacts and runs toward the carbine. He leans over and grabs it, and then catches sight, through the doorway, of the wounded man writhing on the ground moaning, another man coming on the run with his carbine raised and shouting something to the wounded man, and beyond him a third man hitching the wagon with the arms to a horse. Barely taking aim, he shoots. The man who was coming running stumbles, rolls on the ground bellowing, and Galileo takes another shot at him. 'There are two bullets left,' he thinks. He sees Jurema at his side, pushing the door, sees her close it, lower the crossbar, and slip to the back of the shack. He gets to his feet, wondering when it was that she fell to the floor. He is covered with dirt and drenched with sweat, his teeth are chattering, and he is clutching the revolver so tightly that his fingers ache. He peeks out through the palings: the wagon with the arms is disappearing in the distance in a cloud of dust, and in front of the cabin the dog is barking frantically at the two wounded men, who are creeping toward the sheepfold. Taking aim at them, he shoots the last two bullets left in his revolver and hears what seems to him to be a human roar amid the barking and the tinkling sheep bells. Yes, he has hit one of them: the two are lying motionless, halfway between the cabin and the animal pen. Jurema is screaming still and the chickens cackling madly as they fly about in all directions, overturn things, crash into the palings, collide with his body. He slaps them away and looks out again, to the right and the left. If it weren't for those two bodies lying practically one atop the other, it would seem as though nothing had happened. Breathing hard, he staggers amid the chickens to the door. Through the cracks he glimpses the lonely countryside, the sprawling bodies. 'They made away with the rifles,' he thinks. 'I'd be worse off if I were dead,' he thinks. He pants, his eyes opened wide. Finally he lifts the crossbar and pushes the door open. Nothing, nobody.

He runs, half hunched over, to where the wagon has been standing, hearing the tinkle of the sheep bells as the creatures run round and round and back and forth inside the palings of the pen. He feels a knot of anxiety in his stomach, at the nape of his neck: a trail of gunpowder leads to the horizon, where it disappears in the direction of Riacho da Onça. He takes a deep breath, runs his hand over his little reddish beard; his teeth continue to chatter. The mule, tied to the tree trunk, is contentedly lazing about. He slowly walks back toward the cabin. He stops in front of the bodies lying on the ground: they are corpses now. He scrutinizes their tanned, unknown faces, fixed in a rigid grimace. Suddenly his expression turns to one of bitter, uncontrollable rage. He begins to kick the inert forms, viciously, muttering insults. His fury is contagious: the dog begins to bark, leap about, nibble at the two men's sandals. Finally Galileo calms down. Dragging his feet, he goes back into the cabin. He is met by a flurry of hens that makes him raise his hands in front of his face to protect it. Jurema is standing in the middle of the room: a figure trembling all over, her tunic ripped, her mouth half open, her eyes full of tears, her hair disheveled. She is staring in bewilderment at the disorder that reigns all about her, as though unable to fathom what is happening in her house, and, on spying Gall, runs to him and throws her arms about his chest, stammering words he does not understand. He stands there rigid, his mind a blank. He feels the woman huddling against his chest; he looks, in consternation, in fear, at this body clinging to his, this neck palpitating beneath his eyes. He smells the odor of her, and the thought dimly crosses his mind: 'It's the smell of a woman.' His temples pound. With an effort he raises one arm, puts it around Jurema's shoulders. He lets go of the revolver that he is still holding and his fingers awkwardly smooth her ruffled hair. 'They were trying to kill me,' he whispers in Jurema's ear. 'There's no more danger now. They've carried off what they were after.' Little by little the woman calms down. Her sobs die away, her body stops trembling, her hands let go of Gall. But he is still holding her close, still stroking her hair, and when Jurema tries to step away, he will not let her go. *'Don't be afraid,'* he says to her slowly, in English, blinking rapidly. *'They're gone. They . . .'* Something new, ambiguous, urgent, intense, has appeared in his face, something that grows by the moment, something that he is barely aware of. His lips are very close to Jurema's neck. She steps back, vehemently, covering her bosom as she does so. She begins struggling now to free herself from Gall's grasp, but he will not let her go, and as he holds her fast, he whispers over and over the same phrase that she is unable to understand: *'Don't be afraid, don't be afraid.'* Jurema lashes out at him with both fists, scratches his face, manages to free herself and makes her escape. But Galileo runs across the room after her, catches up with her, grabs her, stumbles over the old trunk, and falls to the floor with her. Jurema kicks at him, fights him off with all her strength, but does not scream. The only sounds to be heard are the jagged panting of the two of them, their murmuring voices as they struggle, the cackling of the chickens, the barking of the dog, the tinkling of the sheep bells. Amid leaden clouds, the sun is rising.

He was born with very short legs and an enormous head, so the inhabitants of Natuba thought it would be better for him and for his parents if the Blessed Jesus took him right away, since if he survived he would be crippled and a cretin. Only the first turned out to be so. Because, even though the youngest son of Celestino Pardinas, the horsebreaker, was never able to walk like other people, he had a keen intelligence, a mind eager to know everything and capable, once a piece of knowledge had gone into that massive head that made people laugh, of retaining it forever. Everything about him was unusual: the fact that he had been born deformed in a family as normal as the Pardinases; that despite being a feeble, ridiculous-looking child he did not die or suffer illnesses; that instead of going about on two feet like humans he went about on all fours; and that his head became so monstrously large that it seemed like a miracle that his frail little body could hold it up. But what caused the townspeople of Natuba to begin to murmur among themselves that he had not been fathered by the horsebreaker but by the Devil was the fact that he had learned to read and write without anyone having taught him.

Neither Celestino nor Dona Gaudência had taken the trouble – thinking, probably, that it would be useless – to take him to Dom Asênio, who, besides making bricks, taught Portuguese, a bit of

Latin, and a smattering of religion. But it so happened that the post rider came one day and nailed up on the official announcement board in the main square a decree that he did not bother to read aloud, claiming that he still had to post it in ten other localities before the sun went down. The townspeople were trying to decipher the hieroglyphics when from underfoot they heard the Lion's little piping voice: 'It says that there's an animal epidemic going round, that stables must be disinfected with creosote, all garbage burned, and water and milk boiled before drinking.' Dom Asênio confirmed that that was what it said. Pestered by the villagers to tell them who had taught him to read, the Lion gave an explanation that many of them found suspect: that he had learned by watching those who knew how, men such as Dom Asênio, Felisbelo the overseer, Dom Abelardo the healer, and Zózimo the tinsmith. None of them had given him lessons, but the four of them remembered having often seen the Lion's huge head with its thick mane and his inquisitive eyes appear alongside the stool where they were reading aloud to someone in the town a letter that the person had received or writing one for him at his dictation. The fact is that the Lion had learned and from that time on he could be seen at any hour of the day hunched over in the shade of the blue jasmine trees of Natuba reading and rereading newspapers, prayer books, missals, edicts, and anything printed that he could lay his hands on. He became the person who wrote, with a goose quill he had sharpened himself and a tincture of cochineal and various plants, in large, flowing letters, the birthday greetings, announcements of births, deaths, weddings, news of sickness, or simple gossip that the townspeople of Natuba wanted to send to people in other towns and that the post rider came to collect once a week. The Lion also read aloud to the villagers the letters that were sent them. He served as scribe and reader for the others as a pastime, without charging them a cent, but sometimes he received presents for performing these services.

His real name was Felício, but as frequently happened in those parts, once the nickname took hold, it replaced his Christian name. They called him the Lion as a joke perhaps, a nickname undoubtedly brought to mind by his enormous head, but in time, as if to prove that the jokers hadn't been far from the truth, it in fact came to be covered with a thick mane that hid his ears and tossed about as he moved. Or perhaps the name came from his way of walking, which was unquestionably animal-like, for he used both his feet and his hands to get about (protecting them with leather soles that served as hoofs, so to speak, or horseshoes), although his gait, what with his little short legs and his long arms that touched the ground every so often as he went along, was more like that of a simian than that of a feline predator. He was not doubled over like that all the time: he could stand erect for brief periods and take a few human steps on his ridiculous legs, but both these things were very tiring for him. Because of his peculiar manner of locomotion, he never wore pants, only long robes, like women, missionaries, or the penitents of the Blessed Jesus.

Despite the fact that he took care of their correspondence, the townspeople never completely accepted the Lion. If his own father and mother could scarcely hide their shame at being his procreators and at one time tried to give him away, how could the men and women of Natuba have been expected to look upon this creature as belonging to the same species as they? The dozen Pardinas offspring who were his brothers and sisters wanted nothing to do with him, and it was common knowledge that he did not eat with them at the same table but at a wooden crate by himself. Hence, he knew neither paternal nor fraternal love (although he apparently had glimpses of another sort of love) nor friendship, for youngsters his age were afraid of him at first and later on repelled by him. They threw stones at him, spat on him, insulted him if he dared come near them to watch them play. He, for his part, moreover, rarely attempted to do so. From a very early age, his intuition or his unfailing intelligence told him that others would always be creatures who shunned him or were disagreeable to him, and would often even be his torturers, so that he had best remain apart from everyone. And that was what he did, at least until what happened at the irrigation ditch, and people saw him always warily keeping his distance, even at festivals and market fairs. When a Holy Mission came to Natuba, the Lion listened to the sermons from the rooftop of the Church of Nossa Senhora da Conceição, like a cat. But even this strategy of withdrawal did not suffice to lay his fears to rest. The Gypsy's Circus was the cause of one of his worst scares. It passed through Natuba twice a year with its caravan of monsters: acrobats, fortune-tellers, *cantadores*, clowns. On one of its visits, the Gypsy asked the horsebreaker and Dona Gaudência to let him take the Lion away with him as a circus hand. 'My circus is the only place where he won't attract attention, and he can make himself useful,' he told them. They agreed. The Gypsy took him off with him, but a week later the Lion had escaped and was back in Natuba. From that time on, every time the Gypsy's Circus came to town, he was nowhere to be found.

What he feared, above all else, were drunks, those bands of cowhands who returned to town after a day's work herding, branding, gelding, or cropping, dismounted, and hurried to Dona Epifânia's tavern to quench their thirst. They would come out arm in arm, singing, staggering, happy at times, in a rage at others, and would go looking for him in the narrow back streets to amuse themselves at his expense or let off steam. He had developed an unusually acute sense of hearing and could tell from a long way away, from their boisterous laughter and their swear words, that they were coming, and then, hugging the walls and the façades of buildings so they wouldn't catch sight of him, he would hop on home as fast as he could, or, if he was far from home, he would hide in the brush or on a rooftop till the danger was past. He didn't always manage to escape them. Sometimes, by resorting to a trick – sending someone to tell him, for instance, that So-and-so was asking for him because he needed to draft a petition to be presented to the town magistrate – they would manage to trap him. And they would then torment him for hours, stripping him naked to see if he had other monstrosities hidden underneath his tunic in addition to the ones that were plainly visible, mounting him on a horse, or trying to mate him with a she-goat to see what sort of offspring this crossbreeding would produce.

As a point of honor rather than out of affection, Celestino Pardinas and other members of the family would intervene if they heard about what was happening and threaten the pranksters, and one time his older brothers lashed out with knives and shovels to rescue the scribe from a band of townspeople roaring drunk on cane brandy who had poured molasses over him, rolled him over and over in a garbage heap, and were leading him through the streets at the end of a rope as though he were an animal of an unknown species. But the relatives had had more than enough of these incidents that they found themselves involved in because of this member of the family. The Lion knew this better than anyone else and hence no one ever heard him denounce his tormentors.

The fate of Celestino Pardinas's youngest son took a decided turn for the worse the day that the tinsmith Zózimo's young daughter, Almudia, the only one of his six children to have survived, the others having been stillborn or died within a few days of their birth, fell sick, with a high fever and vomiting. Dom Abelardo's remedies and spells, like her parents' prayers, had proved to be of no avail. The healer solemnly delivered himself of the opinion that the girl was a victim of the evil eye and that any antidote would be ineffective so long as the person who had put the evil eye upon her remained unknown. In despair at the fate that threatened this daughter who was the light of their lives, Zózimo and his wife Eufrásia made the rounds of the huts of Natuba, seeking information. And thus it was that they heard, from the mouths of three persons, the rumor that the girl had been seen in the company of the Lion, in a strange meeting on the bank of the irrigation ditch leading to the Mirândola hacienda. On being questioned, the sick girl confessed, half delirious, that on that particular morning, as she passed by the irrigation ditch on her way to the house of her godfather, Dom Náutilo, the Lion had asked her if he might sing a song that he had composed for her. And he had done so, before Almudia could take to her heels. It was the one time he had ever spoken to her, although before that she had noticed that, as if by chance, she often came across the Lion as she went about the town, and something about the way he hunched over as she passed made her surmise that he wanted to talk to her.

Zózimo grabbed up his shotgun and, accompanied by nephews, brothers-in-law, and *compadres*, also armed, and followed by a crowd of people, went to the Pardinases' house, cornered the Lion, pointed the shotgun straight between his eyes, and demanded that he repeat the song so that Dom Abelardo could exorcise it. The Lion, struck dumb, stared at him wide-eyed, distraught. After repeating several times that if he did not reveal the magic spell he would blow his big ugly head off, the tinsmith cocked his gun. For the space of a second the Lion's big intelligent eyes gleamed in utter panic. 'If you kill me, you'll never learn the magic spell and Almudia will die,' his little piping voice murmured, so terrified it was unrecognizable. A total silence ensued. Zózimo was sweating heavily. His relatives kept Celestino Pardinas and his sons at bay with their shotguns. 'Will you let me go if I tell you what it was?' they heard the piping voice of the monster say. Zózimo nodded. Then, choking up, his voice breaking like an adolescent's, the Lion began to sing. He sang – as the townspeople of Natuba who were present and those who were not but swore that they had been reported, remembered, recounted far and wide – a love song, in which Almudia's name was mentioned. When he finished singing, the Lion's eyes were filled with embarrassment. 'Let me go now,' he roared. 'I'll let you go when my daughter is cured,' the tinsmith answered dully. 'And if she is not cured, I'll burn you to death at her graveside. I swear it on my soul.' He looked round at the Pardinases – father, mother, brothers frozen motionless by the shotguns – and added in a tone of voice that left no doubt in their minds as to his resolve: 'I'll burn you alive even if my family and yours will then be forced to kill each other for centuries on end.'

Almudia died that same night, after vomiting up blood. The

townspeople thought that Zózimo would weep, tear out his hair, curse God, or drink cane brandy till he fell into a stupor. But he did no such thing. His reckless behavior of recent days gave way to cold determination as he planned, at one and the same time, his daughter's funeral and the death of the sorcerer who had cast his spell over her. He had never been a wicked man or a cruel or violent one, but rather a kindly, helpful neighbor. Hence, everyone pitied him, forgave him in advance for what he was about to do, and there were even those who approved of what he intended to do.

Zózimo had a stake set up at the graveside and straw and dry branches brought to the site. The Pardinases remained prisoners in their house. The Lion was in the tinsmith's animal pen, tied hand and foot. He spent the night there, listening to the prayers, the condolences, the litanies, the lamentations of the wake. The following morning, they hoisted him into a cart drawn by burros, and at a distance, as usual, he followed the funeral procession. When they arrived at the cemetery, as the coffin was lowered into the ground and more prayers were being said, in accordance with the tinsmith's instructions two of the latter's nephews tied him to the post and heaped around it the straw and branches that they were about to light to burn him to death. Nearly everyone in the town was there to witness his immolation.

At that moment the saint arrived. He must have set foot in Natuba the night before, or at dawn that morning, and someone must have informed him of what was about to happen. But this explanation was too logical for the townspeople, for whom the supernatural was more believable than the natural. They were later to say that his ability to foresee the future, or the Blessed Jesus, had brought him and his followers to this remote spot in the backlands of Bahia at this precise moment to correct a mistake, to prevent a crime, or simply to offer a proof of his power. He had not come alone, as he had the first time he preached in Natuba, years before, nor had he come accompanied by only two or three pilgrims, as on his second visit, when in addition to giving counsel he had rebuilt the chapel of the abandoned Jesuit convent on the town square. This time he was accompanied by some thirty people, as gaunt and poor as he was, but with eyes filled with happiness. As they followed after him, he made his way through the crowd to the grave just as the last shovelfuls of earth to fill it were raining down.

The man dressed in dark purple turned to Zózimo, standing with downcast eyes gazing at the freshly turned earth. 'Have you buried her in her best dress, in a sturdy coffin?' he asked in an amiable though not affectionate tone of voice. Zózimo nodded, barely moving his head. 'We will pray to the Father, so that He will receive her with rejoicing in the Kingdom of Heaven,' the Counselor said. And he and the penitents thereupon recited litanies and sang hymns at the graveside. Only then did the saint point to the stake to which the Lion had been tied. 'What are you about to do with this boy, my brother?' he asked. 'Burn him to death,' Zózimo replied. And he explained why, amid a silence that seemed to echo. The saint nodded, not blinking an eye. Then he turned to the Lion and gestured to the crowd to step back a bit. Everyone withdrew a few paces. The saint leaned down and spoke in the ear of the youngster tied to the stake and then brought his ear close to the Lion's mouth to hear what he was saying. And thus, as the Counselor bent his head down toward the ear and the mouth of the other, the two of them held a secret conversation. No one moved, awaiting some extraordinary event.

And, in fact, what happened was as amazing as seeing a man frying to death on a funeral pyre. For when the two of them fell silent, the saint, with the serenity that never abandoned him, not moving from the spot, said: 'Come, untie him!' The tinsmith raised his eyes and looked at him in amazement. 'You must loosen his bonds yourself,' the man dressed in dark purple said, in a voice so deep it made people tremble. 'Do you want your daughter to go to hell? Are the flames down there not hotter, more everlasting than the ones that you are seeking to ignite?' his voice roared once more, as though amazed at such stupidity.

'You are filled with superstition, ungodly, a sinner,' he went on. 'Repent of your intentions, come and loosen his bonds, seek his forgiveness, and pray to the Father not to send your daughter to the realm of the Dog because of your cowardice and wickedness, because of your lack of faith in God.' And he stood there, reviling him, urging him, terrifying him at the thought that through his grievous fault Almudia would go to hell, till finally the townspeople saw Zózimo obey him, rather than shoot him or plunge his knife into him or burn him to death along with the monster, and fall to his knees, sobbing, begging the Father, the Blessed Jesus, the Divine One, the Virgin to keep Almudia's innocent soul from descending to hell.

When the Counselor, after remaining for two weeks in the town, praying, preaching, comforting the sick and offering his counsel to the healthy, took off in the direction of Mocambo, Natuba had a cemetery enclosed within a brick wall and new crosses on all the graves. And the ranks of the Counselor's followers had been increased by one, a small figure half animal and half human who, as the little band of pilgrims marched off into the countryside covered with *mandacarus*, seemed to be trotting off alongside the handful of the faithful in rags and tatters like a horse, a goat, a pack mule . . .

Was he thinking, was he dreaming? I am on the outskirts of Queimadas, it is daytime, this is Rufino's hammock. Everything else was confused in his mind: above all, the concatenation of circumstances which, at dawn this morning, had once again turned his life upside down. The amazement that had overcome him as he fell asleep after making love lingered on as he lay there half asleep and half awake.

Yes, for someone who believed that fate was in large part innate and written in the brain case, where skillful hands could palpate it and perspicacious eyes could read it, it was a harrowing experience to confront the existence of that unpredictable margin that other beings could manipulate with a horrifying disregard of one's own will, of one's personal aptitudes. How long had he been resting? His fatigue had disappeared, at any rate. Had the young woman disappeared, too? Had she gone to get help, to fetch people to come take him prisoner? He thought or dreamed: 'My plans went up in smoke as they were about to materialize.' He thought or dreamed: 'Troubles never come singly.' He realized that he was lying to himself; it was not true that this anxiety and this feeling of stunned amazement were due to his having missed meeting Rufino, to his having narrowly escaped death, to his having killed those two men, to the theft of the arms that he was going to take to Canudos. It was that sudden, incomprehensible, irrepressible impulse that had made him rape Jurema after ten years of not touching a woman that was troubling his half sleep.

He had loved a number of women in his youth, he had had comrades – women fighting for the same ideals as he – with whom he had shared short stretches of his life's journey; in his days in Barcelona he had lived with a working-class woman who was pregnant at the time of the attack on the military barracks and who, he learned later after he had fled Spain, had eventually married a banker. But, unlike science or revolution, women had never occupied a prominent place in his life. Like food, sex to him had been something that satisfied a basic need and soon left him surfeited. The most secret decision of his life had been made ten years before. Or was it eleven? Or twelve? Dates danced about in his head, but not the place: Rome. He had hidden out there after escaping from Barcelona, in the house of a pharmacist, a comrade who wrote for the underground anarchist press and had been in prison more than once. There the vivid images were in Gall's memory. He had had certain suspicions first, and then proof: this comrade picked up whores who solicited around the Colosseum, brought them home when Gall was gone, and paid them to let him whip them. Ah, the poor devil's tears the night that Galileo had rebuked him, and then his confession that he could take his pleasure with a woman only by inflicting punishment on her, that he could make love only when he saw a battered, bruised body. He thought or dreamed he heard the pharmacist's voice, once again, asking him for help, and in his half sleep, as on that night, he palpated him, felt the round bulge in the zone of the inferior emotions, the abnormal temperature of the crown, where Spurzheim had located the organ of sexuality, and the deformation, in the lower occipital curve, just above the nape of his neck, of the cavities that represent the destructive instincts. (And at that moment he was suddenly surrounded once again by the warm atmosphere of Mariano Cubí's study, and heard once more the example that Cubí used to cite, that of Jobard le Joly, the Geneva arsonist, whose head he had examined after the decapitation: 'In him this region of cruelty was so enlarged that it looked like an enormous tumor, a pregnant cranium.') Then he heard his own voice, telling the pharmacist-anarchist the remedy again: 'The thing you must rid your life of, comrade, is not vice but sex,' and explaining to him that when he had done so, the sexual path would be blocked and the destructive power of his nature would be channeled toward ethical and social goals, thus multiplying his energy for the fight for freedom and the eradication from this earth of every form of oppression. And without a tremor in his voice, looking him straight in the eye, he again made him the fraternal proposal: 'Let's do it together. I'll make the same decision and abide by it, to prove to you that it's possible. Let us both swear never to touch a woman again, brother.' Had the pharmacist kept his vow? He remembered his look of consternation, his voice that night, and thought or dreamed: 'He was a weak man.' The sun's rays penetrated his closed eyelids, burned his pupils.

He, on the other hand, was not a weak man. He had been able to keep the vow – until this morning – because the power of reason and knowledge served as a firm support, a source of strength for what in the beginning had been merely an impulse, a comradely gesture. Weren't the search for sexual pleasure, the enslavement to instinct a danger to someone engaged in a war without quarter? Weren't sexual urges liable to distract him from the ideal? What tormented Gall in those years was not banishing women from his life, but the thought that his arch-foes, Catholic priests, were doing precisely the same thing that he was, though admittedly in his case the reasons were not obscurantist ones, rooted in sheer prejudice, as in their case, but the desire, rather, to make himself stronger, freer of impediments, more available for this fight to reconcile, to conjoin what they, more than anyone else, had helped to turn into permanent enemies: heaven and earth, matter and spirit. He had never been tempted to break his vow – 'till today,' Galileo Gall dreamed or thought. On the contrary, he firmly believed that this absence of women in his life had been transformed into a greater intellectual appetite, into an ever-increasing ability to act. No: he was lying to himself again. The power of reason had been able to get the better of sex when he was awake, but not when he was asleep. On many nights during these years, tempting female forms slipped into his bed as he slept, clung to his body, stole caresses. He dreamed or thought that these phantasms had been harder to resist than women of flesh and blood, and he remembered that, like adolescents or comrades locked up in jails the world over, he had often made love with these impalpable silhouettes fashioned by his desire.

In anguish, he thought or dreamed: 'How could I have done that?' Why had he flung himself on that young woman? She had been fighting him off and he had struck her. Overcome with anxiety, he asked himself if he had also hit her when she had stopped fighting him off and was allowing him to strip her naked. What had happened, comrade? He dreamed or thought: 'You don't know yourself, Gall.' No, his own head told him nothing. But others had palpated it and found in him highly developed impulsive tendencies and curiosity, inaptitude for the contemplative, for the aesthetic, and in general for everything having no direct bearing on practical action and physical tasks, and no one had ever perceived the slightest sexual anomaly in the receptacle housing his soul. He dreamed or thought something that he had already thought before: 'Science is still only a candle faintly glimmering in a great pitch-dark cavern.'

In what way would what had happened alter his life? Did his decision made in Rome still hold good now? Ought he to renew or alter his vow after this accident? Was it an accident? How to explain scientifically what had occurred as dawn was breaking this morning? Without his being aware of it, during all these years he had been storing up in his soul – no, in his mind; the word 'soul' was contaminated with religious filth – all the appetites he thought he had rooted out, all the energies he had presumed were directed toward better ends than pleasure. And that secret accumulation had exploded this morning, ignited by circumstances, that is to say, nervousness, tension, fear, the surprise of the attack, the theft, the shooting, the deaths. Was that the correct explanation? Ah, if only he could have examined all this as though it were a problem concerning someone else, objectively, with someone like old Cubí. And he remembered those conversations that the phrenologist called Socratic, as they walked about the port area of Barcelona and through the labyrinth of the Barrio Gótico, and felt pangs of nostalgia in his heart. No, it would be imprudent, dimwitted, stupid to hold to the decision made in Rome; it would be paving the way for a repetition in the future of what had happened this morning, or something even worse. He thought or dreamed, with bitter sarcasm: 'You must resign yourself to fornicating, Galileo.'

He thought of Jurema. Was she a thinking being? A little domestic animal, rather. Diligent, submissive, capable of believing that statues of St. Anthony escape from churches and return to the grottoes where they were carved; trained like the baron's other female servants to care for chickens and sheep, to prepare her husband's food, to wash his clothes, and to open her legs only for him. He thought: 'Perhaps she'll be roused from her lethargy now and discover injustice.' He thought: 'I'm your injustice.' He thought: 'Perhaps you've done her a service.'

He thought of the men who had attacked him and made off with the wagon and of the two that he had killed. Were they the Counselor's men? Was their leader the man he'd met at the tannery in Queimadas, the one called Pajeú? Wasn't it more likely that it had been Pajeú, that he'd taken him to be an army spy or a merchant eager to swindle his people and had had him watched, and then, on discovering that he had arms in his possession, had made off with them so as to supply Canudos? He hoped that that was what had happened, that at that very moment the wagon with those rifles was heading up to Canudos at a fast gallop to reinforce the *jagunços* as they prepared to face what would soon be upon them. Why would Pajeú have trusted him? How could he have trusted a stranger who pronounced his language badly and had obscure ideas? 'You've killed two comrades, Gall,' he thought. He was awake: that heat is the morning sun, those sounds the tinkling of the sheep bells. And what if the rifles were in the hands of mere outlaws? They might have followed him and the guide in leather the night before, as they carried the arms off from the hacienda where Epaminondas had handed them over to him. Didn't everyone say that the region was teeming with *cangaceiros*? Had he gone about things in too much of a hurry, been imprudent? He thought: 'I should have unloaded the arms and brought them inside here.' He thought: 'Then you'd be dead now and they'd have made off with them anyway.' He was consumed with doubts. Would he go back to Bahia? Would he still go on to Canudos? Would he open his eyes? Would he get up out of his hammock? Would he finally face reality? He could still hear the sheep bells tinkling, he could hear barking, and now he also heard footsteps and a voice.

VII

When the columns of Major Febrônio de Brito's expeditionary force and the handful of women camp followers who were still tagging along after them converged on the settlement of Mulungu, two leagues away from Canudos, they had no bearers or guides left. The guides recruited in Queimadas and Monte Santo to orient the reconnaissance patrols had turned downright unfriendly the moment they began to come across hamlets that had been set on fire and were still smoking, and all of them had disappeared at once in the gathering dark as the soldiers, collapsing on the ground and lying propped up on each other's shoulders, thought long thoughts about the wounds and perhaps the death that awaited them behind the mountain peaks that they could see outlined against an indigo-blue sky slowly turning black.

Some six hours later, the runaway guides arrived in Canudos, panting, to beg the Counselor's forgiveness for having served the Can. They were taken to the Vilanovas' store, where Abbot João questioned them in minute detail about the soldiers who were coming and then left them in the hands of the Little Blessed One, the person who always received newcomers. The guides had to swear to him that they were not republicans, that they did not accept the separation of Church and State, or the overthrow of the Emperor Dom Pedro II, or civil marriage, or municipal cemeteries, or the metric system, that they would refuse to answer the census questions, and that they would never again steal or get drunk or bet money. Then at his order they made a slight incision in their flesh with their knives as proof of their willingness to shed their blood fighting the Antichrist. Only then were they led – by armed men, through a crowd of people who had been roused from their sleep a short time before by the guides' arrival, and who applauded them and shook their hands – to the Sanctuary. The Counselor appeared at the door. They fell to their knees, crossed themselves, tried to touch his tunic, to kiss his feet. Overcome with emotion, a number of them burst into sobs. Instead of simply giving them his blessing, the Counselor, his eyes gazing through and beyond them, as when he received the newly elect, leaned down, raised them to their feet, and looked at them one by one with his burning black eyes that none of them would ever forget. Then he asked Maria Quadrado and the eight pious women of the Sacred Choir – dressed in blue tunics with linen sashes – to light the lamps in the Temple of the Blessed Jesus, as they did each evening when he mounted to the tower to offer his counsel.

Minutes later he appeared on the scaffolding, with the Little Blessed One, the Lion of Natuba, the Mother of Men, and the women of the Sacred Choir gathered round him, and below him, packed together in a dense throng and breathless with anticipation in the dawn that was breaking, were the men and women of Canudos, aware that this was a more unusual occasion than others. As always, the Counselor came straight to the point. He spoke of transubstantiation, of the Father and the Son who were two and one, and three and one in the Divine Holy Spirit, and in order that what was obscure might be clear, he explained that Belo Monte could also be Jerusalem. With his index finger he pointed in the direction of the hillside of A Favela: the Garden of Olives, where the Son had spent the agonizing night of Judas's betrayal, and a little farther in the distance, the Serra de Canabrava: the Mount of Calvary, where the wicked had crucified Him between two thieves. He added that the Holy Sepulcher lay a quarter of a league away, in Grajaú, amid ash-colored crags, where nameless faithful had erected a cross. He then described in detail to the silent crowd filled with wonder precisely which of the narrow little streets of Canudos were the Way of the Cross, exactly where Christ had fallen for the first time, where He had met His Mother, the spot where the redeemed woman who had sinned wiped the sweat from His face, and the stretch along which Simon of Cyrene had helped Him bear the cross. As he was explaining that the Valley of Ipueiras was the Valley of Jehoshaphat, shots were heard from the other side of the mountain peaks that separated Canudos from the rest of the world. Unhurriedly, the Counselor asked the crowd – torn between the spell of his voice and the sound of gunfire – to sing a hymn composed by the Little Blessed One: 'In Praise of the Cherubim.' Only then did groups of men leave with Abbot João and Pajeú to reinforce the *jagunços* already fighting Major Febrônio de Brito's vanguard in the foothills of Monte Cambaio.

When they arrived on the run to post themselves in the crevices and gullies and on the projecting rock slabs of the mountain that soldiers in red-and-blue and green-and-blue uniforms were trying to scale, there were already men who had died in combat. The *jagunços* posted by Abbot João in the pass that the main troops would be obliged to file through had seen them approaching while it was still dark, and while most of them stayed behind to rest in Rancho das Pedras – some eight cabins that had been razed by the arsonists – they saw a company of infantrymen, commanded by a lieutenant mounted on a piebald horse, marching toward O Cambaio. They allowed them to advance until they were almost upon them and then, at a signal from José Venâncio, rained down fire from carbines, blunderbusses, muskets, rocks, arrows shot from hunting crossbows, and insults – 'dogs,' 'Freemasons,' 'Protestants' – on them. Only then did the soldiers become aware of their presence. They all turned tail and fled, except for three wounded, who were overtaken and finished off by young *jagunços* dodging bullets, and the horse, which reared and threw its rider, rolled down the mountainside amid the rough stones and broke its legs. The lieutenant managed to take refuge behind some boulders and began returning the fire as the animal lay there, neighing mournfully, for several hours as the shooting went on.

Many *jagunços* had been blown to bits by shells from the Krupps, which began to bombard the mountain shortly after the first skirmish, causing landslides and showers of rock shards. Big João, who was posted alongside José Venâncio, realized that it was suicide to stay bunched together, and leaping from one rock slab to another, waving his arms like the sails of a windmill, shouted at them to disperse so as not to offer such a compact target. They obeyed him, jumping from rock to rock or crawling along on their bellies as below them, divided into combat groups led by lieutenants, sergeants, and corporals, the infantrymen climbed up O Cambaio amid a cloud of dust and a flurry of bugle calls. By the time Abbot João and Pajeú arrived with reinforcements, they had gotten halfway up the mountain. Despite their heavy losses, the *jagunços* who were trying to drive them off had not given a foot of ground. The reinforcements who were equipped with firearms began to shoot immediately, accompanying the volleys with loud shouts. The ones who had only machetes and knives, or the sort of crossbows that men of the backlands used to hunt duck and deer, which Antônio Vilanova had had the carpenters of Canudos make dozens of, confined themselves to grouping themselves around those with firearms and handing them gunpowder or charging the muzzle-loading carbines, hoping that the Blessed Jesus would see fit to allow them to inherit a gun or get close enough to the enemy to be able to attack with their bare hands.

The Krupps kept bombarding the heights of the mountain, and the rockslides caused as many casualties as the bullets. As dusk was just beginning to fall and the figures in red-and-blue and green-and-blue uniforms were beginning to break through the lines of the elect, Abbot João convinced the others that they should fall back or they would find themselves surrounded. Several dozen *jagunços* had died and many more were wounded. Those able to hear the order and obey it began to retreat, slipping off via the plain known as O Taboleirinho toward Belo Monte; they numbered just over half as many men as had taken this route in the other direction the night before and that morning. José Venâncio, who was one of the last to fall back, leaning on a stick with his bloody leg bent, was hit in the back by a bullet that killed him before he could cross himself.

From dawn on, that morning, the Counselor never left the Temple, remaining there praying, surrounded by the women of the Sacred Choir, Maria Quadrado, the Little Blessed One, the Lion of Natuba, and a great crowd of the faithful, who also prayed, while at the same time keeping their ears trained on the din, very distinct at times, borne to Canudos on the north wind. Pedrão, the Vilanova brothers, Joaquim Macambira, and the others who had stayed behind readying the city for the attack, were deployed along the Vaza-Barris. They had brought down to its banks all the firearms, powder, and projectiles they were able to find. When old Macambira caught sight of the *jagunços* returning from Monte Cambaio, he murmured that the Blessed Jesus apparently wanted the dogs to enter Jerusalem. None of his sons noticed that he had mixed up the names of the two cities.

But they did not enter. The outcome of the battle was decided that very day, before nightfall, on the plain of O Taboleirinho, where at that moment the troops of Major Febrônio de Brito's three columns were stretching out on the ground, dizzy with fatigue and joy, after seeing the *jagunços* flee from the last spurs of the mountain and being almost able to make out from there the heterogeneous geography of straw rooftops and the two lofty stone towers of what they already regarded as the prize that their victory had won them, less than half a league's distance away. As the *jagunços* still left alive were entering Canudos – their arrival gave rise to anxiety, to agitated conversations, weeping and wailing, shouts, prayers recited at the top of people's lungs – the soldiers were collapsing to the ground, opening their red-and-blue, green-and-blue tunics, removing their leggings, so exhausted that they were not even able to tell each other how overjoyed they were at having defeated the enemy. Meeting in a war council, Major Febrônio and his fourteen officers decided to camp on that bare mountain plateau, alongside a nonexistent lagoon which their maps showed under the name Cipó – Liana – and which, from that day forward, they would show as Lagoa do Sangue – Lagoon of Blood. The following morning, at first light, they would attack the fanatics' lair.

But, before an hour was out, as lieutenants, sergeants, and corporals were still inspecting the benumbed companies and drawing up lists of the dead, wounded, and missing, and soldiers of the rear guard were still arriving, picking their way between the rocks, they were attacked. Sick and healthy, men and women, youngsters and oldsters, all the elect able to fight fell on them like an avalanche. Abbot João had convinced them that they should attack then and there, all of them together, since there wasn't going to be any 'later on' if they didn't do so. The tumultuous mob had followed after him, crossing the plateau like a cattle stampede. They came armed with all the images of the Blessed Jesus, of the Virgin, of the Divine to be found in the city, they were clutching all the cudgels, clubs, sickles, pitchforks, knives, and machetes in Canudos, along with blunderbusses, shotguns, carbines, muskets, and the Mannlichers captured in

Uauá, and as they shot off bullets, pieces of metal, spikes, arrows, stones, they let out war cries, possessed by that reckless courage that was the very air that people of the *sertão* breathed from the day they were born, multiplied in them now by the love of God and the hatred of the Prince of Darkness that the saint had contrived to instill in them. They did not give the soldiers time to recover from their stupefaction at suddenly seeing that yelling, shouting horde of men and women running across the plain toward them as though they had not already been defeated. When fear brought them to, jolted them awake, propelled them to their feet, and they finally grabbed their guns, it was too late. The *jagunços* were already upon them, among them, behind them, in front of them, shooting them, knifing them, stoning them, piercing them with spikes, biting them, tearing away their guns, their cartridge belts, tearing out their hair, their eyes, and above all reviling them with the strangest curses they had ever heard. First a few of them, then others managed to make their escape, bewildered, driven mad, petrified by this sudden insane attack that seemed beyond the human. In the shadows that were falling in the wake of the ball of fire that had just sunk behind the mountaintops, they scattered, one by one or in groups, amid those foothills of O Cambaio that they had climbed with such effort all through the long day – running in all directions, stumbling, falling, getting to their feet again, ripping off their uniforms in the hope that they would not be noticed, and praying that night would finally come and be a dark one.

They might all have died, there might not have been a single officer or infantryman left to tell the world the story of this battle already won and then suddenly lost; every last one of these half a thousand vanquished men running about aimlessly, driven hither and yon by fear and confusion, might have been pursued, tracked down, hemmed in if the victors had known that the logic of war demands the total destruction of the enemy. But the logic of the elect of the Blessed Jesus was not the logic of this earth. The war that they were waging was only apparently that of the outside world, that of men in uniform against men in rags, that of the seacoast against the interior, that of the new Brazil against traditional Brazil. All the *jagunços* were aware that they were merely puppets of a profound, timeless, eternal war, that of good and evil, which had been going on since the beginning of time. Hence they allowed their adversaries to escape, as in the light of oil lamps they recovered their dead and wounded brothers who lay on the plateau or on the slopes of O Cambaio with grimaces of pain or of love of God etched into their faces (provided the enemy's machine guns had spared their faces). They spent the entire night transporting the wounded to the Health Houses of Belo Monte, and taking dead bodies, once they had been dressed in their best clothes and placed in coffins hastily nailed together, to the wake that was held for them in the Temple of the Blessed Jesus and the Church of Santo Antônio. The Counselor decided that they would not be buried until the parish priest from Cumbe could come say a Mass for their souls, and one of the women of the Sacred Choir, Alexandrinha Correa, went to fetch him.

As they waited for him, Antônio the Pyrotechnist prepared a fireworks display, and there was a procession. On the following day, many *jagunços* returned to the site of the battle. They stripped the soldiers and left their naked corpses to rot. Once back in Canudos, they burned the troops' tunics and trousers and everything in the pockets: paper money issued by the Republic, cigars, illustrated cards, locks of hair of wives, sweethearts, daughters, keepsakes they frowned upon. But they put the rifles, the bayonets, the bullets aside, because Abbot João, Pajeú, the Vilanovas had asked them to and because they realized that they would be indispensable if they were attacked again. As some of the *jagunços* still insisted they should be destroyed, the Counselor himself had to ask them to place all the Mannlichers, Winchesters, revolvers, boxes of gunpowder, cartridge belts, cans of grease in the care of Antônio Vilanova. The two Krupp cannons were still at the foot of O Cambaio, in the emplacement from which they had bombarded the mountain. All the parts of them that could be burned – the wheels and the caissons – were set afire, and the steel barrels were hauled to

Canudos by mule team so that the smiths could melt them down.

In Rancho das Pedras, which had been Major Febrônio de Brito's last camp, Pedrão's men found six hungry, disheveled women who had followed the soldiers, cooking for them, washing their clothes, and sleeping with them. They took them to Canudos and the Little Blessed One made them leave, telling them that anyone who had freely chosen to serve the Antichrist could not remain in Belo Monte. But two half-breeds who had belonged to José Venâncio's band and were disconsolate at his death caught one of them, who was pregnant, on the outskirts of Canudos, slit her belly open with a machete, ripped out the fetus, and put a live rooster in its place, convinced that they were thus doing their leader in the other world a favor.

He hears the name Caifás, repeated two or three times, in between words that he doesn't understand, and struggles to open his eyes, and there Rufino's wife is, standing next to the hammock, all excited, moving her mouth, making noises, and it is broad daylight now and the sun is pouring into the cabin through the door and the chinks between the palings. The light hurts his eyes so much that he blinks and rubs his eyelids hard as he gets to his feet. Blurred images come to him through a milky water, and as his head clears and the world comes into focus, Galileo Gall's mind and eyes discover that a metamorphosis has taken place in the room: it has been carefully put back in order; floor, walls, objects look bright and shining, as though everything had been scrubbed and polished. He understands now what Jurema is saying: Caifás is coming, Caifás is coming. He notices that the tracker's wife has changed out of her tunic that he ripped open and is now wearing a dark blouse and skirt, that she is barefoot and frightened, and as he tries to remember where his revolver fell that morning, he tells himself that there is no need to be alarmed, that the man coming is the guide dressed in leather who took him to Epaminondas Gonçalves's and brought him back here with the arms, precisely the person he needs most at this moment. There the revolver is, next to his small valise, at the foot of the print of the Virgin of Lapa hanging on a nail. He picks it up and as the thought occurs to him that there are no more bullets left in it he sees Caifás in the doorway of the cabin.

'*They tried to kill me*,' he blurts out in English, and then, realizing his mistake, switches to Portuguese. 'They tried to kill me. They've stolen the arms. I must go see Epaminondas Gonçalves, right away.'

'Good morning,' Caifás says, raising two fingers to his sombrero with ornamental thongs round the brim without taking it off, addressing Jurema in what strikes Gall as an absurdly solemn manner. Then Caifás turns to him, makes the same gesture, and repeats: 'Good morning.'

'Good morning,' Gall answers, feeling suddenly ridiculous with the revolver in his hand. He tucks it away at his waist, between his trousers and his belly, and takes two steps toward Caifás, noticing the confusion, the abashment, the embarrassment that have come over Jurema on the guide's arrival: she is standing there not moving, staring at the floor, not knowing what to do with her hands.

Galileo points outside. 'Did you see those two dead men out there? There was another one with them, the one who made away with the arms. I must talk to Epaminondas, I must warn him. Take me to him.'

'I saw them,' Caifás says, not wasting words. And he turns to Jurema, who is still standing there with her head down, petrified, flexing her fingers as though she had a cramp in them. 'Soldiers have come to Queimadas. Over five hundred of them. They're looking for guides to take them to Canudos. Anyone who doesn't want to hire on with them they take by force. I came to warn Rufino.'

'He's not here,' Jurema stammers, without raising her head. 'He's gone to Jacobina.'

'Soldiers?' Gall takes another step, bringing him so close to the newcomer that he is practically brushing against him. 'Major Brito's expedition is already here?'

'There's going to be a parade,' Caifás says, nodding. 'They're lined up in formation in the main square. They arrived on the morning train.'

Gall wonders why the man doesn't seem surprised by the dead bodies he saw outside the cabin when he arrived, why he's not asking him any questions as to what's happened, how it happened, why he's still here, so calm, so impassive, so unexpressive, waiting – for what? – and he tells himself once more that the people in these parts are strange, impenetrable, inscrutable, reminding him of Chinese, of Hindustanis. Caifás is a very skinny, bony, bronze-skinned man with prominent cheekbones and wine-dark eyes that are disconcerting because they never blink, whose voice is quite unfamiliar to him, since he scarcely opened his mouth all during the trip back and forth that he made with him, sitting directly alongside him, and whose leather vest and pants, reinforced in the seat and the legs with strips of leather as well, and even his rope sandals appear to be part of his body, a tough additional skin, a crust. Why has his arrival so disconcerted Jurema? Is it because of what has happened between the two of them a few hours before? The little woolly dog appears from somewhere and leaps and gambols and plays about at Jurema's feet, and at that moment Galileo Gall notices that the chickens in the room have all disappeared.

'I saw only three of them. The one who escaped took the arms off with him,' he says, smoothing his disheveled red hair. 'Epaminondas must be told of this as soon as possible; it might be dangerous for him. Can you take me to his hacienda?'

'He's not there any more,' Caifás says. 'You heard him yesterday when he said he was about to leave for Bahia.'

'That's true,' Gall says. There is no getting round it; he, too, will be obliged to go back to Bahia. He thinks: 'The soldiers are already here.' He thinks: 'They're going to come looking for Rufino, they're going to find the dead men, they're going to find me.' He simply must leave, shake off this lassitude, this drowsiness that has overcome him. But he doesn't move.

'Perhaps they were enemies of Epaminondas's, Governor Luiz

Viana's people, the baron's,' he murmurs, as though speaking to Caifás, though he is really talking to himself. 'Why didn't the National Guard come, then? Those three men weren't gendarmes. They could have been brigands, who might have wanted the arms for their depredations, or in order to sell them.'

Jurema is still standing motionless with her head down, and not three feet away from him is Caifás, still calm, quiet, impassive. The little dog leaps about, panting.

'What's more, there's something strange about this whole thing,' Gall says, thinking aloud. And to himself: 'I must hide out till the soldiers leave and then go back to Salvador' – reflecting at the same time that Major Brito's expedition is already there, less than two kilometers away, that it will proceed to Canudos and no doubt put an end to this outbreak of rebellion in which he thought he saw, or fondly believed he saw, the seeds of a revolution. 'They weren't only after arms. They also were out to kill me, there's no doubt of that. And that I don't understand at all. Who could possibly want to kill me here in Queimadas?'

'I could, sir,' he hears Caifás say, in the same toneless voice, as he suddenly feels the knife edge at his throat, but his reflexes are, have always been, very fast, and he has managed to throw his head back, to step a few millimeters away just as the man dressed in leather has leapt upon him, and his knife, instead of burying itself in his throat, misses its mark and wounds him farther down, to the right, where his neck and his shoulder meet, producing in his body a sensation that is more one of cold and surprise than of pain. He has fallen to the floor and is touching the wound, noting that blood is pouring out between his fingers, his eyes opened wide, staring spellbound at the man with the biblical name dressed in leather, whose expression, even now, has not changed, except perhaps for the pupils of his eyes, opaque before and now gleaming brightly. He is holding the bloody knife in his right hand and a small pearl-handled revolver in his left. Leaning over him, he aims it at Galileo's head, offering him more or less of an explanation as he does so: 'I'm acting on orders from Colonel Epaminondas Gonçalves, sir.

I was the one who rode off with the arms this morning; I'm the leader of the men you killed.'

'Epaminondas Gonçalves?' Galileo Gall roars, and now the pain in his throat is agonizing.

'He needs an English corpse,' Caifás says in what sounds like a more or less apologetic tone of voice as he squeezes the trigger, and Gall, who has automatically tilted his head to one side, feels a burning sensation in his jaw and in his hair and another that feels as though his ear is being ripped off.

'I'm a Scotsman and I hate the English,' he manages to murmur, thinking that the second shot will hit him in the forehead, the mouth, or the heart and he will lose consciousness and die, for the man dressed in leather is raising his hand with the revolver again, but instead what he sees is a meteor, a commotion, as Jurema lunges at Caifás, grabs him, and trips him, and then he stops thinking, and discovering strength within himself he no longer knows he possesses, he rises to his feet and also flings himself upon Caifás, vaguely aware that he is bleeding and burning with pain, and before he can think again or try to understand what has happened, what has saved him, he is hitting with the butt of his revolver, with every last ounce of his strength, the man in leather, whom Jurema is still hanging on to. Before seeing him fall senseless, he realizes that Caifás is not looking at him as he defends himself from the blows of his revolver, but at Jurema, and that there is no hatred or anger but only an immeasurable stupefaction in his dark wine-colored pupils, as though he is unable to comprehend what she has done, as though the fact that she has been the one who has flung herself upon him and deflected his arm, thereby permitting his victim to rise to his feet, was something he could not have imagined, could never have dreamed of. But when Caifás, his body going limp, his face swollen from the blows, covered with his own blood or Gall's, lets go of the knife and his miniature revolver and Gall grabs it and is about to shoot him, it is again Jurema who stops him, grabbing his hand, just as she had seized Caifás's before, screaming hysterically.

'Don't be afraid,' Gall says in English, with no strength left to fight. 'I must clear out of here; the soldiers will be coming. Help me onto the mule, woman.'

He opens and closes his mouth several times, certain that he is about to collapse alongside Caifás, who appears to be stirring. His face contorted from the effort, noting that the burning sensation in his neck has grown worse and that now his bones, his fingernails, his hair hurt him too, he walks across the cabin, bumping into the trunks and the furniture, toward the blaze of white light that is the door, thinking: 'Epaminondas Gonçalves,' thinking: 'I'm an English corpse.'

The new parish priest in Cumbe, Dom Joaquim, arrived in the town – no skyrockets were set off, no bells pealed – one cloudy afternoon with a storm threatening. He appeared in an oxcart, with a battered valise and a little umbrella to keep off the rain and the sun. He had had a long journey, from Bengalas, in Pernambuco, where he had been the parish priest for two years. In the months to come, the story was to go round that his bishop had sent him away because he had taken liberties with a girl who was a minor.

The townspeople he met at the entrance to Cumbe took him to the church square and showed him the tumbledown parish house where the priest had lived at the time when Cumbe still had a priest. The dwelling was now a hollow shell with walls but no roof that served as a garbage dump and a refuge for stray animals. Dom Joaquim went into the little Church of Nossa Senhora da Conceição, and by putting the usable benches together made himself a bed and stretched out on it to sleep, just as he was.

He was a young man, short and slightly stoop-shouldered, with a little potbelly and a jovial air about him that made people take a liking to him from the very beginning. If it hadn't been for his habit and his tonsure, no one would have taken him to be a man in active commerce with the world of the spirit, for it sufficed to be in his company just once on some social occasion to realize that he cared about the things of this world (women in particular) just as much, or perhaps more. On the very day that he arrived he showed Cumbe that he was capable of rubbing elbows with people in the town as though he were one of them and that his presence would not interfere in any substantial way with the habits and customs of the population. Nearly every family in Cumbe had gathered in the church square to welcome him when he opened his eyes after sleeping for a fair number of hours. Night had fallen, it had rained and stopped raining, and in the warm damp crickets were chirping and there were myriad stars in the sky. The introductions began, a long line of women filing past who kissed his hand and men who removed their sombreros as they came by, murmuring their names. After only a short time Father Joaquim interrupted the hand-kissing, explaining that he was dying of hunger and thirst. A ceremony then took place that was somewhat reminiscent of the stations of the cross during Holy Week, as the priest dropped in at one house after the other and was offered the choicest viands the householder could provide. Dawn found him still awake, in one of the two taverns of Cumbe, drinking brandy with sour cherries and having a ballad contest with the *caboclo* Matias de Tavares.

He began his priestly functions immediately, saying Masses, baptizing newborn babes, confessing the adults, administering the last rites to the dying, and marrying newly betrothed couples or those who were already living together and wanted to appear upright in the sight of God. As he had a vast territory to look after, he traveled about a great deal. He was active and even self-abnegating when it came to fulfilling his duties as priest of the parish. The fees he asked for many of his services were modest, he didn't mind if people put off paying him or didn't pay at all, for, of the capital vices, the one that he was definitely free of was avarice. Of the others, no, but at least he indulged in all of them without discrimination. He accepted the succulent roast kid offered him by the owner of a hacienda with the same warm thanks and rejoicing as the mouthful of raw sugar that a poor peasant invited him to share, and his throat made no distinction between aged brandy and the throat-scalding raw rum toned down with water that was the usual drink in times of scarcity. As far as women were concerned, nothing seemed to put him off: gummy-eyed crones, silly girls who hadn't yet reached puberty, women punished by nature with warts, harelips, or feeblemindedness. He never tired of flattering them and flirting with them and insisting that they come round to decorate the altar of the church. He would have boisterous romps with them, his face would grow flushed, and he would paw them as though it were the most natural thing in the world. The fact that he was a man of the cloth made fathers, husbands, brothers look upon him as sexless, and they resignedly put up with these audacities on the part of the priest of the parish; had any other male made so bold, they would have had their knives out instantly. Nonetheless, they heaved a sigh of relief when Father Joaquim established a permanent relationship with Alexandrinha Correa, the girl who had remained a spinster because she was a water divineress.

Legend had it that Alexandrinha's miraculous ability came to light when she was still a little girl, the year of the great drought, as the townspeople of Cumbe, desperate because of the lack of water, were going about digging wells everywhere. They had divided up into crews and from dawn on, each day, excavated everywhere where there had once been thick vegetation, thinking that this was an indication of water below ground. The women and children were doing their share of this exhausting work. But the earth that was brought up showed no sign of moisture, and the only thing found at the bottom of the holes was more layers of blackish sand or unbreakable rock. Until one day Alexandrinha, speaking in a vehement rush of words, as though they were being dictated to her with barely enough time for her to get them out, interrupted her father's crew to tell them that instead of digging where they were they should do so farther up, at the beginning of the trail leading to Massacará. No one paid any attention to her. But the little girl kept insisting, drumming her feet on the ground and waving her hands as though inspired. 'All right then, we'll dig just one more hole,' her father said. They went off to put her inspiration to the test, on the flat stretch of yellowish pebbles where the trails to Carnaíba and Massacará fork off. On the second day of digging, after they had brought up nothing but dry clods of earth and stones, the subsoil began to turn a darker color, to show signs of moisture, and finally, amid everyone's excitement, drops of water appeared. Three more wells were found close by, thanks to which Cumbe was less hard hit than other towns by those two years of misery and wholesale death.

From that day on, Alexandrinha Correa became an object of reverence and curiosity. And in the eyes of her parents something else besides: a creature whose intuition they tried to profit from, charging the settlements and the inhabitants round about a fee for divining the place where they should dig to find water. Alexandrinha's talents, however, did not lend themselves to being bought and sold. The little girl was wrong more often than she was right, and many times, after sniffling all about her with her little turned-up nose, she would say: 'I don't know; nothing comes to me.' But neither these blanks of hers nor her mistakes, which were always effaced by the memory of her successes, dimmed the reputation that surrounded her as she grew up. Her talents as a water divineress made her famous but not happy. Once it became known that she possessed this power, a wall went up round about her that isolated her from people. The other youngsters did not feel at ease with her and adults did not treat her as though she were just an ordinary little girl. They stared at her, they asked her strange questions about the future or life after death and brought her to kneel at the bedside of sick people to try to cure them with the powers of her mind. Her efforts to be simply a woman like all the others were of no avail. Men always respectfully kept their distance. They didn't ask her to dance at fiestas or serenade her, and none of them would ever have dreamed of taking her for a wife. It was as though falling in love with her would have been a profanation.

Until the new parish priest arrived in town. Father Joaquim was not a man to allow himself to be intimidated by an aura of sanctity or sorcery when it came to women. Alexandrinha was now past twenty. She was tall and slender, with the same curious nose and restless eyes, and still lived with her parents, unlike her four older sisters, who already had husbands and homes of their own. Because of the religious respect that she inspired and was unable to banish despite her simple, straightforward behavior, her life was a lonely one. Since this spinster daughter of the Correas seldom went out except to attend Sunday Mass, and since she was invited to very few private celebrations (people were afraid that her presence, contaminated as it was by an aura of the supernatural, would put a damper on the festivities), it was a long time before the new parish priest made her acquaintance.

A romance must have begun very gradually, beneath the bushy-topped Malay apple trees of the church square, or in the narrow streets of Cumbe, where the little priest and the water divineress must necessarily have met and then continued on their way, as his impertinent, vivacious, provocative little eyes looked her up and down while at the same time the good-natured smile on his face made this inspection seem less rude. And he must have been the one who spoke first, perhaps asking her about the town festival, on the eighth of December, or why he hadn't seen her at Rosaries or what that story about her and the water was all about. And she must have answered him in that quick, direct, straightforward way of hers, gazing at him unblushingly. And so one casual meeting must have followed upon another, then others less casual, conversations in which, besides chitchat about local happenings, bandits and flying brigades and quarrels and love affairs and exchanges of confidences, little by little guileful and daring remarks must also have entered the picture.

The fact is that one fine day all of Cumbe began slyly commenting on the change in Alexandrinha, an indifferent parishioner who had suddenly become the most diligent one of all. She could be seen, early every morning, dusting the benches in the church, putting the altar to rights, sweeping the doorway. And she also began to be seen in the parish house, which, with the help of the townspeople, now had a roof, doors, and windows once again. That what there was between them was more than kissing and giggling became evident the day that Alexandrinha strode resolutely into the tavern where Father Joaquim had hidden out with a group of friends after a christening feast and was playing the guitar and drinking, happy as a lark. The moment she entered he fell silent. She marched over to him and said to him in a firm tone of voice: 'You're coming with me, right now, because you've had enough to drink.' Without a word, the little priest followed her out.

The first time the saint came to Cumbe, Alexandrinha Correa had already been living for several years in the parish house. In the beginning she had installed herself there to take care of Father Joaquim after he had been wounded in the town of Rosário, where he'd been caught in the middle of a shootout between Satan João's *cangaço* and the police brigade of Captain Geraldo Macedo, known as Bandit-Chaser, and afterward she had stayed on there. They had had three children, whom people referred to only as 'Alexandrinha's kids,' and she was spoken of as Dom Joaquim's 'caretaker.' By her very presence she had a calming effect on the priest's life, although he did not change his habits in the slightest. The townspeople would summon her when, having drunk more than he should have, the little priest became a problem, and once she appeared he was always docile, even when he was drunk to the gills. Perhaps this was one of the reasons why the townspeople tolerated their relationship without making too much of a fuss. When the saint came to Cumbe for the first time, Alexandrinha was so well accepted by the town that even her parents and her brothers and sisters visited her in the parish house and called her children 'grandson,' 'granddaughter,' 'niece,' 'nephew,' without feeling at all uncomfortable.

Hence it was as though a bomb had gone off when, in his first sermon from the pulpit of the church in Cumbe, to which Father Joaquim, with an affable smile, had allowed him to ascend, the tall, gaunt man with flashing eyes and cascading Nazarene locks, dressed in a long flowing dark purple tunic, railed against bad shepherds. A sepulchral silence fell in the crowded nave. No one looked at Dom Joaquim, who had taken a place on the front bench. He had opened his eyes with a more or less violent start, and was sitting there not moving a muscle, staring straight ahead, at the crucifix or at his humiliation. Nor did the townspeople look at Alexandrinha Correa, who was sitting in the third row. Unlike Dom Joaquim, she was gravely contemplating the preacher, her face deathly pale. Apparently the saint had come to Cumbe after enemies of the couple had had a word with him. Solemn, unbending, with a voice that reverberated from the fragile walls and the concave ceiling, he said terrible things about those chosen by the Lord who, despite having been ordained and taken the habit, turned into Satan's lackeys. He mercilessly vituperated all Father Joaquim's sins: the shamefulness of pastors of the Lord's flock who instead of setting an example of sobriety drank cane brandy to the point of delirium; the unseemliness of those who instead of fasting and being frugal stuffed themselves without stopping to think that they lived surrounded by people who had barely enough to eat; the scandal of those who forgot their vow of chastity and took their pleasure with women, whom they did not guide spiritually but instead doomed to perdition by delivering their poor souls over to the Dog of the domains of hell. When the townspeople finally dared to look at their priest out of the corner of their eyes, they saw him still sitting there, still staring straight ahead, his face beet-red.

What had happened – an event that remained the talk of the town for many days – did not prevent the Counselor from continuing to preach in the Church of Nossa Senhora da Conceição during his stay in Cumbe, or again when, months later, he returned accompanied by a retinue of the elect, or on other occasions in the years that followed. The difference was that Father Joaquim usually was absent when these subsequent sermons were delivered. Alexandrinha, however, was not. She was always there, in the third row, with her turned-up nose, listening to the saint's admonishments against worldly wealth and excesses, his defense of austere habits, and his exhortations to prepare the soul for death through sacrifice and prayer. The former water divineress began to show signs of growing religious fervor. She lighted candles in the vaulted niches along the streets, she spent a great deal of time on her knees before the altar in an attitude of profound concentration, she organized acts of thanksgiving, public prayers, Rosaries, novenas. One day she appeared with her head covered with a black kerchief and an amulet with the image of the Blessed Jesus on her breast. Rumor had it that, though they continued to live under the same roof, nothing that would offend God happened now between Father Joaquim and her. When the townspeople dared to ask Dom Joaquim about Alexandrinha, he would change the subject. He seemed bewildered. Although he continued to lead a happy life, his relations with the woman who shared his house and was the mother of his children changed. In public at least, they were as perfectly polite to each other as two people who scarcely knew each other. The Counselor aroused indefinable feelings in the parish priest. Did he fear, respect, envy, pity him? The fact was that every time the saint came to town Father Joaquim opened the church to him, confessed him, gave him Communion, and during his stay in Cumbe was a model of temperance and devotion.

When, on the saint's last visit, Alexandrinha Correa took off with him among his followers, abandoning everything she had, Father Joaquim was the only person in town who did not appear to be surprised.

He thought that he had never feared death and that he didn't fear it now. But his hands trembled, shivers ran up and down his spine, and he kept moving closer and closer to the fire to warm his ice-cold insides. Yet he was sweating. He thought: 'You're dying of fear, Gall.' Those great beads of sweat, those shivers, that icy feeling, that trembling were the panic of one who has a premonition of death. 'You don't know yourself at all well, old pal.' Or had he changed? For he was certain that he had never felt anything like this as a young man, in the jail in Paris when he was waiting to be shot to death by a firing squad, or in Barcelona in the infirmary, while the stupid bourgeois were curing him so that he would be in good health when they executed him by tying him to a post and strangling him with an iron collar. He was about to die: your hour has come, Galileo.

Would his penis get hard at the supreme moment, as was said to happen to men who drowned or were beheaded? That belief straight out of a horror show concealed some tortuous truth, some mysterious affinity between sex and the awareness of death. If such a thing did not exist, what had happened early this morning and what had happened a little while ago would not have occurred. A little while ago? Hours, rather. Night had fallen and there were countless stars in the sky. He remembered that as he was waiting in the boarding house in Queimadas, he had planned to write a letter to *L'Etincelle de la révolte* explaining that the skyscape in this region was infinitely more varied than the landscape, and that this no doubt had a determining influence on the inhabitants' religious bent. He could hear Jurema's breathing, mingled with the crackling of the dying fire. Yes, it had been sniffing death close at hand that had made him fall upon this woman and take her with his stiff penis, twice in the same day. 'A strange relationship based on fear and semen and nothing else,' he thought. Why had she saved his life, by interceding just as Caifás was about to give him the *coup de grâce*? Why had she helped him onto the mule, gone with him, cured him, brought him here? Why was she behaving like this toward someone she must hate?

Fascinated, he recalled that sudden, pressing, uncontrollable urgency, when the animal fell as it was trotting along at full clip, throwing both of them to the ground. 'Its heart must have burst open like a ripe fruit,' he thought. How far were they from Queimadas? Was the little stream where he'd washed and bandaged himself the Rio do Peixe? Had they detoured round Riacho da Onça, leaving it behind, or had they not yet reached it? A host of questions were running riot in his head, but his fear had vanished. Had he been badly frightened when the mule collapsed and he realized that he was falling off, that he was rolling on the ground? Yes. That was the explanation: fear. The instant suspicion that the animal had died not of exhaustion but of a shot through the heart fired by the hired assassins who were following him to turn him into an English cadaver. And it must have been because he was instinctively seeking protection that he had leapt on top of the woman, who had fallen off and was rolling on the ground with him. Had Jurema thought him a madman, or the Devil perhaps? Taking her in such circumstances, at that moment, in that state. Ah, the dismay in the woman's eyes, her trepidation when she realized, from the way that Gall's hands were pawing at her clothes, what he wanted from her. She had not put up any resistance this time, but neither had she hidden her disgust, or, rather, her indifference. Ah, that quiet resignation of her body, which had remained impressed on Gall's mind as he lay on the ground, confused, stunned, overwhelmed with something that might be desire, fear, anxiety, uncertainty, or a blind denial of the trap in which he found himself. Through a mist of sweat, with the wounds in his shoulder and neck hurting as though they had reopened and his life were draining away through them, he saw Jurema in the gathering darkness, examining the mule, opening its eyes and mouth. Still lying on the ground, he then saw her collect branches and leaves and light a fire. And without her saying a word to him, he saw her take out the knife tucked in her belt, slice off strips of flesh from the animal's flanks, thread them on a stick, and put them over the fire to roast. She gave the impression that she was merely performing a routine domestic task, as though nothing out of the way had happened, as though the events of that day had not completely changed her life. He thought: 'They're the most enigmatic people on this planet.' He thought: 'Fatalists, brought up to accept whatever life brings them, whether good, bad, or horrendous.' He thought: 'For her you're the horrendous.'

After a while he had been able to sit up, to drink a few swallows of water, and, with a great effort because of the burning pain in his throat, to chew. The pieces of meat seemed like an exquisite delicacy. As they ate, presuming that Jurema was no doubt bewildered by everything that had happened, he had tried to explain everything to her: who Epaminondas Gonçalves was, his proposal regarding the arms, how Gonçalves had been the one who had planned the attack at Rufino's house so as to steal the rifles he himself had bought and have him, Galileo, killed because he needed a corpse with light skin and red hair. But he realized that she wasn't at all interested in what he was telling her. As she listened, she nibbled the meat with her tiny, even teeth and chased the flies away, without nodding to show she understood or asking a single question, meeting his gaze every so often with eyes that were gradually being swallowed up by the darkness and that were making him feel stupid. He thought: 'I *am* stupid.' That was true; he had amply proved that fact. He had the moral and political obligation to be mistrustful, to suspect that an ambitious bourgeois, capable of mounting a conspiracy against his enemies such as the one involving the arms, was equally capable of mounting another one against him. An English corpse! In other words, what Gonçalves had said about the rifles had not been a mistake, a slip of the tongue: he had told him that they were French, knowing full well that they were English. Galileo had discovered this on arriving at Rufino's cabin, as he was loading the cases in the wagon. The factory mark on the butt leapt to his eye: 'Liverpool, 1891.' The discovery had made him joke to himself: 'France hasn't yet invaded England, as far as I know. These are English rifles, not French ones.' English rifles, an English corpse. What was Gonçalves up to? He could well imagine: his idea was a cold, cruel, daring one, and mayhap even a brilliant one. His chest tightened with anxiety once again and he thought: 'He'll kill me.' This was unknown territory to him, he was wounded, he was an outsider whose trail could easily be pointed out by anyone and everyone in the region. Where was he going to be able to hide out? 'In Canudos.' Yes, of course. He would be safe there, or at least he would not die there with the rueful feeling that he had been stupid. The thought came to him: 'Canudos will justify you, comrade.'

He was shivering from the cold, and his shoulder, his neck, his head hurt. To take his mind off his wounds, he tried to turn his thoughts to the troops under the command of Major Febrônio de Brito. Had they already left Queimadas and headed for Monte Santo? Would they wipe out that hypothetical refuge before he reached it? He thought: 'The bullet isn't lodged in my body, it didn't break the skin, its red-hot fire barely grazed it. The bullet, moreover, must have been very small caliber, like the revolver, meant for killing sparrows.' The serious wound was not the one from the bullet but from the knife thrust: it had penetrated deeply, severing veins, nerves, and that was the source of the burning, stabbing pains mounting to his ear, his eyes, the nape of his neck. Hot and cold shivers were making him shake from head to foot. Are you about to die, Gall? All of a sudden he remembered the snowfalls in Europe, its landscape so thoroughly domesticated by comparison with this untamed nature. He thought: 'Is there geography anywhere in Europe as hostile as this?' In the south of Spain, in Turkey surely, in Russia. He remembered Bakunin's escape, after being chained to the wall of a prison for eleven months. His father had sat him on his lap and told him the story of it: the epic journey across Siberia, the Amur River, California, then back to Europe, and on his arrival in London, the burning question: 'Are there oysters in this country?' He remembered the inns scattered along the roadsides of Europe, where there was always a fire smoking on the hearth, hot soup, and other travelers to smoke a pipe with and share the events of the day's journey. He thought: 'Nostalgia is an act of cowardice, Gall.'

He was allowing himself to be overcome by self-pity and melancholy. Shame on you, Gall! Haven't you even learned yet to die with dignity? What did it matter if it was in Europe, Brazil, or any other bit of ground on this earth! Wouldn't the result be precisely the same? He thought: 'Disintegration, decomposition, the rotting place, the worm brood, and if hungry scavengers don't play their role, a frail frame of yellowish bones covered with a dried-out skin.' He thought: 'You're burning up and dying of cold and that is what is known as fever.' It was not fear, nor the pellet for killing birds, nor the knife wound: it was a sickness. Because he had begun to feel that something was wrong with him even before the attack by the man dressed in leather, when he was on that hacienda with Epaminondas Gonçalves; whatever it was had been secretly eating away at some organ and spreading through the rest of his body. He was ill, not badly wounded. Something else new in your life, old pal. He thought: 'Fate wants to complete your education before you die by subjecting you to experiences you've never had before.' First a rapist and then sick! Because he could not recall ever having been ill, even in earliest childhood. Wounded, yes, a number of times, seriously so that time in Barcelona. But sick: never. He had the feeling that he was about to fall into a faint at any moment. Why this senseless effort to go on thinking? Why this intuition that as long as he kept thinking he would remain alive? He was suddenly aware that Jurema had gone. He listened, terrified: he could still hear the sound of her breathing, to his right. He could no longer see her because the fire had gone out altogether.

He tried to raise his spirits, knowing that it was useless, murmuring that adverse circumstances spurred the true revolutionary on, telling himself that he would write a letter to *L'Etincelle de la révolte* pointing out the analogy between what was happening in Canudos and Bakunin's address to the watchmakers and craftsmen of La Chaux-de-Fonds and the valley of Saint-Imier, in which he maintained that it was not in the most highly industrialized societies that great uprisings would take place, as Marx had prophesied, but in backward, agrarian countries, whose miserable peasant masses had nothing to lose – Spain, for instance, Russia, and, why not? Brazil, and he roused himself to reprove Epaminondas Gonçalves in his mind: 'Your hopes are going to be thwarted, you bourgeois. You should have killed me when I was at your mercy, on the terrace of the hacienda. I'll get well. I'll escape.' He would get well, he would escape, the young woman would guide him, he would steal a mount and would fight in Canudos against what you represented, you bourgeois: selfishness, cynicism, greed, and . . .

II

I

The heat has not let up as the evening shadows have fallen, and unlike other summer nights, there is not so much as the breath of a breeze. Salvador is burning up with the heat in the darkness. It is now pitch black, since at midnight, by municipal ordinance, the gaslights on the street corners go out, and the lamps in the houses of night owls have also gone out some time ago. Only the windows of the *Jornal de Notícias*, up there on the heights of the old city, are still lit, and their brightness makes the fancy Gothic lettering of the name of the newspaper on the windowpanes of the front office even more indecipherable.

Outside the door is a calash, and horse and coachman are both dozing. But Epaminondas Gonçalves's henchmen are awake, smoking, as they lean their elbows on the wall above the escarpment next to the newspaper office. They are talking together in a half whisper, pointing to something down below, there where the massive bulk of the Church of Nossa Senhora de Conceição da Praia and the fringe of foam along the reef are just barely visible in the darkness. The mounted police patrol has passed by on its rounds a while before and will not be back that way till dawn.

Inside, all by himself in the combination copy room and office, is that young, thin, ungainly journalist whose thickened eyeglasses to correct his nearsightedness, his frequent fits of sneezing, and his insistence on writing with a goose-quill pen instead of a metal one make him the laughingstock of the office staff. Leaning over his desk, his ugly head bathed in the halo of light from the little lamp, in a posture that makes him hunch over the desk at an awkward angle, he is writing rapidly, stopping only to dip his pen in the inkwell or to consult a small notebook, which he raises up so close to his eyeglasses that it almost touches them. The scratching of his pen is the only sound in the night. The sea is inaudible tonight and the office of the owner and editor-in-chief, which is also lighted up, is silent, as though Epaminondas Gonçalves had fallen asleep at his desk. But when the nearsighted journalist has set down the last word of his article and swiftly crosses the large outer office and enters the office of the head of the Progressivist Republican Party, he finds him waiting for him with his eyes wide open. His elbows are resting on the desk and his hands are crossed. As he sees the journalist enter, his dark, angular face, whose features and bones are underscored by that inner energy that enables him to spend entire nights without a wink of sleep at political meetings and then work all the following day without the least sign of fatigue, relaxes, as if to say: 'Well, at last.'

'Is it finished?' he murmurs.

'Finished.' The nearsighted journalist holds the sheaf of pages out to him. But Epaminondas Gonçalves does not take them.

'I'd rather you read them aloud to me,' he says. 'If I hear them, I'll have a better idea of how they turned out. Have a seat there, next to the light.'

As the journalist is about to begin to read, he is overcome by a sneeze, and then another, and finally a fit of them that forces him to remove his eyeglasses and cover his mouth and nose with an enormous handkerchief that he pulls out of his sleeve, like a sleight-of-hand artist.

'It's this summer dampness,' he says apologetically, wiping his congested face.

'I know,' Epaminondas Gonçalves cuts him short. 'Please read.'

II

A United Brazil, A Strong Nation

JORNAL DE NOTÍCIAS
(Owner: Epaminondas Gonçalves)
Bahia, January 3, 1897

The Defeat of Major Febrônio de Brito's Expedition in the Hinterland of Canudos
New Developments

THE PROGRESSIVIST REPUBLICAN PARTY ACCUSES THE GOVERNOR AND THE BAHIA AUTONOMIST PARTY OF CONSPIRING AGAINST THE REPUBLIC TO RESTORE THE OUTMODED IMPERIAL ORDER

The corpse of the 'English agent'
Commission of Republicans journeys to Rio to seek intervention of Federal Army to put down rebellion of subversive fanatics

TELEGRAM OF PATRIOTS OF BAHIA TO COLONEL MOREIRA CÉSAR: 'SAVE THE REPUBLIC!'

The defeat of the military expedition under the command of Major Febrônio de Brito and composed of troops from the Ninth, Twenty-sixth, and Thirty-third Infantry Battalions, and the growing signs of complicity between the English Crown and the landowners of the State of Bahia known to have ties to the Autonomist cause and nostalgic leanings, on the one hand, and the fanatics of Canudos, on the other, resulted on Friday evening in yet another stormy session of the Legislative Assembly of the State of Bahia.

Through its President, the Honorable Deputy Dom Epaminondas Gonçalves, the Progressivist Republican Party formally accused the governor of the State of Bahia, the Honorable Dom Luiz Viana, and the groups traditionally affiliated with the Baron de Canabrava – the former Minister of the Empire and former Ambassador of the Emperor Dom Pedro II to the British Crown – of having fomented the uprising in Canudos and of having furnished the rebels arms, thanks to the aid of England, with the aim of bringing about the fall of the Republic and the restoration of the monarchy.

The Deputies of the Progressivist Republican Party demanded that the Federal Government intervene immediately in the State of Bahia in order to snuff out what the Honorable Deputy Dom

Epaminondas Gonçalves called 'a seditious plot on the part of native bluebloods and the greed of Albion aimed against the sovereignty of Brazil.' Moreover, it was announced that a Commission made up of prominent figures of Bahia had departed for Rio de Janeiro to make representations to President Prudente de Morais concerning the public hue and cry in Bahia for troops of the Federal Army to be sent to wipe out Antônio Conselheiro's subversive movement.

The Progressivist Republicans reminded the Assembly that two weeks have now passed since the defeat of the Brito expedition by rebels vastly superior in number and better armed, and that despite this fact, and despite the discovery in the hamlet of Ipupiará of a shipment of English rifles being delivered to Canudos and the corpse of the English agent Galileo Gall, the State authorities, beginning with His Excellency Governor Dom Luiz Viana, have demonstrated a suspect apathy and passivity by not having immediately called for the intervention of the Federal Army, as the patriots of Bahia are demanding, in order to put down this conspiracy that is threatening the very existence of the Brazilian nation.

The Vice-President of the Progressivist Republican Party, the Honorable Deputy Dom Eliseu de Roque, read a telegram sent to the hero of the Republican Army, the officer responsible for crushing the monarchist uprising in Santa Catarina and the eminent collaborator of Marshal Floriano Peixoto, Colonel Moreira César, the text of which consisted of the following terse message: 'Come and save the Republic.' Despite the protests of the deputies of the majority, the Honorable Deputy read the names of the 325 heads of households and Salvador voters who had signed the telegram.

The Vice-President of the Autonomist Party and President of the Legislative Assembly, His Excellency Sir Adalberto de Gumúcio, declared that it was base calumny even to intimate that a man such as the Baron de Canabrava, a leading figure in Bahia, thanks to whom this State has roads, railways, bridges, charity hospitals, schools, and a multitude of public works, might be open to the accusation – leveled against him, moreover, *in absentia* – of conspiring against Brazilian sovereignty.

The Honorable Deputy Dom Floriano Mártir declared that the President of the Assembly preferred to bathe his kinsman and the head of his Party, the Baron de Canabrava, in incense rather than speak of the blood of soldiers shed in Uauá and on Monte Cambaio by degenerate Sebastianists or of the English arms seized in the interior or of the English agent Gall, whose corpse was discovered by the Rural Guard in Ipupiará. And the question was asked: 'Is this sleight of hand perhaps due to the fact that these subjects make the Honorable President of the Assembly uncomfortable?' The Autonomist Party Deputy, the Honorable Dom Eduardo Glicério, declared that in their eagerness for power the Republicans invent Grand Guignol conspiracies, complete with albino-haired spies burned to cinders, that make them the laughingstock of sensible Bahians. And he posed the question: 'Isn't the Baron de Canabrava the prime victim of the rebellion of those merciless fanatics? Are they not occupying land on his estate?' He was thereupon interrupted by the Honorable Deputy Dom Dantas Horcadas, who declared: 'And what if that land has not been usurped but willingly handed over to them?' The Honorable Deputy Dom Eduardo Glicério answered by asking the Honorable Deputy Dom Dantas Horcadas whether they hadn't taught him at the Salesian Fathers' school not to interrupt a gentleman while he is speaking. The Honorable Deputy Dom Dantas Horcadas replied immediately that he had no idea that a gentleman was speaking. The Honorable Deputy Dom Eduardo Glicério exclaimed that this insult would receive its answer on the field of honor unless apologies were forthcoming *ipso facto.* The President of the Assembly, His Excellency Sir Adalberto de Gumúcio, exhorted the Honorable Deputy Dom Dantas Horcadas to present his apologies to his colleague, for the sake of the harmony and dignity of the institution. The Honorable Deputy Dom Dantas Horcadas declared that he had merely meant to say that to his knowledge, strictly speaking, there no longer existed in

Brazil either gentlemen in the sense of chevalier, or barons, or viscounts, because, beginning with the glorious Republican government of Marshal Floriano Peixoto, Worthy Patriot of his country, whose memory will live forever in the hearts of Brazilians, all titles of nobility have become useless pieces of paper. But, he stated, it was not his intention to offend anyone, least of all the Honorable Deputy Dom Eduardo Glicério. The latter accepted this apology.

The Honorable Deputy Dom Rocha Seabra declared that he could not permit a man such as the Baron de Canabrava, who is the honor and glory of the State, to be defamed by resentful men whose records would show that they had not bestowed on Bahia so much as a hundredth part of the benefits conferred on it by the founder of the Autonomist Party. And he added that he failed to understand why telegrams should be sent summoning a Jacobin such as Colonel Moreira César to Bahia, since to judge from the cruelty with which he had put down the uprising of Santa Catarina, his dream was to erect guillotines in every public square in Brazil and become the country's Robespierre. This statement brought an angry protest from the Honorable Deputies of the Progressivist Republican Party, who, having risen to their feet, rousingly acclaimed the Army, Marshal Floriano Peixoto, and Colonel Moreira César, and demanded satisfaction for this insult blackening the name of a hero of the Republic. The Honorable Deputy Dom Rocha Seabra took the floor again to declare that it had not been his intention to cast aspersions upon Colonel Moreira César, whose military virtues he admired, nor to offend the memory of the late Marshal Floriano Peixoto, whose services to the Republic he recognized, but rather to make it clear that he was opposed to the intervention of men of the military in politics, since he did not want to see Brazil suffer the same fate as those South American countries whose history has been nothing but a succession of barrack-room pronunciamentos. The Honorable Deputy Dom Eliseu de Roque interrupted him to remind him that it had been the Brazilian Army that had put an end to the monarchy and installed the Republic, and rising to their feet once more, the Honorable Deputies of the opposition rendered homage to the Army and Marshal Floriano Peixoto and Colonel Moreira César. Continuing his remarks after this interruption, the Honorable Deputy Dom Rocha Seabra declared that it was absurd that federal intervention should be requested when His Excellency Governor Dom Luiz Viana had repeatedly asserted that the State of Bahia had the necessary means to suppress the outbreak of banditry and Sebastianist madness that Canudos represented. The Honorable Deputy Dom Epaminondas Gonçalves reminded the Assembly that the rebels had already decimated two military expeditions in the interior and asked the Honorable Deputy Dom Rocha Seabra how many more expeditionary forces had to be massacred, in his opinion, before federal intervention was justified. The Honorable Deputy Dom Dantas Horcadas declared that patriotism was sufficient justification for him or for anyone else to drag in the mud anyone who devoted his efforts to stirring up mud, that is to say, fomenting restorationist rebellions against the Republic in connivance with Perfidious Albion. The Honorable Deputy Dom Lélis Piedades declared that the most telling proof that the Baron de Canabrava was involved in no way whatsoever in the events brought about by the bloodthirsty rebels of Canudos was the fact that he had been outside of Brazil for several months now. The Honorable Deputy Floriano Mártir declared that his absence, rather than being proof of his lack of involvement, might be regarded as proof of precisely the opposite, and that nobody was fooled by such an alibi since all of Bahia was aware that no one moved a finger in the State without the authorization or an express order from the Baron de Canabrava. The Honorable Deputy Dom Dantas Horcadas declared that it was suspect and illuminative that the Honorable Deputies of the majority stubbornly refused to debate the question of the shipment of English arms and of the English agent Gall, sent by the British Crown to aid the rebels in their evil designs. The Honorable President of the Assembly, His Excellency Sir Adalberto de Gumúcio, declared that speculations and fantasies dictated by hatred and ignorance could readily be dispelled by simply stating the truth. And he announced that within a few days the Baron de Canabrava would be disembarking on Bahian shores, where not only the Autonomists but the entire populace would accord him the triumphal reception that he deserved and that this would be the best possible way of making amends for the lies of those who were attempting to associate his name and that of his Party and that of the authorities of Bahia with the deplorable events to which the banditry and moral degeneration of Canudos had given rise. Whereupon the Honorable Deputies of the majority, having risen to their feet, acclaimed and applauded the name of their President, the Baron de Canabrava, while the Honorable Deputies of the Progressivist Republican Party remained seated and shook their chairs as a sign of their disapproval.

The session was temporarily adjourned to permit the Honorable Deputies to partake of refreshments and to allow tempers to cool down. But during this brief pause in their deliberations, heated discussions and vehement verbal exchanges were heard in the corridors of the Assembly, and the Honorable Deputies Dom Floriano Mártir and Dom Rocha Seabra had to be separated by their respective friends inasmuch as they were on the point of resorting to fisticuffs.

When the session resumed, the Honorable President of the Assembly, His Excellency Sir Adalberto de Gumúcio, proposed that, in view of the lengthy agenda before them that evening, the Assembly proceed to discuss the new budgetary funds requested by the Ministry of the Interior for the laying of new railway lines to open up the remote inland regions of the State. This proposal aroused the ire of the Honorable Deputies of the Progressivist Republican Party, who, rising to their feet with cries of 'Treason!' 'Underhanded maneuver!' demanded a resumption of the debate concerning the most crucial problem confronting Bahia and hence the entire nation. The Honorable Deputy Dom Epaminondas Gonçalves warned that if the majority tried to sidestep debate concerning the Restorationist rebellion of Canudos and the intervention of the British Crown in

Brazilian affairs, he and his fellow members of the opposition would walk out of the Assembly, for they would not tolerate this attempt by the majority to dupe the people by resorting to such farcical maneuvering. The Honorable Deputy Dom Eliseu de Roque declared that the efforts of the Honorable President of the Assembly to prevent debate amounted to a palpable demonstration of what an embarrassment it was to the Autonomist Party to be obliged to discuss the subject of the English agent Gall and the English arms, which was not surprising, since the nostalgic monarchical leanings and the Anglophilic sympathies of the Baron de Canabrava were common knowledge.

The Honorable President of the Assembly, His Excellency Sir Adalberto de Gumúcio, declared that the Honorable Deputies of the opposition would not succeed in intimidating anyone by resorting to such blackmail and that the Bahia Autonomist Party was precisely the one most interested, out of patriotism, in putting down the fanatical Sebastianists of Canudos and in restoring peace and order in the backlands. Moreover, he added, far from avoiding a discussion, they were eager to engage in one.

The Honorable Deputy Dom João Seixas de Pondé declared that only those who lacked a sense of the ridiculous could continue to speak of the supposed English agent Galileo Gall, whose charred corpse had purportedly been found in Ipupiará by the Bahia Rural Guard, a militia that according to *vox populi*, he would like to add, was recruited, financed, and controlled by the Party of the opposition, words that gave rise to furious protests from the Honorable Deputies of the Progressivist Republican Party. The Honorable Deputy Dom João Seixas de Pondé offered the additional information that the British Consulate in Bahia had attested to the fact that, having come by knowledge that the individual who calls himself Gall had a bad record, it had so notified the authorities of the State two months ago in order that they might act accordingly, and that the Police Commissioner of Bahia had confirmed this, and produced the order of expulsion from the country delivered to the aforementioned individual, who was to ready himself to leave on the French boat *La Marseillaise*. The Honorable Deputy further added that the fact that the individual known as Galileo Gall had failed to obey the order of expulsion and been found a month later in the interior of the State with rifles in his possession in no way constituted proof of a political conspiracy or of the intervention of a foreign power; on the contrary, it was proof, at most, that the aforementioned scoundrel was attempting to smuggle arms to buyers certain to pay, being well provided with money from their multiple robberies, namely the fanatical Sebastianists led by Antônio Conselheiro. As the remarks by the Honorable Deputy Dom João Seixas de Pondé provoked hilarious laughter on the part of the Honorable Deputies of the opposition, who made gestures suggesting that he had angel's wings and a saint's halo, the Honorable President of the Assembly, His Excellency Baron Adalberto de Gumúcio, called for order in the house. The Honorable Deputy Dom João Seixas de Pondé declared that it was hypocritical to cause such an uproar over the discovery of a few rifles in the backlands when everyone knew that smuggling and trafficking in arms was unfortunately more or less the general rule in the interior, and if this were not true, could the Honorable Deputies of the opposition explain how the Progressivist Republican Party had armed the *capangas* and *cangaceiros* they had recruited to form the private Army that went by the name of the Bahia Rural Guard, whose intended purpose was to function outside the official institutions of the State? The Honorable Deputy Dom João Seixas de Pondé having been indignantly jeered at for his insulting words by the Honorable Deputies of the Progressivist Republican Party, the Honorable President of the Assembly was obliged to call for order in the house once again.

The Honorable Deputy Epaminondas Gonçalves declared that the Honorable Deputies of the majority were becoming more and more bogged down in their own contradictions and lies, as inevitably happens to those who walk over quicksand. And he thanked heaven that it had been the Rural Guard that had captured the English rifles and the English agent Gall, for it was an independent, sound, patriotic, genuinely Republican corps, which had alerted the authorities of the Federal Government to the seriousness of the events that had taken place and taken all necessary measures to prevent any attempt to hide the proofs of the collaboration of the native monarchists with the British Crown in the plot against Brazilian sovereignty of which Canudos was the spearhead. In fact, had it not been for the Rural Guard, he declared, the Republic would never have learned of the presence of English agents transporting through the backlands shipments of rifles for the restorationists of Canudos. The Honorable Deputy Dom Eduardo Glicério interrupted him to inform him that the only trace of the famous English agent that had been found was a handful of hair that could well have been that of a redheaded woman or a horse's mane, a sally that brought laughter from both the benches of the majority and those of the opposition. Continuing after this interruption, the Honorable Deputy Dom Epaminondas Gonçalves declared that he applauded the sense of humor of the Honorable Deputy who had interrupted him, but that when the sovereign interests of the Country were threatened, and the blood of the patriots who had fallen in defense of the Republic in Uauá and on the slopes of Monte Cambaio was still warm, the moment was perhaps not an appropriate one for jokes, a remark which brought thunderous applause from the Honorable Deputies of the opposition.

The Honorable Deputy Dom Eliseu de Roque reminded the Assembly that there was incontrovertible proof of the identity of the corpse found in Ipupiará, along with the English rifles, and declared that to refuse to admit the existence of such proof was to refuse to admit the existence of the light of day. He reminded the Assembly of the fact that two persons who had met the English spy Galileo Gall and been on friendly terms with him during his stay in Bahia, the citizen Jan van Rijsted and the distinguished physician Dr. José Batista de Sá Oliveira, had identified as being his the English agent's clothes, his frock coat, his trousers belt, his boots, and, most importantly, the bright red hair that the members of the Rural Guard who found the corpse had had the good judgment to cut off. He reminded the Honorable Deputies that both citizens had also testified as to the revolutionary ideas of the Englishman and his obviously conspiratorial intentions with regard to Canudos, and that neither of them had been surprised that his dead body had been found in that region. And, finally, he reminded his hearers that many citizens of towns in the interior had given testimony to the Rural Guard that they had seen the stranger with red hair and an odd way of speaking Portuguese trying to secure guides to take him to Canudos. The Honorable Deputy Dom João Seixas de Pondé stated that no one denied that the individual called Galileo Gall had been found dead, with rifles in his possession, in Ipupiará, but that this was not incontrovertible evidence that he was an English spy, since in and of itself his being a foreigner proved nothing. Why might he not have been a Danish, Swedish, French, or German spy, or one from Cochin China?

The Honorable Deputy Dom Epaminondas Gonçalves declared that hearing the words of the Honorable Deputies of the majority, who, instead of shaking with anger when evidence was put before them that a foreign power was attempting to interfere in the domestic affairs of Brazil to undermine the Republic and restore the old feudal and aristocratic order, tried to divert public attention toward questions of secondary importance and look for excuses and extenuating circumstances to justify the behavior of the guilty parties, constituted the most categorical proof that the Government of the State of Bahia would not lift a finger to put an end to the Canudos rebellion, since, on the contrary, it gave them intimate satisfaction. The Machiavellian machinations of the Baron de Canabrava and of the Autonomists would not succeed, however, for the Army of Brazil was there to thwart them, and just as it had thus far put down all the monarchist insurrections against the Republic in the South of the country, it would also crush that of Canudos. He declared that when the sovereignty of the Country was at stake words were superfluous, and that the very next day the Progressivist Republican Party would open a drive for funds to buy arms to be delivered to the Federal Army. And he proposed to the Honorable Deputies of the Progressivist Republican Party that they leave the halls of the Assembly to those nostalgic for the old order and make a pilgrimage to Campo Grande to renew their vow of Republicanism before the marble plaque commemorating Marshal Floriano Peixoto. They proceeded to do so immediately, to the consternation of the Honorable Deputies of the majority.

Minutes later, the Honorable President of the Assembly, His Excellency Sir Adalberto de Gumúcio, adjourned the session.

Tomorrow we shall report on the patriotic ceremony held at Campo Grande, before the marble plaque commemorating the Iron Marshal, by the Honorable Deputies of the Progressivist Republican Party, at daybreak.

III

'It doesn't need so much as a comma added or taken out,' Epaminondas Gonçalves says. The look on his face is one of relief, even more than of satisfaction, as though he had feared the worst from this article that the journalist had just read aloud to him, straight through without being interrupted even once by a sneezing fit. 'I congratulate you.'

'Whether true or false, it's an extraordinary story,' the journalist, who doesn't seem to have heard him, mutters. 'That a fairgrounds mountebank who went about the streets of Salvador saying that bones are the handwriting of the soul and who preached anarchy and atheism in the taverns should turn out to be an English agent plotting with the Sebastianists to restore the monarchy and end up being burned alive in the backlands – isn't that extraordinary?'

'It is indeed,' the head of the Progressivist Republican Party agrees. 'And what is even more so is that those people who seemed to be a bunch of fanatics could decimate and rout a battalion equipped with cannons and machine guns. Extraordinary, yes. But, above all, terrifying for the future of this country.'

It has become hotter and the nearsighted journalist's face is bathed in sweat. He mops it with the bedsheet that serves him as a handkerchief and then wipes his fogged eyeglasses on his rumpled shirtfront.

'I'll take this to the compositors myself and stay while they set the type,' he says, gathering together the sheets of paper scattered about on the desk top. 'There won't be any printer's errors; don't worry. You may sleep in peace, sir.'

'Are you happier working with me than on the baron's paper?' his boss asks him, point-blank. 'I know that you earn more here than on the *Diário da Bahia*. But I'm referring to the work. Do you like it better here?'

'In all truth, yes.' The journalist puts his eyeglasses back on and stands there for a moment petrified, waiting for the sneeze with his eyes half closed, his mouth half open, and his nose twitching. But it is a false alarm. 'Political reporting is more entertaining than writing about the damage wreaked by fishing with explosives in the Ribeira de Itapagipe or the fire in the Magalhães Chocolate Factory.'

'And, what's more, it's helping build the country, contributing to a worthwhile national cause,' Epaminondas Gonçalves says. 'Because you're one of us, isn't that so?'

'I don't know what I am, sir,' the journalist replies, in that voice that, at times piercingly high-pitched and at times deep and sonorous, is as undependable as the rest of his body. 'I don't have any political convictions and politics don't interest me.'

'I like your frankness.' The owner of the newspaper laughs, rising to his feet and reaching for his briefcase. 'I'm happy with you. Your feature articles are impeccable. They say precisely what needs to be said, in just the right words. I'm glad I turned the most ticklish section over to you.'

He picks up the little desk lamp, blows the flame out, and leaves the office, followed by the journalist, who, on going through the door leading to the outer office, stumbles over a spittoon.

'Well then, I'm going to ask you a favor, sir,' he blurts out. 'If Colonel Moreira César comes to put down the Canudos insurrection, I'd like to accompany him, as the correspondent of the *Jornal de Notícias*.'

Epaminondas Gonçalves has turned around to look at him and scrutinizes him as he puts his hat on.

'I suppose it's possible,' he says. 'You see – you really are one of us, even though politics don't interest you. To admire Colonel Moreira César, a person has to be a republican through and through.'

'To be honest with you, I don't know if it's admiration exactly,' the journalist confesses, fanning himself with the sheaf of paper. 'Seeing a flesh-and-blood hero, being close to someone very famous is a very tempting prospect. It would be like seeing and touching a character in a novel.'

'You'll have to watch your step. The colonel doesn't like journalists,' Epaminondas Gonçalves says. He is already heading toward the door. 'He began his public life by shooting down a penpusher in the streets of Rio because he'd insulted the army.'

'Good night,' the journalist murmurs. He trots to the other end of the building, where a dark passageway leads to the print shop. The compositors, who have stayed on the job till this late hour waiting for his article, will surely invite him to have a cup of coffee with them.

III

I

The train whistles as it enters the Queimadas station, decorated with streamers welcoming Colonel Moreira César. A huge crowd has congregated on the narrow red-tile platform, beneath a large white canvas banner wafting out over the tracks: 'Queimadas Welcomes Heroic Colonel Moreira César and His Glorious Regiment. Long Live Brazil!' A group of barefoot children wave little flags and there are half a dozen men dressed in their best Sunday suits, with the insignia of the Municipal Council on their breasts and hats in hand, surrounded by a horde of miserable people in rags and tatters who are standing looking on with great curiosity as beggars asking for alms and vendors peddling raw brown sugar and fritters move among them.

The appearance of Colonel Moreira César on the steps of the train – there are crowds of soldiers with rifles at all the windows – is greeted with shouts and applause. Dressed in a blue wool uniform with gold buttons and red stripes and piping, a sword at his waist, and boots with gold spurs, the colonel leaps out onto the platform. He is a man of small build, almost rachitic, very agile. Everyone's face is flushed from the heat, but the colonel is not even sweating. His physical frailty contrasts sharply with the force that he appears to radiate round about him, due to the effervescent energy in his eyes or the sureness of his movements. He has the air of someone who is master of himself, knows what he wants, and is accustomed to being in command.

Applause and cheers fill the air all along the platform and the street, where the people gathered there are shielding themselves from the sun with pieces of cardboard. The children toss handfuls of confetti into the air and those carrying flags wave them. The town dignitaries step forward, but Colonel Moreira César does not stop to shake hands. He has been surrounded by a group of army officers. He nods politely to the dignitaries and then, turning to the crowd, shouts: '*Viva* the Republic! *Viva* Marshal Floriano!' To the surprise of the municipal councillors, who were no doubt expecting to hear speeches, to converse with him, to escort him, the colonel enters the station, accompanied by his officers. The councillors try to follow him, but are stopped by the guards at the door, which has just closed behind him. A whinny is heard. A beautiful white horse is stepping off the train, to the delight of the crowd of youngsters. The animal licks itself clean, shakes its mane, and gives a joyous neigh, sensing open countryside nearby. Lines of soldiers now climb down from the train, one by one, through the doors and windows, setting down bundles, valises, unloading boxes of ammunition, machine guns. A great cheer goes up as the cannons appear, gleaming in the sun. The soldiers are now bringing up teams of oxen to pull the heavy artillery pieces. With resigned expressions, the municipal authorities proceed to join the curious who have piled up at the doors and windows to peep inside the station, trying to catch a glimpse of Moreira César amid the group of officers, adjutants, orderlies who are milling about.

The inside of the station is a single large room, divided by a partition, behind which the telegrapher is working. The side of the room opposite the train platform overlooks a three-story building with a sign that reads: Hotel Continental. There are soldiers everywhere along the treeless Avenida Itapicuru, which leads up to the main square. Behind the dozens of faces pressed against the glass, peering inside the station, the troops are eagerly proceeding to detrain. As the regimental flag appears, unfurled and waved with a flourish by a soldier before the eyes of the crowd, another round of applause is heard. On the esplanade between the station and the Hotel Continental, a soldier curries the white horse with the showy mane. In one corner of the station hall is a long table laden with pitchers, bottles, and platters of food, protected by pieces of cheesecloth from the myriad flies that nobody takes any notice of. Little flags and garlands are suspended from the ceiling, amid posters of the Progressivist

Republican Party and the Bahia Autonomist Party, hailing Colonel Moreira César, the Republic, and the Seventh Infantry Regiment of the Brazilian Army.

Amid all this bustling activity, Colonel Moreira César changes out of woolen dress uniform into a field uniform. Two soldiers have strung up a blanket in front of the partition marking off the telegrapher's office, and the colonel tosses out from this improvised dressing room the various articles comprising his parade dress, which an adjutant gathers up and stores away in a trunk. As he dons his field dress, Moreira César speaks with three officers standing at attention outside.

'Report on our effective strength, Cunha Matos.'

With a slight click of his heels, the major announces: 'Eighty-three men who have come down with smallpox and other illnesses,' he says, consulting a sheet of paper. 'One thousand two hundred thirty-five troops ready for combat. The fifteen million rifle rounds and the seventy artillery rounds are intact and ready to fire, sir.'

'Have the order given for the vanguard to leave within two hours at the latest for Monte Santo.' The colonel's voice is trenchant, toneless, impersonal. 'You, Olímpio, present my apologies to the Municipal Council. I will receive them in a while. Explain to them that we are unable to waste time attending ceremonies or banquets.'

'Yes, sir.'

When Captain Olímpio de Castro takes his leave, the third officer steps forward. He is wearing colonel's stripes and is a man advanced in years, a bit on the tubby side, with a calm look in his eye. 'Lieutenant Pires Ferreira and Major Febrônio de Brito are here. They have orders to join the regiment as advisers.'

Moreira César is lost in thought for a moment. 'How fortunate for the regiment,' he murmurs, in a voice that is almost inaudible. 'Escort them here, Tamarindo.'

An orderly, on his knees, helps the colonel don a pair of riding boots, without spurs. A moment later, preceded by Colonel Tamarindo, Febrônio de Brito and Pires Ferreira arrive and stand at attention in front of the blanket. They click their heels, give their name and rank, and announce: 'Reporting for duty, sir.' The blanket falls to the floor. Moreira César is wearing a pistol and sword at his side, his shirtsleeves are rolled up, and his arms are short, skinny, and hairless. He looks the newcomers over from head to foot without a word, with an icy look in his eyes.

'It is an honor for us to place our experience in this region at the service of the most prestigious military leader of Brazil, sir.'

Colonel Moreira César stares into the eyes of Febrônio de Brito, until the latter looks away in confusion.

'Experience that was of no avail to you when you were confronted with a mere handful of bandits.' The colonel has not raised his voice, yet the hall of the railway station seems to be electrified, paralyzed. Scrutinizing the major as he would an insect, Moreira César points a finger at Pires Ferreira: 'This officer was in command of no more than a company. But you had half a thousand men at your command and allowed yourself to be defeated like a tenderfoot. The two of you have cast discredit on the army and hence on the Republic. Your presence in the Seventh Regiment is not welcome. You are forbidden to enter combat. You will remain in the rear guard to take care of the sick and the animals. You are dismissed.'

The two officers are deathly pale. Febrônio de Brito is sweating heavily. His lips part, as though about to say something, but then he decides merely to salute and withdraw with tottering footsteps. The lieutenant stands rooted to the spot, his eyes suddenly red. Moreira César walks by without looking at him, and the swarm of officers and orderlies go on with their duties. On a table maps and a pile of papers are laid out.

'Let the correspondents come in, Cunha Matos,' the colonel orders.

The major shows them in. They have come on the same train as the Seventh Regiment and they are plainly worn out from all the bumping and jolting. There are five of them, of different ages, dressed in leggings, caps, riding pants, and equipped with pencils and notebooks; one of them is carrying a bellows camera and a tripod. The one who most attracts people's notice is the near-sighted young correspondent from the *Jornal de Notícias.* The sparse little goatee that he has grown is in keeping with his threadbare appearance, his extravagant portable writing desk, the inkwell tied to his sleeve, and the goose-quill pen that he nibbles on as the photographer sets up his camera. As he trips the shutter, there is a flash of powder in the pan that brings even louder screams of excitement from the youngsters crouching behind the windowpanes. Colonel Moreira César acknowledges the correspondents' greeting with a slight nod.

'It surprised many people that I did not receive the people of note in Salvador,' he says, without polite formulas or warmth, by way of salutation. 'There is no mystery involved, sirs. It is a question of time. Every minute is precious, in view of the mission that has brought us to Bahia. We shall bring it to a successful conclusion. The Seventh Regiment is going to punish the rebels of Canudos, as it did the insurgents of the Fortress of Santa Cruz and of Laje, and the federalists of Santa Catarina. There will not be any further uprisings against the Republic.'

The clusters of humanity behind the windowpanes have fallen silent, straining to hear what the colonel is saying; officers and orderlies are standing stock-still, listening; and the five journalists are gazing at him with mingled fascination and incredulity. Yes, it is he, he is here at last, in person, just as he appears in caricatures of him: thin, frail, vibrant, with little eyes that flash or drill straight through the person he is addressing, and a forward thrust of his hand as he speaks that resembles the lunge of a fencer. Two days previously, they had been waiting for him in Salvador, with the same curiosity as hundreds of other Bahians, and he had left everyone frustrated, for he did not attend either the banquets or the ball that had been arranged, or the official receptions and ceremonies in his honor, and except for a brief visit to the Military Club and to Governor Luiz Viana, he spoke with no one, devoting all his time to supervising personally the disembarkation of his troops at the port and the transportation of equipment and supplies to the Calçada Station, so as to leave the following day on this train that has brought the regiment to the backlands. He had passed through the city of Salvador as though he were fleeing on the run, as though fearing that he would be infected by some dread disease, and it was only now that he was offering an explanation of his conduct: time. But the five journalists, who are closely watching his slightest gesture, are not thinking about what he is saying at this moment, but recalling what has been said and written about him, mentally comparing that mythical creature, both despised and deified, with the very small-statured, stern figure who is speaking to them as though they were not there. They are trying to imagine him, a youngster still, enrolling as a volunteer in the war against Paraguay, where he received wounds and medals in equal number, and his first years as an officer, in Rio de Janeiro, when his militant republicanism very nearly caused him to be thrown out of the army and sent to jail, or in the days when he was the leader of the conspiracies against the monarchy. Despite the energy transmitted by his eyes, his gestures, his voice, it is hard for them to imagine him killing that obscure journalist, in the Rua do Ouvidor in the capital, with five shots from his revolver, though it is not difficult, on the other hand, to imagine his voice declaring at his trial that he is proud to have done what he did and would do so again if he heard anyone insult the army. But above all they recall his public career, after his years of exile in the Mato Grosso and his return following the fall of the Empire. They remember how he turned into President Floriano Peixoto's right-hand man, crushing with an iron fist all the uprisings that took place in the first years of the Republic, and defending in *O Jacobino*, that incendiary paper, his arguments in favor of a Dictatorial Republic, without a parliament, without political parties, in which the army, like the Church in the past, would be the nerve center of a secular society frantically pursuing henceforth the goal of scientific progress. They are wondering whether it is true that on the death of Marshal Floriano Peixoto he was so overwrought that he fainted as he was reading the eulogy at the cemetery. People have said that with the coming to power of a civilian president,

Prudente de Moraes, the political fate of Colonel Moreira César and the so-called Jacobins is sealed. But, they tell themselves, this must not be true, since, if it were, he would not be here in Queimadas, at the head of the most famous corps of the Brazilian Army, sent by the government itself to carry out a mission from which – who can possibly doubt it? – he will return to Rio with greatly enhanced prestige.

'I have not come to Bahia to intervene in local political struggles,' he is saying, as without looking at them he points to the posters of the Republican Party and the Autonomist Party hanging from the ceiling. 'The army is above factional quarrels, on the sidelines of political maneuvering. The Seventh Regiment is here to put down a monarchist conspiracy. For behind the brigands and fanatical madmen of Canudos is a plot against the Republic. Those poor devils are a mere tool of aristocrats who are unable to resign themselves to the loss of their privileges, who do not want Brazil to be a modern country. And of certain fanatical priests unable to resign themselves to the separation of Church and State because they do not want to render unto Caesar that which is Caesar's. And even of England, apparently, which wants to restore the corrupt Empire that allowed it to buy up the entire output of Brazilian sugar at ridiculously low prices. But they are mistaken. Neither aristocrats nor priests nor England will ever again lay down the law in Brazil. The army will not permit it.'

He has raised his voice little by little and uttered the last sentences in an impassioned tone, with his right hand resting on the pistol suspended from his cartridge belt. As he falls silent there is a reverent hush of expectation in the station hall and the buzzing of insects can be heard as they circle round in mad frustration above the plates of food covered with cheesecloth. The most grizzled journalist, a man who, despite the stifling heat in the room, is still bundled up in a plaid jacket, timidly raises one hand to indicate that he wishes to make a comment or ask a question. But the colonel does not allow him to speak; he has just motioned with his hand to two of his orderlies. Coached beforehand, they lift a box off the floor, place it on the table, and open it: it is full of rifles.

Moreira César begins slowly pacing back and forth in front of the five journalists, his hands clasped behind his back.

'Captured in the backlands of Bahia, gentlemen,' he goes on to say in a sarcastic tone of voice, as though he were making mock of someone. 'These rifles, at least, failed to reach Canudos. And where are they from? They didn't even bother to remove the manufacturer's label. Liverpool, no less! Rifles of this type have never turned up in Brazil before. Moreover, they're equipped with a special device for shooting expanding bullets. That explains the gaping bullet holes that so surprised the army surgeons: wounds ten, twelve centimeters in diameter. They looked more like shrapnel wounds than bullet wounds. Is it likely that simple *jagunços*, mere cattle rustlers, would know about such European refinements as expanding bullets? And furthermore, what is the meaning behind the sudden appearance of so many people whose origins are a mystery? The corpse discovered in Ipupiará. The individual who turns up in Capim Grosso with a pocket full of pounds sterling who confesses to having guided a party of English-speaking horsemen. Foreigners trying to take shipments of provisions and gunpowder to Canudos have even been discovered in Belo Horizonte. Too many apparent coincidences not to point to a plot against the Republic as the source behind them. The enemies of the Republic refuse to give up. But their machinations are of no avail. They failed in Rio, they failed in Rio Grande do Sul, and they will also fail in Bahia, gentlemen.'

He has paced back and forth in front of the five journalists two, three times, taking short, rapid, nervous steps. He has now returned to the same place as before, alongside the table with the maps. As he addresses them once again, his tone of voice becomes imperious, threatening.

'I have agreed to allow you to accompany the Seventh Regiment, but you will be obliged to obey certain rules. The dispatches that you telegraph from here must first have been approved by Major Cunha Matos or by Colonel Tamarindo. The same is true of any reports you send via messengers during the campaign. I must warn you that if any one of you tries to send off an article that has not been approved by my aides, this will be regarded as a serious offense. I hope you understand the situation: any slip, error, imprudence risks serving the enemy's cause. Don't forget that we are at war. May your stay with the regiment be a pleasant one. That is all, gentlemen.'

He turns to his staff officers, who surround him forthwith, and immediately, as though a magic spell had been broken, the hustle and bustle, the din, the milling back and forth begin again in the Queimadas station. But the five journalists stand there looking at each other, disconcerted, dazed, disappointed, unable to understand why Colonel Moreira César is treating them as though they were his potential enemies, why he has not allowed them to ask a single question, why he has not shown them the slightest sign of warmth or at least politeness. The circle surrounding the colonel breaks up as each of his officers, obeying his instructions, clicks his heels and heads off in a different direction. Once he is alone, the colonel gazes all about him, and for a second the five journalists have the impression that he is about to approach them, but they are mistaken. He is looking, as though he had just become aware of them, at the dark, miserable, famished faces pressing against the doors and windows. He observes them with an expression impossible to define, scowling, his lower lip thrust forward. Suddenly he strides resolutely to the nearest door. He flings it wide open and opens his arms to welcome the swarm of men, women, children, oldsters dressed in almost nothing but rags, many of them barefoot, who gaze at him with respect, fear, or admiration. With imperious gestures, he motions to them to come inside, pulls them, drags them in, encourages them, pointing out to them the long table where, beneath clouds of greedy insects, the drinks and viands that the Municipal Council of Queimadas has set out to honor him are sitting untouched.

'Come on in, come on in,' he says, leading them to the table, pushing them, removing with his own hand the pieces of cheesecloth covering the viands. 'You're the guests of the Seventh Regiment. Come on, don't be afraid. All this is for you. You need it more than we do. Drink, eat, and may you enjoy it.'

And now there is no need to urge them on; they have fallen ecstatically, greedily, incredulously, on the plates, glasses, platters, pitchers, and are elbowing each other aside, crowding round, pushing and shoving, fighting with each other for the food and drink, before the colonel's saddened gaze. The journalists stand there, openmouthed. A little old woman, holding a morsel of food that she has grabbed and already bitten into, backs away from the table and stops alongside Moreira César, her face beaming with gratitude.

'May the Blessed Lady protect you, Colonel,' she murmurs, making the sign of the cross in the air.

'This is the lady that protects me,' the journalists hear him answer as he touches his sword.

In its better days, the Gypsy's Circus had included twenty persons, if one could call persons creatures such as the Bearded Lady, the Dwarf, the Spider Man, Pedrim the Giant, and Julião, swallower of live toads. In those days the circus went about in a wagon painted red, with posters of trapeze artists on the side, drawn by the four horses on which the French Brothers did acrobatic tricks. It also had a small menagerie, a counterpart of the collection of human curiosities that the Gypsy had collected in his wanderings: a five-legged sheep, a little two-headed monkey, a cobra (a normal one) which had to be fed small birds, and a goat with three rows of teeth, which Pedrim displayed to the public by opening its mouth with his huge hands. They never had a tent. Performances were given in the main squares of towns, on holidays or the local patron saint's day.

There were feats of strength and balancing acts, magic tricks and mind reading, Solimão the Black swallowed swords, in nothing flat the Spider Man glided up to the top of the greased pole and then offered a fabulous milreis piece to anyone who could do the same, Pedrim the Giant broke chains, the Bearded

Lady danced with the cobra and kissed it on the mouth, and all of them, made up as clowns with burnt cork and rice powder, bent the Idiot, who seemed to have no bones, in two, in four, in six. But the star performer was the Dwarf, who recounted tales, with great sensitivity, vehemence, tender feeling, and imagination: the story of Princess Maguelone, the daughter of the King of Naples, who is abducted by Sir Pierre the knight and whose jewels are found by a sailor in the belly of a fish; the story of the Beautiful Silvaninha, whose own father, no less, wished to marry her; the story of Charlemagne and the Twelve Peers of France; the story of the barren duchess with whom the Devil fornicated, who then gave birth to Robert the Devil; the story of Olivier and Fierabras. His turn was last because it put the audience in a generous mood.

The Gypsy must have been in trouble with the police on the coast, for even in periods of drought he never went down there. He was a violent man; on the slightest pretext, his fists would shoot out and he would mercilessly beat up any creature who annoyed him, be it man, woman, or animal. Despite his mistreatment of them, however, none of the circus people would have dreamed of leaving him. He was the soul of the circus, he was the one who had created it, collecting from all over those beings who, in their towns and their families, were objects of derision, freaks whom others looked upon as punishments from God and mistakes of the species. All of them, the Dwarf, the Bearded Lady, the Giant, the Spider Man, even the Idiot (who could feel these things even though he wasn't able to understand them), had found in the traveling circus a more hospitable home than the one they had come from. In the caravan that went up and down and around the burning-hot backlands, they ceased to live a life filled with fear and shame and shared an abnormality that made them feel that they were normal.

Hence, none of them could understand the behavior of the youngster from Natuba with long tangled locks, lively dark eyes, and practically no legs at all, who trotted around on all fours. When they gave their show in his town, they noticed that he'd caught the Gypsy's eye, that he watched the boy all during the performance. Because there was no getting around the fact that freaks of nature – human or animal – fascinated him for some more profound reason than the money he could make by exhibiting them. Perhaps he felt more normal, more complete, more perfect in the society of misfits and oddities. In any event, when the show was over, he asked people where the youngster lived, found the house, introduced himself to his parents, and persuaded them to give the boy to him so as to make a circus performer of him. The thing the others found incomprehensible was that, a week later, this creature who got about on all fours escaped from the circus, just as the Gypsy had started teaching him a turn as an animal tamer.

Their bad luck began with the great drought, on account of the Gypsy's obdurate refusal to go down to the coast as the circus people begged him to do. They found deserted towns and haciendas that had turned into charnel houses; they realized that they might die of thirst. But the Gypsy was as stubborn as a mule, and one night he said to them: 'I'm giving you your freedom. Clear out if you want to. But if you don't go, I don't want anybody ever to tell me again where the circus should head next.' Nobody took off, no doubt because all of them feared other people more than they feared catastrophe. In Caatinga do Moura, Dádiva, the Gypsy's wife, took sick with fevers that made her delirious, and they had to bury her in Taquarandi. They were forced to begin eating the circus animals. When the rains came again, a year and a half later, Julião and his wife Sabina, Solimão the Black, Pedrim the Giant, the Spider Man, and the Little Star had died. They had lost the wagon with the posters of trapeze artists on the sides and were now hauling their belongings about in two carts that they pulled themselves, until people, water, life returned to the backlands and the Gypsy was able to buy two draft mules.

They began to put on shows again and once more they earned enough to put food in their mouths. But things weren't the same as before. The Gypsy, crazed with grief at the loss of his children, took no interest in the performances now. He had left the three children in the care of a family in Caldeirão Grande, and when he came back to get them after the drought, nobody in the town could tell him anything about the Campinas family or his children. He never gave up hope of finding them, and years later he was still questioning people in the towns as to whether they'd seen them or heard anything about them. The disappearance of his children – everyone else was sure they were dead – turned him from a man who had once been energy and high spirits personified into a creature filled with bitterness, who drank too much and flew into a fury over anything and everything. One afternoon they were putting on a show in the village of Santa Rosa and the Gypsy was doing the turn that Pedrim the Giant used to do in the old days: challenging any spectator to make his shoulders touch the ground. A robust man presented himself and knocked him clean over at the first shove. The Gypsy picked himself up, saying that he'd slipped and that the man would have to try again. The brawny man again sent him sprawling. Getting to his feet once more, the Gypsy, his eyes flashing, asked him if he'd be willing to repeat his feat with a knife in his hand. The man didn't really want to fight it out with him, but the Gypsy, having taken leave of his reason, egged him on in such an insulting way that finally there was nothing else the husky fellow could do but accept the challenge. As effortlessly as he'd knocked him down before, he left the Gypsy lying on the ground, with his throat slit and his eyes turning glassy. They learned later that the Gypsy had had the temerity to challenge Pedrão, the famous bandit.

Despite everything, surviving through simple inertia, as if to prove that nothing dies unless it's meant to (the phrase had come from the Bearded Lady), the circus did not disappear. It was admittedly a mere shadow of the old circus now, huddling round a wagon with a patched canvas top, drawn by a lone burro; folded up inside it was a much-mended tent, which the last remaining performers – the Bearded Lady, the Dwarf, the Idiot, and the cobra – set up and slept under each night. They still gave shows and the Dwarf's stories of love and adventure were still as great a success as in the old days. In order not to tire the burro, they traveled on foot and the only one of them to enjoy the use of the wagon was the cobra, which lived in a wicker basket. In their wanderings hither and yon, the last members of the Gypsy's Circus had met up with saints, bandits, pilgrims, migrants, people with the most startling faces dressed in the most improbable attire. But never, before that morning, had they come across a flaming-red mane of hair such as that of the man stretched out full-length on the ground that they caught sight of as they rounded a bend of the trail that leads to Riacho da Onça. He was lying there motionless, dressed in a black garment covered with patches of white dust. A few yards farther on were the rotting carcass of a mule being devoured by black vultures and a fire that had gone out. And sitting alongside the ashes was a young woman, watching them approach with an expression on her face that did not seem to be a sad one. The burro, as though it had been given an order to do so, stopped in its tracks. The Bearded Lady, the Dwarf, the Idiot, took a close look at the man and spied the purplish wound in his shoulder half hidden by the fiery-red locks, and the dried blood on his beard, ear, and shirt-front.

'Is he dead?' the Bearded Lady asked.

'Not yet,' Jurema answered.

'This place will be destroyed by fire,' the Counselor said, sitting up on his pallet. They had rested only four hours, since the procession the evening before had ended after midnight, but the Lion of Natuba, whose ears pricked up at the slightest sound, heard that unmistakable voice in his sleep and leapt up from the floor to grab pen and paper so as to note down these words which must not be lost. His eyes closed, totally absorbed in the vision, the Counselor added: 'There will be four fires. I shall extinguish the first three, and the fourth I shall leave to the Blessed Jesus.' This time his words awakened the women of the Sacred Choir in the next room as well, for, as he wrote, the Lion of Natuba heard the door open and saw Maria Quadrado, enveloped in her blue tunic, come into the Sanctuary – the only person save for himself and the Little Blessed One who ever entered, either by day or by night, without first asking the Counselor's permission. 'Praised be Our Lord Jesus Christ,' the Superior of the Sacred Choir said, crossing herself. 'Praised be He,' the Counselor answered, opening his eyes. And with a note of sadness in his voice, he said, dreaming still: 'They will kill me, but I shall not betray Our Lord.'

As he wrote, not letting his mind wander for an instant, aware to the very roots of his hair of the transcendent importance of the mission that the Little Blessed One had entrusted him with, thereby allowing him to share the Counselor's every moment, the Lion of Natuba could hear the women of the Sacred Choir in the next room, anxiously awaiting Maria Quadrado's permission to enter the Sanctuary. There were eight of them, and like her, they were dressed in blue tunics with long sleeves and a high neck, tied at the waist with a white girdle. They went about barefoot, and kept their heads covered with kerchiefs that were also blue. Chosen by the Mother of Men because of their spirit of self-abnegation and their devotion, they had one mission, to serve the Counselor, and all eight of them had vowed to live a life of chastity and never return to their families. They slept on the floor, on the other side of the door, and accompanied the Counselor like an aureole as he supervised the construction of the Temple of the Blessed Jesus, prayed in the little Church of Santo Antônio, led processions, presided at Rosaries and funerals, or visited the Health Houses. In view of the saint's frugal habits, their daily tasks were few: washing and mending his dark purple tunic, caring for the little white lamb, cleaning the floor and the walls of the Sanctuary, and vigorously beating his rush mattress. They were entering the Sanctuary now: Maria Quadrado had let them in and closed the door behind them. Alexandrinha Correa was leading the little white lamb. The eight of them made the sign of the cross as they intoned: 'Praised be Our Lord Jesus Christ.' 'Praised be He,' the Counselor replied, gently stroking the lamb. The Lion of Natuba remained squatting on his heels, his pen in hand and his paper on the little bench that served him as a writing desk, and his intelligent eyes – gleaming brightly amid the long filthy mane that fell all about over his face – fixed on the Counselor's lips. The latter was about to pray. He stretched out face downward on the floor, as Maria Quadrado and the eight pious women knelt round him to pray with him. But the Lion of Natuba did not stretch out on the floor or kneel: his mission exempted him even from joining in the devotions. The Little Blessed One had instructed him to remain on the alert, in case one of the prayers that the saint recited turned out to be a 'revelation.' But that morning the Counselor prayed silently in the dawn light, growing brighter by the second as it filtered into the Sanctuary through the chinks in the roof and the walls and the door, strands of gold shot through with motes of dust. Little by little, Belo Monte was waking: roosters, dogs, human voices could be heard. Outside, doubtless, the usual small groups had already begun to gather: pilgrims and members of the community who wished to see the Counselor or ask his favor.

Once the Counselor rose to his feet, the women of the Sacred Choir offered him a bowlful of goat's milk, a bit of bread, a dish of boiled cornmeal, and a basketful of *mangabas*. But all he took was a few sips of the milk. Then the women brought a bucket of water so as to wash him. As they silently, diligently circled round his pallet, never once getting in each other's way, as though they had practiced their movements, sponging his hands and face and vigorously scrubbing his feet, the Counselor sat there without moving, lost in thought or in prayer. As they were placing on his feet his shepherd's sandals that he had removed to take his night's rest, the Little Blessed One and Abbot João entered the Sanctuary.

The outward appearance of those two was so different that the former always looked even frailer, more absorbed in his reflections, and the latter more corpulent, when the two of them were together. 'Praised be the Blessed Jesus,' one of them said, and the other: 'Praised be Our Lord Jesus Christ.' 'Praised be He.'

The Counselor extended his hand, and as they kissed it, he asked them in an anxious tone of voice: 'Is there any news of Father Joaquim?'

The Little Blessed One replied that there was none. Although he was painfully thin, in delicate health, and old before his time, his face revealed that indomitable energy with which he organized all the worship services, took charge of receiving the pilgrims, planned the processions, saw to it that the altars were properly cared for, and found the time to compose hymns and litanies. His dark brown tunic was draped with scapulars and full of holes through which one could see the wire circling his waist, which, people said, he had never once removed since that day in his tender years when the Counselor had first knotted it round him. He stepped forward now to speak, as Abbot João, whom people had started calling Leader of the Town and Street Commander, stepped back.

'João has an idea that's inspired, Father,' the Little Blessed One said in the shy, reverent tone of voice in which he always addressed the Counselor. 'There's been a war, right here in Belo Monte. And while everybody was fighting, you were all alone in the tower. There was nobody protecting you.'

'The Father protects me, Little Blessed One,' the Counselor murmured. 'As He protects you and all of those who believe.'

'Though we may die, you must live,' the Little Blessed One insisted. 'Out of charity toward all mankind, Counselor.'

'We want to organize a guard to watch over you, Father,' Abbot João murmured. He spoke with lowered eyes, searching for words. 'This guard will see to it that no harm comes to you. We will choose it the way Mother Maria Quadrado chose the Sacred Choir. It will be made up of the best and bravest men, those who are entirely trustworthy. They will devote themselves to serving you.'

'As the archangels in heaven serve Our Lord Jesus,' the Little Blessed One said. He pointed to the door, the mounting din. 'Every day, every hour, there are more people. There are a hundred of them out there waiting. We can't be personally acquainted with each and every one of them. And what if the Can's men make their way inside to harm you? The corps of guards will be your shield. And if there's fighting, you'll never be alone.'

The women of the Sacred Choir sat squatting on their heels, quietly listening, not saying a word. Only Maria Quadrado was standing, alongside the two men who had just arrived. The Lion of Natuba had dragged himself over to the Counselor as they talked, and, like a dog that is its master's favorite, laid his head on the saint's knee.

'Don't think of yourself, but of the others,' Maria Quadrado said. 'It's an inspired idea, Father. Accept it.'

'It will be the Catholic Guard, the Company of the Blessed Jesus,' the Little Blessed One said. 'They will be crusaders, soldiers who believe in the Truth.'

The Counselor made a gesture that was almost imperceptible, but all of them understood that he had given his consent. 'Who is to lead it?' he asked.

'Big João, if you approve,' the erstwhile *cangaceiro* answered. 'The Little Blessed One also thinks he might be the right one.'

'He's a firm believer.' The Counselor remained silent for a moment, and when he began to speak again his voice had become completely impersonal and his words did not appear to be addressed to any of them, but rather to a far greater number of listeners, a vast, imperishable audience. 'He has suffered, both in body and in soul. And it is the suffering of the soul, above all, that makes good people truly good.'

Before the Little Blessed One even looked his way, the Lion of Natuba had raised his head from the saint's knees and with feline swiftness had seized pen and paper and written down the words they had just heard. When he had finished, he crawled back on all fours to the Counselor and once more laid his massive head with its tangled locks on his knee. Abbot João had meanwhile begun to recount what had taken place in the last few hours. *Jagunços* had gone out to reconnoiter, others had come back with provisions and news, and still others had set fire to the haciendas of people who refused to help the Blessed Jesus. Was the Counselor listening to him? His eyes were closed, and he remained perfectly silent and motionless, as did the women of the Sacred Choir. His soul had seemingly taken wing to participate in one of those celestial colloquies – as the Little Blessed One called them – following which he would bring back revelations and truths to the inhabitants of Belo Monte. Even though there were no signs that other soldiers were coming, Abbot João had posted men along the roads that led from Canudos to Jeremoabo, Uauá, O Cambaio, Rosário, Chorrochó, Curral dos Bois, and was digging trenches and erecting parapets along the banks of the Vaza-Barris. The Counselor did not ask him any questions, nor did he ask any when the Little Blessed One gave an account of the battles that he for his part was waging. As though reciting one of his litanies, he explained how the pilgrims had poured in the evening before and that morning – from Cabrobó, from Jacobina, from Bom Conselho, from Pombal – and were now in the Church of Santo Antônio, awaiting the Counselor. Would he receive them during the morning before going to see how the work was getting on at the Temple of the Blessed Jesus, or in the evening during the counsels? The Little Blessed One then gave him an account of how the work was going. They had run out of timber for the vaulting and were unable to start on the roof. Two carpenters had gone to Juazeiro to see about getting more. Since, happily, there was no lack of stones, the masons were going on with the bracing of the walls.

'The Temple of the Blessed Jesus must be finished as soon as possible,' the Counselor murmured, opening his eyes. 'That is what matters most.'

'Indeed it is, Father,' the Little Blessed One said. 'Everyone is helping. What's lacking isn't willing hands but building materials. We're running out of everything. But we'll get the timber we need, and if we have to pay for it, we'll do so. People are prepared, one and all, to give whatever money they have.'

'Father Joaquim hasn't come round for many days now,' the Counselor said, with a note of anxiety in his voice. 'There hasn't been a Mass in Belo Monte for quite some time now.'

'It must be the fuses that are delaying him, Father,' Abbot João said. 'We have hardly any left, and he offered to go buy some at the mines in Caçabu. He's no doubt ordered them and is waiting for them to come. Do you want me to send someone out to look for him?'

'He'll be along. Father Joaquim won't let us down,' the Counselor answered. And he looked around for Alexandrinha Correa, who had been sitting with her head hunched over between her shoulders, visibly embarrassed, ever since the name of the parish priest of Cumbe had first been mentioned. 'Come here to me. You mustn't feel ashamed, my daughter.'

Alexandrinha Correa – with the years she had become thinner and her face grown more wrinkled, but she still had her turned-up nose and an intractable air about her that contrasted with her humble manner – crept over to the Counselor without daring to look at him.

Placing one hand on her head as he spoke, he said to her: 'From that evil there came good, Alexandrinha. He was a bad shepherd, and because he had sinned, he suffered, repented, settled his accounts with heaven, and is now a good son of the Father. When all is said and done, you did him a service. And you did your brothers and sisters of Belo Monte one as well, for thanks to Dom Joaquim we are still able to hear Mass from time to time.'

There was sadness in his voice as he spoke these last words, and perhaps he did not notice that the former water divineress bent her head to kiss his tunic before retreating to her corner. In the early days at Canudos, a number of priests used to come to say Mass, baptize babies, and marry couples. But after that Holy Mission of the Capuchin missionary priests from Salvador which ended so badly, the Archbishop of Bahia had forbidden parish priests to offer the sacraments at Canudos. Father Joaquim was the only one who had continued to come nonetheless. He brought not only religious solace but also paper and ink for the Lion of Natuba, candles and incense for the Little Blessed One, and all sorts of things that Abbot João and the Vilanova brothers had asked him to procure for them. What impelled him to defy first the Church and now the civil authorities? Alexandrinha Correa perhaps, the mother of his children, with whom, each time he visited Canudos, he had an austere conversation in the Sanctuary or in the Chapel of Santo Antônio. Or the Counselor perhaps, in whose presence he was always visibly perturbed and seemingly moved to the depths of his soul. Or the hope perhaps (as many people suspected) that by coming he was paying a long-standing debt owed heaven and the people of the backlands.

The Little Blessed One had started to speak again, about the Triduum of the Precious Blood that was to begin that afternoon, when they heard a gentle knock on the door amid all the uproar outside. Maria Quadrado went to open it. With the sun shining brightly behind him and a multitude of heads trying to peek over his shoulders, the parish priest of Cumbe appeared in the doorway.

'Praised be Our Lord Jesus Christ,' the Counselor said, rising to his feet so quickly that the Lion of Natuba was obliged to step aside. 'We were just speaking of you, and suddenly you appear.'

He walked to the door to meet Father Joaquim, whose cassock was covered with dust, as was his face. The saint bent down, took his hand, and kissed it. The humility and respect with which the Counselor always received him made the priest feel ill at ease, but today he was so perturbed that he did not appear to have even noticed.

'A telegram arrived,' he said, as the Little Blessed One, Abbot João, the Mother of Men, and the women of the Sacred Choir kissed his hand. 'A regiment of the Federal Army is on its way here, from Rio. Its commanding officer is a famous figure, a hero who has won every war he's ever led his troops in.'

'Thus far, nobody has ever won a war against the Father,' the Counselor said joyfully.

Crouching over his bench, the Lion of Natuba was writing swiftly.

*

Having finished the job in Itiúba that he had hired on for with the people from the railroad company in Jacobina, Rufino is now guiding a group of cowhands along the rugged back trails of the Serra de Bendengó, that mountain fastness where a stone from heaven once fell to earth. They are tracking cattle rustlers who have stolen half a hundred head from the Pedra Vermelha hacienda belonging to a 'colonel' named José Bernardo Murau, but before they locate the cattle they learn of the defeat of Major Febrônio de Brito's expedition at Monte Cambaio and decide to stop searching so as not to run into *jagunços* or retreating soldiers. Just after parting company with the cowhands, Rufino falls into the hands of a band of deserters, led by a sergeant from Pernambuco, in the spurs of the Serra Grande. They relieve him of his shotgun, his machete, his provisions, and the sack containing the reis that he has earned as a guide for the railway people. But they do not otherwise harm him and even warn him not to go by way of Monte Santo, since Major Brito's defeated troops are regrouping there and might well enlist his services.

The region is in a state of profound unrest because of the war. The following night, near the Rio Cariacá, the guide hears the sound of gunfire and early the next morning discovers that men who have come from Canudos have sacked and razed the Santa Rosa hacienda, which he knows very well. The house, vast and cool, with a wooden balustrade and surrounded by palm trees, has been reduced to a pile of smoking ashes. He catches sight of the empty stables, the former slave quarters, and the peasants' huts, which have also been set on fire, and an old man living nearby tells him that everyone has gone off to Belo Monte, taking with them the animals and everything else that did not go up in flames.

Rufino takes a roundabout way so as to skirt Monte Santo, and the following day a family of pilgrims headed for Canudos warns him to be on his guard, for there are patrols from the Rural Guard scouring the countryside in search of young men to press into army service. At midday he arrives at a chapel half hidden amid the yellowish slopes of the Serra da Engorda, where, by long-standing tradition, men with blood on their hands come to repent of their crimes, and others come to make offerings. It is a very small building, standing all by itself, with no doors and with white walls teeming with lizards slithering up and down. The inside walls are completely covered with ex-votos: bowls containing petrified food, little wooden figurines, arms, legs, heads made of wax, weapons, articles of clothing, all manner of miniature objects. Rufino carefully examines knives, machetes, shotguns, and chooses a long, curved, sharp-honed knife recently left there. Then he goes to kneel before the altar, on which there is nothing but a cross, and explains to the Blessed Jesus that he is merely borrowing this knife. He tells Him how he has been robbed of everything he had on him, so that he needs the knife in order to get back home. He assures Him that it is not at all his intention to take something that belongs to Him, and promises to return it to Him, along with a brand-new knife that will be his offering to Him. He reminds Him that he is not a thief, that he has always kept his promises. He crosses himself and says: 'I thank you, Blessed Jesus.'

He then goes on his way at a steady pace that does not tire him, climbing up slopes or down ravines, traversing scrubland *caatinga* or stony ground. That afternoon he catches an armadillo that he roasts over a fire. The meat from it lasts him two days. The third day finds him not far from Nordestina. He heads for the hut of a farmer he knows, where he has often spent the night. The family receives him even more cordially than in the past, and the wife prepares a meal for him. He tells them how the deserters robbed him, and they talk about what is going to happen after the battle on O Cambaio, in which, so people are saying, a great many men lost their lives. As they talk, Rufino notes that the man and his wife exchange glances, as though there is something they want to tell him though they don't dare come out with it. Then the farmer, coughing nervously, asks him how long it has been since he has had news of his family. Nearly a month. Has his mother died? No. Jurema, then? The couple sit there looking at him. Finally the man speaks up: the news is going round that there has been a shootout and men killed at his house and that his wife has taken off with a red-headed stranger. Rufino thanks them for their hospitality and leaves immediately.

At dawn the following morning the silhouette of the guide stands out against the light on a hill from which his cabin can be seen. He walks through the little copse dotted with boulders and bushes where he first met Galileo Gall and makes his way toward the rise on which his dwelling stands, at his usual pace, a quick trot halfway between walking and running. His face bears the traces of his long journey, of the troubles he has come up against, of the bad news he has had the night before: tense and rigid, the features stand out more sharply, the lines and hollows more deeply etched. The only thing he has with him is the knife that he has borrowed from the Blessed Jesus. Approaching within a few yards of his cabin, he gazes warily about. The gate of the animal pen is open, and it is empty. But what Rufino stands staring at with eyes at once grave, curious, and dumfounded is not the animal pen but the open space in front of the house, where there are now two crosses that were not there before, propped up by two piles of little stones. On entering the cabin, he spies the oil lamp, the casks and jars, the pallet, the hammock, the trunk, the print of the Virgin of Lapa, the cooking pots and the bowls, and the pile of firewood. There doesn't seem to be anything missing, and what is more, the cabin appears to have been carefully tidied up, each thing in its proper place. Rufino looks around again, slowly, as though trying to wrench from these objects the secret of what has happened in his absence. He can hear the silence: no dog barking, no cackling hens, no sheep bells tinkling, no voice of his wife. He finally begins walking about the room, closely examining everything. By the time he finishes, his eyes are red. He leaves the cabin, closing the door gently behind him.

He heads toward Queimadas, gleaming brightly in the distance beneath a sun that is now directly overhead. Rufino's silhouette disappears around a bend of the promontory, then reappears, trotting amid the lead-colored stones, cacti, yellowish brush, the sharp-pointed palisade fence round a corral. Half an hour later he enters the town by way of Avenida Itapicuru and walks up along it to the main square. The sun reflects like quicksilver off the little whitewashed houses with blue or green doors. The soldiers who have beaten a retreat after the defeat at O Cambaio have begun to straggle into town, ragged strangers who can be seen standing about on the street corners, sleeping underneath the trees, or bathing in the river. The guide walks past them without looking at them, perhaps without even seeing them, thinking only of the townspeople: cowhands with tanned, weather-beaten faces, women nursing their babies, horsemen riding off, oldsters sunning themselves, children running about. They bid him good day or call out to him by name, and he knows that after he has passed by, they turn round and stare at him, point a finger at him, and begin to whisper among themselves. He returns their greetings with a nod of his head, looking straight ahead without smiling so as to discourage anyone from trying to have a word with him. He crosses the main square – a dense mass of sunlight, dogs, hustle and bustle – bowing to left and right, aware of the murmurs, the stares, the gestures, the thoughts he arouses. He does not stop till he reaches a little shop with candles and religious images hanging outside, opposite the little Chapel of Our Lady of the Rosary. He removes his sombrero, takes a deep breath as though he were about to dive into water, and goes inside. On catching sight of him, the tiny old woman who is handing a package to a customer opens her eyes wide and her face lights up. But she waits until the buyer has left before she says a word to him.

The shop is a cube with holes through which tongues of sunlight enter. Candles and tapers hang from nails and lie lined up on the counter. The walls are covered with ex-votos and with saints, Christs, Virgins, and devotional prints. Rufino kneels to kiss the old woman's hand: 'Good day, Mother.' She traces the sign of the cross on his forehead with her gnarled fingers with dirty nails. She is a gaunt, grim-faced old woman with hard eyes, all bundled up in a shawl despite the stifling heat. She is holding a rosary with large beads in one hand.

'Caifás wants to see you, to explain to you,' she says. She has difficulty getting the words out, either because she finds the subject painful or because she has no teeth. 'He'll be coming to the Saturday market. He's come every Saturday to see if you're back yet. It's a long journey, but he's come anyway. He's your friend – he wants to explain to you.'

'Meanwhile, Mother, tell me what you know,' the guide mutters.

'They didn't come to kill *you*,' the little old woman answers straightaway. 'Or her either. They were only out to kill the stranger. But he put up a fight and killed two of them. Did you see the crosses there in front of your house?' Rufino nods. 'Nobody claimed the bodies and they buried them there.' She crosses herself. 'May they be received in Thy holy glory, Lord. Did you find your house in order? I've been going out there every so often. So you wouldn't find it all dirty.'

'You shouldn't have gone,' Rufino says. He stands there with his head bowed dejectedly, his sombrero in his hand. 'You can hardly walk. And besides, that house is dirty forever now.'

'So you already know,' the old woman murmurs, her gaze seeking his, but he avoids her eyes and continues to stare down at the floor. The woman sighs. After a moment's silence, she adds: 'I've sold your sheep so they wouldn't be stolen, the way the chickens were. Your money's in that drawer.' She pauses once more, trying to postpone the inevitable, to avoid talking about the only subject that interests her, the only one that interests Rufino. 'People are malicious. They said you weren't going to come back. That they'd conscripted you in the army perhaps, that you'd died in the battle perhaps. Have you seen how many soldiers there are in Queimadas? There were lots of them that died back there, it seems. Major Febrônio de Brito's here, too.'

But Rufino interrupts her. 'The ones who came to kill him – do you know who their leader was?'

'Caifás,' the old woman answers. 'He brought them there.

He'll explain to you. He explained to me. He's your friend. They weren't out to kill you. Or her. Just the redhead, the stranger.'

She falls silent, as does Rufino, and in the burning-hot, dark redoubt the buzzing of bluebottles, of the swarms of flies circling about among the images, can be heard.

Finally the old woman makes up her mind to speak again. 'Lots of people saw them,' she exclaims in a trembling voice, her eyes suddenly blazing. 'Caifás saw them. When he told me, I thought: I've sinned, and God is punishing me. I brought my son misfortune. Yes, Rufino: Jurema, Jurema. She saved his life, she grabbed Caifás's hands. She went off with him, with her arm around him, leaning on him.' She stretches out a hand and points in the direction of the street. 'Everybody knows. We can't live here any longer, son.'

There is not a twitch of a muscle, the blink of an eye in the angular, beardless face darkened by the deep shadow in the room.

The little old woman shakes her tiny gnarled fist and spits scornfully in the direction of the street. 'They came to commiserate with me, to talk to me about you. Their every word was a knife in my heart. They're vipers, my son!' She passes the black shawl across her eyes, as though she were wiping away tears, but her eyes are dry. 'You'll clear your name of the filth they've heaped upon it, won't you? It's worse than if they'd plucked out your eyes, worse than if they'd killed me. Talk with Caifás. He knows the insult to your name, he knows what honor is. He'll explain to you.'

She sighs once again, then kisses the beads of her rosary with fervent devotion. She looks at Rufino, who hasn't moved or raised his head. 'Many people have gone off to Canudos,' she says in a gentler tone of voice. 'Apostles have come. I would have gone, too. But I stayed because I knew you'd come back. The world's going to end, my son. That's why we're seeing what we're seeing. That's why what's happened has happened. Now I can leave. Will my legs hold up for such a long journey? The Father will decide. It is He who decides everything.'

She falls silent, and after a moment Rufino leans over and kisses her hand again. 'It's a very long journey and I advise you not to make it, Mother,' he says. 'There's fighting, fires, nothing to eat on the way. But if that's your wish, go ahead. Whatever you do will always be the right thing to do. And forget what Caifás told you. Don't grieve or feel ashamed on that account.'

When the Baron de Canabrava and his wife disembarked at the Navy Yard of Salvador, after an absence of several months, they could judge from the reception they received how greatly the strength of the once-all-powerful Bahia Autonomist Party and of its leader and founder had declined. In bygone days, when he was a minister of the Empire or the plenipotentiary in London, and even in the early years of the Republic, the baron's returns to Bahia were always the occasion for great celebrations. All the notables of the city and any number of landowners hastened to the port, accompanied by servants and relatives carrying welcome banners. The city officials always came, and there was a band and children from parochial schools with bouquets of flowers for Baroness Estela. The banquet was held in the Palace of Victory, with the governor as master of ceremonies, and dozens of guests applauded the toasts, the speeches, and the inevitable sonnet that a local bard recited in honor of the returning couple.

But this time there were no more than two hundred people at the Navy Yard to applaud the baron and baroness when they landed, and there was not a single municipal or military or ecclesiastical dignitary among them. As Sir Adalberto de Gumúcio and the deputies Eduardo Glicério, Rocha Seabra, Lélis Piedades, and João Seixas de Pondé – the committee appointed by the Autonomist Party to receive their leader – stepped up to shake the baron's hand and kiss the baroness's, from the expressions on their faces one would have thought they were attending a funeral.

The baron and baroness, however, gave no sign that they noticed what a different reception they were receiving this time. They behaved exactly as always. As the baroness smilingly showed the bouquets to her inseparable personal maid Sebastiana, as though she were amazed at having been given them, the baron bestowed backslaps and embraces on his fellow party members, relatives, and friends who filed past to welcome him. He greeted them by name, inquired after their wives, thanked them for having taken the trouble to come meet him. And every so often, as though impelled by some intimate necessity, he repeated that it was always a joy to return to Bahia, to be back with this sun, this clean air, these people. Before climbing into the carriage that awaited them at the pier, driven by a coachman in livery who bowed repeatedly on catching sight of them, the baron bade everyone farewell with both arms upraised. Then he seated himself opposite the baroness and Sebastiana, whose skirts were full of flowers. Adalberto de Gumúcio sat down next to him and the carriage started up the Ladeira da Conceição da Praia, blanketed in luxuriant greenery. Soon the travelers could see the sailboats in the bay, the Fort of São Marcelo, the market, and any number of blacks and mulattoes in the water catching crabs.

'Europe is always an elixir of youth,' Gumúcio congratulated them. 'You look ten years younger than when you left.'

'I owe that more to the ship crossing than to Europe,' the baroness said. 'The three most restful weeks of my life!'

'You, on the other hand, look ten years older.' The baron looked out the little window at the majestic panorama of the sea and the island spread out wider and wider as the carriage climbed higher, ascending the Ladeira de São Bento now, heading for the upper town. 'Are things as bad as all that?'

'Worse than you can possibly imagine.' He pointed to the port. 'We wanted to have a big turnout, to stage a great public demonstration. Everybody promised to bring people, even from the interior. We were counting on thousands. And you saw how many there were.'

The baron waved to some fish peddlers who had removed their straw hats on seeing the carriage pass by the seminary.

'It's not polite to talk politics in the presence of ladies. Or don't you consider Estela a lady?' the baron chided his friend in a mock-serious tone of voice.

The baroness laughed, a tinkling, carefree laugh that made her seem younger. She had chestnut hair and very white skin, and hands with slender fingers that fluttered like birds. She and her maidservant, an amply curved brunette, gazed in rapture at the dark blue sea, the phosphorescent green of the shoreline, the blood-red rooftops.

'The only person whose absence is justified is the governor,' Gumúcio said, as though he hadn't heard. 'We were the ones responsible for that. He wanted to come, along with the Municipal Council. But the situation being what it is, it's better that he remain *au-dessus de la mêlée*. Luiz Viana is still a loyal supporter.'

'I brought you an album of horse engravings,' the baron said, to raise his friend's spirits. 'I presume that political troubles haven't caused you to lose your passion for equines, Adalberto.'

On entering the upper town, on their way to the Nazareth district, the recently arrived couple put on their best smiles and devoted their attention to returning the greetings of people passing by. Several carriages and a fair number of horsemen, some of them having come up from the port and others who had been waiting at the top of the cliff, escorted the baron through the narrow cobblestone streets, amid curious onlookers standing crowded together on the sidewalks or coming out onto the balconies or poking their heads out of the donkey-drawn streetcars to watch them pass. The Canabravas lived in a town house faced with tlles imported from Portugal, a roof of round red Spanish-style tiles, wrought-iron balconies supported by strong-breasted caryatids, and a façade topped by four ornaments in gleaming yellow porcelain: two bushy-maned lions and two pineapples. The lions appeared to be keeping an eye on the boats arriving in the bay and the pineapples to be proclaiming the splendor of the city to seafarers. The luxuriant garden surrounding the mansion was full of coral trees, mangoes, crotons, and ficus sighing in the breeze. The house had been disinfected with vinegar, perfumed with aromatic herbs, and decorated with large vases of flowers to receive its owners. In the doorway, servants in white balloon pants and little black girls in red aprons and kerchiefs stood clapping their hands to greet them. The baroness began to say a few words to them as the baron, taking his place in the entryway, bade those escorting him goodbye. Only Gumúcio and the deputies Eduardo Glicério, Rocha Seabra, Lélis Piedades, and João Seixas de Pondé came inside the house with him. As the baroness went upstairs, followed by her personal maid, the men crossed the foyer, an anteroom with pieces of furniture in wood, and the baron opened the doors of a room lined with shelves full of books, overlooking the garden. Some twenty men fell silent as they saw him enter the room. Those who were seated rose to their feet and all of them applauded.

The first to embrace him was Governor Luiz Viana. 'It wasn't my idea not to appear at the port,' he said. 'In any event, you see here before you the governor and each and every member of the Municipal Council, your obedient servants.'

He was a forceful man, with a prominent bald head and an aggressive paunch, who did not trouble to conceal his concern. As the baron greeted those present, Gumúcio closed the door. There was more cigar smoke than air in the room. Pitchers of fruit punch had been set out on a table, and as there were not enough chairs to seat everyone, some of the men were perched on chair arms and others were standing leaning against the bookshelves. The baron slowly made his way around the room, greeting each man. When he finally sat down, there was a glacial silence. The men looked at him and their eyes betrayed not only concern but also a mute plea, an anxious trustfulness. The expression on the baron's face, until that moment a jovial one, grew graver as he looked about at the others' funereal countenances.

'I can see that the situation is such that it wouldn't be apropos to inform you whether or not the carnival in Nice is the equal of ours,' he said, very seriously, his gaze seeking Luiz Viana's. 'Let's begin with the worst that's happened. What is it?'

'A telegram that arrived at the same time you did,' the governor murmured from an armchair he appeared to be buried in. 'Rio has decided to intervene militarily in Bahia, after a unanimous vote in Congress. A regiment of the Federal Army has been sent to attack Canudos.'

'In other words, the federal government and the Congress are officially accepting the view that a conspiracy is afoot,' Adalberto de Gumúcio interrupted him. 'In other words, the Sebastianist fanatics are seeking to restore the Empire, with the aid of the Count of Eu, the monarchists, England, and, naturally, the Bahia Autonomist Party. All the humbug churned out by the Jacobin breed suddenly turned into the official truth of the Republic.'

The baron showed no sign of alarm. 'Intervention by the Federal Army comes as no surprise to me,' he said. 'At this juncture it was inevitable. What does surprise me is this business of Canudos. Two expeditions roundly defeated!' He gestured in amazement, his eyes seeking Viana's. 'I don't understand, Luiz. Those madmen should have been either left in peace or wiped out the first time round. I can't fathom why the government botched so badly, let those people become a national problem, freely handed our enemies a gift like that . . .'

'Five hundred troops, two cannons, two machine guns – does that strike you as a paltry force to send against a band of scalawags and religious fanatics?' Luiz Viana answered heatedly. 'Who could have imagined that with strength like that Febrônio de Brito could be hacked to pieces by a few poor devils?'

'It's true that a conspiracy exists, but it's not our doing,' Adalberto de Gumúcio interrupted him once more, with a worried frown and nervously clenched hands, and the thought crossed the baron's mind that he had never seen him this deeply upset by a political crisis. 'Major Febrônio is not as inept as he would have us believe. His defeat was a deliberate one, bargained for and decided in advance with the Jacobins in Rio de Janeiro, with Epaminondas Gonçalves as intermediary. So as to bring about the national scandal that they've been looking for ever since Floriano Peixoto left power. Haven't they been continually inventing monarchist conspiracies since then so that the army will adjourn the Congress and set up a Dictatorial Republic?'

'Save your conjectures for later, Adalberto,' the baron interjected. 'First I want to know exactly what's been happening: the facts.'

'There aren't any facts, only wild imaginings and the most incredible intrigues,' Deputy Rocha Seabra broke in. 'They're accusing us of stirring up the Sebastianists, of sending them arms, of plotting with England to restore the Empire.'

'The *Jornal de Notícias* has been accusing us of that and even worse things ever since the fall of Dom Pedro II,' the baron said with a smile, accompanied by a scornful wave of his hand.

'The difference is that now it's not only the *Jornal de Notícias* but half of Brazil,' Luiz Viana put in. The baron saw him squirm nervously in his chair and wipe his bald head with his hand. 'All of a sudden, in Rio, in São Paulo, in Belo Horizonte, all over the country, people are beginning to mouth the egregious nonsense and the calumnies invented by the Progressivist Republican Party.'

Several men spoke up at once and the baron motioned to them with upraised hands not to ride roughshod over each other. From between his friends' heads he could see the garden, and though what he was hearing interested him and alarmed him, from the moment that he entered his study he had been wondering whether or not the chameleon was hiding among the trees – an animal that he had grown fond of as others conceive an affection for dogs or cats.

'We now know why Epaminondas organized the Rural Police,' Deputy Eduardo Glicério was saying. 'So that it would furnish proof at the right moment. Of contraband rifles for the *jagunços*, and even of foreign spies.'

'Ah, you haven't heard the latest news,' Adalberto de Gumúcio said on noting the intrigued expression on the baron's face. 'The height of the grotesque. An English secret agent in the backlands. His body was burned to a cinder when they found it, but he was English. How did they know? Because of his red hair! They exhibited it in the Rio parliament, along with rifles supposedly found alongside his corpse, in Ipupiará. Nobody will listen to us; in Rio, even our best friends are swallowing all this nonsense. The entire country is convinced that the Republic is endangered by Canudos.'

'I presume that I'm the dark genius behind this conspiracy,' the baron muttered.

'You've had more mud slung at you than anyone else,' the owner–publisher of the *Diário da Bahia* said. 'You handed Canudos over to the rebels and took a trip to Europe to meet with the émigrés of the Empire and plan the rebellion. It's even been said that there was a "fund for subversion," that you put up half the money and England the other half.'

'A fifty–fifty partner of the British Crown,' the baron murmured. 'Good heavens, they overestimate me.'

'Do you know who they're sending to put down the restorationist rebellion?' asked Deputy Lélis Piedades, who was sitting on the arm of the governor's chair. 'Colonel Moreira César and the Seventh Regiment.'

The Baron de Canabrava thrust his head forward slightly and blinked.

'Colonel Moreira César?' He sat lost in thought for some time, moving his lips from time to time as though speaking under his breath. Then he turned to Gumúcio and said: 'Perhaps you're right, Adalberto. This might well be a bold maneuver on the part of the Jacobins. Ever since the death of Marshal Floriano, Colonel Moreira César has been their top card, the hero they're counting on to regain power.'

Again he heard all of them trying to talk at once, but this time he did not stop them. As his friends offered their opinions and argued, he sat there pretending to be listening but with his mind elsewhere, a habit he readily fell into when a discussion bored him or his own thoughts seemed to him to be more important than what he was hearing. Colonel Moreira César! It did not augur well that he was being sent to Bahia. He was a fanatic and, like all fanatics, dangerous. The baron remembered the cold-blooded way in which he had put down the federalist revolution in Santa Catarina four years before, and how, when the Federal Congress asked him to appear before that body and give an account of the executions by firing squad that he had ordered, he had answered with a telegram that was a model of terseness and arrogance: 'No.' He recalled that among those sent to their deaths by the colonel there in the South there had been a marshal, a baron, and an admiral that he knew, and that on the advent of the Republic, Marshal Floriano Peixoto had ordered him to purge the army of all officers known to have had ties with the monarchy. The Seventh Infantry Regiment against Canudos! 'Adalberto is right,' he thought. 'It's the height of the grotesque.' He forced himself to listen once more.

'It's not the Sebastianists in the interior he's come to liquidate – it's us,' Adalberto was saying. 'He's coming to liquidate you, Luiz Viana, the Autonomist Party, and hand Bahia over to Epaminondas Gonçalves, who is the Jacobins' man here.'

'There's no reason to kill yourselves, gentlemen,' the baron interrupted him, raising his voice slightly. He was serious now, no longer smiling, and spoke in a firm voice. 'There's no reason to kill yourselves,' he repeated. He looked slowly about the room, certain that his friends would find his serenity contagious. 'Nobody's going to take what's ours away from us. Haven't we present, right here in this room, the political power of Bahia, the municipal government of Bahia, the judiciary of Bahia, the journalism of Bahia? Aren't the majority of the landed property, the possessions, the herds of Bahia right here? Even Colonel Moreira César can't change that. Finishing us off would be to finish off Bahia, gentlemen. Epaminondas Gonçalves and his followers are an outlandish curiosity in these parts. They have neither the means nor the men nor the experience to take over the reins of Bahia even if they were placed square in their hands. The horse would throw them immediately.'

He paused and someone solicitously handed him a glass of fruit punch. He savored each sip, recognizing the pleasantly sweet taste of guava.

'We're overjoyed, naturally, at your optimism,' he heard Luiz

Viana say. 'You'll grant, however, that we've suffered reverses and that we must act as quickly as possible.'

'There is no doubt of that,' the baron agreed. 'We shall do so. For the moment, what we're going to do is send Colonel Moreira César a telegram immediately, welcoming his arrival and offering him the support of the Bahia authorities and of the Autonomist Party. Is it not in fact in our interest to have him come to rid us of the thieves who steal our land, of the fanatics who sack haciendas and won't allow our peasants to work the fields in peace? And this very day we're also going to begin taking up a collection that will be handed over to the Federal Army to be used in the fight against the bandits.'

He waited until the murmur of voices died down, taking another sip of punch. It was hot and his forehead was wet with sweat.

'I remind you that, for years now, our entire policy has been to prevent the central government from interfering too zealously in Bahia affairs,' Luiz Viana finally said.

'That's all well and good, but the only policy left us now, unless we choose to kill ourselves, is to demonstrate to the entire country that we are not the enemies of the Republic or of the sovereignty of Brazil,' the baron said dryly. 'We must put a stop to this intrigue at once and there is no other way to do so. We'll give Moreira César and the Seventh Regiment a splendid reception. It'll be our welcome ceremony – not the Republican Party's.'

He mopped his forehead with his handkerchief and waited once again for the murmur of voices, even louder than before, to die down.

'It's too abrupt a change,' Adalberto de Gumúcio said, and the baron saw several heads behind him nod in agreement.

'In the Assembly, in the press, our entire strategy has been aimed at avoiding federal intervention,' Deputy Rocha Seabra chimed in.

'In order to defend Bahia's interests we must remain in power and in order to remain in power we must change our policy, at least for the moment,' the baron replied softly. And as if the objections that were raised were of no importance, he went on laying down guidelines. 'We landowners must collaborate with the colonel. Quarter his regiment, provide it with guides, furnish it supplies. Along with Moreira César, we'll be the ones who do away with the monarchist conspirators financed by Queen Victoria.' He simulated a smile as he again mopped his forehead with his handkerchief. 'It's a ridiculous farce, but we have no other choice. And when the colonel has liquidated the poor *cangaceiros* and plaster saints of Canudos we'll stage all sorts of grand celebrations to commemorate the defeat of the British Empire and the Bragança dynasty.'

No one applauded him; no one smiled. They were all silent and ill at ease. But as he observed them the baron saw that already there were some who were admitting to themselves, however reluctantly, that there was nothing else they could do.

'I'll go to Calumbi,' the baron said. 'I hadn't planned on doing so just yet. But it's necessary. I myself will place everything that the Seventh Regiment needs at its disposal. All the landowners in the region should do likewise. Let Moreira César see whom that part of the country belongs to, who is in command there.'

The atmosphere was very tense and everyone wanted to ask questions, to reply to these remarks. But the baron deemed that this was not the proper time to discuss the matter further. After they had eaten and drunk throughout the afternoon and into the night, it would be easier to make them forget their doubts, their scruples.

'Let us join the ladies and have lunch,' he proposed, rising to his feet. 'We'll talk afterward. Politics shouldn't be everything in life. Pleasant things ought to have their place too.'

II

Transformed into a camp, Queimadas is a beehive of activity in the strong wind that covers it with dust: orders are barked out and troops hurriedly fall into formation amid cavalrymen with drawn sabers who are shouting and gesticulating. Suddenly bugle calls cleave the dawn and the curious bystanders run along the bank of the Itapicuru to watch the stretch of bone-dry *caatinga* that disappears on the horizon in the direction of Monte Santo: the first corps of the Seventh Regiment are setting out and the wind carries away the marching song that the soldiers are singing at the tops of their lungs.

Inside the railroad station, since first light, Colonel Moreira César has been studying topographical maps, giving instructions, signing dispatches, and receiving the duty reports of the various battalions. The drowsy correspondents are harnessing their mules and horses and loading the baggage cart outside the door of the station – all of them except the scrawny reporter from the *Jornal de Notícias*, who, with his portable desk beneath his arm and his inkwell fastened to his sleeve, is prowling about the place trying to make his way to the colonel's side. Despite the early hour, the six members of the Municipal Council are on hand to bid the commander of the Seventh Regiment farewell. They are sitting waiting on a bench, and the swarm of officers and aides coming and going around them is paying no more attention to them than to the huge posters of the Progressivist Republican Party and the Bahia Autonomist Party that are still hanging from the ceiling. But they are amused as they watch the scarecrow-thin journalist, who, taking advantage of a moment of calm, has finally managed to approach Moreira César.

'May I ask you a question, Colonel?' he says in his thin, nasal voice.

'The press conference was yesterday,' the officer answers, examining him from head to foot as though he were a being from another planet. But the creature's outlandish appearance or his audacity causes the colonel to relent: 'All right, then. What's your question?'

'It's about the prisoners,' the reporter murmurs, both his squint eyes fixed on him. 'It has come to my attention that you are taking thieves and murderers into the regiment. I went down to the jail last night with the two lieutenants, and saw them enlist seven of the inmates.'

'That's correct,' Moreira César says, looking him up and down inquisitively. 'But what's your question?'

'The question is: Why? What's the reason for promising those criminals their freedom?'

'They know how to fight,' Colonel Moreira César says. And then, after a pause: 'A criminal is a case of excessive human energy that flows in the wrong direction. War can channel it in the right one. They know why they're fighting, and that makes them brave, even heroic at times. I've seen it with my own eyes. And you'll see it, too, if you get to Canudos. Because' – he inspects him from head to foot once again – 'from the looks of you, you're likely not to last one day in the backlands.'

'I'll try my best to hold up, Colonel.' The nearsighted journalist withdraws and Colonel Tamarindo and Major Cunha Matos, who were standing waiting behind him, step forward.

'The vanguard has just moved out,' Colonel Tamarindo says.

The major explains that Captain Ferreira Rocha's patrols have reconnoitered the route to Tanquinho and that there is no trace of *jagunços*, but that the road is full of sudden drops and rough stretches that are going to make it difficult to get the artillery through. Ferreira Rocha's scouts are looking to see if there is some way around these obstacles, and in any case a team of sappers has also gone on ahead to level the road.

'Did you make sure the prisoners were separated?' Moreira César asks him.

'I assigned them to different companies and expressly forbade them to see each other or talk to each other,' the major assures him.

'The animal convoy detail has also left,' Colonel Tamarindo says. And after a moment's hesitation: 'Febrônio de Brito was very upset. He had a crying fit.'

'Any other officer would have committed suicide' is Moreira César's only comment. He rises to his feet and an orderly hastens to gather up the papers on the table that the colonel has been using as a desk. Followed by his staff officers, Moreira César heads toward the exit. People rush forward to see him, but before he reaches the door he remembers something, shifts course, and walks over to the bench where the municipal councillors of Queimadas are waiting. They rise to their feet. They are simple folk, farmers or humble tradesmen, who are dressed in their best clothes and have shined their big clumsy shoes as a mark of their respect. They are carrying their sombreros in their hands, and are plainly ill at ease.

'Thanks for your hospitality and collaboration, gentlemen.' The colonel includes all of them in a single conventionally polite, almost blank sweep of his eyes. 'The Seventh Regiment will not forget the warm welcome it received in Queimadas. I trust you will look after the troops that remain here.'

They haven't time to answer, for instead of bidding each of them farewell individually, he salutes the group as a whole, raising his right hand to his kepi, turns round, and heads for the door.

The appearance of Moreira César and his escort outside in the street, where the regiment is lined up in formation – the ranks of men disappear from sight in the distance, one company behind another as far as the railroad tracks – is greeted by applause and cheers. The sentinels stop the curious from coming any closer. The handsome white horse whinnies, impatient to be off. Tamarindo, Cunha Matos, Olímpio de Castro, and the escort mount their horses, and the press correspondents, already in the saddle, surround the colonel. He is rereading the telegram to the Supreme Government that he has dictated: 'The Seventh Regiment beginning this day, 8 February, its campaign in defense of Brazilian sovereignty. Not one case of indiscipline among the troops. Our one fear that Antônio Conselheiro and the Restorationist rebels will not be awaiting us in Canudos. Long live the Republic.' He initials it so that the telegraph operator can send it off immediately. He then signals to Captain Olímpio de Castro, who gives an order to the buglers. They sound a piercing, mournful call that rends the early-morning air.

'It's the regimental call,' Cunha Matos says to the gray-haired correspondent next to him.

'Does it have a name?' the shrill, irksome little voice of the man from the *Jornal de Notícias* asks. He has equipped his mule with a large leather pouch for his portable writing desk, thus giving the animal the air of a marsupial.

'Call to charge and slit throats,' Moreira César answers. 'The regiment has sounded it ever since the war with Paraguay, when for lack of ammunition it was obliged to attack with sabers, bayonets, and knives.'

With a wave of his right hand he gives the order to march. Mules, men, horses, carts, artillery pieces begin moving off, amid clouds of dust that a strong wind sends their way. As they leave Queimadas, the various corps of the column are grouped close together, and only the colors of the pennons carried by their standard-bearers differentiate them. Soon the uniforms of officers and men become indistinguishable, for the strong wind that is blowing forces all of them to lower the visors of their caps and kepis and many of them to tie handkerchiefs over their mouths. Little by little, battalions, companies, and platoons march off in the distance and what appeared on leaving the station to be a compact living creature, a long serpent slithering over the cracked ground, amid dry dead trunks of thornbushes, breaks up into independent members, smaller serpents that in turn draw farther and farther apart, losing sight of each other for a time and then descrying each other again as they wind their way across the tortuous terrain. Cavalrymen constantly move back and forth, establishing a circulatory system of information, orders, inquiries between the parts of that scattered whole whose head, after a few hours' march, can already make out in the distance the first village on their line of march: Pau Seco. The vanguard, as Colonel Moreira César sees through his field glasses, has left traces of its passage there among the huts: a small signal flag, and two men who are doubtless waiting for him with messages.

The cavalry escort rides a few yards ahead of the colonel and his staff officers; behind these latter, exotic parasites on this uniformed body, are the correspondents, who, like many of the officers, have dismounted and are chatting together as they walk along. Precisely in the middle of the column is the battery of cannon, drawn by teams of bullocks that are urged on by some twenty men under the command of an officer wearing on his sleeves the red diamond-shaped emblem of the artillery corps: Captain José Agostinho Salomão da Rocha. The shouts of the men, to spur the animals on or get them back on the trail when they wander off it, are the only sounds to be heard. The troops talk in low voices to save their strength, or march along in silence, scrutinizing this flat, semibarren landscape that they are seeing for the first time. Many of them are sweating, what with the hot sun, their heavy uniforms, and the weight of their knapsacks and rifles, and following orders, they try not to lift their canteens to their mouths too often since they know that the first battle to be waged has already begun: that against thirst. At midmorning they overtake the supply train and leave it behind them; the cattle, sheep, and goats are being herded along by a company of soldiers and cowhands who have started off the night before; at their head, grim-faced, moving his lips as though refuting or setting forth an argument in an imaginary dialogue is Major Febrônio de Brito. At the rear of the line of march is the cavalry troop, led by a dashing, martial officer: Captain Pedreira Franco. Moreira César has been riding along for some time without saying a word, and his adjutants fall silent, too, so as not to interrupt their commanding officer's train of thought. On reaching the straight stretch of road leading into Pau Seco, the colonel looks at his watch.

'At this rate, that Canudos bunch is going to give us the slip,' he says, leaning over toward Tamarindo and Cunha Matos. 'We're going to have to leave the heavy equipment behind in Monte Santo and lighten the men's knapsacks. It's certain that we have more than enough ammunition. It would be too bad to go all the way there and find nothing but vultures.'

The regiment has with it fifteen million rifle cartridges and seventy artillery shells, in carts drawn by mules. This is the principal reason why they are making such slow progress. Colonel Tamarindo remarks that once they have passed Monte Santo they may advance even more slowly, since according to the two engineer corps officers, Domingo Alves Leite and Alfredo do Nascimento, the terrain is even rougher from there on.

'Not to mention the fact that from that point on there are going to be skirmishes,' he adds. He is exhausted from the heat and keeps mopping his congested face with a colored handkerchief. He is past retirement age and nothing obliges him to be here, but he has insisted on accompanying the regiment.

'We mustn't allow them time to get away,' Colonel Moreira César mutters. This is something that his officers have heard him say many times since they boarded the train in Rio. Despite the heat he is not sweating. He has a pale little face, eyes with an intense, sometimes obsessive gaze, and rarely smiles; his voice is very nearly a monotone, thin and flat, as though he were keeping a tight rein on it as is recommended in the case of a skittish horse. 'The minute they discover we're getting close they'll bolt and the campaign will be a resounding failure. We cannot allow that to happen.' He looks once again at his companions, who listen to him without saying a word in reply. 'Southern Brazil has now realized that the Republic is a *fait accompli*. We've brought that home to them. But here in the state of Bahia there are still a great many aristocrats who haven't yet resigned themselves to that fact. Especially since the death of the marshal; with a civilian without ideals heading the country, they think they can turn the clock back. They won't accept the irreversible till they've had a good lesson. And now is the time to give them one, gentlemen.'

'They're scared to death, sir,' Cunha Matos says. 'Doesn't the fact that the Autonomist Party organized the reception for us in Salvador and took up a collection to defend the Republic prove they've got their tails between their legs?'

'The crowning touch was the triumphal arch in the Calçada Station calling us saviors,' Tamarindo recalls. 'Just a few days before, they were violently opposed to the intervention of the Federal Army in Bahia, and then they toss flowers at us in the streets and the Baron de Canabrava sends us word that he's coming to Calumbi to place his hacienda at the disposal of the regiment.'

He gives a hearty laugh, but Moreira César does not find his good humor infectious.

'That means that the baron is more intelligent than his friends,' the colonel replies. 'He couldn't keep Rio from intervening in an out-and-out case of insurrection. So then he opts for patriotism, in order not to be outdone by the Republicans. His aim is to distract and confuse people for the moment so as to be in a position to deal us another blow later. The baron has been well schooled: in the English school, gentlemen.'

They find Pau Seco empty of people, possessions, animals. Two soldiers, standing next to the branchless tree trunk atop which the signal flag left by the vanguard is fluttering, salute. Moreira César reins his mount in and looks around at the mud huts, the interiors of which are visible through the doors left ajar or fallen from their hinges. A toothless, barefoot woman, dressed in a tunic full of holes through which her dark skin shows, emerges from one of the huts. Two rickety children, with glassy eyes, one of whom is naked and has a swollen belly, cling to her, staring at the soldiers in stupefaction. From astride his horse, Moreira César looks down at them: they strike him as the very image of helplessness. His face contorts in an expression in which sadness, anger, and rancor are commingled.

Still looking at them, he gives one of his escorts an order: 'Have some food brought them.' And he turns to his adjutants: 'Do you see the state they keep the people on their lands in?'

His voice trembles and his eyes flash. In an impetuous gesture, he draws his sword from its scabbard and raises it to his face, as though he were about to kiss it. Craning their necks, the press correspondents then see the commanding officer of the Seventh Regiment give, before riding off again, that ceremonial sword salute reserved at parades for the national flag and the highest authority, here addressed to the three miserable inhabitants of Pau Seco.

The incomprehensible words had been pouring out in great bursts ever since they came upon him lying near the sad-faced woman and the dead body of the mule being pecked at by *urubus* – black vultures. Sporadic, vehement, thunderous, or hushed, murmured, furtive, they poured out day and night, at times frightening the Idiot, who began to tremble. After sniffing the redheaded man, the Bearded Lady said to Jurema: 'He has delirious fever, like the one that killed Dádiva. He'll die before the day is out.' But he hadn't died, although at times he turned up the whites of his eyes and appeared to be about to go into the death rattle. After lying for a long time not moving a muscle, he would start tossing and turning again, grimacing and uttering words that were meaningless sounds to them. Now and again, he would open his eyes and look at them in bewilderment. The Dwarf swore that he was talking in gypsy cant and the Bearded Lady insisted it sounded like the Latin of the Mass.

When Jurema asked whether she could come with them, the Bearded Lady consented, perhaps out of compassion, perhaps out of simple inertia. Between the four of them they hoisted the stranger into the wagon alongside the cobra's basket and started off again. Their new companions brought them luck, for as darkness fell they were invited to stay for supper in the farm settlement of Quererá. A little old woman blew smoke over Galileo Gall, placed herbs on his wounds, made him a decoction, and said that he'd get well. That night the Bearded Lady did a turn with the cobra to entertain the cowhands, the Idiot performed his clown act, and the Dwarf told them his stories of knights and chivalry. They went on, and as it turned out, the stranger did begin to swallow the mouthfuls of food they gave him. The Bearded Lady asked Jurema if she was his wife. No, she wasn't: while her husband was away, he had dishonored her, and what else could she do after that except tag along after him? 'Now I understand why you're sad,' the Dwarf said sympathetically.

They went steadily northward, guided by a lucky star, for they found something to eat every single day. On the third day, they gave a show at a village fair. What the villagers liked best was the Bearded Lady: they paid money to prove to themselves that her beard wasn't false and gently felt her tits to make sure she was really a woman. Meanwhile, the Dwarf told them her life story, since the days when she'd been a normal little girl, back in Ceará, who one day became the shame of her family when hair started growing on her back, her arms, her legs, and her face. People began to whisper that there was sin involved somewhere, that she was the daughter of a sacristan or of the Can. The little girl swallowed some ground glass of the sort used to kill rabid dogs. But she didn't die and lived the life of the town laughing-stock till the King of the Circus, the Gypsy, appeared one day, took her off with him, and made a circus performer out of her. Jurema thought the Dwarf was making the whole story up, but he assured her that every word of it was true. They would sit down to talk together sometimes, and as the Dwarf was nice to her and she trusted him, she told him about her childhood on the hacienda at Calumbi as a servant of the wife of the Baron de Canabrava, a very beautiful and kind woman. It was sad that, instead of staying with the baron, Rufino, her husband, had gone off to Queimadas and become a guide, a horrid occupation that kept him away from home a great deal of the time. And what was sadder still, he'd not been able to make her a baby. Why should God have punished her by keeping her from having a baby? 'Who knows?' the Dwarf murmured. God's will was sometimes difficult to understand.

A few days later, they camped at Ipupiará, a hamlet at a cross-roads. A tragedy had just happened. In a fit of madness, a villager had hacked his children and then himself to death with a machete. Since the villagers were holding a funeral for the child martyrs, the circus people did not give a performance, though they announced that there would be one the following evening. The settlement was a tiny one, but it had a general store, where people from all over the region came to buy their provisions.

The following morning the *capangas* arrived. They came galloping into the village, and the pawing and stamping of their mounts awakened the Bearded Lady, who crawled out from under the tent to see who it was. Villagers appeared at the doors of all the huts in Ipupiará, as surprised by this apparition as she was. She saw six armed riders: she could tell, by the way they were dressed and by the clearly visible brand of the same hacienda on the flanks of all their horses, that they were *capangas* and not *cangaceiros* or Rural Police. The one riding in front – a man dressed in leather – dismounted and the Bearded Lady saw him head her way. Jurema had just sat up on her blanket. The Bearded Lady saw her face turn deathly pale and her mouth gape open. 'Is that your husband?' she asked Jurema. 'It's Caifás,' the young woman said. 'Has he come to kill you?' the Bearded Lady asked insistently. But instead of answering her, Jurema crawled out from under the tent on all fours, stood up, and walked over to the *capanga*, who stopped dead in his tracks. The Bearded Lady felt her heart begin to pound, thinking that the man dressed in leather – a swarthy, bony-faced man with cold eyes – was about to strike her, kick her, and maybe plunge his knife into her, and then walk over and plunge it into the back of the redheaded man, whom she could hear tossing about in the wagon. But the man didn't hit her. Quite the contrary: he removed his sombrero and greeted her in an obviously polite and respectful manner. From astride their horses, the five men watched this dialogue that for them, as for the Bearded Lady, was merely lips moving. What were the two of them saying to each other? The Dwarf and the Idiot had awakened and were also watching. After a moment, Jurema turned around and pointed to the wagon where the wounded stranger was sleeping.

With the young woman following after him, the man in leather walked over to the wagon and poked his head underneath the canvas. The Bearded Lady then saw him gaze indifferently at the man, who, asleep or awake, was still talking with his ghosts. The leader of the *capangas* had the dead-calm eyes of those who are used to killing, the same look that the Bearded

Lady had seen in the eyes of the bandit Pedrão that time that he'd beaten the Gypsy in the fight and killed him. Her face deathly pale, Jurema waited for the *capanga* to finish his inspection. He finally turned to her, said something to her. Jurema nodded and the man then signaled to his men to dismount. Jurema came over to the Bearded Lady and asked her for the shears. As she searched about for them, the Bearded Lady whispered: 'Is he going to kill you?' 'No,' Jurema answered. And with the pair of shears that had belonged to Dádiva in her hand, she climbed into the wagon. Leading their horses by the reins, the *capangas* headed for the Ipupiará store, whereupon the Bearded Lady, followed by the Dwarf and the Idiot, went to see what Jurema was up to.

Kneeling alongside the stranger – there was barely room for the two of them in the small space – Jurema was shearing him down to his very scalp, holding his bright-red locks in one hand and the squeaking scissors in the other. There were dried bloodstains, tears, dust, bird droppings on Galileo Gall's black frock coat. He was lying on his back, amid multicolored pieces of cloth and boxes, hoops, lampblack, pointed hats with half-moons and stars. His eyes were closed, he had a growth of beard on which there was also dried blood, his boots had been removed and his long toes with dirty nails were poking out of the holes in his socks. The wound in his neck disappeared from sight beneath a bandage and the healer's herbs. The Idiot burst out laughing, and though the Bearded Lady dug her elbows into his ribs, he went on whooping. Beardless, skinny as a rail, his eyes blank, his mouth open and a thread of spittle hanging from his lips, he writhed with laughter. Jurema paid no attention to him, but the stranger opened his eyes. His face contorted in surprise, pain, or terror at what was being done to him, but he was so weak he was unable to sit up and simply lay there tossing about and uttering one of those sounds that the circus people found incomprehensible.

It took Jurema a long while to finish her task – so long that, before she was done, the *capangas* had had time to go to the store, hear the story of the children murdered by the madman, and go to the cemetery to commit a sacrilege that left the villagers of Ipupiará stupefied: namely, disinterring the corpse of the filicide, loading it, coffin and all, on the back of one of their horses, and carrying it off. Now they were back, standing a few yards away from the circus people, waiting. When Gall's hair was all sheared off, and his skull covered with an uneven iridescence like red shot silk, the Idiot burst out laughing once again. Jurema gathered up the locks of hair that she had carefully laid in her lap, tied them in a bundle with the bit of string with which her own hair was fastened back, and then the Bearded Lady saw her search through the stranger's pockets and take out a little pouch that he had told them contained money, in case they wanted to use it. With the shock of hair in one hand and the pouch in the other, she climbed down out of the wagon and headed past the circus people.

The leader of the *capangas* stepped forward. The Bearded Lady saw him take the stranger's locks that Jurema handed him and, almost without looking at them, put them in his saddlebag. His motionless pupils were threatening, despite the fact that he addressed Jurema in a studiedly courteous, formal manner, picking at his teeth the while with his index finger. This time the Bearded Lady could hear what they said.

'He had this in his pocket,' Jurema said, holding out the pouch. But Caifás did not take it.

'I mustn't,' he said, as though repelled by something invisible. 'That belongs to Rufino, too.'

Not making the slightest objection, Jurema tucked the pouch in her skirts. The Bearded Lady thought that she was about to walk off, but looking Caifás straight in the eye, she asked him softly: 'And what if Rufino's dead?'

Caifás thought for a moment, without changing expression, without blinking. 'If he's dead, there will always be someone to avenge the dishonor done him,' the Bearded Lady heard him say, and she seemed to be hearing the Dwarf and his tales of knights and princes. 'A kinsman, a friend. I myself, if necessary.'

'And what if your boss finds out what you've done?' she asked then.

'He's only my boss,' Caifás replied self-assuredly. 'Rufino's more than that. He wants the stranger dead and the stranger's going to die. Maybe from his wounds, maybe at Rufino's hand. The lie is soon going to become the truth, and this hair is going to be that of a dead man.'

He turned his back on Jurema to mount his horse. Anxiously, she put one hand on the saddle. 'Will he kill me, too?'

The Bearded Lady saw the man dressed in leather gaze down at her without pity and perhaps with a certain contempt. 'If I were Rufino I'd kill you, because it's your fault, too – perhaps more than his,' Caifás said from the back of his mount. 'But since I'm not Rufino, I don't know. He'll know, though.'

He spurred his horse and the *capangas* rode off with their strange, stinking booty, in the same direction from which they had come.

As soon as the Mass celebrated by Father Joaquim in the Chapel of Santo Antônio was over, Abbot João went to the Sanctuary to get the crate full of things that he had asked the priest to bring. There was a question preying on his mind: How many soldiers are there in a regiment? He hoisted the crate onto his shoulder and strode rapidly across the uneven ground of Belo Monte, dodging the people who hurried over to ask if it was true that another army was coming. He answered yes, without stopping, leaping over the chickens, goats, dogs, and children in his way so as not to step on them. He reached the former hacienda steward's house, now turned into a store, with his shoulder aching from the weight of the crate.

The crowd of people standing in the doorway moved aside to let him by, and inside Antônio Vilanova broke off whatever it was he was telling his wife Antônia and his sister-in-law Assunção and hurried across the room to join him. From its swing, a parrot kept frantically repeating: 'Felicity! Felicity!'

'A regiment's coming,' Abbot João said, setting his load down on the floor.

'How many men is that?'

'He brought the fuses!' Antônio Vilanova exclaimed, squatting on his heels, eagerly examining the contents of the crate. He beamed with satisfaction as he discovered, in addition to the packets of fuses, tablets for diarrhea, disinfectants, bandages, calomel, oil, and alcohol.

'There's no way to repay Father Joaquim for what he does for us,' he said, lifting the crate onto the counter. The shelves were full of canned goods and bottles, lengths of material and all manner of wearing apparel, from sandals to sombreros, and sacks and cartons were sitting about everywhere on the floor, with the Sardelinha sisters and other people walking about among them. Lying on top of the counter, a long plank resting on barrels, were several black ledgers, of the sort used by hacienda bookkeepers.

'Father Joaquim also brought news,' Abbot João said. 'Could a regiment be a thousand men?'

'Yes, so I've heard, an army's coming.' Antônio Vilanova nodded, setting the things the priest had brought out on the counter. 'A regiment? More than a thousand men. Two thousand maybe.'

Abbot João realized that Antônio's mind was not on how many soldiers the Can was sending against Canudos this time. He watched the fat, slightly bald, bushy-bearded storekeeper putting packages and bottles away in his usual brisk, efficient way. There was not the slightest trace of anxiety, or even interest, in his voice. 'He has too many other things to do,' Abbot João thought, as he explained that it was necessary to send someone to Monte Santo right away. 'He's right; it's better for him not to have to worry about the war along with everything else.' Because Antônio was perhaps the person who, for years now, had slept the least and worked the most of anyone in Canudos. In the early days, just after the Counselor arrived, he had gone on with his work of buying and selling merchandise, but gradually, with the tacit agreement of everyone, he had taken on in addition the task of organizing the society that was aborning, a responsibility that now occupied most of his time. Without him it would have been hard to eat, sleep, survive as the waves of pilgrims began pouring into Canudos from all over. He was the one who had parceled out the land so that they could build their dwellings and put in their crops, advised them what to grow and what livestock to raise, and it was he who took charge of bartering in the villages round about, exchanging the things Canudos produced for the things it needed, and when donations began to come in, it was he who decided how much would be set aside for the Temple of the Blessed Jesus and how much would go for the purchase of arms and supplies. Once the Little Blessed One gave them permission to stay permanently, the newcomers then went to Antônio Vilanova for help in getting settled. The Health Houses for the old, the sick, and the disabled were his idea, and at the time of the engagements at Uauá and O Cambaio, he was the one who took charge of storing the captured weapons and distributing them, after consulting with Abbot João. He met with the Counselor almost every day to give him an account of everything and learn of his wishes. He had not gone back to traveling all about, and Abbot João had heard Antônia Sardelinha say that this was the most amazing sign of the change that had taken place in her husband, that man once so possessed by the demonic urge to be forever on the move. It was Honório who traveled all over on community business now, and no one could have said whether the elder brother's stay-at-home habits were due to his many important duties in Belo Monte or to the fact that he was thus able to be in the Counselor's company almost every day, if only for a few minutes. He came away from these meetings with renewed energies and a profound peace of heart.

'The Counselor has agreed that there should be a corps of guards to protect him,' Abbot João said. 'He also agreed that Big João should be the head of it.'

This time Antônio was interested in what he had to say and looked at him in relief. 'Felicity!' the parrot screamed again.

'Have Big João come round to see me. I can help him choose his men – I know all of them. If you think I ought to, that is.'

Antônia Sardelinha had approached. 'Catarina came around this morning asking for you,' she said to Abbot João. 'Do you have the time right now to go see her?'

João shook his head: no, he didn't. Tonight, perhaps. He felt abashed, though the Vilanovas understood that with him God came first and his family second: wasn't it the same with them? But in his heart of hearts it distressed him deeply that through force of circumstance, or the will of the Blessed Jesus, he saw less and less of his wife these days.

'I'll go tell Catarina,' Antônia said to him with a smile.

Abbot João left the store thinking how strange things had turned out in his life, as they did in everyone's perhaps. 'Like in the minstrels' stories,' he thought. On meeting up with the Counselor, he had believed that blood would vanish from his path, and here he was involved in a battle that was worse than any he had ever fought. Was that why the Father had made him repent of his sins? So as to go on killing and seeing people die? Yes, that was no doubt why. He sent two kids he ran into on the street to tell Pedrão and old Joaquim Macambira to meet him at the exit from town leading to Jeremoabo, and before going to where Big João was he went to look for Pajeú, who was out digging trenches on the road to Rosário. He found him a few hundred yards past the last huts, covering a trench across the trails with boughs of buckthorn to hide it. A group of men, some of them with shotguns, were bringing tree branches and putting them in place, as women distributed plates of food to other men sitting on the ground who appeared to have just finished their work shift. On seeing him coming, everyone flocked round him, and he found himself in the center of a circle of inquisitive faces. Without a word, one of the women placed in his hands a bowlful of goat meat sprinkled with maize meal; another handed him a jug of water. He was so tired – he had come all the way on the run – that he had to take a deep breath and drink a long swallow of water before he was able to speak. He did so as he ate, without the thought ever occurring to him that a few years before – at the time when his gang and Pajeú's were trying to wipe each other out – the people listening to him would have given anything to have him at their mercy like this so as to subject him to the worst tortures imaginable before killing him.

Luckily, those chaotic days were a thing of the past.

Pajeú didn't turn a hair on hearing of Father Joaquim's news about a second army coming. He did not ask a single question. Did Pajeú know how many men there were in a regiment? No, he didn't know, and neither did any of the others. Abbot João then asked him what he had come to ask him to do: go south to spy on these troops that were coming and harass them. His band of outlaws had marauded in that region for years; he knew it better than anybody else: so wasn't he the best man to patrol the route the soldiers took, to hunt up guides and bearers to infiltrate their ranks, to set up ambushes to delay them and give Belo Monte time to ready its defenses?

Pajeú nodded, still without having opened his mouth. Seeing his yellowish-gray pallor, the enormous scar across his face, and his strong, solid body, Abbot João wondered yet again how old he was, whether he wasn't a man far along in years whose age didn't show.

'All right,' he heard him say. 'I'll send you reports every day. How many of these men am I to take with me?'

'However many you want,' Abbot João answered. 'They're your men.'

'They *were* my men,' Pajeú growled, glancing quickly around at the men surrounding him, a sudden warm gleam in his expressionless, deep-set little eyes. 'They're the Blessed Jesus' men now.'

'We're all His men,' Abbot João replied. And with sudden urgency in his voice: 'Before you leave, have Antônio Vilanova give you ammunition and explosives. We have fuses now. Can Taramela stay here?'

The man whose name had been mentioned stepped forward: he was a tiny little fellow with slanted eyes, scars, wrinkles, and broad shoulders, who had been Pajeú's lieutenant.

'I want to go with you to Monte Santo,' he said to Pajeú in a tart voice. 'I've always looked after you. I bring you good luck.'

'Look after Canudos now. It's worth more than I am,' Pajeú answered brusquely.

'Yes, stay and bring us good luck,' Abbot João said. 'I'll send you more men so you won't feel lonesome. Praised be the Blessed Jesus.'

'Praised be He,' several voices answered.

Abbot João had turned his back to them and was running once more, cutting across the fields toward the looming bulk of O Cambaio, where Big João was. As he ran, he thought about his wife. He hadn't seen her since he had decided to have hiding places and trenches dug along all the trails, an undertaking that had kept him running day and night within a circumference of which Canudos was also the center, as it was of the world. Abbot João had come to know Catarina when he had been one of that handful of men and women – whose number rose and fell like the waters of the river – who entered villages with the Counselor and stretched out on the ground at his side at night after the long, tiring day's journey to pray with him and listen to his counsels. Among them had been a figure so thin she seemed to be a ghost, enveloped in a tunic as white as a shroud. The former *cangaceiro*'s eyes had often found hers fixed on him during their marches, prayers, halts to rest. They made him uncomfortable, and at times they frightened him. They were eyes ravaged by pain, eyes that seemed to threaten him with punishments that were not of this world.

One night, when the pilgrims were already asleep round a campfire, Abbot João crawled over to the woman whose eyes he could see in the firelight, riveted on him. 'I want to know why you keep looking at me,' he whispered. She answered with an effort, as though struggling to overcome great exhaustion or great repugnance. 'I was in Custódia when you came to wreak your vengeance,' she said in a voice that he could barely hear. 'The first man you killed, the one who gave the warning shout, was my father. I saw how you plunged your knife in his belly.' Abbot João remained silent, hearing the sound of the campfire crackling, the insects buzzing, the woman breathing, trying to remember those eyes on that dawn so long ago. After a moment, his voice, too, scarcely more than a whisper, he asked: 'So not all of you in Custódia died that day?' 'There were three of us who didn't,' the woman murmured. 'Dom Matias, who hid in the straw on his roof. Senhora Rosa, whose wounds healed, though her mind was gone. And me. They thought they'd killed me too, and my wound also healed.' It was as though the two of them were speaking of other people, of other happenings, of a different, poorer life. 'How old were you?' the *cangaceiro* asked. 'Ten or twelve, something like that,' she said. Abbot João looked at her: she must still be very young, then, but hunger and suffering had aged her. Continuing to speak very softly so as not to awaken the other pilgrims, the two of them gravely recalled the events of that long-ago night, still so vivid in their memories. She had been raped by three men and later someone had made her kneel in front of a pair of pants that smelled of horse dung, and callused hands had crammed down her throat a member so big it would barely fit in her mouth, and she had been forced to suck it till a gob of his seed spurted out of it and the man ordered her to swallow it. When one of the bandits slashed her with his knife, Catarina felt a great peace come over her. 'Was I the one who slashed you with the knife?' Abbot João whispered. 'I don't know,' she whispered back. 'Even though it was daylight by then, I couldn't tell the faces apart and I didn't know where I was.'

From that night onward, the former *cangaceiro* and the survivor of Custódia always prayed together and walked along together, recounting to each other stories of their past lives that now seemed incomprehensible to them. She had joined the saint in a village in Sergipe, where she had been living on the charity of others. After the Counselor, she was the frailest of the band, and there came a day when she fell into a dead faint as they marched along. Abbot João lifted her up and carried her in his arms till nightfall. He carried her for several days and also took it upon himself to bring her little bits of food soaked in liquid that she could keep down. Then at night, again as he would have done with a child, after they had listened to the Counselor together he told her the tales of chivalry he had heard the *cantadores* recite when he was little, which now – perhaps because his soul had regained its childhood innocence – came back to him with a wealth of detail. She listened to him without interrupting him, and days later, in her voice so faint it was almost inaudible, she asked him questions about the Saracens, Fierabras, and Robert the Devil, whereupon he realized that those phantoms had become as intimate a part of Catarina's life as they had once been of his.

She had recovered and was walking on her own two feet again when one night Abbot João, trembling with embarrassment, confessed before all the pilgrims that he had often felt the desire to possess her. The Counselor called Catarina to him and asked her if she was offended by what she had just heard. She shook her head. Before the silent circle of pilgrims, the Counselor asked her if she still felt bitterness in her heart because of what had happened in Custódia. She shook her head once more. 'You are purified,' the Counselor said. He had both of them join hands and asked all the disciples to pray to the Father for them. One week later the parish priest of Xiquexique married them. How long ago had that been? Four or five years? Feeling that his heart was about to burst, João at last caught sight of the shadows of the *jagunços* on the lower slopes of O Cambaio. He stopped running and went on in that quick, short stride that had taken him so many miles in his endless journeys.

An hour later he was with Big João, telling him the latest news as he drank cool water and ate a plateful of maize. The two of them were by themselves, since after announcing to the rest of the men that a regiment was coming – none of them could tell him how many soldiers that was – he had asked to be alone with Big João. The former slave was barefoot as usual, and wearing a pair of faded pants held up at the waist by a length of rope from which there hung a knife and a machete, and a shirt with all the buttons missing that bared his hairy chest. He had a carbine slung over his shoulder and two bandoleers draped round his neck like necklaces. When Big João heard that a Catholic Guard was to be formed to protect the Counselor and that he was to be the leader of it, he shook his head emphatically.

'Why not?' Abbot João asked.

'I'm not worthy of such an honor,' the black murmured.

'The Counselor says you are,' Abbot João replied. 'He's a better judge than you.'

'I don't know how to give orders,' the black protested. 'And what's more, I don't want to learn how. Let somebody else be the leader.'

'You're the one who's going to be the leader,' the Street Commander said. 'There's no time to argue, Big João.'

Lost in thought, the black stood watching the groups of men scattered about amid the rocks and boulders on the mountainside, beneath a sky that had turned a leaden color.

'Watching over the Counselor is a heavy load on my shoulders,' he finally said.

'Choose the best men, the ones who've been here the longest, the ones you saw fight well at Uauá and here in O Cambaio,' Abbot João said. 'When that army gets here, the Catholic Guard must already exist and serve as a shield for Canudos.'

Big João remained silent, chewing slowly even though his mouth was empty. He stood there gazing at the mountain peaks round about him as though he were seeing the shining warriors of King Dom Sebastião suddenly appear on them: awed, overwhelmed, taken completely by surprise.

'It's you who've chosen me, not the Little Blessed One or the Counselor,' he said dully. 'And you haven't done me any favor.'

'No, I haven't,' Abbot João conceded. 'I didn't choose you so as to do you one, or to do you any harm either. I chose you because you're the best man. Go to Belo Monte and get to work.'

'Praised be Blessed Jesus the Counselor,' the black said. He got up from the rock he was sitting on and started off across the stony ground.

'Praised be He,' Abbot João said. A few seconds later he saw the ex-slave break into a run.

'In other words, you were untrue to your duty, twice,' Rufino says. 'You didn't kill him the way Epaminondas wanted you to. And you lied to Epaminondas, leading him to believe he was dead. Two times.'

'Only the first time is really serious,' Caifás says. 'I handed his hair and a corpse over to him. It was somebody else's dead body, but neither he nor anybody else could tell that it was. And the foreigner will be a corpse soon, if he isn't one already. So that's a minor fault.'

On the reddish bank of the Itapicuru, opposite the one the Queimadas tanneries are on, that Saturday, like every other Saturday, stalls and stands have been set up where vendors from all over the region are hawking their wares. Discussions between buyers and sellers rise above the sea of heads, bare or topped with black sombreros, that dot the marketplace, and mingle with the din of whinnying horses, barking dogs, screaming children, and roistering drunkards. Beggars appeal to people's generosity by exaggerating the contortions of their maimed and crippled limbs, and minstrels accompanying themselves on guitars stand in front of little knots of people, reciting love stories and tales of the wars between Christian crusaders and unbelievers. Shaking their skirts, their arms covered with bracelets, gypsy women, young and old, tell fortunes.

'Anyway, I'm grateful to you,' Rufino says. 'You're a man of honor, Caifás. That's why I've always respected you. That's why everybody respects you.'

'What's a person's greatest duty?' Caifás says. 'Toward his boss or toward his friend? A blind man could have seen that I was obliged to do what I did.'

They walk on side by side, very gravely, indifferent to the colorful, motley throng, the chaotic atmosphere round about them. They rudely push their way through the crowd, forcing people aside with one glaring look or a shove of their shoulders. Every so often someone standing behind a counter or inside a canvas-covered stall greets them, and both of them return the greeting so curtly that no one approaches them. As if by tacit agreement, they head for a place where drinks are being sold – wooden benches, plank tables, an arbor – with fewer customers in it than in the others.

'If I'd finished him off there in Ipupiará I'd have offended you,' Caifás says, as though putting into words something he has long been mulling over in his mind. 'By keeping you from avenging the blot on your honor.'

'Why did you go there to kill him in the first place?' Rufino interrupts him. 'Why at my house?'

'Epaminondas wanted him to die there,' Caifás answered. 'Neither you nor Jurema was to be killed. My men died so as to keep her from getting hurt.' He spits in the air past an eyetooth, and stands there thinking things over in his mind. 'Maybe it was my fault they died. It didn't occur to me that he might defend himself, that he knew how to fight. He didn't look the type.'

'No,' Rufino agrees. 'He didn't.'

They sit down and pull their chairs closer together so as to talk without being overheard. The woman waiting on them hands them two glasses and asks if they'll have cane brandy. Yes. She brings a half-full bottle, the guide pours the two of them a drink, and they down it without offering a toast. Then Caifás takes a turn filling the glasses. He is older than Rufino, and his eyes, with their fixed stare, are dull and lifeless. He is dressed all in leather, as always, from head to foot.

'She was the one who saved him?' Rufino finally says, lowering his eyes. 'She was the one who grabbed your arm?'

'That's how I realized she'd become his woman.' Caifás nods. There are still traces of the surprise on his face. 'When she leapt on me and deflected my aim, when she attacked me at the same moment he did.' He shrugs his shoulders and spits. 'She was already his woman, so what else could she do but defend him?'

'True,' Rufino says.

'I don't understand why the two of them didn't kill me,' Caifás says. 'I asked Jurema why, in Ipupiará, and she couldn't tell me. That foreigner is a strange one.'

'That he is,' Rufino agrees.

Among the people at the market are a number of soldiers.

They are what is left of Major Febrônio de Brito's expedition, troops who have stayed in town waiting, they say, for an army that is to arrive. Their uniforms are in rags, they wander about like lost souls; they sleep in the main square, in the train station, in the gorges of the river. They are here too now, roaming aimlessly about amid the stalls, by twos, by fours, looking longingly at the women, the food, the drinks all round them. The townspeople make it a point not to speak to them, not to listen to them, not to take any note of them.

'Promises tie your hands, don't they?' Rufino says timidly, a deep frown furrowing his forehead.

'That they do,' Caifás concedes. 'How can a person go back on a promise made to the Blessed Jesus or the Virgin?'

'Or to the baron?' Rufino says, thrusting his head forward.

'The baron can release you from one made to him,' Caifás says. He fills their glasses again and they drink. Amid all the hubbub of the market, a violent argument breaks out somewhere in the distance and ends in a chorus of laughter. The sky has clouded over, as though it is about to rain.

'I know how you feel,' Caifás suddenly says. 'I know that you can't sleep, that everything in life is over for you. That even when you're with other people, the way you're with me right now, you're wreaking your vengeance. That's how it is, Rufino. That's how it is when a man values his honor.'

A line of ants heads across the table, detouring around the bottle of *cachaça* that is now empty. Rufino watches them advance and disappear. His hand, still holding the glass, clenches it tightly.

'There's something you ought to keep in mind,' Caifás adds. 'Death isn't enough. It doesn't remove the stain. But a slap, a whiplash, square in the face, does. Because a man's face is as sacred as his mother or his wife.'

Rufino stands up. The woman who owns the place hurries over and Caifás reaches toward his pocket, but the tracker stops him and pays the bill himself. They wait for her to bring the change, neither of them saying a word, each lost in his own thoughts.

'Is it true your mother's gone to Canudos?' Caifás asks. And, as Rufino nods: 'Lots of people are going there. Epaminondas is enlisting more men in the Rural Police. An army's coming and he wants to give it a hand. I have kinfolk who are with the saint, too. It's hard to wage war against a person's own family, isn't that so, Rufino?'

'I've another war to wage,' Rufino murmurs, pocketing the coins the woman hands him.

'I hope you find him, that he hasn't died of illness,' Caifás says.

Their silhouettes disappear amid the tumult of the Queimadas market.

'There's something I don't understand, Baron,' Colonel José Bernardo Murau repeated, relaxing in the rocking chair in which he was swaying slowly back and forth, pushing it with his foot. 'Colonel Moreira César hates us and we hate him. His coming to Bahia is a great victory for Epaminondas and a defeat for the principle we've always upheld: that Rio is not to interfere in our affairs. Yet the Autonomist Party gives him a hero's welcome in Salvador, and now we're competing with Epaminondas to see which party will help Throat-Slitter the most.'

The cool, whitewashed sitting room of the old manor house looked untidy and run-down: the bouquet of flowers in a large copper vase was faded, there were cracks in the wall, and the floor was chipped. Through the windows the cane field could be seen, burning-hot in the sun, and just outside the house a group of servants were hitching up a team of horses.

'The times are out of joint, my dear José Bernardo.' The Baron de Canabrava smiled. 'Even the most intelligent people are unable to make their way through the jungle we're living in.'

'I never was intelligent. That's not a virtue characteristic of landowners,' Colonel Murau growled. He made a vague gesture toward the outdoors. 'I've spent half a century here, only to see everything beginning to fall apart in my old age. My one consolation is that I'm going to die one day soon and won't live to see the total ruin of this country.'

He was indeed a very elderly man, mere skin and bones, with deeply tanned skin and gnarled hands that frequently scratched at his ill-shaven face. He was dressed like a peon, in a pair of faded pants and an open shirt topped by a rawhide vest that had lost all its buttons.

'These bad times will end soon,' Adalberto de Gumúcio said.

'Not for me.' The landowner cracked his knuckles. 'Do you know how many people have left this part of the country in the last few years? Hundreds of families. The drought of '77, the mirage of the coffee plantations in the South, of rubber in the Amazon, and now that accursed Canudos. Do you have any idea how many people are going off to Canudos? Leaving everything behind: houses, animals, work? To go up there to wait for the Apocalypse and the coming of King Dom Sebastião.' He looked at them, overwhelmed by human stupidity. 'I'm not intelligent, but I'll tell you what's going to happen. Moreira César will set Epaminondas up as governor of Bahia and he and his men will give us so much trouble that we'll be forced to sell our haciendas at a sacrifice price, or give them away free, and go off too.'

There was a little table with cool drinks and a basket of sweet biscuits, which no one had touched, in front of the baron and Gumúcio. The baron opened a little box of snuff, offered some to his friends, and inhaled with delectation. He sat there for a moment with his eyes closed.

'We're not going to hand Brazil over to the Jacobins on a platter, José Bernardo,' he said, opening his eyes. 'Despite the fact that they've laid the groundwork very cleverly, they're not going to be able to pull their maneuver off.'

'Brazil is already theirs,' Murau interrupted him. 'The proof is that Moreira César's coming here, by order of the government.'

'He was given command of the expedition because of pressure from the Military Club in Rio, a minor Jacobin stronghold that took advantage of the fact that President Moraes was ill,' the baron said. 'The truth of the matter is that this is a plot against Moraes. It's as plain as day what their plan is. Canudos is the pretext for their man to earn even more glory and prestige.

Moreira César crushes a monarchist conspiracy! Moreira César saves the Republic! Isn't that the best possible proof that only the army can guarantee the safety of the nation? So the army is swept into power, and it's the Dictatorial Republic.' He had been smiling up until then, but now his manner grew grave. 'We are not going to allow that, José Bernardo. Because we're the ones who are going to crush the monarchist conspiracy, not the Jacobins.' He grimaced in disgust. 'We can't act like gentlemen, old boy. Politics is a job for ruffians.'

These words released some spring within old Murau, for his face brightened and he burst out laughing.

'Very well, I surrender, you ruffians,' he exclaimed. 'I'll send Throat-Slitter mules, guides, provisions, and whatever else he needs. Must I also quarter the Seventh Regiment here?'

'I can assure you he won't pass through your land.' The baron thanked him. 'You won't even have to see his face.'

'We can't allow Brazil to believe that we've risen up in rebellion against the Republic and are even plotting with England to restore the monarchy,' Adalberto de Gumúcio said. 'Don't you realize that, José Bernardo? We must put an end to this plot, as quickly as possible. Patriotism isn't a game.'

'It's one Epaminondas has been playing, and playing very well,' Murau muttered.

'That's true,' the baron admitted. 'I, you, Adalberto, Viana, all of us thought that his little game didn't matter. But Epaminondas has proved to be a dangerous adversary.'

'The entire plot against us is cheap, grotesque, and utterly vulgar,' Gumúcio said.

'But it's brought him good results, up to now.' The baron glanced outside: yes, the horses were ready. He announced to his friends that he had best be off again, now that he'd achieved his objective: convincing the most stubborn landowner in all the state of Bahia. He was about to go see if Estela and Sebastiana were ready to leave, when José Bernardo Murau reminded him that a man who'd come from Queimadas had been waiting to see him for two hours. The baron had forgotten all about him.

'That's right, that's right,' he muttered, and had word sent to him to come in.

A moment later Rufino's silhouette appeared in the door. They saw him remove his straw sombrero, nod politely to the owner of the house and Gumúcio, walk over to the baron, bend down and kiss his hand.

'How glad I am to see you, godson,' the latter said to him, patting him affectionately on the back. 'How good of you to come to see us. How is Jurema? Why didn't you bring her with you? Estela would have been so pleased to see her.'

The baron noted that the guide was standing there before him with his head hanging, clutching his sombrero and looking extremely embarrassed. He immediately suspected what the reason for his former peon's visit might be.

'Has something happened to your wife?' he asked. 'Is Jurema ill?'

'Give me leave to break my promise, godfather,' Rufino blurted out. Gumúcio and Murau, whose attention had wandered, took a sudden interest in this conversation between the baron and this man who looked so shamefaced. In the tense, enigmatic silence that ensued, it took the baron some time to realize what those words might mean, to understand what it was that Rufino was asking of him.

'Jurema?' he said, blinking, stepping backward, searching his memory. 'What's she done to you? She hasn't abandoned you, has she, Rufino? Do you mean to say that that's what she's done, that she's gone off with another man?'

The head of straight, dirty hair that was before him nodded almost imperceptibly. The baron then understood why his godson was hiding his eyes from him and realized what an effort this was costing him, how much he was suffering. He felt compassion for him.

'Why are you asking that of me, Rufino?' he said with a pained gesture. 'What good would that do you? You'd be bringing misfortune on yourself twice over instead of once. If she's gone off, in a way she's already dead, she's killed herself without your having had a hand in it. Forget Jurema. Forget Queimadas for a while, too. You'll find yourself another wife who'll be faithful to you. Come with us to Calumbi, where you have so many friends.'

Their curiosity aroused, Gumúcio and José Bernardo Murau awaited Rufino's answer. Gumúcio had poured himself a glass of punch and was holding it to his lips without drinking.

'Give me leave to break my promise, godfather,' the guide said at last, not raising his eyes.

A cordial smile of approval appeared on Adalberto de Gumúcio's face as he continued to listen with bated breath to this conversation between the baron and his former servant. José Bernardo Murau, on the other hand, had started to yawn. The baron told himself that there was no use arguing, that he had to accept the inevitable and say either yes or no, rather than deluding himself that he could change Rufino's mind.

Even so, he tried to stall for time. 'Who stole her from you?' he murmured. 'Who was it that she ran away with?'

Rufino paused a second before answering. 'A foreigner who came to Queimadas,' he said. He paused once again, and then added, speaking very slowly: 'They sent him to my house. He was trying to get to Canudos, to bring the *jagunços* arms.'

The glass fell from Adalberto de Gumúcio's hand and smashed to pieces at his feet, but neither the sound of the glass breaking nor the spattering punch nor the shower of shards distracted the three men as they stared at the guide in wide-eyed amazement. The latter stood there motionless, his head hanging down, saying not a word, seemingly unaware of the effect the words he had just uttered had produced.

The baron was the first to recover from the shock. 'A foreigner was trying to bring arms to Canudos?' The effort he was making to speak in a normal tone of voice made him sound even more surprised.

'That's what he was trying to do, but he didn't get there.' The mop of dirty hair nodded. Still with his head bowed respectfully, Rufino continued to gaze at the floor. 'Colonel Epaminondas

Gonçalves ordered him killed. And he thinks he's dead. But he isn't. Jurema saved him. And now he and Jurema are together.'

Gumúcio and the baron looked at each other dumfounded, and José Bernardo Murau struggled to get up out of his rocking chair, muttering something. The baron was pale and his hands were trembling. Even now the guide did not appear to be aware of how badly he had upset the three men by the story he had recounted.

'In other words, Galileo Gall is still alive,' Gumúcio finally managed to say, striking the palm of one hand with the fist of the other. 'In other words, the corpse burned to a cinder, the severed head, and all the other acts of violence . . .'

'They didn't cut his head off, sir,' Rufino interrupted him, and again an electric silence reigned in the untidy little sitting room. 'They only cut off his long hair. The dead body was a madman who'd murdered his children. The foreigner is still alive.'

He fell silent, and though Adalberto de Gumúcio and José Bernardo Murau asked him several questions at once and pressed him for details and demanded that he answer, Rufino remained stubbornly silent. The baron knew the people from his land well enough to know that the guide had said what he had to say and that there was not anybody or anything that could get another word out of him.

'Is there anything else that you can tell us, godson?' He had put one hand on Rufino's shoulder and was making no effort to conceal his emotion.

Rufino shook his head.

'I thank you for coming,' the baron said. 'You've done me a great service, my son. You've done us all one. And the country, too, even though you don't know it.'

Rufino spoke out once again, his voice more insistent than ever: 'I want to break the promise I made you, godfather.'

The baron nodded, feeling greatly distressed. The thought crossed his mind that he was about to pronounce a death sentence upon someone who was perhaps innocent, or who had acted for compelling reasons, out of estimable motives, and that he was going to feel remorse, repugnance even, for what he was about to say, and yet he could not do otherwise.

'Do what your conscience bids you,' he murmured. 'May God be with you and forgive you.'

Rufino raised his head, sighed. The baron saw that his little eyes were bloodshot and brimming with tears, and that the expression on his face was that of a man who had survived a terrible test. Rufino knelt, and the baron made the sign of the cross on his forehead and extended his hand for him to kiss again. The guide rose to his feet and left the room without so much as a glance at the other two persons in it.

Adalberto was the first to speak. 'I bow to you in due apology,' he said, gazing at the shards of glass scattered all about at his feet. 'Epaminondas is a man of great resources. I willingly concede that we are mistaken about him.'

'Too bad he's not on our side,' the baron added. But despite the extraordinary discovery he had made, he was not thinking about Epaminondas Gonçalves, but about Jurema, the young woman whom Rufino was going to kill, and about how sorrow-stricken Estela would be if she learned of this.

III

'The order has been posted since yesterday,' Moreira César says, pointing with his whip to the official announcement ordering the civilian population to register all firearms in their possession with the Seventh Regiment. 'And this morning, when the column arrived, it was read aloud publicly before the search. So you knew what you were risking, senhores.'

The prisoners are tied back to back, and there are no torture marks either on their faces or on their torsos. Barefoot and bareheaded, they could be father and son, uncle and nephew, or two brothers, since the younger one's features are exactly like the older one's, and both have a similar look in their eyes as they gaze at the little camp table at which the tribunal that has just tried them has sat. Of the three army officers who acted as judges, two are now walking off, with the same haste with which they came and passed sentence on them, toward the companies that are continuing to arrive in Cansanção, in addition to those already camped in the town. Only Moreira César is still there, standing next to the incriminating evidence: two carbines, a box of bullets, a little pouch full of gunpowder. Besides concealing arms, the prisoners have attacked and wounded one of the soldiers who arrested them. The entire population of Cansanção – a few dozen peasants – is in the clearing, behind soldiers with fixed bayonets who are keeping them from coming any closer.

'It wasn't worth the while for this junk.' The colonel's boot brushes the carbines. There is not the slightest animosity in his voice. He turns to a sergeant standing next to him and, as though asking him the time, says to him: 'Give them a swallow of brandy.'

Right next to the prisoners, bunched together in a little group, not saying a word, with a look of fear and stupefaction on their faces, are the correspondents. Those not wearing hats have covered their heads with their handkerchiefs to shield them from the blazing sun. Beyond the clearing, the usual sounds can be heard: the clump of heavy shoes and boots against the earth, the pawing and whinnying of horses, voices shouting orders, creaking noises, bursts of laughter. It would appear that the soldiers who are arriving or who are already there resting couldn't care less about what is about to happen. The sergeant has uncorked a bottle and holds it up to the mouth of each of the prisoners in turn. Both take a long swallow.

'I want to be shot to death, Colonel,' the younger one suddenly pleads.

Moreira César shakes his head. 'I don't waste ammunition on traitors to the Republic,' he says. 'Courage. Die like men.'

He gives a signal and two soldiers unsheathe the knives at their waist and step forward. They move briskly and precisely, their gestures identical: each of them grabs the hair of a prisoner with his left hand, thrusts his head abruptly backward, and slits his throat with a deep slash that cuts short the animal moan of the younger one and the cry of the older one: 'Long live Blessed Jesus the Counselor! Long live Belo . . .'

The soldiers close ranks, as though to block the villagers' path, though they haven't budged. Some of the correspondents have averted their eyes, one of them looks on in utter dejection, and the nearsighted reporter from the *Jornal de Notícias* grimaces. Moreira César gazes at the bloodstained bodies lying on the ground.

'Leave them in plain sight at the foot of the posted order,' he says in a soft voice.

He then appears to put the execution entirely out of his mind. With nervous, rapid strides, he starts off across the clearing toward the hut where a hammock has been put up for him. The group of correspondents takes off after him and catches up. He walks on in their midst, grave, calm, not sweating a drop, unlike the reporters, whose faces are flushed from the heat and the shock of what they have just witnessed. They have not yet recovered from the sight of those throats being slit just a few steps away from them: the meaning of certain words – war, cruelty, suffering, fate – has left the abstract domain in which it dwelt and taken on a measurable, tangible, carnal materiality that has left them speechless. They reach the door of the hut. An orderly hands the colonel a washbasin, a towel. The commanding officer of the Seventh Regiment rinses his hands and pats his face with cool water.

The correspondent who always goes about all bundled up stammers: 'May we send dispatches about this execution, sir?'

Moreira César does not hear or does not deign to answer. 'In the last analysis, the one thing man fears is death,' he says as he dries his hands and face. The words are spoken in a natural tone of voice, without grandiloquence, as in the conversations he has been heard to have at night with certain of his officers. 'Hence it is the only effective punishment. Provided that it is justly administered. It edifies the civilian population and demoralizes the enemy. That sounds cruel, I know. But that is the way wars are won. You have had your baptism of fire today. You now know what to expect, gentlemen.'

He dismisses them with the swift, icy nod that they have learned to recognize as the incontrovertible sign that an interview has ended. He turns his back to them and enters the hut, in which they manage to glimpse uniforms bustling about, a map spread out, and a handful of aides clicking their heels. Troubled, deeply distressed, taken aback, they go back across the clearing to the mess tent, where at each rest halt they receive their rations, identical to those of the officers. But it is certain that none of them will eat a bite today.

The five of them are worn out from the swift pace at which the column advances. They have aching backsides, stiff legs, skin badly burned by the sun of this sandy desert, bristling with cactus and thornbush, that lies between Queimadas and Monte Santo. They wonder how those who march on foot, the vast majority of the regiment, can hold up. But many of them do not hold up: they have seen them collapse and be dumped onto the medics' carts like so many sacks. They know now that these exhausted men, once they have come to, are severely reprimanded. 'Is this what war is?' the nearsighted journalist thinks. For, before this execution, they have seen nothing resembling a war. Hence they do not understand why the commanding officer of the Seventh Regiment is driving his men on so heartlessly. Is this a race toward a mirage? There were admittedly all sorts of rumors about the violent deeds of the *jagunços* in the interior. But where are these rebels? They have come upon nothing but half-deserted villages, whose wretched inhabitants watch them pass with indifferent eyes and who, when questioned, always offer only evasive answers. The column has not been attacked; they have not once heard the sound of gunfire. Is it true that the cattle that have disappeared were stolen by the enemy, as Moreira César assures them? They do not find this intense little man a likable sort, but they are impressed by his self-assurance, his ability to go without eating or sleeping, his inexhaustible energy. As they wrap their blankets around themselves for a bad night's sleep, they see him still up and about, his uniform not yet unbuttoned, the sleeves of it not yet rolled up, going up and down the ranks of soldiers, stopping to exchange a few words with the sentinels, or conversing with his staff officers. And at dawn, when the bugle sounds and they open their eyes, still drunk with sleep, he is there, washed and shaved, interrogating the messengers from the vanguard or inspecting the artillery pieces, as though he hadn't gone to bed at all. Until the execution a moment ago war, for them, was this man. He was the only one to talk constantly of it, with such conviction that he managed to convince them, to make them see themselves surrounded by it, besieged by it. He has persuaded them that many of those undaunted, starving creatures – exactly like the two men executed – who come out of their huts to watch them pass by, are the enemy's accomplices, and that behind those impassive eyes are intelligences that count, measure, calculate, register, and that this information, it too on its way to Canudos, always precedes the column. The nearsighted journalist recalls that the old man shouted 'Long live the Counselor!' before dying and thinks: 'Perhaps it's true. Perhaps all of them are the enemy.'

This time, unlike previous halts, none of the correspondents stretches out to catch a few winks of sleep. Keeping each other company in their confusion and anguish, they linger by the mess tent, smoking, reflecting, and the reporter from the *Jornal de Notícias* is unable to keep his eyes off the dead bodies of the two men stretched out at the foot of the tree trunk on which the order that they have disobeyed flutters in the wind. An hour later the correspondents are again at the head of the column, immediately behind the standard-bearers and Colonel Moreira César, heading toward the war which for them has now really begun.

Another surprise awaits them before they reach Monte Santo, at the crossroads where a small blurred sign indicates the turnoff to the hacienda of Calumbi; the column arrives there six hours after having resumed its march. Of the five correspondents, only the gaunt scarecrow from the *Jornal de Notícias* will witness the incident at close hand. A curious relationship has sprung up between him and the commanding officer of the Seventh Regiment, which it would be inexact to call friendship or even congeniality. It is a question, rather, of a curiosity born of a mutual repulsion, of the attraction exerted by diametrical opposites. In any event, the man who appears to be a caricature of himself, not only when he sits writing at the outlandish portable writing table that he places on his knees or his saddle and dips his pen in the inkwell that looks more like the sort of horn in which the *caboclos* carry about the poison for the arrows of the crossbows when they are out hunting, but also when he walks or rides, continually giving the impression that he is about to collapse, appears to be fascinated, bewitched, obsessed by the little colonel. He keeps watching him every minute, never missing a chance to approach him, and in his conversations with his colleagues, Moreira César is very nearly the only subject that interests him, one that to all appearances matters more to him than Canudos and the war. And what is it about this young journalist that can have aroused the colonel's interest? His eccentric dress and his odd physique perhaps, his resemblance to a walking skeleton, those gangling limbs, that proliferation of hair and fuzz, those long fingernails now black with dirt, that spineless manner, that whole in which there is not the least sign of anything that the colonel would call virile, martial. But the truth remains that there is something about this grotesque figure with the unpleasant voice that, perhaps despite himself, the little officer with fixed ideas and forceful eyes finds attractive. He is the only one whom the colonel is in the habit of addressing when he holds press conferences, and sometimes he converses with him alone after the evening mess. During the marches, the reporter from the *Jornal de Notícias*, as though through his mount's initiative, habitually rides on ahead and joins the colonel. This is what has happened this time, after the column has left Cansanção. The nearsighted journalist, bouncing up and down like a puppet, is lost from sight amid the officers and aides surrounding Moreira César's white horse, when the colonel, on arriving at the turnoff to Calumbi, raises his right hand: the signal to halt.

The escorts gallop off with orders, and the bugler sounds the call that will bring all the companies of the regiment to a halt. Moreira César, Olímpio de Castro, Cunha Matos, and Tamarindo dismount; the journalist slides to the ground. To the rear, the correspondents and a great many soldiers go to dip their faces, arms, and feet in a pool of stagnant water. The major and Tamarindo examine a map and Moreira César scans the horizon with his field glasses. The sun is disappearing behind a lone peak in the distance – Monte Santo – to which it has imparted a spectral form. As he puts away his glasses, the colonel's face has paled. He is visibly tense.

'What is it that's worrying you, sir?' Captain Olímpio de Castro asks.

'Time.' Moreira César speaks as though he had a foreign object in his mouth. 'The possibility that they may take to their heels before we get there.'

'They won't run away,' the nearsighted journalist pipes up. 'They believe that God is on their side. People in these parts like a good fight.'

'As the old saying goes: "Smooth the way for an enemy on the run,"' the captain says jokingly.

'Not in this case.' The colonel has difficulty articulating the words. 'We must teach them a lesson that will put an end to monarchist illusions. And avenge the affront to the army as well.'

He speaks with mysterious pauses between one syllable and another, in a quavering voice. He opens his mouth again to say something, but not a word comes out. He is deathly pale, and his eyes are an angry red. He sits down on a fallen tree trunk and slowly removes his kepi. The reporter from the *Jornal de Notícias* goes over and sits down, too, when he sees Moreira César raise his hands to his face. The colonel's kepi falls to the ground and he leaps to his feet, staggering, his face beet-red, as he frantically rips off the buttons of his blouse, as though suffocating. Moaning and frothing at the mouth, writhing uncontrollably, he rolls about at the feet of Captain Olímpio de Castro and the reporter, who have no idea what has come over him. As they bend over him Tamarindo, Cunha Matos, and several aides rush up.

'Don't touch him,' Colonel Tamarindo shouts with an imperious gesture. 'Quick, a blanket. Call Dr. Souza Ferreiro. Don't anybody come near him! Get back, get back!'

Major Cunha Matos pulls the reporter away and goes with the aides to confront the press. They rudely force the correspondents to keep their distance, as meanwhile a blanket is thrown over Moreira César, and Olímpio de Castro and Tamarindo fold their tunics to serve as a pillow under his head.

'Open his mouth and get hold of his tongue,' the old colonel instructs them, knowing exactly what must be done. He turns around to the two escorts and orders them to put up a tent.

The captain forces Moreira César's mouth open. His convulsions continue for some time. Dr. Souza Ferreiro finally arrives, in a medical corps wagon. They have set up the tent and Moreira César is lying in it on a camp cot. Tamarindo and Olímpio de Castro remain at his side, taking turns keeping his mouth open and seeing that he stays covered. His face drenched with sweat, his eyes closed, tossing and turning, emitting broken moans, from time to time the colonel foams at the mouth. The doctor and Colonel Tamarindo wordlessly exchange glances. The captain explains how the fit came over him, and how long ago, as Souza Ferreiro meanwhile goes on removing his uniform jacket and gestures to an aide to bring his medical kit to the cot. The officers leave the tent so that the doctor may give the patient a thorough examination.

Armed sentinels ring the tent to seal it off from the remainder of the column. Just beyond them are the correspondents, spying on the scene from between the rifles. They have plied the nearsighted journalist with questions, and he has told them what he has seen. Between the sentinels and the camp is a no-man's-land that no officer or soldier crosses unless summoned by Major Cunha Matos. The latter strides back and forth with his hands clasped behind his back. Colonel Tamarindo and Captain Olímpio de Castro join him and the correspondents see them pace round and round the tent. Their faces gradually grow darker as the great twilight conflagration dies away. From time to time, Tamarindo goes inside the tent, comes out again, and the three begin pacing about once more. Many minutes go by, half an hour, an hour perhaps, and then Captain de Castro suddenly walks over to the correspondents and motions to the reporter from the *Jornal de Notícias* to come with him. A bonfire has been lighted and somewhere in the rear the bugler is blowing the evening mess call. The sentinels allow the nearsighted journalist, whom the captain is escorting to the colonel and the major, to pass.

'You know this region. You can help us,' Tamarindo murmurs, in a tone of voice not at all like his usual amiable one, as though struggling to overcome a profound repugnance at being forced to discuss the matter at hand with an outsider. 'The doctor insists that the colonel must be taken to a place where there are certain comforts and conveniences, where he can be well cared for. Is there any sort of hacienda nearby?'

'Certainly,' the high-pitched voice says. 'You know as well as I do that there's one.'

'Apart from Calumbi, I mean,' Colonel Tamarindo corrects himself, ill at ease. 'The colonel refused in no uncertain terms the baron's invitation to quarter the regiment. It's not the proper place to take him.'

'There isn't any other,' the nearsighted journalist says trenchantly, gazing intently through the semidarkness at the field tent and the greenish glow coming from inside it. 'Everything the eye can see between Cansanção and Canudos belongs to the Baron of Canabrava.'

The colonel looks at him in distress. At that moment Dr. Souza Ferreiro comes out of the tent, wiping his hands. He is a man with silver-gray temples and a receding hairline, dressed in an army uniform. The officers surround him, forgetting the journalist, who remains standing there nonetheless, brazenly staring at them with eyes magnified by the lenses of his glasses.

'It's the nervous and physical fatigue of the last few days,' the doctor says querulously, placing a cigarette between his lips. 'Another attack, two years later, in the situation we're in. Bad luck, a trick of the Devil – who can say? I've bled him, for the congestion. But he needs baths, massages, the whole treatment. You decide, gentlemen.'

Cunha Matos and Olímpio de Castro look at Colonel Tamarindo. The latter clears his throat but says nothing. 'Do you insist that we take him to Calumbi, when you know the baron's there?' he finally says.

'I didn't say a word about Calumbi,' Souza Ferreiro shoots back. 'I'm only talking about what the patient needs. And allow me to add one more thing. It's foolhardy to keep him here in these conditions.'

'You know the colonel,' Cunha Matos interjects. 'He'll feel affronted, humiliated in the house of one of the leaders of the monarchist subversion.'

Dr. Souza Ferreiro shrugs. 'I respect your decision. I'm your junior officer. I've fulfilled my responsibility.'

A commotion behind them causes the four officers and the journalist to turn around and look in the direction of the field tent. Moreira César is standing in the doorway, dimly visible in the feeble light from the lamp inside, roaring something they fail to understand. Naked to the waist, leaning on the canvas with his two hands, he has dark, motionless patches on his chest that must be leeches. He has the strength to remain on his feet for only a few seconds. They see him collapse, a querulous moan on his lips. The doctor kneels down to force his mouth open as the officers pick him up by the feet, the arms, the shoulders, to carry him back to the folding cot.

'I assume the responsibility of taking him to Calumbi, sir,' Captain Olímpio de Castro says.

'Very well,' Tamarindo replies. 'Take an escort and accompany Souza Ferreiro. But the regiment will not go to the baron's. It will camp here.'

'May I go with you, Captain?' the nearsighted journalist asks in his importunate voice. 'I know the baron. I worked for his paper before I went over to the *Jornal de Notícias*.'

They stayed in Ipupiará ten days more, after the visit from the *capangas* on horseback, who took with them as their only booty a bright-red shock of hair. The stranger began to get better. One night the Bearded Lady heard him conversing, in labored Portuguese, with Jurema, asking her what country he was in, what month and day it was. The following evening he slid down off the wagon and managed to take a few tottering steps. And two nights later he was in the Ipupiará general store, his fever gone, thin as a rail but in good spirits, plying the storekeeper (who kept looking at his bare skull in amusement) with questions about Canudos and the war. Overcome with a sort of wild exhilaration, he made the man repeat several times that an army of half a thousand men, come from Bahia under the command of Major Febrônio, had been demolished at O Cambaio. The news excited him so much that Jurema, the Bearded Lady, and the Dwarf thought he was about to rave deliriously in a strange tongue again. But after having had a little glass of *cachaça* with the storekeeper, Gall fell into a deep sleep for a good ten hours.

At Gall's insistence, they started out again. The circus people would rather have stayed a while longer in Ipupiará, where they could get themselves enough to eat, if nothing else, by entertaining the villagers with clown acts and stories. But the foreigner was afraid that the *capangas* would come back and carry off his head this time. He had recovered: he talked with such whirlwind energy that the Bearded Lady, the Dwarf, and even the Idiot listened to him dumfounded. They had to guess at part of what he said, and his irresistible urge to talk about the *jagunços* intrigued them. The Bearded Lady asked Jurema if he was one of those apostles of the Blessed Jesus who were wandering about all over. No, he wasn't: he hadn't been to Canudos, he didn't know the Counselor, and he didn't even believe in God. Jurema couldn't understand this mania of his either. When Gall announced to them that he was heading north, the Dwarf and the Bearded

Lady decided to follow him. They wouldn't have been able to explain why. Perhaps it was gravity that was the cause – weak bodies magnetized by strong ones – or simply not having anything better to do, no alternative, no will to oppose that of someone who, unlike themselves, appeared to be following a definite path through life.

They left at dawn and walked all day amid stones and thorny *mandacarus*, not saying a word to each other, with the wagon in front, the Bearded Lady, the Dwarf, and the Idiot alongside, Jurema right next to the wheels, and Galileo Gall drawing up the end of the caravan. To shield himself from the sun, he had put on a sombrero that had once belonged to Pedrim the Giant. He had grown so thin that his pants were baggy and his shirt kept sliding off his shoulders. The red-hot bullet that had grazed him had left a purple mark behind his ear and Caifás's knife a sinuous scar between his neck and his shoulder. His thinness and paleness somehow made his eyes look wilder still. On the fourth day of their trek, at a bend in the road known as the Sítio das Flores, they ran into a band of starving outlaws, who took their burro away from them. They were in a thicket of thistles and *mandacarus*, divided in two by a dry riverbed. In the distance they could see the mountainside of the Serra da Engorda. There were eight bandits, some of them dressed in leather, wearing sombreros decorated with coins, and armed with knives, carbines, and bandoleers. The leader – a short, paunchy man with the profile of a bird of prey and cruel eyes – was called Toughbeard by his men, even though he was beardless. He gave a few terse instructions, and in less time than it takes to tell, his *cangaceiros* killed the burro, skinned it, hacked it up, built a fire, and roasted great chunks of it, which a while later they fell upon voraciously. They must have gone without food for several days, for some of them, overjoyed at this feast, began to sing.

As he watched them, Galileo wondered how long it would take the scavengers and the elements to turn the carcass into the little mounds of polished bones that he had grown accustomed to coming across in the backlands, skeletons, remains, mementos of man or animal that were grim reminders to the traveler of the fate that awaited him in case he fainted from exhaustion or died. He was sitting in the wagon alongside the Bearded Lady, the Dwarf, the Idiot, and Jurema. Toughbeard took off his sombrero, on the brim of which, above his forehead, a sovereign gleamed, and made signs to the circus people to eat. The first to dare to do so was the Idiot, who knelt down and reached his fingers out toward the dense cloud of smoke. The Bearded Lady, the Dwarf, Jurema followed his example. Gall walked over to the fire. Life in the open air had made him as tanned and weather-beaten as a *sertanejo*. From the moment he saw Toughbeard take off his sombrero, his eyes never left the man's head. And Gall kept on looking at him intently as he raised a chunk of meat to his lips. On trying to swallow the first mouthful, he began to retch.

'He can only swallow soft things,' Jurema explained to the men. 'He's been sick.'

'He's a foreigner,' the Dwarf added. 'He talks languages.'

'Only my enemies look at me like that,' the leader of the *cangaço* said in a harsh voice. 'Stop staring at me; it bothers me.'

Because, even as he was vomiting, Gall's eyes had never left him. They all turned toward him. Still scrutinizing the man, Galileo took a few steps forward, thus bringing himself within reach of him. 'The only thing that interests me is your head,' he said very slowly. 'Allow me to touch it.'

The bandit reached for his knife, as though he were about to attack him. Gall calmed him down by giving him a friendly smile.

'Let him touch you,' the Bearded Lady muttered. 'He'll tell you your secrets.'

His curiosity aroused, the outlaw looked Gall over from head to foot. He had a piece of meat in his mouth, but he had stopped chewing. 'Are you a magician?' he asked, the cruelty in his eyes suddenly evaporating.

Gall smiled at him again and took another step forward. He was so close now that his body lightly brushed the bandit's. He was taller than the *cangaceiro*, whose bushy head of hair barely came up to his shoulder. Circus people and bandits alike stared at the two of them, intrigued. Still holding the knife in his hand, Toughbeard seemed wary, but also curious. Galileo raised his two hands, placed them on Toughbeard's head, and began to palpate it.

'At one time I set out to be one,' he answered, pronouncing each syllable carefully as his fingers moved slowly, parting the locks of hair, skillfully exploring the bandit's scalp. 'The police didn't give me time.'

'The flying brigades?' Toughbeard said understandingly.

'We have one thing in common at least,' Gall said. 'We have the same enemy.'

Toughbeard's beady eyes were suddenly full of anxiety, as though he were helplessly trapped. 'I want to know how I'm going to die,' he said in a half whisper, forcing himself to reveal what was preying most on his mind.

Gall's fingers poked about in the outlaw's mane, lingering for an especially long while above and behind his ears. His face was very serious, and his eyes had the same feverish gleam as in his moments of euphoria. Science was not wrong: his fingertips could clearly feel the organ of Combativeness, the organ of those inclined to attack, of those who enjoy fighting, of those who are rash and unruly; it was right there beneath his fingers, a round, contumelious bump, in both hemispheres. But, above all, it was the organ of Destructiveness, the organ of those who are vengeful, given to extremes, cruel, the organ that makes for bloodthirsty monsters when its effects are not counteracted by moral and intellectual powers, that was abnormally prominent: two hard, hot swellings, above the ears. 'The predatory man,' he thought.

'Didn't you hear?' Toughbeard roared, moving his head away from the touch of Gall's fingers with such a violent jerk that it made the latter stagger. 'How am I going to die?'

Gall shook his head apologetically. 'I don't know,' he said. 'It's not written in your bones.'

The band of *cangaceiros* standing watching dispersed, returning to the fire in search of more roast meat. But the circus people stayed where they were, next to Gall and Toughbeard.

The bandit looked pensive. 'There's nothing I'm afraid of,' he said gravely. 'When I'm awake. At night it's different. I see my skeleton sometimes. As though it was there waiting for me, do you follow me?'

He gestured in annoyance, rubbed his hand across his mouth, spat. He was visibly upset, and everyone stood there in silence for a time, listening to the flies, the wasps, the bluebottles buzzing about the remains of the burro.

'It's not a dream I've just had recently,' the brigand added. 'I used to have it as a child back in Cariri, long before I came to Bahia. And also when I was with Pajeú. Sometimes years go by and I don't have that dream. And then, all of a sudden, I start having it again, every night.'

'Pajeú?' Gall said, looking at Toughbeard with a gleam in his eye. 'The one with the scar? The one who . . .?'

'That's right. Pajeú.' The *cangaceiro* nodded. 'I was with him for five years, without our ever having words. He was the best when it came to fighting. The angel's wing brushed him and he got converted. He's now one of the elect of God, up there in Canudos.'

He shrugged, as though he found this difficult to understand, or as though it were a matter of complete indifference to him.

'Have you been to Canudos?' Gall asked. 'Tell me about it. What's happening up there? What's it like?'

'You hear lots of things,' Toughbeard said, spitting. 'That they killed a whole bunch of soldiers who'd come with some man named Febrônio. They strung them up on the trees. If a corpse isn't buried, the Can takes off with it, people say.'

'Are they well armed?' Gall went on insistently. 'Will they be able to hold out against another attack?'

'Yes, they will,' Toughbeard growled. 'Pajeú's not the only one up there. There's also Abbot João, Taramela, Joaquim Macambira and his sons, Pedrão. The most fearful outlaws in these parts. They used to hate each other and kill each other. But now they're brothers and fight for the Counselor. They're going to go to heaven, despite their evil deeds. The Counselor pardoned them.'

The Bearded Lady, the Idiot, the Dwarf, and Jurema had sat down on the ground and were listening spellbound.

'The Counselor gives the pilgrims a kiss on the forehead,' Toughbeard added. 'The Little Blessed One has them kneel and the Counselor lifts them to their feet and kisses them. That's called the kiss of the elect. People weep for joy. Because once you're an elect, you know that you're going to go to heaven. What does death matter after that?'

'You should be in Canudos too,' Gall said. 'They're your brothers too. They're fighting so that heaven will descend on earth. So that the hell that you're so afraid of will disappear.'

'I'm not afraid of hell but of death,' Toughbeard corrected him, with no sign of anger in his voice. 'Or to put it a better way, I'm afraid of the nightmare, the dream of death. That's something different, don't you see what I mean?'

He spat again, with a tortured look on his face. Suddenly he said to Jurema, pointing at Gall: 'Doesn't your husband ever dream of his skeleton?'

'He's not my husband,' Jurema answered.

Big João entered Canudos at a run, his head in a whirl at the responsibility that had just been conferred upon him and that with each passing second seemed to him to be an honor not deserved by a poor sinner such as he, a person who sometimes believed himself to be possessed by the Dog (it was a fear that kept returning, like the seasons). But he had accepted, and he couldn't back down now. He stopped as he reached the first houses, not knowing what to do. He had intended to go to Antônio Vilanova's, to find out from him how to organize the Catholic Guard. But now his bewildered heart told him that what he needed most at this moment was not practical help but spiritual aid. It was dusk; the Counselor would soon be mounting to the tower; if he hurried, perhaps he could still find him in the Sanctuary. He began running again, through narrow winding streets crowded with men, women, and children who were leaving their houses, shanties, caves, holes, and flocking, as they did every evening, to the Temple of the Blessed Jesus to listen to the counsels. As he went by the Vilanovas' store, he saw that Pajeú and some twenty men, equipped for a long journey, were bidding groups of their relatives goodbye. He had great difficulty making his way through the great throng overflowing the open ground adjoining the churches. Darkness was falling and here and there little lamps were already twinkling.

The Counselor was not in the Sanctuary. He had accompanied Father Joaquim as far as the exit on the road to Cumbe so as to say goodbye to the priest as he left town, and then, cradling the little white lamb with one hand and holding his shepherd's crook in the other, he had stopped by the Health Houses to comfort the sick and the aged. Because of the great crowds that dogged his every footstep, these tours of Belo Monte were becoming more and more difficult for the Counselor with each passing day. This time the Lion of Natuba and the women of the Sacred Choir had gone with him to escort him, but the Little Blessed One and Maria Quadrado were there in the Sanctuary.

'I'm not worthy, Little Blessed One,' the former slave said from the doorway, his voice choking. 'Praised be the Blessed Jesus.'

'I've prepared an oath for the Catholic Guard,' the Little Blessed One answered softly. 'More solemn than the one taken by those who come to be saved. The Lion has written it out.' He handed Big João a piece of paper, which disappeared in his huge dark hands. 'You are to learn it by heart and have each man you choose swear to obey it. Then, when the Catholic Guard is formed, they will all take it publicly in the Temple and we'll have a procession.'

Maria Quadrado, who had been standing in one corner of the room, came over to them with a cloth and a vessel full of water. 'Sit down, João,' she said tenderly. 'Have a drink first, and then let me wash you.'

The black obeyed her. He was so tall that even sitting down he was the same height as the Mother Superior of the Sacred Choir. He drank thirstily. He was perturbed and drenched with sweat, and he closed his eyes as Maria Quadrado passed the cool damp cloth over his face, his neck, his kinky locks sprinkled with gray.

Suddenly he reached out an arm and clung to her. 'Help me, Mother Maria Quadrado,' he implored, transfixed with fear. 'I'm not worthy of this honor.'

'You've been the slave of one man,' she said, caressing him as though he were a child. 'Will you not accept being the slave of the Blessed Jesus? He will help you, Big João.'

'I swear that I have not been a republican, that I do not accept the expulsion of the Emperor or his replacement by the Antichrist,' the Little Blessed One recited with intense devotion. 'That I do not accept civil marriage or the separation of Church and State or the metric system. That I will not answer the census questions. That I will never again steal or smoke or drink or make wagers or fornicate out of vice. And that I will give my life for my religion and the Blessed Jesus.'

'I'll learn it, Little Blessed One,' Big João stammered.

At that moment the Counselor arrived, preceded by a great din. Once the tall, dark, gaunt figure entered the Sanctuary, followed by the little lamb, the Lion of Natuba – a vague four-footed shape that seemed to be leaping about – and the Sacred Choir, the impatient clamor of voices continued on the other side of the door. The little lamb came over and licked Maria Quadrado's ankles. The women of the Choir squatted down, their backs against the wall. The Counselor walked over to Big João, who was on his knees with his eyes fixed on the floor. He appeared to be trembling from head to foot; he had been with the Counselor for fifteen years now, and yet each time he was in his presence he still suddenly felt like a worthless creature, a worthless thing almost.

The Counselor took Big João's two hands and obliged him to lift his head. The saint's incandescent pupils stared into the depths of the ex-slave's tear-filled eyes. 'You are still suffering, Big João,' he said softly.

'I'm not worthy to watch over you,' the black sobbed. 'Order me to do anything else you like. Kill me, if need be. I don't want anything to happen to you through any fault of mine. Remember, Father, I've had the Dog in my flesh.'

'You will form the Catholic Guard,' the Counselor answered. 'You will be in command of it. You have suffered a great deal, and you are suffering now. That is why you are worthy. The Father has said that the just man will wash his hands in the blood of the sinner. You are a just man now, Big João.'

He allowed him to kiss his hand and with an absent look in his eyes waited till the black had left off weeping. A moment later, followed by all of them, he left the Sanctuary to mount to the tower once more to counsel the people of Belo Monte. Joining the multitude, Big João heard him offer a prayer and then tell of the miracle of the bronze serpent that, by order of the Father, Moses built in order that anyone who looked upon it might be cured should he be bitten by the snakes that were attacking the Jews, and then prophesy a new invasion of vipers that would come to Belo Monte to exterminate those who believed in God. But, he heard him say, those who kept the faith would survive the serpents' bite. As people began to wend their way home, Big João's heart was at peace. He remembered that years before, during the drought, the Counselor had told of this miracle for the first time, thereby bringing about another miracle in the *sertão* overrun by snakes. The memory reassured him.

He was another person when he knocked on Antônio Vilanova's door. Assunção Sardelinha, Honôrio's wife, let him in, and João found the storekeeper, his wife, and various children and helpers of the two brothers sitting at the counter eating. They made room for him, and handed him a steaming plateful of food that he downed without even noticing what it was that he was eating, with the feeling that he was wasting precious time. He barely listened as Antônio told him that, rather than taking gunpowder with him, Pajeú had chosen to go off with cane whistles and crossbows and poisoned arrows, his idea being that that would be a better way of harassing the soldiers who were coming. The black chewed and swallowed, paying no attention, his mind entirely occupied by his mission.

Once the meal was over, the others went off to bed in the adjoining rooms or trundled off to their hammocks, pallets, or blankets laid down amid the crates and shelves around them. Then, by the light of an oil lamp, João and Antônio talked. They talked for a long time, in low voices at times and much louder ones at others, in perfect accord at times and at others furious with each other. Meanwhile, little by little, fireflies invaded the store, glowing in all the corners. From time to time Antônio opened one of the large ledgers in which he was in the habit of recording the arrivals of pilgrims, births, and deaths, and mentioned certain names. But still João did not allow the storekeeper to go off for his night's rest. After carefully smoothing out a crumpled bit of paper that he had been clutching in his hand, he held it out to him and had him read it over several times until he had memorized the words written on it. As sleep overcame the ex-slave, who had bedded down in a vacant space underneath the counter, so tired he hadn't even taken off his boots, Antônio Vilanova heard him repeating the oath composed by the Little Blessed One for the Catholic Guard.

The next morning, the Vilanova brothers' children and helpers went all about Belo Monte, announcing, whenever they came upon a group of people, that any person not afraid to give his or her life for the Counselor might aspire to become a member of the Catholic Guard. Soon so many candidates gathered in front of the former steward's house of the hacienda that they blocked Campo Grande, the only straight street in Canudos. Sitting on a crate of merchandise, Big João and Antônio received them one by one. The storekeeper checked the name and date of arrival of each one against his ledger, and João asked them one by one if they were willing to give away everything they possessed and abandon their families as Christ's apostles had done for His sake, and subject themselves to a baptism by resistance. All of them fervently consented.

Those who had fought at Uauá and O Cambaio were given

preference, and those incapable of reaming out a rifle, loading a blunderbuss, or cooling an overheated musket were eliminated. The very old and very young were also eliminated, as were those unfit for combat; lunatics and pregnant women, for instance. No one who had ever been a guide for the police flying brigades or a tax collector or a census taker was accepted. Every so often, Big João would take those who had passed all these tests to a vacant lot and order them to attack him as though he were an enemy. Those who hesitated were turned down. He had the rest fight hand to hand with each other to test their bravery. By nightfall, the Catholic Guard had eighteen members, one of whom was a woman who had belonged to Pedrão's band. Big João administered the oath to them in the store, then told them to return to their homes to bid their families farewell, for from the following day on they had only one obligation: to protect the Counselor.

The second day the selection was more rapid, for those already chosen helped Big João test those who presented themselves as candidates and kept order amid all the chaos that ensued. The Sardelinha sisters had meanwhile hunted about and found enough blue cloth to make armbands or kerchiefs for all those chosen. João swore in thirty more on the second day, fifty on the third day, and at the end of the week he had nearly four hundred guards to rely on.

The following Sunday, the Catholic Guard marched through the streets of Canudos, lined on either side by people who applauded them and envied them. The procession began at midday, and as in all the great celebrations, statues from the Church of Santo Antônio and the Temple under construction were carried through the streets, the townspeople brought out those in their houses, skyrockets were shot off, and the air was filled with incense and prayers. As night was falling, in the Temple of the Blessed Jesus, still without a roof, beneath a sky thick with stars that seemed to have come out early so as to witness the joyous ceremony, the members of the Catholic Guard repeated in chorus the oath composed by the Little Blessed One.

And at dawn the following morning a messenger sent by

Pajeú came to tell Abbot João that the Can's army numbered one thousand two hundred men, that it had several cannons, and that the colonel in command was known as Throat-Slitter.

With rapid, spare gestures, Rufino makes the final preparations for yet another journey, its outcome more uncertain this time. He has changed out of the pants and shirt he had worn to go see the baron at the Pedra Vermelha hacienda, into identical ones, and he is taking with him a machete, a carbine, two knives, and a knapsack. He takes a look around the cabin: the bowls, the hammock, the benches, the image of Our Lady of Lapa. His features are drawn and his eyes blink continuously. But after a moment his angular face is again set in an inscrutable expression. With precise movements, he makes a few last preparations. When he has finished, he takes the lighted wick of the oil lamp and sets fire to objects that he has set in different places about the room. The shack begins to go up in flames. He walks unhurriedly to the door, taking with him only the weapons and the knapsack. Once outside, he squats down next to the empty animal pen and from there watches a gentle breeze fan the flames that are devouring his home. The cloud of smoke drifts his way and makes him cough. He rises to his feet. He slings the carbine over his shoulder, tucks the machete into his belt next to the knives, and hoists the knapsack onto his back. He turns around and walks off, knowing that he will never return to Queimadas. As he goes past the station, he does not even notice that people are putting up banners and posters to welcome the Seventh Regiment and Colonel Moreira César.

Five days later, as night is falling, his lean, supple, dusty silhouette can be seen entering Ipupiará. He has made a detour to return the knife that he borrowed from the Blessed Jesus and has walked an average of ten hours a day, taking time out to rest during those moments when it is hottest and darkest. Except for just one day, when he paid for his food, he has trapped or shot everything that he has eaten. Sitting at the door of the general store are a handful of old men who look exactly alike, puffing on identical pipes. The tracker walks over to them, removes his sombrero, greets them. They must know him, for they ask him about Queimadas and all of them want to know if he has seen soldiers and what news he has of the war. Sitting down beside them, he tells them everything he knows, and asks about people in Ipupiará. Some of them have died, others have left for the South to make their fortune, and two families have just gone off to Canudos. When darkness has fallen, Rufino and the old men go into the store to have a little glass of *cachaça.* The stifling heat has now died down to a pleasant warmth. With the appropriate circumlocutions, Rufino now broaches the subject that they all knew the conversation would lead to sooner or later. He employs the most impersonal turns of speech to question them. The old men listen to him without feigning surprise. They all nod their heads and speak in turn. Yes, it has passed this way, more a ghost of a circus than a real one, so wretched-looking it was hard to believe that once upon a time it had been that sumptuous caravan led by the Gypsy. Rufino listens respectfully as they recall the circus shows of the old days. Finally, when there is a pause, he leads the conversation back round to where it began, and this time, as though they had decided that the proprieties had now been observed, they tell him what he has come to learn or confirm: how long it camped just outside the town, how the Bearded Lady, the Dwarf, and the Idiot earned their daily bread by telling fortunes, reciting stories, and putting on clown acts, how the stranger went around asking wild questions about the *jagunços,* how a band of *capangas* had come to cut off his red hair and steal the corpse of the father who had killed his children. He does not ask, nor do they mention the other person who was neither a circus performer nor a stranger. But this eminently present absent person haunts the conversation each time someone touches on the subject of how the wounded stranger was cared for and fed. Are they aware that this specter is Rufino's wife? They surely know or sense this, as they know or sense what can be said and what must be left unsaid. At the end of the conversation, almost by chance, Rufino finds out which direction the circus people were headed when they left. He sleeps in the store that night, on a pallet that the owner offers him, and leaves at dawn at his steady trot.

Neither picking up nor slowing his pace, Rufino traverses a landscape where the only shadow is that of his body, following him at first and then preceding him. With a set expression on his face and half-closed eyes, he makes his way along without hesitating, despite the fact that drifting sand has covered the trail over in places. Night is falling as he arrives at a hut overlooking a sowed field. The tenant farmer, his wife and half-naked kids welcome him as though he were an old friend. He eats and drinks with them, giving them news of Queimadas, Ipupiará, and other places. They talk of the war and the fears it arouses, of the pilgrims who pass by on their way to Canudos, and speculate on the possibility that the world is coming to an end. Only then does Rufino ask them about the circus and the stranger with all his hair lopped off. Yes, they passed by there and headed on toward the Serra de Olhos D'Agua on their way to Monte Santo. The wife remembers best of all the skinny man with no hair and yellowish eyes, who moved like an animal without bones and kept bursting out laughing for no reason at all. The couple find Rufino a hammock to sleep in and the next morning they fill his knapsack, refusing to accept payment.

For a good part of the day, Rufino trots along without seeing anyone, in a landscape cooled by thickets full of flocks of jabbering parrots. That afternoon he begins to come across goatherds, with whom he stops to talk from time to time. A little beyond the Sitio das Flores – the Flower Place, a name that strikes him as a joke since there is nothing to be found there but stones and sunbaked earth – he turns off and heads for a wayside cross fashioned from tree trunks that is surrounded by ex-votos in the form of little carved wooden figurines. A legless woman is keeping vigil at the foot of the cross, lying stretched out on the ground like a snake. Rufino kneels and the woman blesses him. The tracker gives her something to eat and they talk. She hasn't heard of them; she hasn't seen them. Before continuing on his way, Rufino lights a candle and bows his head before the cross.

For three days he loses their trail. He questions peasants and cow-herds and concludes that instead of going on to Monte Santo the circus has turned off somewhere or gone back the way it came. Looking for a market being held, perhaps, so as to take in enough to eat? He goes all about the countryside round Sitio das Flores, in ever-widening circles, asking questions about each one of the people with the circus. Has anyone seen a woman with hair on her face? A dwarf three feet tall? An idiot with a body like rubber? A stranger with reddish fuzz on his skull who speaks in a language that's hard to understand? The answer is always no. Lying in shelters that he has chanced upon, he makes conjectures. Can they have already killed him? Could he have died of his wounds? He goes down to Tanquinho and comes up-country again, without picking up their trail. One afternoon when he has stretched out on the ground exhausted, to sleep for a while, a band of armed men creep up on him, as silent as ghosts. A rope sandal planted on his chest awakens him. He sees that, in addition to carbines, the men are equipped with machetes, cane whistles, bandoleers, and are not bandits, or at any rate no longer bandits. He has difficulty convincing them that he is not a guide who has hired on with the army, that he hasn't seen a single soldier since leaving Queimadas. He shows such a lack of interest in the war that they think he's lying, and at one point one of them puts his knife to his throat. Finally the interrogation turns into a friendly conversation. Rufino spends the night in their company, listening to them talk of the Antichrist, the Blessed Jesus, the Counselor, Belo Monte. He gathers that they have kidnapped, murdered, stolen, and lived on the run from the law, but that now they are saints. They explain to him that an army is advancing like a plague, confiscating people's arms, conscripting men, and plunging knives in the throats of all those who refuse to spit on a crucifix and curse Christ. When they ask him if he wants to join them, Rufino answers no. He explains why and they understand.

The following morning, he arrives in Cansanção at almost the same time as the soldiers. Rufino goes round to see the blacksmith, whom he knows. Standing next to the forge that is throwing out red-hot sparks, drenched in sweat, the man advises him to get out of town as fast as he can because the devils are conscripting all guides. When Rufino explains to him, he, too, understands. Yes, he can help him. Toughbeard has passed that way just a short time before; he'd run into the people Rufino was asking about, and had talked about meeting up with the stranger who reads heads. Where did he run into them? The blacksmith explains and the tracker stays there in the shop chatting with him until nightfall. Then he leaves the village without the sentinels spying him, and two hours later he is back with the apostles from Belo Monte. He tells them that, sure enough, the war has reached Cansanção.

Dr. Souza Ferreiro dipped the cupping glasses in alcohol and handed them one by one to Baroness Estela, who had placed a handkerchief over her head as a coif. She set each glass aflame and skillfully applied it to the colonel's back. The latter was lying so quietly that the sheets were scarcely wrinkled.

'I've had to act as doctor and midwife many a time here in Calumbi,' the baroness said in her lilting voice, addressing the doctor perhaps, or perhaps the patient. 'But, to tell you the truth, it's been years since I've applied cupping glasses. Am I hurting you, Colonel?'

'Not at all, Baroness.' Moreira César did his best to conceal his pain, but did not succeed. 'Please accept my apologies for this invasion, and kindly convey them to your husband as well. It was not my idea.'

'We're delighted to have you.' The baroness had finished applying the cupping glasses and straightened the pillows. 'I was very eager to meet a hero in person. Though, naturally, I would rather it had not been an illness that brought you to Calumbi . . .'

Her voice was friendly, charming, superficial. Next to the bed was a table with pitchers and porcelain basins decorated with royal peacocks, bandages, balls of cotton, a jar full of leeches, cupping glasses, and many vials. The dawn light was filtering into the cool, clean room through the white curtains. Sebastiana, the baroness's personal maid, was standing at the door, motionless. Dr. Souza Ferreiro examined the patient's back, broken out with a rash of cupping glasses, with eyes that showed that he had gone without sleep all night.

'Well, we'll wait half an hour and then it's a bath and massages for you. You won't deny me the fact that you're feeling better, sir: your color has come back.'

'The bath is ready, and I'll be here if you need me,' Sebastiana said.

'I'm at your service, too,' the baroness chimed in. 'I'll leave you two now. Oh, I almost forgot. I asked Dr. Souza's permission for you to have tea with us, Colonel. My husband wants to pay his respects to you. You're invited too, Doctor. And Captain de Castro, and that very odd young man, what's his name again?'

The colonel did his best to smile at her, but the moment the wife of Baron de Canabrava, followed by Sebastiana, had left the room, he exploded: 'I ought to have you shot, Doctor, for having gotten me caught in this trap.'

'If you fall into a fit of temper, I'll bleed you and you'll be obliged to stay in bed for another day.' Dr. Souza Ferreiro collapsed in a rocking chair, drunk with exhaustion. 'And now allow me to rest too, for half an hour. Kindly don't move.'

In precisely half an hour, he opened his eyes, rubbed them hard, and began to remove the cupping glasses. They came off easily, leaving purplish circles where they had gripped the patient's skin. The colonel lay there face downward, with his head buried in his crossed arms, and barely opened his mouth when Captain Olímpio de Castro entered to give him news of the column. Souza Ferreiro accompanied Moreira César to the bathroom, where Sebastiana had readied everything according to his instructions. The colonel undressed – unlike his deeply tanned face and arms, his little body was very white – climbed straight into the bathtub without a word, and remained in it for a long time, clenching his teeth. Then the doctor massaged him vigorously with alcohol, applied a mustard poultice, and made him inhale the vapor from herbs boiling on a brazier. The entire treatment took place in silence, but once the inhalations were over, the colonel, attempting to relieve the tension in the air, remarked that he had the sensation that he had been subjected to practices of witchcraft. Souza Ferreiro remarked that the borderline separating science from magic was invisible. They had made their peace. Back in the bedroom, a tray with fruit, fresh milk, rolls, ham, and coffee awaited them. Moreira César ate dutifully and then dropped off to sleep. When he awoke, it was midday and the reporter from the *Jornal de Notícias* was standing at his bedside with a pack of cards in his hand, offering to teach him how to play ombre, a game that was all the rage in bohemian circles in Bahia. They played for some time without exchanging a word, until Souza Ferreiro, bathed and freshly shaved, came to tell the colonel that he could get up. When the latter entered the drawing room to have tea with his host and hostess, he found the baron and his wife, the doctor, Captain de Castro, and the journalist, the only one of their number who had not made his toilet since the night before, already gathered there.

Baron de Canabrava came over to shake hands with the colonel. The vast room with a red-and-white-tiled floor was furnished in matching jacaranda pieces, straight-backed wooden chairs with woven straw seats that went by the name of 'Austrian chairs,' little tables with kerosene lamps and photographs, glass cabinets with crystalware and porcelain, and butterflies mounted in velvet-lined cases. The walls were decorated with watercolors showing country scenes. The baron asked how his guest was feeling, and the two of them exchanged the usual polite remarks, a game that the baron was more skilled at than the army officer. The windows, flung open to the twilight, afforded a view of the stone columns at the entrance, a well, and on either side of the esplanade opposite, lined with tamarinds and royal palms, what had once been the slave quarter and was now that of the peons who worked on the hacienda. Sebastiana and a maidservant in a checkered apron busied themselves setting out teapots, cups, sweet biscuits, and cakes. As the baroness recounted to the doctor, the journalist, and Olímpio de Castro how difficult it had been down through the years to transport all the materials and furnishings of this house to Calumbi, the baron showed Moreira César an herbarium, remarking that as a young man he had dreamed of science and of spending his life in laboratories and dissecting rooms. But man proposes and God disposes; in the end he had devoted his life to agriculture, diplomacy, and politics, things which never interested him when he was growing up. And what about the colonel? Had he always wanted to be in the military? Yes, an army career had been his ambition ever since he had reached the age of reason, and perhaps even before, back in the little town in the state of São Paulo where he was born: Pindamonhangaba. The reporter had left the other group and was now standing next to them, brazenly listening in on their conversation. 'It came as a surprise to me to see this young man arriving with you.' The baron smiled, pointing to the nearsighted journalist. 'Has he told you that he once worked for me? At the time he admired Victor Hugo and wanted to be a dramatist. He had a very low opinion of journalism in those days.'

'I still do,' the high-pitched, unpleasant voice said.

'That's an outright lie!' the baron exclaimed. 'The truth is that he has a vocation for gossip, treachery, calumny, the cunning attack. He was my protégé, and when he went over to my adversary's paper, he turned into my most contemptible critic. Be on your guard, Colonel. This man is dangerous.'

The nearsighted journalist was radiant, as though he were being showered with praise.

'All intellectuals are dangerous,' Moreira César replied. 'Weak, sentimental, capable of making use of the best of ideas to justify the worst mischief. The country needs them, but they must be handled like animals that can't be trusted.'

The journalist burst into such delighted laughter that the baroness, the doctor, and the captain looked over at him. Sebastiana was serving the tea.

The baron took Moreira César by the arm and led him to a cabinet. 'I have a present for you. It's the custom here in the *sertão* to offer a present to a guest.' He took out a dusty bottle of cognac and with a sly wink showed him the label. 'I know that you are eager to root out all European influences in Brazil, but I presume that your hatred of all things foreign does not extend to cognac.'

Once they were seated, the baroness handed the colonel a cup of tea and slipped two lumps of sugar into it.

'My rifles are French and my cannons German,' Moreira César said in such a solemn tone of voice that the others broke off their conversation. 'I do not hate Europe, nor do I hate cognac. But since I do not take alcohol, it's best not to waste such a gift on someone who is unable to appreciate it.'

'Keep it as a souvenir, then,' the baroness interjected.

'I hate the local landowners and the English merchants who kept this region in the dark ages,' the colonel went on in an icy voice. 'I hate those to whom sugar meant more than the people of Brazil.'

The baroness went on serving her guests, her face not changing expression.

The master of the house, on the other hand, had stopped smiling. His voice, nonetheless, remained cordial. 'Are the Yankee traders that the South is receiving with open arms interested in the people or only in coffee?' he asked.

Moreira César had a ready answer. 'They bring with them the machines, the technology, and the money that Brazil needs in order to progress. Because progress means industry, work, capital, as the United States has demonstrated.' His cold little eyes blinked as he added: 'That is something that slaveowners will never understand, Baron.'

In the silence that fell after these words, spoons were heard stirring cups, and sips that sounded like gargles as the journalist downed his tea.

'It wasn't the Republic that abolished slavery. It was the monarchy,' the baroness recalled, smiling as though the remark were charmingly witty repartee as she offered her guest sweet biscuits. 'By the way, did you know that on my husband's haciendas the slaves were freed five years before the emancipation decree?'

'No, I didn't know that,' the colonel replied. 'A praiseworthy act, certainly.'

He gave a forced smile and took a sip of tea. The atmosphere was tense now, despite the baroness's smiles and Dr. Souza Ferreiro's sudden interest in the butterfly collection and Captain Olímpio de Castro's story of a Rio barrister who had been murdered by his wife.

The tension mounted further as Souza Ferreiro offered the baron a polite compliment. 'The landowners in these parts are abandoning their estates because the *jagunços* are setting fire to them,' he said. 'You, however, are setting an example by returning to Calumbi.'

'I returned so as to place the hacienda at the disposal of the Seventh Regiment,' the baron replied. 'I regret that my aid has not been accepted.'

'Seeing the peace that reigns here, no one would ever suspect that a war is being waged so close at hand,' Colonel Moreira César murmured. 'The *jagunços* haven't touched you. You're a lucky man.'

'Appearances are deceiving,' the baron answered, his tone of voice still calm. 'Many families at Calumbi have left and the land under cultivation has been reduced by half. Moreover, Canudos is land that belongs to me, is that not so? I've had my share of sacrifices forced upon me – more than anyone else in the region.'

The baron was managing to hide the wrath that the colonel's words no doubt aroused in him, but the baroness had turned into another person when she spoke up again. 'I trust you don't believe all that slander about my husband's having supposedly handed Canudos over to the *jagunços*,' she said, her eyes narrowing in indignation.

The colonel took another sip of tea, neither confirming nor denying her statement.

'So they've persuaded you that that infamous lie is true,' the baron murmured. 'Do you really believe I help mad heretics, arsonists, and thieves who steal haciendas?'

Moreira César sat his cup down on the table. He looked at the baron with an icy gaze and ran his tongue rapidly over his lips. 'Those madmen kill soldiers with explosive bullets,' he said very slowly and deliberately, as though fearing that someone might miss a syllable. 'Those arsonists have very modern rifles. Those thieves receive aid from English agents. Who besides the monarchists would be conspiring to stir up an insurrection against the Republic?' He had turned pale and the little cup began to tremble in his hands. Everyone except the journalist looked down at the floor.

'Those people don't steal or murder or set fires when they feel that order reigns, when they see that the world is organized, because nobody has more respect for hierarchy than they,' the baron said in a firm voice. 'But the Republic destroyed our system through unrealistic laws, substituting unwarranted enthusiasms for the principle of obedience. An error of Marshal Floriano's, Colonel, for the social ideal is rooted in tranquillity, not enthusiasm.'

'Are you feeling ill, sir?' Dr. Souza Ferreiro interrupted him, rising to his feet.

But a look from Moreira César made him keep his distance. The colonel was livid now, his forehead beaded with sweat, his lips purplish, as though he had bitten them. He rose from his chair and addressed the baroness, his voice scarcely more than a mumble: 'I beg you to excuse me, Baroness. I know that my manners leave a great deal to be desired. I come from a humble background and the only social circle I have ever frequented is the barracks room.'

He staggered out of the drawing room, weaving from side to side between the pieces of furniture and the glass cabinets. At his back, the voice of the journalist rudely asked for another cup of tea. He and Olímpio de Castro remained in the room, but the doctor went to see what had happened to the commanding officer of the Seventh Regiment. He found him in bed, panting for breath, in a state of great fatigue. He helped him undress, gave him a sedative, and heard him say that he would rejoin the regiment at dawn the next morning: he would entertain no discussion of the matter. This said, he allowed the doctor to apply the cupping glasses again and plunged once more into a tub of cold water, from which he emerged shivering. Massages with turpentine and mustard warmed him up. He ate in his bedroom, but then got up in his bathrobe and spent a few minutes in the drawing room, thanking the baron and baroness for their hospitality. He awoke at five the following morning. As he drank a cup of coffee, he assured Dr. Souza Ferreiro that he had never felt better in his life and warned the nearsighted journalist, who was just waking up, disheveled and yawning, as he sat at his side, that if there was the least little news item about his illness in any paper, he would hold him responsible. As he was about to leave, a manservant came to tell him that the baron would like him to come by his study. He led him to a small room with a large wooden writing desk on top of which a device for rolling cigarettes occupied the place of honor; on the walls, in addition to shelves lined with books, were knives, whips, leather gloves, and sombreros and harnesses. The room had windows with a view, and in the dawning light the men in the colonel's escort could be seen talking with the journalist from Bahia.

The baron was in his bathrobe and slippers. 'Despite our differences of opinion, I believe you to be a patriot who has Brazil's best interests at heart, Colonel,' he said by way of greeting. 'No, I am not trying to win your sympathies by flattering you. Nor do I wish to waste your time. I need to know whether the army, or at least you yourself, are aware of the underhanded maneuver being used against me and against my friends by our adversaries.'

'The army doesn't interfere in local political quarrels,' Moreira César interrupted him. 'I have come to the state of Bahia to put down an insurrection that is endangering the Republic. That is my sole purpose in coming.'

They were standing very close to each other, looking each other straight in the eye.

'That's precisely what their maneuvering has been aimed at,' the baron said. 'Making Rio, the government, the army believe that this is the danger that Canudos represents. Those miserable wretches don't have any sort of modern weapons. The explosive bullets are limonite projectiles, or brown hematite if you prefer the technical term, a mineral found everywhere in the Serra de Bendengó that the people in the backlands have always used as shotgun pellets.'

'Are the defeats undergone by the army in Uauá and on O Cambaio also a maneuver?' the colonel asked. 'And the rifles shipped from Liverpool and smuggled into the region by English agents?'

The baron scrutinized the officer's fearless face, his hostile eyes, his scornful smile. Was he a cynic? At this point he couldn't tell yet: the only thing that was entirely clear was that Moreira César detested him.

'The English rifles are indeed a part of their scheme,' he answered. 'Epaminondas Gonçalves, your most fervent supporter in Bahia, had them brought here so as to accuse us of conspiring with a foreign power and with the *jagunços*. And as for the English spy in Ipupiará, he manufactured him too, by giving men in his hire orders to kill a poor devil who to his misfortune had red hair. Did you know that?'

Moreira César didn't blink, didn't move a muscle. Nor did he open his mouth. He continued to stare straight back at the baron, a look that told the baron more eloquently than words what he thought of him and of the things he had just said.

'So you do know, you're a co-conspirator and perhaps the Gray Eminence of the entire plot.' The baron averted his eyes and stood for a moment with his head down, as though he were thinking hard, but in truth his mind was a blank. Finally recovering from his daze, he said: 'Do you think all this is worth the trouble? All these lies, these intrigues, all these crimes even, in order to establish the Dictatorial Republic? Do you really believe that something born of all that will be the panacea for Brazil's many ills?'

A few seconds passed without Moreira César's opening his mouth. Outside, a reddish glow heralded the rising of the sun; voices and the whinnying of horses were heard; from upstairs came the sound of shuffling feet.

'There are people up in arms here who are refusing to accept the Republic and have routed two military expeditions,' the colonel said suddenly, his firm, curt, impersonal tone of voice not changing in the slightest. 'Objectively, these people are the instruments of those who, like yourself, have accepted the Republic the better to betray it, to seize the reins of power, and by changing a few names maintain the traditional system. You were well on your way to attaining your goal, I grant you. There is now a civilian president, a party rule that divides and paralyzes the country, a parliament where every effort to change things can be delayed and distorted thanks to the ruses of which you people are past masters. You were already crowing in triumph, isn't that true? There is even talk of reducing the army's troop strength by half, isn't that true? What a victory! Well, you people are mistaken. Brazil will not go on being the fief that you have been exploiting for centuries. That's what the army is for. To bring about national unity, to bring progress, to establish equality among all Brazilians, to create a strong, modern country. We are going to remove the obstacles in the way, I promise you: Canudos, you, the English merchants, whoever blocks our path. I am not going to explain to you what we true republicans mean by a republic. You wouldn't understand, because you belong to the past, you are someone who is looking backward. Don't you realize how ridiculous it is to be a baron when in just four years it will be the beginning of the twentieth century? You and I are mortal enemies, the war between us is without quarter, and we have nothing to say to each other.'

He bowed, turned round, and headed for the door.

'I thank you for your frankness,' the baron murmured. Without moving from where he stood, he saw the colonel leave the study and appear again outside the manor house a few moments later. He saw him mount the white horse that his orderly was holding by the bridle, and, followed by his escort, ride off in a cloud of dust.

IV

The sound of the whistles is like the call of certain birds, an unrhythmic lament that pierces the soldiers' eardrums and embeds itself in their nerves, awakening them at night or taking them by surprise during a march. It is a prelude to death, for it is followed by bullets or arrows that rise with a clean hiss and gleam against the sunlit or star-studded sky before striking their target. The sound of the whistles ceases then and the plaintive moans of wounded cattle, horses, mules, goats, or kids is heard. Sometimes a soldier is hit, but this is exceptional because just as the whistles are destined to assail the ears – the minds, the souls – of the soldiers, so the bullets and arrows stubbornly seek out the animals.

The first two head of cattle that were hit have been enough for the soldiers to discover that these victims are not edible, not even for those who have lived through all the campaigns and learned to eat stones. Those who ate the meat from these cattle began to vomit so badly and to suffer from such severe diarrhea that, even before the doctors rendered their opinion, they had realized that the *jagunços'* arrows killed the animals twice over, first taking their lives and then the possibility of their helping those who were herding them along to survive. From that point on, the moment an animal falls, Major Febrônio de Brito pours kerosene over it and sets fire to it. Grown thinner, suffering from eye irritation, in the few short days since the departure of the column from Queimadas the major has become a bitter, sullen man. Of all those in the column, he is probably the one on whom the whistles wreak their intended effect most successfully, keeping him awake and tormenting him. As his ill luck would have it, he is the one responsible for these quadrupeds that fall amid loud bellows of pain, he is the one who must order them to be given the *coup de grâce* and burned, knowing that these deaths herald future pangs of hunger. He has done everything within his power to minimize the effect of the arrows, sending out men to patrol in circles around the herds and shielding the animals with leather and rawhide coverings, but in the very high summer temperature, this protection makes them sweat, lag behind, and sometimes topple over in the heat. The soldiers have seen the major at the head of the patrols which go out to scour the countryside the moment the symphony begins. These are exhausting, depressing incursions that merely serve to prove how elusive, impalpable, ghost-like the attackers are. The earsplitting racket their whistles make suggests that there are many of them, but that cannot possibly be so, for how in the world could they make themselves invisible in this flat terrain with only sparse vegetation? Colonel Moreira César has given them the explanation: the attackers are divided into very small groups, which hole up in key sites and lie in wait for hours, for days, in caves, crevices, animal lairs, thickets, and the sound of the whistles is deceptively amplified by the astral silence of the countryside they are passing through. This trickery should not distract them; it can have no effect on the column.

And on giving the order to resume their march, after receiving the report on the animals that have been lost, he has remarked: 'That's fine. It lightens our burden, and we'll get there that much sooner.'

His serenity impresses the correspondents, before whom, each time he receives reports of more deaths, he permits himself to make some joking remark. The journalists are more and more nervous in the presence of these adversaries who constantly spy on their movements yet are never seen. It is their one subject of conversation. They besiege the nearsighted reporter from the *Jornal de Notícias*, asking him what the colonel really thinks of this relentless attack on the nerves and reserves of the column, and each time the journalist answers that Moreira César doesn't talk about those arrows or hear those whistles because he is entirely preoccupied, body and soul, by one concern: arriving at

Canudos before the Counselor and the rebels can make their escape. He knows, he is certain, that those arrows and whistles have no other object than to distract the Seventh Regiment so as to give the bandits time to prepare their retreat. But the colonel is a clever officer who does not allow himself to be taken in or lose a single day pointlessly scouring the countryside or turn aside a single millimeter from his planned route. He has told the officers who are worried about future provisions that, from this point of view too, what matters most is getting to Canudos as soon as possible, since the Seventh Regiment will find everything it needs there, in the enemy's storehouses, fields, and stables.

How many times since the regiment began marching again have the correspondents seen a young officer clutching a handful of bloody arrows gallop up to the head of the column to report yet another attack? But this time, at midday, a few hours before the regiment enters Monte Santo, the officer sent by Major Febrônio de Brito brings not only arrows but a whistle and a crossbow as well. The column has halted in a ravine, the men's faces drenched with sweat in the beating sun. Moreira César carefully inspects the crossbow. It is a very primitive type, fashioned of unpolished wood and crudely strung, simple to use. Colonel Tamarindo, Olímpio de Castro, and the correspondents crowd round him. The colonel takes one of the arrows, fits it in the crossbow, shows the journalists how it works. Then he raises the whistle, made of a length of sugarcane with notches cut into it, to his mouth, and all of them hear the lugubrious lament.

Only then does the messenger report the earthshaking news. 'We have two prisoners, sir. One of them is wounded, but the other one is able to talk.'

In the silence that ensues, Moreira César, Tamarindo, and Olímpio de Castro exchange looks. The young officer goes on to explain that three patrols stand ready at all times to scour the countryside the minute the whistles are heard, that two hours before, when the whistling started, the three of them headed off in different directions before the arrows started falling, and that one of them spied the archers just as they slipped away behind some rocks. The patrol had given chase, caught up with them, and tried to take them alive, but one of them attacked and was wounded. Moreira César immediately gallops off in the direction of the rear guard, followed by the correspondents, who are wildly excited at the thought of seeing the enemy's face at last. They are not to see it for some time. When they reach the rear guard an hour later, the prisoners are shut up in a hut guarded by soldiers with fixed bayonets who do not allow them to come anywhere near it. They prowl about the vicinity, watch the officers bustling back and forth, receive evasive answers from those of them who have seen the prisoners. Two or perhaps three hours later Moreira César appears, on his way back to his place at the head of the column. They finally learn a little about what was gone on.

'One of them is in rather bad shape,' the colonel tells them. 'He may not last till we get to Monte Santo. A pity. They should be executed there, so that their death might serve as an example. It would be pointless here.'

When the veteran journalist who always goes about all bundled up as though he were recovering from a cold asks if the prisoners have provided any useful information, the colonel shrugs skeptically. 'The usual rigamarole about God, the Antichrist, the end of the world. They're willing to talk endlessly about all that. But not a word out of them about accomplices or instigators. It may well be that they don't know very much, the poor devils. They belong to a band led by a *cangaceiro* named Pajeú.'

The column immediately marches off again, at a hellish pace, and enters Monte Santo as night is falling. There things take a different turn from what they have in other towns, where the regiment has merely made a rapid search for arms. Here, as the correspondents are still dismounting in the town square beneath the tamarinds, at the foot of the mountainside lined with chapels, surrounded by women, children, and old men with looks in their eyes that they have already learned to recognize – apathetic, mistrustful, distant, stubbornly feigning stupidity and total ignorance of what is going on – they see the troops running, by twos and threes, toward the mud huts and entering them with their rifles at the ready, as though expecting to encounter resistance. Alongside them, in front of them, everywhere, as orders and shouts ring out, the patrols kick in doors and windows and force them open with blows of their rifle butts, and the correspondents soon begin to see lines of townspeople being herded into four enclosures guarded by sentinels. There they are interrogated. From where the journalists are standing they can hear insults, protests, bellows of pain, along with the wails and screams of women outside struggling to get past the sentinels. A few short minutes suffice to turn all of Monte Santo into the scene of a strange battle, without charges or exchanges of fire. Abandoned, without a single officer coming to them to explain what is happening, the correspondents wander aimlessly about the town of calvaries and crosses. They go from one enclosure to another, seeing the same thing in each: lines of men hemmed in by soldiers with bayonets. And from time to time they see a prisoner that they are leading away, pushing and shoving him before them, or are dragging out of a hovel, so battered he can scarcely stand on his feet. The correspondents huddle together, terrified at being caught up in this mechanism relentlessly grinding away round about them, not understanding what is happening but suspecting that it is a consequence of what the two prisoners taken that morning have revealed.

And their suspicions are confirmed by Colonel Moreira César, with whom they are able to speak that same night, after the prisoners have been executed. Before the execution, which takes place under the tamarinds, an officer reads the order of the day that spells out that the Republic is obliged to defend itself against those who, out of cupidity, fanaticism, ignorance, or deliberate deception, rise up against it and serve the appetites of a retrograde caste whose interest it is to keep Brazil in a backward state the better to exploit it. Do the townspeople understand this message? The correspondents intuit that these words, proclaimed in a thundering voice by the town crier, are taken by the silent creatures being held back by the guards as mere sound and fury. Once the execution is over and the townspeople are allowed to approach those whose throats have been slit, the journalists accompany the commanding officer of the Seventh Regiment to the dwelling where he will spend the night. The nearsighted reporter from the *Jornal de Notícias* arranges matters, as usual, so that he may be at his side as he receives the press.

'Was it necessary to turn all of Monte Santo against you with those interrogations?' he asks the colonel.

'They're already enemies, the entire populace is a party to the conspiracy,' Moreira César replies. 'Pajeú, the *cangaceiro*, has passed through here recently, with about fifty men. They were feted and given provisions. Do you correspondents see what I mean? Subversion has sunk deep roots among these wretched people, thanks to ground already fertilized by religious fanaticism.'

He does not appear to be alarmed. Oil lamps, candles, bonfires are burning everywhere, and in the dark shadows patrols of the regiment are prowling about like specters.

'To execute all the accomplices, it would have been necessary to slit the throats of every last person in Monte Santo.' Moreira César has reached a small house where Colonel Tamarindo, Major Cunha Matos, and a group of officers are awaiting him. He dismisses the correspondents with a wave of his hand, turns to a lieutenant, and abruptly changes the subject: 'How many animals are left?'

'Between fifteen and eighteen, sir.'

'We'll offer the troops a feast before the enemy poisons the poor beasts. Tell Febrônio to have them all killed once and for all.' The officer leaves on the run and Moreira César turns to his other junior officers. 'After tomorrow, we'll have to tighten our belts.'

He disappears into the rude dwelling and the correspondents head for the mess hut. There they drink coffee, smoke, exchange impressions, and hear the litanies that are drifting down from the chapels on the mountainside where the townspeople are holding a wake for the two dead men. Later on, they watch as the meat is distributed, see the soldiers dig into this splendid repast with gusto, and hear them begin to play guitars and sing, their spirits lifted. Although the journalists also eat the meat and drink cane brandy, they do not share the euphoria that has taken possession of the soldiers as they celebrate what they believe to be imminent victory. A little while later, Captain Olímpio de Castro comes to ask them if they plan to stay in Monte Santo or go on to Canudos. Those who go on will find it difficult to make their way back, for there will not be another intermediate camp set up.

Of the five, two decide to remain in Monte Santo and another to return to Queimadas, since he is not feeling well. The captain suggests to the two who choose to go on with the regiment – the elderly journalist who goes around all bundled up and the nearsighted one – that they go get some sleep, since from now on there will be forced marches.

The following day, when the two correspondents wake up – it is dawn and cocks are crowing – they are told that Moreira César has already left because there has been an incident in the vanguard: three soldiers have raped an adolescent girl. They depart immediately, with a company under the command of Colonel Tamarindo. When they reach the head of the column, they find that the rapists have been tied to tree trunks, one alongside the other, and are being flogged. One of them roars with pain at each lash of the whip; the second one appears to be praying; and the third one keeps his face set in an arrogant expression as his back grows redder and redder and the blood begins to spurt.

They are in a clearing, surrounded by a thicket of *mandacarus*, *velame*, and *calumbi*. The companies of the vanguard are standing amid the bushes and brambles watching the flogging. An absolute silence reigns among the men, whose eyes never leave those receiving the lashing. The screech of parrots and a woman's sobs break the silence from time to time. The one who is weeping is a young albino girl, slightly deformed, barefoot, with bruises showing through the tears in her garments. No one pays any attention to her, and when the nearsighted journalist asks an official if she is the one who has been raped, he nods. Moreira César is standing next to Major Cunha Matos. His white horse idles about a few yards away, without a saddle, its coat fresh and clean as though it had just been curried.

When the flogging is over, two of the soldiers being punished have fainted, but the third one, the arrogant one, makes a show of coming to attention to listen to the colonel's words.

'May this serve as a lesson to you men,' he shouts. 'The army is and must be the most incorruptible institution of the Republic. All of us, from the highest-ranking officer to the humblest private in the ranks, are obliged to act at all times in such a way that civilians will respect the uniform we wear. You know the tradition of this regiment: misdeeds are punished with the greatest severity. We are here to protect the civilian population, not to rival bandits. The next man guilty of rape will meet with the death penalty.'

There is not a murmur, not a movement in response to his words. The bodies of the two men who have fainted lie in ridiculous, comic postures. The albino girl has stopped weeping. She has a mad look in her eyes and every so often breaks into a smile.

'Give this unfortunate creature something to eat,' Moreira César says, pointing to her. And adds, addressing the journalists who have approached him: 'She's a little touched in the head. Would you say that raping her was setting a good example in the eyes of a populace that is already prejudiced against us? Isn't a thing like this the best way to prove that those who call us the Antichrist are right?'

An orderly saddles the colonel's horse and the clearing resounds with orders, the sound of troops on the move. The companies take off, in different directions.

'The important accomplices are beginning to turn up,' Moreira César says, the rape suddenly forgotten. 'Yes indeed, gentlemen. Do you know who the supplier of Canudos is? The curé of Cumbe, a certain Father Joaquim. The cassock: an ideal safe-conduct pass, an open sesame, an immunity! A Catholic priest, gentlemen!'

The expression on his face is more one of self-satisfaction than of wrath.

The circus people proceeded, amid *macambiras* and across stony ground, taking turns pulling the wagon. The landscape round about was parched now and sometimes they made long days' journeys without a thing to eat. After Sítio das Flores they began to meet pilgrims on their way to Canudos, people more wretched than they, carrying all their possessions on their backs and often dragging the disabled along with them as best they could. Wherever circumstances permitted, the Bearded Lady, the Idiot, and the Dwarf told their fortunes, recited romances, and performed clown acts, but these people on the road had very little to give in return. As rumors were going about that the Bahia Rural Guard in Monte Santo had blocked off the road to Canudos and was conscripting every man of fighting age, they took the longest way round to Cumbe. Every once in a while they spied clouds of smoke; according to what people told them, it was the work of the *jagunços*, who were laying waste to the land so that the armies of the Can would die of hunger. They, too, might be victims of this desolation. The Idiot, grown very feeble, had already lost his laugh and his voice.

They pulled the wagon along two by two; the five of them were a pitiful sight to behold, as though they had endured tremendous sufferings.

Every time it came his turn to be a draft animal, the Dwarf grumbled to the Bearded Lady: 'You know it's madness to go to Canudos and yet we're going. There's nothing to eat and people there are dying of hunger.' He pointed to Gall, his face contorted with anger. 'Why are you listening to him?'

The Dwarf was sweating, and since he was bending over and leaning forward to speak he looked even shorter. How old might he be? He himself didn't know. His face was already beginning to wrinkle; the little humps on his back and chest had become more pronounced now that he was so much thinner.

The Bearded Lady looked at Gall. 'Because he's a real man!'

she exclaimed. 'I'm tired of being surrounded by monsters.'

The Dwarf was overcome by a fit of the giggles. 'And what about you? What are you?' he said, doubling over with laughter. 'Oh, I know the answer to that one. You're a slave. You enjoy obeying a man – him now and the Gypsy before him.'

The Bearded Lady, who had burst out laughing too, tried to slap him, but the Dwarf dodged her. 'You like being a slave,' he shouted. 'He bought you the day he felt your head and told you that you'd have been a perfect mother. You believed it, and your eyes filled with tears.'

He was laughing fit to kill and had to take off at a run so the Bearded Lady wouldn't catch him. She threw stones after him for a while. A few minutes later the Dwarf was back walking at her side again. Their quarrels were always like that, more a game or an unusual way of communicating.

They walked along in silence, with no set system for taking turns pulling the wagon or stopping to rest. They halted when one or another of them was too tired to walk another step, or when they came upon a little stream, a spring, or a shady place where they could spend the hottest hour of the day. As they walked along, they kept a sharp eye out at all times, scanning the environs in search of food, and hence from time to time they had been able to catch game. But this was a rare occurrence, and they had to content themselves with chewing on anything that was green. They looked for *imbuzeiros* in particular, a tree that Galileo Gall had taught them to appreciate: the sweetish, refreshing taste of its juicy roots made it seem like real food.

That afternoon, after Algodões, they met a group of pilgrims who had stopped to rest. They left their wagon and joined them. Most of them were people from the village who had decided to go off to Canudos. They were being led by an apostle, an elderly man dressed in a tunic over trousers and shod in rope sandals. He was wearing an enormous scapular, and the people following him looked at him with timid veneration in their eyes, as though he were someone from another world. Squatting at the man's side, Galileo Gall asked him questions. But the apostle looked at him with a distant gaze, not understanding him, and went on talking with his people. Later on, however, the old man spoke of Canudos, of the Holy Books, and of the prophecies of the Counselor, whom he called a messenger of Jesus. His followers would be restored to life in three months and a day, exactly. The Can's followers, however, would die forever. That was the difference: the difference between life and death, heaven and hell, damnation and salvation. The Antichrist could send soldiers to Canudos: but to what avail? They would rot away, they would disappear forever. Believers too might die, but three months and a day later, they would be back, their bodies whole and their souls purified by the brush of angels' wings and the breath of the Blessed Jesus. Gall gazed at him intently, his eyes gleaming, trying his best not to miss a syllable. As the old man paused for a moment, he said that not only faith, but arms as well, were needed to win wars. Was Canudos able to defend itself against the rich people's army? The pilgrims' heads turned round to see who was speaking and then turned back toward the apostle. Though he had not looked at Gall, the latter had listened. When the war was ended, there would no longer be any rich people, or rather, no one would take any notice of them, because everybody would be rich. These stones would become rivers, these hillsides fertile fields, and the sandy ground of Algodões a garden of orchids like the ones that grow on Monte Santo. Snakes, tarantulas, cougars would be friends of man, as it would be now if Adam had not been driven out of Paradise. The Counselor was in this world to remind people of these truths.

Someone began to weep in the semidarkness, with quiet, heartfelt sobs that continued for a long time. The old man began to speak again, with a sort of tenderness. The spirit was stronger than matter. The spirit was the Blessed Jesus and matter was the Dog. The miracles so long awaited would take place: poverty, sickness, ugliness would disappear. His hands touched the Dwarf, lying curled up next to Galileo. He, too, would be tall and beautiful, like all the others. Now other people could be heard weeping, caught up by the contagious sobs of the first person.

The apostle leaned his head against the body of the disciple closest to him and dropped off to sleep. Little by little, the pilgrims quieted down, and one after the other, they, too, fell asleep. The circus people returned to their wagon. Very soon afterward they heard the Dwarf, who often talked in his sleep, snoring away.

Galileo and Jurema slept apart from the others, on top of the canvas tent that they had not set up since Ipupiará. The moon, full and bright, presided over a cortege of countless stars. The night was cool, clear, without a sound, peopled with the shadows of *mandacarus* and *cajueiros.* Jurema closed her eyes and her breathing grew slow and regular, as Gall, lying alongside her, face up with his hands behind his head, contemplated the sky. It would be stupid to end up in this wasteland without having seen Canudos. It might well be something primitive, naive, contaminated by superstition, but there was no doubt of it: it was also something unusual. A libertarian citadel, without money, without masters, without politics, without priests, without bankers, without landowners, a world built with the faith and the blood of the poorest of the poor. If it endured, the rest would come by itself: religious prejudices, the mirage of the beyond, being obsolete and useless, would fade away. The example would spread, there would be other Canudoses, and who could tell . . . He had begun to smile. He scratched his head. His hair was growing out, long enough now for him to grasp with his fingertips. Going around with a shaved head had left him a prey to anxiety, to sudden rushes of fear. Why? It went back to that time in Barcelona when they were taking care of him so as to garrote him. The sick ward, the madmen of the prison. They had had their heads shaved and been put in straitjackets. The guards were common prisoners; they ate the patients' rations, beat them mercilessly, and delighted in hosing them down with ice-cold water. That was the vision that came to life again each time he caught a glimpse of his head reflected in a mirror, a stream, a well: the vision of those madmen tortured by prison guards and doctors alike. Back then he had written an article that he was proud of: 'Against the Oppression of Illness.' The revolution would not only free man of the yoke of capital and religion, but also of the prejudices that surrounded illnesses in a class society: the patient – above all, the mental patient – was a social victim no less long-suffering and scorned than the worker, the peasant, the prostitute, the servant girl. Hadn't that revered old man said, just tonight, thinking that he was speaking of God when in reality he was speaking of freedom, that in Canudos poverty, sickness, ugliness would disappear? Wasn't that the revolutionary ideal? Jurema's eyes were open and she was watching him. Had he been thinking aloud?

'I would have given anything to be with them when they routed Febrônio de Brito,' he said in a whisper, as though uttering words of love. 'I've spent my life fighting and all I've seen in our camp is betrayals, dissensions, and defeats. I would have liked to see a victory, if only just once. To know what it feels like, what it's really like, what a victory for our side tastes like.'

He saw that Jurema was looking at him as she had at other times, at once aloof and intrigued. They lay there, just a fraction of an inch apart, their bodies not touching. The Dwarf had begun to babble deliriously, in a soft voice.

'You don't understand me and I don't understand you,' Gall said. 'Why didn't you kill me when I was unconscious? Why didn't you convince the *capangas* to take my head away with them instead of just my hair? Why are you with me? You don't believe in the things that I believe in.'

'The person who must kill you is Rufino,' Jurema whispered, with no hatred in her voice, as though she were explaining something very simple. 'By killing you, I would have done a worse thing to him than you did.'

'That's what I don't understand,' Gall thought. They had talked about the same thing before and each time he had ended up as much in the dark as ever. Honor, vengeance, that rigorous religion, those punctilious codes of conduct – how to explain their existence here at the end of the world, among people who possessed nothing but the rags and lice they had on them? Honor, a vow, a man's word, those luxuries and games of the rich, of idlers and parasites – how to understand their existence here? He remembered how, from the window in his room at the boarding house of Our Lady of Grace in Queimadas, he had listened one market day to a wandering minstrel recite a story that, though distorted, was a medieval legend he had read as a child and as a young man seen transformed into a light romantic comedy for the stage: Robert the Devil. How had it gotten here? The world was more unpredictable than it appeared to be.

'I don't understand those *capangas'* reasons for carrying off my hair either,' he murmured. 'That Caifás, I mean. Was he sparing my life so as not to deprive his friend of the pleasure of taking his revenge? That's not the behavior of a peasant. It's the behavior of an aristocrat.'

At other times, Jurema had tried to explain, but tonight she remained silent. Perhaps she was now convinced that this stranger would never understand these things.

The following morning, they took to the road again before the Algodões pilgrims. It took them an entire day to cross the Serra da França, and that night they were so tired and hungry they collapsed. The Idiot fainted twice during the day's journey, and the second time he lay there so pale and still they thought he was dead. At dusk they were rewarded for their hard day by the discovery of a pool of greenish water. Parting the water plants, they drank from it, and the Bearded Lady brought the Idiot a drink in her cupped hands and cooled the cobra by sprinkling it with drops of water. The animal did not suffer from hunger, for they could always find little leaves or a worm or two to feed it. Once they had quenched their thirst, they gathered roots, stems, leaves to eat, and the Dwarf laid traps. The breeze that was blowing was balm after the terrible heat they had endured all day long. The Bearded Lady sat down next to the Idiot and took his head in her lap. The fate of the Idiot, the cobra, and the wagon was as great a concern to her as her own; she seemed to believe that her survival depended on her ability to protect that person, animal, and thing that constituted her world.

Gall, Jurema, and the Dwarf chewed slowly, without gusto,

spitting out the little twigs and roots once they had extracted the juice from them. At the feet of the revolutionary was something hard, lying half buried. Yes, it was a skull, yellowed and broken. Ever since he had been in the backlands, he had seen human bones along the roads. Someone had told him that some men in these parts dug up their enemies' dead bodies and left them lying in the open as food for scavengers, because they believed that by so doing they were sending their souls to hell. He examined the skull, turning it this way and that in his hands.

'To my father, heads were books, mirrors,' he said nostalgically. 'What would he think if he knew that I was here in this place, in the state that I'm in? The last time I saw him, I was seventeen years old. I disappointed him by telling him that action was more important than science. He was a rebel, too, though in his own way. Doctors made fun of him, and called him a sorcerer.'

The Dwarf looked at him, trying to understand, as did Jurema. Gall went on chewing and spitting, his face pensive.

'Why did you come here?' the Dwarf murmured. 'Aren't you afraid of dying so far from your homeland? You have no family here, no friends. Nobody will remember you.'

'You're my family,' Gall answered. 'And the *jagunços*, too.'

'You're not a saint, you don't pray, you don't talk about God,' the Dwarf said. 'Why are you so set on getting to Canudos?'

'I couldn't live among foreigners,' Jurema said. 'If you don't have a fatherland, you're an orphan.'

'Someday the word "fatherland" is going to disappear,' Galileo immediately replied. 'People will look back on us, shut up within frontiers, killing each other over lines on a map, and they'll say: How stupid they were.'

The Dwarf and Jurema looked at each other and Gall had the feeling that they were thinking he was the one who was stupid. They chewed and spat, grimacing in disgust every so often.

'Do you believe what the apostle from Algodões said?' the Dwarf asked. 'That one day there'll be a world without evil, without sicknesses . . .'

'And without ugliness,' Gall added. He nodded his head several times. 'I believe in that the way other people believe in God. For a long time now, a lot of people have given their lives so that that might be possible. That's why I'm so doggedly determined to get to Canudos. Up there, in the very worst of cases, I'll die for something that's worth dying for.'

'You're going to get killed by Rufino,' Jurema muttered, staring at the ground. Her voice rose: 'Do you think he's forgotten the affront to his honor? He's searching for us and sooner or later he'll take his revenge.'

Gall seized her by the arm. 'You're staying with me so as to see that revenge, isn't that true?' he asked her. He shrugged. 'Rufino couldn't understand either. It wasn't my intention to offend him. Desire sweeps everything before it: force of will, friendship. We've no control over it, it's in our bones, in what other people call our souls.' He brought his face close to Jurema's again. 'I have no regrets, it was . . . instructive. What I believed was false. Carnal pleasure is not at odds with the ideal. We mustn't be ashamed of the body, do you understand? No, you don't understand.'

'In other words, it might be true?' the Dwarf interrupted, his voice breaking and an imploring look in his eyes. 'People say that he's made the blind see and the deaf hear, closed the wounds of lepers. If I say to him: "I've come because I know you'll work the miracle," will he touch me and make me grow?'

Gall looked at him, disconcerted, and found no truth or lie to offer him in reply. At that moment the Bearded Lady burst into tears, out of pity for the Idiot. 'He hasn't an ounce of strength left,' she said. 'He's not smiling any more, or complaining, he's just dying little little, second by second.' They heard her weeping like that for a long time before falling asleep. At dawn, they were awakened by a family from Carnaíba, who passed some bad news on to them. Rural Police patrols and *capangas* in the hire of hacienda owners in the region were blocking the entrances and exits of Cumbe, waiting for the arrival of the army. The only way to reach Canudos now was to turn north and make a long detour by way of Massacará, Angico, and Rosário.

A day and a half later they arrived in Santo Antônio, a tiny spa on the banks of the greenish Massacará. The circus people had been in the town, years before, and remembered how many people came to cure their skin diseases in the bubbling, fetid mineral springs. Santo Antônio had also been the constant victim of attacks by bandits, who came to rob the sick people. Today it appeared to be deserted. They did not come across a single washerwoman down by the river, and in the narrow cobblestone streets lined with coconut palms, ficus, and cactus there was not a living creature – human, dog, or bird – to be seen. Despite this, the Dwarf's mood had suddenly brightened. He grabbed a cornet, put it to his lips and produced a comic blare, and began his spiel about the performance they would give. The Bearded Lady burst out laughing, and even the Idiot, weak as he was, tried to push the wagon along faster, with his shoulders, his hands, his head; his mouth was gaping open and long trickles of saliva were dribbling out of it. They finally spied an ugly, misshapen little old man who was fastening an eyebolt to a door. He looked at them as though he didn't see them, but when the Bearded Lady threw him a kiss he smiled.

The circus people parked the wagon in a little square with climbing vines; doors and windows started flying open and faces of the townspeople, attracted by the blaring of the cornet, began peeking out of them. The Dwarf, the Bearded Lady, and the Idiot rummaged through their bits of cloth and odds and ends, and a moment later they were busily daubing paint on their faces, blackening them, decking themselves out in bright costumes, and in their hands there appeared the last few remains of a set of props: the cobra cage, hoops, magic wands, a paper concertina. The Dwarf blew furiously into his cornet and shouted: 'The show is about to begin!' Gradually, an audience straight out of a nightmare began to crowd round them. Human skeletons, of indefinable age and sex, most of them with faces, arms, and legs pitted with gangrene sores, abscesses, rashes, pockmarks, came out of the dwellings, and overcoming their initial apprehension, leaning on each other, crawling on all fours, or dragging themselves along, came to swell the circle. 'They don't look like people who are dying,' Gall thought. 'They look like people who've been dead for some time.' All of them, the children in particular, seemed very old. Some of them smiled at the Bearded Lady, who was coiling the cobra round her, kissing it on the mouth, and making it writhe in and out of her arms. The Dwarf grabbed the Idiot and mimicked the number that the Bearded Lady was performing with the snake: he made him dance, contort himself, tie himself in knots. The townspeople and the sick of Santo Antônio watched, grave-faced or smiling, nodding their heads in approval and bursting into applause now and again. Some of them turned around to look at Gall and Jurema, as though wondering when they would put on their act. The revolutionary watched them, fascinated, as Jurema's face contorted in a grimace of repulsion. She did her best to contain her feelings, but soon she whispered that she couldn't bear the sight of them and wanted to leave. Galileo did not calm her down. His eyes had begun to redden and he was deeply shaken. Health, like love, like wealth and power, was selfish: it shut one up within oneself, it abolished all thought of others. Yes, it was better not to have anything, not to love, but how to give up one's health in order to be as one with those brothers who were ill? There were so many problems, the hydra had so many heads, iniquity raised its head everywhere one looked.

He noticed then how repelled and frightened Jurema was, and took her by the arm. 'Look at them, look at them,' he said feverishly, indignantly. 'Look at the women. They were young, strong, pretty once. Who turned them into what they are today? God? No: scoundrels, evildoers, the rich, the healthy, the selfish, the powerful.'

With a look of feverish excitement on his face, he let go of Jurema's arm and strode to the center of the circle, not even noticing that the Dwarf had begun to tell the strange story of Princess Maguelone, the daughter of the King of Naples. The spectators saw the man with reddish fuzz on his scalp and a red beard, a scar on his neck, and ragged pants begin to wave his arms wildly.

'Don't lose your courage, my brothers, don't give in to despair! You are not rotting away here in this life because a ghost hidden behind the clouds has so decided, but because society is evil. You are in the state you are because you have nothing to eat, because you don't have doctors or medicine, because no one takes care of you, because you are poor. Your sickness is called injustice, abuse, exploitation. Do not resign yourselves, my brothers. From the depths of your misery, rebel, as your brothers in Canudos have done. Occupy the lands, the houses, take possession of the goods of those who have stolen your youth, who have stolen your health, your humanity . . .'

The Bearded Lady did not allow him to go on. Her face congested with rage, she shook him and screamed at him: 'You stupid fool! You stupid fool! Nobody's listening to you! You're making them sad, you're boring them, they won't give us money to eat on! Feel their heads, predict their future – do something that'll make them happy!'

His eyes still closed, the Little Blessed One heard the cock crow and thought: 'Praised be the Blessed Jesus.' Without moving, he prayed and asked the Father for strength for the day. The intense activity was almost too much for his frail body: in recent days, what with the ever-increasing numbers of pilgrims pouring in, he sometimes had attacks of vertigo. At night when he collapsed on his straw mattress behind the altar of the Chapel of Santo Antônio, his bones and muscles ached so badly that the pain made rest impossible; he would sometimes lie there for hours, with his teeth clenched, before sleep freed him from this secret torture.

Because, despite being frail, the Little Blessed One had so strong a spirit that nobody noticed the weakness of his body, in this city in which, after the Counselor, he exercised the highest spiritual functions.

He opened his eyes. The cock had crowed again, and the light of dawn appeared through the skylight. He slept in the tunic that Maria Quadrado and the women of the Sacred Choir had mended countless times. He put on his rope sandals, kissed the scapular and the emblem of the Sacred Heart that he wore on his breast, and girded tightly about his waist the length of wire, long since rusted, that the Counselor had given him when he was still a child, back in Pombal. He rolled up the straw mattress and went to awaken the sacristan and sexton who slept at the entrance to the church. He was an old man from Chorrochó; on opening his eyes, he murmured: 'Praised be Our Lord Jesus Christ.' 'Praised be He,' the Little Blessed One replied, and handed him the whip with which each morning he offered the sacrifice of his pain to the Father. The old man took the whip – the Little Blessed One had knelt – and gave him ten lashes, on the back and the buttocks, with all his strength. The Little Blessed One received them without a single moan. The two of them crossed themselves again. Thus the day's tasks began.

As the sacristan went to tidy the altar, the Little Blessed One headed for the door. On drawing near it, he sensed the presence of the pilgrims who had arrived in Belo Monte during the night. The men of the Catholic Guard had undoubtedly been keeping close watch on them until he could decide whether they might stay or were unworthy of so doing. The fear that he might make a mistake, refusing a good Christian or admitting someone whose presence might cause harm to the Counselor, sorely troubled his heart; it was one of those things for which he implored the Father's help with the most anguish. He opened the door and heard a murmur of voices and saw the dozens of creatures camped in front of the portal. Circulating among them were members of the Catholic Guard, with rifles and blue armbands or kerchiefs, who on catching sight of him said in chorus: 'Praised be the Blessed Jesus.' 'Praised be He,' the Little Blessed One answered softly. The pilgrims crossed themselves, and those who were not crippled or ill rose to their feet. There was hunger and happiness in their eyes. The Little Blessed One estimated that there were at least fifty of them.

'Welcome to Belo Monte, the land of the Father and of the Blessed Jesus,' he intoned. 'The Counselor asks two things of those who come in answer to the call: faith and truth. There is no place for unbelievers or liars in this land of the Lord.'

He told the Catholic Guard to begin letting them in. In bygone days, he conversed with each pilgrim, one by one; nowadays he was obliged to speak with them in groups. The Counselor did not want anyone to lend him a hand. 'It is you who are the door, Little Blessed One,' he would answer each time that the latter asked that someone be appointed to share this responsibility.

A blind man, his daughter and her husband, and two of their children entered. They had come from Quererá, a journey that had taken them a month. On the way the husband's mother and the couple's twin sons had died. Had they given them a Christian burial? Yes, in coffins and with the prayer for the dead. As the old man with eyelids glued shut told him about their journey, the Little Blessed One observed them. He remarked to himself that they were a united family in which there was respect for one's elders, for the other four listened to the blind man without interrupting him, nodding their heads to confirm what he was saying. The five faces showed signs of that mixture of fatigue from hunger and physical suffering and that soul's rejoicing that came over pilgrims as they set foot on Belo Monte. Feeling the brush of the angel's wing, the Little Blessed One decided that they were welcome. He nonetheless asked if any one of them ever served the Antichrist. After having them repeat after him the oath whereby they swore that they were not republicans, did not accept the expulsion of the Emperor, nor the separation of Church and State, nor civil marriage, nor the new system of weights and measures, nor the census questions, he embraced them and sent them with a member of the Catholic Guard to Antônio Vilanova's. At the door, the woman whispered something in the blind man's ear, and in fear and trembling he asked when they would see Blessed Jesus the Counselor. The family awaited his answer with such anxiety that the Little Blessed One thought to himself: 'They are elect.' They would see him that evening, in the Temple; they would hear him give counsel and tell them that the Father was happy to receive them into the flock. He saw them leave, giddy with joy. The presence of grace in this world doomed to perdition was purifying. These new residents – the Little Blessed One knew for certain – had already forgotten their three dead and their tribulations and were feeling that life was worth living. Antônio Vilanova would now register their names in his ledgers, and would then send the blind man to a Health House, the woman to help the Sardelinha sisters, and the husband and children out to work as water carriers.

As he listened to another couple – the woman had a bundle in her arms – the Little Blessed One's thoughts dwelt on Antônio Vilanova. He was a man of faith, an elect, one of the Father's sheep. He and his brother were people with schooling, they had had various businesses, cattle, money; they might have devoted their lives to accumulating wealth and acquiring houses, lands, servants. But they had chosen instead to serve God alongside their humble brothers. Was it not a gift from the Father to have someone like Antônio Vilanova here, a man thanks to whose wisdom so many problems were solved? He had just organized the distribution of water, for instance. It was collected from the Vaza-Barris and the reservoirs of the Fazenda Velha and then brought round to the dwellings free of charge. The water carriers were recently arrived pilgrims; in this way, people got to know them, felt they were of service to the Counselor and the Blessed Jesus, and gave them food.

The Little Blessed One finally pieced together, from the man's torrent of words, that the bundle was a newborn baby girl, who had died the evening before as they were coming down the Serra da Canabrava. He raised the bit of cloth and looked: the little body was rigid, the color of parchment. He explained to the woman that it was a blessing from heaven that her daughter had died on the only piece of earth in this world that remained free of the Devil. They had not baptized her, and the Little Blessed One now did so, naming her Maria Eufrásia and praying to the Father to take this little soul to His Glory. He had the couple repeat the oath and sent them to the Vilanovas to arrange for their daughter's burial. Because of the scarcity of wood, burials had become a problem in Belo Monte. A shiver ran up his spine. That was the most terrifying thing he could think of: his body buried in a grave with no coffin to protect it.

As he spoke with more pilgrims, one of the women of the Sacred Choir entered to tidy the chapel and Alexandrinha Correa brought him a little earthenware bowl accompanied by a message from Maria Quadrado: 'For you alone to eat,' because the Mother of Men knew that he was in the habit of giving his rations to those who were starving. As he listened to the pilgrims, the Little Blessed One thanked God for having given him strength of soul such that he never felt the pangs of hunger or thirst: a few sips of water, a mouthful of food sufficed; not even during the pilgrimage through the desert had he suffered the torments of near-starvation that other brothers and sisters had. It was for that reason that only the Counselor had offered up more fasts than he to the Blessed Jesus. Alexandrinha Correa also told him that Abbot João, Big João, and Antônio Vilanova were waiting for him in the Sanctuary.

He remained in the chapel for almost two hours more to receive pilgrims, only one of whom was not granted permission to stay, a grain merchant from Pedrinhas who had been a tax collector. He did not reject former soldiers, guides, or purveyors for the army. But tax gatherers were to depart immediately, never to return, under threat of death. They had bled the poor white, seized their harvests and sold them off, stolen their animals; their greed was implacable, and they risked being the worm that spoils the fruit. The Little Blessed One explained to the man from Pedrinhas that in order to obtain heaven's mercy he must fight the Can, somewhere far away, on his own. After sending word to the pilgrims outside to wait for him, he headed for the Sanctuary. It was mid-morning now, and the bright sunlight made the stones shimmer. Many people tried to detain him, but he explained in gestures that he was in a hurry. He was escorted by members of the Catholic Guard. In the beginning he had refused an escort, but now he realized that one was indispensable. Without these brothers, making his way across the few yards that separated the chapel and the Sanctuary would have taken him hours because of the number of people who assailed him with requests or insisted on having a word with him. As he walked along, the thought came to him that among this morning's pilgrims were some who had come from as far away as Alagoas and Ceará. Wasn't that extraordinary? The crowd that had gathered around the Sanctuary was so dense – people of all ages craning their necks toward the little wooden door where, at one moment of the day or another, the Counselor would appear – that he and the four members of the Catholic Guard were trapped. They waved their bits of blue cloth then and their comrades on duty at the Sanctuary cleared a path for the Little Blessed One. As he walked with hunched shoulders down this narrow passage lined with bodies, he told himself that without the Catholic Guard chaos would have descended upon Belo Monte: that would have been the gate through which the Dog would have entered.

'Praised be Our Lord Jesus Christ,' he said, and heard in answer: 'Praised be He.' He was immediately aware of the peace that the Counselor created round about himself. Even the din outside became music here.

'I'm ashamed at having made you wait for me, Father,' he muttered. 'More and more pilgrims keep pouring in, so many I can't speak with them or remember their faces.'

'All of them have a right to salvation,' the Counselor said. 'Rejoice for them.'

'My heart rejoices to see that there are more and more of them each day,' the Little Blessed One said. 'It's myself I'm angry at, because I can't find the time to get to know them well.'

He sat down on the floor, between Abbot João and Big João, who were holding their carbines across their knees. Besides Antônio Vilanova, his brother Honório was there too, apparently just back from a journey, to judge from the dust he was covered with. Maria Quadrado handed him a glass of water and he drank it down slowly, savoring every drop. Enveloped in his dark purple tunic, the Counselor was sitting, very erect, on his pallet, and at his feet was the Lion of Natuba, his pencil and notebook in his hands, his huge head resting on the saint's knees; one of the latter's hands was buried in his coal-black, tangled hair. The women of the Choir were squatting on their heels along the wall, silent and motionless, and the little white lamb was sleeping. 'He is the Counselor, the Master, the Comely One, the Beloved,' the Little Blessed One thought with fervor. 'We are his children. We were nothing and he made us apostles.' He felt a rush of happiness: again the angel's wing brushing him.

He realized that there was a difference of opinion between Abbot João and Antônio Vilanova. The latter was saying that he was opposed to burning Calumbi, as Abbot João wanted to do, that it would be Belo Monte and not the Evil One who would suffer the consequences if the Baron de Canabrava's hacienda disappeared, since it was their best source of supplies. He spoke as though he were afraid of hurting someone's feelings or of uttering such serious thoughts aloud, in so soft a voice that the Little Blessed One had to strain his ears to hear him. How unquestionably supernatural the Counselor's aura was if a man like Antônio Vilanova was so diffident in his presence, he thought. In everyday life, the storekeeper was a force of nature, whose energy was overpowering and whose opinions were expressed with a conviction that was contagious. And that booming-voiced stentor, that tireless worker, that fountainhead of ideas, became as a little child before the Counselor. 'He's not distressed, though; he's feeling the balm.' Antônio had told him so himself many times in the past, as they had walked and talked together after the counsels. Antônio wanted to know everything about the Counselor, the story of his wanderings, the teachings that he had spread, and the Little Blessed One enlightened him. He thought with nostalgia of those first days in Belo Monte, of the sense of freedom and openness to others that had been lost. He and the shopkeeper used to chat together every day, walking from one end of Canudos to the other, in the days when it was still small and not yet populated. Antônio Vilanova bared his heart to him, revealing how the Counselor had changed his life.

'I was always upset, with my nerves constantly on edge and the sensation that my head was about to explode. Now, just knowing that he's close at hand is enough to make me feel a serenity I've never felt before. It's a balm, Little Blessed One.' But they could no longer have long talks together, for both of them were now enslaved by their respective responsibilities. Thy will be done, Father.

He had been so lost in memories he hadn't even noticed when Antônio Vilanova stopped speaking. Abbot João was now answering him. The news was definite and Pajeú had confirmed it: the Baron de Canabrava was in the service of the Antichrist, he was ordering the landowners to supply the army with *capangas*, provisions, guides, horses, and mules, and Calumbi was being turned into a military camp. The baron's hacienda was the richest, the largest, the one with the best-stocked storehouses, able to provision ten armies. It was necessary to raze it, to leave nothing that could be of use to the Can's troops; otherwise, it would be much more difficult to defend Belo Monte when they arrived. Abbot João stood there with his eyes fixed on the Counselor's lips; Antônio Vilanova did likewise. There was no need to discuss the matter further: the saint would know if Calumbi should be saved or go up in flames. Despite their disagreement – the Little Blessed One had seen the two men argue many times – their feeling of brotherhood would be undiminished. But before the Counselor could open his mouth, there was a knock on the door of the Sanctuary. It was armed men, coming from Cumbe. Abbot João went to see what news they were bringing.

When he had left, Antônio Vilanova began to speak again, though this time it was about the deaths in Belo Monte. With the flood of pilgrims arriving, the number of dead had increased, and the old cemetery, behind the churches, had almost no room left for any more graves. He had therefore sent people out to clear and wall in a plot of ground in O Taboleirinho, between Canudos and O Cambaio, so as to start a new one. Did the Counselor approve? The saint gave a brief nod. As Big João, waving his huge hands, perturbed, his kinky hair gleaming with sweat, was recounting how the Catholic Guard had begun the day before to dig a trench with a double parapet of stones which would run from the banks of the Vaza-Barris to the Fazenda Velha, Abbot João returned. Even the Lion of Natuba raised his huge head and his inquisitive eyes.

'The army troops arrived in Cumbe at dawn this morning. They were asking about Father Joaquim as they came into town, and went looking for him. It would seem that they've slit his throat.'

The Little Blessed One heard a sob, but he did not look around: he knew that it was Alexandrinha Correa. The others did not look at her either, despite the fact that her sobs grew deeper and deeper, till the sound of them filled the Sanctuary.

The Counselor had not moved. 'We shall now pray for Father Joaquim,' he said in a tender voice. 'He is with the Father now. He will continue to help us there, even more than in this world. Let us rejoice for him and for ourselves. Death is a fiesta for the just man.'

As he knelt, the Little Blessed One was filled with envy for the parish priest of Cumbe, safe now from the Can up there in that privileged place that only the martyrs of the Blessed Jesus enter.

Rufino reaches Cumbe at the same time as two army patrols, who behave as though the townspeople were the enemy. They search the houses, strike with their rifle butts anyone who protests, post an order promising death to anyone who conceals firearms, and proclaim it with a rolling of drums. They are looking for the parish priest. Rufino is told that they finally located him, that they had no scruples about entering the church and dragging him out by brute force. After going all about Cumbe asking after the circus people, Rufino finds lodgings for the night in the house of a brick maker. The family comments on the searches, the mistreatment, but they are even more deeply shocked by the sacrilege: invading the church and striking a minister of God! What people are saying must be true then: those wicked men are the Can's servants.

Rufino leaves the town convinced that the stranger has not passed by way of Cumbe. Can he perhaps be in Canudos? Or in the hands of the soldiers? He is about to be taken prisoner at a barricade set up by the Rural Police to block off the road to Canudos. Several of them recognize him and intercede with the others on his behalf: after a time they let him continue on his way. He heads north via a shortcut, and after walking only a little way, he hears a rifle report. He realizes from the dust suddenly raised at his feet that they are shooting at him. He throws himself on the ground, crawls along, locates his attackers: two guards crouching on a rise. They shout to him to throw down his carbine and knife. He leaps up and runs as fast as he can in a zigzag line toward a dead angle. He arrives at this safe spot unhurt, and from there manages to put distance between himself and the guards by darting from rock to rock. But he loses his bearings, and when he is certain that he is no longer being followed, he lies down to rest. He is so exhausted that he sleeps like a log. The sun puts him on the right track to Canudos. Groups of pilgrims flowing in from all directions flock down the muddy trail that a few years before was used only by droves of cattle and poverty-stricken traders. At nightfall, camping among pilgrims, he hears a little old man covered with boils who has come from Santo Antônio tell about a circus show he has seen there. Rufino's heart pounds madly. He lets the old man talk without interrupting him and a moment later he knows that he has picked up the trail.

He arrives in Santo Antônio in the dark and sits down alongside one of the pools along the banks of the Massacará to wait for daylight. He is so impatient he is unable to think. With the sun's first rays, he begins to go from one little house to the next, all of them identical. Most of them are empty. The first villager he comes across shows him where to go. He enters a dark, foul-smelling interior and halts till his eyes adjust to the dim light. He begins to make out the walls, with lines and scrawls and a Sacred Heart of Jesus scratched on them. There are no pictures or furniture, not even an oil lamp, but there is something like a lingering memory of these things that the occupants have carried away with them.

The woman is lying on the floor and sits up on seeing him enter. Round about her are bits of colored cloth, a wicker basket, and a brazier. In her lap is something that he has difficulty recognizing. Yes, it's the head of a snake. The tracker now notices the fuzz that darkens the woman's face and arms. Between her and the wall is someone lying stretched out; he can see half the person's body and his or her feet. He catches a glimpse of the grief that fills the eyes of the Bearded Lady. He bends down and respectfully asks her about the circus. She continues to look at him without seeing him, and finally, dejectedly, she hands him the cobra: he can have it to eat if he likes. Squatting on his heels, Rufino explains to her that he hasn't come to take food away from her but to find out something. The Bearded Lady talks to him about the dead one. He'd been dying by inches and the night before he breathed his last. He listens to her, nodding. She reproaches herself, she is filled with remorse, perhaps she should have killed Idílica before and given her to him to eat. If she'd done that, would it have saved him? She herself says no. The cobra and the dead man had shared her life ever since the beginnings of the circus. Memory brings back to Rufino images of the Gypsy, of Pedrim the Giant, and other performers he saw as a child in Calumbi. The woman has heard that if dead people aren't buried in a coffin they go to hell; this fills her with anguish. Rufino offers to make a coffin and dig a grave for her friend. She asks him point-blank what he wants. His voice trembling, Rufino tells her. The stranger? the Bearded Lady repeats. Galileo Gall? Yes, him. Some men on horseback took him away as they were leaving the village. And she speaks again of the dead man, she couldn't drag him any farther, it was too hard, she'd decided she'd rather stay behind and care for him. Were they soldiers? Rural Police? Bandits? She doesn't know. The ones who cut off his hair in Ipupiará? No, it wasn't the same ones. Were they looking for him? Yes, they didn't bother the circus people. Did they go off in the direction of Canudos? She doesn't know that, either.

Rufino uses the boards over the window to prepare the deceased for burial, tying them around with the bright-colored bits of cloth. He hoists the dubious coffin onto his shoulder and goes outside, followed by the woman. Some villagers show him the way to the cemetery and lend him a shovel. He digs a grave, places the coffin in it and fills it up again, and remains there while the Bearded Lady prays. On returning to the little settlement, she thanks him effusively. Rufino, who has been standing staring into the distance, asks her: Did they also take the woman with them? The Bearded Lady blinks. You're Rufino, she says. He nods. She tells him that Jurema knew he'd be coming. Did they take her away with them, too? No, she went off with the Dwarf, heading for Canudos. A group of sick people and healthy townspeople overhear the conversation and are amused. Rufino is so exhausted he begins to stagger. He is offered hospitality and agrees to go rest in the house that the Bearded Lady is occupying. He sleeps till nightfall. When he wakes up, a man and wife bring him a bowl with a thick substance in it. He has a conversation with them about the war and the upheavals all over the world. When the man and woman leave, he asks the Bearded Lady about Galileo and Jurema. She tells him what she knows and informs him that she, too, is going to Canudos. Isn't she afraid she's entering the lion's den? She is more afraid of being all by herself; up there she'll perhaps meet up with the Dwarf again and they can go on keeping each other company.

The following morning, they bid each other goodbye. The tracker takes off toward the west, since the villagers assure him that that was the way the *capangas* were headed. He makes his way amid bushes, thorns, and thickets and in the middle of the morning he dodges a patrol of scouts who are combing the scrub. He halts often to examine the animal tracks on the ground. He captures no game that day and is obliged to chew on bits of greenery. He spends the night in Riacho de Varginha. Shortly after resuming his journey the next morning, he spies the army of Throat-Slitter, the name that is on everyone's lips. He sees the troops' bayonets gleaming in the dust, hears the creaking of gun carriages rolling along the trail. He breaks into his little trot again but does not enter Zélia till after dark. The villagers tell him that not only have the soldiers passed that way but Pajeú's *jagunços* as well. Nobody, however, remembers having seen a party of *capangas* who have anybody who looks like Gall with them. Rufino hears the cane whistles keening in the distance; they hoot intermittently all night long.

Between Zélia and Monte Santo the terrain is flat, dry, strewn with sharp stones, and without trails. Rufino makes his way cautiously, fearing that he may meet up with a patrol at any moment. He finds water and food at mid-morning. Shortly thereafter, he has the feeling that he is not alone. He looks about, inspects the scrub, walks back and forth: nothing. A while later, however, there is no doubting the fact: he is being watched, by several men. He tries to shake them, changes direction, hides, runs. Useless: they are trackers who know their business and they are still there, invisible and very close by. He walks on resignedly, taking no precautions now, hoping that they'll kill him. A few minutes later, he hears a herd of goats bleating. He finally comes upon a clearing. Before he spies the armed men, he sees the young girl: an albino, deformed, with a mad look in her eyes. Dark bruises show through her ripped garments. She is playing with a handful of animal bells and a cane whistle of the sort that shepherds use to guide their flocks. The men, some twenty of them, allow him to approach them, not saying a word to him. They look more like peasants than *cangaceiros*, but they have machetes, carbines, bandoleers, knives, powder horns. When Rufino reaches them, one of them walks toward the girl, smiling so as not to frighten her. Her eyes open wide and she sits there stock-still. Making gestures the while to reassure her, he takes the little bells and the whistle from her and joins his comrades again. Rufino sees that all of them are wearing little bells and whistles around their necks.

They are sitting more or less in a circle eating. They do not appear to be at all surprised by his arrival, as though they were expecting him. The tracker raises his hand to his straw sombrero:

'Good afternoon.' Some of the men go on eating, others nod, and one of them murmurs with his mouth full: 'Praised be the Blessed Jesus.' He is a husky Indian half-breed with an olive complexion and a scar that has left him with almost no nose at all. 'That's Pajeú,' Rufino thinks. 'He's going to kill me.' This makes him feel sad, for he'll die without having struck in the face the man who dishonored him. Pajeú begins to question him. Without animosity, without even asking him to hand over his weapons: where he's from, who he is working for, where he's going, whom he's seen. Rufino answers without hesitation, falling silent only when he is interrupted by another question. The other men go on eating; only when Rufino explains what it is he's looking for and why, do they turn their heads and scrutinize him from head to foot. Pajeú makes him say again how many times he has guided the flying brigades that hunt down *cangaceiros,* to see if he'll contradict himself. But since Rufino has decided from the beginning to tell the truth, he doesn't give any wrong answers. Did he know that one of those flying brigades was hunting for Pajeú? Yes, he knew that. The former outlaw then says that he remembers that brigade led by Captain Geraldo Macedo, Bandit-Chaser, because he had a hard time shaking it. 'You were a good tracker,' he says. 'I still am,' Rufino answers. 'But your trackers are better. I couldn't get rid of them.' From time to time a silent figure emerges from the brush, comes over to Pajeú to tell him something, and then melts back into the brush like a ghost. Without becoming impatient, without asking what his fate is to be, Rufino watches them finish eating. The *jagunços* rise to their feet, bury the coals of their fire, rub out the traces of their presence with *icó* branches. Pajeú looks at him. 'Don't you want to save your soul?' he asks him. 'I must save my honor first,' Rufino answers. No one laughs. Pajeú hesitates for a few seconds. 'The stranger you're looking for has been taken to Calumbi, to the Baron de Canabrava's,' he mutters. The next moment he rides off with his men. Rufino sees the albino girl, still sitting on the ground, and two black vultures at the top of an *imbuzeiro,* clearing their throats like hoarse old men.

He leaves the clearing immediately and walks on, but before half an hour has gone by, a paralysis overtakes his body, an utter exhaustion that causes him to collapse on the spot. When he awakens, his face, neck, and arms are full of insect bites. For the first time since leaving Queimadas, he feels bitterly discouraged, convinced that what he is doing is all in vain. He sets out again, in the opposite direction. But now, despite the fact that he is passing through an area that he has been back and forth across countless times since the day when he first learned to walk, in which he knows where all the shortcuts are and where to look for water and which are the best places to set traps, the day's journey seems interminable and at each and every moment he must fight off his feeling of dejection. Very often, something that he has dreamed that afternoon comes back to him again: the earth is a thin crust that may split open and swallow him up at any moment. He cautiously fords the river just before Monte Santo, and from there it takes him less than ten hours to reach Calumbi. All through the night, he has not stopped to rest, and at times he has broken into a run. As he crosses the hacienda on which he was born and spent his childhood, he does not notice how overgrown with weeds the fields are, how few people are about, the general state of deterioration. He meets a few peons who greet him, but he does not return their greetings or answer their questions. None of them bars his way and a few of them follow him at a distance.

On the terrace surrounding the manor house, beneath the imperial palms and the tamarinds, in addition to peons going back and forth to the stables, storehouses, and servants' quarters, there are armed men. The blinds at the window are lowered. Rufino walks slowly toward the *capangas*, watching them carefully. Without any sort of order, without a word to each other, they step forward to meet him. There are no shouts, no threats, not even an exchange of questions and answers between them and Rufino. When the tracker reaches them, they take hold of him and pin his arms down. They do not hit him or take his carbine or his machete or his knife away from him, and try not to be brutal with him. They simply block his way. At the same time, they clap him on the back, say hello to him, tell him not to be pigheaded and to listen to reason. The tracker's face is drenched with sweat. He does not hit them either, but he tries to get away. When he gets loose from two of them and takes a step forward, two others immediately force him to step back. This sort of game goes on for quite some time. Rufino finally gives up and hangs his head. The men let go of him. He looks at the two-story building, the round roof tiles, the window of the baron's study. He takes a step forward and immediately the men bar his way again.

The door of the manor house opens and someone he knows comes out: Aristarco, the overseer, the one who gives the *capangas* their orders. 'If you want to see the baron, he'll receive you this minute,' he says to him amicably.

Rufino's chest heaves. 'Is he going to hand the stranger over to me?'

Aristarco shakes his head. 'He's going to hand him over to the army. The army will avenge you.'

'That guy's mine,' Rufino murmurs. 'The baron knows that.'

'He's not yours to kill, and the baron's not going to hand him over to you,' Aristarco repeats. 'Do you want him to explain to you himself?'

His face livid, Rufino answers no. The veins at his temples and neck have swelled, his eyes are bulging, and he is sweating heavily. 'Tell the baron he's not my godfather any more,' he says, his voice breaking. 'And tell that other one that I'm going off to kill the woman he stole from me.'

He spits, turns around, and walks off the way he came.

Through the window of the study, the Baron de Canabrava and Galileo Gall saw Rufino leave and the guards and peons return to their places. Galileo had bathed and been given a shirt and a pair of trousers in better condition than the ones he had on. The baron went back over to his desk, beneath a collection of knives and whips hanging on the wall. There was a cup of steaming-hot coffee on it and he took a sip, with a faraway look in his eye. Then he examined Gall once again, like an entomologist fascinated by a rare species. He had been scrutinizing Gall in that way ever since he had seen him being brought into his study, worn out and famished, by Aristarco and his *capangas*, and, more intently still, ever since he had first heard him speak.

'Would you have ordered them to kill Rufino?' Gall asked, in English. 'If he had insisted on coming inside, if he had become insolent? Yes, I'm certain of it, you'd have ordered him killed.'

'One can't kill dead men, Mr. Gall,' the baron answered. 'Rufino is already dead. You killed him when you stole Jurema from him. If I had ordered him killed I'd have been doing him a favor. I'd have freed him of the anguish of having been dishonored. There is no worse torment for a *sertanejo*.'

He opened a box of cigars and as he lighted one he imagined a headline in the *Jornal de Notícias:* ENGLISH AGENT GUIDED BY BARON'S HENCHMAN. It had been a clever plan to have Rufino serve Gall as a guide: what better proof that he, the baron, was a co-conspirator of the foreigner's?

'The only thing I didn't understand was what pretext Epaminondas had used to attract the supposed agent to the backlands,' he said, moving his fingers as though he had cramps in them. 'It never entered my head that heaven might favor him by putting an idealist in his hands. A strange breed, idealists. I've never met one before, and now, in the space of just a few days, I've had dealings with two of them. The other one is Colonel Moreira César. Yes, he too is a dreamer. Though his dreams and yours don't coincide . . .'

A great commotion outside interrupted him. He went to the window, and through the little squares of the metal grille he saw that it wasn't Rufino who'd come back, but four men with carbines who had arrived and been surrounded by Aristarco and the *capangas*. 'It's Pajeú, from Canudos,' he heard Gall say – that man who was either his prisoner or his guest, though even he himself couldn't say which. He looked closely at the newcomers. Three of them were standing there not saying a word, while the fourth was speaking with Aristarco. He was a *caboclo*, short, heavyset, no longer young, with skin like rawhide. He had a scar all the way across his face: yes, it might be Pajeú. Aristarco nodded several times, and the baron saw him head toward the house.

'This is an eventful day,' he murmured, puffing on his cigar.

Aristarco's face had the same inscrutable expression as always, but the baron could nonetheless tell how alarmed he was.

'Pajeú,' he said laconically. 'He wants to talk to you.'

Instead of answering, the baron turned to Gall. 'I would like you to leave me now, if you will. I'll see you at dinnertime. We eat early here in the country. At six.'

When Gall had left the room, the baron asked the overseer if only those four men had come. No, there were at least fifty *jagunços* round about outside the house. Was he certain that the *caboclo* was Pajeú? Yes.

'What will happen if they attack Calumbi?' the baron asked. 'Can we hold out?'

'We may get ourselves killed,' the *capanga* replied, as though he had asked himself the same question and arrived at that answer. 'There are lots of the men I don't trust any more. They, too, may go off to Canudos at any moment.'

The baron sighed. 'Bring him inside,' he said. 'And I'd like you to be present at this meeting.'

Aristarco went outside and came back a moment later with the newcomer. The *caboclo* from Canudos halted a yard away from the master of the house, removing his hat as he did so. The baron tried to see some hint in those stubborn little eyes, in those weather-beaten features, of the crimes and terrible misdeeds he was said to have committed. The cruel scar, which might have been left by a bullet, a knife, or the claw of a great wild feline, was a reminder of the violent life he had led. Apart from that, he might easily be taken for a peon on his land. But when his peons raised their eyes to his, they always blinked and lowered them. Pajeú's eyes stared straight into his, without humility.

'You're Pajeú?' he finally asked.

'I am,' the man said.

Aristarco was standing behind him, as motionless as a statue.

'You've wreaked as much havoc in these parts as the drought,' the baron said, 'with your robbing and killing and marauding.'

'Those days are past now,' Pajeú answered, without resentment, with heartfelt contrition. 'There are sins I've committed in my life that I will one day be held accountable for. It's not the Can I serve now but the Father.'

The baron recognized that tone of voice; it was that of the Capuchin Fathers of the Sacred Missions, that of the sanctimonious wandering sects who made pilgrimages to Monte Santo, that of Moreira César, that of Galileo Gall. The tone of absolute certainty, he thought, the tone of those who are never assailed by doubts. And suddenly, for the first time, he was curious to hear the Counselor, that individual capable of turning a ruffian into a fanatic.

'Why have you come here?'

'To burn Calumbi down,' the even voice replied.

'To burn Calumbi down?' Stupefaction changed the baron's expression, voice, posture.

'To purify it. After so much hard labor, this earth deserves a rest,' the *caboclo* explained, speaking very slowly.

Aristarco hadn't moved and the baron, who had recovered his self-possession, looked closely at the former *cangaceiro* in the same way that, in quieter days, he had so often examined the butterflies and plants in his herbarium with the aid of a magnifying glass. He was suddenly moved by the desire to penetrate to the innermost depths of this man, to know the secret roots of what he was saying. And at the same time there came to his mind's eye the image of Sebastiana brushing Estela's fair hair amid a circle of flames. The color drained from his face.

'Doesn't that wretch of a Counselor realize what he's doing?' He did his best to contain his indignation. 'Doesn't he see that haciendas burned down mean hunger and death for hundreds of families? Doesn't he realize that such madness has brought war to the state of Bahia?'

'It's in the Bible,' Pajeú explained imperturbably. 'The Republic will come, and the Throat-Slitter: there will be a cataclysm. But the poor will be saved, thanks to Belo Monte.'

'Have you even read the Bible?' the baron murmured.

'The Counselor has read it,' the *caboclo* answered. 'You and your family can leave. The Throat-Slitter has been here and taken guides and livestock off with him. Calumbi is accursed; it has gone over to the Can's side.'

'I will not allow you to raze the hacienda,' the baron said. 'Not only on my account, but on account of the hundreds of people whose survival depends on this land.'

'The Blessed Jesus will take better care of them than you,' Pajeú answered. It was evident that he meant no offense; he was making every effort to speak in a respectful tone of voice; he appeared to be disconcerted by the baron's inability to accept the obvious truth. 'When you leave, everyone will go off to Belo Monte.'

'And in the meanwhile Moreira César will have it wiped off the face of the earth,' the baron said. 'Can't you understand that shotguns and knives are no defense against an army?'

No, he would never understand. It was as useless to try to reason with him as it was to argue with Moreira César or Gall. The baron felt a shiver down his spine; it was as if the world had taken leave of its reason and blind, irrational beliefs had taken over.

'Is that what happens when you people are sent food, livestock, loads of grain?' he asked. 'The agreement with Antônio Vilanova was that you wouldn't touch Calumbi or harm my people. Is that the way the Counselor keeps his word?'

'He is obliged to obey the Father,' Pajeú explained.

'In other words, it's God who ordered you to burn down my house?' the baron murmured.

'No, the Father,' the *caboclo* corrected him vehemently, as if to avoid a very serious misunderstanding. 'The Counselor doesn't want to cause you or your family any harm. All those who wish to do so may leave.'

'That's very kind of you,' the baron answered sarcastically. 'I won't let you burn down this house. I won't leave.'

A shadow veiled the half-breed's eyes and the scar across his face contracted. 'If you don't leave, I'll be forced to attack and kill people whose lives could be spared,' he explained regretfully. 'I'll have to kill you and your family. I don't want all those deaths hanging over my soul. What's more, there'd be hardly anybody left to put up a fight.' His hand pointed behind him. 'Ask Aristarco.'

He waited, his eyes pleading for a reassuring answer.

'Can you give me a week?' the baron finally murmured. 'I can't leave . . .'

'A day,' Pajeú interrupted him. 'You may take whatever you like with you. I can't wait any longer than that. The Dog is on his way to Belo Monte, and I must be there, too.' He put his sombrero back on, turned around, and, with his back to him, added as his parting words as he went out the door, followed by Aristarco: 'Praised be the Blessed Jesus.'

The baron noted that his cigar had gone out. He brushed off the ash, relighted it, and calculated as he puffed on it that there was no possibility of his asking Moreira César to come to his aid within the time limit given him by Pajeú. Then, fatalistically – he too, when all was said and done, was a *sertanejo* – he asked himself how Estela would take the destruction of this house and this land to which their lives were so closely tied.

Half an hour later he was in the dining room, with Estela at his right and Galileo at his left, the three of them seated in the high-backed 'Austrian' chairs. Though darkness had not yet fallen, the servants had lighted the lamps. He watched Gall: he was spooning food into his mouth with no sign of enjoyment and had the usual tormented expression on his face. The baron had told him that if he so desired he could go outside to stretch his legs, but except for the moments he spent conversing with him, Gall had stayed in his room – the same one that Moreira César had occupied – busy writing. The baron had asked him for a written statement of everything that had happened to him since his meeting with Epaminondas Gonçalves. 'If I do what you ask, will I be free again?' Gall had asked him. The baron shook his head. 'You're the best weapon I have against my enemies.' The revolutionary hadn't said another word and the baron doubted that he was writing the confession he had asked him for. What could he be scribbling, then, night and day? In the midst of his depression, he was curious.

'An idealist?' Gall's voice took him by surprise. 'A man reputed to have committed so many atrocities?'

The baron realized that without warning the Scotsman was resuming the conversation they had been having in his study.

'Does it strike you as odd that Colonel Moreira César is an idealist?' he replied, in English. 'He is one, there's no doubt of that. He's not interested in money or honors, and perhaps not even in power for himself. It's abstract things that motivate him to act: an unhealthy nationalism, the worship of technical progress, the belief that only the army can impose order and save this country from chaos and corruption. An idealist of the same stamp as Robespierre . . .'

He fell silent as a servant cleared the table. He toyed with his napkin, thinking that the next night would find everything that surrounded him reduced to rubble and ashes. For the space of an instant, he wished that a miracle would occur, that the army of his enemy Moreira César would suddenly appear at Calumbi and prevent that crime from happening.

'As is the case with many idealists, he is implacable when it comes to realizing his dreams,' he added without his expression betraying what his real feelings were. His wife and Gall looked at him. 'Do you know what he did at the Fortress of Anhato Mirim, at the time of the federalist revolt against Marshal Floriano? He executed one hundred eighty-five people. They had surrendered, but that made no difference to him. He wanted the mass execution to serve as an example.'

'He slit their throats,' the baroness said. She spoke English without the baron's easy command of the language, slowly, pronouncing each syllable cautiously. 'Do you know what the peasants call him? Throat-Slitter.'

The baron gave a little laugh; he was looking down at the plate that had just been served him without seeing it. 'Just think what's going to happen when that idealist has the monarchist, Anglophile insurgents of Canudos at his mercy,' he said in a gloomy voice. 'He knows that they're really neither one, but it's useful to the Jacobin cause if that's what they are, which amounts to the same thing. And why is he doing what he's doing? For the good of Brazil, naturally. And he believes with all his heart and soul that that's so.'

He swallowed with difficulty and thought of the flames that would destroy Calumbi. He could see them devouring everything, could hear them crackling.

'I know those poor devils in Canudos very well,' he said, feeling his palms grow moist. 'They're ignorant and superstitious, and a charlatan can convince them that the end of the world has come. But they're also courageous, long-suffering people, with an unfailing, instinctive dignity. Isn't it an absurd situation? They're going to be put to death for being monarchists and Anglophiles, when the truth of the matter is that they confuse the Emperor Pedro II with one of the apostles, have no idea where England is, and are waiting for King Dom Sebastião to emerge from the bottom of the sea to defend them.'

He raised the fork to his lips again and swallowed a mouthful of food that seemed to him to taste of soot. 'Moreira César said that one must be mistrustful of intellectuals,' he added. 'Even more than of idealists, Mr. Gall.'

The latter's voice reached his ears as though it were coming from very far away. 'Let me leave for Canudos.' A rapt expression had come over his face, his eyes were gleaming, and he appeared to be deeply moved. 'I want to die for what is best in me, for what I believe in, for what I've fought for. I don't want to end my days a stupid idiot. Those poor devils represent the most worthy thing there is on this earth, suffering that rises up in rebellion. Despite the abyss that separates us, you can understand me.'

The baroness gestured to the servant to clear the table and leave the room.

'I'm of no use to you at all,' Gall added. 'I'm naïve perhaps, but I'm not a braggart. What I'm saying isn't blackmail but a fact. It won't get you anywhere to hand me over to the authorities, to the army. I won't say one word. And I'll lie if I have to; I'll swear that I've been paid by you to accuse Epaminondas Gonçalves of something he didn't do. Because, even though he's a rat and you're a gentleman, I'll always prefer a Jacobin to a monarchist. We're enemies, Baron, and you'd best not forget it.'

The baroness made a move to leave the table.

'You needn't go.' The baron stopped her. He was listening to Gall, but all he could think about was the fire that would burn down Calumbi. How was he going to tell Estela?

'Let me leave for Canudos,' Gall repeated.

'But whatever for?' the baroness exclaimed. 'The *jagunços* will take you for an enemy and kill you. Haven't you said that you're an atheist, an anarchist? What does all that have to do with Canudos?'

'The *jagunços* and I have many things in common, Baroness, even though they don't know it,' Gall answered. He fell silent for a moment and then asked: 'May I leave?'

Without realizing it, the baron switched to Portuguese as he addressed his wife. 'We must leave here, Estela. They're going to burn Calumbi down. There's nothing else we can do. I don't have the men to put up a fight and it's not worth committing suicide over losing it.' He saw his wife sitting there stock-still, becoming paler and paler, biting her lips. He thought that she was about to faint. He turned to Gall. 'As you can see, Estela and I have a very serious matter that we must discuss. I'll come up to your room later.'

Gall went upstairs immediately. The master and mistress of Calumbi remained in the dining room, in silence. The baroness waited, not opening her mouth. The baron told her of his conversation with Pajeú. He noted that she was trying her best to appear calm, but was not succeeding very well: she was deathly pale, and trembling. He had always loved her very deeply, and what was more, in moments of crisis he had admired her. He had never seen her lose her courage; behind that delicate appearance of a porcelain doll was a strong woman. The thought came to him that this time, too, she would be his best defense against adversity. He explained to her that they could take almost nothing with them, that they must put all their most precious things in trunks and bury them, that it was best to divide everything else among the house servants and the peons.

'Is there nothing that can be done, then?' the baroness said very softly, as though some enemy might overhear.

The baron shook his head: nothing. 'In reality they're not out to do us harm but to kill the Devil and give the land a rest. There's no reasoning with them.' He shrugged, and as he felt that he was about to be overcome with emotion, he put an end to the conversation. 'We'll leave tomorrow, at noon. That's the time limit they've given me.'

The baroness nodded. Her face was drawn now, her forehead furrowed in a worried frown, her teeth chattering. 'Well then, we shall have to work all night long,' she said, rising to her feet.

The baron saw her leave the room and knew that before doing anything else she had gone off to tell Sebastiana everything. He sent for Aristarco and discussed the preparations for the journey with him. Then he shut himself up in his study and spent a long time destroying notebooks, papers, letters. The things that he would take with him filled no more than two small valises. As he went up to Gall's room, he saw that Sebastiana and Estela had already gone to work. The house was caught up in feverish activity, with maids and menservants rushing all about, carrying things here and there, taking things down from walls, filling baskets, boxes, trunks, and whispering together with panicked expressions on their faces. He entered Gall's room without bothering to knock, and found him sitting writing at the bedside table; on hearing him come into the room, Gall looked up, pen still in hand, and gazed at him with questioning eyes.

'I know it's madness to allow you to leave,' the baron said with a half smile that was really a grimace. 'What I should do is parade you through the streets of Salvador, of Rio, the way they paraded your hair, your fake corpse, the fake English rifles . . .' Too dispirited to go on, he did not finish the sentence.

'Make no mistake about it,' Galileo said. He and the baron were so close now their knees were touching. 'I'm not going to help you solve your problems; I'll never collaborate with you. We're at war, and every weapon counts.'

There was no hostility in his voice, and the baron looked at him as though he were already far away: a tiny figure, picturesque, harmless, absurd.

'Every weapon counts,' he repeated softly. 'That is a precise definition of the times we're living in, of the twentieth century that will soon be upon us, Mr. Gall. I'm not surprised that those madmen think that the end of the world has come.'

He saw so much anguish in the Scotsman's face that he suddenly felt pity for him. He thought: 'The one thing he really wants to do is go die like a dog among people who don't understand him and whom he doesn't understand. He thinks that he's going to die like a hero, and the truth is that he's going to die exactly as he fears he will: like an idiot.' The whole world suddenly seemed to him to be the victim of an irremediable misunderstanding.

'You may leave,' he said to him. 'I'll provide you with a guide to take you there. Though I doubt that you'll get as far as Canudos.'

He saw Gall's face light up and heard him stammer his thanks.

'I don't know why I'm letting you go,' he added. 'I'm fascinated by idealists, even though I don't share their feelings in the slightest. But, even so, perhaps I do feel a certain sympathy for you, inasmuch as you're a man who is irredeemably lost, and your end will be the result of an error.'

But he realized that Gall was not listening to him. He was gathering together the pages filled with his handwriting that lay on the bedside table, and held them out to him. 'They're a summary of what I am, of what I think.' The look in his eyes, his hands, his very skin seemed to quiver with excitement. 'You may not be the best person to leave it with, but there's nobody else around. Read it, and when you've finished, I'd be grateful to you if you'd send it on to this address in Lyons. It's a review, published by friends of mine. I don't know if it's going to continue to come out . . .' He fell silent, as though overcome with shame for some reason or other. 'When may I leave?' he asked.

'This very minute,' the baron answered. 'I needn't warn you of the risk you're taking, I presume. It's more than likely that you'll fall into the army's hands. And in any event, the colonel will kill you.'

'One can't kill dead men, sir, as you yourself said,' Gall answered. 'I've already been killed in Ipupiará, remember . . .'

V

The group of men advance across the stretch of sand, their eyes riveted on the brush. There is hope in their faces, though not in that of the nearsighted journalist who has been thinking ever since they left camp: 'This is going to be useless.' He has not said a word that would reveal the feeling of defeatism against which he has been fighting ever since their water was rationed. The meager food is not a hardship for him, since he never feels hungry. Thirst, on the other hand, is difficult for him to endure. Every so often he finds himself counting the time he must wait till he takes the next sip of water, in accordance with the rigid schedule he has set for himself. Perhaps that is why he has chosen to go out with Captain Olímpio de Castro's patrol. The sensible thing to do would have been to take advantage of the hours in camp and rest. This scouting excursion is certain to tire him, poor horseman that he is, and naturally it is going to make him thirstier. But if he stayed behind there in the camp, he'd be overcome with anxiety, filled with gloomy thoughts. Here at least he is obliged to concentrate on his arduous struggle not to fall off his horse. He knows that among themselves the soldiers poke fun at his eyeglasses, his dress, his appearance, his portable writing desk, his inkwell. But this does not bother him.

The guide who is leading the patrol points to the water well. The expression on the man's face suffices for the journalist to realize that this well, too, has been filled in by the *jagunços*. The soldiers hurry over to it with their canteens, pushing and shoving; he hears the sound of the tin hitting the stones at the bottom and sees how disappointed, how bitter the men are. What is he doing here? Why isn't he back in his untidy little house in Salvador, surrounded by his books, smoking a pipeful of opium, feeling its great peace steal over him?

'Well, this was only to be expected,' Captain Olímpio de Castro murmurs. 'How many other wells are there in the vicinity?'

'Only two that we haven't been to yet.' The guide gestures skeptically. 'I don't think it's worth the trouble seeing if there's water in them.'

'Go take a look anyway,' the captain interrupts him. 'And the patrol is to be back before dark, Sergeant.'

The officer and the journalist accompany the patrol for a time, and once they have left the thicket far behind and are again out on the bare sun-baked mesa they hear the guide murmur that the Counselor's prophecy is coming true: the Blessed Jesus will trace a circle round about Canudos, beyond which all animal, vegetable, and, finally, human life will disappear.

'If you believe that, what are you doing here with us?' Olímpio de Castro asks him.

The guide raises his hand to his throat. 'I'm more afraid of the Throat-Slitter than I am of the Can.'

Some of the soldiers laugh. The captain and the journalist part company with the patrol. They gallop along for a while, until the officer, taking pity on his companion, slows his horse to a walk. Feeling relieved, the journalist takes a sip of water from his canteen despite his timetable. Three-quarters of an hour later they catch sight of the camp.

They have just passed the first sentinel when the dust raised by another patrol coming from the north overtakes them. The lieutenant in command, a very young man, covered with dust from head to foot, has a happy look on his face.

'Well, then?' Olímpio de Castro greets him. 'Did you find him?'

The lieutenant points to him with his chin. The nearsighted journalist spies the prisoner. His hands are bound together, he has a terrified expression on his face, and the long, tattered garment he is dressed in must have been his cassock. He is a short-statured, robust little man with a potbelly and white locks at his temples. His eyes gaze about in all directions. The patrol proceeds on its way, followed by the captain and the journalist. When it reaches the tent of the commanding officer of the Seventh Regiment, two soldiers shake the prisoner down. His arrival causes a great commotion and many soldiers approach to have a better look at him. The little man's teeth chatter and he looks about in panic, as though fearing that he will be beaten. The lieutenant pushes him inside the tent and the journalist slips in behind the others.

'Mission accomplished, sir,' the young officer says, clicking his heels.

Moreira César rises to his feet from behind a folding table, where he is sitting between Colonel Tamarindo and Major Cunha Matos. He walks over to the prisoner and his cold little eyes look him over from head to foot. His face betrays no emotion, but the nearsighted journalist notices that he is biting his lower lip, as is his habit whenever he is taken by surprise.

'Good show, Lieutenant,' he says, extending his hand. 'Go take a rest now.'

The nearsighted journalist sees the colonel's eyes meet his for the space of an instant and fears that he will order him to leave. But he does not do so.

Moreira César slowly studies the prisoner. They are very nearly the same height, though the colonel is much thinner. 'You're half dead with fear.'

'Yes, sir, I am,' the prisoner stammers. He is trembling so

badly he can scarcely speak. 'I've been badly mistreated. My office as a priest . . .'

'Has not prevented you from placing yourself in the service of the enemies of your country,' the colonel silences him, pacing back and forth in front of the curé of Cumbe, who has lowered his head.

'I am a peace-loving man, sir,' he moans.

'No, you're an enemy of the Republic, in the service of a monarchist insurrection and a foreign power.'

'A foreign power?' Father Joaquim stammers, so stupefied that he forgets how terrified he is.

'In your case, I shall not allow you to use superstition as an excuse,' Moreira César adds in a soft voice, his hands behind his back. 'All that foolishness about the end of the world, about God and the Devil.'

Those present watch, without a word, as the colonel paces back and forth. The nearsighted journalist feels the itch at the end of his nose that precedes a sneeze, and for some reason this alarms him.

'Your fear tells me that you know what's going on, my good man,' Moreira César says in a harsh tone of voice. 'And it so happens that we have ways of making the bravest *jagunços* talk. So don't make us waste time.'

'I have nothing to hide,' the parish priest stammers, beginning to tremble once more. 'I don't know if I've done the right thing or the wrong thing, I'm all confused . . .'

'In particular, the relations with conspirators outside,' the colonel interrupts him, and the nearsighted journalist notes that the officer is nervously twining and untwining his fingers behind his back. 'Landowners, politicians, military advisers, either native or English.'

'English?' the priest exclaims, completely taken aback. 'I never saw a foreigner in Canudos, only the poorest and humblest people. What landowner or politician would ever set foot amid all that wretchedness? I assure you, sir. There are people who have come from a long way away, I grant you. From Pernambuco, from O Piauí. That's one of the things that amazes me. How so many people have been able . . .'

'How many?' the colonel interrupts him, and the little parish priest gives a start.

'Thousands,' he murmurs. 'Five thousand, eight thousand, I couldn't say. The poorest of the poor, the most helpless. And I know whereof I speak, for I've seen endless misery hereabouts, what with the drought, the epidemics. But it's as though those worst off had agreed to congregate up there, as though God had gathered them together. The sick, the infirm, all the people with no hope left, living up there, one on top of the other. Wasn't it my obligation as a priest to be there with them?'

'It has always been the policy of the Catholic Church to be where it believes it to be to its advantage to be,' Moreira César answers. 'Was it your bishop who ordered you to aid the rebels?'

'And yet, despite their misery, those people are happy,' Father Joaquim stammers, as though he hadn't heard the question. His eyes fly back and forth between Moreira César, Tamarindo, and Cunha Matos. 'The happiest people I've ever seen, sir. It's difficult to grant that, even for me. But it's true, absolutely true. He's given them a peace of mind, a resigned acceptance of privations, of suffering, that is simply miraculous.'

'Let's discuss the explosive bullets,' Moreira César says. 'They penetrate the body and then burst like a grenade, making wounds like craters. The army doctors had never seen wounds like that in Brazil. Where do those bullets come from? Are they some sort of miracle, too?'

'I don't know anything about arms,' Father Joaquim stammers. 'You don't believe it, but it's true, sir. I swear it, by the habit I wear. Something extraordinary is happening up there. Those people are living in the grace of God.'

The colonel gives him a sarcastic look. But there in his corner, the nearsighted journalist has forgotten how thirsty he is and is hanging on the parish priest's every word, as though what he is saying is a matter of life and death to him.

'Saints, the just, people straight out of the Bible, the elect of

God? Is that what you're expecting me to swallow?' the colonel says. 'Those people who burn down haciendas, murder people, and call the Republic the Antichrist?'

'I haven't made myself clear, sir,' the prisoner says in a shrill voice. 'They've committed terrible deeds, certainly. But . . .'

'But you're their accomplice,' the colonel mutters. 'What other priests are helping them?'

'It's difficult to explain.' The curé of Cumbe hangs his head. 'In the beginning, I went up there to say Mass for them, and I had never seen such fervor, such participation. The faith of those people is incredible, sir. Wouldn't it have been a sin for me to turn my back on them? That's why I continued to go up there, even though the archbishop had forbidden it. Wouldn't it have been a sin to deprive the most wholehearted believers I've ever seen of the sacraments? Religion is everything in life to them. I'm baring my conscience to you. I know that I am not worthy of being a priest, sir.'

The nearsighted journalist suddenly wishes he had his portable writing desk, his pen, his inkwell, his paper with him.

'I had a woman who cohabited with me,' the parish priest of Cumbe stammers. 'I lived like a married man for many years. I have children, sir.'

He stands there with his head hanging down, trembling, and undoubtedly, the nearsighted journalist thinks to himself, he does not notice Major Cunha Matos's little snicker. And undoubtedly, he also thinks to himself, his face is beet-red with shame beneath the crust of dirt on it.

'The fact that a priest has children isn't going to keep me awake nights,' Moreira César says. 'On the other hand, the fact that the Catholic Church is with the insurgents may cause me a good many sleepless nights. What other priests are helping Canudos?'

'And he taught me a lesson,' Father Joaquim says. 'When I saw how he was able to give up everything, to devote his entire life to the spirit, to what is most important. Shouldn't God, the soul, be what comes first?'

'The Counselor?' Moreira César asks sarcastically. 'A saint, no doubt?'

'I don't know, sir,' the prisoner says. 'I've been asking myself that every day of my life, since the very first moment I saw him come into Cumbe, many years ago now. A madman, I thought at the beginning – just as the Church hierarchy did. The archbishop sent some Capuchin friars to look into the matter. They didn't understand at all, they were frightened, they, too, said he was crazy. But then how do you explain what's happened, sir? All those conversions, that peace of mind, the happiness of so many wretched people?'

'And how do you explain the crimes, the destruction of property, the attacks on the army?' the colonel interrupts him.

'I agree, I agree, there's no excuse for them,' Father Joaquim concedes. 'But they don't realize what they're doing. That is to say, they're crimes that they commit in good faith. For the love of God, sir. It's admittedly all very confused in their minds.'

He looks all around in terror, as though he has just said something that may lead to tragedy.

'Who put the idea into those wretches' heads that the Republic is the Antichrist? Who turned all that wild religious nonsense into a military movement against the regime? That's what I'd like to know, padre.' Moreira César's voice is sharp and shrill now. 'Who enlisted those people in the service of the politicians whose aim is to restore the monarchy in Brazil?'

'They aren't politicians. They don't know anything at all about politics,' Father Joaquim squeaks. 'They're against civil marriage; that's what the talk about the Antichrist is about. They're pure Christians, sir. They can't understand why there should be such a thing as civil marriage when a sacrament created by God already exists . . .'

But at that point he gives a little groan and suddenly falls silent, for Moreira César has taken his pistol out of its holster. He calmly releases the safety catch and points the gun at the prisoner's temple. The nearsighted journalist's heart is pounding like a bass drum and he is trying so hard not to sneeze that his temples ache.

'Don't kill me! Don't kill me, in the name of what you hold dearest, sir, Colonel, Your Excellency!' He has dropped to his knees.

'Despite my warning, you're wasting our time, padre,' the colonel says.

'It's true: I brought them medicines, supplies, things they'd asked me to bring up to them,' Father Joaquim whimpers. 'And explosives, gunpowder, sticks of dynamite, too. I bought them for them at the mines in Caçabu. It was doubtless a mistake. I don't know, sir, I wasn't thinking. They cause me such uneasiness, such envy, on account of that faith, that peace of mind that I've never known. Don't kill me.'

'Who are the people who are helping them?' the colonel asks. 'Who's giving them arms, supplies, money?'

'I don't know who they are, I don't know,' the priest moans. 'I do know, that is to say, that it's lots of landowners. It's the custom, sir – like with the bandits. To give them something so they won't attack, so they move on to other people's land.'

'Do they also receive help from the Baron de Canabrava's hacienda?' Moreira César interrupts him.

'Yes, I suppose they get things from Calumbi, too, sir. It's always been the custom. But that's changed now that so many people have left. I've never seen a landowner or a politician or a foreigner in Canudos. Just poor people. I'm telling you everything I know. I'm not like them. I don't want to be a martyr; don't kill me.'

His voice breaks and he bursts into sobs, his shoulders sagging.

'There's paper over there on that table,' Moreira César says. 'I want a detailed map of Canudos. Streets, entrances into the town, how and where it's defended.'

'Yes, yes.' Father Joaquim crawls over to the little camp table. 'Everything I know. I have no reason to lie to you.'

He climbs up onto the chair and begins to draw. Moreira César, Tamarindo, and Cunha Matos stand around him. Over in his corner, the correspondent from the *Jornal de Notícias* feels relieved. He is not going to see the little priest's head blown off. He gazes at the curé's anxious profile as he draws the map they've asked him for. He hears him hasten to answer questions about trenches, traps, blocked streets. The nearsighted journalist sits down on the floor and sneezes, two, three, ten times. His head is spinning and he is beginning to feel unbearably thirsty again. The colonel and the other officers are talking with the prisoner about 'nests of sharpshooters' and 'outposts' – the latter does not appear to have a very good idea of what they are – and he unscrews his canteen and takes a long swallow, thinking to himself that he has failed once again to stick to his schedule. Distracted, dazed, uninterested, he hears the officers discussing the vague information that the priest is giving them, and the colonel explaining where the machine guns and the cannons will be placed, and how the regimental companies must be deployed in order to close in on the *jagunços* in a pincers movement. He hears him say, 'We must leave them no avenue of escape.'

The interrogation is over. Two soldiers enter to take the prisoner away. Before he leaves, Moreira César says to him, 'Since you know this region, you will help the guides. And you will help us identify the ringleaders when the time comes.'

'I thought you were going to kill him,' the nearsighted journalist pipes up from where he is sitting on the floor, once the priest has been led away.

The colonel looks at him as though he had not noticed his presence in the room until that very moment. 'That priest will be useful to us in Canudos,' he answers. 'Moreover, it will be worthwhile to let the word get around that the Church's adherence to the Republic is not as sincere as some people believe.'

The nearsighted journalist leaves the tent. Night has fallen, and the camp is bathed in the light of the big yellow moon. As he walks toward the hut that he shares with the old journalist who is always chilly, the mess call is heard. The sound of the bugle echoes in the distance. Fires have been lighted here and there, and he passes among groups of soldiers heading over to them to get their meager evening rations. He finds his colleague in the hut. As usual, he has his muffler wound round his neck. As they stand in line for their food, the correspondent from the *Jornal de Notícias* tells him everything he has seen and heard in the colonel's tent. Their rations that night are a thick substance with a vague taste of manioc, a little flour, and two lumps of sugar. They are also given coffee that tastes wonderful to them.

'What is it that's impressed you so?' his colleague asks him.

'We don't understand what's happening in Canudos,' he replies. 'It's more complicated, more confused than I'd thought.'

'Well, I for one never thought there were emissaries of Her Britannic Majesty running around in the backlands, if that's what you mean,' the old journalist growls. 'But neither am I prepared to believe that little priest's story that the only thing behind all this is love of God. Too many rifles, too many skirmishes, tactics far too well planned for all of this to be the work of illiterate Sebastianists.'

The nearsighted journalist says nothing. They go back to their hut, and the veteran correspondent immediately bundles up and drops off to sleep. But his colleague stays up, writing by the light of a candle, with his portable desk on his knees. He collapses on his blanket when he hears taps sounded. In his mind's eye he can see the troops who are sleeping in the open, fully dressed, with their rifles, stacked by fours, at their feet, and the horses in their corral alongside the artillery pieces. He lies awake for a long time, thinking of the sentries making their rounds at the edge of camp, who will signal to each other all night long by blowing whistles. But, at the same time, something else is preying on his mind, below the surface: the priest taken prisoner, his stammerings, the words he has spoken. Are his colleague and the colonel right? Can Canudos be explained in terms of the familiar concepts of conspiracy, rebellion, subversion, intrigues of politicians out to restore the monarchy? Listening to that terrified little priest today, he has had the certainty that all that is not the explanation. Something more diffuse, timeless, extraordinary, something that his skepticism prevents him from calling divine or diabolical or simply spiritual. What is it, then? He runs his tongue across the mouth of his empty canteen and a few moments later falls asleep.

When first light appears on the horizon, the tinkling of little bells and bleating are heard at one end of the camp, and a little clump of bushes begins to stir. A few heads are raised, in the company covering that flank of the regiment. The sentry who has just passed by swiftly retraces his steps. Those who have been awakened by the noise strain their eyes, cup their hands behind their ears. Yes, bleating, bells tinkling. A look of joyous anticipation comes over their sleepy, hungry, thirsty faces. They rub their eyes, signal to each other not to make a sound, rise cautiously to their feet, and run toward the bushes, from which the bleating, tinkling noises are still coming. The first men to reach the thicket spy the sheep, an off-white blur in the deep shadow tinged with blue: baaa, baaa . . . They have just caught one of the animals when the shooting breaks out, and moans of pain are heard from those sent sprawling on the ground, hit by bullets from carbines or arrows from crossbows.

Reveille sounds from the other end of the camp, signaling that the column is to move on.

The casualties resulting from the ambush are not very heavy – two dead and three wounded – and though the patrols who take out after the *jagunços* do not catch them, they bring back a dozen sheep that are a welcome addition to their scanty rations. But perhaps because of the growing difficulties in securing food and water, perhaps because they are now so close to Canudos, the troops' reaction to the ambush betrays a nervousness of which there has been no sign up until now. The soldiers of the company to which the victims belong ask that the prisoner be executed in reprisal. The nearsighted journalist notes the change in attitude of the men who have crowded round the white horse of the commander of the Seventh Regiment: contorted faces, eyes filled with hate. The colonel gives them permission to speak, listens to them, nods, as they all talk at once. He finally explains to them that this prisoner is not just another *jagunço* but someone whose knowledge will be precious to the regiment once they are in Canudos.

'You'll get your revenge,' he tells them. 'And very soon now. Save your rage for later: don't waste it.'

That noon, however, the soldiers have the revenge they are so eager for. The regiment is marching past a rocky promontory, on which there can be seen – a frequent sight – the head and carcass of a cow that black vultures have stripped of everything edible. A sudden intuition causes one of the soldiers to remark that the dead animal is a blind for a lookout post. He has barely gotten the words out when several men break ranks, run over, and, shrieking with excitement, watch as a *jagunço* who is a little more than skin and bones crawls out from his hiding place underneath the cow. The soldiers fall on him, sink their knives, their bayonets into him. They decapitate him and carry the head back to Moreira César to show it to him. They tell him that they are going to load it into a cannon and send it flying into Canudos so the rebels will see the fate that awaits them. The colonel remarks to the nearsighted journalist that the troops are in fine fettle for combat.

Although he had ridden all night, Galileo Gall did not feel sleepy. The mounts were old and skinny, but showed no signs of tiring till after daylight. Communication with Ulpino, the guide, a man with a rough-hewn face and copper-colored skin who chewed tobacco, was not easy. They barely said a word to each other till midday, when they halted to eat. How long would it take them to get to Canudos? Spitting out the wad he was chewing on, the guide gave him a roundabout answer. If the horses held up, two or three days. But that was in normal times, not in times like this . . . They would not be heading for Canudos in a straight line, they'd be backtracking every so often so as to keep out of the way of both the *jagunços* and the soldiers, since either would make off with their horses. Gall suddenly felt very tired, and fell asleep almost immediately.

A few hours later, they rode off again. Shortly thereafter, they were able to cool off a bit in a tiny rivulet of brackish water. As they rode on amid stony hillsides and level stretches of ground bristling with prickly pears and thistles, Gall was beside himself with impatience. He remembered that dawn in Queimadas when he might well have died and the stirrings of sex had flooded back into his life. Everything was lost now in the depths of his memory. He discovered to his astonishment that he had no idea what the date was: neither the day nor the month. Only the year: it was probably still 1897. It was as though in this region that he kept continually journeying through, bouncing back and forth, time had been abolished, or was a different time, with its own rhythm. He tried to remember how the sense of chronology had revealed itself in the heads that he had palpated here. Was there such a thing as a specific organ that revealed man's relationship to time? Yes, of course there was. But was it a tiny bone, an imperceptible depression, a temperature? He could not remember its exact location, though he could recall the capacities or incapacities that it revealed: punctuality or the lack of it, foresight or continual improvisation, the ability to organize one's life methodically or existences undermined by disorder, overwhelmed by confusion . . . 'Like mine,' he thought. Yes, he was a typical case of a personality whose fate was chronic tumult, a life falling into chaos on every hand . . . He had had proof of that at Calumbi, when he had tried feverishly to sum up what it was he believed in and the essential facts of his life story. He had had the demoralizing feeling that it was impossible to order, to hierarchize that whole dizzying round of travels, surroundings, people, convictions, dangers, high points, and low ones. And it was more than likely that those papers that he had left in the hands of the Baron de Canabrava did not make sufficiently clear what was surely an enduring factor in his life, that loyalty that had been unfailing, something that could provide a semblance of order amid all the disorder: his revolutionary passion, his great hatred of the misery and injustice that so many people suffered from, his will to help somehow to change all that. 'Nothing of what you believe in is certain, nor do your ideals have anything to do with what is happening in Canudos.' The baron's phrase rang in his ears once more, and irritated him. How could an aristocratic landowner who lived as if the French Revolution had never taken place understand the ideals he lived by? Someone for whom 'idealism' was a bad word? How could a person from whom *jagunços* had seized one estate and were about to burn down another have any understanding of Canudos? At this moment, doubtless, Calumbi was going up in flames. He, Galileo Gall, could understand that conflagration, he knew very well that it was not a product of fanaticism or madness. The *jagunços* were destroying the symbol of oppression. Dimly but intuitively, they had rightly concluded that centuries of the rule of private property eventually came to have such a hold on the minds of the exploited that that system would seem to them of divine origin and the landowners superior beings, demigods. Wasn't fire the best way of proving that such myths were false, of dispelling the victims' fears, of making the starving masses see that it was possible to destroy the power of the landowners, that the poor possessed the strength necessary to put an end to it? Despite the dregs of religion they clung to, the Counselor and his men knew where the blows must be aimed. At the very foundations of oppression: property, the army, the obscurantist moral code. Had he made a mistake by writing those autobiographical pages that he had left in the baron's hands? No, they would not harm the cause. But wasn't it absurd to entrust something so personal to an enemy? Because the baron was his enemy. Nonetheless, he felt no enmity toward him. Perhaps because, thanks to him, he now felt he understood everything he heard and other people understood everything he said: that was something that hadn't happened to him since he'd left Salvador. Why had he written those pages? Why did he know that he was going to die? Had he written them in an excess of bourgeois weakness because he didn't want to end his days without leaving a single trace of himself in the world? All of a sudden the thought occurred to him that perhaps he had left Jurema pregnant. He felt a sort of panic. The idea of his having a child had always caused him a visceral repulsion, and perhaps that had influenced his decision in Rome to abstain from sexual relations. He had always told himself that his horror of fathering a child was a consequence of his revolutionary convictions. How can a man be available at all times for action if he has an offspring that must be fed, clothed, cared for? In that respect, too, he had been single-minded: neither a wife nor children nor anything that might restrict his freedom and sap his spirit of rebellion.

The stars were already out when they dismounted in a little thicket of *velame* and *macambira*. They ate without saying a word and Galileo fell asleep before he'd drunk his coffee. His sleep was very troubled, full of images of death. When Ulpino awakened him, it was still pitch-dark and they heard a mournful wail that might have been a fox. The guide had warmed up the coffee and saddled the horses. He tried to start up a conversation with Ulpino. How long had he worked for the baron? What did he think of the *jagunços*? The guide's answers were so evasive that he gave up trying. Was it his foreign accent that immediately aroused these people's mistrust? Or was it an even more profound lack of communication, between his entire way of feeling and thinking and theirs?

At that moment Ulpino said something he didn't understand. He asked him to repeat it, and this time each word was clear: Why was he going to Canudos? 'Because there are things going on up there I've fought for all my life,' he told him. 'They're creating a world without oppressors or oppressed up there, a world where everybody is free and equal.' He explained, in the simplest terms he could, why Canudos was important for the world, how certain things that the *jagunços* were doing coincided with an old ideal for which many men had given their lives. Ulpino did not interrupt him or look at him as he spoke, and Gall could not help feeling that what he said slid off the guide as wind blows over rocks, without leaving the slightest trace. When he fell silent, Ulpino tilted his head a little to one side, and in what struck Gall as a very odd tone of voice murmured that he thought that Gall was going to Canudos to save his wife's life. And as Gall stared at him in surprise, he went doggedly on: Hadn't Rufino said he was going to kill her? Didn't he care if

Rufino killed her? Wasn't she his wife? Why else would he have stolen her from Rufino? 'I don't have a wife. I haven't stolen anybody,' Gall replied vehemently. Rufino had been talking about someone else; Ulpino was the victim of a misunderstanding. The guide withdrew into his stubborn silence once more.

They did not speak again till hours later, when they met a group of pilgrims, with carts and water jugs, who offered them a drink. When they had left them behind, Gall felt dejected. It was because of Ulpino's totally unexpected questions, and his reproachful tone of voice. So as not to let his mind dwell on Jurema and Rufino, he thought about death. He wasn't afraid of it; that was why he had defied it so many times. If the soldiers captured him before he reached Canudos, he would put up such a fight that they would be forced to kill him; in that way he would not have to endure the humiliation of being tortured and of perhaps turning out to be a coward.

He noted that Ulpino seemed uneasy. They had been riding through a dense stretch of *caatinga,* amid breaths of searing-hot air, for half an hour, when suddenly the guide began to peer intently at the foliage around them. 'We're surrounded,' he whispered. 'We'd best wait till they come out.' They climbed down from their horses. Gall tried in vain to see any sign that would indicate that there were human beings close by. But, a few moments later, men armed with shotguns, crossbows, machetes, and knives stepped out from among the trees. A huge black, well along in years, naked to the waist, greeted them in words that Gall could not follow and asked where they were coming from. From Calumbi, Ulpino answered, on their way to Canudos. He then indicated the roundabout route they'd taken, so as, he said, to avoid meeting up with the soldiers. The exchange was tense, but it did not strike Gall as unfriendly. He then saw the black grab the reins of Ulpino's horse and mount it, as one of the others mounted his. He took a step toward the black, and immediately all those who had shotguns aimed them at him. He gestured to show his peaceful intentions and asked them to listen to him. He explained that he had to get to Canudos immediately, to talk with the Counselor, to tell him something important, that he was going to help them fight the soldiers . . . but he fell silent, disconcerted by the men's distant, set, scornful faces. The black waited a moment, but on seeing that Gall was not going to go on, he said something that the latter didn't understand this time either, whereupon they all left, as silently as they had appeared.

'What did he say?' Gall murmured.

'That the Father, the Blessed Jesus, and the Divine are defending Belo Monte,' Ulpino answered. 'They don't need any more help.'

And he added that they were not very far away now, so there was no need for him to worry about having lost the horses. They immediately set out again. And in fact they made their way through the tangled scrub as fast on foot as they would have on horseback. But the loss of the horses had also meant the loss of the saddlebags with their provisions, and from that moment on they ate dry fruits, shoots, and roots to appease their hunger. As Gall had noted that, since leaving Calumbi, remembering the incidents of the most recent period of his life opened the doors of his mind to pessimism, he tried – it was an old remedy – to lose himself in abstract, impersonal reflections. 'Science against an uneasy conscience.' Didn't Canudos represent an interesting exception to the historical law according to which religion had always served to lull the masses and keep them from rebelling against their masters? The Counselor had used religious superstition to incite the peasants to rise up against bourgeois order and conservative morality and to stir them up against those who traditionally had taken advantage of religious beliefs to keep them enslaved and exploited. In the very best of cases, as David Hume had written, religion was a dream of sick men; that was doubtless true, yet in certain cases, such as that of Canudos, it could serve to rouse the victims of society from their passivity and incite them to revolutionary action, in the course of which rational, scientific truths would gradually take the place of irrational myths and fetishes. Would he have a chance to send a letter on the subject to *L'Etincelle de la révolte*? He tried once again to start up a conversation with the guide. What did Ulpino think of Canudos? The latter chewed for a good while without answering. Finally, with serene fatalism, as though it were of no concern to him, he said: 'All of them are going to get their throats slit.' Gall decided that they had nothing more to say to each other.

On leaving the *caatinga*, they found themselves on a plateau covered with *xiquexiques*, which Ulpino split open with his knife; inside was a bittersweet pulp that quenched their thirst. That day they came upon more groups of pilgrims going to Canudos, whom they soon left behind. Meeting up with these people in the depths of whose tired eyes he could glimpse a profound enthusiasm stronger than their misery did Gall's heart good. They restored his optimism, his euphoria. They had left their homes to go to a place where a war was about to break out. Didn't that mean that the people's instinct was always right? They were going there because they had intuited that Canudos embodied their hunger for justice and freedom. He asked Ulpino when they would arrive. At nightfall, if nothing untoward happened. Nothing untoward? What did he mean? They had nothing left that could be stolen from them, wasn't that so? 'We could be killed,' Ulpino answered. But Gall did not allow his spirits to flag. And, after all, he thought to himself with a smile, the stolen horses were a contribution to the cause.

They stopped to rest in a deserted farmhouse that bore traces of having been set afire. There was no vegetation or water. Gall massaged his legs, stiff and sore after the long day's trek on foot. Ulpino suddenly muttered that they had crossed the circle. He pointed in the direction where there had been stables, animals, cowherds and now there was only desolation. The circle? The one that separated Canudos from the rest of the world. People said that inside it the Blessed Jesus reigned, and outside it the Can. Gall said nothing. In the last analysis, names did not matter; they were wrappings, and if they helped uneducated people to identify the contents more easily, it was of little moment that instead of speaking of justice and injustice, freedom and oppression, classless society and class society, they talked in terms of God and the Devil. He thought that when he arrived in Canudos he would see something he'd seen as an adolescent in Paris: a people bubbling over with revolutionary fervor, defending their dignity tooth and nail. If he could manage to make himself heard, understood, he could indeed help them, by at least sharing with them certain things they did not know, things he had learned in his years of roaming the world.

'Doesn't it really matter to you at all whether Rufino kills your wife or not?' he heard Ulpino ask him. 'Why did you steal her from him, then?'

He felt himself choke with anger. Stumbling over his words, he roared that he didn't have a wife: how dare he ask him something that he'd already answered? He felt hatred of him mounting, and a desire to insult him.

'It's beyond all understanding,' he heard Ulpino mutter.

His legs ached so and his feet were so swollen that shortly after they started walking again, he said he needed to rest a while more. As he sank to the ground, he thought: 'I'm not the man I was.' He had also grown much thinner; as he looked at the bony forearm on which his head was resting, it seemed to be someone else's.

'I'm going to see if I can find something to eat,' Ulpino said. 'Get a little sleep.'

Gall saw him disappear behind some leafless trees. As he closed his eyes he caught sight of a wooden board mounted on a tree trunk, with half the nails fallen out and a faint inscription: Caracatá. The name kept going round and round in his head as he dropped off to sleep.

Pricking up his ears, the Lion of Natuba thought: 'He's going to speak to me.' His little body trembled with joy. The Counselor lay on his pallet, absolutely silent, but the scribe of Canudos could tell from the way he was breathing whether he was awake or asleep. He began to listen again in the darkness. Yes, he was still awake. His deep eyes must be closed, and beneath his eyelids he must be seeing one of those apparitions that descended to speak to him or that he ascended to visit above the tall clouds: the saints, the Virgin, the Blessed Jesus, the Father. Or else he must be thinking of the wise things that he would say the following day, things that the Lion would note down on the paper that Father Joaquim brought him and that believers of the future would read as believers today read the Gospels.

The thought came to him that since Father Joaquim wouldn't be coming to Canudos any more, his stock of writing paper would run out soon and he would then have to write on those big sheets of wrapping paper from the Vilanovas' store that made the ink run. Father Joaquim had rarely spoken to him, and ever since the day he first saw him – the morning he entered Cumbe, scooting along at the Counselor's heels – he had noted in the priest's eyes, too, many times, that surprise, uneasiness, repugnance that his person always aroused, and that rapid movement of his head to avert his eyes and put the sight of him out of his mind. But the priest's capture by the Throat-Slitter's soldiers and his probable death had saddened him because of the effect that the news had had on the Counselor. 'Let us rejoice, my sons,' he had said that evening as he gave his counsel from the tower of the new Temple. 'Belo Monte has its first saint.' But later, in the Sanctuary, the Lion of Natuba had been aware of the sadness that had come over him. He refused the food that Maria Quadrado brought him, and as the women of the Choir made his toilet he did not stroke, as he usually did, the little lamb that Alexandrinha Correa (her eyes swollen from weeping) held within his reach. On resting his head on the Counselor's knees, the Lion did not feel his hand on his hair, and later he heard him sigh: 'There won't be any more Masses; we are orphans now.' The Lion had a foreboding of catastrophe.

Hence he, too, was having difficulty falling asleep. What was going to happen? War was close at hand once again, and this time it would be worse than when the elect and the dogs had clashed at O Taboleirinho. There would be fighting in the streets, there would be more dead and wounded, and he would be one of the first to die. No one would come to his rescue, as the Counselor had rescued him in Natuba. He had gone off with him out of gratitude, and out of gratitude he had followed the saint everywhere, despite the superhuman effort those long journeys meant for him, since he was obliged to hop about on all fours. The Lion understood why many followers missed those bygone days of wandering. There were only a handful of them then, and they had the Counselor all to themselves. How things had changed! He thought of the thousands who envied him for being able to be at the saint's side night and day. Even he, however, no longer had a chance to be by himself with the Counselor and speak alone with the only man who had always treated him as though he were like everyone else. For the Lion had never noticed the slightest sign that the Counselor saw him as that creature with a crooked back and a giant head who looked like a strange animal born by mistake among human beings.

He remembered the night on the outskirts of Tepidó, many years before. How many pilgrims were with the Counselor then? After they had prayed, they had begun to make confession aloud. When his turn came, in an unexpected rush of emotion the Lion of Natuba suddenly said something that nobody had ever heard him say before: 'I don't believe in God or in religion. Only in you, Father, because you make me feel human.' There was a deep silence. Trembling at his temerity, he felt the shocked gaze of all the pilgrims fall upon him. He now heard once again the Counselor's words that night: 'You have suffered much more than even devils must suffer. The Father knows that your soul is pure because your every moment is an expiation. You have nothing to repent, Lion: your life is a penance.'

He repeated in his mind: 'Your life is a penance.' But in it were also moments of incomparable happiness. Finding something new to read, for example, a few lines of a book, a page of a magazine, some little bit of printed matter, and learning the fabulous things that letters said. Or imagining that Almudia was still alive, still the beautiful young girl in Natuba, and that he sang to her, and instead of bewitching her and killing her, his songs made her smile. Or resting his head on the Counselor's knees and feeling his fingers making their way through his thick locks, separating them, rubbing his scalp. It was soothing; a warm sensation came over him from head to foot, and he felt that, thanks to that hand in his hair and those bones against his cheek, he was receiving his recompense for the bad moments he had had in his life.

He was unfair; the Counselor was not the only one to whom he owed a debt of gratitude. Hadn't the others carried him in their arms when his strength had given out? Hadn't they all prayed fervently, the Little Blessed One especially, that he be given faith? Wasn't Maria Quadrado good, kind, generous to him? He tried to feel tenderness in his heart toward the Mother of Men as he thought of her. She had done everything possible to gain his affection. In their days as pilgrims, when she saw that he was worn out, she would massage his body for a long time, just as she massaged the limbs of the Little Blessed One. And when he had attacks of fever, she had him sleep in her arms to keep him warm. She found him the clothes he wore, and the ingenious combination glove and shoe, of wood and leather, that made walking on all fours easier for him had been her idea. Why, then, didn't he love her? No doubt because he had also heard the Superior of the Sacred Choir accuse herself, when the pilgrims would halt for the night in the desert, of having felt repugnance for the Lion of Natuba and of having thought that his ugliness came from the Evil One. Maria Quadrado wept as she confessed these sins and, beating her breast, begged his forgiveness for being so wicked. He would always say that he forgave her, and called her Mother. But in his heart of hearts he knew he hadn't forgiven her. 'I still bear her a grudge,' he thought. 'If there is a hell, I shall burn forever and ever.' At other times the very thought of fire terrified him. Tonight it did not trouble him.

He wondered, remembering the last procession, whether he should attend any more of them. How frightened he had been! How many times he had been nearly smothered to death, trampled to death by the crowd trying to get closer to the Counselor!

The Catholic Guard had all it could do not to be overrun by believers who wanted to reach out their hands and touch the saint amid the torches and the incense. The Lion found himself being badly jostled, then pushed to the ground, and had to yell to the Catholic Guard to lift him up just as the human tide was about to engulf him. In recent days, he hardly dared set foot outside the Sanctuary, for it had become dangerous for him to be out on the streets. People rushed up to touch his crooked back, believing that it would bring them luck, and snatched him away from each other as though he were a doll; or else they kept him at their houses for hours asking him questions about the Counselor. Would he be obliged to spend the rest of his days shut up between these four adobe walls? There was no bottom to unhappiness; the stores of suffering were inexhaustible.

He could hear by the Counselor's breathing that he was asleep now. He turned an ear in the direction of the cubicle where the women of the Choir spent the nights all huddled together: they, too, were sleeping, even Alexandrinha Correa. Was it the thought of the war that was keeping him awake? It was imminent: neither Abbot João nor Pajeú nor Macambira nor Pedrão nor Taramela nor those who were guarding the roads and the trenches had come to the counsels, and the Lion had seen the armed men behind the parapets erected around the churches and the ones going back and forth with blunderbusses, shotguns, bandoleers, crossbows, clubs, pitchforks, as though they were expecting the attack at any moment.

He heard the cock crow; day was breaking between the reeds. When the water carriers began to blow their conch shells to announce that water was being distributed, the Counselor awakened and fell to his knees. Maria Quadrado came into the Sanctuary immediately. The Lion was already up, despite the sleepless night he had spent, ready to record the saint's thoughts. The latter prayed for a long time, then sat with his eyes closed as the women washed his feet with a damp cloth and put his sandals on his feet. He drank the little bowl of milk that Maria Quadrado handed him, however, and ate a maize cake. But he did not stroke the little lamb. 'It's not just because of Father Joaquim that he's so sad,' the Lion of Natuba thought. 'It's also because of the war.'

At that moment Abbot João, Big João, and Taramela entered. It was the first time that the Lion had seen the latter in the Sanctuary. When the Street Commander and the head of the Catholic Guard rose to their feet after kissing the Counselor's hand, Pajeú's lieutenant remained on his knees.

'Taramela received news last night, Father,' Abbot João said.

It occurred to the Lion that the Street Commander had no doubt not slept a wink all night either. He was sweaty, dirty, preoccupied. Big João downed with gusto the bowl of milk that Maria Quadrado had just handed him. The Lion imagined the two men running all night long from trench to trench, from one entrance to the town to another, bringing gunpowder, inspecting weapons, talking the situation over. 'It'll be today,' he thought. Taramela was still on his knees, crushing his leather hat in his hand. He had two shotguns and so many bandoleers around his neck that they looked like festive carnival necklaces. He was biting his lips, unable to get a word out. Finally, he stammered that Cíntio and Cruzes had arrived, on horseback. One of the horses had been ridden so hard it died. The other one might be dead now, too, for when he had last seen it there were rivers of sweat running down its flanks. The two men had galloped for two days without stopping. They, too, had nearly died of exhaustion. He fell silent, abashed, not knowing what to say next, his little almond eyes begging Abbot João for help.

'Tell the Father Counselor the message that Cíntio and Cruzes brought from Pajeú,' the former *cangaceiro* prompted him. He spoke with his mouth full, for Maria Quadrado had given him a bowl of milk and a little corn cake, too.

'The order has been carried out, Father,' Taramela reported. 'Calumbi was burned down. The Baron de Canabrava has gone off to Queimadas, with his family and some of his *capangas*.'

Struggling to overcome the timidity he felt in the saint's presence, he explained that, instead of going on ahead of the soldiers after he'd burned the hacienda down, Pajeú had positioned himself behind Throat-Slitter so as to fall upon him from the rear as he attacked Belo Monte. And then, without pausing, Taramela began to talk about the dead horse again. He had ordered that it be butchered for the men in his trench to eat, and that if the other one died it was to be given to Antônio Vilanova, so that he could distribute . . . But as at that moment the Counselor opened his eyes, he suddenly fell silent. The saint's deep, dark gaze made Pajeú's lieutenant feel even more unnerved; the Lion could see how hard his hand was crushing his sombrero.

'It's all right, son,' the Counselor murmured. 'The Blessed Jesus will reward Pajeú and those who are with him for their faith and courage.'

He held out his hand and Taramela kissed it, holding it for a moment in his and looking at the saint with fervent devotion. The Counselor blessed him and he crossed himself. Abbot João gestured to him to leave. Taramela stepped back, nodding reverently the while, and before he left the Sanctuary, Maria Quadrado gave him some milk, in the same bowl that Abbot João and Big João had drunk out of.

The Counselor looked at them questioningly.

'They're very close, Father,' the Street Commander said, squatting on his heels. He spoke in such a solemn tone of voice that the Lion of Natuba was suddenly frightened and felt the women shiver, too. Abbot João took out his knife, traced a circle, and then added lines leading to it to represent the roads along which the soldiers were advancing.

'There is no one coming from this side,' he said, pointing to the entrance to town, on the Jeremoabo road. 'The Vilanovas are taking a great many of the old and the sick there so as to get them out of the line of fire.'

He looked at Big João to indicate that he should tell the rest. The black pointed at the circle with one finger. 'We've built a shelter for you here, between the stables and the Mocambo,' he murmured. 'A deep one, parapeted, with lots of stones so that it will be bulletproof. You can't stay here in the Sanctuary, because they're coming from this direction.'

'They're bringing cannons with them,' Abbot João said. 'I saw them, last night. The guides sneaked me into Throat-Slitter's camp. They're big long-range ones. The Sanctuary and the churches are sure to be their first target.'

The Lion of Natuba was so drowsy that the pen slipped out of his fingers. His head was buzzing, and he pushed the Counselor's arms apart and managed to rest his great mane on his knees. He barely heard the saint's words: 'When will they be here?'

'Tonight at the very latest,' Abbot João replied.

'I'm going to go to the trenches, then,' the Counselor said softly. 'Have the Little Blessed One bring out the saints and the Christs and the glass box with the Blessed Jesus, and have him take all the statues and the crosses to the roads along which the Antichrist is coming. Many people are going to die, but there is no need for tears. Death is bliss for the faithful believer.'

For the Lion of Natuba, bliss arrived at that very moment: the Counselor's hand had just come to rest on his head. He immediately fell fast asleep, reconciled with life.

As he turns his back on the manor house of Calumbi, Rufino feels relieved: breaking the tie that bound him to the baron has suddenly given him the feeling of having more resources at his disposal to achieve his goal. Half a league farther on, he accepts the hospitality of a family he has known since he was a youngster. Without asking after Jurema or inquiring as to the reason for his having come to Calumbi, they give ample demonstration of their affection for him, and send him off the following morning with provisions for his journey.

He walks all day, and every so often along the way meets pilgrims heading for Canudos, who invariably ask him for something to eat. Hence by nightfall his provisions are all gone. He sleeps near some caves that he used to come to with other children from Calumbi to burn the bats with torches. On the following day, a peasant warns him that an army patrol has passed that way and that *jagunços* are prowling all about the region. He walks on, with a feeling of foreboding.

At dusk he reaches the outlying countryside round Caracatá, a handful of shacks in the distance, scattered about amid bushes and cacti. After the burning-hot sun, the shade of the *cajueiros* and *cipós* is a blessing. At that moment he senses that he is not alone. He is surrounded by a number of shadowy figures who have stealthily crept out of the *caatinga.* They are men armed with carbines, crossbows, and machetes and wearing little animal bells and cane whistles around their necks. He recognizes several *jagunços* from Pajeú's old band, but the half-breed is not with them. The barefoot man with Indian features who is in command puts a finger to his lips and motions to him to follow them. Rufino hesitates, but a look from the *jagunço* tells him that he must go with them, that they are doing him a favor. He immediately thinks of Jurema and the expression on his face betrays him, for the *jagunço* nods. He spies other men hiding amid the trees and brush. Several of them are camouflaged from head to foot in mantles of woven grass. Crouching down, squatting on their heels, stretched out on the ground, they are keeping a close watch on the trail and the village. They motion to Rufino to hide, too. A moment later the tracker hears a noise.

It is a patrol of ten men in red-and-gray uniforms, headed by a young fair-haired sergeant. They are being led by a guide who, Rufino thinks to himself, is no doubt an accomplice of the *jagunços.* As though he had a sudden presentiment of danger, the sergeant begins to take precautions. Keeping his finger on the trigger of his rifle, he dashes from one tree to the other, followed by his men, who also take cover behind tree trunks. The guide moves forward down the middle of the trail. The *jagunços* around Rufino appear to have vanished. Not a leaf stirs in the *caatinga.*

The patrol reaches the first shack. Two soldiers knock the door down and go inside as the other men cover them. The guide crouches down behind the soldiers and Rufino notes that he is beginning to move back. After a moment, the two soldiers reappear and motion with their hands and heads to indicate to the sergeant that there is no one inside. The patrol advances to the next shack and goes through the same procedure, with the same result. But suddenly, in the door of a shack that is larger than the others, a woman with tousled hair appears, and then another, peering out in terror. When the soldiers spy them and point their rifles at them, the women make peaceable gestures, accompanied by shrill little cries. Rufino feels as dazed as when he heard the Bearded Lady mention the name Galileo Gall. Taking advantage of the sudden confusion, the guide disappears in the underbrush.

The soldiers surround the shack and Rufino sees that they are talking with the women. Finally, two men from the patrol follow them into the shack, while the rest of the men wait outside, rifles at the ready. A few moments later, the two who have gone inside come out again, making obscene gestures and egging the others to go in and do as they have done. Rufino hears laughter, shouts, and sees all the soldiers head into the house with gleeful, excited looks on their faces. But the sergeant orders two of them to stay outside to guard the door.

The *caatinga* round about him begins to stir. The men in hiding crawl out on all fours and stand up. He realizes that there are at least thirty of them. He follows them, breaking into a run, and overtakes the leader. 'Is the woman who used to be my wife there?' he hears himself saying. 'There's a dwarf with her, isn't that right?' Yes. 'It must be her, then,' the *jagunço* says. At that moment a hail of bullets mows down the two soldiers guarding the door, immediately followed by shouts, screams, the sound of feet running, a shot from inside the shack. As he runs forward with the *jagunços*, Rufino draws his knife, the only weapon he has left, and sees soldiers at the doors and windows firing at them or trying to make their escape. They manage to take no more than a few steps before they are hit by arrows or bullets or thrown to the ground by the *jagunços*, who finish them off with their knives and machetes. Just then, Rufino slips and falls. As he gets to his feet again, he hears the piercing wail of the whistles and sees the *jagunços* tossing out one of the windows the bloody corpse of a soldier whose uniform they have ripped off. The naked body hits the ground with a dull thud.

When Rufino enters the shack, he is stunned by the violent spectacle that meets his eye. On the floor are dying soldiers, on whom knots of men and women are venting their fury with knives, clubs, stones, striking and pounding them without mercy, aided by *jagunços* who continue to pour into the shack. It is the women, four or five of them, who are screaming at the top of their lungs, and they who are ripping the uniforms off their dead or dying victims so as to insult them by baring their privates. There is blood, a terrible stench, and gaping holes between the floorboards where the *jagunços* must have been lying in wait for the patrol. Underneath a table is a woman with a head wound, writhing in pain and moaning.

As the *jagunços* strip the soldiers naked and grab their rifles and knapsacks, Rufino, certain now that what he is looking for is not in that room, makes his way toward the bedrooms. There are three of them, in a row. The door of the first one is open, but he sees no one inside. Through the cracks in the door of the second he spies a plank bed and a woman's legs lying on the floor. He pushes the door open and sees Jurema. She is alive, and on catching sight of him, her face contorts in a deep frown and her entire body hunches over in shocked surprise. Huddled next to Jurema is the grotesquely terror-stricken, minuscule figure of the Dwarf, whom Rufino seems to have known as long as he can remember, and on the bed, the fair-haired sergeant. Despite the fact that he is lying there limp and lifeless, two *jagunços* are still plunging their knives into him, roaring with each blow and spattering Rufino with blood. Jurema, motionless, stares at him, her mouth gaping, her face fallen, the ridge of her nose standing out sharply, and her eyes full of panic and resignation. Rufino realizes that the barefoot *jagunço* with Indian features has entered the room and is helping the others hoist the sergeant off the bed and throw him out the window into the street. They leave the room, taking with them the dead man's uniform, rifle, and knapsack. As he walks past Rufino, the leader mutters, pointing to Jurema: 'You see? It was her.' The Dwarf begins to utter disjointed phrases that Rufino hears but fails to understand. He stands calmly in the doorway, his face once again expressionless. His heart quiets down, and the vertigo he has felt at first is succeeded by a feeling of complete serenity. Jurema is still lying on the floor, too drained of strength to get to her feet. Through the window the *jagunços*, both the men and the women, can be seen moving off into the *caatinga*.

'They're leaving,' the Dwarf stammers, his eyes leaping from one to the other. 'We should leave, too, Jurema.'

Rufino shakes his head. 'She's staying,' he says softly. 'You go.'

But the Dwarf doesn't leave. Confused, afraid, not knowing what to do, he wanders about the empty house, amid the blood and the stench, cursing his lot, calling out to the Bearded Lady, crossing himself, vaguely praying to God. Meanwhile, Rufino searches the bedrooms, finds two straw mattresses, and drags them to the room in the front of the shack, from which he can see the one street and the dwellings of Caracatá. He has brought out the mattresses mechanically, not knowing what he intends to do with them, but now that they are there, he knows: sleep. His body is like a soft sponge sopping up water. He grabs some ropes dangling from a hook, goes to Jurema, and orders: 'Come.' She follows him, without curiosity or fear. He sits her down next to the mattresses and ties her hand and foot. The Dwarf is there, his eyes bulging in terror. 'Don't kill her, don't kill her!' he screams.

Rufino lies down on his back and without looking at him orders: 'Go stand over there, and if you see anybody coming, wake me up.'

The Dwarf blinks, disconcerted, but a second later he nods and hops to the door. Rufino closes his eyes. Before dropping off to sleep, he asks himself whether he hasn't killed Jurema yet because he wants to see her suffer or because now that he's finally caught up with her his hatred has subsided. He hears her lie down on the other mattress, a few feet away from him. He peers stealthily at her from beneath lowered eyelashes: she is much thinner, her sunken eyes are dull and resigned, her clothes torn, her hair disheveled. There is a deep scratch on her arm.

When Rufino wakes up, he leaps from the mattress as though

he were fleeing from a nightmare. But he does not remember having had a dream. Without so much as a glance at Jurema, he goes over to the Dwarf, who is still guarding the door and looking at him with mingled fear and hope in his eyes. Can he go with him? Rufino nods. They do not say a word to each other as the guide searches about outside for something to assuage his hunger and thirst. 'Are you going to kill her?' the Dwarf asks him as they are returning to the shack. He does not answer. He takes grass, roots, leaves, stems out of his knapsack and lays them down on the mattress. He does not look at Jurema as he unties her, or looks at her as though she weren't there. The Dwarf raises a handful of grass to his mouth and doggedly chews. Jurema also begins to chew and swallow, mechanically; every so often she rubs her wrists and ankles. They eat in silence, as outside the dusk turns to darkness and the buzz of insects grows louder. Rufino thinks to himself that the stench is like the one he smelled the night he once spent in a trap, alongside the dead body of a jaguar.

Suddenly he hears Jurema say: 'Why don't you kill me and get it over with?'

Rufino continues to stare into space, as though he has not heard her. But he is listening intently to that voice that is growing more and more exasperated, more and more broken: 'Do you think I'm afraid of dying? I'm not. On the contrary, I've been waiting for you to end my life. Don't you think I'm sick and tired of all this? I would have killed myself before this if God didn't forbid it, if it wasn't a sin. When are you going to kill me? Why don't you do it now?'

'No, no,' the Dwarf stammers, his voice choking.

The tracker sits there, without moving, without answering. The room is now nearly pitch-dark. A moment later, Rufino hears her crawling over to touch him. His entire body tenses, a prey to a feeling that is at once one of disgust, desire, contempt, rage, nostalgia. But he allows his face to betray none of this.

'Forget, I beg you, forget what's happened, in the name of the Virgin, of the Blessed Jesus,' he hears her implore, feeling her body tremble. 'He took me by force, it wasn't my fault, I tried to fight him off. Don't suffer any more, Rufino.'

She clings to him and immediately the guide pushes her away, though not violently. He rises to his feet, feels about for the ropes, and ties her up again without a word. He sits down again in the same place as before.

'I'm hungry, I'm thirsty, I'm tired, I don't want to live any longer,' he hears her sob. 'Kill me and get it over with.'

'I'm going to,' he says. 'But not here. In Calumbi. So people will see you die.'

A long time goes by, as Jurema's sobs grow quieter and finally die away altogether.

'You're not the Rufino you were,' he hears her murmur.

'You're not the woman you were either,' he says. 'You have a milk inside you now that isn't mine. I know now why God punished you for so long, not letting you get pregnant.'

The light of the moon suddenly filters obliquely into the room through the doors and windows, revealing the motes of dust suspended in the air. The Dwarf curls up at Jurema's feet and Rufino stretches out on his mattress. How long does he lie there with clenched teeth, thinking, remembering? When he hears the two of them talking, it's as though he were waking up, but he hasn't closed his eyes.

'Why are you staying here if nobody's forcing you to?' Jurema is asking the Dwarf. 'How can you bear this stench, the thought of what's going to happen? Go off to Canudos instead.'

'I'm afraid to go and I'm afraid to stay,' the Dwarf whimpers. 'I don't know how to be by myself, I've never been alone since the Gypsy bought me. I'm afraid of dying, like everybody else.'

'The women who were waiting for the soldiers weren't afraid,' Jurema says.

'Because they were sure they'd rise from the dead,' the Dwarf squeals. 'If I were that sure, I wouldn't be afraid either.'

'I'm not afraid of dying and I don't know if I'm going to rise from the dead,' Jurema declares, and Rufino understands that she is not speaking to the Dwarf now but to him.

Something awakens him when the dawn is scarcely more than a faint blue-green glow. The whipping of the wind? No, something else. Jurema and the Dwarf both open their eyes at the same moment, and the latter begins to stretch and yawn, but Rufino shuts him up: 'Shhh, shhh.' Crouching behind the door, he peeks out. The elongated silhouette of a man, without a shotgun, is coming down Caracatá's one street, poking his head in each of the shacks. As the man is almost upon them, Rufino recognizes him: Ulpino, the guide from Calumbi. He sees him cup both hands about his mouth and call: 'Rufino! Rufino!' He steps out from behind the door and shows himself. When he recognizes him, Ulpino's eyes open wide with relief and he calls to him. Rufino goes out to meet him, gripping the handle of his knife. He doesn't utter a single word of greeting. He can see, from the looks of him, that he has come a long way on foot.

'I've been searching for you since early last evening,' Ulpino exclaims in a friendly tone of voice. 'I was told you were on your way to Canudos. But then I met up with the *jagunços* who killed the soldiers. I've been walking all night long.'

Rufino listens to him without opening his mouth, his face grave. Ulpino looks at him sympathetically, as though reminding him that they have been friends. 'I've brought him to you,' he murmurs slowly. 'The baron ordered me to guide him to Canudos. But I talked things over with Aristarco and we decided that if I could find you, he was for you.'

Rufino's face betrays his utter astonishment, his disbelief. 'You've brought him to me? The stranger?'

'He's a bastard without honor.' To emphasize his disgust, Ulpino spits on the ground. 'He doesn't care if you kill his woman, the one he took away from you. He didn't want to talk about it. He lied and said she wasn't his.'

'Where is he?' Rufino blinks and passes his tongue over his lips. 'It's not true,' he thinks, 'he hasn't brought him.'

But Ulpino explains in great detail where he can be found. 'Though it's none of my business, there's something I'd like to know,' he adds. 'Have you killed Jurema?'

He makes no comment when Rufino shakes his head in reply. For a moment he appears to be ashamed of his curiosity. He points to the *caatinga* stretching out in the distance behind him.

'A nightmare,' he says. 'They hung the ones they killed here in the trees. The *urubus* are pecking them to pieces. It makes your hair stand on end.'

'When did you leave him?' Rufino cuts him off abruptly.

'Yesterday evening,' Ulpino says. 'He probably hasn't budged. He was dead tired. And what's more, he had no place to go. He not only lacks honor but endurance as well, and doesn't have any idea how to find his bearings . . .'

Rufino grabs him by the arm and squeezes it. 'Thanks,' he says, looking him straight in the eye.

Ulpino nods and frees his arm from Rufino's grasp. The tracker runs back into the shack, his eyes gleaming. The Dwarf and Jurema rise to their feet in bewilderment as he rushes into the room. He unties Jurema's feet but not her hands, and with swift, dexterous movements passes the same rope around her neck. The Dwarf screams and covers his face with his hands. But he is not hanging her, only making a loop in the rope so as to drag her along behind him. He forces her to follow him outside. Ulpino has gone. The Dwarf hops along behind. Rufino turns around to him. 'Don't make any noise,' he orders. Jurema stumbles on the stones, gets tangled in the brush, but doesn't open her mouth and matches Rufino's pace. Behind them, the Dwarf rambles on deliriously about the soldiers strung up on the trees who are being devoured by vultures.

'I've seen many awful things in my life,' Baroness Estela said, gazing down at the chipped tiles of the living-room floor. 'There in the country. Things that would terrify people in Salvador.' She looked at the baron, balancing back and forth in a rocking chair, unconsciously keeping time with old Colonel José Bernardo Murau, his host, as he swayed back and forth in his. 'Do you remember the bull that went mad and charged the children as they were coming out of catechism? I didn't fall into a faint, did

I? I'm not a weak woman. During the great drought, for example, we saw dreadful things, isn't that so?'

The baron nodded. José Bernardo Murau and Adalberto de Gumúcio – the latter had come from Salvador to meet the baron and baroness at the Pedra Vermelha hacienda and had been with them barely two hours – were trying their best to act as though it were an entirely normal conversation, but they could not hide how uncomfortable they were at seeing the baroness's agitation. That discreet woman, invisible behind her impeccable manners, whose smiles served as an impalpable wall between herself and others, was now rambling on and on, carrying on an endless monologue, as though she were suffering from some malady that had affected her speech. Even Sebastiana, who came from time to time to cool her forehead with eau de cologne, was unable to make her stop talking. And neither her husband nor her host nor Gumúcio had been able to persuade her to go to her room to rest.

'I'm prepared for terrible catastrophes,' she went on, her white hands reaching out toward them beseechingly. 'Seeing Calumbi burn down was worse than seeing my mother die in agony, hearing her scream with pain, giving her with my own hands the doses of laudanum that slowly killed her. Those flames are still burning here inside me.' She touched her stomach and doubled over, trembling. 'It was as though the children I lost when they were born were being burned to cinders.'

She looked in turn at the baron, Murau, Gumúcio, begging them to believe her. Adalberto de Gumúcio smiled at her. He had tried to change the subject, but each time the baroness brought the talk round again to the fire at Calumbi.

He tried once more to take her mind off this memory. 'And yet, my dear Estela, one resigns oneself to the worst tragedies. Did I ever tell you what Adelinha Isabel's murder at the hands of two slaves was like for me? What I felt when we found my sister's badly decomposed body, with so many dagger wounds in it that it was unrecognizable?' He cleared his throat as he stirred restlessly in his chair. 'That is why I prefer horses to blacks.

There are depths of barbarism and infamy in inferior classes and races that give one vertigo. And yet, my dear Estela, in the end one accepts the will of God, resigns oneself, and discovers that, even with all its calvaries, life is full of beautiful things.'

The baroness's right hand came to rest on Gumúcio's arm. 'I am so sorry to have brought back the memory of Adelinha Isabel,' she said tenderly. 'Please pardon me.'

'You didn't bring back the memory of her, because I never forget her.' Gumúcio smiled, taking the baroness's hands in his. 'Twenty years have gone by, and yet it's as though it had been this morning. I'm talking to you about Adelinha Isabel so you'll see that the destruction of Calumbi is a wound that will heal.'

The baroness tried to smile, but the smile turned into a pout, as though she were about to weep. At that moment Sebastiana came into the room, carrying the little vial of cologne. As she cooled the baroness's forehead and cheeks, patting her skin very delicately with one hand, she smoothed her mistress's ruffled hair with the other. 'Between Calumbi and here she has ceased to be the beautiful, courageous young woman she was,' the baron thought to himself. She had dark circles under her eyes, a gloomy frown, her features had gone slack, and her eyes had lost the vivacity and self-possession that he had always seen in them. Had he asked too much of her? Had he sacrificed his wife to his political interests? He remembered that when he had decided to return to Calumbi, Luiz Viana and Adalberto de Gumúcio had advised him not to take Estela with him, because of the turmoil that Canudos was causing in the region. He felt extremely uneasy. Through his thoughtlessness and selfishness he had perhaps done irreparable harm to his wife, whom he loved more dearly than anyone else in the world. And yet, when Aristarco, who was riding at his side, alerted them: 'Look, they've already set fire to Calumbi,' Estela had not lost her composure; on the contrary, she had remained incredibly calm. They were on the crest of a hill, where the baron used to halt when he was out hunting, to look out across his land, the place he took visitors to show them the hacienda, the lookout point that everybody flocked to after floods or plagues of insects to see how much damage had been done. Now, in the starry night with no wind, they could see the flames – red, blue, yellow – gleaming brightly, burning to the ground the manor house to which the lives of all those present were linked. The baron heard Sebastiana sobbing and saw Aristarco's eyes brim with tears. But Estela did not weep, he was certain of that. She held herself very straight, gripping his arm, and at one moment he heard her murmur: 'They're burning not only the house but the stables, the horse barns, the storehouse.' The next morning she had begun talking about the fire, and since then there had been no way of calming her down. 'I shall never forgive myself,' the baron thought.

'Had it been my hacienda, I'd be there now: dead,' José Bernardo Murau suddenly said. 'They would have had to burn me, too.'

Sebastiana left the room, murmuring, 'Please excuse me.' The baron thought to himself that the old man's fits of rage must have been terrible, worse than Adalberto's, and that before emancipation, he had undoubtedly tortured disobedient and runaway slaves.

'Not that Pedra Vermelha is worth all that much any more,' he grumbled, looking at the peeling walls of his living room. 'I've sometimes thought of burning it down myself, seeing all the grief it's causing me. A person has the right to destroy his own property if he feels like it. But I'd never have allowed a band of infamous, demented thieves to tell me that they were going to burn my land so it could have a rest, because it had worked hard. They would have had to kill me.'

'They wouldn't have given you any choice in the matter. They'd have burned you to death before they set fire to the hacienda,' the baron said, trying to make a joke of it.

'They're like scorpions,' he thought. 'Burning down haciendas is like stinging themselves with their own tails to cheat death. But to whom are they offering this sacrifice of themselves, of all of us?' He was pleased to note that the baroness was yawning. Ah, if only she could sleep, it would be the best possible thing to quiet her nerves. Estela hadn't slept a wink in these last few days. When they had stopped over in Monte Santo, she had refused even to stretch out on the bed in the parish house and had sat weeping in Sebastiana's arms all night long. That was when the baron began to be alarmed, for Estela was not a woman given to weeping.

'It's curious,' Murau said, exchanging a look of relief with the baron and Gumúcio, for the baroness had closed her eyes. 'When you came by here on your way to Calumbi, my hatred was principally directed against Moreira César. But now I almost feel sorry for him. I have a more violent hatred of the *jagunços* than I ever had of Epaminondas and the Jacobins.' When he was very upset, he moved his hands in a circle and scratched his chin: the baron was waiting for him to do so. But the old man just sat there with his arms crossed in a hieratic posture. 'What they've done to Calumbi, to Poço da Pedra, to Suçurana, to Juá and Curral Novo, to Penedo and Lagoa is heinous, beyond belief! Destroying the haciendas that provide them with food, the centers of civilization of the entire region! God will not forgive such a thing. It's the work of devils, of monsters.'

'Well, at last,' the baron thought: Murau had finally made his usual gesture. A swift circle traced in the air with his gnarled hand and his outstretched index finger, and now he was furiously scratching his goatee.

'Don't raise your voice like that, José Bernardo,' Gumúcio interrupted him, pointing to the baroness. 'Shall we carry her to her bedroom?'

'When she's sleeping more soundly,' the baron answered. He had risen to his feet and was arranging the cushion so that his wife could lie back against it. He then knelt and put her feet up on a footstool.

'I thought the best thing would be to take her back to Salvador as quickly as possible,' Adalberto de Gumúcio said in a low voice. 'But I wonder if it's not imprudent to subject her to another long journey.'

'We'll see how she feels when she wakes up in the morning.'

The baron had sat back down and synchronized the swaying of his rocking chair with that of his host.

'Burning down Calumbi! People who owe you so much!' Murau again traced one of his circles in the air and scratched his chin. 'I hope that Moreira César makes them pay dearly for it. I'd like to be there when he starts slitting throats.'

'Isn't there any news of him yet?' Gumúcio interrupted him. 'He should have finished off Canudos some time ago.'

'Yes, I've been making calculations,' the baron said, nodding. 'Even with lead in his feet, he must have reached Canudos many days ago. Unless . . .' He noted that his friends were looking at him, intrigued. 'I mean to say, another attack, like the one that forced him to seek refuge in Calumbi. Perhaps he's had yet another one.'

'That's all we need – to have Moreira César die of illness before he's put an end to this iniquity,' José Bernardo Murau growled.

'It's also possible that there aren't any telegraph lines left in the region,' Gumúcio said. 'If the *jagunços* burn the fields so as to let them have a little nap, they doubtless destroy the telegraph wires and the poles so as to keep them from having headaches. The colonel may have no way of getting a message out.'

The baron gave a labored smile. The last time they had been gathered together here, Moreira César's arrival had seemed like the death announcement of the Bahia Autonomist Party.

And now they were consumed with impatience to learn the details of the colonel's victory against those whom he was trying his best to pass off as restorationists and agents of the English Crown. The baron reflected on all this without taking his eyes off the sleeping baroness: she was pale, but the expression on her face was calm.

'Agents of the English Crown?' he suddenly exclaimed. 'Horsemen who burn down haciendas so that the earth may have a rest! I heard it and still don't believe it. A *cangaceiro* like Pajeú, a murderer, a rapist, a thief, a man who cuts off people's ears, who sacks towns, suddenly become a religious crusader! I saw him with my own eyes. It's hard to believe I was born in these parts, and spent a good many years of my life here. It's a strange land to me now. These people aren't the same ones I've known as long as I can remember. Maybe that Scottish anarchist understands them better than I do. Or the Counselor. It's quite possible that only madmen understand other madmen . . .' He gestured in despair and left his sentence unfinished.

'Speaking of the Scottish anarchist,' Gumúcio said. The baron felt intensely uneasy: he knew the question would be asked, and had been expecting it for two hours now. 'You surely know that I have never doubted your good judgment when it comes to politics. But I fail to understand why you would let the Scotsman go like that. He was a valuable prisoner, the best weapon we had against our number-one enemy.' He looked at the baron, his eyes blinking. 'Isn't that so?'

'Our number-one enemy is no longer Epaminondas, or any other Jacobin,' the baron murmured dispiritedly. 'It's the *jagunços.* The economic breakdown of Bahia. That's what's going to happen if there's not a stop put to this madness. The lands will remain uncultivatable, and everything's going to go to hell. The livestock is being eaten, the cattle are disappearing. And what's worse still, a region where the lack of manpower has always been a problem is going to be depopulated. People are leaving in droves and we aren't going to be able to bring them back. We must halt at any price the ruin that Canudos is bringing down upon our heads.'

He saw Gumúcio's and José Bernardo's surprised and reproving looks and felt uncomfortable. 'I know I haven't answered your question about Galileo Gall,' he murmured. 'By the way, that isn't even his real name. Why did I let him go? Perhaps it's another sign of the madness of the times, my contribution to the general folly.' Without noticing, he traced a circle like Murau's with his hand. 'I doubt that he would have been of any use to us, even if our war with Epaminondas goes on . . .'

'Goes on?' Gumúcio growled. 'It hasn't let up for a second, as far as I know. With the arrival of Moreira César, the Jacobins in Salvador have become more arrogant than ever. The *Jornal de*

Notícias is demanding that parliament try Viana and appoint a special tribunal to judge our conspiracies and shady deals.'

'I haven't forgotten the harm done us by the Progressivist Republicans,' the baron interrupted him. 'But at the moment things have taken a different turn.'

'You're mistaken,' Gumúcio said. 'They're just waiting for Moreira César and the Seventh Regiment to enter Bahia with the Counselor's head to turn Viana out of office, close down parliament, and begin the witch-hunt against us.'

'Has Epaminondas Gonçalves lost anything at the hands of the monarchist restorationists?' The baron smiled. 'In addition to Canudos, I for my part have lost Calumbi, the oldest and most prosperous hacienda in the interior. I have more reasons than he does to welcome Moreira César as our savior.'

'Nonetheless, none of this explains why you allowed the English corpse to escape your grasp in such cavalier fashion,' José Bernardo said. The baron realized what a great effort it was costing the old man to utter these phrases. 'Wasn't he living proof of Epaminondas's lack of scruples? Wasn't he a prize witness to bring forward to testify to that ambitious man's scorn for Brazil?'

'In theory, yes,' the baron agreed. 'In the realm of hypotheses.'

'We would have paraded him in the same places that they paraded his famous mop of red hair,' Gumúcio murmured in an equally severe, hurt tone of voice.

'But not in practice,' the baron went on. 'Gall is not a normal madman. No, don't laugh. He's a special type of madman: a fanatic. He would not have testified in our favor but against us. He would have confirmed Epaminondas's accusations, and made us appear utterly ridiculous.'

'I must contradict you again, I regret to say,' Gumúcio said. 'There are any number of ways to get the truth out of both sane men and madmen.'

'Not out of fanatics,' the baron shot back. 'Not out of those whose beliefs are stronger than their fear of dying. Torture would have no effect on Gall; it would merely reinforce his convictions. The history of religion provides many examples . . .'

'In that case, it would have been preferable to put a bullet through him and deliver his dead body,' Murau muttered. 'But simply to let him go . . .'

'I'm curious to know what happened to him,' the baron said. 'To know who killed him. The guide, so as not to take him to Canudos? The *jagunços*, so as to rob him? Or Moreira César?'

'The guide?' Gumúcio's eyes opened wide in surprise. 'In addition to everything else, you gave him a guide?'

'And a horse.' The baron nodded. 'I had a weak spot in my heart for him. I felt compassion, sympathy for him.'

'Compassion? Sympathy?' José Bernardo Murau repeated, rocking furiously in his chair. 'For an anarchist who dreams of setting the world on fire, of wholesale bloodshed?'

'One who's already left a number of dead bodies in his wake, to judge from his papers,' the baron said. 'Unless they're fake, which is also possible. The poor fellow was convinced that Canudos represents universal brotherhood, a materialist paradise. He spoke of the *jagunços* as though they were his political comrades, fellow believers. It was impossible not to feel affection for him.'

He noted that his friends were staring at him in greater and greater stupefaction.

'I have his testament,' he told them. 'Difficult reading, full of all sorts of nonsense, but interesting. It includes a detailed account of the plot cooked up by Epaminondas: how the latter hired him, then tried to kill him, and so on.'

'It would have been better if he'd told his story publicly, in person,' Adalberto de Gumúcio said indignantly.

'Nobody would have believed him,' the baron replied. 'The story dreamed up by Epaminondas Gonçalves, with its secret agents and arms smugglers, is more believable than the real one. I'll translate a few paragraphs from it for you, after dinner. It's in English, naturally.' He paused for a few seconds as he looked over at the baroness, who had sighed in her sleep. 'Do you know why he gave me that testament? So I'd send it on to some anarchist rag in Lyons. Just think, I'm no longer conspiring with the British Crown but with French terrorists fighting for world revolution.'

He laughed as he watched his friends' rage mounting by the second.

'As you see, we are unable to share your good humor,' Gumúcio said.

'I find that amusing, too, since it's my property that's been burned down.'

'Never mind your bad jokes, and explain to us once and for all what you're up to,' Murau said reprovingly.

'It's no longer important to do Epaminondas any harm whatsoever. He's a boor, a country bumpkin,' the Baron de Canabrava said. 'What's important now is to reach an accommodation with the republicans. The war between us is over; circumstances have put an end to it. It's not possible to wage two wars at the same time. The Scotsman was of no use to us, and in the long run he would only have complicated matters.'

'An accommodation with the Progressivist Republicans, you said?' Gumúcio stared at him in stupefaction.

'I said accommodation, but what I was thinking of was an alliance, a pact,' the baron answered. 'It's difficult to understand, and even more difficult to bring off, but there's no other way. Well then, I think we may carry Estela to her room now.'

VI

Drenched to the skin, curled up on a blanket indistinguishable from the mud, the nearsighted correspondent from the *Jornal de Notícias* hears the cannons roar. Partly because of the rain and partly because battle is imminent, no one is asleep. He pricks up his ears: are the bells of Canudos still pealing in the darkness? All he can hear is the cannons firing at intervals and bugles blowing the call to charge and slit throats. Have the *jagunços* also given a name to the symphony of whistles with which they have tortured the Seventh Regiment ever since Monte Santo? He is overcome with anxiety, frightened, shivering from the cold. He is soaked to his very bones from the rain. He thinks of his colleague, the elderly journalist who feels the cold so badly; on being left in the rear with the half-naked soldier boys, he said to him: 'There's many a slip 'twixt the cup and the lip, my young friend.' Is he dead? Have he and those youngsters met the same fate as the fair-haired sergeant and the soldiers of his patrol whose corpses they came upon late yesterday afternoon in the foothills of this mountain range? At that very moment the bells down below answer the bugles of the regiment, a dialogue in the dark, rainy shadows that are a prelude to the one that will take place between shotguns and rifles as soon as day breaks.

He might well have shared the fate that befell the fair-haired sergeant and his patrol: he had been about to agree when Moreira César suggested that he accompany them. Was it his fatigue that had saved him? A presentiment? Chance? That was just yesterday, but in his memory it seems a very long time ago, because all during the day just past, Canudos seemed like somewhere they would never reach. The head of the column stops and the nearsighted journalist remembers that his ears were ringing, that his legs were trembling, that his lips were chapped. The colonel is leading his horse by the reins and the officers are indistinguishable from the soldiers and the guides, for they all look the same on foot. He notes the fatigue, the dirt, the deprivation all around him. A dozen soldiers break ranks, step swiftly forward, and stand at attention before the colonel and Major Cunha Matos. The one who is to lead the patrol is the young sergeant who brought the parish priest of Cumbe in as a prisoner.

He hears him click his heels, repeat his orders. 'Take up a commanding position at Caracatá; close off the ravine with cross fire once the assault has begun.' The sergeant has the same resolute, healthy, optimistic spirit that he has noted in him at all times during the march. 'Have no fear, sir, no outlaw is going to escape by way of Caracatá.'

Was the guide who lined up alongside the sergeant the same

one who accompanied the patrols that went out to search for water? It was their guide at any rate who led the sergeant and his men into the ambush, and the nearsighted journalist thinks to himself that it is only by a sheer miracle that he is here, his mind in a daze. Colonel Moreira César spies him sitting on the ground, completely worn out, stiff and aching all over, with his portable writing desk on his knees. 'Do you want to go with the patrol? You'll be safer in Caracatá than you will be with us.'

What had made him say no, after a few seconds' hesitation? He remembers that the young sergeant and he had talked together a number of times: he had asked him questions about the *Jornal de Notícias* and his work; Colonel Moreira César was the person he admired most in the world – 'even more than Marshal Floriano' – and like the colonel, he believed that civilian politicians were a catastrophe for the Republic, a source of corruption and divisiveness, and that only men bearing swords and uniforms were capable of regenerating the Fatherland debased by monarchical rule.

Has it stopped raining? The nearsighted journalist turns over onto his back, without opening his eyes. Yes, it is no longer pouring; that fine penetrating mist is being driven their way by the wind sweeping down the hillside. The cannon fire has also stopped and his mental image of the young sergeant is replaced by that of the elderly journalist who suffers from the cold: his straw-colored hair that had turned almost white, his kindly face that had taken on a sickly cast, his muffler, his fingernails that he so often contemplated as though they were an aid to meditation. Was he, too, hanging dead from a tree? Not long after the patrol has left, a messenger has come to tell the colonel that something is happening among the youngsters. The company of youngsters! he thinks. It's all written down, it's in the bottom of the pouch he's lying on top of so as to protect it from the rain, four or five pages telling the story of those adolescents, barely past childhood, that the Seventh Regiment recruits without asking them how old they are. Why does it do that? Because, according to Moreira César, youngsters have a surer aim, steadier nerves than adults. He has seen, has spoken with these soldiers fourteen or fifteen years old who are known as the youngsters. Hence, when he hears the messenger say that something is happening among them, the nearsighted journalist follows the colonel to the rear guard. Half an hour later they come upon them.

In the rain-drenched shadows, a shiver runs down his body from head to foot. The bugles and the bells ring out again, very loud now, but in the late-afternoon sun he continues to see the eight or nine soldier boys, squatting on their heels or lying exhausted on the gravel-strewn ground. The companies of the rear guard are leaving them behind. They are the youngest ones, they seem to be wearing masks, and are obviously dying of hunger and exhaustion. Dumfounded, the nearsighted journalist spies his colleague among them. A captain with a luxuriant mustache, who appears to be the victim of warring feelings – pity, anger, hesitation – greets the colonel: they refused to go any farther, sir. What should I do? The journalist does his best to spur his colleague on, to persuade him to get up, to pull himself together. 'I needn't have tried to reason with him,' he thinks. 'If he'd had an ounce of strength left, he'd have gone on. He remembers how his legs were all sprawled out, how pale his face was, how he lay there panting like a dog. One of the boys is whimpering: they'd rather you ordered them killed, sir, the blisters on their feet are infected, their heads are buzzing, they can't go a single step farther. The youngster is sobbing, his hands joined as though in prayer, and little by little those who are not weeping also burst into tears, hiding their faces in their hands and curling up in a ball at the colonel's feet.

He remembers the look in Moreira César's cold little eyes as they sweep back and forth over the group. 'I thought that it would make real men of you sooner if I put you in the ranks. You're going to miss out on the best part of all. You boys have disappointed me. To keep you from being carried on the rolls as deserters, I'm giving you your discharge. Hand over your rifles and your uniforms.'

The nearsighted journalist gives half his water ration to his colleague, who immediately thanks him with a smile, as the youngsters, leaning weakly on each other, take off their high-buttoned tunics and kepis and hand their rifles over to the armorers.

'Don't stay here, it's too open,' Moreira César says to them. 'Try to get back to the rocky hilltop where we halted to rest this morning. Hide there till a patrol comes past. There isn't much chance of that, however.'

He turns on his heels and returns to the head of the column. As his farewell words to him, his colleague whispers to the journalist: 'There's many a slip 'twixt the cup and the lip, my young friend.' With his absurd muffler wound around his neck, the old man stays behind, sitting there like a class monitor amid half-naked, bawling kids. He thinks: 'It rained back there, too.' He imagines the surprise, the happiness, the resurrection that this sudden downpour, sent by heaven seconds after it was hidden from sight by dark, lowering clouds, must have been for the old man and the youngsters. He imagines their disbelief, their smiles, their mouths opening greedily, joyously, their hands cupping to catch the drops; he imagines the boys rising to their feet, hugging each other, refreshed, encouraged, restored body and soul. Have they begun marching again, perhaps catching up with the rear guard? Hunching over till his chin is touching his knees, the nearsighted journalist tells himself that this isn't so: their mental and physical states were such that not even the rain would have been capable of getting them on their feet again.

How many hours has it been raining now? It began at nightfall, as the vanguard was starting to take up positions on the heights of Canudos. There is an indescribable explosion of joy throughout the regiment; men from the ranks and officers leap about, clap each other on the back, drink out of their kepis, stand with outstretched arms beneath the deluge from the sky; the colonel's white horse whinnies, shakes its mane, stamps its hoofs in the mud that is beginning to form. The nearsighted journalist manages only to raise his head, close his eyes, open his mouth, his nostrils, incredulous, sent into ecstasies by these drops that are pelting his very bones. He is so absorbed, so overjoyed that he hears neither the shots nor the cries of the soldier, rolling about on the ground alongside him, moaning with pain and clutching his face. When he finally becomes aware of the chaos round about him, he stoops over, picks up the portable writing desk and the leather pouch, and puts them over his head. From this miserable refuge he sees Captain Olímpio de Castro shooting his revolver and soldiers running for shelter or flinging themselves face down in the mud. And between the muddy legs scissoring back and forth he sees – the image is frozen in his memory like a daguerreotype – Colonel Moreira César grabbing the reins of his horse, leaping into the saddle, and with saber unsheathed charging, not knowing if any of his men are following him, toward the patch of scrub from which the shots have come. 'He was shouting "Long live the Republic," "Long live Brazil,"' he thinks to himself. In the lead-colored light, amid the pouring rain and the wind whipping the trees back and forth, officers and men break into a run, echoing the colonel's shouts, and – forgetting the cold and his panic for a moment, the correspondent from the *Jornal de Notícias* laughs to himself, remembering – he suddenly finds himself running, too, right alongside them, toward the thicket, to confront the invisible enemy, too. He remembers thinking as he stumbled along how stupid he was to be running toward a battle that he was not going to fight. What would he have fought it with? His portable writing desk? The leather pouch containing his changes of clothes and his papers? His empty inkwell? But the enemy, naturally, never appears.

'What did appear was worse,' he thinks, and another shiver runs down his spine, like a lizard. Once again he sees the landscape, in the ashen afternoon that is beginning to turn to dusk, become a phantasmagoria, with strange human fruit hanging from the *umburanas* and the thornbushes, and boots, scabbards, tunics, kepis dangling from the branches. Some of the corpses are already skeletons picked clean of eyes, bellies, buttocks, muscles, privates by vultures or rodents, and their nakedness stands out sharply against the spectral greenish-gray of the trees and the dark-colored earth. Standing rooted to the spot for an instant by the incredible sight, he then walks in a daze amid these remains of men and uniforms adorning the *caatinga*. Moreira César has dismounted and is surrounded by the officers and men who have followed him as he charged. They are petrified. The shouts and the mad dashes of a moment before have been succeeded by a deep silence, a tense motionlessness. They are all standing staring at the sight before them, and on their faces stupefaction, fear gradually give way to sadness, anger. The young fair-haired sergeant's head is still intact – though the eyes are gone – and his body a mass of dark purple bruises and protruding bones, with swollen wounds that seem to be bleeding as the rain streams down. He sways back and forth, very slowly. From that moment on, even before being overcome with pity and horror, the nearsighted journalist has thought about what he cannot help thinking about, what is gnawing at him this minute and preventing him from sleeping: the stroke of luck, the miracle that kept him from being there too, naked, hacked to pieces, castrated by the knives of the *jagunços* or the beaks of the vultures, hanging amid the cacti. Someone breaks into sobs. It is Captain Olímpio de Castro, who raises his arms to his face, his pistol still in his hand. In the half shadow, the nearsighted journalist sees that other officers and men are also weeping for the fair-haired sergeant and his patrol, whom they have begun taking down. Moreira César remains there, witnessing this operation that is taking place in the gathering dark, his face set in a stony expression he has never seen on it before. Wrapped in blankets, the corpses are buried immediately, side by side, by soldiers who present arms in the darkness and fire a rifle volley in their honor.

After the bugler has blown taps, Moreira César points with his sword at the mountainside before them and delivers a very short speech. 'The murderers have not fled, men. They are there, awaiting punishment. I say no more now, in order that bayonets and rifles may speak.'

He hears the roar of the cannon again, closer this time, and gives a start, wide awake now. He remembers that in the last few days he has hardly sneezed once, not even in this rainy dampness, and he tells himself that the expedition will have been worthwhile to him for one reason at least: the nightmare of his life, the fits of sneezing that drove his fellow workers at the newspaper mad and often kept him awake all night long, have become less frequent, have perhaps disappeared altogether. He remembers that he began to smoke opium, not so much because he wanted to have the dreams it brings as because he wanted to sleep without sneezing, and he says to himself: 'What a dull clod I am.' He turns over on his side and looks up at the sky: a black expanse without a spark of light. It is so dark he cannot make out the faces of the soldiers lying next to him, to his right and to his left. But he can hear their heavy breathing, the words that escape their lips. Every so often, some of them get up and others lie down as the former climb up to the top of the mountain to take their places. He thinks: 'It's going to be terrible.' Something that can never be faithfully reproduced in writing. He thinks: 'They are filled with hatred, intoxicated by their desire for vengeance, the desire to make someone pay for their exhaustion, hunger, thirst, the horses and animals lost, and above all for the mutilated, outraged dead bodies of the comrades they saw leave a few short hours before to take Caracatá.' He thinks: 'It was what they needed to reach a fever pitch. That hatred is what has enabled them to scale the rocky mountainsides at a frenetic pace, clenching their teeth, and what must be causing them to lie there unable to sleep now, clutching their weapons, looking down obsessively from the crest at the shadows below where their prey awaits them, hated in the beginning out of duty but hated intimately and personally now, like enemies from whom it is their duty to collect a debt of honor owed them.'

Because of the mad cadence at which the Seventh Regiment stormed up the hillsides, he was unable to remain at the head of the column with the colonel, his staff officers, and his escort. He was prevented from doing so by the fading light, his constant stumbling and falling, his swollen feet, his heart that seemed to be about to burst, his pounding temples. What made him hold out, struggle back to his feet again and again, go on climbing? He thinks: fear of being left all by myself, curiosity as to what is going to happen. In one of his many falls he lost track of his portable writing desk, but a soldier with a bare scalp – they shave all the hair off those infested with lice – hands it to him a few minutes later. He has no use for it any more; his ink is all gone and his last goose-quill got broken the evening before. Now that the rain has stopped, he hears various sounds, a rattling of stones, and wonders if the companies are continuing to deploy in all directions during the night, if the cannons and machine guns are being hauled to a new emplacement, or if the vanguard has dashed down the mountainside without waiting for daybreak.

He has not been left behind all by himself; he has arrived before many of the troops. He feels a childish joy, the elation of having won a wager. The featureless silhouettes are no longer advancing now; they are eagerly opening bundles of supplies, slipping off their knapsacks. Their fatigue, their anxiety disappear. He asks where the command post is, goes from one group of men to another, wanders back and forth till he comes upon a canvas shelter stretched between poles, lighted by a feeble oil lamp. It is now pitch-dark, it is still raining buckets, and the nearsighted journalist remembers the feeling of safety, of relief that came over him as he crawled to the tent and spied Moreira César. The latter is receiving reports, giving orders; an atmosphere of feverish activity reigns around the little table on which the oil lamp sputters. The nearsighted journalist collapses on the ground at the entrance, as he has on previous occasions, thinking that his position, his presence there are akin to a dog's, and doubtless Colonel Moreira César associates him in his mind, first and foremost, with a dog. He sees mud-spattered officers go in and out, he hears Colonel Tamarindo discussing the situation with Major Cunha Matos, and Colonel Moreira César giving orders. The colonel is enveloped in a black cape and in the smoky light he looks strangely deformed. Has he had another attack of his mysterious malady? For at his side is Dr. Souza Ferreiro.

'Order the artillery to open fire,' he hears him say. 'Have the Krupps send them our visiting cards, so as to soften them up before we launch our attack.'

As the officers begin to leave the tent, he is obliged to move aside to keep from being trampled underfoot.

'Have the regimental call sounded,' the colonel says to Captain Olímpio de Castro.

Shortly thereafter, the nearsighted journalist hears the long, lugubrious, macabre bugle call that he heard as the column marched off from Queimadas. Moreira César has risen to his feet and walks toward the door of the tent, half buried in his cape. He shakes hands with the officers who are leaving and wishes them good luck.

'Well, well! So you managed to get to Canudos,' the colonel says as he catches sight of him. 'I confess that I'm surprised. I never thought you'd be the only correspondent to accompany us this far.'

And then, immediately losing all interest in him, he turns to Colonel Tamarindo. The call to charge and slit throats echoes back in the rain from different directions. As a silence falls, the nearsighted journalist suddenly hears bells pealing wildly. He remembers thinking what all the others were no doubt thinking: 'The *jagunços*' answer.' 'Tomorrow we will lunch in Canudos,' he hears the colonel say. He feels his heart skip a beat, for tomorrow is already today.

He was awakened by a painful burning sensation: lines of ants were running up both his arms, leaving a trail of red marks on his skin. He slapped them dead with his hand as he shook his drowsy head. Studying the gray sky, the light growing fainter and fainter, Galileo Gall tried to guess what time it was. He had always envied Rufino, Jurema, the Bearded Lady, all the people in these parts for the certainty with which, after a mere glance at the sun or the stars, they could tell precisely what hour of the day or night it was. How long had he slept? Not long, since Ulpino hadn't come back yet. When he saw the first stars appear he gave a start. Could something have happened? Could Ulpino have lighted out, afraid to take him all the way to Canudos? He suddenly felt cold, a sensation it seemed to him he hadn't felt for ages.

A few hours later, in the clear night, he was certain that Ulpino was not going to come back. He rose to his feet and, with no idea where he was heading, started off in the direction indicated on a wooden sign that said Caracatá. The little trail disappeared amid a labyrinth of thorny bushes that scratched him. He went back to the clearing. He managed to fall asleep, overcome with anxiety, and had nightmares that he remembered vaguely on awaking the next morning. He was so hungry that he forgot all about the guide for a good while and spent a fair time chewing on grasses till he had calmed the empty feeling in his belly. Then he explored his surroundings, convinced that the only solution was to find his own way. After all, it should not be all that difficult: all he needed to do was find a group of pilgrims and follow them. But where were they to be found? The thought that Ulpino had deliberately gotten him lost upset him so much that the moment this suspicion crossed his mind he instantly rejected it. In order to clear a path through the vegetation he had a stout branch; his double saddlebag was slung over his shoulder. Suddenly it began to rain. Drunk with elation, he was licking the drops falling on his face when he caught sight of figures amid the trees. He shouted to them and ran toward them, splashing through the water, muttering 'At last' to himself, when he recognized Jurema. And Rufino. He stopped dead in his tracks. Through a curtain of water, he saw the calm expression on the tracker's face and noted that he was leading Jurema along by a rope tied around her neck, like an animal. He saw him let go of the rope and spied the terrified face of the Dwarf. The three of them looked at him and he suddenly felt totally disconcerted, unreal. Rufino had a knife in his hand; his eyes were gleaming like burning coals.

'If it had been you, you wouldn't have come to defend your wife,' he heard him say to him, with more scorn than rage. 'You have no honor, Gall.'

His feeling of unreality grew even more intense. He raised his free hand and made a peaceable, friendly gesture. 'There's no time for this, Rufino. I can explain to you what happened. There's something that's much more urgent now. There are thousands of men and women who risk being killed because of a handful of ambitious politicians. It's your duty . . .'

But he realized he was speaking in English. Rufino was coming toward him and Galileo began to step back. The ground between them was a sea of mud. Behind Rufino, the Dwarf was trying to untie Jurema. 'I'm not going to kill you yet,' he thought he heard Rufino say, and apparently he added that he was going to slap him full in the face to dishonor him. Galileo felt like laughing. The distance between the two of them was growing shorter by the moment and he thought: 'He's deaf to reason and he always will be.' Hatred, like desire, canceled out intelligence and reduced man to a creature of sheer instinct. Was he about to die on account of such a stupid thing as a woman's cunt? He continued to make pacifying gestures and assumed a fearful, pleading expression. At the same time, he calculated the distance, and when Rufino was almost upon him, he suddenly lashed out at him with the stout stick he was clutching in his fist. The guide fell to the ground. He heard Jurema scream, but by the time she reached his side, he had already hit Rufino over the head twice more; the latter, stunned, had let go of his knife, which Gall picked up. He held Jurema off, indicating with a wave of his hand that he was not going to kill Rufino.

In a fury, shaking his fist at the man lying on the ground, he roared: 'You blind, selfish, petty traitor to your class – can't you see beyond your vainglorious little world? Men's honor doesn't lie in faces or in women's cunts, you idiot. There are thousands of innocents in Canudos. The fate of your brothers is at stake: can't you understand?'

Rufino shook his head as he came to.

'You try to make him understand,' Gall shouted to Jurema before he walked off. She stared at him as though he were mad, or someone she had never seen in her life before. Again he had the feeling that everything was absurd and unreal. Why hadn't he killed Rufino? The imbecile would pursue him to the end of the earth, he was certain. He ran, panting, through the scrub, raked by the thorns, amid torrents of rain, getting covered with mud, with no idea where he was going. He still had the stick and his double saddlebag, but he had lost his sombrero and could feel the drops bouncing off his skull. A while later – it might have been a few minutes or an hour – he stopped, then went on again, at a slow walk. There was no sort of trail, no reference point amid the brambles and the cacti, and his feet sank into the mud, holding him back. He could feel that he was sweating beneath the pouring rain. He silently cursed his luck. The light was fading and he could scarcely believe that it was already dusk. He finally realized that he was looking all around as though he were about to plead with those gray, barren trees, with barbs instead of leaves, to help him. He gestured, half in pity and half in desperation, and broke into a run again. But after just a few meters he stopped dead in his tracks, utterly unnerved by his helplessness. A sob escaped his lips.

'Rufinoooo, Rufinoooo!' he shouted, cupping his hands around his mouth. 'Come on, come on, I'm here, I need you! Help me, take me to Canudos, let's do something useful, let's not be stupid. You can take your revenge, kill me, slap my face afterward. Rufinoooo!'

He heard his shouts echoing amid the splash of the raindrops. He was soaked to the skin, dying of cold. He went on walking aimlessly, his mouth working, slapping his legs with the stick. It was dusk, night would soon be falling, all this was perhaps just a nightmare – and suddenly the earth gave way beneath his feet. Before he hit bottom, he realized that he had stepped on a mat of branches concealing a deep pit. The fall did not knock him senseless: the earth at the bottom of the pit was soft from the rain. He stood up, felt his arms, his legs, his aching shoulder. He fumbled about for Rufino's knife, which had fallen out of his belt, and the thought occurred to him that he had had a chance to plunge it into Rufino. He tried to climb out of the hole, but his feet slipped and he fell back in. He sat down on the wet dirt, leaned back against the wall, and, with a feeling of something like relief, dropped off to sleep. He was awakened by a faint rustling of branches and leaves being trampled underfoot. He was about to give a shout when he felt a puff of air go past his shoulder and in the semidarkness saw a wooden dart bury itself in the dirt.

'Don't shoot, don't shoot!' he yelled. 'I'm a friend, a friend.'

There were murmurs, voices, and he went on shouting till a lighted length of wood was thrust into the hole and he dimly made out human heads behind the flame. They were armed men, camouflaged in long cloaks made of woven grass. Several hands reached down and pulled him to the surface. There was a look of rapturous excitement on Galileo Gall's face as the *jagunços* examined him from head to foot by the light of torches sputtering in the dampness left by the recent rain. With their caparisons of grass, their cane whistles around their necks, their carbines, their machetes, their crossbows, their bandoleers, their rags, their scapulars and medals with the Sacred Heart of Jesus, they looked as though they were in disguise. As they peered at him, sniffed at him, with expressions that betrayed their surprise at coming upon this creature whom they were unable to classify as belonging to any of the varieties of humans known to them, Galileo Gall asked insistently to be taken to Canudos: he could be of service to them, help the Counselor, explain to them the machinations of corrupt bourgeois politicians and military officers of which they were victims. He gesticulated violently so as to lend emphasis and eloquence to his words and fill in the gaps in his faltering Portuguese, looking first at one and then at another, wild-eyed with excitement; he had had long experience as a revolutionary, comrades, he had fought many a time at the side of the people, he wanted to share their destiny.

'Praised be the Blessed Jesus,' he seemed to hear someone say.

Were they making fun of him? He began to stammer, to trip

over his words, to struggle against the feeling of helplessness that was coming over him little by little as he realized that the things he was saying were not exactly the ones he wanted to say, the ones that they might have been able to understand. He was demoralized, above all, on seeing by the flickering light of the torches that the *jagunços* were exchanging knowing glances and gestures, and smiling at him pityingly, revealing mouths with either teeth missing or a tooth or two too many. Yes, what he was saying sounded like nonsense, but they had to believe him! He had had incredible difficulties getting to Canudos, but was here now to help them. Thanks to them, a fire that the oppressor believed to have been extinguished in the world had been rekindled. He fell silent again, disconcerted, disheartened by the complacent attitude of the men in the grass cloaks, who showed no signs of anything save curiosity and compassion. He stood there with outstretched hands and felt tears well up in his eyes. What was he doing here? How had he managed to fall into this trap, from which there was no escape, believing the while that he was contributing his might to the great undertaking of making the world a less barbarous place? Someone said helpfully that he mustn't be afraid: those people he spoke of were nothing but Freemasons, Protestants, servants of the Antichrist, and the Counselor and the Blessed Jesus had more power than they did. The man who was speaking had a long, narrow face and beady eyes, and pronounced each word slowly and distinctly: when the time came, a king called Sebastião would rise up out of the sea and ascend to Belo Monte. He mustn't weep, the innocents had been brushed by the wings of the angel and the Father would bring him back to life if the heretics killed him. He would have liked to answer that they were right, that beneath the deceptive verbal formulas they used to express themselves, he was able to hear the overwhelmingly evident truth of a battle under way, between good, represented by the poor, the long-suffering, the despoiled, and evil, championed by the rich and their armies, and that once this battle had ended, an era of universal brotherhood would begin. But he was unable to find the right words and could feel them sympathetically patting him on the back now to console him, for they could see that he was sobbing. He half understood a few words and bits of phrases: the kiss of the elect, someday he'd be rich, he should pray.

'I want to go to Canudos,' he managed to say, grabbing the arm of the man who was speaking. 'Take me with you. May I follow you?'

'That's not possible,' one of the *jagunços* answered, pointing in the direction of the mountaintop. 'The dogs are up there. They'd slit your throat. Hide somewhere. You can come to Canudos later, when they're dead.'

With reassuring gestures, they vanished round about him, leaving him in the dark of night, bewildered, with a phrase echoing in his ears like a mocking joke: 'Praised be the Blessed Jesus.' He took a few steps, trying to follow them, but all of a sudden a meteor blocked his path and knocked him to the ground. He realized it was Rufino only after he was already fighting with him, and as he hit out and was hit back, the thought came to him that the little bright spots gleaming like quicksilver that he had glimpsed behind the *jagunços* had been the tracker's eyes. Had he been waiting until the men from Canudos left, so as to attack him? They did not exchange insults as they struck each other, panting in the mire of the *caatinga*. It was raining again and Gall heard the thunder, the splashing drops, and for some reason the animal violence of the two of them freed him of his despair and for the moment gave his life meaning. As he bit, kicked, scratched, butted, he heard a woman screaming, doubtless Jurema calling to Rufino, and mingled with her cries the Dwarf's shrill voice, calling to Jurema. But soon all these sounds were drowned out by the repeated blare of bugles coming from the heights and a pealing of church bells in answer. It was as though those bugles and bells, whose meaning he sensed, were of help to him; he was fighting with more energy now, feeling neither pain nor fatigue. He kept falling and getting up again, not knowing whether what he felt trickling over his skin was sweat, rain, or blood. All of a sudden, Rufino slipped out of his hands, sunk from sight, and he heard the dull thud of the body hitting the bottom of the hole. Gall lay there panting, feeling with his hand the edge of the pit that had decided the fight, thinking that this was the first good thing that had happened to him in several days.

'Opinionated fool! Madman! Conceited, pigheaded bastard!' he shouted, choking with rage. 'I'm not your enemy, your enemies are the men who are blowing those bugles. Can't you hear them? That's more important than my semen, than your wife's cunt, where you've placed your honor, like a stupid bourgeois.'

He realized that, once again, he'd spoken in English. With an effort he rose to his feet. It was raining buckets and the water that fell into his open mouth felt good. Limping because he'd hurt his leg, perhaps when he fell into the pit, perhaps in the fight, he walked on through the *caatinga,* feeling his way through the branches and sharp thorns of the trees, stumbling. He tried to take his bearings from the slow, sad, funereal call of the bugles or the solemn peal of the bells, but the sounds seemed to keep shifting direction. And at that moment something grabbed his feet and sent him rolling on the ground, feeling mud between his teeth. He kicked, trying to free himself, and heard the Dwarf moan.

Clinging to him in terror, the Dwarf cried in his shrill voice: 'Don't abandon me, Gall, don't leave me by myself. Don't you hear those whooshing sounds? Don't you see what they are, Gall?'

Once again he experienced that sensation that it was all a nightmare, unreal, absurd. He remembered that the Dwarf could see in the dark and that sometimes the Bearded Lady called him 'cat' and 'owl.' He was so exhausted that he continued to lie there, letting the Dwarf cling to him, listening to him whimper over and over that he didn't want to die. He raised a hand to his shoulder and rubbed it as he strained his ears to hear. There was no doubt about it: they were cannon reports. He had been hearing them at intervals for some time now, thinking that they were deep drumrolls, but now he was certain that they were artillery fire. From cannons, no doubt small ones, or perhaps only mortars, but even so they were enough to blow Canudos sky-high. He was so worn out that he either fainted or fell dead asleep.

The next thing he knew, he was trembling with cold in the feeblest of first light. He heard the Dwarf's teeth chattering and saw his big eyes rolling in terror. The little fellow must have slept propped up on Gall's right leg, for it had gone numb. He gradually roused himself, blinked, looked around: hanging from the trees were bits and pieces of uniforms, kepis, field boots, greatcoats, canteens, knapsacks, saber and bayonet scabbards, and a few crude crosses. It was these tattered objects hanging from the trees that the Dwarf was staring at spellbound, as though he were not seeing these belongings but the ghosts of those who had worn them. 'At least they defeated these men,' he thought.

He listened. Yes, more cannon fire. It had stopped raining a good many hours before, since everything around him was dry by now, but the cold gnawed his very bones. Weak and aching all over, he managed to struggle to his feet. He spied the knife in his belt and thought to himself that it had never crossed his mind to use it as he was fighting with Rufino. Why had he not tried to kill him this second time either? He heard yet another cannonade, very distinctly now, and a din of bugles, that lugubrious call that sounded like funeral taps. As though in a dream, he saw Rufino and Jurema appear from between the trees. The tracker was badly hurt, or exhausted, for he was leaning on her for support, and Gall knew intuitively that Rufino had spent the night tirelessly searching for him in the darkness of the thicket. He felt hatred for the man's obstinacy, for his single-minded, unshakable determination to kill him.

They looked each other straight in the eye and Gall felt himself tremble. He pulled the knife out of his belt and pointed in the direction from which the bugle calls were coming. 'Do you hear that?' he said in a slow, deliberate voice. 'Your brothers are under artillery fire, they're dying like flies. You kept me from going to join them and dying with them. You've made a stupid clown of me . . .'

Rufino had a sort of wooden dagger in his hand. He saw him let go of Jurema, push her away, crouch down to attack. 'What a wretched bastard you are, Gall,' he heard him say. 'You talk a lot about the poor, but you betray a friend and dishonor the house where you're given hospitality.'

He shut him up by throwing himself on him, blind with rage. They began hacking each other to pieces as Jurema watched in a daze, overcome with anguish and fatigue. The Dwarf doubled over in terror.

'I won't die for my own wretchedness, Rufino,' Gall roared. 'My life is worth more than a little semen, you miserable creature.'

They were rolling over and over together on the ground when the two soldiers appeared, running hard. On catching sight of them, they stopped short. Their uniforms were half torn away, and one of them had lost his boots, but they were holding their rifles at the ready.

The Dwarf hid his head. Jurema ran to them, stepped in their line of fire, and begged: 'Don't shoot! They're not *jagunços* . . .'

But the soldiers fired point blank at the two adversaries and then threw themselves upon her, grunting, and dragged her into the dry underbrush. Badly wounded, the tracker and the phrenologist went on fighting.

'I should be happy, since this means that my bodily suffering will be over, that I shall see the Father and the Blessed Virgin,' Maria Quadrado thought. But she was transfixed with fear, though she tried her best not to let the women of the Sacred Choir see that she was. If they noticed, they, too, would be paralyzed by fear and the entire structure devoted to caring for the Counselor would collapse. And in the hours to come, she was certain, the Sacred Choir would be needed more than ever. She asked God's forgiveness for her cowardice and tried to pray as she always had, and had taught the women to do, as the Counselor met with the apostles. But she found herself unable to concentrate on the Credo. Abbot João and Big João were no longer insisting on taking the Counselor to the refuge, but the Street Commander was endeavoring to dissuade him from making the rounds of the trenches: the battle might take you by surprise, out in the open, with no protection, Father.

The Counselor never argued, and he did not do so now. He gently removed the head of the Lion of Natuba from his knees and placed it on the floor without disturbing the Lion's sleep. He rose to his feet and Abbot João and Big João also stood up. He had become thinner still in recent days and looked even taller now. A shiver ran down Maria Quadrado's spine as she saw how greatly troubled he was: his eyes narrowed in a deep frown, his mouth half open in a grimace that was like a terrible premonition.

She decided then and there to accompany him. She did not always do so, especially in recent weeks when, because of the press of the crowds in the narrow streets, the Catholic Guard was obliged to form such an unyielding wall around the Counselor that it had been difficult for her and the women of the Choir to stay close to him. But now she suddenly felt it absolutely necessary to go with him. She gestured and the women of the Choir flocked to her side. They followed the men out, leaving the Lion of Natuba fast asleep in the Sanctuary.

The appearance of the Counselor in the doorway of the Sanctuary took the crowd gathered there by surprise, so much so that they did not have time to block his path. At a signal from Big João, the men with blue armbands stationed in the open space between the small Chapel of Santo Antônio and the Temple under construction, to keep order among the pilgrims who had just arrived, ran to surround the saint, who was already striding down the little Street of the Martyrs toward the path leading to As Umburanas. As she trotted after the Counselor, surrounded by the women of the Choir, Maria Quadrado remembered her journey from Salvador to Monte Santo, and the young *sertanejo* who had raped her, for whom she had felt compassion. It was a bad sign: she remembered the greatest sin of her life only when she was greatly dejected. She had repented of this sin countless times, had confessed it publicly and whispered it in the ears of parish priests, and done every manner of penance for it. But her grievous fault still lay there in the depths of her memory, rising periodically to the surface to torture her.

She realized that amid the cries of 'Long live the Counselor' there were voices calling her by name – 'Mother Maria Quadrado! Mother of Men!' – seeking her out, pointing her out. This popularity seemed to her to be a trap set by the Devil. In the beginning, she had told herself that those who sought her intercession were pilgrims from Monte Santo who had known her there. But in the end she realized that she owed the veneration of which she was the object to the many years that she had devoted to serving the Counselor, that people believed that he had thereby imbued her with his own saintliness.

The feverish bustle, the preparations that she could see in the narrow winding paths, and the huts crowded together on Belo Monte gradually made the Superior of the Sacred Choir forget her worries. The spades and hoes, the sounds of hammering meant that Canudos was preparing for war. The village was being transformed, as though a battle were about to take place in each and every dwelling. She saw men erecting on the rooftops those little platforms that she had seen amid the treetops in the *caatinga*, where hunters lay in wait for jaguars. Even inside the dwellings, men, women, and children, who stopped their work to cross themselves, were digging pits or filling sacks with earth. And all of them had carbines, blunderbusses, pikes, clubs, knives, bandoleers, or were piling up pebbles, odds and ends of iron, stones.

The path leading down to As Umburanas, an open space on either side of a little stream, was unrecognizable. The Catholic Guard had to guide the women of the Choir across this terrain riddled with holes and crisscrossed with countless trenches. Because, in addition to the trench that she had seen when the last procession had passed by this way, there were now pits dug everywhere, with one or two men inside them, surrounded by parapets to protect their heads and serve as supports for their rifles.

The arrival of the Counselor caused great rejoicing. Those who were digging pits or carrying loads of earth came hurrying over to listen to his words. Standing below the cart that the saint had climbed up on, behind a double row of Catholic Guards, Maria Quadrado could see dozens of armed men in the trench, some of whom, fast asleep in ridiculous postures, did not awaken despite all the commotion. In her mind's eye, she saw them, awake the whole night watching, working, preparing to defend Belo Monte against the Great Dog, and felt affection for all of them, the desire to wipe their foreheads, to give them water and fresh-baked bread and tell them that for their abnegation the Most Holy Mother and the Father would forgive them all their sins.

The Counselor had begun to speak, whereupon all the din ceased. He did not speak of dogs or elect, but of the waves of pain that arose in the Heart of Mary when, in obedience to the law of the Jews, she brought her son to the Temple, eight days after his birth, to shed his blood in the rite of circumcision. The Counselor was describing, in accents that touched Maria Quadrado's soul – and she could see that all those present were equally moved – how the Christ Child, immediately after being circumcised, raised his arms toward the Holy Mother, seeking to be comforted, and how his bleatings of a little lamb pierced the soul of Our Lady and tortured her, when suddenly it began to rain. The murmur of the crowd, the people falling on their knees before this proof that even the elements were moved by what the Counselor was recounting, told Maria Quadrado that the brothers and sisters realized that a miracle had just taken place. 'Is it a sign, Mother?' Alexandrinha Correa murmured. Maria Quadrado nodded. The Counselor said that they should hear how Mary moaned on seeing so lovely a flower baptized in blood at the dawn of His precious life, and that the tears He shed were a symbol of those Our Lady shed daily for the sins and cowardice of men who, like the priest of the Temple, made Jesus bleed. At that moment the Little Blessed One arrived, followed by a procession bearing the statues from the churches and the glass case with the countenance of the Blessed Jesus.

Among those who had just arrived was the Lion of Natuba, almost lost from sight in the crowd, his back as curved as a scythe, soaking wet. The Little Blessed One and the scribe were lifted up and carried bodily to their rightful places by the Catholic Guard.

When the procession started off again, toward the Vaza-Barris, the rain had turned the ground into a quagmire. The elect floundered in the mud, and in a few moments the statues, standards, canopies, and banners were lead-colored lumps and strips of cloth. As the rain pelted the surface of the river, the Counselor, standing atop an altar of barrels, spoke of something, the war perhaps, in a voice that those closest to him could barely hear, but what they heard they repeated to those behind them, who passed it on to those farther back, and so on, in a series of concentric circles.

Referring to God and His Church, he said that in all things the body must be united to the head, otherwise it would not be a living body nor would it live the life of the head, and Maria Quadrado, her feet buried in the warm mud, feeling the little lamb that Alexandrinha Correa was holding by its rope brush against her knees, understood that he was speaking of the indissoluble union that there must be between the elect and himself and the Father, the Son, and the Divine in the battle. And she had only to look at the faces around her to know that all of them understood, just as she did, that he was thinking of them when he said that the faithful believer had the wariness of the serpent and the innocence of the dove. Maria Quadrado trembled on hearing him psalmodize: 'I pour myself out like water and all my bones are dislocated. My heart has turned to wax and is melting into my bowels.' She had heard him softly chant this same psalm – was it four, five years ago? – on the heights of Masseté, the day of the confrontation that put an end to the pilgrimages.

The multitude went along the river's edge, following in the Counselor's footsteps, amid plots of ground that the elect had worked, sowing them with maize and manioc, putting goats, kids, lambs, cows out to pasture. Was all this about to disappear, swept away by heresy? Maria Quadrado also saw pits that had been dug in the middle of the cultivated fields, with armed men in them. From a little rise of ground, the Counselor was now speaking explicitly of the war. Would the rifles of the Freemasons spit out water instead of bullets? She knew that the Counselor's words were not to be taken literally, because they were often comparisons, symbols whose meaning was hard to puzzle out, whose relationship to events could be seen clearly only after the latter had taken place. It had stopped raining and torches were now lit. A smell of freshness filled the air. The Counselor explained that the fact that the Throat-Slitter had a white horse came as no surprise to the believer, for wasn't it written in the Apocalypse that such a horse would come and that its rider would be carrying a bow and a crown so as to conquer and rule? But his conquests would end at the gates of Belo Monte through the intercession of Our Lady.

And he made his way in this fashion from the exit to Jeremoabo to the one to Uauá, from O Cambaio to the Rosário entrance, from the road to Chorrochó to O Curral dos Bois, bringing men and women the fire of his presence. He stopped at all the trenches, and in all of them he was received and sent on his way again with cheers and applause. It was the longest procession that Maria Quadrado could remember, amid heavy downpours that would suddenly start and as suddenly stop, abrupt changes in the sky overhead, ups and downs that matched those of her spirits, which all through the day had gone from panic to serenity and from pessimism to enthusiasm.

It was dark now, and at the Cocorobó exit the Counselor drew a comparison between Eve, in whom curiosity and disobedience predominated, and Mary, all love and willing submission, who had never succumbed to the temptation of the forbidden fruit responsible for man's Fall. In the faint light, Maria Quadrado saw the Counselor standing amid Abbot João, Big João, the Little Blessed One, the Vilanovas, and the thought came to her that, just like herself, Mary Magdalene, there in Judea, had seen the Blessed Jesus and his disciples, men as humble and good as these, and had thought, just as she was thinking at this moment, how generous it was of the Lord to elect, so that history might take a different direction, not rich landowners and *capangas*, but a handful of the humblest of men. She suddenly realized that the Lion of Natuba was not among the apostles. Her heart skipped a beat. Had he fallen and been trampled underfoot, was he lying on the muddy ground somewhere, with his tiny body like a child's and his eyes of a wise man? She reproached herself for not having paid more attention to him and ordered the women of the Choir to go look for him. But they could scarcely move in the dense crowd.

On the way back, Maria Quadrado managed to make her way to Big João, and was telling him that he must find the Lion of Natuba when the first cannon report rang out. The multitude stopped to listen and many pairs of eyes scanned the heavens in consternation. At that moment there came another roar of cannon fire and they saw a dwelling in the cemetery section blow up, reduced to splinters and cinders. In the stampede that ensued round about her, Maria felt a shapeless body press against hers, seeking refuge. She recognized the Lion of Natuba by his great mane and his tiny frame. She put her arms around him, held him close, kissed him tenderly, as she murmured in his ear: 'My son, my little son, I thought you were lost, your mother is happy, so happy.' A bugle call in the distance, long and lugubrious, spread more panic in the night. The Counselor strode on, at the same pace, toward the heart of Belo Monte. Trying to shield the Lion of Natuba from the pushing and shoving, Maria Quadrado did her best to stay as close as possible to the ring of men who, once the first moment of confusion was past, closed in around the Counselor again. But as the two of them made their way along, stumbling and falling, the crowd pushed and shoved its way past them, and by the time they finally reached the esplanade between the churches, it was filled with people. Drowning out the cries of people calling to each other or pleading for heaven's protection, Abbot João's great booming voice ordered all the lamps in Canudos extinguished. Soon the city was a pit of darkness in which Maria Quadrado could not even make out the scribe's features.

'The fear has left me,' she thought. The war had begun; at any moment another shell might fall right here and turn her and the Lion into the shapeless heap of bone and muscle that the people who had lived in the destroyed house must now be. And yet she was no longer afraid. 'Thank you, Father, Blessed Mother,' she prayed. Holding the scribe in her arms, she dropped to the ground, like the others. She listened for gunfire. But there were no shots. Why this darkness, then? She had spoken aloud, for the Lion's voice sang out in answer: 'So they can't take aim at us, Mother.'

The bells of the Temple of the Blessed Jesus rang out and their metallic echo drowned out the blare of bugles with which the Dog was trying to terrorize Belo Monte. This pealing of bells, which was to go on all the rest of the night, was like a great gale of faith, of relief. 'He's up there in the bell tower,' Maria Quadrado said. There was a roar of grateful thanks, of affirmation, from the multitude gathered in the square, as people felt themselves bathed in the defiant, restorative ringing of the bells. And Maria Quadrado thought of how the Counselor in his wisdom had known, amid the panic, precisely what to do to establish order among the believers and bring them hope.

Another shell landing filled the entire square with yellow light. The explosion lifted Maria Quadrado off the ground, set her back down again, and made her head ring. In the second of light she caught a glimpse of the faces of women and children looking up at the sky as though gazing into hell. She suddenly realized that the bits and pieces that she had seen flying through the air were what had been the house of Eufrásio the shoemaker, from Chorrochó, who lived close by the cemetery with a swarm of daughters, sons-in-law, and grandchildren. A silence followed the explosion, and this time no one ran. The bells went on pealing as joyously as before. It did her heart good to feel the Lion of Natuba huddling next to her, so close it was as though he were trying to hide inside her aged body.

There was a sudden stir, shadows clearing a path before them and shouting: 'Water carriers! Water carriers!' She recognized Antônio and Honório Vilanova and realized where they were going. Two or three days before, the storekeeper had explained to the Counselor that, among the other measures being taken in preparation for combat, the water carriers had been instructed that when the fighting began they were to pick up the wounded and take them to the Health Houses and take the dead to a stable that had been converted into a morgue, so as to give them Christian burial later. Stretcher-bearers and gravediggers now, the water carriers were setting to work. Maria Quadrado prayed for them, thinking: 'Everything is happening as we were told it would.'

Not far off, someone was weeping. There was, apparently, no one in the square except women and children. Where were the men? They must have run to clamber up onto the platforms in the trees, to crouch down in the trenches and behind the parapets, and had doubtless now joined Abbot João, Macambira, Pajeú, Big João, Pedrão, Taramela, and the other leaders, armed with their carbines and rifles, with their pikes, knives, machetes, and clubs, out somewhere peering into the darkness, waiting for the Antichrist. She felt gratitude, love for these men who were about to be bitten by the Dog and perhaps die. Lulled by the bells in the tower, she prayed for them.

And so the night passed, amid brief thunderstorms that drowned out the pealing of the bells, and spaced cannon shots that pulverized one or two shacks and started fires that the next thunderstorm put out. A cloud of smoke that made people's throats and eyes burn drifted over the city, and Maria Quadrado, as she drowsed with the Lion of Natuba cradled in her arms, could hear people around her coughing and hawking. Suddenly someone shook her. She opened her eyes and saw that she was surrounded by the women of the Sacred Choir, in a light as yet still very faint, struggling to dispel the darkness. The Lion of Natuba was propped up against her knees, fast asleep. The bells were still ringing. The women embraced her; they had been looking for her, calling her in the darkness; she was so weary and numb she could barely hear them. She woke the Lion up: his huge eyes gazed at her, gleaming brightly, from behind the jungle of his wild locks. The two of them struggled to their feet.

Part of the square was empty now, and Alexandrinha Correa explained to her that Antônio Vilanova had ordered those women for whom no more room was left in the churches to go back to their houses, to hide in the trenches, because now that day was about to break, cannonades would rake the esplanade. Surrounded by the women of the Choir, the Lion of Natuba and Maria Quadrado made their way to the Temple of the Blessed Jesus. The Catholic Guard let them in. It was still dark within the labyrinth of beams and half-erected walls. But the Superior of the Sacred Choir could make out, not only women and children curled up like cats, but armed men as well, and Big João, running about with a carbine and bandoleers about his neck. She felt herself being pushed, dragged, guided toward the scaffolding with knots of people standing on it peering out. She climbed up, aided by strong sinewy arms, hearing people call her Mother, without letting go of the Lion, who every so often very nearly slipped out of her arms. Before reaching the bell tower, she heard yet another burst of cannon fire, very far off.

Finally she spied the Counselor, on the bell platform. He was on his knees, praying, inside a barrier of men who were allowing no one to climb up the little ladder leading to the platform. But they let her and the Lion come up. She threw herself on the planks and kissed the Counselor's feet, or rather, the crust of dried mud on them, for he had long since lost his sandals. When she stood up again she noted that it was fast growing light. She walked over to the embrasure of stone and wood, and, blinking her eyes, saw on the hills a dim gray-red-blue blur, with bright glints here and there, coming down toward Canudos. She did not ask the silent, frowning men taking turns ringing the bells what the blur was, for her heart told her that it was the dogs. Filled with hatred, they were descending on Belo Monte to perpetrate another massacre of the innocents.

*

'They're not going to kill me,' Jurema thinks. She allows herself to be dragged along by the soldiers who are holding her wrists in an iron grip and force her to enter the labyrinth of branches, thorns, tree trunks, and mud. She slips and scrambles to her feet again, looking apologetically at the men in ragged uniforms in whose eyes and on whose parted lips she perceives what she first came to know on that morning that changed her life, there in Queimadas, when after the shooting Galileo Gall threw himself upon her. She thinks, with a serenity that astonishes her: 'As long as they have that look in their eyes, as long as that's what they want, they won't kill me.' She forgets Rufino and Gall and thinks only of saving her life, of holding them up for a while, of pleasing them, of pleading with them, of doing anything she has to so that they won't kill her. She slips again, and this time one of them lets go of her and falls on top of her, on his knees with his legs open. The other one also lets go of her and steps back a pace to watch, all excited. The one who is on top of her brandishes his rifle, warning her that he'll beat her face to a pulp if she screams. Clear-sighted, obedient, she calms down instantly, goes limp, nods gently to reassure him. It is the same look, the same ravenous, bestial expression as that other time. With her eyes half closed she sees him feel about inside his trousers, unbutton them, as he tries to lift her skirt up with the hand that has just let go of the rifle. She helps him as best she can, hunching up, stretching out one leg, but even so it gets in his way and finally he rips it away. All sorts of ideas sputter in her head and she also hears thunder, bugles, bells, behind the soldier's panting. He is lying on top of her, hitting her with one of his elbows until she understands and moves the leg that is in his way aside, and now she feels, between her thighs, the hard, wet rod, struggling to enter her. She feels asphyxiated by the weight of the man, and each of his movements seems to break one of her bones. She makes an intense effort not to betray the repugnance that comes over her when the bearded face rubs against hers, and a mouth, green from the blades of grass that it is still chewing, flattens itself against hers and forces her to separate her lips so as to voraciously shove in a tongue that works hers over. She is concentrating so hard on not doing anything that might irritate him that she does not see the men draped in cloaks of grass arrive, nor does she notice when they put a knife to the soldier's throat and give him a kick that rolls him off her. It is only when she feels free of the weight of him and can breathe again that she sees them. There are twenty, thirty of them, perhaps more, and they fill the entire *caatinga* around her. They bend down, pull her skirt around her, cover her, help her to sit up, to rise to her feet. She hears kind words, sees faces that are trying their best to appear friendly.

It seems to her that she is waking up, that she is coming back from a very long journey, that no more than a few minutes have gone by since the soldiers fell upon her. What has become of Rufino, Gall, the Dwarf? As though it were a dream, she remembers the two men fighting, remembers the soldiers shooting at them. A few paces away, the soldier who had been on top of her is being interrogated by a short, sturdy *caboclo* well along in years, whose dull yellowish-gray features are cruelly mutilated by a scar running from his mouth to his eyes. She thinks: Pajeú. For the first time that day she feels afraid. A look of terror has come over the soldier's face, he is answering every question he is asked as fast as he can get the words out, and is begging, pleading, with his eyes, mouth, hands, for as Pajeú interrogates him others are stripping him naked. They remove his tattered tunic, his frayed trousers, without manhandling him, and Jurema – feeling neither happy nor sad, as though she were still dreaming – sees the *jagunços*, once they have stripped him naked, at a simple gesture from that *caboclo* people tell such terrible stories about, plunge several knives into him, in the belly, in the back, in the neck, and sees the soldier topple over dead without even having had the time to scream. She sees one of the *jagunços* bend down, take hold of the soldier's penis, soft and now very small, cut it off with one stroke of his knife and in the same motion stuff it into his mouth. He then wipes his knife on the corpse and thrusts it back into his belt. She feels neither joy nor sadness nor revulsion.

She realizes that the *caboclo* without a nose is speaking to her. 'Are you on your way to Belo Monte alone or with other pilgrims?' He pronounces each word slowly, as though she might not understand him, hear him. 'Where are you from?'

She finds it hard to speak. In a voice that seems to be another woman's, she stammers that she has come from Queimadas.

'A long journey,' the *caboclo* says, looking her up and down, obviously curious. 'And what's more, by the same route the soldiers were following.'

Jurema nods. She ought to thank him, say something nice to him for having rescued her, but she is too terrified of this famous outlaw. All the other *jagunços* are standing round about her, and with their grass cloaks, their weapons, their whistles, they impress her as being not real live men but creatures out of a fairy tale or a nightmare.

'You can't get to Belo Monte from this direction,' Pajeú tells her, with a grimace that must be his way of smiling. 'There are Protestants all about in these hills. Go around them instead, till you get to the road from Jeremoabo. There aren't any soldiers on that side.'

'My husband,' Jurema murmurs, pointing to the thicket.

Her voice catches in a sob. She hurries off, overcome with anxiety as the memory of what was happening when the soldiers arrived on the scene suddenly comes back to her and she recognizes the other one, the one who was watching as he waited for his turn: he is the naked, bloody corpse hanged by the neck from a tree, swaying back and forth alongside his uniform, which has also been hung up in the branches. Jurema knows which way to go, for she hears a noise to guide her, and indeed in just a few moments she comes upon Galileo Gall and Rufino, in the part of the *caatinga* decorated with uniforms. The two men have taken on the same color as the muddy earth, and must be dying, yet they are still fighting. They are tattered wrecks locked together, hitting out at each other with their heads, with their feet, biting and scratching each other, but so slowly it is as if they are playing. Jurema halts in front of them and the *caboclo* and the *jagunços* gather round in a circle to watch the fight. It is a contest that is nearing its end, two shapes covered with mud, unrecognizable, inseparable, who are barely moving and give no sign that they have noticed that they are surrounded by dozens of people who have just arrived on the scene. They lie there panting, bleeding, ripping off bits and pieces of each other's clothes.

'You're Jurema, you're the wife of the guide from Queimadas,' Pajeú says at her side, in an excited voice. 'He found you, then. And found that poor fool who was at Calumbi.'

'That's the lunatic who fell into the trap last night,' someone on the other side of the circle says. 'The one who was so terrified of the soldiers.'

Jurema feels a hand in hers, a tiny chubby one, squeezing tightly. It is the Dwarf. He looks at her with eyes full of hope and joy, as though she were about to save his life. Covered with mud, he clings to her.

'Stop them, stop them, Pajeú,' Jurema says. 'Save my husband, save . . .'

'Do you want me to save both of them?' Pajeú says mockingly. 'Do you want to stay with both of them?'

Jurema hears other *jagunços* laugh at these words from the *caboclo* without a nose.

'This is men's business, Jurema,' Pajeú calmly explains to her. 'You got them into this. Leave them in the mess you got them into, and let them settle the matter between them the way two men should. If your husband gets out of it alive, he'll kill you, and if he dies you'll be to blame for his death and you'll have to account for yourself to the Father. In Belo Monte the Counselor will tell you what you must do to redeem yourself. So be off with you now, because war is coming this way. Praised be Blessed Jesus the Counselor!'

The *caatinga* stirs, and in seconds the *jagunços* disappear in the scrub. The Dwarf continues to squeeze her hand as he stands there watching with her. Jurema sees that there is a knife plunged halfway into Gall's ribs. She can still hear bugles, bells, whistles. Suddenly the struggle ends, for with a roar Gall rolls a few yards away from Rufino. Jurema sees him grab hold of the knife and pull it out of his side with another roar. She looks at Rufino, who looks back at her as he lies there in the mud, his mouth open, his eyes lifeless.

'You still haven't slapped my face,' she hears Galileo say, urging Rufino on with the hand that is clutching the knife.

Jurema sees Rufino nod and thinks: 'They understand each other.' She doesn't know what the thought means and yet she feels that it is altogether true. Rufino drags himself toward Gall, very slowly. Will he reach him? He pushes himself along with his elbows, with his knees, rubs his face in the mud, like an earthworm, and Gall urges him on, waving the knife. 'Men's business,' Jurema thinks. She thinks: 'The blame will fall on me.' Rufino reaches Gall, who tries to plunge the knife into him, as the guide strikes him in the face. But the slap has no momentum behind it by the time it lands, for Rufino has no energy left or has entirely lost heart. The hand lingers on Gall's face, like a sort of caress. Gall strikes too, once, twice, and then his hand rests quietly on the guide's head. They lie dying in each other's arms, gazing into each other's eyes. Jurema has the impression that the two faces, a fraction of an inch apart, are smiling at each other. The bugle calls and the whistles have been succeeded now by heavy gunfire. The Dwarf says something that she does not understand.

'You struck him in the face, Rufino,' Jurema thinks. 'What did you gain by that, Rufino? What use was there in getting your revenge if you've died, if you've left me all alone in the world, Rufino?' She does not weep, she does not move, she does not take her eyes from the two motionless men. That hand on Rufino's head reminds her that in Queimadas, when to the misfortune of all of them God willed that the stranger should come to offer her husband work, he had once felt Rufino's head and read its secrets for him, just as Porfírio the sorcerer read them in coffee grounds and Dona Cacilda in a basin of water.

*

'Did I tell you who turned up in Calumbi among the people accompanying Moreira César?' the Baron de Canabrava said. 'That reporter who once worked for me and was lured away by Epaminondas to the *Jornal de Notícias.* That disaster on two feet with glasses like the goggles of a diving suit who stumbled about scribbling and wore some sort of clown costume. Do you remember him, Adalberto? He wrote poetry and smoked opium.'

But neither Colonel José Bernardo Murau nor Adalberto de Gumúcio was listening. The latter was rereading the papers that the baron had just translated for them, bringing them up close to the candelabrum lighting the dining-room table, from which their empty coffee cups had not yet been removed. Old Murau, swaying back and forth in his high-backed chair at the table as though he were still in his rocking chair in the little sitting room, appeared to have fallen asleep. But the baron knew that he was thinking about what his guest had read to the two of them.

'I'm going to see Estela,' the baron said, rising to his feet.

As he walked through the ramshackle manor house, plunged in shadow, to the bedroom where they had put the baroness to bed shortly before dinner, he calculated the impression that that sort of testament left with him by the Scottish adventurer had made on his friends. As he stumbled on a broken tile in the hallway onto which bedrooms on either side opened, he thought: 'There will be more questions in Salvador. And each time I explain why I let him go, I'll have the same feeling that I'm lying.' Why exactly had he let Galileo Gall go? Out of stupidity? Out of weariness? Out of disgust at everything that had happened? Out of sympathy? 'I have a weak spot in my heart for odd specimens, for what's abnormal,' he thought, remembering Gall and the nearsighted journalist.

From the doorway, in the feeble reddish glow of the night lamp on the bedside table, he saw Sebastiana's profile. She was sitting at the foot of the bed, in an armchair with cushions, and though she had never been a cheerful, smiling woman, her expression now was so grave that the baron was alarmed. She had risen to her feet on seeing him enter the room.

'Has she gone on sleeping quietly?' the baron asked, raising the mosquito netting and bending over to look at his wife. Her eyes were closed and in the semidarkness her face, though very pale, looked serene. The sheets rose and fell gently with her breathing.

'Sleeping, yes, but not all that quietly,' Sebastiana said in a low voice, accompanying him to the door of the bedroom. She lowered her voice even more, and the baron noted the concern lurking deep in her black eyes. 'She's dreaming. She keeps talking in her sleep – always about the same thing.'

'Sebastiana doesn't dare mention the words "burning down," "fire," "flames,"' the baron thought with a heavy heart. Would they become taboo, would he be obliged to give orders that any words that Estela might associate with the holocaust at Calumbi never be uttered in their home? He had taken her by the arm, trying to calm her, but could find nothing to say to her. He felt the maidservant's smooth, warm skin beneath his fingers.

'My mistress cannot stay here,' she muttered. 'Take her to Salvador. Doctors must see her, give her something, free her mind of those memories. She can't go on suffering such anguish night and day.'

'I know, Sebastiana,' the baron assured her. 'But it's such a long, hard journey. It strikes me as too great a risk to expose her to more traveling in the state she's in. Though I grant that it may be even more dangerous to keep her from getting medical treatment. We'll see tomorrow. You must go get some rest now. You haven't slept a wink either for several days now.'

'I'm going to spend the night here with my mistress,' Sebastiana answered in a defiant tone of voice.

As he saw her settle herself in the armchair at Estela's bedside, the thought ran through the baron's mind that she was still a woman with a firm, beautiful, admirably preserved figure. 'Just like Estela,' he said to himself. And in a wave of nostalgia he remembered that in the first years of their marriage he had come to feel such intense jealousy that it kept him awake nights on seeing the camaraderie, the inviolable intimacy that existed between the two women. He went back to the dining room, and saw through a window that the night sky was covered with clouds that hid the stars. He remembered, smiling, that because of his feelings of jealousy he had one day asked Estela to dismiss Sebastiana; the argument that had ensued had been the most serious one of their entire married life. He entered the dining room with the vivid, painful image, still intact, of the baroness, her cheeks on fire, defending her maidservant and repeating over and over that if Sebastiana left, she was leaving, too. This memory, which had long remained a spark setting his desire aflame, moved him to the depths now. He felt like weeping. He found his friends absorbed in conjectures as to whether what he had read to them could possibly be true.

'A braggart, a dreamer, a rascal with a lively imagination, a first-rate confidence man,' Colonel Murau was saying. 'Even heroes in novels don't have that many adventures. The only part I believe is where he tells about the agreement with Epaminondas to take arms to Canudos. A smuggler who invented that story about anarchism as a pretext and a justification.'

'A pretext and a justification?' Adalberto de Gumúcio bounced up and down in his chair. 'An aggravating circumstance, rather.'

The baron sat down next to him and tried to take an interest in the discussion.

'Does attempting to do away with property, religion, marriage, morality impress you as being a mitigating circumstance?' Gumúcio said, pressing his point. 'That's far more serious than trafficking in arms.'

'Marriage, morality,' the baron thought. And he wondered if Adalberto would have permitted in his home as intimate a relationship as that between Estela and Sebastiana. His heart sank again as he thought about his wife. He decided to leave the following morning. He poured himself a glass of port and took a long sip of it.

'I'm inclined to believe that the story is true,' Gumúcio said. 'Because of the natural way in which he tells of all those extraordinary things – the escapes, the murders, his voyages as a freebooter, his sexual abstinence. He doesn't realize that there is anything out of the ordinary about them. This makes me think that he really experienced them and that he believes the horrendous things he says against God, the family, and society.'

'There's no doubt that he believes them,' the baron said, savoring the sweetish afterglow left by the port. 'I heard him tell them many times, at Calumbi.'

Old Murau filled their glasses again. They had not drunk during dinner, but after the coffee their host had brought out this decanter full of port that was now nearly half empty. Was drinking till he fell into a stupor what he needed to keep his mind off Estela's health? the baron wondered.

'He confuses reality and illusion, he has no idea where the one ends and the other begins,' he said. 'It may be that he recounts those things in all sincerity and believes every word. It doesn't matter. Because he doesn't see them with his eyes but through the filter of his ideas, his beliefs. Don't you recall what he says about Canudos, about the *jagunços*? It must be the same with all the rest. It's quite possible that to him a street fight among ruffians in Barcelona or a raid on smugglers by the police in Marseilles is a battle waged by the oppressed against the oppressors in the war to shatter the chains binding humanity.'

'And what about sex?' José Bernardo Murau said: his face was congested, his little eyes gleaming, his tongue thick. 'Do you two swallow that story about his ten years of chastity? Ten years of chastity to store up energy to be released in revolution?'

His tone of voice was such that the baron suspected that at any moment he would begin to tell off-color stories.

'What about priests?' he asked. 'Don't they live in chastity out of love of God? Gall is a sort of priest.'

'José Bernardo judges men by his own example,' Gumúcio joked, turning to their host. 'You couldn't have remained chaste for ten years for anything in the world.'

'Not for anything in the world.' Murau laughed. 'Isn't it stupid to give up one of the few compensations life has to offer?'

One of the tapers in the candelabrum began to sputter and give off a little cloud of smoke, and Murau rose to his feet to blow it out. While he was up, he poured all of them another glass of port, leaving the decanter completely empty.

'During all those years of abstinence he must have accumulated enough energy to cover a she-donkey and leave her pregnant,' he said, his eyes aglow. He gave a vulgar laugh and staggered over to a buffet to get out another bottle of port. The remaining tapers in the candelabrum were going out and the room had grown dark. 'What does the guide's wife, the woman who caused him to renounce chastity, look like?'

'I haven't seen her for some time,' the baron said. 'She was a little bit of a thing, docile and timid.'

'A good behind?' Colonel Murau said thickly, raising his glass to his lips with a trembling hand. 'In these parts, that's the best thing they've got. They're weak little things and they age fast. But they all have first-class asses.'

Adalberto de Gumúcio hurriedly changed the subject. 'It's going to be hard to make a peace pact with the Jacobins as you suggest,' he remarked to the baron. 'Our friends won't want to work with those who have been attacking us for so many years.'

'Of course it's going to be hard,' the baron answered, grateful to Adalberto for bringing up another subject. 'Above all, persuading Epaminondas, who thinks he's won. But in the end they'll all realize that there's no other way. It's a question of survival . . .'

He was interrupted by the sound of hoofbeats and whinnies very close by and, a moment later, by loud knocking at the door. José Bernardo Murau frowned in irritation. 'What the devil is going on?' he grumbled, struggling to his feet. He shuffled out of the dining room, and the baron filled their glasses again.

'You drinking: that's something new, I must say,' Gumúcio commented. 'Is it because Calumbi was burned down? That's not the end of the world, you know. Just a temporary setback.'

'It's on account of Estela,' the baron said. 'I'll never forgive myself. It was my fault, Adalberto. I asked too much of her. I shouldn't have taken her to Calumbi, just as you and Viana warned me. It was selfish, stupid of me.'

They heard the bolt of the front door slide open, and men's voices.

'It's a passing crisis that she'll soon recover from,' Gumúcio said. 'It's absurd of you to blame yourself.'

'I've decided to go on to Salvador tomorrow,' the baron said. 'It's more of a risk keeping her here, without medical attention.'

José Bernardo Murau reappeared in the doorway. He seemed to have sobered up all of a sudden, and had such an odd expression on his face that Gumúcio and the baron hurried to his side.

'News of Moreira César?' The baron took him by the arm, trying to bring him back to reality.

'Incredible, incredible,' the old cattle breeder muttered, as though he'd just seen ghosts.

VII

The first thing the nearsighted journalist notices in the early dawn light as he shakes the crusted mud off himself is that his body aches more than it did the evening before, as though he had received a terrible beating during his sleepless night. Secondly, the feverish activity, the movement of uniforms that is taking place without any orders being given, in a silence that is a sharp contrast to the sound of cannon fire, bells, and bugles that has assailed his ears all night long. He throws his big leather pouch over his shoulder, tucks the portable writing desk under his arm, and, with pins and needles in his legs and the tickle of an imminent sneeze in his nose, begins to climb the slope toward Colonel Moreira César's tent. 'The humidity,' he thinks, overcome by a fit of sneezing that makes him forget the war and everything save those internal explosions that bring tears to his eyes, stop up his ears, dizzy his brain, and turn his nostrils into anthills. Soldiers brush by him and push him aside as they hurry past, buckling on their knapsacks, rifles in hand, and he can now hear voices shouting orders.

Arriving at the top, he spies Moreira César, surrounded by officers, standing on something, looking down the mountainside through field glasses. Round about him, enormous confusion reigns. The white horse, saddled and ready, rears amid soldiers and buglers who bump into officers coming or going on the run, shouting phrases that the journalist, his ears buzzing from his sneezes, barely catches. He hears the colonel's voice: 'What's happening with the artillery, Cunha Matos?' The reply is drowned out by the blare of bugle calls. Ridding himself of his pouch and writing desk, the journalist steps forward to have a look at Canudos below.

He has not seen it the night before, and the thought crosses his mind that within minutes or hours no one will ever see it again. He hurriedly wipes the fogged lenses of his glasses on the tail of his undershirt and observes the scene that lies at his feet. The light, of a hue between dark blue and leaden, suffusing the mountain peaks, has not yet reached the hollow in which Canudos lies. He finds it hard to make out where the hillsides, the fields, and the stony ground end and the jumble of huts and shacks, huddled together one atop the other over a wide area, begins. But he immediately spies two churches, one of them small and the other very tall, with imposing towers, separated by a quadrangular open space. He is squinting, trying to make out in the half light the area bounded by a river which appears to be at high water, when a cannonade begins that makes him start and clap his hands over his ears. But he does not close his eyes, staring in fascination as flames suddenly appear below and several shacks are reduced to a shower of planks, bricks, laths, straw mats, unidentifiable objects that fly to pieces and disappear. The cannon fire grows heavier and Canudos vanishes from sight beneath a cloud of smoke that ascends the hillsides and opens up, here and there, to form craters from which there come flying out bits of rooftops and walls blown to pieces by exploding shells. The stupid thought crosses his mind that if the cloud of smoke continues to rise it will reach his nose and send him into another fit of sneezing.

'What is the Seventh waiting for! And the Ninth! And the Sixteenth!' he hears Moreira César's voice say, so close to him that he turns around to look, and finds the colonel and the group around him practically at his side.

'The Seventh is charging down there, sir,' Captain Olímpio de Castro answers just a few steps away.

'And the Ninth and the Sixteenth,' someone hastily adds from behind him.

'You are witness to a spectacle that will make you famous.' Colonel Moreira César claps him on the back as he passes him. He is left no time to answer, for the colonel and his staff leave him standing there and proceed to station themselves a bit farther down the mountainside, on a little promontory.

'The Seventh, the Ninth, the Sixteenth,' he thinks. 'Battalions? Platoons? Companies?' But the light dawns immediately. From three directions on the mountainsides round about, regimental corps are descending – bayonets gleaming – toward the smoke-filled hollow in which Canudos lies. The cannons have ceased to roar, and in the silence the nearsighted journalist suddenly hears bells pealing. The troops are running, slipping, leaping down the hillsides, shooting. The slopes, too, begin to be covered with smoke. Moreira César's red-and-blue kepi nods approvingly. The journalist picks up his leather pouch and his portable writing desk and walks down the few yards that separate him from the commander of the Seventh Regiment; he settles down in a cleft in the rock, between the colonel and his staff and the white horse that an orderly is holding by the bridle. He feels strange, hypnotized, and the absurd idea passes through his mind that he is not really seeing what he is seeing.

A breeze begins to dispel the lumpy leaden-colored clouds that veil the city; he sees them grow wispier, break up, move off, driven by the wind in the direction of the open terrain where the road from Jeremoabo must be. He is now able to follow the movements of the troops. Those on his right have reached the bank of the river and are crossing it; the little red, green, blue figures are turning gray, disappearing and reappearing on the other bank, when suddenly a wall of dust rises between them and Canudos. A number of the figures fall to the ground.

'Trenches,' someone says.

The nearsighted journalist decides to approach the group surrounding the colonel, who has taken a few steps downhill and is observing the scene below, having exchanged his field glasses for a spyglass. The red ball of the sun has risen a few moments before and is now illuminating the theater of operations. Almost without realizing what he is doing, the correspondent from the *Jornal de Notícias,* who has not stopped trembling, clambers up onto a projecting rock in order to see better. He then has at least a vague idea of what is going on. The first ranks of soldiers to ford the river have been blown to bits from a series of hidden defenses, and there is now heavy gunfire down there. Another of the assault units, which is deploying almost at his feet as it attacks, is also being stopped by a heavy burst of fire from ground level. The sharpshooters are entrenched in holes dug in the earth. He sees the *jagunços.* They are those heads – wearing hats? headcloths? – that suddenly pop up out of the ground, emitting smoke, and although the cloud of dust blurs their features and silhouettes, he can make out men who have been hit by the rounds of fire or are sliding down into the holes where they are no doubt already engaged in hand-to-hand combat.

He is convulsed by a fit of sneezing so prolonged that for a moment he thinks he is going to faint. Doubled over, with his eyes closed, his glasses in his hand, he sneezes, opens his mouth, gasps desperately for air. He is finally able to straighten up, to breathe, and realizes that he is being pounded on the back. He puts his glasses back on and sees the colonel.

'We thought you'd been wounded,' Moreira César says, to all appearances in an excellent humor.

The journalist is surrounded by officers and doesn't know what to say, for the idea that anyone could think he was wounded amazes him, as though it never would have entered his head that he, too, is part of this war, that he, too, is under fire.

'What's happening? What's happening?' he stammers.

'The Ninth has entered Canudos and now the Seventh is going in,' the colonel says, the field glasses at his eyes.

Panting, his temples pounding, the nearsighted journalist has the sensation that everything has come closer, that he can reach out and touch the war. On the outskirts of Canudos there are houses in flames and two lines of soldiers are entering the town, amid puffs of cloud that must be gunsmoke. They disappear, swallowed up in a labyrinth of rooftops made of tiles, of straw, of corrugated tin, of palings, from which flames leap up from time to time. 'They are pumping all those who escaped the cannon fire full of bullets,' he thinks. And he imagines the fury with which officers and men are no doubt avenging the corpses strung up in the *caatinga*, avenging themselves for those ambushes and whistles that have kept them awake nights all the way from Monte Santo.

'There are nests of sharpshooters in the churches,' he hears the colonel say. 'What's Cunha Matos waiting for? Why doesn't he take them?'

The bells have been pealing continually and he has been hearing them all this time, like background music amid the cannonades and the fusillades. In the narrow winding streets between the dwellings he makes out figures running, uniforms scurrying every which way. 'Cunha Matos is in that hell,' he thinks. 'Running, stumbling, killing.' And Tamarindo and Olímpio de Castro? He looks for them and can't see the old colonel, but the captain is among the officers with Moreira César. For some reason, he feels relieved.

'Have the rear guard and the Bahia police attack on the other flank,' he hears the colonel order.

Captain Olímpio de Castro and three or four escorts run up the mountainside and several buglers begin to sound calls until similar calls answer in the distance. Only now does he realize that orders are passed on by means of bugles. He would like to note this down so as not to forget it. But several officers cry out something, in unison, and he begins to watch again. In the open space between the churches, ten, twelve, fifteen red-and-blue uniforms are running behind two officers – he can make out their unsheathed sabers, and tries to identify those lieutenants or captains whom he must have seen many times now – with the obvious intention of capturing the Temple with very tall white towers surrounded by scaffolding, when they are met with heavy fire from all over the building which downs the majority of them; a handful turn and disappear in the dust.

'They should have protected themselves with rifle charges,' he hears Moreira César say in an icy tone of voice. 'There's a redoubt there . . .'

Many figures have come running out of the churches; they make for the soldiers who have fallen and throw themselves on them. 'They are finishing them off, castrating them, plucking out their eyes,' he thinks, and at that instant he hears the colonel murmur: 'Those demented fools, they're undressing them.' 'Undressing them?' he repeats mentally. And he again sees the corpses of the fair-haired sergeant and his men hanging from the trees. He is half dead from the cold. The open space is still enveloped in a cloud of dust. The journalist's eyes peer about in different directions, trying to make out what is happening down below. The soldiers of the two corps that have entered Canudos, one on his left and the other at his feet, have disappeared in that taut web, while a third corps, on his right, continues to pour into the city, and he is able to measure their progress by the whirlwinds of dust that precede them and rise in their wake along the narrow alleyways, little streets, twists and turns, meanders in which he can imagine the clashes, the thrusts, the blows of rifle butts smashing doors, knocking down planks, palings, staving in roofs, episodes in the war which, on breaking down into encounters in a thousand huts, turns into utter confusion, hand-to-hand combat of one against one, one against two, two against three.

He has not taken a single swallow of water this morning, nor has he eaten anything the night before, and in addition to the hollow feeling in his stomach his guts are writhing. The bright sun is at its zenith. Can it possibly be noon, can so many hours already have gone by? Moreira César and his staff officers walk a few yards farther down the mountainside, and the nearsighted journalist follows along after them, tripping and falling, till he catches up with them. He grabs Olímpio de Castro by the arm and asks him what is happening, how many hours the battle has been going on.

'The rear guard and the Bahia police are there now,' Moreira César says, the field glasses at his eyes. 'The enemy is hemmed in on that flank.'

The nearsighted journalist makes out, on the far side of the little houses half hidden by the dust, some blue, greenish, gold-colored patches, advancing in this sector that thus far has been spared, with no smoke, no fires, no people visible. The attack now encompasses all of Canudos; there are dwellings in flames everywhere.

'This is taking too long,' the colonel says, and the nearsighted journalist notes his impatience, his indignation. 'Have the cavalry squadron come to the aid of Cunha Matos.'

He immediately detects – from the officers' surprised, disconcerted faces – that the colonel's order is unexpected, risky. None of them protests, but the looks they exchange are more eloquent than words.

'What is it?' Moreira's eyes sweep round the circle of officers and light on Olímpio de Castro. 'What is the objection?'

'None, sir,' the captain says. 'Except that . . .'

'Except what?' Moreira César replies sternly. 'That's an order.'

'The cavalry squadron is our only reserve, sir,' the captain goes on to end his sentence.

'What do we need it up here for?' Moreira César points downhill. 'Isn't the fighting down there? When those who are still alive see our cavalrymen they'll come pouring out in terror and we can finish them off. Let them charge immediately!'

'I request your permission to charge with the squadron,' Olímpio de Castro stammers.

'I need you here,' the colonel answers curtly.

The nearsighted journalist hears more bugle calls, and minutes later the cavalrymen, in troops of ten and fifteen, appear at the summit, with an officer at the head of the squadron; as they gallop past Moreira César they salute him with upraised sabers.

'Clear out the churches, drive the enemy north!' the colonel shouts to them.

The journalist is thinking that those tense young faces – white, dark-skinned, black, Indian – are about to enter the whirlwind, when he is convulsed by another fit of sneezing, worse than the one before. His glasses shoot off his nose, and he thinks in terror, as he feels asphyxia set in, his chest and temples explode, his nose itch, that they have been broken, that somebody may step on them, that his remaining days will be a perpetual fog. When the attack is over, he falls on his knees, gropes all about him in anguish till he comes across them. He discovers, to his joy, that they are intact. He cleans them, puts them back on, looks through them. The hundred or so cavalrymen have reached the bottom of the slope. How can they have descended so quickly? But something is happening to them down by the river. They cannot manage to get across it. Their mounts enter the water and then appear to rear, to rebel, despite the fury with which they are urged on with whips, spurs, saber blows. It is as if the river terrified them. They turn round in midstream, and some of them throw their riders.

'They must have set traps in the water,' one officer says.

'They're being fired on from that dead angle,' another one murmurs.

'My mount!' Moreira César cries, and the nearsighted journalist sees him hand his field glasses to an orderly. As he mounts the horse, he adds in irritation: 'The boys need to have an example set them. I'm leaving you in command, Olímpio.'

His heart beats faster as he sees the colonel unsheathe his saber, put the spurs to his mount, and begin to descend the slope at a fast gallop. But he has not gone fifty yards when he sees him slouch over in the saddle, leaning on the neck of his horse, which stops dead in its tracks. He sees the colonel turn it around – to come back up to the command post? – but as though it were receiving contradictory orders from its rider, the animal wheels round twice, three times. And now he sees why officers and escorts are uttering exclamations, shouting, running downhill with their revolvers unholstered. Moreira César rolls to the ground and almost at the same moment he is hidden from sight by the captain and the others, who have lifted him up and are carrying him up the hill toward him, as quickly as they can. There is a deafening uproar, voices shouting, shots, all sorts of noises.

He stands there stunned, unable to move, as he watches the group of men trotting up the mountainside, followed by the white horse, its reins dragging. He has been left all by himself. The terror that overcomes him drives him up the slope, slipping and falling, struggling to his feet, crawling on all fours. When he reaches the summit and bounds toward the tent, he vaguely notes that there are almost no soldiers in the area. Except for a group crowded around the entrance to the tent, the only ones in sight are a sentinel or two, looking in his direction with fear-stricken expressions. He hears the words 'Can you help Dr. Souza Ferreiro?' and although the person speaking to him is Captain Olímpio de Castro, he does not recognize his voice and barely recognizes his face. He nods, and the captain pushes him forward with such force that he collides with a soldier. Inside the tent, he sees Dr. Souza Ferreiro's back, bending over the camp cot and the colonel's feet.

'A medical corpsman?' Souza Ferreiro wheels around, and on catching sight of him a sour look comes over his face.

'I've told you already – there aren't any medical corpsmen,' Captain de Castro shouts at him, pushing the nearsighted journalist forward. 'They're all with the battalions down below. Let this fellow help you.'

The nervousness of the two of them is contagious, and he feels like screaming, like stamping his feet.

'The projectiles must be removed or infection will be the end of him in no time,' Dr. Souza Ferreiro whines, looking all about as though awaiting a miracle.

'Do the impossible,' the captain says as he leaves. 'I can't abandon my post, I'm in command, I must send word to Colonel Tamarindo to take . . .' He goes out of the tent without finishing the sentence.

'Roll up your sleeves and rub yourself with this disinfectant,' the doctor roars.

He obeys as fast as he can in the daze that has come over him, and a moment later he finds himself kneeling on the ground soaking bandages with spurts of ether – a smell that brings back memories of carnival balls at Politeama – which he then places over Colonel Moreira César's nose and mouth to keep him asleep while the doctor operates. 'Don't tremble, don't be an idiot, keep the ether over his nose,' the doctor barks at him twice. He concentrates on his task – opening the flacon, wetting the cloth, placing it over that fine-drawn nose, those lips that are contorted in a grimace of interminable agony – and he thinks of the pain that this little man must be feeling as Dr. Souza Ferreiro bends over his belly as though he were about to sniff it or lick it. Every so often he takes a quick glance, despite himself, at the spatters of blood on the doctor's hands and smock and uniform, the blanket on the bed, and his own pants. How much blood inside such a small body! The smell of ether dizzies him and makes him retch. He thinks: 'I've nothing to throw up.' He thinks: 'Why is it I'm not hungry or thirsty?' The wounded man's eyes remain closed, but from time to time he stirs and then the doctor grumbles: 'More ether, more ether.' But the last of the little flacons is almost empty now and he says so, feeling guilty.

Orderlies enter, bringing steaming basins in which the doctor washes lancets, needles, sutures, scissors, with just one hand. Several times, as he applies the ether-soaked bandages, he hears Dr. Souza Ferreiro talking to himself, dirty words, insults, imprecations, curses on his own mother for ever having borne him. He becomes more and more drowsy and the doctor reprimands him severely: 'Don't be an idiot, this is no time to be napping.' He stammers an apology and the next time they bring the basin he begs them to get him a drink of water.

He notes that they are no longer alone in the tent: the shadow that brings a canteen to his lips is Captain Olímpio de Castro. Colonel Tamarindo and Major Cunha Matos are there too, their backs leaning against the canvas, their faces grief-stricken, their uniforms in tatters. 'More ether?' he says, and feels stupid, for the flacon has been empty for some time now. Dr. Souza Ferreiro bandages Moreira César and is now covering him with the blanket. He thinks in astonishment: 'It's nighttime already.' There are shadows round about them and someone hangs a lantern on one of the tent poles.

'How is he?' Colonel Tamarindo says in a low voice.

'His belly is ripped to shreds.' The doctor sighs. 'I'm very much afraid that . . .'

As he rolls down his shirtsleeves, the nearsighted journalist thinks: 'If it was dawn, noon, just a moment ago, how is it possible for time to go by that fast?'

'I doubt that he'll even come to,' Souza Ferreiro adds.

As though in answer to him, Colonel Moreira César begins to stir. All of them move to his bedside. Are his bandages comfortable? He blinks. The nearsighted journalist imagines him seeing silhouettes, hearing sounds, trying to understand, to remember, and he himself remembers, like something from another life, certain awakenings after a night's peace induced by opium. The colonel's return to reality must be just as slow, as difficult, as hazy. Moreira César's eyes are open and he is gazing anxiously at Tamarindo, taking in his torn uniform, the deep scratches on his neck, his dejection.

'Did we take Canudos?' he articulates in a hoarse voice.

Colonel Tamarindo lowers his eyes and shakes his head. Moreira César's eyes search the embarrassed faces of the major, the captain, of Dr. Souza Ferreiro, and the nearsighted journalist sees that he is also examining him, as though performing an autopsy on him.

'We tried three times, sir,' Colonel Tamarindo stammers. 'The men fought till their last ounce of strength was gone.'

Colonel Moreira César sits up, his face even paler now than before, and angrily waves a clenched fist. 'Another attack, Tamarindo. Immediately! That's an order!'

'There are heavy casualties, sir,' the colonel murmurs shamefacedly, as though everything were his fault. 'Our position is untenable. We must retreat to a safe place and send for reinforcements . . .'

'You will be court-martialed for this,' Moreira César interrupts him, raising his voice. 'The Seventh Regiment retreat in the face of good-for-nothing rascals? Surrender your sword to Cunha Matos.'

'How can he move, how can he writhe about like that with his belly slit wide open?' the nearsighted journalist thinks. In the prolonged silence that follows, Colonel Tamarindo looks at the other officers, wordlessly pleading for their help. Cunha Matos steps closer to the camp cot.

'There are many deserters, sir; the regiment has fallen apart. If the *jagunços* attack, they'll take the camp. Order a retreat.'

Peering past the doctor and the captain, the nearsighted journalist sees Moreira César's shoulders fall back onto the cot. 'You're a traitor, too?' he murmurs in desperation. 'You all know how important this campaign is to our cause. Do you mean to tell me that I have compromised my honor in vain?'

'We've all compromised our honor, sir,' Colonel Tamarindo says.

'You know that I had to resign myself to conspiring with corrupt petty politicians.' Moreira César's voice rises and falls abruptly, absurdly. 'Do you mean to tell me that we've lied to the country in vain?'

'Listen to what's happening outside, sir,' Major Cunha Matos says in a shrill voice, and the nearsighted journalist tells himself that he has been hearing that cacophony, that clamor, those running feet, that confusion for some time, but has refused to realize what it means, so as not to feel more frightened still. 'It's a rout.

They may finish off the entire regiment if we don't make an orderly retreat.'

The nearsighted journalist makes out the sound of the cane whistles and the little bells amid the running footfalls and the voices. Colonel Moreira César looks at them one by one, his face contorted, his mouth agape. He says something that no one hears. The nearsighted journalist realizes that the flashing eyes in that livid face are fixed on him. 'You there, you,' he hears. 'Paper and pen, you hear? I want to dictate a statement concerning this infamy. Come, scribe, are you ready?'

At that moment the nearsighted journalist suddenly remembers his portable writing desk, his leather pouch, and as though bitten by a snake frantically searches all about for them. With the sensation that he has lost part of his body, an amulet that protected him, he recalls that he did not have them when he ran up the mountainside, they are still lying on the slope down below, but he can think no further because Olímpio de Castro, his eyes full of tears, thrusts some paper and a pencil into his hand, and Major Souza Ferreiro holds the lantern above him to give him light.

'I'm ready,' he says, thinking that he won't be able to write, that his hands will tremble.

'I, Colonel Moreira César, commanding officer of the Seventh Regiment, being in possession of all my faculties, hereby state that the retreat from the siege of Canudos is a decision that is being taken against my will, by subordinates who are not capable of assuming their responsibility in the face of history.' Moreira César sits up on the camp cot for a moment and then falls back once more. 'Future generations will judge. I am confident that there will be republicans to defend me. My entire conduct has been aimed at the defense of the Republic, which must make its authority felt in every corner of the country if it wishes it to progress.'

When the voice, so low that he can scarcely hear it, stops speaking, it takes him a moment to realize this, for he has fallen behind as he takes down the dictation. Writing, that manual labor, like that of placing cloths soaked in ether over the wounded man's nose, is a boon to him, for it has kept him from torturing himself with questions as to how it can have happened that the Seventh Regiment failed to take Canudos and must now beat a retreat. When he raises his eyes, the doctor has put his ear to the colonel's chest and is taking his pulse. He straightens up and makes a gesture fraught with meaning. Chaos immediately ensues, and Cunha Matos and Tamarindo begin to argue in loud voices as Olímpio de Castro tells Souza Ferreiro that the colonel's remains must not be desecrated.

'A retreat now, in darkness, is insane,' Tamarindo shouts. 'Where to? Which way? How can I ask any more of exhausted men who have fought for an entire day? Tomorrow . . .'

'Tomorrow not even the dead will still be around down there,' Cunha Matos says with a wave of his hand. 'Don't you see that the regiment is disintegrating, that there's no one in command, that if the men aren't regrouped now they'll be hunted down like rabbits?'

'Regroup them, do whatever you like. I'm staying here till dawn, to carry out a retreat in good and proper order.' Colonel Tamarindo turns to Olímpio de Castro. 'Try to reach the artillery. Those four cannons must not fall into the enemy's hands. Have Salomão da Rocha destroy them.'

'Yes, sir.'

The captain and Cunha Matos leave the tent together and the nearsighted journalist follows them like an automaton. He hears what they are saying and cannot believe his ears.

'Waiting is madness, Olímpio. We must retreat now or by morning there won't be anybody left alive.'

'I'm going to try to get to the artillery,' Olímpio de Castro cuts him short. 'It's madness perhaps, but it is my duty to obey the new commanding officer.'

The nearsighted journalist tugs at the captain's arm, muttering: 'Your canteen, I'm dying of thirst.'

He drinks avidly, choking, as the captain advises him: 'Don't stay with us. The major is right. Things are going to end badly. Clear out.'

Clear out? Take off by himself, through the *caatinga*, in the dark? Olímpio de Castro and Cunha Matos disappear, leaving him confused, afraid, petrified. Around him are men running or walking very fast. He takes a few steps in one direction, then another, starts toward the tent, but someone gives him a shove that sends him off in another direction. 'Let me come with you, don't go away,' he cries, and without turning around, one soldier urges him on: 'Run, run, they're coming up the mountainside right now. Can't you hear the whistles?' Yes, he hears them. He starts running behind them, but he trips and falls several times and is left behind. He leans against a shadow that appears to be a tree, but the moment he touches it he feels it moving. 'Untie me, for the love of God,' he hears a voice say. And he recognizes it as that of the parish priest of Cumbe, the same voice in which he answered when he was interrogated by Moreira César, yelping now with the same panic: 'Untie me, untie me, the ants are eating me alive.'

'Yes, yes,' the nearsighted journalist stammers, joyous at having found company. 'I'll untie you, I'll untie you.'

'Let's get out of here this minute,' the Dwarf begged her. 'Let's go, Jurema, let's go. Now that the cannons have stopped firing.'

Jurema had been sitting there, looking at Rufino and Gall, without realizing that the sun was tingeing the *caatinga* with gold, drying up the raindrops and evaporating the humidity in the air and the underbrush. The Dwarf shook her.

'Where are we going to go?' she answered, feeling great fatigue and a heavy weight in the pit of her stomach.

'To Cumbe, to Jeremoabo, anywhere,' the Dwarf insisted, tugging at her skirt.

'And which way is it to Cumbe, to Jeremoabo?' Jurema murmured. 'Do we have any idea? Do you know?'

'It doesn't matter! It doesn't matter!' the Dwarf yelped, pulling at her. 'Didn't you hear the *jagunços*? They're going to fight here, there's going to be shooting here, we're going to be killed.'

Jurema rose to her feet and took a few steps toward the mantle of woven grass that the *jagunços* had put over her when they rescued her from the soldiers. It felt damp. She threw it over the corpses of the guide and the stranger, trying to cover the parts of their bodies that had been battered worst: their torsos and their heads. Then, suddenly determined to overcome her apathy, she set out in the direction that she remembered seeing Pajeú take off in. She immediately felt a chubby little hand in her right hand.

'Where are we going?' the Dwarf asked. 'And what about the soldiers?'

She shrugged. The soldiers, the *jagunços*: what did she care? She had had enough of everything and everybody, and her one desire was to forget everything she'd seen. As they walked on, she gathered leaves and little twigs to suck the sap from them.

'Shots,' the Dwarf said. 'Shots, shots.'

It was heavy fire. In a few seconds the din filled the dense, serpentine *caatinga,* which seemed to multiply the bursts and volleys. But not a single living creature was to be seen anywhere about: only rising ground covered with brambles and leaves torn off the trees by the rain, mud puddles, and thickets of *macambiras* with branches like claws and *mandacarus* and *xique-xiques* with sharp thorns. She had lost her sandals at some point during the night, and though she had gone about barefoot for a good part of her life, she could feel how badly cut and bruised her feet were. The hillside grew steeper and steeper. The sun shone full in her face and seemed to mend her limbs, to bring them back to life. She realized that something was up when the Dwarf's fingernails dug into her flesh. Some four yards away a short-barreled, wide-mouthed blunderbuss was aimed straight at them, held in the hands of a man from the vegetable kingdom, with bark for skin, limbs that were branches, and hair that was tufts of grass.

'Clear out of here,' the *jagunço* said, poking his face out of his mantle. 'Didn't Pajeú tell you that you should go to the Jeremoabo entrance?'

'I don't know how to get there,' Jurema answered.

'Shh, shhh,' she heard voices say at this moment, as though the bushes and the cacti had started to speak. Then she saw men's heads appear amid the branches.

'Hide them,' she heard Pajeú order, without being able to tell where his voice was coming from, and felt herself being shoved to the ground, crushed beneath the body of a man who whispered to her as he enveloped her with his mantle of woven grasses: 'Shhh, shhh.' She lay there motionless, with her eyes half closed, stealing cautious glances. She could feel the *jagunço*'s breath in her ear and wondered if the same thing had happened to the Dwarf as had happened to her. She spied the soldiers. Her heart skipped a beat on seeing how close they were. They were marching in a column, two abreast, in their trousers with red stripes and their blue tunics, their black boots and their rifles with naked bayonets. She held her breath, closed her eyes, waiting for the shots to ring out, but as nothing happened, she opened them again and the soldiers were still there, passing by them. She could see their eyes, feverish with anxiety or bloodshot from lack of sleep, their faces, undaunted or terrified, and make out a few scattered words of what they were saying. Wasn't it incredible that so many soldiers should pass by without discovering that there were *jagunços* so close that they could almost touch them, so close that they were almost stepping on them?

And at this moment a great blinding flash of exploding gunpowder filled the *caatinga*, reminding her for a second of the fiesta of Santo Antônio, in Queimadas, when the circus came to town and fireworks were set off. Amid the fusillade, she caught sight of a rain of silhouettes dressed in grass cloaks falling or flinging themselves upon the men dressed in uniforms, and amid the smoke and the roar of gunfire she found herself free of the weight of the *jagunço* pinning her down, lifted up, dragged along, as voices said to her: 'Crouch down, crouch down.' She obeyed, hunching over, tucking her head between her shoulders, and ran as fast as her legs would carry her, expecting at any moment to feel the smack of bullets hitting her in the back, almost wishing that that would happen. The dash left her dripping with sweat and feeling as though she were about to spit up her heart.

Just then she spied the *caboclo* without a nose standing alongside her, looking at her with gentle mockery in his eyes: 'Who won the fight? Your husband or the lunatic?'

'The two of them killed each other,' she panted.

'All the better for you,' Pajeú commented with a smile. 'You can look for another husband now, in Belo Monte.'

The Dwarf was at her side, gasping for breath, too. She caught a glimpse of Canudos. It was spread out there in front of her, the entire length and breadth of it, shaken by explosions, licked by tongues of fire, drifted over with scattered clouds of smoke, as overhead a clear blue sky belied this disorder and a bright sun beat down. Her eyes filled with tears and she felt a sudden hatred against that city and those men, killing each other in those narrow little streets like burrows. Her misfortunes had begun because of this place; the stranger had come to her house because of Canudos, and that had been the start of the misadventures that had left her without anything or anybody in the world, lost in the midst of a war. She wished with all her heart for a miracle, for nothing to have happened, for Rufino and her to be as they had been before, back in Queimadas.

'Don't cry, girl,' the *caboclo* said to her. 'Don't you know the dead are going to be brought back to life? Haven't you heard? There's such a thing as the resurrection of the flesh.'

His voice was calm, as though he and his men had not just had a gunfight with the soldiers. She dried her tears with her hand and looked around, reconnoitering the place. It was a shortcut between the hills, a sort of tunnel. To her left was an overhanging wall of stones and rocks without vegetation that hid the mountain from view, and to her right the somewhat sparse *caatinga* descended till it gave way to a rocky stretch of ground which, beyond a broad river, was transformed into a jumble of little jerry-built dwellings with reddish roofs. Pajeú placed something in her hand, and without looking to see what it was, she raised it to her mouth. She ate the soft, sour fruit in little bites.

The men in the grass mantles were gradually scattering, hugging the bushes, disappearing in hiding places dug in the ground. Again the chubby little hand sought hers. She felt pity and tenderness toward this familiar presence. 'Hide in here,' Pajeú ordered, pushing aside some branches. Once the two of them had crouched down in the ditch, he explained to them, pointing to the rocks: 'The dogs are up there.' In the hole was another *jagunço*, a toothless man who hunched up to make room for them. He had a crossbow and a quiver full of arrows.

'What's going to happen?' the Dwarf whispered.

'Be still,' the *jagunço* said. 'Didn't you hear? The heretics are right above us.'

Jurema peeked out through the branches. The shots continued, sparse and intermittent now, followed by puffs of smoke and the flames of fires, but from their hiding place she could not see the little uniformed figures she'd spied crossing the river and disappearing into the town. 'Don't move,' the *jagunço* said, and for the second time that day soldiers appeared out of nowhere. This time they were cavalrymen, two abreast, mounted on whinnying brown, black, bay, speckled horses, who suddenly emerged, incredibly close at hand, below the rock wall on her left and galloped on toward the river. They appeared to be about to roll down the almost vertical slope, but the animals kept their balance, and she saw them pass swiftly by, using their hind legs to brake themselves. She was dizzied by the succession of cavalrymen's faces flashing by and the sabers that the officers were brandishing to point the way, when suddenly there was a stir in the *caatinga*. The men in grass mantles emerged from the holes, the branches, and fired their shotguns, or, like the *jagunço* who had been with them and was now creeping downhill, riddled them with arrows that hissed like snakes. She heard, very distinctly, Pajeú's voice: 'Go after the horses, those of you who have machetes.' She could no longer see the cavalrymen, but she imagined them splashing in the river – amid a fusillade and a distant pealing of bells she could hear whinnying – and being struck in the back, without knowing where they were coming from, by those arrows and bullets that she could see and hear the *jagunços* scattered about her shooting. Some of them, standing upright, were steadying their carbines or crossbows on branches of the *mandacarus*. The *caboclo* with the nose missing was not shooting. He was standing directing his men to the right or to the left. At that moment the Dwarf clutched her belly so tightly that she could barely breathe. She could feel him trembling, put her two arms round him, and rocked him back and forth: 'They've passed now, they're gone, look!' But when she looked herself, there was another cavalryman there, on a white horse, its mane ruffled by the wind as it galloped down the slope. The little officer riding it was holding its reins with one hand and brandishing a saber in the other. He was so close that she could see his frowning face, his burning eyes, and a moment later she saw him hunch over, his face suddenly blank. Pajeú had his carbine aimed at him and she thought that he was the one who had shot at him. She saw the white horse caracole, wheel about in one of those pirouettes that cowboys put their mounts through to impress the crowds at fairs, and saw it climb back up the slope with its rider clinging to its neck. As it disappeared from sight, she saw Pajeú aiming once again and doubtless getting off another shot.

'Let's get out of here, let's get out of here. We're in the midst of the battle,' the Dwarf whimpered, huddling up next to her again.

'Shut up, you stupid idiot, you coward,' Jurema insulted him. The Dwarf fell silent, drew away, and stared at her in terror, his eyes begging forgiveness. The din of explosions, gunfire, bugle calls, pealing bells continued and the men in grass mantles disappeared, running or crawling down the wooded slope that descended in the distance to the river and Canudos. She looked around for Pajeú and he, too, was no longer there. The two of them were all alone now. What should she do? Stay where she was? Follow the *jagunços*? Look for a trail that would lead her away from Canudos? She felt dead tired, a stiffness in her every joint and muscle, as though her body were protesting against the mere idea of budging from the spot. She leaned her back against the damp side of the pit and closed her eyes. She felt herself drifting, falling into sleep.

When awakened by the Dwarf shaking her, murmuring apologies for rousing her, she found herself barely able to move. Her bones ached and she was obliged to massage the nape of her neck. Darkness was already falling, to judge from the slanting shadows and the fading light. The deafening din that assailed her ears was not a dream. 'What's happening?' she asked, her tongue feeling parched and swollen. 'They're coming this way. Can't you hear them?' the Dwarf murmured, pointing down the slope. 'We must go have a look,' Jurema said. The Dwarf clung to her, trying to hold her back, but when she climbed out of the pit, he followed her on all fours. She walked down to the rocks and brambles where Pajeú had disappeared from sight, and squatted on her heels. Despite the cloud of dust, she spied a swarm of dark ants moving about on the foothills below her and thought it was more soldiers descending to the river, but she soon realized that they were not moving downward but upward, that they were fleeing from Canudos. Yes, there was no doubt of it, they were emerging from the river, on the run, making for the heights, and on the far side of it she saw groups of men shooting and chasing after isolated soldiers who ran out from between the huts, trying to reach the riverbank. Yes, the soldiers were fleeing, and it was the *jagunços* now who were pursuing them. 'They're coming this way,' the Dwarf whined, and her blood froze as she noticed that because she had been watching the hillsides opposite, she had not realized that there was a battle going on at her feet as well, on both banks of the Vaza-Barris. That was where the uproar that she had thought she'd dreamed had been coming from.

She glimpsed – in a dizzying confusion, half blotted out by the dust and the smoke that deformed bodies, faces – horses that had fallen and been stranded on the riverbanks, some of them dying, for they were moving their long necks as though asking for help to get themselves out of that muddy water in which they were about to drown or bleed to death. A riderless horse with only three legs was wheeling about, maddened with pain, trying to bite its tail, amid soldiers who were fording the river with their rifles over their heads, as others appeared, running and screaming from amid the walls of Canudos. They burst out by twos and threes, some of them running backward like scorpions, and plunged into the water, trying to reach the slope where she and the Dwarf were. They were being shot at from somewhere, because some of them fell, howling, wailing, but others of those in uniform were beginning to clamber up the rocks.

'They're going to kill us, Jurema,' the Dwarf whimpered.

Yes, she thought, they're going to kill us. She scrambled to her feet, grabbed the Dwarf, and shouted: 'Run, run!' She dashed up the slope, toward the densest part of the *caatinga*. She was soon exhausted but found the strength to go on by remembering the soldier who had flung himself upon her that morning. When she could not run another step, she slowed down to a walk. She thought with pity how worn out the Dwarf must be, with his short little legs, though she had not heard him complain even once and he had kept up with her all the way, holding tightly to her hand. By the time they halted, darkness was falling. They found themselves on the other side of the mountain. The terrain was flat in places here and the vegetation a denser tangle. The din of the war was far in the distance now. She collapsed on the ground and automatically groped about for grasses, raised them to her mouth, and slowly chewed them till she tasted their acid juice on her palate. She spat the wad out, gathered another handful, and gradually assuaged her thirst somewhat. The Dwarf, a motionless lump, did likewise. 'We've run for hours,' he said to her, but she did not hear him and doubtless thought that he, too, did not have enough strength left to talk. He touched her arm and squeezed her hand in gratitude. They sat there, catching their breath, chewing and spitting out fibers, till the stars came out between the sparse branches of the scrub. Seeing them, Jurema remembered Rufino, Gall. All through the day the *urubus*, the ants, and the lizards had no doubt been devouring their remains and by now they must be beginning to rot. She would never again see their two dead bodies, perhaps lying only a few yards away, locked in each other's arms. At that moment she heard voices, very close by, and reached out and found the Dwarf's little trembling hand. One of the two silhouettes had just stumbled over him, and the Dwarf was screaming as though he'd been stabbed.

'Don't shoot, don't kill us,' a voice from very close by screamed. 'I'm Father Joaquim, the parish priest of Cumbe, we're peaceable people!'

'We're a woman and a dwarf, Father,' Jurema said, not moving. 'We're peaceable people, too.'

This time, she had the strength to speak the words aloud.

On hearing the roar of the first cannon shell that night, Antônio Vilanova's reaction, after an instant of stunned surprise, was to protect the saint with his body. Abbot João and Big João, the Little Blessed One and Joaquim Macambira and his brother Honório all had the same reaction, so that he found himself standing arm in arm with them, surrounding the Counselor, and calculating the trajectory of the shell, which must have fallen somewhere in São Cipriano, the little street where the healers, sorcerers, practitioners of smoke cures, and herb doctors of Belo Monte lived. Which of the shacks of old women who could ward off the evil eye with potions of *jurema* and *manacá*, or of bonesetters who put things back in their place by yanking and pulling on people's bodies, had been sent flying through the air? The Counselor brought them out of their paralysis: 'Let us go to the Temple.' As they headed up Campo Grande, arms linked, in the direction of the churches, Abbot João began to call out to people to darken their houses, for oil lamps and open fires helped the enemy locate their targets. His orders were repeated, passed along from house to house, and obeyed: as they left behind them Espírito Santo, Santo Agostinho, Santo Cristo, Os Papas, and Maria Madalena, narrow little streets meandering off from the edges of Campo Grande, the little shacks were gradually swallowed up in darkness. As they came opposite the slope that had been named the Hill of Martyrs, Antônio Vilanova heard Big João say to the Street Commander: 'Go lead the battle. We'll get him to the Temple safe and sound.' But the former *cangaceiro* was still with them when the second shell exploded, causing them to let go of each other's arms and see, in the great flash that lighted up all of Canudos, planks and debris, roof tiles, remains of animals or people suspended for an instant in the air. The shells seemed to have landed in Santa Inês, where the peasants who looked after the fruit orchards lived, or in the section of town next to it where so many *cafuzos*, mulattoes, and blacks had settled that it was called O Mocambo – the Slave Refuge.

The Counselor separated from the group at the door of the Temple of the Blessed Jesus and went inside, followed by a multitude. In the pitch-dark outside, Antônio Vilanova sensed that the esplanade was crowded with people who had followed the procession, for whom there was no room left in the churches. 'Am I afraid?' he thought, surprised at his weakness. No, it was not fear he felt. In his years as a merchant, traveling all through the hinterland transporting goods and carrying money on him, he had run a great many risks and not been afraid. And here in Canudos, as the Counselor reminded him, he had learned to count, to find a meaning in things, an ultimate reason for everything he did, and that had freed him from a fear which, before, on certain sleepless nights, had made icy sweat run down his back. It was not fear but sadness.

A hand shook him roughly. 'Can't you hear, Antônio Vilanova?' Abbot João's voice said. 'Can't you see that they're here? Haven't we been getting ready to greet them? What are you waiting for?'

'Excuse me,' he murmured, rubbing his hand over his half-bald head. 'I'm in a daze. Yes, yes, I'm going.'

'These people have to be moved out of here,' the ex-*cangaceiro* said, shaking him. 'Otherwise, they'll be blown to bits.'

'I'm going, I'm going, don't worry, everything will go as we planned,' Antônio replied. 'I won't fall down on the job.'

He shouted for his brother as he stumbled through the crowd, and in a moment or two heard him call out: 'I'm over here, *compadre*.' But as he and Honório went into action, exhorting people to go to the shelters they had dug inside their houses and calling to the water carriers to come get stretchers, and then headed back down the Campo Grande toward the store, Antônio was still fighting against a sadness that rent his soul. There were already several water carriers at the store waiting for him. He distributed the stretchers that had been made of cactus fiber and strips of bark, and sent some of them in the direction that the explosions had come from and ordered others to wait. His wife and sister-in-law had left for the Health Houses and Honório's children were in the trench in As Umburanas. He opened the storehouse that had once been a stable and was now the arsenal of Canudos, and his helpers took the boxes of explosives and projectiles to the back room of the store. He instructed them to hand ammunition over only to Abbot João or men sent by him. He left Honório in charge of the distribution of gunpowder and with three helpers ran through the meanders of Santo Elói and São Pedro to the Menino Jesus forge, where the smiths, following his instructions, had for the past week stopped making horseshoes, hoes, sickles, knives, and worked day and night turning nails, tin cans, hooks, iron tools, and every sort of metal object that could be found into bullets for blunderbusses and muskets. He found the smiths in a state of confusion, not knowing whether the order to put out all lamps and fires also applied to them. He had them relight the smithy furnace and go back to work, after helping them stop up the cracks in the walls on the side facing the hills. When he returned to the store, with a case of ammunition that smelled of sulfur, two shells crossed the sky and landed in the distance, out toward the animal pens. The thought crossed his mind that a number of kids no doubt had their bellies and legs blown off, and perhaps a few shepherds too, and that many she-goats had probably run off in panic and were doubtless breaking their legs and getting badly scratched in the brambles and cacti. At that moment he realized why he was sad. 'Everything is going to be destroyed yet again, everything is going to be lost,' he thought. He felt a taste of ashes in his mouth. He thought: 'Like the time of the plague in Assaré, like the time of the drought in Juazeiro, like the time of the flood in Caatinga do Moura.' But those who were shelling Belo Monte that night were worse than hostile elements, more deadly than plagues and natural catastrophes. 'Thank you for having made me feel so certain of the existence of the Dog,' he prayed. 'Thank you, for thus I know that you exist, Father.' He heard the bells, ringing very loudly, and their pealing did his heart good.

He found Abbot João and some twenty men carrying away the ammunition and the gunpowder: they were faceless creatures, shapes moving silently about as the rain poured down once more, making the roof shake. 'Are you taking everything?' he asked him in surprise, for Abbot João himself had been adamant that the store should be the distribution center for arms and provisions. The Street Commander led him to the esplanade, by now a quagmire. 'They're deploying from here to there,' he said, pointing to A Favela and O Cambaio. 'They're going to attack from those two sides. If Joaquim Macambira's men don't hold out, this sector will be the first to fall. It's better to distribute the ammunition now.' Antônio nodded. 'Where are you going to be?' he asked. 'All over,' the ex-*cangaceiro* answered.

The men were waiting with the boxes and the sacks in their arms.

'Good luck, João,' Antônio said. 'I'm going to the Health Houses. Any message for Catarina?'

The ex-*cangaceiro* hesitated. Then he said slowly: 'If I die, I'd like her to know that even though she's forgiven what happened in Custódia, I haven't.' He disappeared in the damp night, in which another shell had just exploded.

'Did you understand João's message to Catarina, *compadre*?' Honório asked him.

'It's a story that goes back a long way, *compadre*,' he answered.

By the light of a candle, in silence, listening to the dialogue between the churchbells and the bugles and from time to time the roar of the cannon, they went on getting provisions, bandages, medicines ready. A little while later a little boy sent by Antônia Sardelinha came to tell them that many injured had been brought to the Santa Ana Health House. He picked up one of the boxes containing iodoform, substrate of bismuth, and calomel that Father Joaquim had procured for him and set out for the Health House with it, after telling his brother to rest for a while since the worst would come at dawn.

The Health House on the Santa Ana slope was a madhouse. There was weeping and wailing on every hand, and Antônia Sardelinha, Catarina, and the other women who went there regularly to cook for the aged, the disabled, and the sick could scarcely move amid the crowd of relatives and friends of the injured who kept tugging at them and demanding that they attend to this victim or that. The injured were lying on the floor, one atop the other, and at times being stepped on. With the help of the water carriers, Antônio forced the intruders to leave, then had the men stand guard at the door while he went off to help treat the injured and bandage them. The shells had blown off fingers and hands, left gaping wounds in bodies, and one woman had had her leg ripped off. How can she still be alive, Antônio wondered as he gave her spirits to inhale. She must be suffering so terribly that one could only hope death would come take her as quickly as possible. The apothecary arrived as the woman was breathing her last in his arms. He had come, he said, from the other Health House, where there were as many victims as in this one, and immediately ordered that all the dead bodies, which he recognized at a single glance, be taken out to the henhouse. He was the one person in Canudos who had any sort of medical training and his presence calmed everyone. Antônio Vilanova found Catarina sponging the forehead of a boy wearing the armband of the Catholic Guard; a shell splinter had put out one of his eyes and slashed his cheek to the bone. He was clinging to her like a baby as she hummed softly to him.

'João gave me a message,' Antônio said to her. And he passed the *cangaceiro*'s words on to her. Catarina merely gave a little nod. This thin, sad, silent woman was a mystery to him. She was an obliging, devoted disciple, yet at the same time seemed withdrawn from everything and everybody. She and Abbot João lived on the Rua do Menino Jesus, in a little hut squeezed in between two wood houses, and they preferred to be by themselves. Antônio had seen them, many a time, walking together down by the little cultivated plots behind O Mocambo, deep in a conversation that never seemed to end. 'Are you going to see João?' she asked him. 'Maybe. What would you like me to tell him?' 'That if he suffers eternal damnation, I want to, too.'

Antônio spent the rest of the night setting up infirmaries in two dwellings on the road to Jeremoabo, after having moved their inhabitants to neighbors' houses. As he and his aides cleared each place out and had wooden stands, cots, blankets, buckets of water, medicines, bandages brought, he was overcome with sadness once again. It had been such hard work to make this land productive again, to lay out and dig irrigation ditches, to break and fertilize this stony ground so that maize and beans, broad beans and sugarcane, melons and watermelons would grow in it, and it had been such hard work bringing goats and kids, raising them, breeding them. It had taken so much work, so much faith, so much dedication on the part of so many people to make these fields and pens what they were. And now the cannon fire was destroying them and soldiers were about to enter Canudos to destroy people who had gathered together there to live in the love of God and help each other since no one else had ever helped them. He forced himself to banish from his mind these thoughts that provoked in him that wrath against which the Counselor had so often preached. An aide came to tell him that the dogs were coming down the hillside.

It was dawn; there was a blare of bugles; the slopes swarmed with red-and-blue forms. Taking his revolver from its holster, Antônio Vilanova headed on the run to the store on Campo Grande. Just as he arrived he saw, fifty yards farther on, that ranks of soldiers had already crossed the river and were overrunning old Joaquim Macambira's trench, firing in all directions.

Honório and half a dozen aides had barricaded themselves

inside the store, behind barrels, counters, cots, crates, and sacks of dirt, over which Antônio and his men clambered on all fours, with those inside pulling them in. Panting, he found himself a place that gave him a clear aim outside. The gunfire was so heavy that he could not hear his brother, even though they were elbow to elbow. He peered through the barricade of various objects: clouds of dust coming from the direction of the river were advancing along Campo Grande and the slopes of São Jose and Santa Ana. He saw smoke, flames. They were setting the houses on fire, trying to fry all of them to a crisp. The thought crossed his mind that his wife and sister-in-law were down there, in Santa Ana, being asphyxiated and burned to death along with the wounded in the Health House, and once again he was overcome with rage. Several soldiers emerged from the clouds of smoke and dirt, looking wildly to right and left. The bayonets of their long rifles gleamed; they were dressed in blue tunics and red trousers. One of them tossed a torch over the barricade. 'Put it out,' Antônio roared to the lad at his side as he aimed his revolver at the chest of the closest soldier. He fired away, almost blindly because of the dense cloud of dust, his eardrums nearly bursting, till there were no bullets left in his revolver. As he reloaded it, with his back against a barrel, he saw that Pedrim, the boy he had ordered to smother the torch, was lying on top of the end of wood smeared with tar, with blood on his back. But he was unable to go to him, for the barricade gave way on his left and two soldiers squeezed through the breach, getting in each other's way. 'Watch out, watch out!' he shouted to the others, firing at the soldiers till once again he heard the click of the hammer on the empty chamber of his revolver. The two soldiers had fallen to the floor and by the time he reached them, knife in hand, three aides were finishing them off with theirs, each thrust accompanied by an insult. He looked around and was overjoyed to see Honório unharmed and smiling. 'Everything all right, *compadre*?' he asked him, and his brother nodded. He went to have a look at Pedrim. He was not dead, but in addition to the wound in his back he had burned his hands.

He carried him to the next room and laid him down on some blankets. His face was wet with tears. He was an orphan whom he and Antônia had taken in shortly after settling in Canudos. Hearing the fusillade begin again outside, he covered him and left his side, telling him: 'I'll be back to take care of you, Pedrim.'

At the barricade, his brother was shooting with a rifle that had belonged to one of the soldiers, and the aides had plugged up the breach. Antônio reloaded his revolver and installed himself next to Honório, who said to him: 'About twenty of them just went by.' The deafening fusillade seemed to be coming from all sides. He looked to see what was happening on the Santa Ana slope and heard Honório's voice saying, 'Do you think Antônia and Assunção are still alive, *compadre*?' At that moment he spied, lying in the mud in front of the barricade, a soldier with a rifle lightly cradled in one arm and a saber in his other hand. 'We need those weapons,' he said. They made an opening in the barricade for him and he dashed into the street. As he leaned over to pick up the rifle, the soldier tried to raise his saber. Without a moment's hesitation, he sank his knife into the man's belly and flung himself on top of him with all his weight. The soldier's body beneath his gave a sort of belch, grunted something, went limp, and stopped moving. As he pulled his knife out of him and grabbed the man's saber, rifle, and knapsack, he examined the ashen face with a yellowish tinge, the sort of face that he had often seen among the peasants and cowhands, and for the space of an instant he felt bitter regret. Honório and the aides were outside on the street, stripping another soldier of his weapons. And at that moment he recognized Abbot João's voice. The Street Commander had arrived as though driven by the wind, followed by two men. All three were covered with bloodstains.

'How many of you are there?' he asked, gesturing to them at the same time to hug the façade of the building.

'Nine,' Antônio answered. 'And Pedrim's inside, wounded.'

'Come on,' Abbot João said, turning around. 'Be careful, there are soldiers inside lots of the houses.'

But the *cangaceiro* himself was not at all cautious, for, holding himself erect, he strode rapidly down the middle of the street, as he went on to explain that they were attacking the churches and the cemetery from the direction of the river and that the soldiers must be prevented from approaching from this way as well, since that would leave the Counselor isolated. He wanted to close Campo Grande off with a barrier at Mártires, almost at the corner of the Chapel of Santo Antônio.

Some three hundred yards separated them from there, and Antônio was surprised to see how much damage had been done: houses demolished, torn from their foundations, riddled with holes, rubble, heaps of debris, broken roof tiles, charred planks with scattered corpses lying in the middle of them, and clouds of smoke and dust that blurred, effaced, dissolved everything. Here and there, like markers of the soldiers' advance, were tongues of fire from burning buildings. Striding up to Mártires at Abbot João's side, he repeated Catarina's message to him. The *cangaceiro* nodded without turning his head. Suddenly they came upon a patrol of soldiers at the entrance to the Rua Maria Madalena, and Antônio saw João take a running jump and send his knife flying through the air, as in marksmanship contests. He, too, broke into a run, shooting. The bullets whined all around him and a moment later he stumbled and fell to the ground. But he was able to get to his feet and dodge the bayonet that he saw coming at him and drag the soldier down into the mud with him. He traded blows with the man, not knowing whether he had his knife in his hand or not. All of a sudden he felt the soldier double over and go limp. Abbot João helped Antônio to his feet.

'Gather up the dogs' weapons,' he ordered at the same time. 'The bayonets, the bullets, the knapsacks.'

Honório and two aides were bending over Anastácio, another aide, trying to lift him.

Abbot João stopped them. 'Don't bother. He's dead. Drag the bodies along with you. We can use them to block the street.'

And setting the example, he grabbed the nearest corpse by one foot and started walking in the direction of Mártires. At the entrance to the street were many *jagunços*, already busy erecting the barricade with everything they could find at hand. Antônio Vilanova set to work along with them. They could hear shots, bursts of gunfire, and a few moments later a youngster from the Catholic Guard appeared to tell Abbot João, who was helping Antônio bring up the wheels of a cart, that the heretics were again advancing on the Temple of the Blessed Jesus. 'Everybody back there,' Abbot João shouted, and the *jagunços* followed along behind him on the run. They entered the square just as several soldiers, led by a fair-haired young man brandishing a saber and discharging a revolver, came out onto it from the cemetery. A heavy fusillade from the chapel and the towers and rooftop of the Temple under construction kept the soldiers from advancing. 'Follow them, follow them,' Antônio heard Abbot João roar. Dozens of men poured out of the churches to join in the pursuit. He saw Big João, immense, barefoot, catch up with the Street Commander and talk to him as he ran. The soldiers had entrenched themselves behind the cemetery, and on entering São Cipriano the *jagunços* were met with a hail of bullets. 'He's going to get killed,' Antônio, who had flung himself headlong onto the ground, thought as he saw Abbot João standing in the middle of the street gesturing to those following him to take cover in the houses or hit the dirt.

Then he walked over to Antônio, squatted down alongside him, and said in his ear: 'Go back to the barricade and secure it. We have to dislodge those troops from here and push them back to where Pajeú is going to pounce on them. Go back and see that they don't sneak in from the other side.'

Antônio nodded and a moment later ran back, followed by Honório, the aides, and ten other men, to the intersection of Mártires and Campo Grande. He seemed to be coming to at last, to be coming out of his stupor. 'You know how to organize things,' he said to himself. 'And that's what's needed now, precisely that.' He ordered the men to take the dead bodies and the rubble on the square back to the barricade and helped them till, amid all the hurrying back and forth, he heard shouts inside one of the buildings. He was the first one in, kicking a hole in the wall and shooting at the soldier squatting on his heels. To his stupefaction, he realized that the soldier he had killed had been eating: in his hand was a piece of jerked beef that he had doubtless just grabbed off the stove. The owner of the house, an old man, lay dying alongside him, a bayonet thrust into his belly, and three little children were screaming in terror. 'How hungry he must have been,' he thought, 'to have forgotten everything and gotten himself killed for a mouthful of jerked beef.' He and five men searched all the houses between the end of the street and the square. All of them looked like a battlefield: disorder, roofs with gaping holes, walls ripped apart, objects smashed to bits. Women, oldsters, children armed with shovels and pitchforks greeted them with looks of relief on their faces, or began to chatter frantically. In one house he found two buckets of water, and after he and the men had had a drink, he toted them back to the barricade. He could see how joyfully Honório and the others drank the water down.

Climbing up onto the barricade, he peeked out between various objects and dead bodies. The only straight street in all of Canudos, Campo Grande, was deserted. To his right there was heavy gunfire amid the burning buildings. 'Things are rough in O Mocambo, *compadre*,' Honório said. His face was crimson and dripping with sweat. Antônio smiled at him. 'The dogs aren't going to be able to get us out of here, right?' he said. 'Of course they're not, *compadre*,' Honório replied. Antônio sat down on a cart and as he was reloading his revolver – there were almost no bullets left in the cartridge belts wound around his middle – he noticed that most of the *jagunços* were now armed with rifles taken from soldiers. They were winning the war.

He suddenly remembered the Sardelinha sisters, down below, on the lower slope of Santa Ana. 'Stay here, and tell João that I've gone to the Health House to see how things are going there,' he said to his brother.

He climbed to the top of the barricade, stepping on corpses swarming with flies, and leapt down on the other side. Four *jagunços* followed him. 'Who ordered you to come with me?' he shouted at them. 'Abbot João,' one of them answered. He didn't have time to argue, for at São Pedro they found themselves caught in a fusillade: there was fighting in the doorways, on the rooftops, and inside the houses along the street. They turned back to Campo Grande and were able to make their way down to Santa Ana from that direction, without encountering soldiers. But there was shooting in Santa Ana. They crouched down behind a house going up in smoke and the storekeeper took a look around. Up by the Health House there was another cloud of smoke; the shooting was coming from there. 'I'm going to go closer. Wait here,' he said, but as he crawled off, he saw that the four *jagunços* were crawling along at his side. A few yards farther on he finally spied half a dozen soldiers, directing their fire not at them but at the houses. He stood up and ran toward them as fast as his legs could carry him, his finger on the trigger of his revolver, but he did not shoot until one of the soldiers turned. He fired all six bullets at him and threw his knife at another one who came at him. He fell to the ground and grabbed his attacker's legs, or those of another soldier, and somehow found himself strangling him, with all his strength. 'You've killed two dogs, Antônio,' one of the *jagunços* said. 'Their rifles, their bullets – take all of them' was his answer. The doors of the houses opened and people came pouring out, coughing, smiling, waving. Antônia, his wife, was there, and Assunção, and behind them Catarina, Abbot João's wife.

'Look at them,' one of the *jagunços* said, giving him a shake. 'Look at them jumping into the river.'

Above the jumble of rooftops on the slope of Santa Ana, to the right, to the left, were other uniformed figures, clambering frantically up the hillside; others were leaping into the river, a number of them having first thrown away their rifles. But what drew his attention even more was the gathering darkness. Night would soon be upon them. 'We're going to take their arms away from them,' he shouted at the top of his lungs. 'Come on, boys, we can't leave the job half finished.' Several of the *jagunços* ran toward the river with him, and one of them began to shout:

'Down with the Republic and the Antichrist! Long live the Counselor and the Blessed Jesus!'

In that dreaming that is and is not, a dozing that blurs the borderline between waking and sleeping and that reminds him of certain opium nights in his disorderly little house in Salvador, the nearsighted correspondent from the *Jornal de Notícias* has the sensation that he has not slept but has spoken and listened, told those faceless presences that are sharing the *caatinga*, hunger, and uncertainty with him that for him the worst part is not being lost, with no idea of what will happen when day breaks, but having lost his big leather pouch and the rolls of paper covered with his scribbling that he has wrapped up in his few clean clothes. He is certain that he has also told them things that he is ashamed of: that two days before, when his ink was all gone and his last goose-quill pen broken, he had a fit of weeping, as though a member of his family had died. And he is certain – certain in the uncertain, disjointed, cottony way in which everything happens, is said, or is received in the world of opium – that all night long he has chewed, without repulsion, the handfuls of grasses, leaves, little twigs, insects perhaps, the unidentifiable bits of matter, dry or moist, viscous or solid, that he and his companions have passed from hand to hand. And he is certain that he has listened to as many intimate confessions as he believes that he himself has made. 'Except for her, all of us are immensely afraid,' he thinks. Father Joaquim, whom he has served as a pillow and who in turn has served as his, has acknowledged as much: that he discovered what real fear was only the day before, tied to that tree over there, waiting for a soldier to come slit his throat, hearing the shooting, watching the goings and comings, the arrival of the wounded, a fear infinitely greater than he had ever felt before, of anything or anybody, including the Devil and hell. Did the curé say those things, moaning and every so often begging God's forgiveness for having said them? But the one who is more frightened still is the one she has said is a dwarf. Because, in a shrill little voice as deformed as his body must be, he has not stopped whimpering and rambling on about bearded women, gypsies, strong men, and a boneless man who could tie himself in knots. What can the Dwarf look like? Can she be his mother? What are the two of them doing here? How can she possibly not be afraid? What is she feeling that's worse than fear? For the nearsighted journalist has noted something even more destructive, disastrous, distressing in the woman's soft-spoken voice, in the sporadic murmur in which she has never once spoken of the one thing that has any meaning, the fear of dying, but only of the stubbornness of someone who is dead, left unburied, getting soaked, freezing, being devoured by all sorts of creatures. Can she be a madwoman, someone who is no longer afraid because she was once so afraid that she went mad?

He feels someone shaking him. He thinks: 'My glasses.' He sees a faint greenish light, moving shadows. And as he pats his body, feels all about him, he hears Father Joaquim: 'Wake up, it's already light, let's try to find the road to Cumbe.' He finally locates them, between his legs, unbroken. He cleans them, stands up, stammers 'All right, all right,' and as he puts his glasses on and the world comes into focus he sees the Dwarf: a real one, as small as a ten-year-old boy but with a face furrowed with wrinkles. He is holding the hand of a woman of indeterminate age, with her hair falling round her shoulders, so thin she seems nothing but skin and bones. Both of them are covered with mud, their clothes are in tatters, and the nearsighted journalist wonders whether he too, like the two of them and the robust little curé who has begun walking determinedly in the direction of the rising sun, gives the same impression of disarray, forlornness, vulnerability. 'We're on the other side of A Favela,' Father Joaquim says. 'If we go this way we should come out onto the trail to Bendengó. God grant there won't be any soldiers . . .' 'But there will be,' the nearsighted journalist thinks. 'Or else *jagunços*. We're not anything. We're in neither the one camp nor the other. We're going to be killed.' He walks along, surprised that he isn't tired, seeing in front of him the woman's scrawny silhouette and the Dwarf hopping along after her so as not to fall behind. They go on for a long time in that order, not exchanging a word. In the sunny dawn they hear birds singing, insects buzzing, and a confusion of many sounds, indistinct, dissimilar, growing louder and louder: isolated shots, bells, the wail of a bugle, an explosion perhaps, human voices perhaps. The little priest wanders neither right nor left; he appears to know where he is going, The *caatinga* begins to thin out, dwindling down to brambles and cacti, and eventually turns into steep, open country. They walk along parallel to a rocky ridge that blocks their view on their right. Half an hour later they reach the crest line of this rocky outcropping and at one and the same time the nearsighted journalist hears the curé's exclamation and sees the cause of it: soldiers, almost on top of them, and behind them, in front of them, on either side of them, *jagunços*. 'Thousands,' the nearsighted journalist murmurs. He feels like sitting down, closing his eyes, forgetting everything. 'Jurema, look, look!' the Dwarf screeches. To make himself less visible against the horizon, the priest falls to his knees, and his companions also squat down. 'We've ended up right in the middle of the battle,' the Dwarf whispers. 'It's not a battle,' the nearsighted journalist thinks. 'It's a rout.' The spectacle unfolding on the hillside below makes him forget his fear. So they didn't heed Major Cunha Matos's advice; they didn't retreat last night and are doing so only now, as Colonel Tamarindo wished.

The masses of soldiers swarming over a wide area down below, in no order or formation, bunched together in places and in others spread far apart, in utter chaos, dragging the carts of the medical corps behind them and carrying stretchers, with their rifles slung over their shoulders any which way, or using them as canes and crutches, bear no resemblance whatsoever to the Seventh Regiment of Colonel Moreira César that he remembers, that highly disciplined corps, scrupulous in dress and demeanor. Have they buried the colonel up there on the heights behind them? Are they bringing his mortal remains down on one of those stretchers, one of those carts?

'Can they have made their peace with each other?' the curé murmurs at his side. 'An armistice perhaps?'

The idea of a reconciliation strikes him as unthinkable, but it is quite true that something bizarre is happening down there below: there is no fighting. And yet soldiers and *jagunços* are very close to each other, closer and closer by the moment. His myopic, avid gaze leaps, as in some wild dream, from one group of *jagunços* to another, that indescribable mass of humanity in outlandish dress, armed with shotguns, carbines, clubs, machetes, rakes, hunting crossbows, stones, with bits of cloth tied round their heads, that seems to be the embodiment of disorder, of confusion, like those whom they are pursuing, or rather, escorting, accompanying.

'Can the soldiers have surrendered?' Father Joaquim says. 'Can they be taking them prisoner?'

The large groups of *jagunços* are mounting the slopes, on either side of the drunkenly meandering current of soldiers, pressing in upon them, closer and closer. But there are no shots. Not, in any event, the sort of gunfire there had been the day before in Canudos, heavy fusillades and bursting shells, though scattered reports reach his ears now and then. And echoes of insults and imprecations: what else could those snatches of voices be? The nearsighted journalist suddenly recognizes Captain Salomão da Rocha in the rear guard of the wretched column. The little group of soldiers tagging along far behind the rest, with four cannons drawn by mules that they are pitilessly whipping, finds itself completely isolated when suddenly a group of *jagunços* descends upon it from the flanks and cuts it off from the other troops. The cannons stop dead and the nearsighted journalist is certain that the officer in command – he has a saber and a pistol, runs from one of his men to the next as they huddle against the mule teams and the cannons, doubtless giving them orders, urging them on, as the *jagunços* close in on them – is Salomão da Rocha. He remembers his little clipped mustache – his fellow officers called him the Fashion Plate – and his incessant talk about the technical advances announced in the Comblain catalogues, the precision of Krupp artillery pieces and of the cannons to which he has given a name and surname. On seeing little puffs of smoke, the nearsighted journalist realizes that they are firing at each other, at point-blank range, even though he and the others are unable to hear the rifle reports because the wind is blowing in another direction. 'They've been shooting at each other, killing each other, hurling insults at each other all this time, and we haven't heard a thing,' he thinks, and then stops thinking, for the group of soldiers and cannons is suddenly lost from view as the *jagunços* surrounding it descend upon it. Blinking his eyes, batting his eyelids, his mouth gaping open, the nearsighted journalist sees the officer with the saber withstand for the space of a few seconds the attack of clubs, pikes, hoes, sickles, machetes, or whatever else those dark objects might be, before disappearing from sight, like his men, beneath the hordes of assailants now leaping upon them, no doubt with shouts that do not reach his ears. He does hear, however, the braying of the mules, though they, too, are lost from sight.

He realizes that he has been left all by himself on the rocky ledge at the crest line from which he has seen the capture of the artillery corps of the Seventh Regiment and the certain death of the soldiers and the officer serving in it. The parish priest of Cumbe is trotting down the slope, some twenty or thirty yards farther below, followed by the woman and the Dwarf, heading straight toward the *jagunços*. He hesitates to the depths of his being. But the fear of remaining there all by himself is worse, and he scrambles to his feet and begins running down the slope after them. He stumbles, slips, falls, gets up again, tries to keep his balance. Many *jagunços* have seen them, there are faces tipped back, raised toward the slope as he comes down it, feeling ridiculous at being so clumsy and unsteady on his feet. The curé of Cumbe, ten yards in front of him now, says something, shouts, makes signs and gestures at the *jagunços*. Is he betraying him, denouncing him? In order to curry favor with them, will he tell them that he's a soldier, will he . . .? And he starts to roll downhill again, in a spectacular fashion. He somersaults, turns over and over like a barrel, feeling neither pain nor shame, his one thought being his eyeglasses, which by some miracle remain firmly hooked over his ears when he finally stops and tries to stand up. But he is so battered and bruised, so stunned and terrified that he cannot manage to do so until several pairs of arms lift him up bodily. 'Thanks,' he murmurs, and sees Father Joaquim being clapped on the back, embraced, kissed on the hand by smiling, surprised, excited *jagunços*. 'They know him,' he thinks. 'If he asks them not to, they won't kill me.'

'It's really me, João,' Father Joaquim says to a tall, sturdy, mud-stained man with weathered skin standing in the middle of a group of men with bandoleers about their necks who have flocked round him. 'Me in the flesh, not my ghost. They didn't kill me – I escaped. I want to go to Cumbe, Abbot João, I want to get out of here. Help me . . .'

'Impossible, Father, it's dangerous. Can't you see that there's shooting on all sides?' the man answers. 'Go to Belo Monte till the war is over.'

'Abbot João?' the nearsighted journalist thinks. 'Abbot João's in Canudos, too?' He hears sudden loud rifle reports from every direction and his blood runs cold. 'Who's that four-eyes?' he hears Abbot João say, pointing to him. 'Ah, yes, he's a journalist, he helped me escape, he's not a soldier. And this woman and this . . .' But the curé is unable to end his sentence because of the gunfire. 'Go to Belo Monte, Father, we've cleared them out of there,' Abbot João says as he starts down the slope at a run, followed by the *jagunços* who have been standing round him. The nearsighted journalist suddenly spies Colonel Tamarindo in the distance, clutching his head in his hands in the midst of a stampede of soldiers. There is total disorder and confusion: the column appears to be scattered all over, to have completely disintegrated. The soldiers are dashing about helter-skelter, their pursuers close behind. From the ground, his mouth full of mud, the nearsighted journalist sees the troops, spreading like a stain, dividing, mingling, figures falling, struggling, and his eyes return again and again to the spot where old Tamarindo has fallen. Several *jagunços* are bending down – killing him? But they linger too long for that, squatting there on their heels, and the nearsighted journalist, his eyes burning from straining so hard to make out what is happening, finally sees that they are stripping him naked.

He is suddenly aware of a bitter taste in his mouth, begins to choke, and realizes that, like an automaton, he is chewing the dirt that got into his mouth when he threw himself to the ground. He spits, not taking his eyes off the rout of the soldiers, amid a terrific wind that has risen. They are scattering in all directions, some of them shooting, others tossing weapons, boxes of ammunition, stretchers onto the ground, into the air, and though they are now a long way off, he can nonetheless see that in their frantic, panic-stricken retreat they are also tossing away their kepis, their tunics, their bandoleers, their chest belts. Why are they, too, stripping naked, what sort of madness is this that he is witnessing? He intuits that they are ridding themselves of anything that might identify them as soldiers, that they are hoping to pass themselves off as *jagunços* in the melee. Father Joaquim gets to his feet and, just as he had a moment before, begins to run again. In a strange fashion this time, moving his head, waving his hands, speaking and shouting to pursued and pursuers alike. 'He's going down there amid all the shooting, the knifing, the killing,' the journalist thinks. His eyes meet the woman's. She looks back at him in terror, mutely pleading for his counsel. And then he too, obeying an impulse, stands up, shouting to her: 'We must stay with him. He's the only one who can help us.' She gets to her feet and starts running, dragging the Dwarf along with her, his eyes bulging, his face covered with dirt, screeching as he runs. The nearsighted journalist soon loses sight of them, for his long legs or his fear give him an advantage over them. He runs swiftly, bent over, his hips jerking grotesquely back and forth, his head down, thinking hypnotically that one of those red-hot bullets whistling past has his name written on it, that he is running directly toward it, and that one of those knives, sickles, machetes, bayonets that he glimpses is waiting for him in order to put an end to his mad dash. But he keeps running amid clouds of dust, glimpsing now and again the robust little figure of the curé of Cumbe, his arms and legs whirling like windmill blades, losing him from sight, spying him again. Suddenly he loses sight of him altogether. As he curses and rages, he thinks: 'Where is he going, why is he running like that, why does he want to get himself killed and get us killed?' Though he is completely out of breath – he runs along with his tongue hanging out, swallowing dust, almost unable to see because his glasses are now covered with dirt – he goes on running for all he is worth; the little strength he has left tells him that his life depends on Father Joaquim.

When he falls to the ground, because he stumbles or because his legs give way from fatigue, he has a curious feeling of relief. He leans his head on his arms, tries to force air into his lungs, listens to his heart beat. Better to die than keep on running. Little by little he recovers, feels the pounding in his temples slow down. He is sick to his stomach and retches, but does not vomit. He takes his glasses off and cleans them. He puts them back on. He is surrounded by people. He is not afraid, and nothing really matters. His exhaustion has freed him from fears, uncertainties, chimeras. Moreover, no one appears to be paying any attention to him. Men are gathering up the rifles, the ammunition, the bayonets, but his eyes are not deceived and from the first moment he knows that the groups of *jagunços* here, there, everywhere, are also beheading the corpses with their machetes, with the same diligence with which they decapitate oxen and goats, and throwing the heads in burlap bags, threading them on pikes and on the same bayonets that the dead were carrying to run *jagunços* through, or carrying them off by the hair, while others light fires where the headless corpses are already beginning to sizzle, crackle, curl up, burst open, char. One fire is very close by and he sees that men with blue headcloths are throwing other remains on top of the two bodies already roasting on it. 'It's my turn now,' he thinks. 'They'll come, cut my head off, carry it away on a pole, and toss my body in that fire.' He goes on drowsing, immunized against everything by his utter exhaustion. Even though the *jagunços* are talking, he doesn't understand a word they are saying.

At that moment he spies Father Joaquim. He is not going but coming, he is not running but walking, in long strides, emerging from that cloud of wind-blown dirt that has already begun to produce that tickling in the journalist's nostrils that precedes a sneezing fit, still making gestures, grimaces, signs, to anybody and everybody, including the dead that are roasting. He is spattered with mud, his clothes are in tatters, his hair disheveled. The nearsighted journalist rises up as the priest walks by him and says: 'Don't go, take me with you, don't let them chop my head off, don't let them burn me . . .' Does the curé of Cumbe hear him? He is talking to himself or with ghosts, repeating incomprehensible things, unrecognizable names, making sweeping gestures. He walks along at his side, very close to him, feeling his proximity revive him. He notes that the barefoot woman and the Dwarf are walking along with them on the right. Pale and wan, covered with dirt, worn out, they look to him like sleepwalkers.

Nothing of what he is seeing and hearing surprises him or frightens him or interests him. Is this what ecstasy is? He thinks: 'Not even opium, in Salvador . . .' He sees as he passes by that *jagunços* are hanging kepis, tunics, canteens, capes, blankets, cartridge belts, boots on the thornbushes dotting both sides of the path, as though they were decorating Christmas trees, but the sight leaves him completely indifferent. And when, as they descend toward the sea of rooftops and rubble that is Canudos, he sees heads of dead soldiers lined up on either side of the trail, looking across at each other, being riddled by insects, his heart does not pound wildly, nor his fear return, nor his imagination race madly. Even when an absurd figure, one of those scarecrows that farmers place in sowed fields, blocks their path and he recognizes the naked, corpulent form impaled on a dry branch as the body and face of Colonel Tamarindo, he does not turn a hair. But a moment later he stops short, and with the serenity that he has attained, he takes a close look at one of the heads crawling with flies. There is no possible doubt: it is the head of Moreira César.

The fit of sneezing overtakes him so completely that he does not have time to raise his hands to his face, to hold his glasses on: they fly off, and as one burst of sneezes follows another and he doubles over, he is sure he hears them hit the pebbles underfoot. As soon as he is able to, he squats down and fumbles about. He finds them immediately. Now, yes, on running his fingers over them and feeling that the lenses are smashed to smithereens, the nightmare of last night, of this morning at dawn, of a few moments ago returns.

'Stop! Stop!' he shouts, putting the glasses on, looking out at a shattered, cracked, crazed world. 'I can't see anything. Please, I beg you.'

He feels in his right hand a hand that – from its size, from its pressure – can only be that of the barefoot woman. She pulls him along, without a word, guiding him in this world suddenly become inapprehensible, blind.

The first thing that surprised Epaminondas Gonçalves on entering the town house of the Baron de Canabrava, in which he had never before set foot, was the odor of vinegar and aromatic herbs that filled the rooms through which a black servant led him, lighting his way with an oil lamp. He showed him into a study with shelves full of books, illuminated by a lamp with green glass panels that lent a sylvan appearance to the oval writing desk, the easy chairs, and the little tables with bibelots. He was examining an old map, on which he managed to read the name Calumbi in ornate Gothic letters, when the baron entered the room. They shook hands without warmth, like two persons who scarcely know each other.

'I thank you for coming,' the baron said, offering him a chair. 'Perhaps it would have been better to hold this meeting in a neutral place, but I took the liberty of proposing my house to you because my wife is not feeling well and I prefer not to go out.'

'I wish her a prompt recovery,' Epaminondas Gonçalves said, refusing a cigar from the box the baron held out to him. 'All of Bahia hopes to see her very soon in as radiant health and as beautiful as ever.'

The baron looked much thinner and older, and the owner–publisher of the *Jornal de Notícias* wondered whether those wrinkles and that dejection were due to the ravages of time or of recent events.

'As a matter of fact, Estela is physically well; her body has recovered,' the baron said sharply. 'It's her mind that is still affected. The fire that destroyed Calumbi was a great shock to her.'

'A disaster that concerns all us Bahians,' Epaminondas murmured. He raised his eyes to follow the baron, who had risen to his feet and was pouring them two glasses of cognac. 'I said as much in the Assembly and in the *Jornal de Notícias.* The destruction of property is a crime that affects all of us, allies and adversaries alike.'

The baron nodded. He handed Epaminondas his cognac and they clinked glasses in silence before drinking. Epaminondas set his glass down on the little table and the baron held his between his palms, warming the reddish liquid and swirling it about the glass. 'I thought it would be a good idea for us to talk together,' he said slowly. 'The success of the negotiations between the Republican Party and the Autonomist Party depends on the two of us reaching an agreement.'

'I must warn you that I have not been authorized by my political friends to negotiate anything tonight,' Epaminondas interrupted him.

'You don't need their authorization,' the baron replied with an ironic smile. 'My dear Epaminondas, let's not put on a Chinese shadow play. There isn't time. The situation is extremely serious and you know it. In Rio, in São Paulo, monarchist papers are being attacked and their owners being lynched. The ladies of Brazil are raffling off their jewels and locks of their hair to raise money for the army that's coming to Bahia. Let us put our cards on the table. There's nothing else for us to do – except commit suicide.' He took another sip of cognac.

'Since you're asking me to speak frankly, I'll confess to you that were it not for what happened to Moreira César in Canudos,

I wouldn't be here, nor would there be any conversations between our two parties,' Epaminondas conceded.

'We're agreed on that point, then,' the baron said. 'I presume that we also agree on what this military mobilization on a grand scale that is being carried out by the federal government throughout the country means for Bahia politically.'

'I don't know if we see eye to eye on that subject.' Epaminondas picked up his glass, took a sip, savored the aftertaste, and added coldly: 'For you and your friends, it's the end, naturally.'

'It's the end for you and yours above all, Epaminondas,' the baron replied amiably. 'Haven't you realized? With Moreira César's death, the Jacobins have suffered a mortal blow. They've lost the only prestigious figure they could count on. Yes, my friend, the *jagunços* have done President Prudente de Moraes and the parliament – that government of "pedants" and "cosmopolites" that you people wanted to overthrow in order to set up your Dictatorial Republic – a favor. Moraes and the politicians in São Paulo are going to take advantage of this crisis to clear all the Jacobins out of the army and the administration. There were always very few of them and now they're without a head. You, too, will be swept out in this purge. That's why I sent for you. What with the huge army that's coming to Bahia, we're going to find ourselves in trouble. The federal government will name a military and political leader to take over this state, someone whom Prudente de Moraes trusts, and the Assembly will lose all its power, or even be closed down, since it will no longer serve any purpose. Every form of local power will disappear from Bahia and we'll be a mere appendix of Rio. However strong a supporter of centralism you may be, I imagine that you're not a strong enough one to be willing to see yourself eliminated from political life.'

'That's one way of looking at things,' Epaminondas murmured imperturbably. 'Can you tell me how this common front that you're proposing would avert this danger?'

'The union of our two parties will force Moraes to negotiate and come to terms with us and will save Bahia from being tied hand and foot beneath the control of a military viceroy,' the baron answered. 'And, moreover, it will give you the possibility of reaching power.'

'Along with . . .' Epaminondas Gonçalves said.

'Alone,' the baron corrected him. 'The governorship of the state is yours. Luiz Viana will not run again and you will be our candidate. We will present joint lists of candidates for the Assembly and the Municipal Councils. Isn't that what you've been fighting for all this time?'

Epaminondas Gonçalves's face flushed. Was this sudden glow produced by the cognac, the heat, what he had just heard, or what he was thinking? He remained silent for a few seconds, lost in thought. 'Are your supporters in agreement with all this?' he finally asked in a low voice.

'They will be when they realize what it is they're obliged to do,' the baron answered. 'I'll persuade them – I give you my word. Are you satisfied?'

'I need to know what you're going to ask of me in return,' Epaminondas Gonçalves replied.

'That landed property and urban businesses not be touched,' the Baron de Canabrava replied immediately. 'Our people and your people will fight any attempt to confiscate, expropriate, interfere with, or impose immoderate taxes on landed property or businesses. That is the only condition.'

Epaminondas Gonçalves took a deep breath, as though he needed air. He drank the rest of his cognac in one swallow. 'And you, Baron?'

'Me?' the baron murmured, as though he were speaking of a ghost. 'I am about to retire from political life. I shall not trouble you in any way. Moreover, as you know, I am leaving for Europe next week. I shall remain there for an indefinite time. Does that ease your mind?'

Instead of answering, Epaminondas Gonçalves rose to his feet and paced about the room with his hands clasped behind his back. The baron affected indifference. The owner–publisher of the *Jornal de Notícias* did not try to conceal the indefinable feeling that had taken possession of him. He was both gravely thoughtful and excited, and in his eyes, along with his usual restless energy, there was also uneasiness, curiosity. 'Though I may not have your experience, at this point I'm not a greenhorn either,' he said defiantly, looking the baron square in the eye. 'I know you're putting one over on me, that there's a trap somewhere in what you're proposing.'

His host nodded, without showing the least sign of irritation. He rose from his chair to pour another finger of cognac in their empty glasses. 'I understand your misgivings,' he said, glass in hand, starting on a tour around the room that ended at the window overlooking the garden. He opened it: a breath of pleasantly warm air entered the study along with the loud chirping of crickets and the sound of a distant guitar. 'That's only natural. But there isn't any sort of trap, I assure you. The truth is that, given the way things are going, I've become convinced that the person best suited to be the political leader of Bahia is you.'

'Ought I to take that as a compliment?' Epaminondas Gonçalves asked in a sarcastic tone of voice.

'I believe that we've seen the end of a style, of a certain way of conducting politics,' the baron went on, as though he had not heard him. 'I admit that I've become obsolete. I functioned better in the old system, when it was a question of getting people to follow established customs and practices, of negotiating, persuading, using diplomacy and politesse. That's all over and done with today, of course. The hour has come for action, daring, violence, even crimes. What is needed now is a total dissociation of politics from morality. Since this is how things stand at present, the person best suited to maintain order in this state is you.'

'I suspected that you weren't paying me a compliment,' Epaminondas Gonçalves said, going back to his chair.

The baron sat down next to him. Along with the chirping of the crickets, sounds of coaches, the legato call of a night watchman, a foghorn, barking dogs came in through the window.

'In a certain way, I admire you.' The baron looked at him with a fleeting gleam in his eye. 'I've been able to appreciate your fearlessness, the complexity and cold-bloodedness of your political maneuvers. Yes, nobody in Bahia has your qualifications for confronting the situation we shall find ourselves in all too soon.'

'Will you tell me once and for all what it is you want of me?' the leader of the Republican Party said. There was a dramatic note in his voice.

'To replace me,' the baron stated emphatically. 'Will it put an end to your distrust of me if I tell you that I feel defeated by you? Not factually speaking, since the Autonomists have more possibilities than the Bahia Jacobins of coming to an understanding with Moraes and the Paulistas in the federal government. But psychologically speaking, yes, Epaminondas.'

He took a sip of cognac and his eyes stared into space. 'Things have happened that I never would have dreamed of,' he said. 'The best regiment in Brazil routed by a bunch of fanatical beggars. How to explain it? A great military strategist wiped out in the first encounter . . .'

'It's beyond explaining, I agree,' Epaminondas Gonçalves said. 'I was with Major Cunha Matos this afternoon. It's much worse than what's been revealed officially. Are you aware of the figures? They're unbelievable: between three hundred and four hundred casualties, three-quarters of the troops. Dozens of officers massacred. All the arms lost, from cannons to knives. The survivors are arriving in Monte Santo naked, in their underwear, delirious. The Seventh Regiment! You were close at hand, there in Calumbi. You saw them. Whatever is happening in Canudos, Baron?'

'I don't know and I don't understand,' the baron said gloomily. 'It's beyond anything I could imagine. And yet I thought I knew those parts, those people. The fanaticism of a few starving wretches is not a sufficient explanation for the rout. There has to be something else behind it.' He looked at him again, in utter bewilderment. 'I've come to think that that fantastic lie you people spread about there being English officers and monarchist arms might have had an element of truth in it. No, we won't even discuss the subject. It's water under the bridge. I merely mention it to you so that you'll see how stunned I am by what happened to Moreira César.'

'I'm not so much stunned as frightened,' Epaminondas said. 'If those men can pulverize the best regiment in Brazil, they're also capable of spreading anarchy throughout this entire state and the neighboring ones, of coming as far as Salvador . . .' He shrugged and made a vague, catastrophic gesture.

'The only explanation is that thousands of peasants, including ones from other regions, have joined that band of Sebastianists,' the baron said. 'Impelled by ignorance, superstition, hunger. Because there are no restraints these days to keep such madness in check, as there once were. This means war, the Brazilian Army installing itself here, the ruin of Bahia.' He grabbed Epaminondas Gonçalves by the arm. 'That is why you must replace me. Given the present situation, someone with your talents is needed to bring the right people together and defend the interests of Bahia amid the cataclysm. There's resentment in the rest of Brazil against Bahia, because of what happened to Moreira César. They say that the mobs that attacked the monarchist dailies in Rio were shouting "Down with Bahia."'

He paused for a long moment, nervously swirling the cognac in his glass. 'There are many who have already been ruined there in the interior,' he said. 'I've lost two haciendas. A great many more people are going to be wiped out and killed in this civil war. If your people and mine go on destroying each other, what will the result be? We'll lose everything. The exodus toward the South and Maranhão will become vaster still. What will become of the state of Bahia then? We must make our peace, Epaminondas. Forget your shrill Jacobin rhetoric, stop attacking the poor Portuguese, stop demanding the nationalization of businesses, and be practical. Jacobinism died with Moreira César. Assume the governorship and let us defend civil order together amid this hecatomb. Let us keep our Republic from turning into what so many other Latin American republics have: a grotesque witches' sabbath where all is chaos, military uprisings, corruption, demagogy . . .'

They sat in silence for some time, glasses in hand, thinking or listening. From time to time, footsteps, voices could be heard somewhere inside the house. A clock struck nine.

'I thank you for inviting me here,' Epaminondas said, rising to his feet. 'I'll keep everything you've told me well in mind and think it over. I can't give you an answer now.'

'Of course not,' the baron said, getting to his feet, too. 'Give it thought and we'll talk again. I would like to see you before I leave, naturally.'

'You will have my answer the day after tomorrow,' Epaminondas said as he started for the door. As they were going through the reception rooms, the black servant with the oil lamp appeared. The baron accompanied Epaminondas as far as the street.

At the front gate he asked him: 'Have you had any news of your journalist, the one who was with Moreira César?'

'The freak?' Epaminondas said. 'He hasn't turned up again. I suppose he must have been killed. As you know, he wasn't a man of action.'

They took their leave of each other with a bow.

IV

I

When a servant informed him who was asking for him, the Baron de Canabrava, rather than sending him back, as was his habit, to tell the person who had appeared on the doorstep that he neither made nor received unannounced visits, rushed downstairs, walked through the spacious rooms that the morning sun was flooding with light, and went to the front door to see if he had heard correctly: it was indeed he, no mistake about it. He shook hands with him without a word and showed him in. There leapt to his mind instantly what he had been trying his best to forget for months: the fire at Calumbi, Canudos, Estela's crisis, his withdrawal from public life.

Overcoming his surprise at this visit and the shock of this resurrection of the past, he silently guided the caller to the room in which all important conversations took place in the town house: the study. Though it was still early in the day, it was hot. In the distance, above the crotons, the branches of the mango, ficus, guava, and *pitangueira* trees in the garden, the sun was turning the sea as blinding white as a sheet of steel. The baron drew the curtain shut and the room fell into shadow.

'I knew that my visit would come as a surprise to you,' the caller said, and the baron recognized the little piping voice that always sounded like a comic actor speaking in falsetto. 'I learned that you had returned from Europe, and had . . . this impulse. I'll tell you straight out: I've come to ask you for work.'

'Have a seat,' the baron said.

He had heard the voice as in a dream, paying no attention to the words, entirely absorbed in studying the man's physical appearance and comparing it with his mental image of what he had looked like the last time he had set eyes on him: the scarecrow he had watched leaving Calumbi that morning with

Colonel Moreira César and his little escort. 'It's the same person and it isn't,' he thought. Because the journalist who had worked for the *Diário da Bahia* and later for the *Jornal de Notícias* had been a youngster and this man with the thick glasses, who on sitting down appeared to collapse into four or six sections, was an old man. His face was lined with myriad wrinkles, his hair was streaked with gray, his body looked brittle. He was wearing an unbuttoned shirt, a sleeveless jacket with worn spots or grease stains, a pair of trousers with frayed cuffs, and big clumsy cowherd's boots.

'I remember now,' the baron said. 'Someone wrote me that you were still alive. I was in Europe when I received the letter. "A ghost has turned up." That's what it said. Nonetheless, I continued to think of you as having disappeared, as having died.'

'I didn't die, nor did I disappear,' the thin, nasal voice said, without a trace of humor. 'After hearing ten times a day the same thing that you've just said, I realized people were disappointed that I was still in this world.'

'If I may say so frankly, I don't give a damn whether you're alive or dead,' the baron heard himself say, surprised at his own rudeness. 'I might even prefer you to be dead. I detest everything that reminds me of Canudos.'

'I heard about your wife,' the nearsighted journalist said, and the baron sensed that an impertinent remark would inevitably follow. 'That she lost her mind, that it's a great tragedy in your life.'

The baron looked at him in such a way that he was cowed and shut his mouth. He cleared his throat, blinked, and took off his glasses to wipe them on the tail of his shirt.

The baron was glad that he had resisted the impulse to throw him out. 'It's all coming back to me now,' he said amiably. 'The letter was from Epaminondas Gonçalves, two months or so ago. It was from him that I learned you'd returned to Salvador.'

'Do you correspond with that miserable wretch?' the thin nasal voice piped. 'Ah, yes, it's true that the two of you are allies now.'

'Is that any way to speak of the Governor of Bahia?' The baron smiled. 'Did he refuse to take you back at the *Jornal de Notícias*?'

'On the contrary: he even offered to raise my salary,' the near-sighted journalist retorted. 'On condition, however, that I forget all about the story of Canudos.'

He gave a little laugh, like that of an exotic bird, and the baron saw it turn into a gale of sneezes that made him bounce up and down in his chair.

'In other words, Canudos made a real journalist out of you,' the baron said mockingly. 'Or else you've changed. Because my ally Epaminondas is the same as he's always been. He hasn't changed one iota.'

He waited for the journalist to blow his nose on a blue rag that he quickly pulled out of his pocket.

'In that letter, Epaminondas said that you turned up with a strange person. A dwarf or something of the sort, is that right?'

The nearsighted journalist nodded. 'He's my friend. I'm indebted to him. He saved my life. Shall I tell you how? By telling me about Charlemagne, the Twelve Peers of France, Queen Maguelone. By reciting the Terrible and Exemplary Story of Robert the Devil.'

He spoke rapidly, rubbing his hands together, twisting and turning in his chair. The baron was reminded of Professor Tales de Azevedo, a scholar friend of his who had visited him in Calumbi many years before: he would spend hour after hour listening, in rapt fascination, to the minstrels at fairs, have them dictate to him the words that he heard them sing and recite, and assured him that they were medieval romances, brought to the New World by the first Portuguese and preserved in the oral tradition of the backlands. He noticed the look of anguish on his visitor's face.

'His life can still be saved,' he heard him say, a pleading look in his ambiguous eyes. 'He has tuberculosis, but it's operable. Dr. Magalhães, at the Portuguese Hospital, has saved many people. I want to do that for him. It's another reason why I need work. But above all . . . in order to eat.'

The baron saw the look of shame that came over his face, as though he had confessed to some ignominious sin.

'I don't know of any reason why I should help that dwarf,' the baron murmured. 'Nor why I should help you.'

'There isn't any reason, of course,' his myopic visitor said, pulling on his fingers. 'I just decided to try my luck. I thought I might be able to touch your heart. In the past you were known to be a generous man.'

'A banal tactic employed by a politician,' the baron said. 'I have no further need of it now that I've retired from politics.'

And at that moment, through the window overlooking the garden, he spied the chameleon. He very seldom caught a glimpse of it, or, better put, seldom recognized it, since it always blended so perfectly with the stones, the grass, or the bushes and branches of the garden that more than once he had nearly stepped on it. The evening before, he had taken Estela, accompanied by Sebastiana, out of doors for a breath of fresh air, beneath the mango trees and ficuses, and the chameleon had been a wonderful diversion for the baroness, who, from her wicker rocking chair, had amused herself by pointing out exactly where the creature was, recognizing it amid the plants and on the bark of trees as readily as in days gone by. The baron and Sebastiana had seen her smile when it ran off as they approached it to see if she had guessed correctly. It was there now, at the foot of one of the mangoes, an iridescent greenish-brown, barely distinguishable from the grass, its little throat palpitating. He spoke to it, in his mind: 'Beloved chameleon, elusive little creature, my good friend. I thank you with all my heart for having made my wife laugh.'

'The only things I own are the clothes on my back,' the near-sighted journalist said. 'When I returned from Canudos I found that the woman who owned my place had sold all my things to get the rent I owed. The *Jornal de Notícias* refused to pay for the upkeep while I was gone.' He fell silent for a moment and then added: 'She also sold off my books. Sometimes I recognize one or another of them in the Santa Bárbara market.'

The thought crossed the baron's mind that the loss of his books must have been heartbreaking for this man who ten or twelve years before had assured him that he would someday be the Oscar Wilde of Brazil.

'Very well,' he said. 'You may have your old job back at the *Diário da Bahia*. All in all, you weren't a bad writer.'

The nearsighted journalist removed his glasses and nodded several times, his face very pale, unable to express his thanks in any other way. 'It's a matter of little importance,' the baron thought. 'Am I doing this for him or for that dwarf? I'm doing it for the chameleon.' He looked out the window, searching for it, and felt disappointed: it was no longer there, or else, sensing that it was being spied on, it had disguised itself perfectly by blending with the colors round it.

'He's someone who's terrified at the thought of dying,' the nearsighted journalist murmured, putting his glasses back on. 'It's not out of a love of life, you understand. He's had a miserable existence. He was sold as a child to a gypsy for whom he was a circus attraction, a freak to be put on exhibition. But he has such a great, such a fabulous fear of death that it has enabled him to survive. And me as well, incidentally.'

The baron suddenly regretted having given him work, for in some indefinable way this established a bond between him and this individual. And he did not want to feel any sort of tie to anyone so closely linked to the memory of Canudos. But, instead of intimating to his caller that their conversation had ended, he blurted out: 'You must have seen terrible things.' He cleared his throat, feeling uncomfortable at having yielded to his curiosity, but added nonetheless: 'When you were up there in Canudos.'

'As a matter of fact, I didn't see anything at all,' the emaciated little figure replied immediately, doubling over and then straightening up. 'I broke my glasses the day they destroyed the Seventh Regiment. I stayed up there for four months, seeing nothing but shadows, vague shapes, phantoms.'

His voice was so ironic that the baron wondered whether he was saying this to irritate him, or whether it was his rude, unfriendly way of letting him know that he didn't want to talk about it.

'I don't know why you haven't laughed at me,' he heard him say in an even more aggressive tone of voice. 'Everybody laughs when I tell them that I didn't see what happened in Canudos because I broke my glasses. It's quite comical, I'm sure.'

'Yes, it is,' the baron said, rising to his feet. 'But it's something that doesn't interest me. Hence . . .'

'But even though I didn't see them, I felt, heard, smelled the things that happened,' the journalist said, his eyes following him from behind his glasses. 'And I intuitively sensed the rest.'

The baron heard him laugh once more, with a sort of impishness now, fearlessly looking him straight in the eye. He sat down again. 'Did you really come here to ask me for work and talk to me about that dwarf?' he said. 'Does that dwarf dying of tuberculosis exist?'

'He's spitting up blood and I want to help him,' the visitor said. 'But I came for another reason as well.'

He bowed his head, and as the baron's gaze fell upon his disheveled salt-and-pepper locks flecked with dandruff, he visualized in his mind his watery eyes fixed on the floor. He had the inexplicable intuition that his visitor was bringing him a message from Galileo Gall.

'People are forgetting Canudos,' the nearsighted journalist said, in a voice that sounded like an echo. 'The last lingering memories of what happened there will fade in the air and mingle with the music of the next carnival ball in the Politeama Theater.'

'Canudos?' the baron murmured. 'Epaminondas is right not to want people to talk about what happened there. It's better to forget it. It's an unfortunate, unclear episode. It's not good for anything. History must be instructive, exemplary. In this war, nobody has covered himself with glory. And nobody has understood what happened. People have decided to ring down a curtain on it. And that's a sensible, healthy reaction.'

'I shall not allow them to forget,' the journalist said, his dim eyes gazing steadily up at him. 'That's a promise I've made myself.'

The baron smiled. Not because of his visitor's sudden solemnity but because the chameleon had just materialized, beyond the desk and the curtains, in the bright green of the plants in the garden, beneath the gnarled branches of the *pitangueira* tree. Long, motionless, greenish, with its profile reminiscent of the topography of sharp mountain peaks, almost transparent, it gleamed like a precious stone. 'Welcome, friend,' the baron thought.

'How will you do that?' he said, for no particular reason, simply to fill the silence.

'In the only way in which things are preserved,' he heard his caller growl. 'By writing of them.'

The baron nodded. 'I remember that, too. You wanted to be a poet, a dramatist. And you're going to write the story of Canudos that you didn't see?'

'What fault of this poor devil is it that Estela is no longer that lucid, intelligent creature she once was?' the baron thought.

'As soon as I was able to get rid of the cheeky and curious strangers who besieged me, I started going to the Reading Room of the Academy of History,' the myopic journalist said. 'To look through the papers, all the news items about Canudos. The *Jornal da Notícias*, the *Diário de Bahia, O Republicano.* I've read everything written about it, everything I wrote. It's something . . . difficult to put into words. Too unreal, do you follow me? It seems like a conspiracy in which everyone played a role, a total misunderstanding on the part of all concerned, from beginning to end.'

'I don't understand.' The baron had forgotten the chameleon and even Estela and was watching in fascination this person sitting all doubled over, his chin brushing his knee, as though he were straining to get his words out.

'Hordes of fanatics, bloodthirsty killers, cannibals of the backlands, racial mongrels, contemptible monsters, human scum, base lunatics, filicides, spiritual degenerates,' the visitor recited, lingering over each syllable. 'Some of those terms were mine. I not only wrote them, I also believed them.'

'Are you going to pen an apology for Canudos?' the baron asked. 'You always did strike me as being a bit crazy. But I find it hard to believe that you're crazy enough to ask my help in such an undertaking. You're aware of what Canudos cost me, are you not? That I lost half my possessions? That on account of Canudos the worst misfortune of all happened to me, since Estela . . .'

He could hear his voice quavering and fell silent. He looked out the window, searching for help. And he found it: the creature was still there, perfectly still, beautiful, prehistoric, eternal, halfway between the animal and vegetable kingdoms, serene in the radiant morning light.

'But those terms were preferable. They at least kept people thinking about Canudos,' the journalist said, as though he had not heard him. 'And now, not a word. Is there talk of Canudos in the cafés on the Rua Chile, in the marketplaces, in the taverns? No, people are talking instead of the orphan girls deflowered by the director of the Santa Rita de Cássia hospice. Or of Dr. Silva Lima's anti-syphilis pill or of the latest shipment of Russian soap and English shoes just arrived at Clark's Department Store.' He looked the baron straight in the eye and the latter saw that there was fury and panic in those myopic orbs. 'The last news item about Canudos appeared in the papers two days ago. Do you know what it was about?'

'I don't read the papers now that I've left politics,' the baron said. 'Not even my own.'

'The return to Rio de Janeiro of the commission sent by the Spiritualist Center of the capital to aid the forces of law and order, through the use of its mediumistic powers, to wipe out the *jagunços*. Well, the commission has now come back to Rio, on the steamer *Rio Vermelho*, with its ouija boards and its crystal balls and what have you. Since then, not a single line. And it hasn't even been three months yet.'

'I don't want to hear any more,' the baron said. 'I've already told you that Canudos is a painful subject to me.'

'I need to know what you know,' the journalist interrupted him in a hurried, conspiratorial voice. 'You know many things. You sent them flour and also cattle. You had contacts with them. You talked with Pajeú.'

Blackmail? Had he come to threaten him, to get money out of him? The baron was disappointed that the explanation of all that enigmatic, empty talk had turned out to be something so vulgar.

'Did you really give Antônio Vilanova that message for me?' Abbot João asks, rousing himself from the warm drowsiness he feels as Catarina's long slender fingers bury themselves in his mane, searching for nits.

'I don't know what message he gave you,' Catarina answers, her fingers continuing to explore his head.

'She's happy,' Abbot João thinks. He knows her well enough to sense, from furtive inflections of her voice or sparks in her dark eyes, when she is feeling unhappy. He is aware that people talk of Catarina's mortal sadness, since no one has ever seen her laugh and very few have ever heard her say a word. But why try to show them that they're wrong? He knows: he has seen her smile and laugh, though always as if in secret.

'That if I'm condemned to eternal damnation, you want to be, too,' he murmurs.

His wife's fingers stop moving, just as they do each time they come across a louse nesting in his hair, whereupon she crushes it between her fingernails. After a moment, they go on with their task and João again immerses himself in the welcome peace of simply being where he is, without his shoes on, his torso bare, lying on the rush pallet of the tiny dwelling made of boards held together with mud, on the Rua do Menino Jesus, with his wife kneeling at his back, removing the lice from his hair. He feels pity for the blindness of others. Feeling no need to speak to each other, he and Catarina tell each other more things than the worst chatterboxes in Canudos. It is mid-morning and the sunlight filtering in through the cracks between the planks of the door and the tiny holes in the length of blue cloth covering the only window brightens the one room of the cabin. Outside, voices can be heard, the sound of children running about, the hustle and bustle of people going about their business, as though this were a world at peace, as though there had not been so many people killed that it took Canudos an entire week to bury its dead and carry off to the outskirts of town all the soldiers' corpses so the vultures would devour them.

'It's true,' Catarina says in his ear, her breath tickling it. 'If you go to hell, I want to go there with you.'

João reaches out his arm, takes Catarina by the waist, and sits her on his knees. He does so with the greatest possible gentleness, as always when he touches her, for, because she is so thin or because he feels such remorse, he always has the distressing feeling that he is going to hurt her, and because the thought always crosses his mind that he must let go of her immediately since he will encounter that resistance that always is evident the moment he even tries to take her by the arm. He knows that she finds physical contact unbearable and he has learned to respect her feelings, fighting his own impulses, because he loves her. Although they have lived together for many years, they have very seldom made love together, or at least given themselves to each other completely, Abbot João thinks, without those interruptions on her part that leave him panting, bathed in sweat, his heart pounding. But this morning, to his surprise, Catarina does not push him away. On the contrary, she curls up on his lap and he feels her frail body, with its protruding ribs, its nearly non-existent breasts, pressing against his.

'There in the Health House, I was afraid for you,' Catarina says. 'As we were caring for the wounded, as we saw the soldiers passing by, shooting and throwing torches. I was afraid. For you.'

She does not say this in a fervent, passionate tone of voice, but rather in a cold, impersonal one, as though she were speaking of other people's reactions. But Abbot João feels deeply moved, and then a sudden desire for her. He thrusts his hand beneath Catarina's wrapper and caresses her back, her sides, her tiny nipples, as his mouth with all its front teeth missing brushes her neck, her cheek, seeking her lips. Catarina allows him to kiss her, but she does not open her mouth, and when João tries to lay her down on the pallet, her body stiffens. He immediately frees her from his embrace, breathing deeply, closing his eyes. Catarina rises to her feet, pulls her wrapper about her, picks up the blue cloth that has fallen to the floor, and covers her head with it once again. The roof of the cabin is so low that she is obliged to bend over in the corner of the room where provisions are stored (when there are any): beef jerky, manioc flour, beans, raw brown sugar. João watches her preparing the meal and calculates how many days – or weeks? – it has been since he has had the opportunity to be alone with her like this, with no thought in either of their minds of the war and of the Antichrist.

Shortly thereafter, Catarina comes over and sits down beside him on the pallet, with a wooden bowl full of beans sprinkled with manioc and a wooden spoon in her hands. They eat, handing the spoon to each other, with him taking two or three mouthfuls to her one.

'Is it true that Belo Monte was saved from the Throat-Slitter by the Indians from Mirandela?' Catarina murmurs. 'That's what Joaquim Macambira says.'

'And also by the blacks from the Mocambo and the others,' Abbot João answers. 'But it's quite true, the Indians from Mirandela were really brave. They had neither carbines nor rifles.'

They had not wanted to have them, out of caprice, superstition, mistrust, or some other unfathomable reason. He himself, the Vilanova brothers, Pedrão, Big João, the Macambiras had tried several times to give them firearms, petards, explosives. The chief shook his head emphatically, thrusting his hands out before him with something like disgust. Shortly before the arrival of Throat-Slitter, he himself had offered to show them how to load, clean, and shoot muskets, shotguns, rifles. The answer had been no. Abbot João concluded that the Cariri Indians would not fight this time either. They had not gone to confront the dogs at Uauá, and when the expedition had come by way of O Cambaio they had not even left their huts, as though that battle had been no business of theirs either. 'Belo Monte is not defended on that flank,' Abbot João had said. 'Let's pray to the Blessed Jesus that they don't come from that direction.' But they had also come from that way. 'The only side where they were unable to break through,' Abbot João thinks. It had been those surly, distant, incomprehensible creatures, fighting with only bows and arrows, lances, and knives, who had stopped them. A miracle perhaps?

His eyes seeking his wife's, João asks: 'Do you remember when we entered Mirandela for the first time, with the Counselor?'

She nods. They have finished eating and Catarina takes the bowl and the spoon to the corner of the stove. Then João sees her come back toward him – very thin, grave, barefoot, her head brushing the ceiling covered with soot – and lie down beside him on the pallet. He places his arm underneath her back and carefully makes room for her to settle down comfortably. They lie there quietly, listening to the sounds of Canudos, near and far. They can lie that way for hours and these are perhaps the most profound moments of the life they share.

'At that time I hated you as much as you used to hate Custódia,' Catarina murmurs.

Mirandela, a village of Indians herded together there in the eighteenth century by the Capuchin missionaries of the Massacará mission, was a strange enclave in the backlands of Canudos, separated from Pombal by four leagues of sandy ground, dense and thorny scrub impenetrable in places, and air so burning hot that it chapped people's lips and turned their skin to parchment. Since time immemorial the village of Cariri Indians, perched on top of a mountain, in rugged country, had been the scene of bloody fights – sometimes turning into veritable massacres – between the Indians and the whites of the region for the possession of the best pieces of land. The Indians lived grouped together in the village, in scattered cabins around the Church of the Ascension of Our Lord, a stone building two centuries old, with a straw roof and a blue door and windows, and the bare stretch of ground that was the village square, in which there was nothing but a handful of coconut palms and a wooden cross. The whites stayed on their haciendas round about the village and this proximity was not coexistence but rather a permanent state of undeclared war that periodically took the form of reciprocal incursions, violent incidents, sackings, and murders. The few hundred Indians of Mirandela went around half naked, speaking a local dialect seasoned with little spurts of spit, and hunting with bows and poisoned arrows. They were surly, wretched specimens of humanity, who kept entirely to themselves within their circle of huts thatched with *icó* leaves, with their maize fields between, and so poor that neither the bandits nor the flying brigades of Rural Police entered Mirandela to sack it. They had become heathens again. It had been years since the Capuchin and Lazarist Fathers had been able to preach a Holy Mission in the village, for the moment the missionaries appeared in the vicinity, the Indians and their wives and children vanished into the *caatinga,* till the Fathers finally gave up and resigned themselves to preaching the mission only for the whites. Abbot João doesn't remember when it was that the Counselor decided to go to Mirandela. For him the disciples' time of wandering is not linear, with a *before* and an *after*, but circular, a repetition of interchangeable days and events. He does remember, on the other hand, how it came about. After having restored the chapel of Pombal, the Counselor took off toward the North one morning, heading across a succession of razor-backed hills that led directly to the Indian redoubt, where a family of whites had just been massacred. No one said a word to him, for no one, ever, questioned the Counselor's decisions. But during the long day's journey, with the blazing sun seemingly trepanning their skulls, many of the disciples, Abbot João among them, thought that they would be greeted by a deserted village or by a shower of arrows.

Neither thing happened. The Counselor and his followers climbed up the mountainside at dusk and entered the village in procession, singing hymns in praise of Mary. The Indians received them without taking fright, without hostility, in an attitude of apparent indifference. They saw the pilgrims install themselves on the open space in front of their huts, light a bonfire, and throng round it. Then they saw them enter the Church of the Ascension of Our Lord and pray at the stations of the cross, and then later, from their cabins and little animal pens and fields, those men whose faces were covered with ritual scars and green-and-white stripes listened to the Counselor give his evening counsel. They heard him speak of the Holy Spirit, which is freedom, and of Mary's sorrow, extol the virtues of frugality, poverty, and sacrifice, explain that every suffering offered to God becomes a reward in the life to come. They then heard the pilgrims of the Blessed Jesus recite a Rosary to the Mother of Christ. And the next morning, still without having approached them, still without giving them so much as a smile or making a single friendly gesture, the Indians saw them leave by the path to the cemetery, where they stopped to tidy the graves and cut the grass.

'The Counselor was inspired by the Father to go to Mirandela that time,' Abbot João says. 'He sowed a seed and it finally flowered.'

Catarina doesn't say anything, but João knows that she is remembering, as he is, how one day some hundred Indians suddenly turned up in Belo Monte, bringing with them, along the road from Bendengó, their belongings, their old people, some of them on stretchers, their wives and their children. Years had gone by, but no one doubted that the surprising appearance of these half-naked people daubed with paint meant that they were returning the Counselor's visit. The Cariris entered Canudos, accompanied by a white from Mirandela, Antônio the Pyrotechnist, as though they were entering their own house, and installed themselves in the open country adjoining the Mocambo that Antônio Vilanova assigned them. They built huts there and planted their crops between them. They went to hear the counsels and spoke just enough broken Portuguese to make themselves understood by the others, but they remained a world apart. The Counselor often used to go to see them – they would receive him by stamping their feet on the ground, that strange way of theirs of dancing – as did the Vilanova brothers, through whom they traded their produce for other provisions. Abbot João had always thought of them as strangers. But not any more. Because the day of the invasion by Throat-Slitter had seen them withstand three infantry charges launched directly on their quarter, two from the Vaza-Barris side and the other via the road from Jeremoabo. When he and some twenty men from the Catholic Guard went to reinforce this sector, he had been astonished at the number of attackers circulating among the huts and at the Indians' stubborn resistance, riddling them with arrows from the rooftops, shooting rocks at them with their slings, flinging themselves upon them with their stone axes and wooden pikes. The Cariris fought hand-to-hand with the invaders, and their women leapt upon them too, biting them and scratching them and trying to snatch their rifles and bayonets out of their hands, forthrightly shouting insults and curses at them the while. At least a third of the infantrymen had been killed or wounded by the end of the encounter.

A knock at the door rouses Abbot João from his thoughts. Catarina removes the plank, held fast by a length of wire, that bars the door, and one of Honório Vilanova's children appears amid a cloud of dust, white light, and noise.

'My uncle Antônio wants to see the Street Commander,' he says.

'Tell him I'll be right there,' Abbot João replies.

Such happiness was bound not to last, he thinks, and he can tell from his wife's face that she is thinking the same thing. He pulls on his coarse cotton pants fastened with leather thongs, his rope sandals, his blouse, and goes out into the street. The bright light of midday blinds him. As always, the women, children, old people sitting at the doors of the dwellings greet him and he waves back. He walks on amid knots of women grinding maize in their mortars together, men conversing in loud voices as they assemble reed flats and fill in the chinks with handfuls of mud to replace walls that have fallen. He even hears a guitar somewhere. He does not need to see them to know that at this moment hundreds of other people are on the banks of the Vaza-

Barris and at the Jeremoabo exit, squatting on their haunches clearing the land, tidying up the orchards, ridding the animal pens of rubble. There is almost no debris in the streets, and many huts that were burned down have been rebuilt. 'That's Antônio Vilanova's doing,' he thinks. The moment the procession celebrating the triumph of Belo Monte over the heretics of the Republic was ended, Antônio Vilanova had taken charge of the squads of volunteers and people from the Catholic Guard, and was out organizing the burial of the dead, the removal of rubble, the rebuilding of the huts and workshops, and the rescue of the sheep, goats, and kids that had scattered in terror. 'It's their doing, too,' Abbot João thinks. 'They've accepted the situation. They're heroes.' There they are, untroubled, greeting, smiling at him, and this evening they will hurry to the Temple of the Blessed Jesus to hear the Counselor, as if nothing had happened, as if all these families did not have someone who had been shot to death, run through with a lance, or burned to death in this war, and someone among the countless wounded lying moaning in the Health Houses and in the Church of Santo Antônio now turned into an infirmary.

And then something makes him stop short. He closes his eyes to listen. He is not mistaken; he is not dreaming. The even, harmonious voice goes on reciting. From the depths of his memory, a cascade that swells and becomes a river, something stirring takes shape, materializes in a rush of swords and a dazzle of palaces and luxurious chambers. 'The battle of Sir Olivier with Fierabras,' he thinks. It is one of the episodes from the tales of the Twelve Peers of France that he is fondest of, a duel that he hasn't heard the story of for years and years. The voice of the minstrel is coming from the intersection of Campo Grande and Divino, where many people have gathered. He draws closer, and on recognizing him, people move aside for him. The one who is singing of Olivier's imprisonment and his duel with Fierabras is a child. No, a dwarf. Tiny, very thin, he is pretending to be strumming a guitar and at the same time is miming the clash of the lances, the knights galloping on their steeds, the courtly bows to Charlemagne the Great. Seated on the ground, with a tin can on her lap, is a woman with long hair, and at her side a bony, bent, mud-spattered creature with the sightless gaze of blind men. He recognizes them: they are the three who appeared with Father Joaquim, the ones whom Antônio Vilanova allows to sleep in the store. He reaches out and touches the little man, who immediately falls silent.

'Do you know the Terrible and Exemplary Story of Robert the Devil?' he asks him.

After a moment's hesitation, the Dwarf nods.

'I would like to hear you recite it sometime,' the Street Commander says in a reassuring tone of voice. And he breaks into a run to make up for lost time. Here and there, there are shell holes along Campo Grande. The façade of the former steward's house of Canudos is riddled with bullet holes.

'Praised be the Blessed Jesus,' Abbot João murmurs, sitting down on top of a barrel next to Pajeú. The expression on the *caboclo*'s face is inscrutable, but he notes that Antônio and Honório Vilanova, old Macambira, Big João, and Pedrão are all scowling. Father Joaquim is standing in the middle of them, covered with mud from head to foot, his hair disheveled, and with a growth of beard.

'Did you find out anything in Juazeiro, Father?' he asks him. 'Are there more troops coming?'

'As he offered to, Father Maximiliano came from Queimadas and brought me the complete list,' Father Joaquim replies in a hoarse voice. He takes a paper out of his pocket and reads out, panting for breath: 'First Brigade: Seventh, Fourteenth, and Third Infantry Battalions, under the command of Colonel Joaquim Manuel de Medeiros. Second Brigade: Sixteenth, Twenty-fifth, and Twenty-seventh Infantry Battalions, under the command of Colonel Inácio Maria Gouveia. Third Brigade: Fifth Artillery Regiment and Fifth and Ninth Infantry Battalions, under the command of Colonel Olímpio da Silveira. Chief of Division: General João da Silva Barboza. Field Commander: General Artur Oscar.'

He stops reading, exhausted and in a daze, and looks at Abbot João. 'How many soldiers does that add up to, Father?' the former *cangaceiro* asks.

'Some five thousand men, it would appear,' the little priest stammers. 'But those are only the ones that are in Queimadas and Monte Santo. Others are coming from the North, via Sergipe.' He begins reading again, in a quavering voice. 'Column under the command of General Cláudio da Amaral Savaget. Three brigades: Fourth, Fifth, and Sixth. Made up of the Twelfth, Thirty-first, and Thirty-third Infantry Battalions, one artillery division, and the Thirty-fourth, Thirty-fifth, Fortieth, Twenty-sixth, Thirty-second Battalions, and another artillery division. Four thousand more men, approximately. They disembarked in Aracaju and are advancing on Jeremoabo. Father Maximiliano was unable to obtain the names of the officers in command. I told him it didn't matter. It really doesn't matter, does it, João?'

'Of course not, Father Joaquim,' Abbot João answers. 'You've managed to obtain excellent information. God will repay you.'

'Father Maximiliano is a good believer,' the little priest murmurs. 'He confessed to me that it scared him to do that. I told him that I was more scared than he was.' He gives a forced laugh and immediately adds: 'They have a great many problems there in Queimadas, he told me. Too many mouths to feed. They haven't organized their train yet. They don't have the wagons, the mule teams to transport the enormous amount of matériel they have. He says it may be weeks before they're ready to move.'

Abbot João nods. No one speaks. They all appear to be concentrating on the buzzing of the flies and the acrobatics of a wasp that finally lands on Big João's knee. The black removes it with a flick of his finger. Abbot João is surprised all of a sudden at the chatter of the Vilanovas' parrot.

'I also met with Dr. Águiar do Nascimento,' Father Joaquim adds. 'He said to tell you that the only thing you could do was to disperse people and send them back to their villages before all that armory gets here.' He pauses and takes a fearful sidelong glance at the seven men looking at him respectfully and attentively. 'But that if, despite everything, you are going to fight it out with the soldiers, then, yes, he has something to offer you.' He lowers his head, as though fatigue or fear will permit him to say no more.

'A hundred Comblain rifles and twenty-five cases of ammunition,' Antônio Vilanova says. 'From the army, brand-new and in their factory cases. They can be brought via Uauá and Bendengó, the road is clear.' He is sweating heavily and wipes his forehead as he speaks. 'But there aren't enough hides or oxen or goats in Canudos to pay the price he's asking.'

'There are silver and gold jewels,' Abbot João says, reading in the merchant's eyes what he must have said or thought already, before he arrived.

'They belong to the Virgin and her Son,' Father Joaquim says in an almost inaudible voice: 'Isn't that sacrilege?'

'The Counselor will know whether it is or not,' Abbot João says. 'We must ask him.'

'It is always possible to feel even more afraid,' the nearsighted journalist thought. That was the great lesson of these days without hours, of figures without faces, of lights veiled with clouds that his eyes struggled to penetrate until they burned so badly that it was necessary for him to close them and remain in the dark for a while, overcome with despair: discovering what a coward he was. What would his colleagues on the staff of the *Jornal de Notícias*, the *Diário da Bahia*, *O Republicano* say if they knew that? He had won the reputation among them of being a fearless reporter, ever in search of new experiences: he had been one of the first to attend *candomblé* rites – voodoo ceremonies – in whatever out-of-the-way back street or hamlet they might be held, in an era in which the religious practices of blacks aroused only fear or disgust among the whites of Bahia, a dogged frequenter of sorcerers and witches, and one of the first to take up smoking opium. Had it not been his spirit of adventure that had led him to volunteer to go to Juazeiro to interview the survivors of Lieutenant Pires Ferreira's military expedition, was it not he himself who had proposed to Epaminondas Gonçalves that he accompany Moreira César? 'I'm the greatest coward in the whole world,' he thought. The Dwarf went on recounting the adventures, the misadventures, the gallant deeds of Olivier and Fierabras. The vague shapes – he was unable to make out whether they were men or women – stood there, not moving, and it was evident that the recital of the tale held them spellbound, outside of time and outside of Canudos. How was it possible that here, at the very end of the world, he was hearing, recited by a dwarf who no doubt did not know how to read, a romance from the Round Table cycle brought here centuries before by some sailor or some young graduate of Coimbra? What other surprises did the *sertão* hold in store for him?

His stomach growled and he wondered whether the audience would give them enough money for a meal. That was another discovery he had made in these days that had taught him so many lessons: the fact that food could be a primary concern, capable of occupying all his thoughts for hours on end, and at times a greater source of anxiety than the semi-blindness in which the breaking of his glasses had plunged him, that state in which he stumbled over everything and everyone, which left his body full of bruises from crashing into indiscernible objects and shapes that got in his way and obliged him to continually apologize, saying I'm sorry, I can't see, I beg your pardon, to appease any possible anger that might be forthcoming.

The Dwarf interrupted his recital and indicated that in order to go on with the story – the journalist pictured in his mind his imploring gestures, the pleading expressions on his face – he required nourishment. The journalist's entire body went into action. His right hand moved toward Jurema and touched her. He did this many times a day, every time something new happened, since it was on the threshold of the novel and unpredictable that his fear – always lurking – would again take possession of him. It was merely a quick brush of his fingertips, to reassure him, for this woman was his only hope now that Father Joaquim seemed to be definitely out of reach; she was the one who looked after him and made him feel less helpless. He and the Dwarf were a bother to Jurema. Why didn't she go off and leave them? Out of generosity? No, out of apathy doubtless, out of that terrible indolence into which she seemed to have sunk. But with his clowning the Dwarf at least managed to obtain for them those handfuls of maize flour or sun-dried goat meat that kept them alive. He himself was the only totally useless one, whom sooner or later the woman would get rid of.

After making a few jokes that no one laughed at, the Dwarf went back to reciting the story of Olivier. The nearsighted journalist felt the touch of Jurema's hand and instantly opened his. He immediately put the vague shape that appeared to be a hard crust of bread in his mouth. He chewed stubbornly, greedily, his entire mind concentrated on that pap that gradually formed in his mouth, that he swallowed with difficulty and with a happy heart. He thought: 'If I survive, I shall hate her, I shall curse even the flowers that have the same name she does.' Because Jurema knew the extent of his cowardice, the extremes to which it could drive him. As he chewed, slowly, avidly, happily, fearfully, he remembered the first night in Canudos, the half-blind, exhausted person with legs of sawdust that he had been, stumbling, falling, dazed and deafened by the tumult of voices shouting 'Long live the Counselor.' He had suddenly been caught up in a swirling confusion of smells, sputtering, oily points of light, and the swelling chorus of litanies. Then, just as suddenly, complete silence fell. 'It's him, it's the Counselor.' He gripped that hand he had not let go of all day so tightly that the woman said: 'Let go of me, let me go.' Later, when the hoarse voice stopped speaking and the crowd began to disperse, he, Jurema, and the Dwarf collapsed right in the middle of the open square between the churches. They had lost the curé of Cumbe, who had been joyously swept along by the crowd as they entered Canudos. During his sermon, the Counselor thanked heaven for bringing him back to Canudos, for restoring him to life, and the nearsighted journalist presumed that Father Joaquim was there at the saint's side on the dais, platform, or tower from which he was preaching. Moreira César was right, after all: the little priest was a *jagunço*, he was one of them. It had been at that moment that he had begun to cry. He had sobbed his heart out, as he could not even imagine himself having done as a child, begging the woman to help him get out of Canudos. He offered her clothes, a house, anything if she would promise not to abandon him, half blind and half dead from hunger. Yes, she knew that fear turned him into a despicable creature capable of anything in order to arouse her compassion.

The Dwarf had finished the story. The journalist heard scattered applause and the audience began to wander off. Tensely, he tried to make out whether people stretched out a hand, left them a little something before going off, but he had the distressing impression that no one did so.

'Nothing?' he murmured, when he sensed that they were alone.

'Nothing,' the woman answered with her usual indifference, rising to her feet.

The nearsighted journalist stood up too, and on noting that she had begun walking – a slight little figure, with her hair hanging and her blouse in tatters, whom he could see in his mind's eye – he followed along after her. The Dwarf came scrambling along at his side, his head at the height of his elbow.

'They're scrawnier than we are,' he heard the Dwarf mutter. 'Do you remember Cipó, Jurema? There are even more human wrecks here. Have you ever seen so many people who are one-armed, blind, crippled, palsied, albinos, so many who are missing ears, a nose, hair, so full of scabs and blotches? You haven't noticed, Jurema. But I have. Because here I feel normal.'

He laughed merrily, and the nearsighted journalist heard him whistle a happy tune for some time as they walked along.

'Will they give us maize flour again today?' he asked all of a sudden in an anxious voice. But he was thinking of something else, and added bitterly: 'If it's true that Father Joaquim has gone off somewhere, we don't have anybody who'll help us now. Why did he do that to us? Why did he abandon us?'

'Why wouldn't he abandon us?' the Dwarf said. 'What are we to him? Did he know us? Be grateful that we have a roof over our heads at night to sleep under, thanks to him.'

It was true, he had helped them; thanks to him, they had a roof over their heads. It was surely thanks to his intercession that the morning after they had slept out in the open all night, as they were waking up with all their bones and muscles aching, a powerful, efficient-sounding voice, which appeared to belong to the solid bulk, the bearded face above them, had said: 'Come on, you can sleep in the storehouse. But don't leave Belo Monte.'

Were they prisoners? Neither he nor Jurema nor the Dwarf asked any questions of this man with the commanding air who, with a simple phrase, took over their lives. Without another word he took them to a place the nearsighted journalist sensed was vast, dark, warm, and chock-full of things, and before disappearing – without questioning them as to who they were, or what they were doing there, or what they wanted to do – told them once more that they could not leave Canudos and warned them not to touch the arms. The Dwarf and Jurema explained to him that they were surrounded by rifles, powder, mortars, sticks of dynamite. He realized that these were the arms that had been seized from the Seventh Regiment. Wasn't it absurd that they were going to sleep there in the middle of all these spoils of war? No, life had ceased to be logical, and therefore nothing was absurd. It was life: one had to accept it as it was or kill oneself.

He had had the thought that, here, something different from reason governed things, men, time, death, something that it would be unfair to call madness and too general to call faith, superstition, ever since the night on which he had first heard the Counselor, immersed in that multitude which, as it listened to the deep, booming, strangely impersonal voice, had taken on a granite immobility, amid a silence one could touch. More than by the man's words and his majestic voice, the journalist was struck, stunned, overwhelmed by that stillness, that silence in which they listened to him. It was like . . . it was like . . . He searched desperately for that similarity with something that he knew lay stored in the depths of his memory, because, he was sure, once it came to the surface it would explain what he was feeling. Yes: the *candomblés*. Sometimes, in those humble huts of the blacks of Salvador, or in the narrow streets behind the Calçada Railroad Station, attending the frenetic rites of those sects that sang in forgotten African languages, he had caught a glimpse of an organization of life, a collusion of things and men, of time, space, and human experience as totally devoid of logic, of common sense, of reason, as the one which, in that rapidly falling darkness that was beginning to blur people's silhouettes, he perceived in these creatures who were being given comfort, strength, and a sense of roots by that deep, cavernous hoarse voice, so contemptuous of material necessities, so proudly centered on the spirit, on everything that could not be eaten or worn or used: thoughts, emotions, feelings, virtues. As he listened to that voice, the nearsighted journalist thought he had a sudden intuitive understanding of the *why* of Canudos, the *why* of the continued existence of that aberration, Canudos. But when the voice ceased and the crowd emerged from its ecstasy, his bewilderment was again as great as it had been before.

'Here's a little flour for you,' he heard the wife of either Antônio or Honório Vilanova saying: their voices were identical. 'And some milk.'

He stopped thinking, letting his mind wander, and was nothing but a ravenous creature who raised little mouthfuls of maize flour to his lips with his fingertips, wet them with saliva, and kept them between his palate and his tongue for a long time before swallowing them, an organism that felt gratitude each time a sip of goat's milk brought this feeling of well-being to his insides.

When they finished, the Dwarf belched and the nearsighted journalist heard him give a happy laugh. 'If he eats he's happy, and if he doesn't he's sad,' he thought. It was the same with him: his happiness or unhappiness now largely depended on his gut. That elemental truth reigned in Canudos, and yet could these people be called materialists? Because another persistent idea of his in recent days was that this society had come, by way of obscure paths and perhaps through simple error or accident, to rid itself of concerns about bodily needs, about economics, about everyday life, and everything that was primordial in the world he had come from. Would this sorry paradise of spirituality and wretchedness be his grave? During his first days in Canudos he had had illusions, had imagined that the little curé of Cumbe would remember him, would secure him guides, a horse, and that he would be able to get back to Salvador. But Father Joaquim had not come back to see them, and people now said that he was away on a journey. He no longer appeared at dusk on the scaffolding of the Temple under construction, and no longer celebrated Mass in the mornings. He had never been able to get close to him, to make his way through the group of armed men and women with blue headcloths standing shoulder to shoulder to guard the Counselor and his most intimate disciples, and now nobody knew if Father Joaquim would be back. Would his lot have been different if he had managed to speak with him? What would he have said to him? 'Father Joaquim, I'm afraid of staying here amid *jagunços*, get me out of here, take me where there are soldiers and police who will offer me some security'? He could almost hear the little curé's answer: 'And what security do they offer *me*, senhor journalist? Have you forgotten that only a miracle kept me from losing my life at the hands of Throat-Slitter? Do you really imagine that I could go back where there are soldiers and police?' He burst out laughing uncontrollably, hysterically. He heard his laughter, and immediately took fright, thinking that it might offend those blurred beings who lived in this place. Finding his laughter infectious, the Dwarf, too, burst into a loud guffaw. He could see him in his mind, a tiny, deformed creature, contorted with merriment. It irritated him that Jurema remained as sober as ever.

'Well, it's a small world! We meet again,' a rasping male voice said, and the nearsighted journalist was aware that dim silhouettes were approaching. One of them, the shorter of the two, with a red patch that must be a neckerchief, planted himself in front of

Jurema. 'I thought the dogs had killed you up there on the mountain.'

'They didn't kill me,' Jurema answered.

'I'm glad,' the man said. 'That would have been too bad.'

'He wants her for himself. He's going to take her off with him,' the nearsighted journalist thought instantly. The palms of his hands began to sweat. He would take her away with him and the Dwarf would tag along after them. He started to tremble: he imagined how it would be all by himself, totally helpless in his semi-blindness, dying of starvation, of crashing into things, of terror.

'I see you've gotten yourself another escort besides the dwarf,' he heard the man say in a half-fawning, half-mocking tone of voice. 'Well, see you later. Praised be the Blessed Jesus.'

Jurema didn't answer and the nearsighted journalist stood there, his body tense, on the alert, expecting – he didn't know why – a kick, a slap, spit in his face.

'These aren't all,' said a voice different from the one that had been speaking, and after a second he realized that it was Abbot João. 'There are more in the storeroom where the hides are.'

'These are enough,' the first man said, his tone of voice neutral now.

'No, they're not,' Abbot João replied. 'They're not enough if eight or nine thousand men are coming. Even two or three times as many wouldn't be enough.'

'That's true,' the first voice said.

He heard them moving about in front of them and behind them, and guessed that they were fingering the rifles, hefting them, handling them, raising them to their eyes to see if the sights were properly lined up and the bores clean. Eight, nine thousand troops were coming?

'And besides, some of these can't even be used, Pajeú,' Abbot João said. 'See this one? The barrel's twisted, the trigger's broken, the breech is split.'

Pajeú? So the one who was there moving about, having a conversation with Abbot João, the one who had been talking to

Jurema, was Pajeú. The two men were saying something about the Virgin's jewels, speaking of someone named Dr. Águiar do Nascimento; their voices came and went along with their footsteps. All the bandits of the *sertão* were here; they'd all turned into fervent believers. How could that be explained? They walked past him and the nearsighted journalist could see two pairs of legs within reach of his hand.

'Do you want to hear the Terrible and Exemplary Story of Robert the Devil?' he heard the Dwarf ask. 'I know it, I've told it a thousand times. Shall I recite it to you, sir?'

'Not now,' Abbot João answered. 'But I'd be pleased to hear it some other day. Why do you call me sir, though? Don't you know my name?'

'Yes, I know it,' the Dwarf murmured. 'I beg your pardon . . .'

The sound of the men's footsteps died away. The nearsighted journalist had been set to thinking: 'The man who cut off ears and noses, the one who castrated his enemies and tattooed them with his initials. The one that murdered everyone in a village to prove he was Satan. And Pajeú, the butcher, the cattle rustler, the killer, the rogue.' They'd been right there next to him. He was dumfounded, and wanted badly to write.

'Did you see how he talked to you, how he looked at you?' he heard the Dwarf say. 'How lucky you are, Jurema. He'll take you to live with him and you'll have a house and food on the table. Because Pajeú is one of those in charge here.'

But what was going to happen to *him*?

'There aren't ten flies per inhabitant – there are a thousand,' Lieutenant Pires Ferreira thinks. 'They know nobody can kill them all. That's why they don't budge when the naive newcomer tries to shoo them away.' They were the only flies in the world that didn't move when a hand waved past within millimeters of them, trying to chase them away. Their multiple eyes looked at the miserable wretch, defying him. He could easily squash them, without the least bit of trouble. But what would be gained by such a disgusting act? Ten, twenty of them inevitably materialized in the place of the one crushed to death. It was better to resign oneself to their company, the way the *sertanejos* did. They allowed them to walk all over their clothing and dishes, leave their houses and food black with flyspecks, live on the bodies of their newborn babes, confining themselves to brushing them off the raw sugar lump they were about to bite into or spitting them out if they got into their mouths. They were bigger than the ones in Salvador, the only fat creatures in this country where men and beasts appeared to be reduced to their minimal expression.

He is lying naked on his bed at the Hotel Continental. Through the window he can see the station and the sign: Vila Bela de Santo Antônio das Queimadas. Which does he hate more: the flies or Queimadas, where he has the feeling that he is going to spend the rest of his days, bored to death, disillusioned, whiling away the hours philosophizing about flies? This is one of those moments in which bitterness makes him forget that he is a privileged man, for he has a little room all to himself here in the Hotel Continental which is the envy of thousands of officers and men who are squeezed in together, by twos, by fours, in houses requisitioned or rented by the army, and of those – the great majority – quartered in huts erected on the banks of the Itapicuru. He has the good fortune to occupy a room in the Hotel Continental by right of seniority. He has been here ever since the Seventh Regiment passed through Queimadas and Colonel Moreira César limited his responsibilities to the humiliating duty of taking care of the sick, in the rear guard. From this window he has witnessed the events that have convulsed the backlands, Bahia, Brazil in the last three months: Moreira César's departure in the direction of Monte Santo and the sudden return of the survivors from the disaster, still wide-eyed with panic or stupefaction; since then he has seen the train from Salvador spew out, week after week, professional soldiers, brigades of police, and regiments of volunteers come from every part of the country to this town held in thrall by flies, to avenge the dead patriots, vindicate the honor of humiliated institutions, and restore the sovereignty of the Republic. And, from this same Hotel Continental, Lieutenant Pires Ferreira has seen how those dozens and dozens of companies, so high-spirited, so eager for action, have been caught in a spiderweb that is keeping them inactive, immobilized, distracted by nagging problems that have nothing to do with the generous ideals that have brought them here: incidents, thefts, the lack of lodging, food, transport, enemies, women. The evening before, Lieutenant Pires Ferreira attended a staff meeting of officers of the Third Infantry Battalion, called because of a major scandal – the disappearance of a hundred Comblain rifles and twenty-five cases of ammunition – and Colonel Joaquim Manuel de Medeiros, after reading an order warning that unless they were returned immediately those found responsible for this robbery would be summarily executed, has told them that the great problem – transporting to Canudos the tremendous amount of matériel accompanying the expeditionary force – has still not been resolved and that therefore no definite date has been set for departure.

There is a knock at the door and Lieutenant Pires Ferreira says: 'Come in.' It is his orderly, come to remind him that Private Queluz is awaiting punishment. As he dresses, yawning, he tries to remember the face of this infantryman whom he has already flogged once, he is sure, a week or a month or so before, perhaps for the same offense. Which one? He knows them all: petty thefts from the regiment or the families that have not yet cleared out of Queimadas, fights with soldiers from other corps, attempted desertion. The captain of the company often orders him to administer the floggings with which he tries to preserve discipline, which is deteriorating by the day because of the boredom and the privations his men are suffering. Giving a man a lashing is not something that Lieutenant Pires Ferreira ordinarily likes doing. But now it is something that he does not dislike doing, either. It has become part of the daily routine here in Queimadas, along with sleeping, dressing and undressing, eating, teaching the men the nomenclature of a Mannlicher or a Comblain, explaining what a defensive or offensive square is, or philosophizing about flies.

On leaving the Hotel Continental, Lieutenant Pires Ferreira takes the Avenida de Itapicuru, the name of the stony incline that leads up to the Church of Santo Antônio, his eyes surveying, above the rooftops of the little houses painted green, white, or blue, the hillsides covered with bone-dry brush surrounding Queimadas, and pitying the poor infantry companies being drilled on those burning-hot slopes. He has taken recruits out there a hundred times to practice digging in, and has seen them run with sweat and sometimes faint dead away. Most often it is the volunteers from cold country who topple over like tenpins after just a few hours of marching through this desert terrain with their knapsacks on their backs and their rifles slung over their shoulders.

At this time of day the streets of Queimadas are not the teeming anthill of uniforms, the sample collection of all the accents of Brazil that they turn into at night, when officers and men pour out into them to chat together, to strum guitars, to listen to songs from their villages, to enjoy a few sips of cane brandy that they have managed to come by at exorbitant prices. Here and there he comes across knots of soldiers with their blouses unbuttoned, but he does not spy a single townsman as he makes his way to the main square, with towering *ouricuri* palms that are always swarming with birds. There are hardly any townspeople around. Except for a handful of cowhands here and there, too elderly, ailing, or apathetic to have left, who stand looking out with undisguised hatred from the doorways of the houses they are forced to share with the intruders, everyone else in Queimadas has gradually taken off.

At the corner on which there stands the boarding house of Our Lady of Grace – on the façade of which is a sign that reads: 'Entry forbidden unless shirts are worn' – Lieutenant Pires Ferreira recognizes, his face a blur in the blinding sunlight, Lieutenant Pinto Souza, an officer attached to his battalion, coming his way. He has been here only a week, and still has the high spirits of those recently arrived in town. They have made friends with each other and fallen into the habit of whiling away their evenings together.

'I've read the report you wrote about Uauá,' Pinto Souza says, falling in step with him as he heads for the camp. 'What a terrifying experience.'

Lieutenant Pires Ferreira looks at him, shielding his eyes from the sun's glare with one hand. 'For those of us who survived it, yes, no doubt. For poor Dr. Antônio Alves dos Santos especially,' he says. 'But what happened in Uauá is nothing by comparison with what happened to Major Febrônio and Colonel Moreira César.'

'I don't mean the dead, but what you report about the uniforms and the arms,' Lieutenant Pinto Souza explains.

'Oh, I see,' Lieutenant Pires Ferreira murmurs.

'I don't understand it,' his friend exclaims in consternation. 'The officers of the General Staff haven't done anything.'

'The same thing happened to the second and third expeditionary forces as happened to us,' Pires Ferreira says. 'They, too, were defeated not so much by the *jagunços* as by the heat, the thorns, and the dust.'

He shrugs. He wrote that report just after his arrival in Juazeiro following the defeat, with tears in his eyes, hoping that the account of his experiences would prove useful to his comrades-at-arms. He explained, with a wealth of detail, how the uniforms had been reduced to tatters by the sun, the rain, and the dust, how flannel jackets and woolen trousers had turned into poultices and been torn to ribbons by the branches of the *caatinga.* He told how the soldiers lost their forage caps and boots and had to go barefoot most of the time. But above all he was explicit, scrupulous, insistent with regard to the subject of weapons: 'Despite its magnificent precision, the Mannlicher very frequently misfires; a few grains of sand in the magazine are enough to prevent the bolt from functioning. Moreover, if many shots are fired in rapid succession, the heat expands the barrel and the magazine then shrinks in size and the six-cartridge chargers cannot be introduced into it. The extractor jams from the effect of the heat and spent cartridges must be removed by hand. And finally, the breech is so delicate that it breaks apart at the first blow.' He not only has written this; he has reported it all to the investigating commissions that have questioned him and has repeated it in dozens of private conversations. And what good has all that done?

'In the beginning I thought that they didn't believe me,' he says. 'That they were convinced I'd written that to excuse my defeat. I know now, though, why the officers of the General Staff aren't doing anything.'

'Why is that?' Lieutenant Pinto Souza asks.

'Are they going to change the uniforms of every last corps of the Brazilian Army? Aren't all of them made of flannel and wool? Are they going to throw all the boots on the dump heap? Toss all the Mannlichers we have in the sea? We have to go on using them, whether they're any good or not.'

They have arrived at the camp of the Third Infantry Battalion, on the right bank of the Itapicuru. It is close by the town, whereas the other camps are farther away from Queimadas, upriver. The huts are lined up facing the hillsides of reddish earth, strewn with great dark rocks, at the bottom of which the blackish-green waters of the river flow. The soldiers of the company are waiting for him; floggings are always well attended since they are one of the battalion's very few diversions. Private Queluz is all ready for his punishment, standing with his back bared in the middle of a circle of soldiers who are teasing him. He wisecracks back, laughing. As the two officers walk up to them, their faces grow serious, and in the eyes of the man about to be disciplined Pires Ferreira sees a sudden fear, which he tries his best to hide beneath his insolent, mocking manner.

'Thirty blows,' he reads in the daily report. 'That's a lot. Who put you on report?'

'Colonel Joaquim Manuel de Medeiros, sir,' Queluz mutters.

'What did you do?' Pires Ferreira asks. He is putting on the leather glove so that the friction of the cane will not raise blisters on his palm as he whips the man. Queluz blinks in embarrassment, looking right and left out of the corner of his eye. There are snickers, murmurs from the hundred soldiers standing in a circle watching.

'Nothing, sir,' he answers, swallowing hard.

Pires Ferreira eyes the bystanders questioningly.

'He tried to rape a bugler from the Fifth Regiment,' Lieutenant Pinto Souza says disgustedly. 'A kid who's not yet fifteen. It was the colonel himself who caught him. You're a pervert, Queluz.'

'That's not true, sir, that's not true,' the soldier says, shaking his head. 'The colonel misunderstood my intentions. We were just innocently bathing in the river. I swear to you.'

'And was that why the bugler started yelling for help?' Pinto Souza says. 'Don't be impudent.'

'The fact is, the bugler also misunderstood my intentions, sir,' the soldier says, looking very earnest. But as these words are greeted by a general guffaw, he, too, finally bursts out laughing.

'The sooner we begin, the sooner we'll be finished,' Pires Ferreira says, seizing the first cane from among a number of them that his orderly is holding within reach of his hand. He tries it in the air, and as the flexible rod comes whistling down, the circle of soldiers steps back. 'Shall we tie you up or will you take your punishment like a man?'

'Like a man, sir,' Private Queluz says, turning pale.

'Like a man who buggers buglers,' someone adds, and there is another burst of laughter.

'Turn around, then, and grab your balls,' Lieutenant Pires Ferreira orders.

The first blows he gives him are hard ones, and he sees him stagger as the rod turns his back red; then, as the effort leaves him too drenched with sweat, he lets up a little. The group of soldiers sings out the number of strokes. Before they have reached twenty the purple welts on Queluz's back begin to bleed. With the last one, the soldier falls to his knees, but he rises to his feet immediately and turns toward the lieutenant, reeling. 'Thank you very much, sir,' he murmurs, his face dripping with sweat and his eyes bloodshot.

'You can console yourself with the thought that I'm as worn out as you are,' Pires Ferreira pants. 'Go to the infirmary and have them put a disinfectant on you. And leave buglers alone.'

The group disperses. A few of the men walk off with Queluz, and one of them throws a towel over him, while others climb down the steep clay bank to cool off in the Itapicuru. Pires Ferreira rinses his face off in a bucket of water that his orderly brings over to him. He signs the report indicating that he has administered the punishment. Meanwhile, he answers Lieutenant Pinto Souza's questions; the latter is still obsessed by his report on Uauá. Were those rifles old ones or ones recently purchased?

'They weren't new ones,' Pires Ferreira says. 'They'd been used in 1884, in the São Paulo and Paraná campaign. But it's not because they're old that they're defective. The problem is the way the Mannlicher is built. It was designed and developed in Europe, for a very different climate and combat conditions, for an army with a capability for maintaining them that ours doesn't have.'

He is interrupted by the sound of many bugles blowing, in all the camps at once.

'Officers' assembly,' Pinto Souza says. 'That's not on the order of the day.'

'It must be the theft of those hundred Comblain rifles. It's driving the senior officers mad,' Pires Ferreira says. 'Maybe they've discovered who the thieves are and are going to shoot them.'

'Or maybe the Minister of War has arrived,' Pinto Souza says. 'His visit's been announced.'

They head for the assembly area of the Third Battalion, but on arriving there they are informed that they will also be meeting with the officers of the Seventh and Fourteenth; in other words, the whole First Brigade. They run to the command post, set up in a tannery on the Itapicuru, a quarter of a league upstream. On their way there, they notice an unusual hustle and bustle in all the camps, and the bugles have set up such a din now that it is difficult to decipher what the calls are. In the tannery they find several dozen officers already assembled. Some of them must have been surprised in the middle of their afternoon siesta, for they are still putting on their blouses or buttoning their tunics. The commanding officer of the First Brigade, Colonel Joaquim Manuel de Medeiros, standing on top of a bench, is speaking, with many gestures, but Pires Ferreira and Pinto Souza are unable to hear what he is saying, for all around them are cheers, shouts of 'Long live Brazil' and 'Hurray for the Republic,' and some of the officers are tossing their kepis in the air to show their joy.

'What's happening? What's happening?' Lieutenant Pinto Souza asks.

'We're leaving for Canudos within two hours!' an artillery captain shouts back at him euphorically.

II

'Madness? Misunderstandings? That's not enough. It doesn't explain everything,' the Baron de Canabrava murmured. 'There has also been stupidity and cruelty.'

He had a sudden image of the kindly face of Gentil de Castro, with his pink cheeks and his blond sideburns, bending over to kiss Estela's hand on some festive occasion at the Palace, when he was a member of the Emperor's cabinet. He was as dainty as a lady, as naïve as a child, good-hearted, obliging. What else besides imbecility and wickedness could explain what had happened to Gentil de Castro?

'I suppose they're what lies behind not only Canudos but all of history,' he said aloud, grimacing in displeasure.

'Unless one believes in God,' the nearsighted journalist interrupted him, his harsh voice reminding the baron of his existence. 'As they did up there. Everything was crystal-clear. Famine, the bombardments, the men with their bellies ripped open, those who died of starvation. The Dog or the Father, the Antichrist or the Blessed Jesus. They knew immediately which of the two was responsible for any given event, whether it was a blessing or a curse. Don't you envy them? Everything becomes easy if one is capable of identifying the good or the evil behind each and every thing that happens.'

'I suddenly remembered Gentil de Castro just now,' the Baron de Canabrava murmured. 'The stupefaction he must have felt on learning why his newspaper offices were being burned down, why they were destroying his house.'

The nearsighted journalist thrust his head forward. The two of them were sitting face to face in the leather armchairs, separated by a little table with a pitcher full of papaya-and-banana punch on it. The morning was going by quickly; the light that beat down on the garden was already a noon light. Cries of peddlers hawking food, parrots, prayers, services came over the tops of the walls.

'This part of the story can be explained,' the man with loose-hinged limbs said in his piercing voice. 'What happened in Rio de Janeiro, in São Paulo, is logical and rational.'

'Logical and rational that the mob should pour out into the streets to destroy newspaper offices, to attack private houses, to murder people unable to point out on a map where Canudos is located, because a handful of fanatics thousands of kilometers away defeated an expeditionary force? That's logical and rational?'

'They were roused to a frenzy by propaganda,' the nearsighted journalist insisted. 'You haven't read the papers, Baron.'

'I learned what happened in Rio from one of the victims,' the latter replied. 'He came within a hair's breadth of being killed himself.'

The baron had met the Viscount de Ouro Preto in London. He had spent an entire afternoon with the former monarchist leader, who had taken refuge in Portugal after hurriedly fleeing from Brazil following the terrifying uprisings that had taken place in Rio de Janeiro when the news of the rout of the Seventh Regiment and the death of Moreira César had reached the city. Incredulous, dumfounded, frightened out of his wits, the elderly ex-dignitary had witnessed, from the balconies of the town house of the Baroness de Guanabara, where he had chanced to pay a call, a crowd of demonstrators parade down the Rua Marquês from the Military Club, carrying posters calling for his head as the person responsible for the defeat of the Republic at Canudos. Shortly thereafter, a messenger had come to inform him that his house had been sacked, along with those of other well-known monarchists, and that the offices of *A Gazeta de Notícias* and *A Liberdade* were burning down.

'The English spy at Ipupiará. The rifles being sent to Canudos that were discovered in the backlands. The Kropatchek projectiles used by the *jagunços* that could only have been brought by British ships. And the explosive bullets. The lies that have been harped on night and day have turned into truths.'

'You are overestimating the audience of the *Jornal de Notícias*.' The Baron de Canabrava smiled.

'The Epaminondas Gonçalves of Rio de Janeiro is named Alcindo Guanabara and his daily *A República*,' the nearsighted journalist stated. 'Since Major Febrônio's defeat, *A República* hasn't let a single day go by without presenting conclusive evidence of the complicity between the Monarchist Party and Canudos.'

The baron barely heard him, for he was hearing in his mind what the Viscount de Ouro Preto, wrapped in a blanket that barely left his mouth free, had told him: 'What's pathetic is that we never took Gentil de Castro seriously. He was a nobody in the days of the Empire. He never was awarded a title, an honor, an official post. His monarchism was purely sentimental; it had nothing to do with reality.'

'The conclusive evidence, for example, with regard to the cattle and arms in Sete Lagoas, in the state of Minas Gerais,' the nearsighted journalist went on to say. 'Weren't they being sent to Canudos? Weren't they being convoyed there by Manuel João Brandão, the known leader of thugs in the hire of monarchist *caudilhos*? Hadn't Brandão been in the service of Joaquim Nabuco, of the Viscount de Ouro Preto? Alcindo gives the names of the police who arrested Brandão, prints word for word his statements confessing everything. What does it matter if Brandão never existed and such a consignment of arms was never discovered? It appeared in print, so it was true. The story of the spy of Ipupiará all over again, blown up to even greater proportions. Do you see how logical, how rational all that is? You weren't lynched, Baron, because there aren't any Jacobins in

Salvador. The only thing that excites Bahians is carnival time. They couldn't care less about politics.'

'Well, I see you're ready to work for the *Diário da Bahia,*' the baron said jokingly. 'You already know all about our adversaries' vile deeds.'

'You aren't any better than they are,' the nearsighted journalist muttered. 'Have you forgotten that Epaminondas is your ally and that your former friends are members of the government?'

'You're discovering a little too late that politics is a dirty business,' the baron said.

'Not for the Counselor,' the nearsighted journalist answered. 'It was a clean and clear-cut one for him.'

'It was for poor Gentil de Castro, too.' The baron sighed.

On returning to Europe, he had found on his desk a letter sent from Rio several months before, in which Gentil de Castro himself had asked him, in his careful handwriting: 'What is this Canudos affair all about, my dear Baron? What is happening there in your beloved lands in the Northeast? They are laying all sorts of conspiratorial nonsense at our doorstep, and we are not able even to defend ourselves because we haven't the least idea what is going on. Who is Antônio Conselheiro? Does he even exist? Who are these Sebastianist despoilers with whom the Jacobins insist on linking us? I would be much obliged to you if you would enlighten me in this regard . . .' And now the elderly man whom the name of Gentil fit so well was dead because he had organized and financed a rebellion aimed at restoring the Empire and making Brazil the slave of England. Years before, when he had first begun receiving copies of *A Gazeta de Notícias* and *A Liberdade,* the Baron de Canabrava wrote to the Viscount de Ouro Preto, asking him what sort of absurd business all this was, putting out two papers nostalgically yearning for a return to the good old days of the monarchy, at a time when it was obvious to everyone that the Empire was forever dead and buried. 'What can I tell you, my dear friend? . . . It wasn't my idea, or João Alfredo's, or any of your friends' here; on the contrary, it was Colonel Gentil de Castro's idea, and his alone. He's decided to throw away his money by bringing out these publications in order to defend the names of those of us who served the Empire from the contumely to which we are subjected. We are all of the opinion that it is quite untimely to seek to restore the monarchy at this juncture, but how to put a damper on poor Gentil de Castro's passionate enthusiasm? I don't know if you remember him. A good man, but never an outstanding figure . . .'

'He wasn't in Rio but in Petrópolis when the news arrived in the capital,' the viscount said. 'I sent word to him through my son, Afonso Celso, that he shouldn't even think of returning to Rio, that his newspaper offices had been burned to the ground and his house destroyed, and a mob in the Rua do Ouvidor and the Largo de São Francisco was demanding his death. That was enough to make Gentil de Castro decide to return.'

The baron pictured him, pink-cheeked, packing his valise and heading for the railway station, as meanwhile in Rio, in the Military Club, twenty officers or so mingled their blood before a square and compass and swore to avenge Moreira César, drawing up a list of traitors to be executed. The name heading it: Gentil de Castro.

'In Meriti Station, Afonso Celso bought him the daily papers,' the Viscount de Ouro Preto went on. 'Gentil de Castro was able to read about everything that had happened the day before in the federal capital. The demonstrations, the closing of stores and theaters, the flags at half staff and the black crepe on the balconies, the attacks on newspaper offices, the assaults. And, naturally, the sensational news in *A República*: "The rifles found at *A Gazeta de Notícias* and *A Liberdade* are of the same manufacture and the same caliber as those in Canudos." And what do you think his reaction was?

'"I have no choice save to send my seconds to Alcindo Guanabara," Colonel Gentil de Castro muttered, smoothing his white mustache. "His infamy has taken him beyond the pale."'

The baron burst out laughing. 'He wanted to fight a duel,' he thought. 'The one thing that occurred to him was to challenge Epaminondas Gonçalves to a duel from Rio. As the mob was searching for him to lynch him, he was thinking of seconds dressed in black, of swords, of duels to end only with the drawing of first blood or death.' He laughed till tears came to his eyes, and the nearsighted journalist stared at him in surprise. As all that was happening, the baron had been journeying to Salvador, admittedly stunned by Moreira César's defeat, though at the same time able to think only of Estela, to count how many hours it would be before the doctors of the Portuguese Hospital and the Faculty of Medicine could put his mind at ease by assuring him that it was a crisis that would pass, that the baroness would once again be a happy, lucid woman, full of life. He had been so dazed by what was happening to his wife that his memories of the events of recent months seemed like a dream: his negotiations with Epaminondas Gonçalves and his feelings on learning of the vast national mobilization to punish the *jagunços*, the sending of battalions from all the states, the forming of corps of volunteers, the fairs and the public raffles at which ladies auctioned off their jewels and locks of their hair to raise money to outfit new companies about to march off to defend the Republic. He felt once again the vertigo that had overtaken him on realizing the enormity of all that had happened, the labyrinth of mistakes, mad whims, barbarities.

'On arriving in Rio, Gentil de Castro and Afonso Celso slipped to the house of friends, near the São Francisco Xavier Station,' the Viscount de Ouro Preto added. 'My friends took me there out of sight and out of the hand of the mobs that were still in the streets. It took some time for all of us to persuade Gentil de Castro that the only thing left for us to do was flee Rio and Brazil at the earliest possible moment.'

It was agreed that the group of friends would take the viscount and the colonel to the station, their faces hidden by their capes, arriving seconds before six-thirty in the evening, the hour of the departure of the train to Petrópolis. Once they had arrived there, they were to remain on a hacienda while arrangements were being made for their flight abroad.

'But fate was on the side of the assassins,' the viscount murmured. 'The train was half an hour late. That was more than enough time for the group of us, standing with our faces hidden in our capes, to attract attention. Demonstrators running up and down the platform shouting "Long life to Marshal Floriano and death to the Viscount de Ouro Preto" started toward us. We had just climbed onto the train when a mob armed with revolvers and daggers surrounded us. A number of shots rang out just as the train pulled out. All the bullets hit Gentil de Castro. I don't know why or how I escaped with my life.'

The baron pictured in his mind the elderly man with pink cheeks, his head and chest riddled with bullets, trying to cross himself. Perhaps meeting his death in that way would not have displeased him. It was a death befitting a gentleman, was it not?

'That may well be,' the Viscount de Ouro Preto said. 'But I am certain that his burial didn't please him.'

He had been buried secretly, on the advice of the authorities. Minister Amaro Cavalcanti warned the family that, in view of the agitation in the streets, the government could not guarantee their security if they tried to hold an elaborate graveside ceremony. No monarchist attended the burial rites and Gentil de Castro was taken to the cemetery in an ordinary carriage, followed by a coach bearing his gardener and two nephews. The latter did not allow the priest to finish the prayers for the dead, fearing that the Jacobins might appear at any moment.

'I see that the death of that man, there in Rio, moved you deeply.' The nearsighted journalist's voice had once again roused him from his thoughts. 'Yet you're not moved at all by the other deaths. Because there were others, there in Canudos.'

At what moment had his caller risen to his feet? He was now standing in front of the bookshelves, bent over, contorted, a human puzzle, looking at him – in fury? – from behind the thick lenses of his glasses.

'It's easier to imagine the death of one person than those of a hundred or a thousand,' the baron murmured. 'When multiplied, suffering becomes abstract. It is not easy to be moved by abstract things.'

'Unless one has seen first one, then ten, a hundred, a thousand, thousands suffer,' the nearsighted journalist answered. 'If the death of Gentil de Castro was absurd, many of those in Canudos died for reasons no less absurd.'

'How many?' the baron said in a low voice. He knew that the number would never be known, that, as with all the rest of history, the figure would be one that historians and politicians would increase and decrease in accordance with their doctrines and the advantage they could extract from it. But he could not help wondering nonetheless.

'I've tried to find out,' the journalist said, walking toward him with his usual unsteady gait and collapsing in the armchair. 'No precise figure has been arrived at.'

'Three thousand? Five thousand dead?' the baron murmured, his eyes seeking his.

'Between twenty-five and thirty thousand.'

'Are you including the wounded, the sick, in that figure?' the baron muttered testily.

'I'm not talking about the army dead,' the journalist said. 'There exists an exact accounting of them. Eight hundred twenty-three, including the victims of epidemics and accidents.'

A silence fell. The baron lowered his eyes. He poured himself a little fruit punch, but scarcely touched it because it had lost its chill and reminded him of lukewarm broth.

'There couldn't have been thirty thousand souls living in Canudos,' he said. 'No settlement in the *sertão* can house that many people.'

'It's a relatively simple calculation,' the journalist answered. 'General Oscar had a count made of the dwellings. You didn't know that? The number has been published in the papers: five thousand seven hundred eighty-three. How many people lived in each one? Five or six at the very least. In other words, between twenty-five and thirty thousand dead.'

There was another silence, a long one, broken by the buzzing of bluebottle flies.

'There were no wounded in Canudos,' the journalist said. 'The so-called survivors, those women and children that the Patriotic Committee organized by your friend Lélis Piedades parceled out all over Brazil, had not been in Canudos but in localities in the vicinity. Only seven people escaped from the siege.'

'Are you certain of that, too?' the baron said, raising his eyes.

'I was one of the seven,' the nearsighted journalist said. And as though to avoid a question, he quickly added: 'It was a different statistic that was of greatest concern to the *jagunços*. How many of them would be killed by bullets and how many finished off by the knife.'

He remained silent for some time; he tossed his head to chase away an insect. 'It's a figure that it's impossible to arrive at, naturally,' he continued, wringing his hands. 'But there is someone who could give us a clue. An interesting individual, Baron. He was in Moreira César's regiment and returned with the fourth expeditionary force as commanding officer of a company from Rio Grande do Sul. Second Lieutenant Maranhão.'

The baron looked at the journalist. He could almost guess what he was about to say.

'Did you know that slitting throats is a gaucho specialty? Second Lieutenant Maranhão and his men were specialists. It was something the lieutenant was both skilled at and greatly enjoyed doing. He would grab the *jagunço* by the nose with his left hand, lift his head up, and draw his knife across his throat. A fifteen-inch slash that cut through the carotid: the head fell off like a rag doll's.'

'Are you trying to move me to pity?' the baron asked.

'If Second Lieutenant Maranhão told us how many *jagunços* he and his men slit the throats of, we'd be able to know how many *jagunços* went to heaven and how many to hell,' the journalist said with a sneeze. 'That was another drawback of having one's throat slit. The dead man's soul apparently went straight to hell.'

The night he leaves Canudos, at the head of three hundred armed men – many more than he has ever been in command of before – Pajeú orders himself not to think about the woman. He knows how important his mission is, as do his comrades, chosen from among the best walkers in Canudos (because they are going to have to go a long way on foot). As they pass the foot of A Favela they halt for a time. Pointing to the spurs of the mountainside, barely visible in the darkness alive with crickets and frogs, Pajeú reminds them that it is up there that the soldiers are to be drawn, driven, surrounded, so that Abbot João and Big João and all those who have not headed off to Jeremoabo with Pedrão and the Vilanovas to meet the troops coming from that direction can shoot at them from the neighboring hills and plateaus, where the *jagunços* have already taken up their positions in trenches full of ammunition. Abbot João is right; that is the way to deal that accursed brood a mortal blow: push them toward this bare slope. 'Either the soldiers fall in the trap and we tear them to pieces, or we fall,' the Street Commander has said. 'Because if they surround Belo Monte we won't have either the men or the arms to keep them from entering. It depends on you, boys.' Pajeú advises the men to hoard the ammunition, to aim always at those dogs who have stripes on their sleeves, or have sabers and are mounted on horseback, and to keep out of sight. He divides them up into four groups and arranges for everyone to meet the following day at dusk, at Lagoa da Laje, not far from Serra de Aracati, where, he calculates, the avant-garde that left Monte Santo yesterday will be arriving about then. None of the groups must fight if they run into enemy patrols; they must hide, let them go on, and at most have a tracker follow them. No one, nothing must make them forget their one responsibility: drawing the dogs to A Favela.

The group of eighty men that remains with him is the last to set out again. Headed for war again. He has gone off in the night like this so many times since he reached the age of reason, hiding out so as to pounce or keep from being pounced on, that he is no more apprehensive this time than he was the others. To Pajeú that is what life is: fleeing an enemy or going out to meet one, knowing that before and behind, in space and in time, there are, and always will be, bullets, wounded, and dead.

The woman's face steals once again – stubbornly, intrusively – into his mind. The *caboclo* tries his best to banish the image of her pale cheeks, her resigned eyes, her lank hair dangling down to her shoulders, and anxiously searches for something different to think about. At his side is Taramela, a short, energetic little man, chewing on something, happy to be marching along with him, as in the days of the *cangaço.* He suddenly asks him if he has with him that egg-yolk poultice that is the best remedy against snake bite. Taramela reminds him that when they were separated from the other groups he himself handed round a bit of it to Joaquim Macambira, Mané Quadrado, and Felício. 'That's right, I did,' Pajeú says. And as Taramela looks at him, saying nothing, Pajeú wonders aloud whether the other groups will have enough *tigelinhas*, those little clay lamps that will allow them to signal to each other at a distance at night if need be. Taramela laughs and reminds him that he himself has supervised the distribution of *tigelinhas* at the Vilanovas' store. Pajeú growls that his forgetfulness is a sign that he's getting old. 'Or that you're falling in love,' Taramela teases. Pajeú feels his cheeks burn, and the memory of the woman's face, which he has managed to drive out of his mind, comes back again. Feeling oddly abashed, he thinks: 'I don't know her name, or where she's from.' When he gets back to Belo Monte, he'll ask her.

The eighty *jagunços* walk behind him and Taramela in silence, or talking so quietly that the sound of their voices is drowned out by the crunching of little stones and the rhythmic shuffle of sandals and espadrilles. Among these eighty are some who were with him in his *cangaço,* along with others who were marauders in Abbot João's band or Pedrão's, old pals who once served in the police flying brigades, and even onetime rural guards and infantrymen who deserted. That men who were once irreconcilable enemies are now marching together is the work of the Father, up there in heaven, and of the Counselor, here below. They've worked the miracle of reconciling Cains, turning the hatred that reigned in the backlands into brotherhood.

Pajeú steps up the pace and keeps it brisk all night long. When, at dawn, they reach the Serra de Caxamango and halt to eat, with a palisade of *xiquexiques* and *mandacarus* for cover, all of them are stiff and sore.

Taramela awakens Pajeú some four hours later. Two trackers have arrived, both of them very young. Their voices choke as they speak and one of them massages his swollen feet as they explain to Pajeú that they have followed the troops all the way from Monte Santo. It's true: there are thousands of soldiers. Divided into nine corps, they are advancing very slowly because of the difficulty they are having dragging along their arms, their carts, their portable field huts, and because of the enormous hindrance represented by a very long cannon they are bringing, which keeps getting stuck in the sand and obliges them to widen the trail as they go along. It is being drawn by no less than forty oxen. They are making, at most, five leagues a day. Pajeú interrupts them: what interests him is not how many of them there are but where they are. The youngster rubbing his feet reports that they made a halt at Rio Pequeno and bivouacked at Caldeirão Grande. Then they headed for Gitirana, where they halted, and finally, after many hitches, they arrived at Juá, where they encamped for the night.

The route the dogs have taken surprises Pajeú. It is not that of any of the previous expeditions. Do they intend to come via Rosário, instead of via Bendengó, O Cambaio, or the Serra de Canabrava? If that is their plan, everything will be easier, for with a few skirmishes and ruses on the part of the *jagunços*, this route will take them to A Favela.

He sends a tracker to Belo Monte, to repeat what he has just been told to Abbot João, and they begin marching again. They go on without stopping till dusk, through stretches of scrub that are a tangle of *mangabeiras, cipós,* and thickets of *macambiras.* The groups led by Mané Quadrado, Macambira, and Felício are already at Lagoa da Laje. Mané Quadrado's has run into a mounted patrol that was scouting the trail from Aracati to Jueté. Squatting down behind a hedge of cacti, they saw them go by, and then come back that way a couple of hours later. There is no question, then: if they are sending patrols out toward Jueté it means that they've chosen to take the Rosário road. Old Macambira scratches his head: why choose the longest way round? Why take this indirect route that will mean a march fourteen or fifteen leagues longer?

'Because it's flatter,' Taramela says. 'There are almost no uphill or downhill stretches if they go that way. It'll be easier for them to get their cannons and wagons through.'

They agree that that is the most likely reason. As the others rest, Pajeú, Taramela, Mané Quadrado, Macambira, and Felício exchange opinions. As it is almost certain that the troop will be coming via Rosário, they decide that Mané Quadrado and Joaquim Macambira will go post themselves there. Pajeú and Felício will track them from Serra de Aracati on.

At dawn, Macambira and Mané Quadrado take off with half the men. Pajeú asks Felício to go ahead of him with his seventy *jagunços* to Aracati, posting them along the half-league stretch of road so as to scout the movements of the battalions in detail. He will remain where they are now.

Lagoa da Laje is not a lagoon – though it may have been one in the very distant past – but a damp ravine where maize, cassava, and beans used to grow, as Pajeú remembers very well from having spent many a night in one or other of the little farmhouses now burned to the ground. There is only one with the façade still intact and a complete roof. One of his *jagunços*, a man with Indian features, points to it and says that the roof tiles could be used for the Temple of the Blessed Jesus. No roof tiles are being turned out in Belo Monte these days because all the kilns are being used to make bullets. Pajeú nods and orders the tiles taken down. He stations his men all round the house. He is giving instructions to the tracker that he is about to send to Canudos when he hears hoofbeats and a whinny. He drops to the ground and slips away among the rocks. Once under cover, he sees that the men have had time to take cover, too, before the patrol appeared – all of them except the ones removing the tiles from the roof of the little house. He sees a dozen troopers pursuing three *jagunços* who are running off in a zigzag line in different directions. They disappear amid the rocks, apparently without being wounded. But the fourth one does not have time to leap down from the roof. Pajeú tries to see who it is: no, he can't, he is too far away. After looking down for a few moments at the cavalrymen aiming their rifles at him, the man raises his hands to his head as though he were surrendering. But all of a sudden he leaps down on top of one of the cavalrymen. Was he trying to get possession of the horse and gallop off to safety? If so, his trick doesn't come off, for the cavalryman drags him to the ground with him. The *jagunço* hits out right and left till the squad leader fires at him point-blank. It is obvious that he is annoyed at having had to kill him, that he would rather have taken a prisoner to bring in to his superiors. The patrol rides off, followed by the eyes of those hiding in the brush. Pajeú tells himself, in satisfaction, that the men have resisted the temptation to kill that bunch of dogs.

He leaves Taramela in Lagoa da Laje to bury the dead man, and goes to take up a position on the heights halfway to Aracati. He does not allow his men to advance in groups now; he orders them to stay a fair distance apart and well off to the side of the road. Shortly after reaching the crags – a good lookout point – he spies the avant-garde approaching. Pajeú can feel the scar on his face: a drawing sensation, as though the old wound were about to open again. This happens to him at crucial moments, when he is having some extraordinary experience. Soldiers armed with picks, shovels, machetes, and handsaws are clearing the trail, leveling it, felling trees, removing rocks. They must have had hard work of it in the Serra de Aracati, a steep, rugged climb; they are moving along with their torsos bared and their blouses tied around their waists, three abreast, with officers on horseback at the head of the column. There are lots and lots of dogs coming, that's certain, if more than two hundred have been sent ahead to clear the way for them. Pajeú also spies one of Felício's trackers following close behind these engineer corpsmen.

It is early in the afternoon when the first of the nine army corps comes by. When the last one passes, the sky is full of stars scattered about a round moon that bathes the *sertão* in a soft yellow glow. They have been passing by, grouped together at times, at times separated by kilometers, dressed in uniforms that vary in color and type – gray-green, blue with red stripes, gray, with gilt buttons, with leather bandoleers, with kepis, with cowboy hats, with boots, with shoes, with rope sandals – on foot and on horseback. In the middle of each corps, cannon drawn by oxen. Pajeú – he has not ceased for a moment to be aware of the scar on his face – tots up the train of ammunition and supplies: seven wagons drawn by bullocks, forty-three donkey carts, some two hundred bearers (many of them *jagunços*) bent double beneath their burdens. He knows that these wooden cases are full of rifle bullets, and his head whirls trying to calculate how many bullets per inhabitant of Belo Monte they add up to.

His men do not move: it is as though they'd even stopped breathing, blinking, and not one of them opens his mouth. Dead silent, motionless, become one with the rocks, the cacti, the bushes that hide them, they listen to the bugles passing on orders from battalion to battalion, see the banners of the escorts fluttering, hear the servers of the artillery pieces shouting to urge the bullocks, the mules, the burros on. Each corps advances in three separate sections, the one in the center waiting for each of the two on the flanks to move forward and only then advancing in turn. Why are they going through this maneuver that holds them up and appears to be as much a retreat as an advance? Pajeú realizes that it is to keep from being surprised from the flank, as happened to the Throat-Slitter's animals and men, which the *jagunços* were able to attack from the edge of the trail. As he listens to the deafening din, contemplating the multicolored spectacle slowly unfolding at his feet, he keeps asking himself the same questions: 'What route are they planning to take to Canudos? And what if they fan out so as to enter Belo Monte from ten different places at once?'

After the rear guard has passed by, he eats a handful of flour and raw brown sugar and he and his men head for Jueté, two leagues away, to wait for the soldiers. On their way there, a trek that takes them about two hours, Pajeú hears his men grimly commenting on the size of the great long cannon, which they have baptized A Matadeira – the Killer. He shuts them up. They are right, though, it is enormous, doubtless capable of blowing several houses to smithereens with one shell, and perhaps of piercing the wall of the Temple under construction. He will have to warn Abbot João about A Matadeira.

As he has calculated, the soldiers bivouac in Lagoa da Laje. Pajeú and his men pass so close to the field huts that they hear the sentinels talking over the day's happenings. They meet up with Taramela before midnight, in Jueté. They find there a messenger sent by Mané Quadrado and Macambira; the two of them are already in Rosário. On the way there, they have seen cavalry patrols. As the men get water to drink and rinse their faces by the light of the moon in the little lagoon of Jueté to which the shepherds in the region used to bring their flocks in the old days, Pajeú dispatches a tracker to Abbot João and stretches out on the ground to sleep, between Taramela and an old *jagunço* who is still talking about A Matadeira. It would be a good idea if the dogs were to capture a *jagunço* who would tell them that all the ways into Belo Monte are well defended, except for the slopes of A Favela. Pajeú turns the thought over in his mind till he falls asleep. The woman visits him in his dreams.

As it is beginning to get light, Felício's group arrives. He has been surprised by one of the patrols of soldiers protecting the flanks of the convoy of cattle and goats trailing along behind the column. Felício's men scattered and did not suffer any casualties, but it took them a long time to regroup, and there are still three men missing. When they learn what happened in Lagoa da Laje, a half-breed Indian boy, who can't be more than thirteen and whom Pajeú uses as a messenger, bursts into tears. He is the son of the *jagunço* who had been removing the tiles on the rooftop of the little house when the dogs surprised and killed him.

As they are advancing toward Rosário, split up into very small groups, Pajeú goes over to the youngster, who is trying his best to hold back his tears though every so often a sob escapes him. Without preamble, he asks him if he would like to do something for the Counselor, something that will help avenge his father. The youngster looks at him with such determination in his eyes that he needs no other reply. He explains to him what he wants him to do. A circle of *jagunços* gathers round to listen, looking by turns at him and at the boy.

'There's more to it than just letting yourself be caught,' Pajeú says. 'They have to think that that was the last thing you wanted. And there's more to it than just starting to blab. They have to think they made you talk. In other words, you must let them beat you and even torture you with knives. They have to think you're terrified. That's the only way they'll believe you. Can you do that?'

The boy is dry-eyed and the look on his face is that of an adult, as though he had grown five years older in five minutes. 'I can, Pajeú.'

They meet up with Mané Quadrado and Macambira on the outskirts of Rosário, in the ruins of what were once the slave quarters and the manor house of the hacienda. Pajeú deploys the men in a ravine that lies at a right angle to the trail, with orders to fight just long enough for the dogs to see them turn tail and head in the direction of Bendengó. The boy is at his side, his hands on the shotgun that is very nearly as tall as he is. The engineer corpsmen pass by without seeing them, and a while later, the first battalion. The fusillade begins and raises a cloud of gunsmoke. Pajeú waits for it to disperse a little before shooting. He does so calmly and deliberately, aiming carefully, firing at intervals of several seconds the six Mannlicher bullets that he has had with him since Uauá. He hears the din of whistles, bugle calls, shouts, sees the troops' disorder. Once they have overcome their confusion somewhat, the soldiers, urged on by their officers, begin to fall to their knees and return fire. There is a frantic flurry of bugle calls; reinforcements will soon be arriving. He can hear the officers ordering their men to enter the *caatinga* in pursuit of their attackers.

He then reloads his rifle, rises to his feet, and, followed by other *jagunços*, steps out into the center of the trail, facing the soldiers, fifty yards away, head on. He aims at them and shoots. His men, who have taken their stand all round him, do likewise. More *jagunços* emerge from the brush. The soldiers, finally, advance toward them. The youngster, still at his side, shoulders his shotgun, closes his eyes, and shoots. The backfire of the buckshot leaves him blood-spattered.

'Take my piece, Pajeú,' he says, handing it to him. 'Take care of it for me. I'll escape and make my way back to Belo Monte.'

He throws himself on the ground and begins to scream in pain, clutching his face in his hands. Pajeú breaks into a run – bullets are whistling by from all directions – and disappears into the *caatinga*, followed by the *jagunços*. A company of soldiers plunges into the scrub after them and they allow themselves to be pursued for quite some time; they get the company completely disoriented in the thickets of *xiquexiques* and tall *mandacarus*, till suddenly it finds itself being sniped at from behind by Macambira's men. The soldiers decide to retreat. Pajeú also falls back. Dividing his men up into the four usual groups, he orders them to turn around, get ahead of the troops, and wait for them in Baixas, half a league from Rosário. On the way there, all of them talk of how plucky the youngster is. Have the Protestants been fooled into believing they've wounded him? Are they interrogating him? Or are they so furious at being ambushed that they're hacking him to pieces with their sabers?

A few hours later, from the dense brush on the clayey plateau of Baixas – they have rested, eaten, counted their men, discovered that there are two missing and eleven wounded – Pajeú and Taramela see the vanguard approaching. At the head of the column, in the midst of a group of soldiers, hobbling after a cavalryman who is leading him along on a rope, is the youngster. He is walking along with his head hanging down, a bandage round it. 'They've believed him,' Pajeú thinks. 'If he's up there in the front of the column, it's because they're making him act as a guide.' He feels a sudden wave of affection for the young half-breed.

Taramela nudges him and whispers that the dogs are no longer disposed in the same marching order as at Rosário. It is true: the banners of the escorts of the head of the column are red and gold instead of blue, and the cannons – A Matadeira among them – are now in the vanguard. In order to protect them, there are companies out combing the *caatinga*; if the *jagunços* stay where they are, they will soon find themselves nose to nose with one or another of them. Pajeú tells Macambira and Felício to go ahead to Rancho do Vigário, where the troops will doubtless bivouac. Crawling on all fours without a sound, without their movements so much as stirring a leaf, Felício's band and old Macambira's take off and disappear from sight. Shortly thereafter, shots ring out. Have they been discovered? Pajeú doesn't move a muscle: through the bushes he has spied, just five yards away, a mounted squad of Freemasons, armed with long lances tipped with metal. On hearing the shots, the cavalrymen step up the pace; he hears horses galloping, bugles blowing. The fusillade continues, grows heavier. Pajeú does not look at Taramela, does not look at any of the *jagunços* hugging the ground, curled up in a ball amid the branches. He knows that the hundred fifty men are there all around him, like himself not breathing, not moving, thinking that Macambira and Felício are perhaps being wiped out . . . The sudden deafening roar of the cannon sets him shaking from head to foot. But what frightens him more than the cannon report is the little cry that it calls forth, despite himself, from a *jagunço* behind him. He does not turn round to reprimand him: what with the whinnying of the horses and the shouts of the cavalry troops, it is not likely that they have heard him. After the cannon report, the shooting stops.

In the hours that follow, Pajeú's scar seems to become incandescent, emitting red-hot waves that reach his brain. His choice of a place to rendezvous has been a bad one; twice, patrols pass by just behind him, accompanied by men in peasant dress armed with machetes who swiftly hack the brush away. Is it a miracle that the patrols do not spy his men, even though they pass by so close they almost step on them? Or are those machete-wielders elect of the Blessed Jesus? If they are discovered, few will escape, for with all those thousands of soldiers it will be no trick at all to surround them. It is the fear of seeing his men decimated, without having fulfilled his mission, that is turning his face into a live wound. But it would be madness to change place now.

As dusk begins to fall, by his count twenty-two donkey carts have passed by; half the column is yet to come. For five hours he has seen troops, cannons, animals go past. He would never have dreamed that there were that many soldiers in the whole world. The red ball in the sky is rapidly setting; in half an hour it will be pitch-dark. He orders Taramela to take half the men with him to Rancho do Vigário and arranges to meet him in the caves where there are arms hidden. Squeezing his arm, he whispers to him: 'Be careful.' The *jagunços* move off, bending over so far that their chests touch their knees, by threes, by fours.

Pajeú stays there where he is till stars appear in the sky. He counts ten carts more, and there is no doubt now: it is obvious that no battalion has taken another route. Raising his cane whistle to his mouth, he gives one short blast. He has not moved for so long a time that his body aches all over. He vigorously massages the calves of his legs before he starts walking. As he reaches up to pull his sombrero over his ears, he discovers that he is bareheaded. He remembers then that he lost it at Rosário: a bullet knocked it off, a bullet whose heat he felt as it went past.

The journey on foot to Rancho do Vigário, two leagues from Baixas, is slow, tiring: they proceed along the edge of the trail, single file, halting again and again to drop down and crawl like worms across the open stretches. It is past midnight when they arrive. Bypassing the mission that has given the place its name, Pajeú detours westward, heading for the rocky defile leading to hills dotted with caves. That is where all of them are to rendezvous. They find waiting for them not only Joaquim Macambira and Felício, who have lost only three men in the skirmish with the soldiers. Abbot João is there, too.

Sitting on the ground in a cave with the others, around a little lamp, as he drinks from a leather pouch full of brackish water that tastes wonderful to him and eats mouthfuls of beans with their still-fresh savor of oil, Pajeú tells Abbot João what he has seen, done, feared, and suspected since leaving Canudos. João listens to him without interrupting, waiting for him to drink or chew before asking questions. Sitting round him are Taramela, Mané Quadrado, and old Macambira, who joins in the conversation to put in a few words about the frightening prospects that A Matadeira represents. Outside the cave, the *jagunços* have stretched out on the ground to sleep. It is a clear night, filled with the chirping of crickets. Abbot João reports that the column mounting from Sergipe and Jeremoabo numbers only half as many troops as this one, a mere two thousand men. Pedrão and the Vilanovas are lying in wait for it at Cocorobó. 'That's the best place to fall upon it,' he says. And then he immediately returns to the subject that weighs most heavily on their minds. He agrees with them: if it has advanced as far as Rancho do Vigário, the column will cross the Serra da Angico tomorrow. Because otherwise it would have to veer ten leagues farther west before finding another way to get its cannons through.

'It's after Angico that we're endangered,' Pajeú grumbles.

As in the past, João makes traces on the ground with the point of his knife. 'If they veer off toward O Taboleirinho, all our plans will have gone awry. Our men are waiting for them to come via A Favela.'

Pajeú pictures in his mind how the slope forks off in two directions after the rocky, thorny ascent to Angico. If they fail to take the fork leading to Pitombas, they will not go by way of A Favela. Why would they take the one to Pitombas? They might very well take the other one, the one that leads to the slopes of O Cambaio and O Taboleirinho.

'Except for the fact that if they go that way they'll run into a hail of bullets,' Abbot João explains, holding up the lamp to light his scratches in the dirt. 'If they can't get through that way, the only thing they can do is go via Pitombas and As Umburanas.'

'We'll wait for them then as they come down from Angico,' Pajeú agrees. 'We'll lay down gunfire all along their route, from the right. They'll see that that route is closed to them.'

'And that's not all,' Abbot João says. 'After that, you have to allow yourselves enough time to reinforce Big João, at O Riacho. There are enough men on the other side. But not at O Riacho.'

Fatigue and tension suddenly overcome Pajeú, and Abbot João sees him slump over on Taramela's shoulder, fast asleep. Taramela slides him gently to the floor and takes away his rifle and the half-breed youngster's shotgun, which Pajeú has been holding on his knees. Abbot João says goodbye with a quickly murmured 'Praised be Blessed Jesus the Counselor.'

When Pajeú wakes up, day is breaking at the top of the ravine, but it is still pitch-dark around him. He shakes Taramela, Felício, Mané Quadrado, and old Macambira, who have also slept in the cave. As a bluish light comes over the hills, they busy themselves replenishing their store of ammunition, used up at Rosário, from the cases buried by the Catholic Guard in the cave. Each *jagunço* takes three hundred bullets with him in his big leather pouch. Pajeú makes each of them repeat what it is he must do. The four groups leave separately.

As they climb the bare rock face of the Serra do Angico, Pajeú's band – it will be the first to attack, so that the troops will pursue them through these hills to Pitombas, where the others will be posted – hears, in the distance, the bugles blowing. The column is on the march. He leaves two *jagunços* at the summit and descends with his men to the foot of the other face, directly opposite the steep slope down which the column must come, since it is the only place wide enough for the wheels of their wagons to slip through. He scatters his men about among the bushes, blocking the trail that forks off toward the west, and tells them once more that this time they are not to start running immediately. That comes later. First they must stand their ground and withstand the enemy's fire, so that the Antichrist will be led to believe that there are hundreds of *jagunços* confronting him. Then they must let themselves be seen, be put on the run, be followed to Pitombas. One of the *jagunços* he has left at the summit comes down to tell him that a patrol is coming. It is made up of six men; they let them pass by without shooting at them. One of them falls from his horse, for the rock slope is slippery, especially in the morning, because of the dew that has collected in the night. After that patrol, two more go by, preceding the engineer corps with their picks, shovels, and handsaws. The second patrol heads off toward O Cambaio. A bad sign. Does it mean that they are going to deploy at this point? Almost immediately thereafter the vanguard appears, close on the heels of those who are clearing the way. Will all nine corps be that close together?

Pajeú has already put his gun to his shoulder and is aiming at the elderly cavalryman who must be the leader when a shot rings out, then another, then several bursts of fire. As he observes the disorder on the slope, the Protestants piling up on top of each other, and begins shooting in his turn, he tells himself that he will have to find out who started the fusillade before he had fired the first shot. He empties his magazine slowly, taking careful aim, thinking that through the fault of the man who started shooting the dogs have had time to withdraw and take refuge at the summit.

The gunfire ceases once the slope is empty. At the summit red-and-blue caps, the gleam of bayonets can be seen. The troops, under cover behind the rocks, try to spot them. He hears the sound of arms, men, animals, occasional curses. All of a sudden a cavalry squad, headed by an officer pointing to the *caatinga* with his saber, dashes down the slope. Pajeú sees that he is digging his spurs mercilessly into the flanks of his nervous, pawing bay. None of the cavalrymen falls on the slope, all of them arrive at the foot of it despite the heavy fire. But they all fall, riddled with bullets, the moment they enter the *caatinga*. The officer with the saber, hit several times, roars: 'Show your faces, you cowards!' 'Show our faces so you can kill us?' Pajeú thinks. 'Is that what atheists call courage?' A strange way of looking at things; the Devil is not only evil but stupid. He reloads his overheated rifle. The slope is swarming with soldiers now, and more are pouring down onto the rock face. As he takes aim, still calm and unhurried, Pajeú calculates that there are at least a hundred, perhaps a hundred fifty, of them.

He sees, out of the corner of his eye, that one of the *jagunços* is fighting hand to hand with a soldier, and he wonders how the dog got there. He puts his knife between his teeth; that is how he has always gone into the fray, ever since the days of the *cangaço.* The scar makes itself felt and he hears, very close by, very loud and clear, shouts of 'Long live the Republic!' 'Long live Marshal Floriano!' 'Death to the English!' The *jagunços* answer: 'Death to the Antichrist!' 'Long live the Counselor!' 'Long live Belo Monte!'

'We can't stay here, Pajeú,' Taramela says to him. A compact mass is descending the slope now: soldiers, bullock carts, a cannon, cavalrymen, protected by two companies of infantrymen that charge into the *caatinga.* They fling themselves into the scrub and sink their bayonets in the bushes in the hope of running their invisible enemy through. 'Either we get out now or we won't get out, Pajeú,' Taramela insists, but there is no panic in his voice. Pajeú wants to make sure that the soldiers are really heading toward Pitombas. Yes, there is no question of it, the river of uniforms is definitely flowing northward; nobody except the men who are combing the brush veers off toward the west. He keeps shooting till all his bullets are gone before taking the knife out of his mouth and blowing the cane whistle with all his might. *Jagunços* instantly appear here and there, crouching over, crawling on all fours, turning tail, leaping from one refuge to another, some of them even slipping right through a soldier's legs, all of them decamping as fast as they can. He blows his whistle again and, followed by Taramela, beats a hasty retreat, too. Has he waited too long? He does not run in a straight line but in a ragged tracery of curves, back and forth, so as to make himself a difficult target to aim at; he glimpses, to his right and his left, soldiers shouldering their rifles or running with fixed bayonets after *jagunços.* As he heads into the *caatinga*, as fast as his legs can carry him, he thinks of the woman again, of the two men who killed each other because of her; is she one of those women who bring bad luck?

He feels exhausted, his heart about to burst. Taramela is panting, too. It is good to have this loyal comrade here with him, his friend for so many years now, with whom he has never had the slightest argument. And at that moment four uniforms, four rifles suddenly confront him. 'Hit the dirt, hit the dirt,' he shouts to Taramela. He throws himself to the ground and rolls, hearing at least two of them shoot. By the time he manages to get himself in a squatting position he has his rifle already aimed at the infantryman coming toward him. The Mannlicher has jammed: the pin hits the head of the cartridge but does not fire. He hears a shot and one of the Protestants falls to the ground, clutching his belly. 'Yes, Taramela, you're my good luck,' he thinks as he flings himself upon the three soldiers who have been thrown into confusion for a moment on seeing their comrade wounded, using his rifle as a bludgeon. He strikes one of them and sends him staggering, but the others leap on top of him. He feels a burning, shooting pain. Suddenly blood spurts all over the face of one of the soldiers and he hears him howl with pain. Taramela is there, landing in their midst like a meteor. The enemy that it falls to Pajeú's lot to deal with is not a real adversary to Pajeú's way of thinking: very young, he is dripping with sweat, and the uniform he is bundled up in barely allows him to move. He struggles till Pajeú gets his rifle away from him and then takes to his heels. Taramela and the other soldier are fighting it out on the ground, panting. Pajeú goes over to them and with a single thrust buries his knife in the soldier's neck up to the handle; he gurgles, trembles, and stops moving. Taramela has a few bruises and Pajeú's shoulder is bleeding. Taramela rubs egg poultice on it and bandages it with the shirt of one of the dead soldiers. 'You're my good luck, Taramela,' Pajeú says. 'That I am,' Taramela agrees. They are unable to run now, for each of them is now carrying not only his own knapsack and rifle but also those of one of the soldiers.

Shortly thereafter they hear gunfire. It is scattered at first, but soon grows heavier. The vanguard is already in Pitombas, being fired on by Felício and his men. He imagines the rage the soldiers must feel on finding, hanging from the trees, the uniforms, the boots, the caps, the leather chest belts of the Throat-Slitter's troops, the skeletons picked clean by the vultures. During nearly all of their trek to Pitombas, the fusillade continues and Taramela comments: 'Anybody who's got all the bullets in the world, the way those soldiers do, can shoot just to be shooting.' The fusillade suddenly ceases. Felício must have started falling back, so as to lure the column into following them along the road to As Umburanas, where old Macambira and Mané Quadrado will greet them with another hail of bullets.

When Pajeú and Taramela – they must rest awhile, for the weight of the soldiers' rifles and knapsacks plus their own is twice as tiring – finally reach the scrubland of Pitombas, there are still scattered *jagunços* there. They are firing sporadically at the column, which pays no attention to them and continues to advance, amid a cloud of yellow dust, toward the deep depression, once a riverbed, that the *sertanejos* call the road to As Umburanas.

'It must not hurt you very much when you laugh, Pajeú,' Taramela says.

Pajeú is blowing his cane whistle to let the *jagunços* know he's arrived, and thinks to himself that he has the right to smile. Aren't the dogs taking off down the ravine, battalion after battalion of them, on the road to As Umburanas? Won't that road take them, inevitably, to A Favela?

He and Taramela are on a wooded promontory overlooking the bare ravines; there is no need to hide themselves, for they are not only standing at a dead angle but are shielded by the sun's rays, which blind the soldiers if they look in this direction. They can see the column below them turn the gray earth red, blue. They can still hear occasional shots. The *jagunços* appear, climbing on all fours, emerging from caves, letting themselves down from lookout platforms hidden in the trees. They crowd around Pajeú, to whom someone hands a leather flask full of milk, which he drinks in little sips and which leaves a little white trickle at the corners of his mouth. No one questions him about his wound, and in fact they avert their eyes from it, as though it were something indecent. Pajeú then eats a handful of fruit they give him: *quixabas*, quarters of *umbu, pinhas.* At the same time, he listens to the report of two men whom Felício left there when he went off to reinforce Joaquim Macambira and Mané Quadrado in As Umburanas. Constantly breaking in on each other, they tell how the dogs did not react immediately to being fired upon from the promontory, because it seemed risky to climb up the slope and present a target to the *jagunço* sharpshooters or because they guessed that the latter were such small groups as to be insignificant. Nonetheless, when Felício and his men advanced to the edge of the ravine and the atheists saw that they were beginning to suffer casualties, they sent several companies to hunt them down. That's how it had gone for some time, with the companies trying to climb the slope and the *jagunços* withstanding their fire, until finally the soldiers slipped away through one opening or another in the brush and disappeared. Felício had left shortly thereafter.

'Till just a little while ago,' one of the messengers says, 'it was swarming with soldiers around here.'

Taramela, who has been counting the men, informs Pajeú that there are thirty-five of them there. Should they wait for the others?

'There isn't time,' Pajeú answers. 'We're needed.'

He leaves a messenger to tell the others which way they've gone, hands out the rifles and knapsacks they've brought, and heads straight for the ravines to meet up with Mané Quadrado, Felício, and Macambira. The rest he has had – along with having had something to eat and drink – has done him good. His muscles no longer ache; the wound burns less. He walks fast, not hiding himself, along the broken path that forces them to zigzag back and forth. Below him, the column continues to advance. The head of it is now far in the distance, perhaps climbing A Favela, but even in spots where the view is unobstructed he is unable to catch a glimpse of it. The river of soldiers, horses, cannons, wagons is endless. 'It's a rattlesnake,' Pajeú thinks. Each battalion is a ring, the uniforms the scales, the powder of its cannons the venom with which it poisons its victims. He would like to be able to tell the woman what has happened to him.

At that moment he hears rifle reports. Everything has turned out as Abbot João has planned it. They are up ahead shooting at the serpent from the rocks of As Umburanas, giving it one last push toward A Favela. On rounding a hill, they see a squad of cavalry coming up. Pajeú begins shooting, aiming at their mounts to make them roll down into the ravine. What fine horses, how easily they scale the very steep slope! The burst of fire downs two of them, but a number of them reach the top. Pajeú gives the order to clear out, knowing as he runs that the men must resent his having deprived them of an easy victory.

When they finally reach the ravines where the *jagunços* are deployed, Pajeú realizes that his comrades are in a tough spot. Old Macambira, whom it takes him some time to locate, explains to him that the soldiers are bombarding the heights, causing rockslides, and that every corps that passes by sends out fresh companies to hunt them down. 'We've lost quite a few men,' the old man says as he energetically unfouls his rifle and carefully loads it with black powder that he extracts from a horn. 'At least twenty,' he grumbles. 'I don't know if we'll withstand the next charge. What shall we do?'

From where he is standing, Pajeú can see, very close by, the range of hills of A Favela, and beyond them, Monte Mário. Those hills, gray and ocher, have now turned bluish, reddish, greenish, and are moving, as though they were infested with larvae.

'They've been coming up for three or four hours now,' old Macambira says. 'They've even gotten the cannons up. And A Matadeira, too.'

'Well then, we've done what we had to do,' Pajeú says. 'So let's all go now to reinforce O Riacho.'

When the Sardelinha sisters asked her if she wanted to go with them to cook for the men who were waiting for the soldiers in Trabubu and Cocorobó, Jurema said yes. She said it mechanically, the way she said and did everything. The Dwarf reproached her for it and the nearsighted man made that noise, halfway between a moan and a gargle, that came from him every time something frightened him. They had been in Canudos for more than two months now and were never apart.

She thought that the Dwarf and the nearsighted man would stay behind in the city, but when the convoy of four pack mules, twenty porters, and a dozen women was ready to leave, both of them fell in alongside her. They took the road to Jeremoabo. No one was bothered by the presence of these two intruders who were carrying neither weapons nor pickaxes and shovels for digging trenches. As they passed by the animal pens, now rebuilt and full once more of goats and kids, everyone began singing the hymns that people said had been composed by the Little Blessed One. Jurema walked along in silence, feeling the rough stones of the road through her sandals. The Dwarf sang along with the others. The nearsighted man, concentrating on seeing where he was stepping, was holding to his right eye the tortoiseshell frame of his glasses, to which he had glued little shards of the shattered lenses. This man who seemed to have more bones than other people, to stagger about in a daze, holding this artifact made of slivers up to his eye, who approached persons and things as though he were about to bump into them, at times kept Jurema from dwelling on her unlucky star. In the weeks during which she had been his eyes, his cane, his consolation, she had thought of him as her son. Thinking of this gangling beanpole of a man as 'my son' was her secret game, a notion that made her laugh. God had brought strange people into her life, people she never dreamed existed, such as Galileo Gall, the circus folk, and this pitiful creature alongside her who had just tripped and fallen headlong.

Every so often they would run into armed groups of the Catholic Guard in the scrub on the mountainsides and stop to give them flour, fruit, brown sugar, jerky, and ammunition. From time to time messengers appeared, who on spying them stopped short to talk with Antônio Vilanova. Rumors spread in whispers through the convoy after they had gone on. They were always about the same thing: the war, the dogs that were on their way. She finally pieced together what had been happening. There were two armies approaching, one of them by way of Queimadas and Monte Santo and the other by way of Sergipe and Jeremoabo. Hundreds of *jagunços* had taken off in those two directions in recent days, and every afternoon, during the counsels, which Jurema had faithfully attended, the Counselor exhorted his flock to pray for them. She had seen the anxiety that the imminent threat of yet another war had aroused. Her one thought was that, because of this war, the robust, mature *caboclo*, the one with the scar and the little beady eyes that frightened her, would not be back for some time.

The convoy arrived in Trabubu as night was falling. They distributed food to the *jagunços* entrenched amid the rocks and three women stayed behind with them. Then Antônio Vilanova ordered the rest of the convoy to go on to Cocorobó. They covered the last stretch in darkness. Jurema led the nearsighted man along by the hand. Despite her help, he stumbled and fell so many times that Antônio Vilanova had him ride a pack mule, sitting on top of the sacks of maize. As they started up the steep pass to Cocorobó, Pedrão came to meet them. He was a giant of a man, nearly as stout and tall as Big João, a light-skinned mulatto well along in years, with an ancient carbine slung over his shoulder that he never removed even to sleep. He was barefoot, with pants that reached down to his ankles and a sleeveless jacket that left his huge sturdy arms bare. He had a round belly that he kept scratching as he spoke. On seeing him, Jurema felt apprehensive, because of the stories that had circulated about his life in Várzea da Ema, where he had perpetrated many a bloody deed with the band that had never left his side, men with the fearsome faces of outlaws. She had the feeling that being around people such as Pedrão, Abbot João, or Pajeú was dangerous, even though they were saints now – like living with a jaguar, a cobra, and a tarantula who, through some dark instinct, might claw, bite, or sting at any moment.

Right now, Pedrão seemed harmless enough, lost in the shadows talking with Antônio and Honório Vilanova, the latter having materialized like a ghost from behind the rocks. A number of silhouettes appeared with him, suddenly popping up out of the brambles to relieve the porters of the burdens they were carrying on their backs. Jurema helped light the braziers. The men busied themselves opening cases of ammunition and sacks of gunpowder, distributing fuses. She and the other women began preparing a meal. The *jagunços* were so hungry they seemed scarcely able to wait for the pots to come to a boil. They congregated around Assunção Sardelinha, who filled their bowls and tins with water, as other women handed out fistfuls of manioc; as things became somewhat disorderly, Pedrão ordered the men to calm down.

Jurema worked all night long, putting the pots back on the fire to warm again and again, frying pieces of meat, reheating the beans. The men showed up in groups of ten, of fifteen, and when one of them recognized his wife among the women cooking, he took her by the arm and they withdrew to talk together. Why had it never occurred to Rufino, as it had to so many other *sertanejos*, to come to Canudos? If he had done so, he would still be alive.

Suddenly they heard a clap of thunder. But the air was dry; it couldn't be a sign of a rainstorm about to break. She realized then that it was the boom of a cannon; Pedrão and the Vilanova brothers ordered the fires put out and sent the men who were eating back to the mountaintops. Once they had left, however, the three stayed there talking. Pedrão said that the soldiers were on the outskirts of Canche; it would be some time before they arrived. They did not march by night; he had followed them from Simão Dias on and knew their habits. The moment darkness fell, they set up their portable huts and posted sentinels and stayed put till the following day. At dawn, before leaving, they fired a cannon shot in the air. That must have been what the cannon report was; they must just be leaving Canche.

'Are there many of them?' a voice from the ground that resembled the screeching of a bird interrupted him. 'How many of them are there?'

Jurema saw him rise to his feet and stand, frail and spindly, in profile between her and the men, trying to see though his monocle of splinters. The Vilanovas and Pedrão burst out laughing, as did the women who were putting away the pots and the food that was left. She refrained from laughing. She felt sorry for the nearsighted man. Was there anyone more helpless and terrified than her son? Everything frightened him: the people who brushed past him, cripples, madmen, and lepers who begged for alms, a rat running across the floor of the store. Everything made him give that little scream of his, made him turn deathly pale, made him search for her hand.

'I didn't count them.' Pedrão guffawed. 'Why should I have, if we're going to kill all of them?'

There was another wave of laughter. On the heights, it was beginning to get light.

'The women had best leave here,' Honório Vilanova said.

Like his brother, he was wearing boots and carrying a pistol as well as a rifle. In their dress, their speech, and even their physical appearance, they seemed to Jurema to be quite different from the other people in Canudos. But no one treated them as though they were any different.

Forgetting about the nearsighted man, Pedrão motioned to the women to follow him. Half the bearers had already gone up the mountainside, but the rest were still there, with their loads on their backs. A red arc was rising behind the slopes of Cocorobó. The nearsighted man stayed where he was, shaking his head, when the convoy set out to take up positions amid the rocks behind the combatants. Jurema took him by the hand: it was soaking wet with sweat. His glassy, unfocused eyes looked at her gratefully. 'Let's go,' she said, tugging at him. 'They're leaving us behind.' They had to wake the Dwarf, who was sleeping soundly.

As they reached a sheltered hillock near the crest, the advance guard of the army was entering the pass and the war had begun.

The Vilanovas and Pedrão disappeared, and the women, the nearsighted man, and the Dwarf stayed behind amid the weathered rocks, listening to the gunfire. It seemed to be scattered and far off. Jurema could hear the shots on the right and on the left, and she thought to herself that the wind must be carrying the sound away from them, for from there it was very muffled. She could not see anything; a wall of mossy stones hid the sharpshooters from sight. The war, despite being so close, seemed very far away. 'Are there many of them?' the nearsighted man stammered. He was still clutching her hand tightly. She answered that she didn't know and went to help the Sardelinha sisters unload the pack mules and set out the earthen jars full of water, pots full of food, strips of cloth and rags to make bandages, and poultices and medicines that the apothecary had packed in a wooden box. She saw the Dwarf climbing up toward the crest. The nearsighted man sat down on the ground and hid his face in his hands, as though he were weeping. But when one of the women shouted to him to gather branches to make an overhead shelter, he hastily rose to his feet and Jurema saw him set to work eagerly, feeling all around for stems, leaves, grass, and stumbling back to hand them to the women. That little figure moving back and forth, tripping and falling and picking himself up again and peering at the ground with his outlandish monocle, was such a funny sight that the women finally began pointing at him and making fun of him. The Dwarf disappeared amid the rocks.

Suddenly the shots sounded louder, closer. The women stood there not moving, listening. Jurema saw that the crackle of gunfire, the continuous bursts had instantly sobered them: they had forgotten all about the nearsighted man and were thinking of their husbands, their fathers, their sons who were the targets of this fire on the slope opposite. The shooting dazed her but it did not frighten her. She felt that this war did not concern her and that the bullets would therefore respect her. She felt such drowsiness come over her that she curled up against the rocks, at the Sardelinha sisters' side. She slept though not asleep, a lucid sleep, aware of the gunfire that was shaking the mountain slopes of Cocorobó, dreaming twice of other shots, those of that morning in Queimadas, that dawn when she had been about to be killed by the *capangas* and the stranger who spoke in some odd language had raped her. She dreamed that, since she knew what was going to happen, she begged him not to do it because that would be the ruin of her and of Rufino and of the stranger himself, but not understanding her language, he had paid no attention to her.

When she awoke, the nearsighted man, at her feet, looked at her the way the Idiot from the circus had. Two *jagunços* were drinking from one of the earthen jugs, surrounded by the women. She rose to her feet and went to see what was happening. The Dwarf had not come back, and the gunfire was deafening. The *jagunços* had come to get more ammunition; they were so tense and exhausted they could barely speak: the pass was crawling with atheists, who were dropping like flies every time they tried to take the mountainside. They had charged twice, and each time they had been pushed back before they were even halfway up the slope. The man speaking, a short little man with a sparse beard sprinkled with white, shrugged: the only thing was, there were so many of them that there was no way to force them to withdraw. What was more, the *jagunços* were beginning to run out of ammunition.

'And what will happen if they take the slopes?' Jurema heard the nearsighted man stammer.

'They won't be able to stop them in Trabubu,' the other *jagunço* said in a hoarse voice. 'There are almost no men left there. They've all come here to give us a hand.'

As though that had reminded them of the need to leave immediately, the two men murmured 'Praised be the Blessed Jesus,' and Jurema saw them scale the rocks and disappear. The Sardelinha sisters said that the food should be reheated, since more *jagunços* would be turning up at any moment. As she helped them, Jurema felt the nearsighted man tremble as he clung to her skirts. She sensed how terrified, how panicked he was at the thought that all of a sudden uniformed men might spring out from amid the rocks, shooting and bayoneting anyone who got in their way. In addition to the rifle fire, there was cannonading; each time a shell landed, it was followed by an avalanche of stones that roared down the mountainside. Jurema remembered her poor son's indecision all these many weeks, not knowing what to do with himself, whether to stay or try to get away. He wanted to leave, that was what he yearned to do, and as they lay on the floor of the store at night, listening to the Vilanova family snore, he told her so, trembling all over: he wanted to get out of there, to escape to Salvador, to Cumbe, to Monte Santo, to Jeremoabo, to a place where he could find help, where he could get word to people who were his friends that he was still alive. But how to get away if they had forbidden him to leave? How far could he get all by himself and half blind? They would catch up with him and kill him. In these whispered dialogues in the dark of the night, he sometimes tried to persuade her to lead him to some hamlet where he could hire guides. He would offer her every reward conceivable if she helped him, but then a moment later he would correct himself and say that it was madness to try to escape since they would find them and kill them. As he had once trembled with fear of the *jagunços*, he now trembled with fear of the soldiers. 'My poor son,' she thought. She felt sad and disheartened. Would the soldiers kill her? It didn't matter. Was it true that when any man or woman of Belo Monte died, angels would come to carry off their soul? True or not, death in any event would be a repose, a sleep with no sad dreams, something not as bad as the life that she had been leading after what had happened in Queimadas.

All the women suddenly looked up. Her eyes followed to see what they were watching: ten or twelve *jagunços* leaping down the slope from the crest. The cannonade was so heavy that it seemed to Jurema that shells were bursting inside her head. Like the other women, she ran to meet the men and heard them say that they needed ammunition: they had none left to shoot back with and were in a desperate rage. When the Sardelinha sisters answered, 'What ammunition?' since the last case of it had been carried off by the two *jagunços* a while before, the men looked at each other and one of them spat and stamped his feet in fury. The women offered them something to eat, but they took time only to have a drink of water, passing a dipper from hand to hand: the moment they had all had a drink, they ran back up the mountainside. The women watched them drink and take off again, dripping with sweat, frowning, the veins at their temples standing out, their eyes bloodshot, and did not ask them a single question.

The last one to leave turned to the Sardelinha sisters and said: 'You'd best go back to Belo Monte. We can't hold out much longer. There are too many of them, and we've no bullets left.'

After a moment's hesitation, instead of heading for the pack mules, the women also began scrambling up the mountainside. Jurema scarcely knew what to make of it. They were not going to war because they were madwomen; their men were up there, and they wanted to know if they were still alive. Without another thought, she ran after them, shouting to the nearsighted man – standing there petrified, his mouth gaping open – to wait for her.

As she clambered up the slope she scratched her hands and twice she slipped and fell. It was a steep climb; her heart began to pound and she found herself short of breath. Up above, she saw great ocher, lead-colored, orange-tinted clouds that the wind drove together, drove apart, drove together again, and along with scattered gunfire, close at hand, she could hear unintelligible shouts. She crawled down a slope without stones, trying to see. She came upon two big rocks leaning against each other and peered out from behind them at the clouds of dust. Little by little she was able to see, intuit, guess. The *jagunços* were not far off, but it was hard to make them out because they blended in with the slope. She gradually located them, curled up behind boulders or clumps of cacti, or hiding in hollows with only their heads peeking out. On the slopes opposite, whose broad outlines she managed to make out in the dust, there were also many *jagunços*, spread out, buried in the dirt, shooting. She had the impression that she was about to go deaf, that the ear-splitting gunfire was the last thing she would ever hear.

And at that moment she realized that the dark spot, like a thicket, that the slope turned into fifty yards down was soldiers. Yes, there they were: a splotch climbing farther and farther up the mountainside, in which there were glints, bright spots, reflections, little red stars that must be rifle shots, bayonets, swords, and glimpsed faces that appeared and disappeared. She looked to both sides, and on the right the splotch had now climbed as high as the place where she was. She felt her stomach writhe, retched, and vomited across her arm. She was alone in the middle of the slope and that tide of uniforms was about to flood over her. Without thinking, she let herself slide, sitting down, to the nearest nest of *jagunços*: three sombreros, two leather ones and one straw one, in a hollow. 'Don't shoot, don't shoot,' she shouted as she slid. But not one of them turned around to look at her as she leapt into the hole protected by a parapet of stones. She then saw that two of the three men inside were dead. One of them had been hit by a projectile that had turned his face into a vermilion blob. He was lying in the arms of the other one who was dead, his eyes and mouth full of flies. They were holding each other up like the two big rocks behind which she had hidden herself. After a moment, the *jagunço* who was still alive looked at her out of the corner of one eye. He was aiming with his other eye closed, calculating before shooting, and with each shot the rifle recoiled and hit him in the shoulder. Without halting his fire, he mumbled something. Jurema did not understand what he said. She crawled toward him, to no avail. The buzzing in her ears was still the only thing she could hear. The *jagunço* motioned to her, and she finally realized that he wanted the pouch that was lying next to the dead body without a face. She handed it to him and saw the *jagunço,* sitting with his legs crossed, clean the barrel of his rifle and calmly reload it, as though he had all the time in the world.

'The soldiers are right on top of us,' Jurema screamed. 'Heaven help us, what's going to become of us?'

He shrugged and took up his position behind the parapet again. Should she leave this trench, go back to the other side of the slope, flee to Canudos? Her body would not obey her, her legs had gone as limp as rags, if she stood up she would fall down. Why didn't the soldiers appear with their bayonets, what were they waiting for if they'd spied them only a few yards away? The *jagunço* moved his lips again, but all she could hear was that buzzing in her ears and now, too, metallic sounds: bugles?

'I can't hear a thing, not a thing,' she shouted at the top of her lungs. 'I've gone deaf.'

The *jagunço* nodded and motioned to her, as though indicating that someone was moving off. He was a young man, with long kinky hair tumbling out from under the brim of his leather sombrero with a greenish tinge, and wearing the armband of the Catholic Guard. 'What?' Jurema shouted. He gestured to her to look over the parapet. Pushing the two dead bodies aside, she peeked out of one of the openings between the stones. The soldiers were now lower down on the slope. It was they who were moving off. 'Why are they going off if they've won?' she wondered, watching them being swallowed up by the swirls of dust. Why were they moving off downhill instead of climbing up the hill to kill off the survivors?

When Sergeant Frutuoso Medrado – First Company, Twelfth Battalion – hears the bugle command to retreat, he thinks he is going mad. His squad of chasseurs is at the head of the company and the company at the head of the battalion as they launch a bayonet charge, the fifth one of the day, on the western slopes of Cocorobó. The fact that this time – when they have taken three-quarters of the mountainside, flushing out, with bayonet and saber, the English from the hiding places from which they were sniping at the patriots – they are being given orders to retreat is simply beyond all understanding as Sergeant Frutuoso sees it, even though he has a good head for such things. But there is no doubt about it: there are now many bugles ordering them to withdraw. His eleven men are crouching down looking at him, and in the windblown dust enveloping them Sergeant Medrado sees that they are as taken aback as he is. Has the field commander lost his mind, robbing them of victory when only the heights remained to be cleared of the enemy? The English are few in number and have almost no ammunition; glancing up toward the crest, Sergeant Frutuoso Medrado spies those of them who have managed to escape from the waves of soldiers breaking over them, and sees that they are not shooting: they are simply brandishing their knives and machetes, throwing stones. 'I haven't gotten myself my Englishman yet,' Frutuoso thinks.

'What are your men waiting for? Why aren't they obeying the order?' the commanding officer of the company, Captain Almeida, who suddenly materializes at his side, shouts in his ear.

'First squad of chasseurs! Retreat!' the sergeant immediately yells, and his eleven men dash down the slope.

But he is in no hurry; he starts back down at the same pace as Captain Almeida. 'The order took me by surprise, sir,' he murmurs, placing himself on the officer's right. 'What sense is there in retreating at this point?'

'It is not our duty to understand but to obey,' Captain Almeida growls, sliding downhill on his heels, leaning on his saber as though it were a cane. But a moment later he adds, without trying to hide his anger: 'I don't understand it either. All we had to do was to kill them off – mere child's play.'

Frutuoso Medrado thinks to himself that one of the few disadvantages of this military life that he relishes so is the mysterious nature of certain command decisions. He has taken part in the five charges on the heights of Cocorobó, and yet he is not tired. He has been fighting for six hours, ever since his battalion, marching in the vanguard of the column, suddenly found itself caught in a cross fire early this morning at the entrance to the Compass. In the first charge, the sergeant was behind the Third Company and saw how Second Lieutenant Sepúlveda's chasseurs were mowed down by bursts of rifle fire whose source no one was able to pin down. In the second, the death toll was also so heavy that they were obliged to fall back. The third charge was made by two battalions of the Sixth Brigade, the Twenty-sixth and the Thirty-second, but Colonel Carlos Maria da Silva Telles ordered Captain Almeida's company to carry out an enveloping movement. It was not successful, for after scaling the spurs of the mountainside they discovered that they were being slashed to ribbons by the thorny brush along the razorback crest. As he was coming back down, the sergeant felt a burning sensation in his left hand: a bullet had just blown off the tip of his little finger. It didn't hurt him, and once back in the rear guard, as the battalion doctor was applying a disinfectant, he cracked jokes so as to raise the morale of the wounded being brought in by the stretcher-bearers. He took part in the fourth charge as a volunteer, arguing that he wanted to wreak his vengeance for that bit of finger he had lost and kill himself an Englishman. They had managed to get halfway up the slope, but with such heavy losses that once again they were forced to fall back. But in this last charge they had defeated the enemy all along the line: so why withdraw? Perhaps so that the Fifth Brigade could finish them off and thus allow Colonel Donaciano de Araújo Pantoja, General Savaget's favorite subordinate, to reap all the glory? 'That might be why,' Captain Almeida mutters.

At the foot of the slope, where there are infantrymen from companies trying to regroup, pushing and shoving each other about, troops trying to yoke the draft animals to cannons, carts, and ambulance wagons, contradictory bugle commands, wounded screaming, Sergeant Frutuoso Medrado discovers the reason for the sudden retreat: the column coming from Queimadas and Monte Santo has fallen into a trap, and the second column, instead of invading Canudos from the north, must now make a forced march and get them out of the trap they are caught in.

The sergeant, who entered the army at the age of fourteen, fought in the war against Paraguay, and in the campaigns to put down the uprisings that broke out in the South following the fall of the monarchy, does not blanch at the idea of withdrawing through unknown territory after having spent the entire day fighting. And what a battle! The bandits are courageous, he must admit. They have withstood several heavy cannonades without budging an inch, forcing the troops to rout them out with bayonets and fight it out in fierce hand-to-hand combat: the bastards are as tough as the Paraguayans. Unlike himself – he feels refreshed and ready for action again after a few swallows of water and a couple of pieces of hardtack – his men look exhausted. They are raw troops, recruited in Bagé in the last six months; this has been their baptism of fire. They have behaved well; he has not seen a single one panic. Can they be more afraid of him than of the English? He is a strict disciplinarian; at their first breach of conduct, his men have him personally to deal with. Instead of the regulation punishments – loss of leave, the stockade, floggings – the sergeant is partial to clouts on the head, ear-pulling, kicks in the behind, or a flying trip into a muddy pigpen. They are well trained, as they have proved today. All of them are safe and sound, with the exception of Private Coríntio, who has tripped over some rocks and is limping. A skinny little runt, he is walking bent over double beneath the weight of his knapsack. A good sort, Coríntio, timid, obliging, an early bird, and Frutuoso Medrado shows certain favoritism toward him because he is Florisa's husband. The sergeant feels a sudden itch and laughs to himself. 'What a hot bitch you are, Florisa – here I am, miles away in the middle of a war, and still you've made me get a hard-on,' he thinks. He feels like bursting out laughing at the silly things that pop into his head. He looks at Coríntio, limping along all hunched over, and remembers the day he first presented himself, as cool as you please, at the laundress's hut: 'Either you sleep with me, Florisa, or Coríntio will be confined to barracks every weekend, without visitors' rights.' Florisa held out for a month; she gave in at first so as to be able to see Coríntio, but now, Frutuoso believes, she continues to sleep with him because she likes it. They do it right there in the hut or at the bend in the river where she goes to do her washing.

It is a relationship that makes him feel as proud as a peacock when he's drunk. Does Coríntio suspect anything? No, not a thing. Or does he simply let it pass, for what can he do when he's up against a man like the sergeant, who, on top of everything else, is his superior?

He hears shots on his right, and so he goes looking for Captain Almeida. The order is to keep moving on, to rescue the first column, to keep the fanatics from wiping it out. Those shots are a tactic to distract them; the bandits have regrouped in Trabubu and are trying to pin them down. General Savaget has dispatched two battalions from the Fifth Brigade to answer the challenge, while the others meanwhile are continuing the forced march to the place where General Oscar is trapped. Captain Almeida looks so down in the mouth that Frutuoso asks him if something has gone wrong.

'Many casualties,' the captain says in a low voice. 'More than two hundred wounded, seventy dead, among them Major Tristão Sucupira. Even General Savaget is wounded.'

'General Savaget?' the sergeant says. 'But I just saw him ride by on horseback, sir.'

'Because he's a brave man,' the captain answers. 'He has a bad bullet wound in the belly.'

Frutuoso goes back to his squad of chasseurs. With so many dead and wounded, they've been lucky: except for Coríntio's knee and the sergeant's little finger, not one of them has a scratch. He looks at his finger. It doesn't hurt but it's bleeding; the bandage has turned a dark red. The doctor who treated him, Major Neri, laughed when the sergeant wanted to know if he'd be invalided out of the army. 'Haven't you noticed how many officers and men in the army are maimed?' Yes, he's noticed. His hair stands on end when he thinks that they might discharge him. What would he do then? Since he has no wife, no children, no parents, the army is all of these things to him.

During the march, as they skirt the mountains that surround Canudos, the infantry, artillery, and cavalry troops of the second column hear shots, coming from the direction of the brush, several times. One or another of the companies drops back to launch a few volleys, as the rest go on. At nightfall, the Twelfth Battalion finally halts. The three hundred men unburden themselves of their knapsacks and rifles. They are worn out. This is not like all the other nights since they left Araçaju and marched to this spot via São Cristóvão, Lagarto, Itaporanga, Simão Dias, Jeremoabo, and Canche. On each of the other nights when they halted to bivouac, they butchered animals and went out searching for water and wood, and the darkness was full of the sound of guitars, songs, voices chatting. Now no one says a word. Even the sergeant is tired.

The rest does not last long for him. Captain Almeida calls the squad leaders together to find out how many cartridges they still have left and replace the ones that have been used up, so that all the men can leave with two hundred rounds each in their knapsacks. He announces to them that the Fourth Brigade, to which they belong, will now be in the vanguard and their battalion in the vanguard of the vanguard. The news restores Frutuoso's enthusiasm, but knowing that they will be the spearhead does not arouse the slightest reaction among his men, who begin marching again with great yawns and without comment.

Captain Almeida has said that they will make contact with the first column at dawn, but it is not yet two o'clock in the morning when the advance units of the Fourth Brigade spy the dark bulk of A Favela, where, according to General Oscar's messengers, he is encircled by the bandits. The sound of bugles blowing cleaves the warm night without a breath of wind, and shortly thereafter they hear other bugles answering in the distance. A chorus of cheers runs through the battalion: their buddies, the men in the first column, are there. Sergeant Frutuoso sees that his men are excited too, waving their kepis in the air and shouting: 'Long live the Republic!' 'Long live Marshal Floriano!'

Colonel Silva Telles gives orders to proceed to A Favela. 'It goes against the official rules of military tactics to leap into the lion's mouth in unknown terrain,' Captain Almeida snorts to the lieutenants and the sergeants as he gives them their final instructions. 'Advance like scorpions, first one little step here, then another and another, keep your proper distance apart, and watch out for surprises.' It doesn't strike Sergeant Frutuoso as an intelligent move either to proceed like this in the dark since they know that the enemy is somewhere between the first column and their own. All of a sudden, the proximity of danger occupies his mind entirely; from his position at the head of his squad he sniffs the stony expanse to the right and to the left.

The fusillade begins all at once, very close, intense, drowning out the sound of the bugle commands from A Favela that are guiding them. 'Get down, get down!' the sergeant roars, flattening himself against the sharp stones. He pricks up his ears: are the shots coming from the right? Yes, from the right. 'They're on your right,' he roars. 'Fire away, boys!' And as he shoots, supporting himself on his left elbow, he thinks to himself that thanks to these English bandits he is seeing strange things, such as withdrawing from a skirmish that's already been won and fighting in the dark, trusting that God will guide the bullets they are firing against the invaders. Won't they end up hitting their own troops instead? He remembers several maxims that he has drilled into his men: 'A wasted bullet weakens the one who wastes it; shoot only when you can see what you're shooting at.' His men must be laughing like anything. From time to time, amid the gunfire, curses and groans can be heard. Finally the order comes to cease fire; the bugles blow again from A Favela, summoning them. Captain Almeida orders the company to hug the ground till he is certain that the bandits have been driven off. Sergeant Frutuoso Medrado's chasseurs lead the march.

'Eight yards between companies. Sixteen between battalions. Fifty between brigades.' Who can maintain the proper distance in the dark? The Official Rule Book of Tactics also states that a squad leader must go to the rear of his unit during an advance, to the head during a charge, and to the center when in square formation. The sergeant nonetheless goes to the head of his squad, thinking that if he positions himself in the rear his men may lose courage, nervous as they are at marching in this darkness where every so often the shooting starts again. Every half hour, every hour, perhaps every ten minutes – he can no longer tell, since these lightning attacks, which last almost no time at all, which tell on their nerves much more than on their bodies, have made him lose all notion of time – a rain of bullets forces them to hit the dirt and respond with another just like it, more for reasons of honor than of effectiveness. He suspects that the attackers are few in number, perhaps only two or three men. But the fact that the darkness gives the English an advantage, since they can see the patriots while the latter can't see them, makes the sergeant feel edgy and tires him badly. And what can it be like for his men if he, with all his experience, feels that way?

At times, the bugle calls from A Favela seem to be coming from farther away. The calls and the ones in answer set the cadence of the march. There are two brief halts, so that the soldiers may drink a little water and casualties may be counted. Captain Almeida's company has suffered none, unlike Captain Noronha's, in which there are three wounded.

'You see, you lucky bastards, you're leading a charmed life,' the sergeant says to raise his men's spirits.

Day is beginning to break, and in the dim light the feeling that the nightmare of the shooting in the dark is over, that now they'll be able to see where they're setting their feet down and where their attackers are, brings a smile to his lips.

The last stretch is child's play by comparison to what has gone before. The mountain spurs of A Favela are very near, and in the glow of the rising sun the sergeant can make out the first column, some bluish patches, some little dots that little by little turn into human figures, animals, wagons. There seems to be vast disorder, enormous confusion. Frutuoso Medrado tells himself that this piling up of one unit on top of another is also scarcely what is laid down in the Official Rule Book. And just as he is remarking to Captain Almeida – the squads have regrouped and the company is marching four abreast at the head of the battalion – that the enemy has vanished into thin air, all of a sudden, out of the ground just a few steps away, amid the branches and bushes of the scrub, there pop up heads, arms, barrels of rifles and carbines all spitting fire at once. Captain Almeida struggles to remove his revolver from its holster and doubles over, his mouth gaping open as though gasping for air, and Sergeant Frutuoso Medrado, his thoughts racing in that big head of his, realizes almost instantly that throwing himself flat on the ground would be suicide since the enemy is very close, as would turning tail, since that would make him a perfect target. So, rifle in hand, he shouts to his men at the top of his lungs: 'Charge, charge, charge!' and sets them an example by leaping in the direction of the trenchful of Englishmen whose opening yawns wide behind a little low parapet of stones. He falls inside it and has the impression that the trigger of his rifle is jammed, but he is sure that the blade of his bayonet has sunk into a body. It is now stuck fast in it and he is unable to pull it out. He tosses the rifle aside and flings himself on the figure closest to him, going for the neck. He keeps shouting 'Charge, charge, fire away!' as he hits, butts, grapples, bites, and is caught up in a milling mass of men in which someone is reciting elements which, according to the Official Rule Book of Tactics, constitute a properly executed attack: reinforcement, support, reserves, cordon.

When he opens his eyes, a minute or a century later, his lips are repeating: reinforcement, support, reserves, cordon. That is the mixed attack, you sons of bitches. What convoy are they talking about? He is lucid. Not in the trench, but in a dry gorge; he sees in front of him the steep side of a ravine, cacti, and overhead the blue sky, a reddish ball. What is he doing here? How did he get here? At what point did he leave the trench? Something about a supply train rings in his ears again, repeated in an anguished, sobbing voice. It costs him a superhuman effort to turn his head. He then spies the little soldier. He feels relieved; he was afraid it was an Englishman. The little soldier is lying face down, less than a yard away, delirious, and the sergeant can barely make out what he is saying because the man's mouth is against the ground. 'Do you have any water?' he asks him. Pain stabs the sergeant's brain like a red-hot iron. He closes his eyes and tries his best to control his panic. Has he been hit by a bullet? Where? With another enormous effort, he looks at himself: a sharp-edged root is sticking out of his belly. It takes him a while to realize that the curved lance has not only gone straight through him but has pinned him to the ground. 'I'm run through, I'm nailed down,' he thinks. He thinks: 'They'll give me a medal.' Why can't he move his hands, his feet? How have they been able to carve him up like this without his seeing or hearing? Has he lost much blood? He doesn't want to look at his belly again.

He turns to the little soldier. 'Help me, help me,' he begs, feeling his head splitting. 'Pull this out of me. Unpin me. We have to climb up the ravine, let's help each other.'

All of a sudden, it strikes him as stupid to be talking about climbing up that ravine when he can't even move a finger.

'They took all the supplies, and all the ammunition, too,' the little soldier whimpers. 'It's not my fault, sir. It's Colonel Campelo's fault.'

He hears him sob like a babe in arms and it occurs to him that he's drunk. He feels hatred and anger toward this bastard who's sniveling instead of pulling himself together and going to fetch help. The little soldier lifts his head and looks at him.

'Are you from the Second Infantry?' the sergeant asks him, noticing as he speaks how stiff his tongue feels. 'From Colonel Silva Telles's brigade?'

'No, sir,' the little soldier says, screwing up his face and weeping. 'I'm from the Fifth Infantry of the Third Brigade. Colonel Olímpio da Silveira's brigade.'

'Don't cry, don't be stupid, come over here and help me get this thing out of my belly,' the sergeant says. 'Come here, you son of a bitch.'

But the little soldier buries his head in the dirt and weeps.

'In other words, you're one of those we came to rescue from the English,' the sergeant says. 'Come over here and save me now, you idiot.'

'They took everything we had away from us! They stole everything!' the little soldier whimpers. 'I told Colonel Campelo that the convoy shouldn't fall so far behind, that we could be cut off from the column. I told him, I told him! And that's what happened, sir! They even stole my horse!'

'Forget the convoy they robbed you of, pull this thing out of me!' Frutuoso calls out. 'Do you want us to die like dogs? Don't be an idiot – think about it!'

'The porters double-crossed us! The guides double-crossed us!' the little soldier whines. 'They were spies, sir, they fired on us with shotguns, too. Count things up for yourself. Twenty carts with ammunition, seven with salt, flour, sugar, cane brandy, alfalfa, forty sacks of maize. And they made off with more than a hundred head of cattle, sir! Do you see what an insane thing Colonel Campelo did? I warned him. I'm Captain Manuel and I never lie, sir: it was his fault.'

'You're a captain?' Frutuoso Medrado stammers. 'A thousand pardons, sir. Your gold braid isn't showing.'

The reply is a death rattle. His neighbor is silent and motionless. 'He's dead,' Frutuoso Medrado thinks. He feels a shiver run down his spine. He thinks: 'A captain! I took him for a raw recruit.' He, too, is going to die at any moment. The Englishmen got the better of you, Frutuoso. Those goddamned foreign bastards have killed you. And just then he sees two figures silhouetted on the edge of the ravine. The sweat running into his eyes keeps him from making out whether or not they are wearing uniforms, but he shouts 'Help, help!' nonetheless. He tries to move, to twist about, so that they'll see that he's alive and come down. His big head is a brazier. The silhouettes leap down the side of the ravine and he feels that he is about to burst into tears when he realizes that they're dressed in light blue and are wearing army boots. He tries to shout: 'Pull this stick out of my belly, boys.'

'Do you recognize me, Sergeant? Do you know who I am?' says the soldier who, like an imbecile, instead of squatting down to unpin him, stands there resting the tip of his bayonet on his neck.

'Of course I recognize you, Coríntio,' he roars. 'What did you think, you idiot? Pull this thing out of my belly! What are you doing, Coríntio? Coríntio!'

Florisa's husband is plunging his bayonet into his neck beneath the revolted gaze of the other one, whom Frutuoso Medrado also recognizes: Argimiro. He manages to say to himself that Coríntio did know, after all.

III

'Why wouldn't those who took to the streets to lynch monarchists have believed it, down there in Rio, in São Paulo, if those who were at the very gates of Canudos and could see the truth with their own eyes believed it?' the nearsighted journalist asked.

He had slid out of the leather armchair and was now sitting on the floor with his knees doubled up and his chin resting on one of them, speaking as though the baron weren't there. It was early in the afternoon and the study was filled with sunlight, so warm it made one drowsy, filtering through the lace curtains of the window overlooking the garden. The baron had become used to the journalist's habit of suddenly changing the subject without warning, in obedience to his own urgent inner promptings, and was no longer bothered by a conversation with him that proceeded by fits and starts, intense and sparkling for a time, then bogged down in the long empty periods that ensued when he, or the journalist, or both, lapsed into silence to reflect or remember.

'The press correspondents,' the nearsighted journalist explained, contorting himself in one of his unpredictable movements that made his skeleton-like frame shake all over and appeared to make each one of his vertebrae shudder. His eyes blinked rapidly behind his glasses. 'They could see and yet they didn't see. All they saw was what they'd come to see. Even if there was no such thing there. It wasn't just one or two of them. They all found glaring proof of a British-monarchist conspiracy. How to explain that?'

'People's credulity, their hunger for fantasy, for illusion,' the baron said. 'There had to be some explanation for the inconceivable fact that bands of peasants and vagabonds routed three army expeditions, that they resisted the armed forces of this country for months on end. The conspiracy had to exist: that's why they invented it and why they believed it.'

'You should read the dispatches my replacement sent back to the *Jornal de Notícias*,' the nearsighted journalist said. 'The one sent up there as a correspondent when Epaminondas Gonçalves thought I was dead. A good man. Honest, with no imagination, no passionate biases, no convictions. The ideal man to provide an impassive, objective version of what happened up there.'

'They were dying and killing on both sides,' the baron murmured, gazing at him with pity. 'Are impassivity and objectivity possible in a war?'

'In his first dispatch, the officers of General Oscar's column come upon four fair-haired observers in well-cut suits mingled with the *jagunços*,' the journalist said slowly. 'In the second, General Savaget's column finds among the dead *jagunços* an individual with white skin, blond hair, an officer's leather shoulder belt, and a hand-knitted cap. No one can identify his uniform, which has never been worn by any of this country's military units.'

'One of Her Gracious Majesty's officers, no doubt?' The baron smiled.

'And in the third dispatch he quotes the text of a letter, found in the pocket of a *jagunço* taken prisoner, which is unsigned but written in an unmistakably aristocratic hand,' the journalist went on, not even hearing his question. 'Addressed to the Counselor, explaining to him why it is necessary to reestablish a conservative, God-fearing monarchy. Everything points to the fact that the person who wrote that letter was you.'

'Were you really so naïve as to believe everything you read in the papers?' the baron asked him. 'You, a journalist?'

'And there is also the dispatch of his about signaling with lights,' the nearsighted journalist went on, without answering him. 'Thanks to such signals, the *jagunços* were able to communicate with each other at night over great distances. The mysterious lights blinked on and off, transmitting a code so clever that army signal corps technicians were never able to decipher the messages.'

Yes, there was no doubt about it, despite his bohemian pranks, despite the opium, the ether, the *candomblés*, there was something ingenuous and angelic about him. This was not strange; it was often the case with intellectuals and artists. Canudos had changed him, naturally. What had it made of him? An embittered man? A skeptic? A fanatic, perhaps? The myopic eyes stared at him intently from behind the thick lenses.

'The important thing in these dispatches are the intimations,' the metallic, incisive, high-pitched voice said. 'Not what they say but what they suggest, what's left to the reader's imagination. They went to Canudos to see English officers. And they saw them. I talked with my replacement for an entire afternoon. He never once lied deliberately, he just didn't realize he was lying. The simple fact is that he didn't write what he saw but what he felt and believed, what those all around him felt and believed. That's how that whole tangled web of false stories and humbug got woven, becoming so intricate that there is now no way to disentangle it. How is anybody ever going to know the story of Canudos?'

'As you yourself see, the best thing to do is forget it,' the baron said. 'It isn't worth wasting your time over it.'

'Cynicism is no solution, either,' the nearsighted journalist said. 'Moreover, I can scarcely believe that this attitude of yours, this proud disdain for what really happened, is sincere.'

'It is indifference, not disdain,' the baron corrected him. The thought of Estela had been far from his mind for some time, but it was there again now and with it the pain, as mordant as acid, that turned him into a completely crushed, cowed being. 'I've already told you that what happened at Canudos doesn't matter to me in the slightest.'

'It does matter to you, Baron,' the vibrant voice of the nearsighted journalist interjected. 'For the same reason it matters to me: because Canudos changed your life. Because of Canudos your wife lost her mind, because of Canudos you lost a large part of your fortune and your power. Of course it matters to you. It's for that reason that you haven't thrown me out, for that reason that we've been talking together for so many hours now . . .'

Yes, perhaps he was right. The Baron de Canabrava was suddenly aware of a bitter taste in his mouth; although he had had more than enough of the man and there was no reason to prolong the conversation, he found himself unable to dismiss him. What was keeping him from it? He finally admitted the truth to himself: it was the idea of being left all alone, alone with Estela, alone with that terrible tragedy.

'But they didn't merely see what didn't exist,' the nearsighted journalist went on. 'Besides that, none of them saw what was really there.'

'Phrenologists?' the baron murmured. 'Scottish anarchists?'

'Priests,' the nearsighted journalist said. 'Nobody mentions them. And there they were, spying for the *jagunços* or fighting shoulder to shoulder with them. Relaying information or bringing medicine, smuggling in saltpeter and sulfur to make explosives. Isn't that surprising? Wasn't that of any importance?'

'Are you certain of that?' the baron said, pricking up his ears.

'I knew one of those priests. I might even go so far as to say that we became friends,' the nearsighted journalist said, nodding his head. 'Father Joaquim, the parish priest of Cumbe.'

The baron looked closely at his caller. 'That little curé who's fathered a whole pack of kids? That toper who regularly commits all the seven capital sins was in Canudos?'

'It's an excellent index of the Counselor's powers of persuasion,' the journalist asserted, nodding again. 'He not only turned thieves and murderers into saints; he also catechized the corrupt and simoniacal priests of the *sertão*. A disquieting man, wouldn't you say?'

That episode from years back seemed to leap to the baron's mind from the depths of time. He and Estela, escorted by a small band of armed *capangas*, had just entered Cumbe and had headed immediately for the church on hearing the bells ring summoning people to Sunday Mass. Try as he might, the notorious Father Joaquim was unable to hide the traces of what must have been a night of debauchery – guitars, cane brandy, womanizing – without a wink of sleep. The baron remembered how vexed the baroness had been on seeing the priest stumble over the liturgy and make mistakes, begin to retch violently right in the middle of Mass, and dash from the altar to go vomit outside. He could even see vividly once again in his mind's eye the face of the curé's concubine: wasn't it the young woman whom people called 'the water divineress' because she knew how to detect unsuspected underground wells? So that rake of a curé had also become one of the Counselor's faithful followers, had he?

'Yes, one of his faithful followers, and also something of a hero.' The journalist broke into one of those bursts of laughter that sounded like light stones sliding down his throat; as usually happened, this time, too, his laughter turned into a fit of sneezing.

'He was a sinful curé but he wasn't an idiot,' the baron reflected. 'When he was sober, one could have a decent conversation with him. A man with a lively mind and one who was even fairly well read. I find it difficult to believe that he, too, would fall under the spell of a charlatan, like the unlettered people of the backlands . . .'

'Culture, intelligence, books have nothing to do with the story of the Counselor,' the nearsighted journalist said. 'But that's the least of it. The surprising thing is not that Father Joaquim became a *jagunço.* It's that the Counselor made a brave man of him, when before he'd been a coward.' He blinked in stupefaction. 'That's the most difficult, the most miraculous conversion of all. I can personally testify to that, for I know what fear is. And the little curé of Cumbe was a man with enough imagination to know what it's like to be seized with panic, to live in terror. And yet . . .'

His voice grew hollow, emptied of substance, and the expression on his face became a grimace. What had happened to him all of a sudden? The baron saw that his caller was doing his utmost to calm down, to break through something that was holding him back. He tried to help him go on. 'And yet . . .?' he said encouragingly.

'And yet he spent months, years perhaps, going all about the villages, the haciendas, the mines, buying gunpowder, dynamite, fuses. Making up elaborate lies to justify these purchases that must have attracted a great deal of attention. And when the *sertão* began to swarm with soldiers, do you know how he risked his neck? By hiding powder kegs in his coffer containing the sacred objects of worship, the tabernacle, the ciborium with the consecrated Hosts, the crucifix, the chasuble, the vestments that he carried about to say Mass. And smuggling them into Canudos right under the noses of the National Guard, of the army. Can you have any idea of what that means when you're a coward, trembling from head to foot, bathed in cold sweat? Can you have any idea of how strong a conviction that takes?'

'The catechism is full of stories like that, my friend,' the baron murmured. 'Martyrs pierced with arrows, devoured by lions, crucified . . . But, I grant you, it is difficult for me to imagine Father Joaquim doing things like that for the Counselor.'

'It requires total conviction,' the journalist repeated. 'Profound, complete certainty, a faith that doubtless you have never felt. Nor I . . .'

He shook his head once more like a restless hen and hoisted himself into the armchair with his long, bony arms. He played with his hands for a few seconds, focusing all his attention on them, and then went on. 'The Church has formally condemned the Counselor as a heretic, a believer in superstition, a disseminator of unrest, and a disturber of the conscience of the faithful. The Archbishop of Bahia has forbidden parish priests to allow him to preach in their pulpits. If one is a priest, it takes absolute faith in the Counselor to disobey the Church and one's own archbishop and run the risk of being condemned for helping him.'

'What is it you find so distressing?' the baron asked. 'The suspicion that the Counselor was really another Christ, come for the second time to redeem men?'

He said this without thinking, and the minute the words were out of his mouth he felt uncomfortable. Had he been trying to make a joke? Neither he nor the nearsighted journalist smiled, however. He saw the latter shake his head, which might have been a reply in the negative or a gesture to chase a fly away.

'I've thought about that, too,' the nearsighted journalist said. 'If it was God, if God sent him, if God existed . . . I don't know. In any event, this time there were no disciples left to spread the myth and bring the good news to the pagans. There was only one left, as far as I know; I doubt that that's sufficient . . .'

He burst out laughing again and the ensuing sneezes occupied him for some time. When he had finished, his nose and eyes were badly irritated.

'But more than of his possible divinity, I thought of the spirit of solidarity, of fraternity, of the unbreakable bond that he was able to forge among those people,' the nearsighted journalist said in a pathetic tone of voice. 'Amazing. Moving. After July 18, the only trails left open were the ones to Chorrochó and Riacho Seco. What would have been the logical thing to do? For people to try to get away, to escape along those trails, isn't that true? But exactly the opposite happened. People tried to come to Canudos, they kept flocking in from all over, in a desperate hurry to get inside the rat trap, the hell, before the soldiers completely encircled Canudos. Do you see? Nothing was normal there . . .'

'You spoke of priests in the plural,' the baron interrupted him. This subject, the *jagunços'* solidarity and their collective will to sacrifice themselves, was disturbing to him. It had turned up several times in the conversation, and each time he had skirted it, as he did again now.

'I didn't know the other ones,' the journalist replied, as though he, too, were relieved at having been obliged to change the subject. 'But they existed. Father Joaquim received information and help from them. And at the end they, too, may very well have been there, scattered about, lost among the multitudes of *jagunços*. Someone told me of a certain Father Martinez. Do you know who it was? Someone you knew, a long time ago, many years ago. The filicide of Salvador – does that mean anything to you?'

'The filicide of Salvador?' the baron said.

'I was present at her trial, when I was still in short pants. My father was a public defender, a lawyer for the poor, and it was he who was her defense attorney. I recognized her even though I couldn't see her, even though twenty or twenty-five years had gone by. You read the papers in those days, didn't you? The entire Northeast was passionately interested in the case of Maria Quadrado, the filicide of Salvador. The Emperor commuted her death sentence to life imprisonment. Don't you remember her? She, too, was in Canudos. Do you see how the whole thing is a story that never ends?'

'I already knew that,' the baron said. 'All those who had accounts to settle with the law, with their conscience, with God, found a refuge thanks to Canudos. It was only natural.'

'That they should take refuge there, yes, I grant you that, but not that they should become different people altogether.' As though he didn't know what to do with his body, the journalist flexed his long legs and slid back down onto the floor. 'She was the saint, the Mother of Men, the Superior of the devout women who cared for the Counselor's needs. People attributed miracles to her, and she was said to have wandered everywhere with him.'

The story gradually came back to the baron. A celebrated case, the subject of endless gossip. She was the maidservant of a notary and had suffocated her newborn baby to death by stuffing a ball of yarn in his mouth, because he cried a great deal and she was afraid that she would be thrown out in the street without a job on account of him. She kept the dead body underneath her bed for several days, till the mistress of the house discovered it because of the stench. The young woman confessed everything immediately. Throughout the trial, her manner was meek and gentle, and she answered all the questions asked her willingly and truthfully. The baron remembered the heated controversy that had arisen regarding the personality of the filicide, with one side arguing that she was 'catatonic and therefore not responsible' and the other maintaining that she was possessed of a 'perverse instinct.' Had she escaped from prison, then?

The journalist had changed the subject once more. 'Before July 18 a great many things had been hideous, but in all truth it was not until that day that I touched and smelled and swallowed the horror till I could feel it in my guts.' The baron saw the journalist pound his fist on his stomach. 'I met her that day, I talked with her, and found out that she was the filicide that I had dreamed about so many times as a child. She helped me, for at that point I had been left all alone.'

'On July 18 I was in London,' the baron said. 'I'm not acquainted with all the details of the war. What happened that day?'

'They're going to attack tomorrow,' Abbot João said, panting for breath because he'd come on the run. Then he remembered something important: 'Praised be the Blessed Jesus.'

The soldiers had been on the mountainsides of A Favela going on a month, and the war was dragging on and on: scattered rifle shots and cannon fire, generally at the hours when the bells rang. At dawn, noon, and dusk, people walked about only in certain places. Men gradually grow accustomed to almost anything, and establish routines to deal with it, is that not true? People died every day and every night there were burials. The blind bombardments destroyed countless houses, ripped open the bellies of oldsters and of toddlers, that is to say, the ones who didn't go down into the trenches. It seemed as though everything would go on like that indefinitely. No, it was going to get even worse, the Street Commander had just told them. The nearsighted journalist was all alone, for Jurema and the Dwarf had gone off to take food to Pajeú, when the war leaders – Honório Vilanova, Big João, Pedrão, Pajeú himself – met in the store. They were worried; you could smell it; the atmosphere in the place was tense. And yet no one was surprised when Abbot João announced that the dogs were going to attack the next day. He knew everything. They were going to shell Canudos all night long, to soften up its defenses, and at 5 a.m. the assault would begin. He knew exactly which places they would charge. The *jagunço* leaders were talking quietly, deciding the best posts for each of them to take, you wait for them here, the street has to be blockaded there: we'll raise barriers here, I'd better move from over there in case they send dogs this way. Could the baron imagine what he felt like, hearing that? At that point the matter of the paper came up. What paper? One that one of Pajeú's 'youngsters' had brought, running as fast as his legs could carry him. They all put their heads together and then asked him if he could read it. He did his best, peering through his monocle of shards, in the light of a candle, to decipher what it said. But he was unable to. Then Abbot João sent someone to fetch the Lion of Natuba.

'Didn't any of the Counselor's lieutenants know how to read?' the baron asked.

'Antônio Vilanova did, but he wasn't in Canudos just then,' the journalist answered. 'And the person they sent for also knew how to read. The Lion of Natuba. Another intimate, another apostle of the Counselor's. He could read and write; he was Canudos's man of learning.'

He fell silent, interrupted by a great gust of sneezes that made him double over, clutching his stomach.

'I was unable to see in detail what he looked like,' he said afterward, gasping for breath. 'Just the vague outline, the shape of him, or, rather, the lack of shape. But that was enough for me to get a rough idea of the rest. He walked about on all fours, and had an enormous head and a hump on his back. Someone went to fetch him and he came with Maria Quadrado. He read them the paper. It was the instructions from the High Command for the assault at dawn.'

That deep, melodious, normal voice read out the battle plan, the disposition of the regiments, the distances between companies, between men, the signals, the bugle commands, and meanwhile he for his part grew more and more panic-stricken, more and more anxious for Jurema and the Dwarf to return. Before the

Lion of Natuba had finished reading, the first part of the battle plan was already being carried out: the bombardment to soften them up.

'I now know that at that moment only nine cannons were bombarding Canudos and that they never shot more than sixteen rounds at a time,' the nearsighted journalist said. 'But it seemed as if there were a thousand of them that night, as if all the stars in the sky had begun bombarding us.'

The din made the sheets of corrugated tin on the roof of the store rattle, the shelves and the counter shake, and they could hear buildings caving in, falling down, screams, feet running, and in the pauses, the inevitable howling of little children. 'It's begun,' one of the *jagunços* said. They went outdoors to see, came back in, told Maria Quadrado and the Lion of Natuba that they wouldn't be able to get back to the Sanctuary because the only way there was being swept with cannon fire, and the journalist heard the woman insist on going back. Big João finally dissuaded her by swearing that the moment the barrage let up he would come and take them back to the Sanctuary himself. The *jagunços* left, and he realized that Jurema and the Dwarf – if they were still alive – were not going to be able to get back from Rancho do Vigário to where he was either. He realized, in his boundless fear, that he would have to go through the coming attack with no one for company except the saint and the quadrumanous monster of Canudos.

'What are you laughing at now?' the Baron de Canabrava asked.

'Something I'd be ashamed to own up to,' the nearsighted journalist stammered. He sat there lost in thought and then suddenly raised his head and exclaimed: 'Canudos changed my ideas about history, about Brazil, about men. But above all else about myself.'

'To judge from your tone of voice, it hasn't been a change for the better,' the baron murmured.

'You're right there,' the journalist said, lower still. 'Thanks to Canudos, I have a very poor opinion of myself.'

Wasn't that also his own case, to a certain degree? Hadn't Canudos turned his life, his ideas, his habits topsy-turvy, like a hostile whirlwind? Hadn't his convictions and illusions fallen to pieces? The image of Estela, in her rooms upstairs, with Sebastiana at her side in her rocking chair, perhaps reading aloud to her passages from the novels that she had been fond of, perhaps combing her hair, or getting her to listen to the Austrian music boxes, and the blank, withdrawn, unreachable face of the woman who had been the great love of his life – the woman who to him had always been the very symbol of the joy of living, beauty, enthusiasm, elegance – again filled his heart with bitterness.

With an effort, he seized on the first thing that passed through his mind. 'You mentioned Antônio Vilanova,' he said hurriedly. 'The trader, isn't that right? A moneygrubber and a man as calculating as they come. I used to see a lot of him and his brother. They were the suppliers for Calumbi. Did he become a saint, too?'

'He wasn't there to do business.' The nearsighted journalist had recovered his sarcastic laugh. 'It was difficult to do business in Canudos. The coin of the Republic was not allowed to circulate there. It was the money of the Dog, of the Devil, of atheists, Protestants, Freemasons, don't you see? Why do you think the *jagunços* made off with the soldiers' weapons but never with their wallets?'

'So the phrenologist wasn't all that crazy, after all,' the baron thought. 'In a word, thanks to his own madness Gall was able to intuit something of the madness that Canudos represented.'

'Antônio Vilanova wasn't someone who went around continually crossing himself and beating his breast in remorse for his sins,' the nearsighted journalist went on. 'He was a practical man, eager to achieve concrete results. He was constantly bustling about organizing things – he reminded you of a perpetual-motion machine. All during those five endless months he took it upon himself to ensure that Canudos had enough to eat. Why would he have done that, amid all the bullets and dead bodies? There's no other explanation: the Counselor had struck some secret chord within him.'

'As he did you,' the baron said. 'He barely missed making you a saint, too.'

'He went out to bring food back till the very end,' the nearsighted journalist went on, paying no attention to what the baron had said. 'He would steal off, taking just a few men with him. They would make their way through the enemy lines, attack the supply trains. I know how they did that. They would set up an infernal racket with their blunderbusses so as to make the animals stampede. In the chaos that ensued, they would drive ten, fifteen of the bullocks to Canudos. So that those who were about to give their lives for the Blessed Jesus could fight on for a little while more.'

'Do you know where those animals came from?' the baron interrupted him.

'From the convoys that the army was sending out from Monte Santo to A Favela,' the nearsighted journalist said. 'The same place the *jagunços*' arms and ammunition came from. That was one of the oddities of this war: the army provided the supplies both for its own forces and for the enemy.'

'What the *jagunços* stole was stolen property,' the baron sighed. 'Many of those cattle and goats were once mine. Very few of them had been bought from me. Almost always they'd been cut out of my herds by gaucho rustlers hired on by the army. I have a friend who owns a hacienda, old Murau, who has filed suit against the state for the cows and sheep that the army troops ate. He's asking for seventy contos in compensation, no less.'

In his half sleep, Big João smells the sea. A warm sensation steals over him, something that feels to him like happiness. In these years in which, thanks to the Counselor, he has found relief for that painful boiling in his soul from the days when he served the Devil, there is only one thing he sometimes misses. How many years is it now that he has not seen, smelled, heard the sea in his body? He has no idea, but he knows that it has been a long, long time since he last saw it, on that high promontory amid cane fields where Mistress Adelinha Isabel de Gumúcio used to come to see sunsets. Scattered shots remind him that the battle is not yet over, but he is not troubled: his consciousness tells him that even if he were wide awake it would make no difference, since neither he nor any of the men in the Catholic Guard huddled in the trenches round about him have a single Mannlicher bullet left, not one load of shotgun pellets, not one grain of powder to set off the explosive devices manufactured by the blacksmiths of Canudos whom necessity has turned into armorers.

So why are they staying, then, in these caves on the heights, in the ravine at the foot of A Favela where the dogs are waiting, crowded one atop the other? They are following Abbot João's orders. After making sure that all the units of the first column have arrived at A Favela and are now pinned down by the fire from the *jagunço* sharpshooters who are all around on the mountainsides and are raining bullets down on them from their parapets, their trenches, their hiding places, Abbot João has gone off to try to capture the soldiers' convoy of ammunition, supplies, cattle and goats which, thanks to the topography and the harassment from Pajeú and his men, has fallen far behind. Hoping to take the convoy by surprise at As Umburanas and divert it to Canudos, Abbot João has asked Big João to see to it that the Catholic Guard, at whatever cost, keeps the regiments at A Favela from retreating. In his half sleep, the former slave tells himself that the dogs must be stupid or must have lost many men, since thus far not a single patrol has tried to make its way back to As Umburanas to see what has happened to the convoy. The Catholic Guards know that if the soldiers make the slightest move to abandon A Favela, they must fling themselves upon them and bar their way, with knives, machetes, bayonets, tooth and nail. Old Joaquim Macambira and his men, hiding in ambush on the other side of the trail cleared for the infantry and the wagons and cannons to advance on A Favela, will do likewise. The soldiers won't try to retreat; they are too intent on answering the fire in front of them and on their flanks, too busy bombarding Canudos to tumble to what is happening at their backs. 'Abbot João is more intelligent than they are,' he thinks in his sleep. Wasn't it his brilliant idea to lure the dogs to A Favela? Wasn't he the one who thought of sending Pedrão and the Vilanova brothers to wait for the other devils in the narrow pass at Cocorobó? There, too, the *jagunços* must have wiped them out. As he breathes in the smell of the sea it intoxicates him, takes him far away from the war, and he sees waves and feels the caress of the foamy water on his skin. This is the first time he has had any sleep, after forty-eight hours of fighting.

At two in the morning a messenger from Joaquim Macambira awakens him. It is one of Joaquim's sons, young and slender, with long hair, crouching patiently in the trench, waiting for Big João to rouse himself from his sleep. The boy's father needs ammunition; his men have almost no bullets or powder left. With his tongue still thick with sleep, Big João explains that his men don't have any left either. Have they had any news from Abbot João? None. And from Pedrão? The youngster nods: he and his men have had to fall back from Cocorobó; they have no ammunition left and have had heavy losses. And they have not been able to stop the dogs in Trabubu either.

Big João feels wide awake at last. Does that mean that the army advancing by way of Jeremoabo is coming here?

'Yes,' Joaquim Macambira's son answers. 'Pedrão and all the men of his who aren't dead are already back in Belo Monte.'

Maybe that is what the Catholic Guard should do: go back to Canudos to defend the Counselor from the attack that now seems inevitable if the other army is coming this way. What is Joaquim Macambira going to do? The youngster doesn't know. Big João decides to go talk to the boy's father.

It is late at night and the sky is studded with stars. After instructing his men not to budge from where they are, the former slave slips silently down the rocky slope, alongside young Macambira. Unfortunately, with so many stars out, he is able to see the dead horses with their bellies ripped open, being pecked at by the black vultures, and the body of the old woman. All the day before and part of the night he has kept coming across these officers' mounts, the first victims of the fusillade. He is certain that he himself has killed a number of them. He had to do it, for the sake of the Father and Blessed Jesus the Counselor and Belo Monte, the most precious thing in his life. He will do it again, as many times as necessary. But something within his soul protests and suffers when he sees these animals fall with a great whinny, agonize for hour after hour, with their insides spilling out on the ground and a pestilential stench in the air. He knows where this sense of guilt, of committing a sin, that possesses him every time he fires on the officers' horses comes from. It stems from the memory of the great care that was taken of the horses on the hacienda, where Master Adalberto de Gumúcio had instilled the veritable worship of horses in his family, his hired hands, his slaves. On seeing the shadowy bulks of the animals' carcasses scattered about as he goes along the trail, crouching at young Macambira's side, he wonders whether it is the Father who makes certain things that go back to the days when he was a sinner – his homesickness for the sea, his love of horses – linger so long and so vividly in his memory.

He sees the dead body of the old woman at the same time, and feels his heart pound. He has glimpsed her for only a few seconds, her face bathed in moonlight, her eyes staring in mad terror, her two remaining teeth protruding from her lips, her hair disheveled, her forehead set in a tense scowl. He has no idea what her name is, but he knows her very well; she came to settle in Belo Monte long ago, with a large family of sons, daughters, grandchildren, nieces and nephews, and homeless waifs that she had taken in, in a little mud hut on the Coração de Jesus, a narrow back street. It was the first dwelling to have been blown to bits by the Throat-Slitter's cannons. The old woman had been in the procession, and when she returned home, her hut was a heap of rubble beneath which were three of her daughters and all her nieces and nephews, a dozen young ones who slept one on top of the other on the floor and in a couple of hammocks. The woman had climbed up to the trenches at As Umburanas with the Catholic Guard when it went up on the heights there three days ago to wait for the soldiers. She had cooked and brought water to the *jagunços* from the nearby water source, along with the rest of the women, but when the shooting began, Big João and his men saw her take off amid the dust, stumble down the gravel slope, and reach the trail at the bottom where – slowly, without taking any precautions – she began wandering about among the wounded soldiers, giving them the *coup de grâce* with a little dagger. They had seen her poke about among the uniformed corpses, and before the hail of bullets blew her to pieces, she had managed to strip some of them naked, lop off their privates, and stuff them in their mouths. All during the fighting, as he saw infantrymen and cavalrymen pass by, saw them die, fire their rifles, fall over each other, trample their dead and wounded underfoot, flee from the rain of gunfire and run for their lives along the slopes of A Favela, the only way left open, Big João's eyes kept constantly looking back toward the dead body of that old woman that he has just left behind.

As he approaches a bog dotted with thornbushes, cacti, and a few scattered *imbuzeiros*, young Macambira raises the cane whistle to his lips and blows a shrill blast that sounds like a parakeet's screech. An identical blast comes in reply. Grabbing João by the arm, the youngster guides him through the bog, their feet sinking into it up to the ankles, and soon afterward the former slave is drinking from a leather canteen full of fresh sweet water, squatting on his heels alongside Joaquim Macambira beneath a shelter of boughs beyond which are many pairs of gleaming eyes.

The old man is consumed with anxiety, but Big João is surprised to discover that the one source of his anxiety is the big, extra-long, shining cannon drawn by forty bullocks that he has seen on the Jueté road. 'If A Matadeira goes into action, the dogs will blow up the towers and the walls of the Temple of the Blessed Jesus and Belo Monte will disappear,' he mutters gloomily. Big João listens to him attentively. He reveres Joaquim

Macambira; he has the air of a venerable patriarch. He is very old, his white locks fall in curls that reach down to his shoulders, his little snow-white beard sets off his dark weather-beaten face with a nose like a gnarled vine shoot. His eyes buried in deep wrinkles sparkle with uncontainable energy. He was once the owner of a large plot of land where he grew manioc and maize, between Cocorobó and Trabubu, in the region known in fact as Macambira. He worked that land with his eleven sons and had many a fight with his neighbors over boundary lines. But one day he abandoned everything and moved with his enormous family to Canudos, where they occupy half a dozen dwellings opposite the cemetery. Everyone in Belo Monte approaches the old man very warily because he has the reputation of being a fiercely proud, touchy man.

Joaquim Macambira has sent messengers to ask Abbot João whether, in view of the situation, he should continue to mount guard at As Umburanas or withdraw to Canudos. He has had no answer as yet. What does Big João think? The latter shakes his head sadly: he doesn't know what to do. On the one hand, what seems most urgent is to hasten back to Belo Monte so as to protect the Counselor in case there is an attack from the north. But, on the other hand, hasn't Abbot João said that it is essential that they protect his rear?

'Protect it with what?' Macambira roars. 'With our hands?'

'Yes,' Big João says humbly. 'If that's all there is.'

They decide that they will stay at As Umburanas until they receive word from the Street Commander. They bid each other goodbye with a simultaneous 'Praised be Blessed Jesus the Counselor.' As he starts to wade through the bog again, alone this time, Big João hears the whistles that sound like the screeching of parakeets, signaling to the *jagunços* to let him through. As he splashes through the mud and feels mosquitoes biting his face, arms, and chest, he tries to picture A Matadeira, that war machine that so alarms Macambira. It must be enormous, deadly, a thundering steel dragon that vomits fire, if it frightens as brave a man as old Macambira. The Evil One, the Dragon, the

Dog is really tremendously powerful, with endless resources, since he can keep hurling more and more enemies, better and better armed, into the battle against Canudos. For how long a time would the Father continue to test the faith of the believers of Belo Monte? Hadn't they suffered enough? Hadn't they endured enough hunger, death, privation, sorrow? No, not yet. The Counselor has told them as much: our penance will be as great as our sins. Since João's burden of sin is heavier than that of the others, he will doubtless have to pay more. But it is a great consolation to be fighting for the right cause, on St. George's side, not the Dragon's.

By the time he gets back to the trench, dawn has begun to break; the sentinels have climbed up to their posts on the rocks, but all the rest of the men, lying on the ground on the slope, are still sleeping. Big João curls up in a ball and feels himself beginning to drowse when the sound of hoofbeats causes him to leap to his feet. Enveloped in a cloud of dust, eight or ten horsemen are approaching. Scouts, the vanguard of troops come to protect the convoy? In the still-dim light a rain of arrows, stones, lances descends upon the patrol from the hillsides and he hears shots from the bog where Macambira is. The horsemen wheel their mounts around and gallop toward A Favela. Yes, he is certain now that the troops reinforcing the convoy will be appearing at any moment, countless numbers of them, too many to be held off by men whose only remaining weapons are hunting crossbows, bayonets, and knives, and Big João prays to the Father that Abbot João will have time to carry out his plan.

They appear an hour later. By this time the Catholic Guard has so thoroughly blockaded the ravine with the carcasses of horses and mules and the dead bodies of soldiers, and with flat rocks, bushes, and cacti that they roll down from the slopes, that two companies of engineers are obliged to move up to clear the trail again. It is not an easy task for them, since in addition to the curtain of fire laid down by Joaquim Macambira and his band with their very last ammunition, which forces them to fall back several times just as the engineers have started clearing the obstacles away with dynamite, Big João and some hundred men crawl over to them on their hands and knees and engage them in hand-to-hand combat. Before more soldiers appear, João and his men wound and kill a number of them and also manage to make off with several rifles and some of their precious knapsacks full of cartridges. By the time Big João gives a blast on his whistle and shouts out the order to fall back, several *jagunços* are lying on the trail, dead or dying. Once back on the slope above, protected by the stone-slab parapet against the hail of bullets from below, the former slave has time to see if he's been wounded, and finds himself unharmed. Spattered with blood, yes, but it is not his blood; he scrubs it off with fine sand. Is it the hand of Divine Providence that in three days of fighting he has not received so much as a scratch? Lying on his belly on the ground, panting for breath, he sees that the soldiers are now marching four abreast along the trail, cleared at last, headed toward the spot where Abbot João has posted himself. They go past by the dozens, by the hundreds. They're no doubt on their way to protect the convoy, since despite all the harassment from the Catholic Guard and from Macambira and his men, they are not even bothering to climb up the slopes or venture into the bog. They merely rake the slopes on both flanks with rifle fire from little groups of snipers who rest one knee on the ground as they shoot. Big João hesitates no longer. There is nothing more he can do here to help the Street Commander. He makes certain that the order to fall back reaches everyone, leaping from one crag and hillock to another, making his way from trench to trench, going over the crest line and down the other side to make sure that the women who came to cook for the men have left. They are no longer there. Then he, too, heads back toward Belo Monte.

He does so by following a meandering branch of the Vaza-Barris, which fills up only during big floods. Walking in the stony riverbed with only a trickle of water in it, João feels the chill morning air grow warmer. He works his way to the rear, checks how many dead there are, foreseeing how sad the Counselor, the Little Blessed One, the Mother of Men will be when they learn that those brothers' bodies will rot in the open air. It pains him to remember those boys, many of whom he taught to shoot a rifle, to know that they will turn into food for vultures, without a burial or a prayer over their graves. But how could they have rescued their mortal remains?

All the way back they hear shots, coming from the direction of A Favela. One *jagunço* says that it seems odd that Pajeú, Mané Quadrado, and Taramela, who are firing on the dogs from that front, should be doing so much shooting. Big João reminds him that when the ammunition was divided up, most of it was given to the men posted in those trenches forming a bulwark between Belo Monte and A Favela. And that even the blacksmiths went out there with their anvils and their bellows so as to go on melting lead for bullets right alongside the combatants. However, the moment they spy Canudos beneath little clouds of smoke which must be grenades exploding – the sun is now high in the sky and the towers of the Temple and the whitewashed dwellings are giving off dazzling reflections – Big João suddenly guesses the good news. He blinks, looks, calculates, compares. Yes, they are firing continuous rounds from the Temple of the Blessed Jesus, from the Church of Santo Antônio, from the parapets at the cemetery, as well as from the ravines of the Vaza-Barris and the Fazenda Velha. Where has all that ammunition come from? Moments later, a 'youngster' brings him a message from Abbot João.

'So he got back to Canudos!' the former slave exclaims.

'With more than a hundred head of cattle and loads of guns,' the lad says enthusiastically. 'And cases of rifle cartridges and grenades, and big drums of gunpowder. He stole all that from the dogs, and now everyone in Belo Monte is eating meat.'

Big João places one of his huge paws on the youngster's head and contains his emotion. Abbot João wants the Catholic Guard to go to the Fazenda Velha to reinforce Pajeú, and the former slave to meet him at the Vilanovas'. Big João guides his men past the line of shacks along the Vaza-Barris, a dead angle that will protect them from the gunfire from A Favela, to the Fazenda

Velha, a maze of trenches and dugouts a kilometer long, constructed by taking advantage of the twists and turns and accidents of the terrain, that is the first line of defense of Belo Monte, barely fifty yards away from the soldiers. Since his return, the *caboclo* Pajeú has been in command on this front.

When he arrives back in Belo Monte, Big João can hardly see a thing because of the dense cloud of dust that blurs everything. The gunfire is very heavy, and he hears not only the deafening rifle reports but also the sound of roof tiles breaking, walls collapsing, and sheets of corrugated tin clanging. The 'youngster' takes him by the hand: he knows where there are no bullets falling. In these two days of fusillades and cannonades people have learned the geography of safety and go back and forth only along certain streets and certain angles of each street so as to be sheltered from the heavy fire. The cattle that Abbot João has brought in are being butchered in the narrow Rua do Espírito Santo, which has been converted into a cattle pen and an abattoir, and there is a long line of oldsters, women, and children waiting there for their share, while Campo Grande resembles a military encampment because of the number of cases of ammunition and barrels and kegs of powder amid which a great many *jagunços* are bustling back and forth. The pack mules that have hauled in this load are clearly marked with regimental brands and some of them have bloody whiplashes; they are braying in terror at the din. Big João sees a dead burro that emaciated dogs are devouring amid swarms of flies. He spies Antônio and Honório Vilanova, standing on a wooden platform; with shouts and gestures, they are supervising the distribution of the cases of ammunition, which are being carried off by pairs of young *jagunços*, who take off with them on the run, hugging the sides of the dwellings facing south; some of them are little more than children, like the 'youngster' with him, who will not allow him to go see the Vilanovas even for a moment and imperiously herds him toward the onetime steward's house of Canudos, where, he tells him, the Street Commander is waiting for him. It was Pajeú's idea to have the kids of Belo Monte serve as messengers, now known as 'youngsters.' When he proposed this, right here in the Vilanovas' store, Abbot João said that it was risky; they weren't responsible and their memories couldn't be trusted. But Pajeú insisted, claiming the contrary: in his experience, children had been swift, efficient, and also loyal and steadfast. 'It was Pajeú who was right,' the former slave thinks, seeing the little hand that does not let go of his until he has led him straight to Abbot João, who is leaning on the counter calmly eating and drinking as he listens to Pedrão, along with a dozen other *jagunços* around him. When he catches sight of Big João he motions to him to come over and gives him a hearty handshake. Big João wants to tell him how he feels, to thank him, to congratulate him for having brought in those arms, that ammunition and food, but as always, something holds him back, intimidates him, embarrasses him: only the Counselor is able to break through that barrier which ever since childhood has prevented him from sharing his intimate feelings with people. He greets the others, nodding or patting them on the back. He suddenly feels dead tired and squats down on his heels. Assunção Sardelinha places a bowlful of roast meat and manioc meal and a jug of water in his hands. For a time he forgets the war and who he is, and eats and drinks with gusto. When he is through, he notices that Abbot João, Pedrão, and the others are standing there silently, waiting for him to finish, and he feels embarrassed. He stammers an apology.

He is in the middle of explaining to them what has happened in As Umburanas when the indescribable roar lifts him off the floor and jolts every bone in his body. For a few seconds they all remain motionless, crouching with their hands over their ears, feeling the stones, the roof, the merchandise on the shelves of the store shake, as though everything were about to shatter into a thousand pieces from the interminable aftershock of the explosion.

'See what I mean, all of you?' old Joaquim Macambira, covered with so much mud and dust that he is barely recognizable, bellows as he enters the store. 'Do you see now what a monstrous thing A Matadeira is, Abbot João?'

Instead of answering him, the latter orders the 'youngster' who has brought Big João there – and who has been thrown into Pedrão's arms by the explosion, from which he emerges with his face transfixed with fear – to go see if the cannon blast has damaged the Temple of the Blessed Jesus or the Sanctuary. Then he motions to Macambira to sit down and have something to eat. But the old man is all upset, and as he nibbles on the chunk of meat that Antônia Sardelinha hands him, he goes on and on about A Matadeira, his voice full of fear and hatred. Big João hears him mutter: 'If we don't do something, it'll bury us.'

And all of a sudden Big João sees before him, in a peaceful dream, a troop of spirited chestnut horses galloping down a sandy beach and leaping into the white sea-foam. The scent of cane fields, of fresh molasses, of crushed cane perfumes the air. But the joy of seeing these horses with their shining coats, whinnying joyfully in the cool ocean waves, is soon ended, for suddenly the long muzzle of the deadly war machine emerges from the bottom of the sea, spitting fire like the Dragon that Oxóssi, in the voodoo rites of the Mocambo, slays with a gleaming sword. Someone says in a booming voice: 'The Devil will win.' His terror awakens him.

Through eyelids sticky with sleep, in the flickering light of an oil lamp, he sees three people eating: the woman, the blind man, and the dwarf who came to Belo Monte with Father Joaquim. Night has fallen, there is no one left in the store, he has slept for hours. He feels such remorse that it brings him wide awake. 'What's happened?' he cries, leaping to his feet. The blind man drops a chunk of meat and he sees his fingers fumble all about on the floor for it.

'I told them they should let you sleep,' he hears Abbot João's voice say and sees his sturdy silhouette emerge from the shadow. 'Praised be Blessed Jesus the Counselor,' the former slave murmurs and starts to apologize, but the Street Commander cuts him short: 'You needed sleep, Big João – nobody can live without sleeping.' He sits down on top of a barrel alongside the oil lamp, and the former slave sees that he is exhausted, his face deathly pale, his eyes sunken, his forehead deeply furrowed. 'While I was lost in dreams of horses, you were out fighting, running, helping,' he thinks. He feels so guilty that he scarcely notices when the Dwarf comes over to them with a tinful of water. After he has drunk from it, Abbot João passes it to him.

The Counselor is safe and sound in the Sanctuary, and the atheists have not budged from A Favela; from time to time there is a burst of gunfire. There is a worried expression on Abbot João's tired face. 'What's happening, João? Is there something I can do?' The Street Commander looks at him affectionately. Though they seldom talk together, the former slave has known, ever since their days of wandering all about with the Counselor, that the former *cangaceiro* esteems him: he has demonstrated the respect and admiration he feels for him many a time.

'Joaquim Macambira and his sons are going to climb to the top of A Favela to silence A Matadeira,' he says to him. The three persons sitting on the floor stop eating and the blind man cranes his neck, his right eye glued to that monocle of his that is a patchwork of slivers of glass glued together. 'They'll have trouble getting up there. But if they manage to, they can put it out of commission. It's easy. All they have to do then is smash the detonating mechanism or blow up the chamber.'

'Can I go with them?' Big João breaks in. 'I'll ram powder down the barrel and blow it to pieces.'

'You can help the Macambiras get up there,' Abbot João answers. 'But you can't go all the way with them, Big João. Just help them get up there. It's their plan, their decision. Come on, let's go.'

As they are leaving, the Dwarf goes over to Abbot João and says to him in a sweet, fawning voice: 'Whenever you'd like, I'll recite the Terrible and Exemplary Story of Robert the Devil for you, Abbot João.' The former *cangaceiro* pushes him aside without answering.

Outside, it is pitch-dark and foggy. There is not one star in the sky. There is no gunfire to be heard, and not a soul in sight on Campo Grande. Nor a single light in any of the dwellings. The captured animals have been taken, once night fell, to pens behind the Mocambo. The narrow street of Espírito Santo reeks of butchered meat and dried blood, and as he listens to the Macambiras' plan, Big João is aware of the countless flies hovering above the remains of the slaughtered animals that the dogs are poking through. They go up Campo Grande to the esplanade between the churches, fortified on all four sides with double and triple barriers of bricks, stones, large wooden boxes full of dirt, overturned carts, barrels, doors, tin drums, stakes, behind which hordes of armed men are posted. They are stretched out on the ground resting, talking together around little braziers, and on one of the street corners a group of them are singing, accompanied by a guitar. 'Why is it men can't resist staying up all night without sleeping even if what's at stake is saving their souls or burning in hell forever?' he thinks in torment.

At the door of the Sanctuary, hidden behind a tall parapet of sandbags and boxes filled with dirt, they talk with the men of the Catholic Guard as they wait for the Macambiras. The old man, his eleven sons, and their wives are with the Counselor. Big João mentally selects which of the sons the father will be taking with him and thinks to himself that he would like to hear what the Counselor is saying to his family about to make this sacrifice for the Blessed Jesus. When they come out, the old man's eyes are shining. The Little Blessed One and Mother Maria Quadrado accompany them as far as the parapet and bless them. The Macambiras embrace their wives, who cling to them and burst into tears. But Joaquim Macambira puts an end to the scene by saying that it is time to leave. The women go off with the Little Blessed One to the Temple to pray.

As they head for the trenches at Fazenda Velha, they pick up the equipment that Abbot João has ordered: crossbars, wedges, petards, axes, hammers. The old man and his sons hand them round without a word, as Abbot João explains to them that the Catholic Guards will distract the dogs by making a feigned attack while the Macambiras are crawling up to A Matadeira. 'Let's see if the "youngsters" have located it,' he says.

Yes, they have located it. Pajeú confirms that they have, on meeting João and his men at Fazenda Velha. A Matadeira is on the first rise, immediately behind Monte Mário, alongside the first column's other cannons. They have placed them in a line, between bags and barrels filled with stones. Two 'youngsters' have crawled up there and, after crossing through no-man's-land and the line of dead sharpshooters, counted three sentry posts on the almost vertical sides of A Favela.

Big João leaves Abbot João and the Macambiras with Pajeú and slips through the labyrinth that has been excavated along this stretch of land bordering the Vaza-Barris. From these tunnels and dugouts the *jagunços* have inflicted their worst punishment on the soldiers who, once they reached the heights and spied Canudos, rushed down the mountainsides to the city lying at the bottom of them. The terrible fusillade stopped them in their tracks, made them turn tail, run about in circles, collide with each other, knock each other down, trample each other as they discovered that they could neither retreat nor advance nor escape on the flanks and that their only choice was to throw themselves flat on the ground and set up defenses. Big João picks his way between sleeping *jagunços*; every so often, a sentry jumps down from the parapets to talk to him. He awakens forty men of the Catholic Guard and explains to them what they are to do. He is not surprised to learn that there have been practically no casualties in this maze of trenches; Abbot João had foreseen that the topography would offer the *jagunços* more protection there than anywhere else.

On his return to Fazenda Velha with the forty Catholic Guards, he finds Abbot João and Joaquim Macambira in the midst of an argument. The Street Commander wants the Macambiras to put on soldiers' uniforms, claiming that this will better their chances of getting to the cannon. Joaquim Macambira indignantly refuses.

'I don't want to be condemned to hell,' he growls.

'You won't be. It's so that you and your sons will get back alive.'

'My life and my sons' are our business,' the old man thunders.

'Do as you please,' Abbot João says resignedly. 'May the Father be with you, then.'

'Praised be Blessed Jesus the Counselor,' the old man says in farewell.

As they are entering no-man's-land, the moon comes out. Big João swears under his breath and he hears his men muttering. It is an enormous round yellow moon whose pale light drives away the shadows and reveals the stretch of bare ground, without vegetation, that disappears from sight in the pitch-blackness of A Favela above. Pajeú accompanies them to the foot of the slope. Big João cannot help mulling over the same thought as before: how could he have slept when everyone else was still awake? He takes a sidelong glance at Pajeú's face. How many days has he gone without sleep now – three, four? He has harassed the dogs all the way from Monte Santo, he has sniped at them at Angico and at As Umburanas, has gone back to Canudos to harry them from there, which he has been doing for two days now, and here he is, still fresh, calm, distant, guiding him and the others along with the two 'youngsters' who will take his place to guide them up on the slope. 'He wouldn't have fallen asleep,' Big João thinks. 'The Devil made me fall asleep,' he thinks. He gives a start; despite the many years that have gone by and the peace the Counselor has brought him, every so often he is tormented by the suspicion that the Demon that entered his body on that long-ago afternoon when he killed Adelinha de Gumúcio is still lurking in the dark shadows of his soul, waiting for the right moment to damn him again.

The steep, nearly vertical face of the mountain suddenly looms up before them. João wonders if old Macambira will be able to scale it. Pajeú points to the line of dead sharpshooters, clearly visible in the moonlight. There are many of them; they were the vanguard and they all fell at the same height on the mountainside, mowed down by the *jagunços'* fusillade. Big João can see the studs on their chest belts, the gilt emblems on their caps gleaming in the half light. Pajeú takes his leave of the others with an almost imperceptible nod and the two 'youngsters' begin to clamber up the slope on all fours. Big João and Joaquim Macambira follow after them, also on all fours, and after them the Catholic Guards. They climb so cautiously that even João can't hear them. What little noise they make, the clatter of the pebbles they send rolling down the mountainside, seems to be the work of the wind. At his back, down below, he can hear a constant murmur rising from Belo Monte. Are they reciting the Rosary in the church square? Is it the hymns that Canudos sings as it buries the day's dead each night? He can now see figures, lights, and hear voices up ahead of him, and tenses all his muscles, ready for whatever may happen.

The 'youngsters' signal to them to halt. They are near a sentry post; four soldiers standing, and behind them many soldiers silhouetted against the glow of a campfire. Old Macambira crawls over to him and Big João hears his labored breathing and the words: 'When you hear the whistle, fire away.' He nods. 'May the Blessed Jesus be with you all, Dom Joaquim.' He sees the shadows swallow up the twelve Macambiras, bent under the crushing weight of their hammers, crowbars, and axes, and the 'youngster' who is guiding them. The other 'youngster' stays behind with Big João and his men.

His every nerve taut, he waits there among them for the whistle signaling that the Macambiras have reached A Matadeira. It is a long time coming, so long that it seems to Big João that he is never going to hear it. When – a sudden long wail – it drowns out all the other sounds, he and his men all fire at once at the sentries. An earsplitting fusillade begins all round him. Chaos ensues, and the soldiers put out their campfire. They shoot back from above, but they have not spotted them, for the shots are not aimed in their direction.

Big João orders his men to advance, and a moment later they are shooting and setting off petards in the dark against the camp, where they hear feet running, voices, confused orders. Once he has emptied his rifle, João crouches down and listens. There also seems to be shooting up above, in the direction of Monte Mário.

Are the Macambiras having a skirmish with the artillerymen? In any event, it's no use going up there; his men, too, have used up all their ammunition. With his whistle, he gives the order to withdraw.

Halfway down the mountainside, a slight little figure catches up with them, running hard. Big João puts his hand on the long, tangled locks.

'Did you take them to A Matadeira?' he asks the boy.

'Yes, I did,' he answers.

There is loud rifle fire behind them, as though the war was raging all over A Favela. The boy says no more and Big João thinks, yet again, of the strange habits of *sertanejos*, who would rather keep still than talk.

'And what happened to the Macambiras?' he finally asks.

'They were killed,' the boy says softly.

'All of them?'

'I think so.'

They have already reached no-man's-land, halfway back to the trenches.

The Dwarf found the nearsighted man hunched over in a fold in the terrain of Cocorobó weeping as Pedrão's men were withdrawing. He took him by the hand and guided him along among the *jagunços* hurrying back to Belo Monte as fast as they could, convinced that the soldiers of the second column, once they had broken through the Trabubu barrier, would attack the city. The following morning, as they were going along a trench in front of the goat pens, they came upon Jurema in the midst of a great throng: she was walking along between the Sardelinha sisters, prodding an ass loaded with panniers. Filled with emotion, the three of them embraced each other, and the Dwarf felt the touch of Jurema's lips on his cheek. That night, as they lay on the floor of the store behind the barrels and boxes, listening to the gunfire raking Canudos without letup, the Dwarf told them that, as far as he could recall, that kiss was the very first one anyone had ever given him.

How many days was it that the cannons roared, rifles cracked, grenades exploded, blackening the air and chipping the towers of the Temple? Three, four, five? They wandered around the store, saw the Vilanova brothers and the others come in by day and by night, heard them talking together and giving orders, and didn't have the least idea what was going on. One afternoon, as the Dwarf was filling little pouches and horns with gunpowder for the blunderbusses and flintlock muskets, he heard one of the *jagunços* say, pointing to the explosives: 'I hope your walls are solid, Antônio Vilanova. Just one bullet could set all this off and blow the whole neighborhood to bits.' The Dwarf did not pass that on to his companions. Why make the nearsighted man more terrified than he already was? The things they had lived through together up here had made him feel an affection for the two of them that he had never felt even for the circus people with whom he got along best.

During the bombardment he went out twice, in search of food. Hugging the walls, like everyone else out in the streets, he went begging from door to door, blinded by the dust in the air, deafened by the gunfire. On the Rua da Madre Igreja he saw a child die. The little boy had come chasing after a hen that was running down the street flapping its wings, and after just a few steps his eyes opened wide and his feet suddenly left the ground, as though he had been yanked up by the hair. The bullet hit him in the belly, killing him instantly. He carried the dead body into the house that he had seen the boy run out of, and since there was no one there he left it in the hammock. He was unable to catch the hen. The morale of the three of them, despite the uncertainty and the death toll, improved once they had food again, thanks to the animals that Abbot João had brought back to Belo Monte.

Night had fallen, there was a letup in the barrage, the sound of prayers in the church square had died away, and they were lying awake on the floor of the store, talking together. All of a sudden, a silent figure appeared in the doorway, with a little clay lamp in its hands. The Dwarf recognized by the scar and the steely eyes that it was Pajeú. He had a shotgun over his shoulder, a machete and a dagger in his belt, and two cartridge belts across his shirt.

'With all due respect,' he murmured, 'I would like you to be my wife.'

The Dwarf heard the nearsighted man moan. It struck him as an extraordinary thing for that man – so reserved, so gloomy, so glacial – to have said. He sensed a great anxiety behind that face pulled taut by the scar. No shooting, barking of dogs, reciting of litanies could be heard, only the buzzing of a bumblebee bumping against the wall. The Dwarf's heart was pounding; it was not fear but a feeling of warmth and compassion toward that man with the disfigured face who was staring intently at Jurema by the light of the little lamp, waiting. He could hear the nearsighted man's anxious breathing. Jurema did not say a word. Pajeú began to speak again, uttering each word slowly and distinctly. He had not been married before, not in the way the Church, the Father, the Counselor demanded. His eyes never left Jurema, they didn't even blink, and the Dwarf thought that it was stupid of him to feel pity for a man so greatly feared. But at that moment Pajeú seemed like a terribly lonely man. He had had passing love affairs, of the sort that leave no trace, but no family, no children. His way of life had not permitted such a thing: always moving about, fleeing, fighting. Hence he understood the Counselor very well when he explained that the weary earth, exhausted from being made to bring forth the same thing again and again, one day asks to rest in peace. That was what Belo Monte had been for Pajeú, something like the earth's repose. His life had been empty of love. But now . . . The Dwarf noticed that he was swallowing hard and the thought crossed his mind that the Sardelinha sisters had awakened and were lying in the dark listening to Pajeú. It was a worry of his, something that woke him up in the night: had his heart hardened forever for lack of love? He stammered and the Dwarf thought: 'Neither the blind man nor I exist for him.' No, it had not hardened: he had seen Jurema in the *caatinga* and suddenly realized that. Something strange happened to his scar: it was the flame of the little lamp, which as it flickered made his face look even more disfigured. 'His hand is trembling,' the Dwarf thought in amazement. That day his heart, his feelings, his soul began to speak. Thanks to Jurema he had discovered that he was not hard inside. Her face, her body, her voice were always present here and here. With a brusque gesture, he touched his head and his breast, and the little flame went up and down. Again he fell silent, waiting, and the bee could again be heard buzzing and thudding against the wall. Jurema still said nothing. The Dwarf looked at her out of the corner of his eye: sitting there all hunched up as though to protect herself, she was gravely meeting the *caboclo*'s gaze.

'We can't get married right now. Right now I have another obligation,' Pajeú added, as though in apology. 'When the dogs have gone away.'

The Dwarf heard the nearsighted man moan. This time, too, the *caboclo*'s eyes never left Jurema to look at her neighbor. But there was one thing . . . Something he'd thought a lot about, these days, as he tracked the atheists and shot them down. Something that would gladden his heart. He fell silent, was overcome with embarrassment, struggled to get the words out: would Jurema bring food, water, to him at Fazenda Velha? It was something he envied the others for, something that he, too, would like to have. Would she do that?

'Yes, yes, she'll do it, she'll bring them to you,' the Dwarf, to his stupefaction, heard the nearsighted man say. 'She'll do it, she'll do it.'

But even this time the *caboclo*'s eyes did not turn his way. 'What is he to you?' the Dwarf heard him ask Jurema, his voice as cutting as a knife now. 'He's not your husband, is he?'

'No,' she answered very softly. 'He's . . . like my son.'

The night rang with shots. First one volley, then another, extremely heavy fire. They heard shouts, feet running, an explosion.

'I'm happy to have come, to have talked to you,' the *caboclo* said. 'I must go now. Praised be the Blessed Jesus.'

A moment later the store was plunged into total darkness again and instead of the bumblebee they heard scattered shots, far off, then closer. The Vilanova brothers were in the trenches and appeared only for the meetings with Abbot João; the Sardelinha sisters spent most of the day working in the Health Houses and taking food to the combatants. The Dwarf, Jurema, and the nearsighted man were the only ones who stayed in the store all the time. It was again full of ammunition and explosives from the convoy that Abbot João had brought in, and sandbags and stones were piled against the façade to protect it.

'Why didn't you answer him?' the Dwarf heard the blind man say in an agitated voice. 'He was terribly nervous, and was forcing himself to tell you all those things. Why didn't you answer him? In the state he was in, his love might have turned to hatred, he might have beaten you, killed you, and us, too – didn't you see that?'

He suddenly fell silent so as to sneeze, once, twice, ten times. By the time his sneezing fit had ended, the shooting had ended, too, and the nocturnal bumblebee was hovering round above their heads.

'I don't want to be Pajeú's wife,' Jurema said, as though it were not the two of them she was speaking to. 'If he forces me to be, I'll kill myself. The way a woman at Calumbi killed herself, with a *xiquexique* thorn. I'll never be his wife.'

The nearsighted man had another sneezing fit, and the Dwarf felt panic-stricken: if Jurema died, what would become of him?

'We should have made our escape while we still had a chance to,' he heard the blind man moan. 'We'll never get out of here now. We'll die a horrible death.'

'Pajeú said the soldiers would go away,' the Dwarf said softly. 'From his tone of voice, he was convinced of that. He knows what he's talking about, he's fighting, he can see how the war is going.'

At other times in the past, the blind man argued with him: had he gone mad like all these poor deluded dreamers, did he, too, imagine that they could win a war against the Brazilian Army? Did he believe, as they did, that King Dom Sebastião would appear to fight on their side? But he said nothing now. The

Dwarf was not as certain as the nearsighted man was that the soldiers were invincible. Hadn't they been able to enter Canudos? Hadn't Abbot João managed to steal their arms and their cattle? People said that they were dying like flies on A Favela, being shot at from all directions, without food, and using up the last of their ammunition.

Nonetheless, the Dwarf, whose nomad existence in the past made it impossible for him to stay cooped up and drove him out of doors despite the shooting, could see, in the days that followed, that Canudos did not have the air of a victorious city. He frequently came across someone lying dead or wounded in the streets; if there was heavy gunfire, hours would go by before they could be brought to the clinics, which were all located on Santa Inês now, near the Mocambo. Except for the times when he helped the medical aides transport them to these new Health Houses, the Dwarf avoided that section of town, for during the day the dead bodies piled up along Santa Inês – they could only be buried at night because the cemetery was in the line of fire – and the stench was overpowering, not to mention the moans and groans of the wounded in the Health Houses and the sad spectacle of the little old men, the disabled and infirm unfit for combat who had been assigned the task of keeping off the black vultures and the dogs from devouring the corpses swarming with flies. The burials took place after the Rosary and the counsels, which were held regularly each evening at the same hour once the bell of the Temple of the Blessed Jesus had called the faithful together. But they took place in the dark now, without the sputtering candles of the time before the war. Jurema and the nearsighted man always went with him to the counsels. But unlike the Dwarf, who then went out with the funeral processions to the cemetery, the two of them returned to the store once the Counselor had delivered his last words of the evening. The Dwarf was fascinated by these burials, by the curious concern of the families of the dead that their loved one be buried with some bit of wood above the mortal remains. Since there was no longer anyone available to make coffins because everyone's time was taken up by the war, the bodies were buried in hammocks, sometimes two or three in a single one. The relatives placed a little end of board, a tree branch, any and every sort of wooden object in the hammock to show the Father their sincere desire to give their departed a proper burial, in a coffin, though the adverse circumtances of the moment prevented them from doing so.

On his return to the store from one of his trips outside, the Dwarf found Jurema and the blind man talking with Father Joaquim. Since their arrival, months before, they had never once been alone with him. They would often see him standing at the Counselor's right in the tower of the Temple of the Blessed Jesus reciting Mass, leading the multitude in reciting the Rosary in the church square, in processions, surrounded by a ring of Catholic Guards, and at graveside services, chanting the prayers for the dead in Latin. They had heard that his disappearance meant that he was off on travels that took him all over the backlands, doing errands for the *jagunços* and bringing them the things they needed. After war broke out again, he could often be seen in the streets of Canudos, in the Santa Inês quarter in particular, on his way to confess and give the last sacraments to those on their death-beds in the Health Houses. Although he had run into him several times, the Dwarf had never had a conversation with him; but on seeing the Dwarf come into the store, the little priest had held out his hand and spoken a few kindly words to him. The curé was now perched on a milking stool, and sitting cross-legged in front of him were Jurema and the nearsighted man.

'Nothing is easy, not even what seems to be the easiest thing in the world,' Father Joaquim said to Jurema, in a discouraged tone of voice, clucking his cracked lips. 'I thought I'd be bringing you great joy. That this time I would be received in people's houses as a bearer of glad tidings.' He paused and wet his lips with his tongue. 'And all I do is visit houses with the holy oils, close the eyes of the dead, watch people suffer.'

The Dwarf thought to himself that the curé had aged a great deal in the last few months and was now a little old man. He had almost no hair left and his tanned, freckled scalp now showed through the tufts of white fuzz above his ears. He was terribly thin; the neck opening of his frayed cassock faded to a dark blue bared his protruding collar-bones; the skin of his face hung down in yellow folds covered with a milky-white stubble of beard. His eyes betrayed not only hunger and old age but also immense fatigue.

'I won't marry him, Father,' Jurema said. 'If he forces me to, I'll kill myself.'

She spoke in a calm voice, with the same quiet determination as on that night when she had talked with them, and the Dwarf realized that the curé of Cumbe must have already heard her say the same thing, for he did not look surprised.

'He's not trying to force you,' he mumbled. 'It's never once entered his mind that you would refuse him. Like everyone else, he knows that any woman in Canudos would be happy to have been chosen by Pajeú to form a home and family. You know who Pajeú is, don't you, my girl? You've surely heard the stories people tell about him?'

He sat there staring down at the dirt floor with a regretful look on his face. A little centipede crawled between his sandals, through which his thin yellowish toes, with long black nails, peeked out. Instead of stepping on it, he allowed it to wander off and disappear among the rows of rifles lined up one next to the other.

'All those stories are true, or, rather, they fall short of the truth,' he added, in a dispirited tone of voice. 'The violent crimes, the murders, the thefts, the sackings, the blood vengeances, the gratuitous acts of cruelty, such as cutting off people's ears, their noses. That whole life of hell and madness. And yet here he is, he too, like Abbot João, like Taramela, Pedrão, and the others . . . The Counselor brought about that miracle, he turned the wolf into the lamb, he brought him into the fold. And because he turned wolves into lambs, because he gave people who knew only fear and hatred, hunger, crime, and pillaging reasons to change their lives, because he brought spirituality where there had been cruelty, they are sending army after army to these lands to exterminate these people. How has Brazil, how has the world been overcome with such confusion as to commit such an abominable deed? Isn't that sufficient proof that the Counselor is right, that Satan has indeed taken possession of Brazil, that the Republic is the Antichrist?'

His words were not tumbling out in a rush, he had not raised his voice, he was neither furious nor sad. Simply overwhelmed.

'It's not that I'm stubborn or that I hate him,' the Dwarf heard Jurema say in the same firm tone of voice. 'Even if it were someone else besides Pajeú, I wouldn't say yes. I don't want to marry again, Father.'

'Very well, I understand,' the curé of Cumbe sighed. 'We'll see that things turn out all right. You don't have to marry him if you don't want to, and you don't have to kill yourself. I'm the one who marries people in Belo Monte; there's no such thing as civil marriage here.' A faint smile crossed his lips and there was an impish little gleam in his eyes. 'But we can't break the news to him all at once. We mustn't hurt his feelings. People like Pajeú are so sensitive that it's like a terrible malady. Another thing that's always amazed me about people like him is their touchy sense of honor. It's as though they were one great open wound. They don't have a thing to their names, but they possess a surpassing sense of honor. It's their form of wealth. So then, we'll start by telling him that you've been left a widow too recently to enter into another marriage just yet. We'll make him wait. But there is one thing you can do. It's important to him. Take him his food at Fazenda Velha. He's talked to me about that. He needs to feel that a woman is taking care of him. It's not much. Give him that pleasure. As for the rest, we'll discourage him, little by little.'

The morning had been quiet; now they began to hear shots, scattered gunfire far in the distance.

'You've aroused a passion,' Father Joaquim added. 'A great passion. He came to the Sanctuary last night to ask the Counselor's permission to marry you. He also said that he would take in these two, since they're your family, that he would take them to live with him . . .' He rose to his feet abruptly.

The nearsighted man went into a sneezing fit that made him shake all over and the Dwarf burst into joyous laughter, delighted at the idea of becoming Pajeú's foster son: he would never lack for food again.

'I wouldn't marry him for that reason or for any other,' Jurema said, as unyielding as ever. She added, however, lowering her eyes: 'But if you think I should, I'll bring his food to him.'

Father Joaquim nodded and had turned to leave when suddenly the nearsighted man leapt to his feet and grabbed his arm. On seeing the anxious expression on his face, the Dwarf guessed what he was about to say.

'You can help me,' he whispered, peering all about fearfully. 'Do it because of what you believe in, Father. I have nothing at all to do with what is happening here. It's by accident that I'm in Canudos; you know that I'm not a soldier or a spy, that I'm a nobody. Help me, I implore you.'

The curé of Cumbe looked at him with commiseration. 'To get out of here?' he murmured.

'Yes, yes,' the nearsighted man stammered, nodding his head. 'They've forbidden me to leave. It isn't right . . .'

'You should have made your escape,' Father Joaquim whispered. 'While it was still possible; when there weren't soldiers all over everywhere.'

'Can't you see the state I'm in?' the nearsighted man whined, pointing to his bulging, watery, unfocused red eyes. 'Can't you see that without my glasses I'm totally blind? Could I have escaped by myself, fumbling my way through the backlands?' His little voice rose to a screech: 'I don't want to die like a rat in a trap!'

The curé of Cumbe blinked several times and the Dwarf felt a chill down his spine, as he always did whenever the nearsighted man predicted the imminent death of all of them.

'I don't want to die like a rat in a trap either,' the little priest said, lingering over each syllable and grimacing. 'I, too, have nothing to do with this war. And yet . . .' He shook his head, as though to banish an image from his mind. 'I can't help you, even though I'd like to. The only ones to leave Canudos are armed bands, to fight. I trust you don't think I could join one of them?' He gave a bitter little wave of his hand. 'If you believe in God, put yourself in His hands. He is the only one who can save us now. And if you don't believe in Him, I'm afraid that there's no one who can help you, my friend.'

He went off, his feet dragging, stoop-shouldered and sad. They did not have time to discuss his visit since at that moment the Vilanova brothers came into the store, followed by several men. From their conversation, the Dwarf gathered that the *jagunços* were digging a new line of trenches to the west of Fazenda Velha, following the curve of the Vaza-Barris opposite O Taboleirinho, for part of the troops had pulled out of A Favela and were gradually encircling O Cambaio, probably to take up positions in that sector. When the Vilanovas left, taking arms with them, the Dwarf and Jurema consoled the nearsighted man, who was so upset by his conversation with Father Joaquim that tears were running down his cheeks and his teeth were chattering.

That same evening the Dwarf accompanied Jurema as she went to take food to Pajeú at Fazenda Velha. She had asked the nearsighted man to come with her too, but he was so terrified by the *caboclo* and the thought of the risk he'd be running by going all the way across Canudos that he refused. The food for the *jagunços* was prepared in the little street of São Cipriano, where they slaughtered the cattle still left from Abbot João's raid. They stood in a long line till they reached Catarina, Abbot João's gaunt wife, who, along with the other women, was handing out chunks of meat and manioc flour and water from leather canteens that 'youngsters' went to the water source of São Pedro to fill. The Street Commander's wife gave them a basket full of food and they joined the line of people going out to the trenches. They had to go along the little narrow street of São Crispim and then hunch over or crawl on all fours along the ravines of the Vaza-Barris, whose dips and hollows served them as cover from the bullets. From the river on, the women could no longer make their way in groups, but instead went on one by one, running in a zigzag line, or – the most prudent of them – crawling on their hands and knees. It was about three hundred yards from the ravines to the trenches, and as he ran along, clinging to Jurema's skirts, the Dwarf could see the towers of the Temple of the Blessed Jesus, crawling with sharpshooters, on his right, and on his left the mountainsides of A Favela, where he was certain there were thousands of rifles aimed at them. Drenched with sweat, he reached the edge of the trench, and two arms lifted him down into it. He caught sight of Pajeú's disfigured face.

The former *cangaceiro* did not seem surprised to see him there. He helped Jurema down into the trench, picking her up as though she were as light as a feather and greeting her with a nod of his head, without smiling, his manner so natural that anyone would have thought she had been coming there for many days now. He took the basket and motioned to them to move to one side, since they were in the way of the women who were working. The Dwarf walked about amid *jagunços* who were squatting on their heels eating, talking with the women who had just arrived, or peeking out through lengths of pipe or hollowed-out tree trunks that allowed them to shoot without being seen. The redoubt finally widened out into a semicircular space. There was room for more people there, and Pajeú sat down in one corner. He motioned to Jurema to come sit down alongside him. Seeing the Dwarf hesitate, not knowing whether to join them, Pajeú pointed to the basket. So the Dwarf sat down next to them and shared the water and food in it with Jurema and Pajeú.

For some time, the *caboclo* didn't say a word, sitting there eating and drinking without even looking at the two beside him. Jurema did not look at him either, and the Dwarf thought to himself that it was stupid of her to refuse to marry this man who could solve all her problems. Why should she care if he was ugly-looking? Every so often, he looked at Pajeú. He found it hard to believe that this man who was sitting there coldly and doggedly chewing, with an indifferent expression on his face – he had leaned his rifle against the side of the trench but did not remove the knife and the machete tucked into his belt or the cartridge belts across his chest – was the same man who had said all those things about love to Jurema in a trembling, desperate voice. There was no steady gunfire at the moment, only occasional shots, something the Dwarf's ears had grown accustomed to. What he couldn't get used to was the shelling. The deafening explosions always left in their wake clouds of dirt and dust, falling debris, great gaping craters in the ground, the terrified wails of children and, often, dismembered corpses. When a cannon roared, he was the first to fling himself headlong and lie there with his eyes closed, drenched with cold sweat, clinging to Jurema and the nearsighted man if they were close by, and trying to pray.

To break this silence, he timidly asked whether it was true that Joaquim Macambira and his sons had destroyed A Matadeira before they were killed. Pajeú answered no. But A Matadeira blew up on the Freemasons a few days later, and apparently three or four of the gun crew were blown up with it. Maybe the Father had done this to reward the Macambiras for their martyrdom. The *caboclo*'s eyes avoided Jurema's, and she did not seem to hear what he said. Still addressing him, Pajeú added that the situation of the atheists on A Favela was becoming worse and worse; they were dying of hunger and thirst and desperate at suffering so many casualties at the hands of the Catholics. Even here, they could be heard moaning and weeping at night. Did that mean, then, that they'd be going away soon?

Pajeú looked dubious. 'The problem lies back there,' he murmured, pointing toward the south with his chin. 'In Queimadas and Monte Santo. More Freemasons, more rifles, more cannons, more livestock, more grain shipments keep arriving. There's another convoy on the way with reinforcements and food. And we're running out of everything.'

The scar puckered slightly in his pale yellow face. 'I'm the one who's going to stop the convoy this time,' he said, turning to Jurema. The Dwarf suddenly felt as though he'd dismissed him, sent him many leagues away. 'It's a pity I must leave just at this time.'

Jurema gazed back at the former *cangaceiro* with a docile, absent expression on her face, and said nothing.

'I don't know how long I'll be away. We're going to take them by surprise up around Jueté. Three or four days, at least.'

Jurema's lips parted but she did not say anything. She had not spoken a word since she arrived.

At that moment there was a commotion in the trench, and the Dwarf saw a whole crowd of *jagunços* coming their way, with much yelling and shouting. Pajeú leapt to his feet and grabbed his rifle. In a rush, knocking over others sitting down or squatting on their heels, several of the *jagunços* reached their side. They surrounded Pajeú and stood there for a moment looking at him, none of them saying a word.

Finally an old man with a hairy mole on the nape of his neck spoke up. 'Taramela's dead,' he said. 'He got a bullet through the ear as he was eating.' He spat, and looking down at the ground he growled: 'You've lost your good luck, Pajeú.'

'They rot before they die,' young Teotônio Leal Cavalcanti says aloud, believing that he's merely thinking to himself, not speaking out loud. But there is no danger of his being overheard by the wounded. Even though the field hospital of the first column, which has been set up in a cleft between the peaks of A Favela and Monte Mário, is well protected from gunfire, the din of the fusillades and, above all, of the artillery fire echoes and reechoes down here, amplified by the semivault formed by the mountainsides, and it is one torture more for the wounded, who must shout to make themselves heard. No, no one has heard him.

The idea of rotting torments Teotônio Leal Cavalcanti. He was a student in his last year of medical school at the University of São Paulo when, out of fervor for the republican cause, he enrolled as a volunteer in the army that was leaving to defend the Fatherland up in Canudos; so this, naturally, is not the first time that he has seen people injured, dying, dead. But those anatomy classes, those autopsies in the dissecting room at the School of Medicine, the injured in the hospitals where he was learning to do surgery – how could they be compared to the inferno that this rat trap of A Favela has turned into? What stupefies him is how quickly wounds become infected, how in just a few hours a sudden restless activity can be seen in them, the writhing of worms, and how a fetid suppuration immediately begins.

'It will be of help in your career,' his father said to him at the São Paulo railroad station as he was seeing him off. 'You will have intensive practice in administering first aid.' What it has been, however, is intensive practice in carpentry. He has learned one thing at any rate in these three weeks: more men die of gangrene than of the wounds they have received, and those who have the best chance of pulling through are those with a bullet or bayonet wound in an arm or a leg – parts of the body that a man can do without – so long as the limb is amputated and cauterized in time. There was enough chloroform to perform amputations humanely only for the first three days; on those days it was Teotônio who broke the ampoules open, soaked a wad of cotton in the liquid that made him light-headed, and held it against the nostrils of the wounded man as the chief field surgeon, Alfredo Gama, a doctor with the rank of captain, sawed away, panting. When their supply of chloroform ran out, the anesthetic was a glass of cane brandy, and now that the brandy has run out, they operate cold, hoping that the victim will faint dead away immediately, so the surgeon can operate without the distraction of hearing the man scream. It is Teotônio Leal Cavalcanti who is now sawing and lopping off feet, legs, hands, and arms in which gangrene has set in, as two medical aides keep the victim pinned down till he has lost consciousness. And it is he who, after having finished amputating, cauterizes the stumps by sprinkling a little gunpowder on them and setting it afire, or pouring boiling-hot grease on them, the way Captain Alfredo Gama taught him before that stupid accident.

Stupid, yes, that's the right word. Because Captain Gama knew there are plenty of artillerymen but there aren't anywhere near enough doctors. Above all, doctors like himself, with a great deal of experience in the sort of medicine practiced in the field, which he learned in the jungles of Paraguay, where he served as a volunteer when he was in medical school, just as young Teotônio has come to serve in Canudos. But in the war against Paraguay, Dr. Alfredo Gama unfortunately caught, as he himself confessed, 'the artillery bug.' It was a bug that killed him a week ago, leaving his young assistant saddled with the crushing responsibility of caring for two hundred sick, wounded, and dying who are lying one on top of the other, half naked, stinking, gnawed by worms, on the bare rock – only a few of them have so much as a blanket or a straw mat – in the field hospital. The medical corps of the first column has been divided into five teams, and the one to which Captain Alfredo Gama and Teotônio were assigned is in charge of the north zone of the hospital.

Dr. Alfredo Gama's 'artillery bug' kept him from concentrating exclusively on his patients. Often he would abruptly break off a treatment to go feverishly clambering up to the Alto do Mário, the area on the very crest line to which all the cannons of the first column had been hauled up hand over hand. The artillerymen would let him fire the Krupps, even A Matadeira. Teotônio remembers his mentor prophesying: 'It is a surgeon who will make the towers of Canudos come tumbling down.' The captain returned to the cleft in the mountainsides below with his spirits refreshed. He was a stout, ruddy, jovial man, devoted to his calling, who took a great liking to Teotônio Leal Cavalcanti from the first day he saw him enter the barracks. His outgoing personality, his cheery good spirits, his adventurous life, his picturesque anecdotes so charmed the student that on the way to Canudos he thought seriously of staying in the army once he received his medical degree, as his idol had. During the regiment's brief stay in Salvador, Dr. Gama showed Teotônio around the medical school at the University of Bahia, in the Praça da Basílica Cathedral, and opposite the yellow façade with tall blue ogival windows, beneath the coral trees, the coconut palms, and the crotons, the doctor and the student had sat drinking sweetish brandy in front of the kiosks set up on the black-

and-white mosaic pavement, amid the vendors hawking trinkets and women selling hot foods from braziers. They went on drinking till dawn, which found them, beside themselves with happiness, in a brothel of mulattas. As they climbed onto the train to Queimadas, Dr. Gama had his disciple down an emetic potion, 'to ward off African syphilis,' he explained to him.

Teotônio mops the sweat from his brow as he gives quinine mixed with water to a patient with smallpox who is delirious from fever. To one side of him is a soldier with his elbow joint exposed to the air, and on the other a soldier with a bullet wound in his lower belly and his sphincter shot away so that his feces are leaking out. The smell of excrement mingles with that of the scorching flesh of the corpses being burned in the distance. Quinine and carbolic acid are the only things left in the pharmacopoeia of the field hospital. The iodoform ran out at the same time as the chloroform, and for lack of antiseptics the doctors have been making do with subnitrate of bismuth and calomel. But now these are gone, too. Teotônio Leal Cavalcanti now cleanses wounds with a solution of water and carbolic acid. He squats down to do so, dipping the solution out of the basin in his cupped hands. He gives others a bit of quinine in half a glass of water. They have a large supply of quinine on hand, since many cases of malaria were expected. 'The great killer of the war against Paraguay,' Dr. Gama used to say. It had decimated the army there. But malaria is nonexistent in this extremely dry climate, where mosquitoes do not breed except around the very few places where there is standing water. Teotônio knows that quinine will do the wounded no good, but it at least gives them the illusion that they are being treated. It was on the day of the accident, in fact, that Captain Gama had begun giving out quinine, for lack of any other medicines.

Teotônio thinks of how the accident happened, of how it must have happened. He was not there; they have told him about it, and since then, this and the dream about the rotting bodies have been the nightmares that have most disturbed the few short hours of sleep that he manages to snatch. In the nightmare the jolly, energetic surgeon-captain ignites the fuse of the Krupp 34 cannon. In his haste he has failed to close the breech properly, and when the fuse detonates the charge, the explosion in the half-open breech ignites a barrel of projectiles standing next to the cannon. He has heard the artillerymen tell how Dr. Alfredo Gama was catapulted several yards off the ground and fell some twenty paces away, a shapeless mass of flesh. First Lieutenant Odilon Coriolano de Azevedo, Second Lieutenant José A. do Amaral, and three artillerymen were also killed, and five artillerymen received burns in the explosion. When Teotônio arrived at Alto do Mário, the dead bodies were being cremated, in accordance with a procedure suggested by the medical corps in view of the difficulty of burying the dead: digging a grave in this ground that is living rock represents a tremendous expenditure of energy, for the shovels and pickaxes become dented and shatter on the solid rock without breaking it up. The order to burn corpses has given rise to an extremely heated argument between General Oscar and the chaplain of the first column, Father Lizzardo, a Capuchin, who calls cremation 'a Masonic perversion.'

Young Teotônio has a memento of Dr. Alfredo Gama that he treasures: a miraculous ribbon of Our Lord of Bonfim, sold to them that afternoon in Bahia by the tightrope walkers in the Praça da Basílica Cathedral. He is going to take it to his chief's widow, if he ever gets back to São Paulo. But Teotônio doubts that he will ever again set eyes on the city where he was born, went to school, and enlisted in the army in the name of a romantic ideal: serving his country and civilization.

In these past months, certain beliefs of his that seemed rock-solid have been profoundly undermined. His notion of patriotism, for instance, a sentiment which, when he volunteered, he had believed ran in the blood of all these men come from the four corners of Brazil to defend the Republic against obscurantism, a perfidious conspiracy, and barbarism. His first disillusionment came in Queimadas, in that long two months of waiting, in the chaos that had resulted when that hamlet in the backlands had been turned into the general headquarters of the first column. In the medical facilities, where he had worked with Captain Alfredo Gama and other physicians and surgeons, he discovered that many men were trying to get out of combat duty by malingering. He had seen them feign illnesses, learn the symptoms by heart and recite them with the consummate skill of professional actors so as to get themselves declared unfit for service in the front lines. The doctor and would-be artillery officer taught him to see through their stupid tricks for making themselves run fevers, vomit, suffer attacks of diarrhea. The fact that there were among them not only troops of the line – that is to say, men of no education or background – but also officers had come as a great shock to Teotônio.

Patriotism was not as widespread as he had supposed. This idea has been borne in on him in the three weeks that he has been in this rat hole. It is not that the men don't fight; they have fought, and they are fighting now. He has seen how bravely they have withstood, ever since Angico, the attacks of that slippery, cowardly enemy that refuses to show its face, that does not know the laws and customs of warfare, that lies in ambush, that attacks from odd angles, from hiding places, and vanishes into thin air when the patriots go to meet them head-on. In these three weeks, despite the fact that one-fourth of the expeditionary troops have been killed or wounded, despite the lack of rations, despite the fact that all of them are beginning to lose hope that the convoy of reinforcements will ever arrive, the men have gone on fighting.

But how to reconcile patriotism with business deals? What kind of love for Brazil is it that leaves room for this sordid traffic between men who are defending the most noble of causes, that of their country and civilization? This is yet another reality that demoralizes Teotônio Leal Cavalcanti: the way in which everyone makes deals and speculates because everything is in such short supply. In the beginning, it was only tobacco that was sold and resold at more and more astronomical prices. Just this morning, he has seen a cavalry major pay twelve milreis for a mere handful . . . Twelve milreis! Ten times more than what a box of fine tobacco costs in the city! Since those first days, the price of everything has reached dizzying heights, everything has become something to be auctioned off to the highest bidder. Since they are receiving almost no rations at all – the officers are being handed out ears of green maize, without salt, and the soldiers the feed for the horses – food is fetching fantastic prices: a quarter of a goat is going for thirty and forty milreis, a loaf of hard brown sugar for twenty, a cupful of manioc flour for five, an *imbuzeiro* root or a 'monk's head' cactus with edible pulp for one and even two milreis. The cigars known as *fuzileiros* are bringing a milreis, and a cup of coffee, five. And, worst of all, he, too, has succumbed to this trafficking. Driven by hunger and his craving for tobacco, he has been spending all the money he has, paying five milreis, for instance, for a spoonful of salt, a commodity he has never before realized a person could miss that badly. What disgusts him most of all is knowing that a good part of these things that are being trafficked have been come by dishonestly, either stolen from the column's quartermaster stores or as thefts of thefts . . .

Isn't it surprising that in circumstances such as these, when they are risking their lives at every second, in this hour of truth that should purify them, leaving within them only what is most lofty and most noble, they should give proof of such a base urge to make deals and accumulate money? 'It is not what is most sublime, but what is most sordid and abject, the hunger for filthy lucre, greed, that is aroused in the presence of death,' Teotônio thinks. His image of humanity has abruptly darkened in these past weeks.

He is roused from his thoughts by someone weeping at his feet. Unlike the others, who are openly sobbing, this one is weeping in silence, as though ashamed of his tears. He kneels down beside him. The man is an old soldier who has found his itching unbearable.

'I've been scratching myself, sir,' he murmurs. 'I don't give a damn any more whether it gets infected – or whatever, Doctor.'

He is one of the victims of that diabolical weapon of those cannibals that has eaten away the epidermis of a fair number of patriots: the ants known as *caçaremas*. At first it appeared to be a natural phenomenon, simply a terrible misfortune that these fierce insects which perforate the skin, produce rashes and a hideous burning sensation, should leave their nests in the cool of the night to attack sleeping men. But it has been discovered that their anthills, spherical structures built of mud, are being brought up to the camp by the *jagunços* and smashed there so that the savage swarms thus let loose wreak their cruel havoc on sleeping patriots . . . And the ones the cannibals send creeping into the camp to deposit the anthills there are mere youngsters! One of them has been captured: young Teotônio has been told that the 'little *jagunço*' struggled like a wild beast in his captors' arms, insulting them like the most foul-mouthed ruffian imaginable . . .

On raising the old soldier's shirt to examine his chest, Teotônio finds that what yesterday were black-and-blue spots are now a huge bright-red patch with pustules teeming with activity. Yes, the ants are there, reproducing, burrowing under his skin, gnawing the poor man's innards. Teotônio has learned to dissimulate, to lie, to smile. The bites are better, he tells the soldier, he must try not to scratch himself. He gives him half a cup of water with quinine to drink, assuring him that this will lessen the itching.

He continues on his rounds, imagining the youngsters whom those degenerates send into the camp at night with the anthills. Barbarians, brutes, savages: only utterly depraved people could pervert innocent children as they have done. But young Teotônio's ideas about Canudos have also changed. Are they really monarchists bent on restoration? Are they really working hand in glove with the House of Bragança and former slaveowners? Is it true that those savages are merely a tool of Perfidious Albion? Although he hears them shouting 'Death to the Republic,' Teotônio Leal Cavalcanti is no longer so sure of all this. Everything has become confused in his mind. He expected to find English officers here, advising the *jagunços*, teaching them how to handle the completely modern, up-to-date arms known to have been smuggled in by way of the shores of Bahia. But among the wounded that he is pretending to treat are victims of *caçarema* ants, and also of poisoned arrows and of sharp-pointed stones hurled with slings, the weapons of cavemen! So that business about a monarchist army, reinforced by English officers, now seems to him to be some sort of fantastic story invented out of whole cloth. 'What we're up against is primitive cannibals,' he thinks. 'Yet we're losing the war; we would already have lost it if the second column hadn't arrived to reinforce us when they ambushed us in these hills.' How to explain such a paradox?

A voice interrupts his train of thought. 'Teotônio?' It is a first lieutenant whose tattered tunic bears the still decipherable insignia of his rank and unit: Ninth Infantry Battalion, Salvador. He has been in the field hospital since the day the first column arrived in A Favela; he was in one of the vanguard corps of the First Brigade, the ones that Colonel Joaquim Manuel de Medeiros led in a mad charge down the mountainside of A Favela to attack Canudos. The carnage dealt them by the *jagunços* from their invisible trenches was frightful; the front line of soldiers can still be seen, lying frozen in death, halfway up the slope where it was mowed down. First Lieutenant Pires Ferreira was hit square in the face by a projectile; the explosion ripped off his two raised hands and left him blind. As it was the first day, Dr. Alfredo Gama was able to anesthetize him with morphine as he sutured the stumps and disinfected his face wounds. Lieutenant Pires Ferreira is fortunate: his wounds are protected by bandages from the dust and the insects. He is an exemplary patient, whom Teotônio has never heard weep or complain. Every day, when he asks him how he is feeling, his answer is: 'All right.' And 'Nothing' is his answer when he asks if there is anything he wants. Teotônio has fallen into the habit of coming to talk with him at night, stretching out alongside him on the stony ground, gazing up at the myriad stars that always stud the sky of Canudos. That is how he has learned that Lieutenant Pires Ferreira is a veteran of this war, one of the few who have served in the four expeditions sent by the Republic to fight against the *jagunços*; that is how he has found out that for this unfortunate officer this tragedy is the culmination of a series of humiliations and defeats. He has thus realized the reason for the bitterness that haunts the lieutenant's thoughts, why he endures so stoically sufferings that destroy other men's morale and dignity. In his case the worst wounds are not physical.

'Teotônio?' Pires Ferreira says again. The bandages cover half his face, but not his mouth or his chin.

'Yes,' the medical student says, sitting down alongside him. He motions to the two aides with the medicine kit and the canteens of water to take a rest; they go off a few paces and collapse on the gravel. 'I'll keep you company for a while, Manuel da Silva. Is there anything you need?'

'Can they hear us?' the officer in bandages says in a low voice. 'This is confidential, Teotônio.'

At that moment the bells ring out on the hillside opposite. Young Leal Cavalcanti looks up at the sky: yes, it is getting dark, it is time for the bells calling the people of Canudos together for the Rosary. They peal every evening, with a magic punctuality, and without fail, a little while later, if there are no fusillades and no cannonades, the fanatics' Ave Marias can be heard even up in the camps on A Favela and Monte Mário. A respectful cessation of all activity occurs at this hour in the field hospital; many of the sick and wounded cross themselves on hearing the bells ring and their lips move, reciting the Rosary at the same time as their enemies. Even Teotônio, who has been a lukewarm Catholic, cannot help feeling a curious, indefinable sensation each evening, what with all the prayers and ringing bells, something that, if it is not faith, is a nostalgia for faith.

'That means the bell ringer is still alive,' he murmurs, without answering First Lieutenant Pires Ferreira. 'They still haven't been able to pick him off.'

Captain Alfredo Gama used to talk a lot about the bell ringer. Several times he had caught sight of him climbing up to the belfry of the little chapel. He said that he was an insignificant, imperturbable little old man, swinging back and forth pulling on the clapper, indifferent to the fusillade from the soldiers in answer to the bells. Dr. Gama had told him that knocking down those defiant bell towers and silencing that provoking bell ringer is the obsessive ambition of all the artillerymen up there on the Alto do Mário, and that all of them shoulder their rifles to take aim at him at the hour of Angelus. Haven't they been able to kill him yet, or is it a new bell ringer?

'What I'm going to ask you is not the product of despair,' Lieutenant Pires Ferreira says. 'It is not the request of a man who has lost his reason.'

His voice is firm and calm. He is lying completely motionless on the blanket separating him from the stony ground, with his head resting on a pillow of straw, and the bandaged stumps of his arms on his belly.

'You mustn't despair,' Teotônio says. 'You'll be among the very first to be evacuated. The moment the reinforcements arrive and the convoy heads back, they'll take you in an ambulance cart to Monte Santo, to Queimadas, to your home. General Oscar promised as much the day he visited the field hospital. Don't despair, Manuel da Silva.'

'I beg you in the name of what you respect most in this world,' Pires Ferreira's mouth says, in a low, firm voice. 'In the name of God, your father, your vocation. Of that fiancée to whom you write verses, Teotônio.'

'What is it you want, Manuel da Silva?' the young medical student from São Paulo murmurs, turning his eyes away from the wounded man, deeply upset, absolutely certain what the words he is about to hear will be.

'A bullet in the head,' the firm, quiet voice says. 'I beg you from the depths of my soul.'

He is not the first to have begged him to do such a thing and Teotônio knows that he will not be the last. But he is the first to have begged him so serenely, so undramatically.

'I can't do it when I've no hands,' the man in bandages explains. 'You do it for me.'

'A little courage, Manuel da Silva,' Teotônio says, noting that he is the one whose voice is charged with emotion. 'Don't ask me to do something that's against my principles, against the oath of my profession.'

'One of your aides, then,' Lieutenant Pires Ferreira says. 'Offer them my wallet. There must be some fifty milreis in it. And my boots, which don't have any holes in them.'

'Death may be worse than what has happened to you already,' Teotônio says. 'You'll be evacuated. You'll recover, you'll come to love life again.'

'With no eyes and no hands?' he asks quietly. Teotônio feels ashamed. The lieutenant's mouth is half open. 'That isn't the worst part, Teotônio. It's the flies. I've always hated them, I've always been revolted by them. And now I'm at their mercy. They walk all over my face, they get in my mouth, they crawl in under the bandages to my wounds.' He falls silent.

Teotônio sees him run his tongue over his lips. He has been so moved at hearing these words from this exemplary patient that it hasn't even occurred to him to ask the aides for the canteen of water to quench the wounded man's thirst.

'It has become a personal matter between the bandits and me,' Pires Ferreira says. 'I don't want them to get away with this. I won't allow them to have turned me into this creature before you, Teotônio, I refuse to be a useless monster. Ever since Uauá, I've known that something tragic crossed my path. A curse, an evil spell.'

'Would you like some water?' Teotônio says gently.

'It's not easy to kill yourself when you have no hands and no eyes,' Pires Ferreira goes on. 'I've tried hitting my head against the rock. It didn't work. Nor does licking the ground, because there aren't any stones the right size to swallow, and . . .'

'Be quiet, Manuel da Silva,' Teotônio says, putting his hand on his shoulder. But he finds it absurd to be calming someone who seems to be the calmest man in the world, who never raises his voice, whose words are never hurried, who speaks of himself as though he were another person.

'Are you going to help me? I beg you in the name of our

friendship. A friendship born here is something sacred. Are you going to help me?'

'Yes,' Teotônio Leal Cavalcanti whispers. 'I'm going to help you, Manuel da Silva.'

IV

'His head?' the Baron de Canabrava repeated. He was standing at the window overlooking the garden; he had walked over to it on the pretext of opening it because the study was growing warmer and warmer, but in reality he wanted to locate the chameleon, whose absence worried him. His eyes searched the garden in all directions, looking for it. It had become invisible again, as though it were playing a game with him. 'They decapitated him. There was an article in *The Times* about it. I read it, in London.'

'They decapitated his corpse,' the nearsighted journalist corrected him.

The baron went back to his armchair. He felt distressed, but nonetheless found that what his visitor was saying had attracted his interest once again. Was he a masochist? All this brought back memories, scratched the wound and reopened it. Nevertheless, he wanted to hear it.

'Did you ever find yourself alone with him and talk to him?' he asked, his eyes seeking the journalist's. 'Were you able to gather any impression of what sort of man he was?'

They had found the grave only two days after the last redoubt fell. They managed to get the Little Blessed One to tell them where he was buried. Under torture, naturally. But not just any torture. The Little Blessed One was a born martyr and he would not have talked had he been subjected to such ordinary brutalities as being kicked, burned, castrated, or having his tongue cut off or his eyes put out – because they sometimes sent *jagunço* prisoners back that way, without eyes, a tongue, sex organs, thinking that such a spectacle would demoralize those who were still holding out. It had precisely the opposite effect, of course. But for the Little Blessed One they hit upon the one torture that he was unable to withstand: dogs.

'I thought I knew all the leaders of that band of villains,' the baron said. 'Pajeú, Abbot João, Big João, Taramela, Pedrão, Macambira. But the Little Blessed One?'

Dogs were another matter. So much human flesh, so many dead bodies to feast on during the long months of siege, had made them as fierce as wolves and hyenas. Packs of bloodthirsty dogs made their way into Canudos, and doubtless into the camp of the besiegers as well, in search of human flesh.

'Weren't those packs of dogs the fulfillment of the prophecies, the infernal beasts of the Apocalypse?' the nearsighted journalist muttered, clutching his stomach. 'Someone must have told them that the Little Blessed One had a particular horror of dogs, or rather of the Dog, Evil Incarnate. They no doubt confronted him with a rabid pack of the beasts, and faced with the threat of being dragged down to hell in pieces by the Can's messengers, he guided them to the place where he'd been buried.'

The baron forgot the chameleon and Baroness Estela. In his mind, raging packs of mad dogs pawed through heaps of corpses, buried their muzzles in bellies gnawed by worms, sank their fangs in skinny kneecaps, fought, snarling, over tibias, spines, skulls. In addition to ravaging the dead, other packs suddenly descended on villages, hurling themselves upon cowherds, shepherds, washerwomen, in search of fresh flesh and bones.

They might have guessed that he was buried in the Sanctuary. Where else could they have buried him? They dug where the Little Blessed One told them to and at a depth of some ten feet – that deep – they found him, dressed in his dark purple tunic and rawhide sandals, with a straw mat wrapped around him. His hair had grown and was wavy: this is what is stated in the notarized certificate of exhumation. All the top army officers were there, beginning with General Artur Oscar, who ordered the artist-photographer of the first column, Senhor Flávio de Barros, to photograph the corpse. This took half an hour, during which all of them remained in the Sanctuary despite the stench.

'Can you imagine what those generals and colonels must have felt on seeing, at last, the corpse of the enemy of the Republic, of the insurgent who massacred three military expeditions and shook the state to its foundations, of the ally of England and the House of Bragança?'

'I met him,' the baron murmured and his visitor remained silent, his watery eyes gazing at him inquisitively. 'But more or less the same thing happens with me as happened to you in Canudos, because of your glasses. I can't picture him clearly, my image of him is blurred. It was some fifteen or twenty years ago. He turned up at Calumbi, with a little band of followers, and it seems we gave them something to eat and some old clothes, because they'd tidied up the tombs and cleaned the chapel. I remember them more as a collection of rags than as a group of men and women. Too many people passing themselves off as saints came by Calumbi. How could I have guessed that, of all of them, he was the important one, the one that would make people forget all the others, the one who would attract to him thousands upon thousands of *sertanejos*?'

'The land of the Bible was also full of illuminati, of heretics,' the nearsighted journalist said. 'That's why so many people were taken to be the Christ. You didn't understand, you didn't see . . .'

'Are you serious?' The baron thrust his head forward. 'Do you believe that the Counselor was really sent by God?'

But the nearsighted journalist's dull voice plodded on.

A notarized statement was drawn up describing the exhumed corpse, which was so decomposed that they were all sick to their stomachs and had to hold their hands and their handkerchiefs over their noses. The four doctors present measured him, noted down that he was 1.78 meters tall, that he had lost all his teeth, and had not died of a bullet wound since the only mark on his skeleton-thin body was a bruise on his left leg, caused by the friction of a bone splinter or a stone. After a brief consultation, it was decided that he should be decapitated, so that science might study his cranium. It was brought to the medical school of the University of Bahia in order that Dr. Nina Rodrigues might examine it. But before beginning to saw the Counselor's head off, they slit the throat of the Little Blessed One. They did so right there in the Sanctuary, while the artist-photographer Flávio de Barros took a photograph, and then threw his body into the hole dug in the floor, along with the Counselor's headless corpse. A happy fate for the Little Blessed One, no doubt: to be buried together with the person he so revered and so faithfully served. But there was one thing that must have terrified him at the last instant: knowing that he was about to be buried like an animal, without any sort of wood covering him. Because those were the things that preyed on people's minds up there.

He was interrupted by another fit of sneezing. But once he recovered from it he went on talking, more and more excitedly, until at times he couldn't even manage to get the words out and his eyes rolled in desperate agitation behind the lenses of his glasses.

There had been some argument as to which of the four doctors was to do it. It was Major Miranda Cúrio, the chief of the medical field corps, who took saw in hand, while the three others held the body down. They tried to submerge the head in a container full of alcohol, but since the remains of hair and flesh were beginning to fall apart, they placed it in a sack of lime. That is how it was transported to Salvador. The delicate mission of transporting it was entrusted to First Lieutenant Pinto Souza, the hero of the Third Infantry Battalion, one of the few surviving officers of this unit, which had been decimated by Pajeú in the first encounter. Lieutenant Pinto Souza delivered it to the Faculty of Medicine and Dr. Nina Rodrigues headed the committee of scientists which observed it, measured it, and weighed it. There are no reliable reports as to what was said in the dissecting room during the examination. The official announcement was irritatingly brief. The person responsible for this was apparently none other than Dr. Nina Rodrigues himself. It was he who drafted the few scant lines that so disappointed the public since the announcement merely stated that science had noted no evident abnormality in the conformation of the cranium of Antônio Conselheiro.

'All that reminds me of Galileo Gall,' the baron said, glancing hopefully at the garden. 'He, too, had a mad faith in craniums as indexes of character.'

But Dr. Nina Rodrigues's opinion was not shared by all his colleagues in Salvador. Dr. Honorato de Albuquerque, for instance, was about to publish a study disagreeing with the conclusion reached in the report of the committee of scientists. He maintained that, according to the classification of the Swedish naturalist Retzius, the cranium was typically brachycephalic, with tendencies toward mental rigidity and linearity (fanaticism, for example). Moreover, the cranial curvature was precisely the same as that pointed out by Benedikt as typical of those epileptics who, as Samt wrote, had the missal in their hands, the name of God on their lips, and the stigmata of crime and brigandage in their hearts.

'Don't you see?' the nearsighted journalist said, breathing as though he were exhausted from some tremendous physical effort. 'Canudos isn't a story; it's a tree of stories.'

'Do you feel ill?' the baron inquired coldly. 'I see that it's not good for you either to speak of these things. Have you been going around visiting all those doctors?'

The nearsighted journalist was bent double like an inchworm, all hunched over and looking as though he were freezing to death. Once the medical examination was over, a problem had arisen. What to do with the bones? Someone proposed that the skull be sent to the National Museum, as a historic curiosity. But there had been violent opposition. On the part of whom? The Freemasons. People already had Our Lord of Bonfim, they said, and that was quite enough; there was no need for another orthodox place of pilgrimage. If that skull was exposed in a glass case in the National Museum, it would become a second Church of Bonfim, a heterodox shrine. The army agreed: it was necessary to keep the skull from becoming a relic, a seed of future uprisings. It had to be made to disappear. How? How?

'Not by burying it, obviously,' the baron murmured.

Obviously, since the fanaticized people would sooner or later discover where it had been buried. What safer and more remote place than the bottom of the sea? The skull was placed in a gunnysack weighted with rocks, sewed up, and spirited away, by night in a boat, by an army officer, to a place in the Atlantic equidistant from the Fort of São Marcelo and the island of Itaparica, and sent to the muddy sea bottom for coral to build on. The officer entrusted with this secret operation was none other than Lieutenant Pinto Souza: and that's the end of the story.

He was sweating so hard and had turned so pale that the baron thought to himself: 'He's about to faint.' What did this ridiculous jumping jack feel for the Counselor? A morbid fascination? The simple curiosity of the gossipmongering journalist? Had he really come to believe him to be a messenger from heaven? Why was he suffering and torturing himself so over Canudos? Why didn't he do what everyone else had done – try to forget?

'Did you say Galileo Gall?' he heard him say.

'Yes.' The baron nodded, seeing those mad eyes, that shaved head, hearing his apocalyptic speeches. 'Gall would have understood that story. He thought that the secret of character lay in the bones of people's heads. Did he ever get to Canudos, I wonder. If he did, it would have been terrible for him to discover that that wasn't the revolution he'd been dreaming of.'

'It wasn't, and yet it was,' the nearsighted journalist said. 'It was the realm of obscurantism, and at the same time a world of brotherhood, of a very special sort of freedom. Perhaps he wouldn't have been all that disappointed.'

'Did you ever find out what happened to him?'

'He died somewhere not very far from Canudos,' the journalist answered. 'I saw a lot of him, before all this. In "The Fort," a tavern in the lower town. He was a great talker, a picturesque character, a madman; he felt people's heads, he prophesied vast upheavals. I thought he was a fraud. Nobody would have guessed that he would turn out to be a tragic figure.'

'I have some papers of his,' the baron said. 'A sort of memoir, or testament, that he wrote in my house, at Calumbi. I was to have seen that it got to some fellow revolutionaries of his. But I wasn't able to. It's not that I wasn't willing to, because I even went to Lyons to do as he'd asked.'

Why had he taken that trip, from London to Lyons, to hand Gall's text over personally to the editors of *L'Etincelle de la révolte*? Not out of affection for the phrenologist, in any event; what he had felt for him in the end was curiosity, a scientific interest in this unsuspected variety of the human species. He had taken the trouble to go to Lyons to see what those revolutionary comrades of his looked like, to hear them talk, to find out whether they were like him, whether they said and believed the same things he did. But the trip had been a waste of time. The only thing he was able to find out was that *L'Etincelle de la révolte*, a sheet that appeared irregularly, had ceased publication altogether some time before, and that it had been put out by a small press whose owner had been sent to prison for printing counterfeit bills, some three or four years earlier. It fitted Gall's destiny very well to have sent articles to what might well have been ghosts and to have died without anyone he'd known during his life in Europe ever finding out where, how, and why he died.

'A story of madmen,' he muttered. 'The Counselor, Moreira César, Gall. Canudos drove all those people mad. And you, too, of course.'

But a thought made him shut his mouth and not say a word more. 'No, they were mad before that. It was only Estela who lost her mind because of Canudos.' He had to keep a tight rein on himself so as not to burst into tears. He didn't remember having cried as a child, or as a young man. But after what had happened to the baroness, he had wept many a time, in his study, on nights when he couldn't sleep.

'It's not so much a story of madmen as a story of misunderstandings,' the nearsighted journalist corrected him again. 'I'd like to know one thing, Baron. I beg you to tell me the truth.'

'Ever since I left politics, I almost always tell the truth,' the baron murmured. 'What is it you'd like to know?'

'Whether there were contacts between the Counselor and the monarchists,' he answered, watching the baron's reaction closely. 'I don't mean the little group who missed the Empire and were naïve enough to proclaim that fact in public, people such as Gentil de Castro. I'm talking about people like you and your party, the Autonomists, the monarchists through and through who nonetheless hid that fact. Did they have contacts with the Counselor? Did they encourage him?'

The baron, who had listened with a look of cynical amusement on his face, burst out laughing. 'Didn't you find out the answer to that in all those months in Canudos? Did you see any politicians from Bahia, São Paulo, Rio among the *jagunços*?'

'I've already told you that I didn't see much of anything,' the unpleasant voice answered. 'But I did find out that you had sent maize, sugar, livestock from Calumbi.'

'Well then, you doubtless also know that I did so against my will, that I was forced to do so,' the baron said. 'All of us landowners in the region had to, so that they wouldn't burn our haciendas down. Isn't that how we deal with bandits in the *sertão*? If you can't kill them, you buy them off. If I'd had the least influence on them, they wouldn't have destroyed Calumbi and my wife would be of sound mind. The fanatics weren't monarchists and they didn't even know what the Empire was. It's beyond belief that you didn't see that, despite . . .'

The nearsighted journalist didn't allow him to go on this time either. 'They didn't know what it was, but they were monarchists nonetheless – in their own way, which no monarchist would have understood,' he blurted, blinking. 'They knew that the monarchy had abolished slavery. The Counselor praised Princess Isabel for having granted the slaves their freedom. He seemed convinced that the monarchy fell because it abolished slavery. Everyone in Canudos believed that the Republic was against abolition, that it wanted to restore slavery.'

'Do you think my friends and I planted such a notion in the Counselor's head?' The baron smiled again. 'If anyone had proposed any such thing to us we would have taken him for an imbecile.'

'That, nonetheless, explains many things,' the journalist said, his voice rising. 'Such as the hatred of the census. I racked my brains, trying to understand the reason for it, and that's the explanation. Race, color, religion. Why would the Republic want to know what race and color people are, if not to enslave blacks again? And why ask their religion if not to identify believers before the slaughter?'

'Is that the misunderstanding that explains Canudos?' the baron asked.

'One of them.' The nearsighted journalist panted. 'I knew that the *jagunços* hadn't been taken in by just any petty politician. I merely wanted to hear you say so.'

'Well, there you are,' the baron answered. What would his friends have said had they been able to foresee such a thing? The humble men and women of the *sertão* rising up in arms to attack the Republic, with the name of the Infanta Dona Isabel on their lips! No, such a thing was too farfetched for it to have occurred to any Brazilian monarchist, even in his dreams.

Abbot João's messenger catches up with Antônio Vilanova on the outskirts of Jueté, where the former storekeeper is lying in ambush with fourteen *jagunços*, waiting for a convoy of cattle and goats. The news the messenger brings is so serious that Antônio decides to return to Canudos before he has finished the task that has brought him there: securing food supplies. It is one that he has set out to do three times now since the soldiers arrived, and been successful each time: twenty-five head of cattle and several dozen kids the first time, eight head the second, and a dozen the third, plus a wagonload of manioc flour, coffee, sugar, and salt. He has insisted on leading these raids to procure food for the *jagunços* himself, claiming that Abbot João, Pajeú, Pedrão, and Big João are indispensable in Belo Monte. For three weeks now he has been attacking the convoys that leave from Queimadas and Monte Santo to bring provisions to A Favela via Rosário.

It is a relatively easy operation, which the former storekeeper, in his methodical and scrupulous way and with his talent for organization, has perfected to the point that it has become a science. He owes his success above all to the information he receives, to the men serving as the soldiers' guides and porters, the majority of whom are *jagunços* who have hired themselves out to the army or been conscripted in various localities, from Tucano to Itapicuru. They keep him posted on the convoy's movements and help him decide where to provoke the stampede, the key to the whole operation. In the place that they have chosen – usually the bottom of a ravine or a section of the mountains with dense brush – and always at night, Antônio and his men suddenly descend on the herd, raising a terrible racket with their blunderbusses, setting off sticks of dynamite, and blowing their whistles so that the animals will panic and bolt off into the *caatinga.* As Antônio and his band distract the troops by sniping at them, the guides and porters round up all the animals they can and herd them along shortcuts that they've decided on beforehand – the shortest and safest trail, the one from Calumbi, has yet to be discovered by the soldiers – to Canudos. Antônio and the others catch up with them later.

This is what would have happened this time, too, if the messenger hadn't brought the news he had: that the dogs will be attacking Canudos at any moment. With clenched teeth and furrowed brows, hurrying along as fast as their legs will carry them, Antônio and his fourteen men have but a single thought in their minds which spurs them on: to be back in Belo Monte with the others, surrounding the Counselor, when the atheists attack. How has the Street Commander learned that they plan to attack? The messenger, an old guide marching along at his side, tells Antônio Vilanova that two *jagunços* dressed in soldiers' uniforms who have been prowling about A Favela have brought the news. He tells this simply and straightforwardly, as though it were quite natural for the sons of the Blessed Jesus to go about among devils disguised as devils.

'They've gotten used to the idea; they don't even notice any more,' Antônio Vilanova thinks to himself. But the first time that Abbot João tried to persuade the *jagunços* to wear soldiers' uniforms to disguise themselves he had very nearly had a rebellion on his hands. The proposal left Antônio himself with a taste of ashes in his mouth. The thought of putting on the very symbol of everything that was wicked, heartless, and hostile in this world turned his stomach, and he understood very well why the men of Canudos should violently resist dying decked out as dogs. 'And yet we were wrong,' he thinks. 'And, as usual, Abbot João was right.' For the information that the valiant 'youngsters' who stole into the camps to let ants, snakes, scorpions loose, to throw poison in the troops' leather canteens, provided could never be as accurate as that of full-grown men, especially those who had been let out of the army or had deserted. It had been Pajeú who had solved the problem, in the trenches of Rancho do Vigário one night when they were having an argument, by turning up dressed in a corporal's uniform and announcing that he was going to slip through the enemy lines. Everyone knew that Pajeú of all people would not get through unnoticed. Abbot João asked the *jagunços* then if it seemed right to them that Pajeú should sacrifice his life so as to set them an example and rid them of their fear of a few rags with buttons. Several men from Pajeú's old *cangaço* then offered to disguise themselves in uniforms. From that day on, the Street Commander had no difficulty sneaking *jagunços* into the camps.

After a few hours, they halt to rest and eat. It is beginning to get dark, and they can just make out O Cambaio and the jagged Serra da Canabrava standing out against the leaden sky. Sitting in a circle with their legs crossed, the *jagunços* open their sacks of woven rope and take out handfuls of hardtack and jerky. They eat in silence. Antônio Vilanova feels the tiredness in his cramped, swollen legs. Is he getting old? It's a feeling he's begun to have in these last months. Or is it the tension, the frantic activity brought on by the war? He has lost so much weight that he has punched new holes in his belt, and Antônia Sardelinha has had to take in his two shirts, which fitted him as loosely as night-shirts. But isn't the same thing happening to all the men and women in Belo Monte? Haven't Big João and Pedrão, those two sturdy giants, become as skinny as beanpoles? Isn't Honório stoop-shouldered and gray-haired now? And don't Abbot João and Pajeú look older, too?

He listens to the roar of the cannon, toward the north. A brief pause, and then several cannon reports in a row. Antônio and the *jagunços* leap to their feet and set off again, loping along in long strides.

They approach the city by way of O Taboleirinho, as dawn is breaking, after five hours during which the rounds of cannon fire have followed one upon the other almost without a break. At the water source, where the first houses are, they find a messenger waiting to take them to Abbot João. He is in the trenches at Fazenda Velha, now manned by twice as many *jagunços* as before, all of them with their finger on the trigger of their rifle or their long-barreled musket, keeping a close watch on the foothills of A Favela in the dim dawn light, waiting to see if the Freemasons will come pouring down from there. 'Praised be Blessed Jesus the Counselor,' Antônio murmurs, and without answering him Abbot João asks if he has seen soldiers along the way. 'No, not even a patrol.'

'We don't know where the attack will come from,' Abbot João says, and the former storekeeper sees how deeply worried he is. 'We know everything, except the most important thing of all.'

The Street Commander calculates that they are going to attack in this sector, the shortest way into Belo Monte, and hence he has come with three hundred *jagunços* to reinforce Pajeú in this line of trenches that stretches in a curve, a quarter of a league long, from the foot of Monte Mário to O Taboleirinho.

Abbot João explains to him that Pedrão is covering the eastern flank of Belo Monte, the area in which the corrals and the cultivated fields are located, and the wooded slopes up which the trails to Trabubu, Macambira, Cocorobó, and Jeremoabo wind their way. The city, defended by Big João's Catholic Guard, has been further fortified by new parapets of stone and sandbags erected in the narrow alleyways and at the intersections of the main streets and the square bounded by the churches and the Sanctuary, that center on which the assault troops will converge, as will the shells of their cannons.

Although he is eager to ply him with questions, Vilanova realizes that there isn't time. What is it that he must do? Abbot João tells him that he and Honório will be responsible for defending the area parallel to the ravines of the Vaza-Barris, to the east of the Alto do Mario and the exit leading to Jeremoabo. Without taking time to explain in more detail, he asks him to send word immediately if soldiers appear in that sector, because what is most important is to discover from which direction they are going to try to enter the city. Vilanova and the fourteen men take off at a run.

His fatigue has disappeared as if by magic. It must be another sign of the divine presence, another manifestation of the supernatural within his person. How otherwise to explain it, if it is not the work of the Father, of the Divine, or of the Blessed Jesus? Ever since he first learned of the attack, he has done nothing but walk or run as fast as he possibly could. A little while ago, as he was crossing the Lagoa do Cipó, his legs started to give way and his heart was pounding so hard he was afraid he'd collapse in a dead faint. And here he is now, running over this rugged stony ground, up hill and down dale, at the end of a long night now filled with the blinding light and deafening thunder of the sudden intense barrages being laid down by the enemy troops. Yet he feels rested, full of energy, capable of any and every effort, and he knows that the fourteen men running at his side feel exactly the same way. Who but the Father could bring about such a change, renew their strength in this way, when circumstances so require? This is not the first time that such a thing has happened to him. Many times in these last weeks, when he has thought that he was about to collapse, he has suddenly felt a great surge of strength that seemed to lift him up, to renew him, to breathe a great gust of life into him.

In the half hour that it takes them to reach the trenches along the Vaza-Barris – running, walking, running – Antônio Vilanova sees the flames of fires flare up back in Canudos. His first concern is not whether one of the fires may be burning his house to the ground, but rather: is the system that he has thought of so that fires won't spread working? For that purpose, hundreds of barrels and boxes of sand have been placed along the streets and at the intersections. The people who have remained in the city know that the moment a shell explodes they must run to put out the flames by throwing pailfuls of sand on them. Antônio himself has organized things so that in each block of dwellings there are women, children, and old men responsible for this task.

In the trenches, he finds his brother Honório and his wife and sister-in-law as well. The Sardelinha sisters are installed with other women in a lean-to, amid things to eat and drink, medicines and bandages. 'Welcome, *compadre*,' Honório says, embracing him. Antônio lingers with him for a moment as he downs with relish the food that the Sardelinha sisters ladle out to the men who have just arrived. Once he finishes this brief repast, the former trader posts his fourteen comrades round about, advises them to get some sleep, and goes with Honório to have a look around the area.

Why has Abbot João entrusted this front to them, of all the warriors, the two men least experienced in the ways of war? Doubtless because this is the front farthest away from A Favela: the enemy will not come this way. They would have three or four times farther to go than if they went straight down the slopes and attacked Fazenda Velha; moreover, before reaching the river, they would have to cross rough terrain bristling with thorny brush that would force the battalions to break ranks and scatter. And that is not the way the atheists fight. They do so in compact blocks, forming those squares of theirs that make such a good target for the *jagunços* holed up in their trenches.

'We're the ones who dug these trenches,' Honório says. 'Do you remember, *compadre*?'

'Of course I remember. Thus far, they haven't had their baptism of fire.'

Yes, they were the ones who had directed the crews that had dotted this plot of ground that winds between the river and the cemetery, without a single tree or clump of brush, with little holes big enough for two or three sharpshooters. They had dug the first of these shelters a year ago, after the encounter at Uauá. After each enemy expedition they have made more holes, and lately little passageways between each of them that allow the men to crawl from one to the other without being seen. They are indeed defenses that have never undergone their baptism of fire: never once has there been any fighting in this sector.

A bluish light, with yellow tinges at the edges, creeps down from the horizon. Cocks can be heard crowing. 'The cannon salvos have stopped,' Honório says, guessing the thought in Antônio's mind. Antônio finishes his brother's sentence: 'That means that they're on their way, *compadre*.' The dugouts are some fifteen to twenty feet apart, spread out over an area half a kilometer long and a hundred or so meters wide. The *jagunços*, crouching down elbow to elbow in the holes by twos and threes, are so well hidden that the Vilanova brothers can see them only when they lean down to exchange a few words with them. Many of them have lengths of pipe, thick cane stalks, and hollowed-out tree trunks that allow them to see outside without poking their heads out. Most of them are sleeping or dozing, curled up in a ball with their Mannlichers, Mausers, and blunderbusses, and their bullet pouch or powder horn within reach of their hand. Honório has posted lookouts along the Vaza-Barris; several of them have gone scouting along the ravines and the riverbed – completely dry there – and on the other side without running into any enemy patrols.

They return to the lean-to, talking together as they walk back. The silence broken only by the crowing of the cocks seems strange after the many hours of bombardment. Antônio remarks that the attack on Canudos has appeared to him to be inevitable ever since the column of reinforcements – more than five hundred troops, apparently – arrived at A Favela intact, despite desperate efforts on the part of Pajeú, who had harried them all the way from Caldeirão but had managed only to steal a few head of their cattle. Honório asks if it is true that the expeditionary force has left companies posted at Jueté and Rosário, places they merely passed through before. Yes, it is true.

Antônio unbuckles his belt and, using his arm as a pillow and covering his face with his sombrero, curls up in the dugout that he is sharing with his brother. His body relaxes, grateful for the rest, but his ears remain alert, listening for any sound of soldiers in the day that is dawning. In a little while he forgets about them, and after drifting along on different fuzzy images, his mind suddenly focuses on this man whose body is touching his. Two years younger than he, with light curly hair, calm, self-effacing, Honório is more than his brother twice over, by blood and by marriage: he is also his comrade, his crony, his confidant, his best friend. They have never separated, they have never had a serious disagreement. Is Honório in Belo Monte, as he is, because he believes with all his heart in the Counselor and everything he represents, religion, truth, salvation, justice? Or is he here only out of loyalty to his brother? In all the years that they have been in Canudos, the question has never entered his mind before. When the angel's wing brushed him and he abandoned his own affairs to take those of Canudos in hand, he naturally presumed that his brother and sister-in-law, like his wife, would willingly accept this change in their lives, as they had each time that misfortune had made them set out in new directions. And that was what had happened: Honório and Assunção acceded to his will without the slightest complaint. It had been when Moreira César attacked Canudos, on that endless day that he spent fighting in the streets, that for the first time he began to have the gnawing suspicion that perhaps Honório was going to die there at his side, not because of something he believed in, but out of respect for his older brother. Whenever he ventures to discuss the subject with Honório, his brother pokes fun at him: 'Do you think I'd risk my neck just to be with you? How vain you've become, *compadre*!' But instead of placating his doubts, these jibes only make him all the more troubled. He has told the Counselor: 'Out of selfishness, I have done as I pleased with Honório and his family without ever finding out what it was that they wanted, as though they were pieces of furniture or goats.' The Counselor provided balm for this wound: 'If that is how it has been, you have helped them accumulate merit to gain heaven.'

He feels someone shaking him, but it takes him a while to open his eyes. The sun is up, shining brightly, and Honório is standing there with his finger on his lips, motioning him to be still. 'They're here, *compadre*,' he says in a very soft voice. 'It's fallen to our lot to receive them.'

'What an honor, *compadre*,' he answers in a voice thick with sleep.

He kneels down in the dugout. From the ravines on the other side of the Vaza-Barris a sea of blue, lead-gray, red uniforms, with glints of sunlight glancing off their brass buttons and their swords and bayonets, is sweeping toward them in the bright morning light. So that is what his ears have been hearing for some time now: the roll of drums, the blare of bugles. 'It looks as though they're coming straight toward us,' he thinks. The air is clear, and though they are still a long way away, he can see the troops very distinctly; they are deployed in three corps, one of which, the one in the center, appears to be heading directly toward the trenches. Something in his mouth that feels pasty keeps him from getting a single word out. Honório tells him that he has already sent two 'youngsters' to Fazenda Velha and to the Trabubu exit to bring Abbot João and Pedrão the news that the enemy troops are coming this way.

'We have to hold them off,' he hears himself say. 'Hold them off as best we can till Abbot João and Pedrão can fall back to Belo Monte.'

'Provided they aren't attacking via A Favela at the same time,' Honório growls.

Antônio doesn't believe they are. Opposite him, coming down the ravines of the dry river, are several thousand soldiers, more than three thousand, perhaps four, which must be all the troops the dogs can field. The *jagunços* know, because of what the 'youngsters' and spies have reported, that there are more than a thousand sick and wounded in the field hospital set up in the valley between A Favela and the Alto do Mário. Some of the troops must have stayed behind there, guarding the hospital, the artillery, and the installations. The soldiers in front of them must constitute the entire attack force. He says as much to Honório, without looking at him, eyes fixed on the ravines as he checks with his fingers to make sure the cylinder of his revolver is fully loaded. Though he has a Mannlicher, he prefers this revolver, the weapon that he has fought with ever since he has been in Canudos. Honório, on the other hand, has his rifle propped on the edge of the trench, with the sight raised and his finger on the trigger. That is how all the other *jagunços* must be waiting in their dugouts, remembering their instructions: Don't shoot till the enemy is practically on top of you, so as to save ammunition and have the advantage of taking them by surprise. That is the only thing that will be in their favor, the only thing that can compensate for the disproportion in numbers of men and equipment.

A youngster bringing them a leather canteen full of hot coffee and some maize cakes crawls up to the dugout and jumps in. Antonio recognizes those bright twinkling eyes, that twisted body. The lad's name is Sebastião, and he is already a battle-hardened veteran, for he has served both Pajeú and Big João as a messenger. As he drinks the coffee, which restores his body, Antônio sees the youngster disappear, slithering along with his canteens and knapsacks, as swiftly and silently as a lizard.

'If only they all advance at once, in a single compact unit,' Antônio thinks. How easy it would be then, in this terrain without trees, bushes, or rocks, to mow them down at point-blank range. The natural depressions will not be of much use to them since the *jagunços'* dugouts are on rises of ground from which they can fire down on them. But they are not advancing in a single unit. The center corps is marching forward more rapidly, like a prow; it is the first to cross the dry riverbed and scale the ravines on the other side. Figures like toy soldiers, in blue, with red stripes down their trouser legs and gleaming bits of metal, appear, less than two hundred paces away from Antônio. It is a company of scouts, some hundred men, all of them on foot, who regroup in two compact formations, five abreast, and advance swiftly, not taking the slightest precautions. He sees them crane their necks, keeping a sharp eye on the towers of Belo Monte, completely unaware of the sharpshooters in the dugouts who have them in their sights.

'What are you waiting for, *compadre*?' Honório says. 'For them to see us?' Antônio shoots, and the next instant, like a multiple echo, earsplitting shots ring out, drowning out the drums and bugles. Thrown into confusion, the soldiers mill about amid the smoke and dust. Antônio squeezes off his shots slowly till his revolver is empty, aiming with one eye closed at the soldiers who have now turned tail and are running away as fast as their legs will carry them. He manages to make out four other corps which have crossed the ravines and are approaching in three, four different directions. The shooting stops.

'They haven't seen us yet,' his brother says to him.

'They have the sun in their eyes,' he answers. 'In an hour they won't be able to see a thing.'

Both of them reload. They can hear scattered shots, from *jagunços* trying to finish off the wounded whom Antônio sees crawling over the stones, trying to reach the ravines. Heads, arms, bodies of soldiers keep emerging from these. The lines of soldiers curve, break up, scatter as they advance across the uneven, shifting terrain. The soldiers have begun to shoot, but Antônio has the impression that they still have not located the dugouts, that they are aiming above their heads, toward Canudos, believing that the hail of gunfire that mowed down the spearhead has come from the Temple of the Blessed Jesus. The shooting makes the cloud of dust and gunsmoke even denser and every so often earth-colored whirlwinds envelop and hide the atheists, who keep advancing, crouching over, bunched together, rifles raised and bayonets fixed, to the sound of drums rolling and bugles blaring and voices shouting out 'Infantry! Advance!'

The former trader empties his revolver twice. It gets hot and burns his hand, so he puts it back in its holster and begins to use his Mannlicher. He aims and shoots, seeking out each time, amid the enemy troops, those who – because of their sabers, their gold braid, or their attitudes – appear to be the commanding officers. Suddenly, seeing these heretics and pharisees with their panicked faces who are falling by ones, by twos, by tens, struck by bullets that seem to be coming out of nowhere, he feels compassion. How can he possibly feel pity for men who are trying to destroy Belo Monte? Yes, at this moment, as he sees them fall to the ground, hears them moan, and aims at them and kills them, he does not hate them: he can sense their spiritual wretchedness, their sinful human nature, he knows they are victims, blind, stupid instruments, prisoners caught fast in the snares of the Evil One. Might that not have been the fate of all the *jagunços*? His, too – if, thanks to that chance meeting with the Counselor, he had not been brushed by the wings of the angel.

'To the left, *compadre,*' Honório says, nudging him in the ribs.

He looks that way and sees: cavalrymen with lances. Some two hundred of them, perhaps more. They have crossed the Vaza-Barris half a kilometer to his right and are grouping in squads to attack this flank, amid the frantic din of a bugle. They are outside the line of trenches. In a second, he sees what is going to happen. The lancers will cut across the rolling hillside to the cemetery, and since in that sector there is no line of trenches to stop them they will reach Belo Monte in just a few minutes. On seeing the way clear, the foot soldiers will follow them into the city. Neither Pedrão nor Big João nor Pajeú has had time yet to get back to Belo Monte to reinforce the *jagunços* behind the parapets on the rooftops and towers of Santo Antônio and the Temple of the Blessed Jesus and the Sanctuary. So, not knowing what exactly he is going to do, guided by the madness of the moment, he grabs his ammunition pouch and leaps out of the dugout, shouting to Honório: 'We must stop them, follow me, follow me!' He breaks into a run, bending over, the Mannlicher in his right hand, the revolver in his left, the ammunition pouch slung over his shoulder; it is as though he were dreaming, or drunk. At that moment, the fear of death – which sometimes wakes him up at night drenched with sweat or makes his blood run cold in the middle of a trivial conversation – disappears and a proud scorn for the very thought that he might be wounded or disappear from among the living takes possession of him. As he runs straight toward the cavalrymen – who, grouped now in squads, are beginning to trot in a zigzag line, raising dust, whom he can see at one moment only to lose sight of them the next because of the dips and rises in the terrain – ideas, memories, images fly up in his head like sparks in a forge. He knows that these cavalrymen belong to the battalion of lancers from the South, gauchos, whom he has spied roaming about behind A Favela in search of cattle. He thinks that none of these horsemen will ever set foot in Canudos, that Big João and the Catholic Guard, the blacks of the Mocambo or the Cariri archers will kill their mounts, magnificent white horses that will make excellent targets. And he thinks of his wife and his sister-in-law, wondering if they and the other women have been able to get back to Belo Monte. Among these faces, hopes, fantasies, Assaré appears, his native village in the state of Ceará, to which he has not returned since he fled from it because of the plague. His town often comes to mind in moments like this when he feels that he has reached a limit, that he is about to step over a line beyond which there lies nothing but a miracle or death.

When his legs refuse to move a step farther, he sinks to the ground, and stretching out flat, without seeking cover, he steadies his rifle in the hollow of his shoulders and begins to shoot. He will not have time to reload, and therefore he aims carefully each time. He has covered half the distance separating him from the cavalrymen. They pass in front of him, in a cloud of dust, and he wonders how they can have failed to see him when he has come running across open terrain and is now shooting at them. Yet none of the lancers even looks his way. Now, however, as though his thought of a moment before has alerted them, the lead squad suddenly veers to the left. He sees a cavalryman make a circular motion with his dress sword, as though calling to him, as though saluting him, and then sees the dozen lancers gallop in his direction. His rifle is empty. He grabs his revolver in his two hands, leaning on his elbows, determined to save these last bullets till the horses are right on top of him. There the faces of the devils are, contorted with rage, their spurs digging cruelly into the flanks of their mounts, their long lances quivering, their balloon pants billowing in the wind. He shoots one, two, three bullets at the one with the saber without hitting him, thinking that nothing will save him from being run through by those lances, from being crushed to death by those hoofs pounding on the stones. But something happens, and again he senses the presence of the supernatural. Many figures suddenly appear from behind him, shooting, brandishing machetes, knives, hammers; they fling themselves upon the animals and their riders, shooting at them, knifing them, hacking at them, in a dizzying whirlwind. He sees *jagunços* hanging on to the cavalrymen's lances and legs and cutting the reins; he sees horses roll over onto the ground and hears roars of pain, whinnies, curses, shots. At least two lancers ride across him without trampling him before he manages to rise to his feet and join the fray. He shoots the last two bullets in his revolver, and using the Mannlicher as a club, he runs toward the nearest atheists and *jagunços* fighting hand to hand on the ground. He swings the rifle butt at a soldier who has a *jagunço* pinned to the ground and lashes out at him till he topples over and stops moving. He helps the *jagunço* to his feet and the two of them rush to rescue Honório, who is being pursued by a cavalryman with his lance outstretched. When he sees them coming toward him, the gaucho puts spurs to his mount and gallops off in the direction of Belo Monte. For some time, Antônio runs from one place to another amid the cloud of dust, helping those who have fallen to their feet, loading and emptying his revolver. Some of his comrades are badly wounded and others dead, run through with lances. One of them is bleeding profusely from a deep saber cut. He sees himself, as though in a dream, bludgeoning unhorsed gauchos to death with the butt of his rifle, as others are doing with their machetes. When the hand-to-hand combat ends for lack of enemies and the *jagunços* regroup, Antônio tells them they must go back to the dugouts, but as he is saying that he notices, when the clouds of reddish dust part for a moment, that the spot where they were lying in ambush before is now being overrun by companies of Freemasons, spread out in formation as far as the eye can see.

There are not more than fifty men around him. What about the others? Those who were able to drag themselves about have gone back to Belo Monte. 'But there weren't many of them,' a toothless *jagunço*, Zózimo the tinsmith, growls. Antônio is surprised to see him among the combatants, when his age and his infirmities should have kept him in Belo Monte putting out fires and helping to bring the wounded to the Health Houses. There is no sense in staying here where they are; a new cavalry charge would be the end of them.

'We're going to go give Big João a hand,' he tells them.

They break up into groups of three or four, and offering those who are limping an arm to lean on, taking cover in folds in the terrain, they start back to Belo Monte. Antônio falls to the rear, alongside Honório and Zózimo. Perhaps the great clouds of dust, perhaps the sun's rays, perhaps the enemy's eagerness to invade Canudos, suffice to explain why neither the troops advancing on their left nor the lancers they spy on their right come to finish them off. Since they can manage to see the dogs now and again, it is not possible that the dogs do not see them, too, now and again. He asks Honório about the Sardelinha sisters. Honório answers that before leaving the dugouts he sent word to all the women to leave. They still have a thousand paces to go before they reach the nearest dwellings. It will be difficult, with the slow progress that they are making, to get there safe and sound. But his trembling legs and his pounding heart tell him that neither he nor any of the other survivors is in any condition to walk faster. Seized by a momentary dizzy spell, old Zózimo is staggering. Antônio gives him a reassuring pat on the back and helps him along. Can it be true that before the angel's wing brushed him this old man was once about to burn the Lion of Natuba alive?

'Look over by Antônio the Pyrotechnist's hut, *compadre*.'

A heavy, deafening fusillade is coming from the jumble of dwellings across from the old cemetery, a section whose narrow little streets, as difficult as a labyrinth to wind one's way through, are the only ones in Canudos not named after saints but after minstrels' stories: Queen Maguelone, Robert the Devil, Silvaninha, Charlemagne, Peers of France. The new pilgrims are all grouped together in this district. Are they the ones who are shooting like that at the atheists? Rooftops, doorways, street entrances are spitting fire at the soldiers. All of a sudden, amid the *jagunços* lying flat on the ground, standing, or squatting, he spies an unmistakable figure, Pedrão, leaping from one spot to another with his musketoon, and he is certain he can distinguish, amid the deafening din of all the firearms, the loud boom of the giant mulatto's ancient weapon. Pedrão has always refused to exchange this old piece of his, dating back to his days as a bandit, for a Mannlicher or a Mauser repeating rifle, despite the fact that these guns can fire five shots in a row and can be very quickly reloaded, whereas every time he fires his musketoon he is obliged to sponge the barrel, pour powder down it, and ram it in before shooting off one of the absurd missiles he loads it with: bits of iron, limonite, glass, wax, and even stone. But Pedrão is amazingly dexterous and performs this entire operation so fast it seems like magic, as does his incredible marksmanship.

It makes him happy to see him there. If Pedrão and his men have had time to get back, so have Abbot João and Pajeú, and hence Belo Monte is well defended. They have now less than two hundred paces to go before reaching the first dwellings, and the *jagunços* who are in the lead are waving their arms and shouting out their names so the defenders won't shoot at them. Some of them are running; he and Honório start running too, then slow down again because old Zózimo is unable to keep up with them. They each grab an arm and drag him along between them, staggering along all hunched over beneath a rain of gunfire that seems to Antônio to be aimed straight at the three of them. They finally reach what was once the entrance to a street and is now a wall of stones, tin drums filled with sand, planks, roof tiles, bricks, and all manner of objects, on top of which Antônio spies a solid line of sharpshooters. Many hands reach out to help them climb up. Antônio feels himself being lifted up bodily, lowered down, deposited on the other side of the barricade. He sits down in the trench to rest. Someone hands him a leather canteen full of water, which he drinks in little sips with his eyes closed, feeling mingled pain and pleasure as the liquid wets his tongue, his palate, his throat, which seem to be made of sandpaper. The ringing in his ears stops for a moment every so often and he can then hear the gunfire and the shouts of 'Death to the Republic and the atheists!' and 'Long live the Counselor and the Blessed Jesus!' But at one of these moments – his tremendous fatigue is going away little by little, and soon he'll be able to get to his feet – he realizes that it can't be the *jagunços* who are yelling: 'Long live the Republic!' 'Long live Marshal Floriano!' 'Death to traitors!' 'Down with the English!' Is it possible that the dogs are so close that he can hear their voices? The bugle commands are right in his ears. Still sitting there, he places five bullets in the cylinder of his revolver. As he loads the Mannlicher, he sees that he is down to his last ammunition pouch. Making an effort that he feels in his every bone, he gets to his feet and, helping himself up with his knees and elbows, climbs to the top of the barricade. The others make room for him. Less than twenty yards away, countless soldiers, rank upon rank of them, in close order, are charging. Without aiming, without seeking out officers, he fires off all the bullets in the revolver and then all the ones in the Mannlicher, feeling a sharp pain in his shoulder each time the rifle butt recoils. As he hurriedly reloads the revolver he looks around. The Freemasons are attacking on all sides, and in

Pedrão's sector they are even closer than here; a few bayonets are already within reach of the barricades and *jagunços* armed with clubs and knives suddenly spring up, dealing the attackers furious blows. He does not see Pedrão. To his right, in a giant cloud of dust, the wave upon wave of uniforms advance upon Espirito Santo, Santa Ana, São José, Santo Tomás, Santa Rita, São Joaquim. If they take any of these streets, in a matter of minutes they will reach São Pedro or Campo Grande, the heart of Belo Monte, and will be able to launch an attack on Santo Antônio, the Temple of the Blessed Jesus, and the Sanctuary. Someone tugs on his leg. A very young man shouts to him that the Street Commander wants to see him, at São Pedro. The young man takes his place on the barricade.

As he goes up the steep incline of São Crispim, he sees women on both sides of the street filling buckets and crates with sand and carrying them away on their shoulders. All round him are people running, dust, chaos, amid dwellings with the roofs caved in, façades riddled with bullet holes and blackened from smoke, and others that have collapsed or been gutted by fire. The frantic hustle and bustle has a center, he discovers on reaching São Pedro, the street parallel to Campo Grande that cuts through Belo Monte from the Vaza-Barris to the cemetery. The Street Commander is there, with two carbines slung over his shoulders, erecting barricades to close off the area on all the corners facing the river. Abbot João shakes hands with him and without preamble – but also, Antônio thinks, without undue haste, so calmly and deliberately that he will understand precisely – he asks him to take charge of closing off the side streets that lead into São Pedro, using all the men available.

'Wouldn't it be better to reinforce the defenses down below?' Antônio Vilanova asks, pointing to the place he has just come from.

'We won't be able to hold out very long down there. It's open terrain,' the Street Commander replies. 'Up here they won't know which way to go and will get in each other's way. It's going to have to be a real wall, a good solid high one.'

'Don't worry, Abbot João. Carry on, and I'll take care of it.' But as Abbot João turns away, he adds: 'What's with Pajeú?'

'He's still alive,' João answers without turning around. 'He's at Fazenda Velha.'

'Defending the water supply,' Vilanova thinks. If they're driven out of there, Canudos will be left without a drop of water. After the churches and the Sanctuary, that is what matters most if they are to survive: water. The former *cangaceiro* disappears in the cloud of dust, striding down the slope leading to the river. Antônio turns his eyes toward the towers of the Temple of the Blessed Jesus. Out of a superstitious fear that they might no longer be there in their place, he has not looked that way since returning to Belo Monte. And there they are, chipped but still standing, their solid stone armature having withstood the dogs, bullets, shells, dynamite. The *jagunços* perched in the bell tower, on the rooftops, on the scaffolding are keeping up a steady fire, and others, squatting on their heels or sitting, are doing the same from the rooftop and the bell tower of Santo Antônio. Amid the little groups of sharpshooters of the Catholic Guard firing from the barricades surrounding the Sanctuary, he spies Big João. All that suddenly uplifts his heart, fills him with faith, banishes the panic that has mounted from the soles of his feet on hearing Abbot João say that the soldiers are bound to get through the trenches down below, that there is no hope of stopping them there. Without losing any more time, he shouts to the swarms of women, children, and old men, ordering them to begin tearing down all the dwellings on the corners of São Crispim, São Joaquim, Santa Rita, Santo Tomás, Espirito Santo, Santa Ana, São José, so as to turn all that section of Belo Monte into an inextricable maze. He takes the lead, using his rifle butt as a battering ram. Making trenches, erecting barricades means constructing, organizing, and those are things that Antônio Vilanova is better at than making war.

Since all the rifles, cases of ammunition, and explosives had been taken away, the general store seemed to have tripled in size. The huge empty space made the nearsighted journalist feel even more lonely. The shelling made him lose all sense of time. How long had he been shut up here in the storeroom with the Mother of Men and the Lion of Natuba? He had listened to the Lion read the paper about the plans for attacking the city with a gnashing of teeth that still hadn't stopped. Since then, the night must have gone by, day must be dawning. It wasn't possible that the cannonading had been going on for less than eight, ten hours. But his fear made each second longer, made the minutes stop dead. Perhaps not even an hour had gone by since Abbot João, Pedrão, Pajeú, Honório Vilanova, and Big João had left on the run, on hearing the first explosions of what the paper had called 'the softening-up.' He remembered their hasty departure, the argument between the men and the woman who wanted to go back to the Sanctuary, how they'd obliged her to stay behind.

Nonetheless, all that was encouraging. If they'd left these two intimates of the Counselor's in the store, it meant that they were better protected here than elsewhere. But wasn't it ridiculous to think of safe places at a time like this? The 'softening-up' was not a matter of shooting at specific targets; it involved, rather, blind cannon salvos whose purpose was to cause fires, destroy dwellings, leave corpses and rubble strewn all over the streets, thereby so badly demoralizing the townspeople that they would not have the courage to stand up to the soldiers when they invaded Canudos.

'Colonel Moreira César's philosophy,' he thought to himself. What idiots, what idiots, what idiots. They hadn't the slightest notion of what was happening here, they hadn't the least idea of what these people were like. The only one who was being softened up by the interminable barrage of the pitch-dark city was himself. He thought: 'Half of Canudos must have disappeared, three-quarters of Canudos.' But thus far not a single shell had hit the store. Dozens of times, closing his eyes, clenching his teeth, he thought: 'This is the one, this is the one.' His body bounced up and down as the roof tiles, the sheets of galvanized tin, the wooden planks shook, as that cloud of dust rose amid which everything appeared to shatter, to tear apart, to fall to pieces over him, under him, around him. But the store remained standing, holding up despite being rocked to its foundations by the explosions.

The woman and the Lion of Natuba were talking together. All he could hear was the murmur of their voices, not what they were saying. He pricked up his ears. They had not said one word since the beginning of the shelling, and at one point he thought that they'd been hit by the bullets and that he was keeping vigil over their dead bodies. The cannonade had deafened him; he could hear a loud bubbling sound, tiny internal explosions. And what about Jurema? And the Dwarf? They had gone in vain to Fazenda Velha to take food to Pajeú, since as they were going out there he was coming back to the meeting in the store. Were they still alive? A sudden wave of affection, aching loneliness, passionate concern washed over him as he imagined them in Pajeú's trench, cringing beneath the shells, surely missing him as much as he missed them. They were part of him and he was part of them. How was it possible for him to feel such a great affinity, such boundless love for those two beings with whom he had nothing in common, whose social background, education, sensibility, experience, culture were in fact altogether different from his? What they had been through together for all these months had forged this bond between them, the fact that without ever imagining such a thing, without deliberately seeking it, without knowing how or why, through the sort of strange, fantastic concatenation of cause and effect, of chance, accident, and coincidence that constitute history, the three of them had been catapulted together into the midst of these extraordinary events, into this life at the brink of death. That was what had created this tie between them. 'I'm never going to be separated from them again,' he thought. 'I'll go with them to take food to Pajeú, I'll go with them to . . .'

But he had the feeling that he was being ridiculous. After this night, would their daily routine be exactly the same as in the past? If they lived through this bombardment, safe and sound, would they survive the second part of the program that the Lion of Natuba had read aloud? He could already see in his mind the dense, solid lines of thousands and thousands of soldiers coming down from the mountaintops with bayonets fixed, pouring down all the streets of Canudos, and felt a cold blade in the thin flesh of his back. He would shout to them to tell them who he was and they wouldn't hear him, he would shout to them 'I'm one of you, a civilized person, an intellectual, a journalist,' and they wouldn't believe him or understand him, he would shout to them 'I have nothing to do with these madmen, with these barbarians,' but it would be useless. They wouldn't give him time to open his mouth. Dying as a *jagunço*, amid the anonymous mass of *jagunços*: wasn't that the height of the absurd, the flagrant proof of the innate stupidity of the world? He missed Jurema and the Dwarf with all his heart, he felt an urgent need to have them close at hand, to talk to them and listen to them.

As though both his ears had suddenly become unstopped, he heard, very clearly, the voice of the Mother of Men: there were faults that could not be expiated, sins that could not be redeemed. In that hard, resigned, tormented voice full of conviction was a suffering that seemed to come from the depths of time itself. 'There's a place in the fire waiting for me,' he heard her repeat. 'I can't close my eyes to that, my child.'

'There is no crime that the Father cannot pardon,' the Lion of Natuba answered promptly. 'Our Lady has interceded in your behalf and the Father has forgiven you. Don't torture yourself, Mother.'

That was a voice with a good timbre, steady, fluent, full of the music of the heart. The journalist thought to himself that that normal, lilting voice always seemed to belong to a strong, handsome man, standing straight and tall, not to the man who was speaking.

'He was tiny, defenseless, a tender little newborn lamb,' the woman chanted. 'His mother's milk had dried up; she was a wicked woman who'd sold her soul to the Devil. Then, on the pretext that she couldn't bear to see him suffer, she stuffed a skein of wool in his mouth. It's not a sin like the others, my child. It is the unpardonable sin. You'll see me burning in hell forever.'

'Don't you believe the Counselor?' the scribe of Canudos said consolingly. 'Doesn't he speak to the Father? Hasn't he said that . . .?'

A deafening explosion drowned out his words. The journalist's body went rigid and he closed his eyes and trembled as the whole building shook, but the sound of the woman's voice lingered on as he associated what he had heard with a dim memory of long ago which, beneath the spell of her words, was rising to the surface from the depths where it lay buried. Was it she? Once again he heard the voice that he had heard in the courtroom, twenty years before: soft, sorrowful, detached, impersonal.

'You're the filicide of Salvador,' he said.

He did not have time to feel alarmed at having said that, for suddenly there were two explosions, one after the other, and the store creaked violently, as though it were about to fall in. A cloud of windblown dust blew in, all of which seemed to settle in his nostrils. He began sneezing, a crescendo of ever more violent, ever more desperate sneezes, closer and closer together, that made him writhe on the floor. His chest was about to burst for lack of air and he pounded it with both hands as he sneezed, and at the same time, as in a dream, he caught a glimpse of blue between the cracks: day had dawned at last. With his temples stretched to the bursting point, the thought came to him that this was the end, he was going to die of asphyxiation, of a sneezing fit, a stupid way to die but preferable to being bayoneted by soldiers. He collapsed on the floor and lay on his back, still sneezing. A second later his head was resting on a warm, affectionate, protecting lap. The woman sat him on her knees, wiped the sweat from his forehead, cradled him in her arms as mothers do to rock their children to sleep.

The sneezes, his discomfort, his near-suffocation, his weakness had the virtue of freeing him from fear. The roar of the cannons sounded as though it had nothing to do with him, and the idea of dying seemed a matter of complete indifference to him. The woman's hands, her voice softly murmuring, her breath, her fingers stroking the top of his head, his forehead, his eyes, filled him with peace, took him back to a dim childhood. He had stopped sneezing but the tickling sensation in his nostrils – two open wounds – told him that he might have another attack at any moment. In that fuzzy, drunken state, he remembered other attacks when he had also been certain that it was the end, those bohemian nights in Bahia which the sneezing fits brutally interrupted, like a censorious conscience, to the hilarious amusement of his friends, those poets, musicians, painters, journalists, parasites, actors, and night owls of Salvador among whom he had wasted his life. He remembered how he had begun to inhale ether because it brought him relief after these attacks that left him exhausted, humiliated, his every nerve on edge, and how, later, opium saved him from sneezing fits by bringing on a lucid, transitory death. The caresses, the soft whispering, the consolation, the warm odor of this woman who had killed her baby, back in the days when he was a cub reporter still in his teens, and who was now the priestess of Canudos, were like opium and ether: something gentle that brought on drowsiness, a pleasing absence, and he wondered whether when he was little that mother whom he did not remember had caressed him like this, making him feel invulnerable and indifferent to the world's dangers. There passed before his mind the classrooms and courtyards of the school of the Salesian Fathers where, thanks to his sneezes, he had been – like the Dwarf no doubt, like the monstrous creature here in the room who had read the paper – a laughingstock and a victim, the butt of cruel jokes. Because of his fits of sneezing and his poor eyesight, he had been treated like an invalid, kept from sports, violent games, outings. That was why he had become such a timid person; on account of that accursed, uncontrollable nose of his, he had had to use handkerchiefs as big as bed-sheets, and because of it and his squint eyes he had never had a sweetheart, a fiancée, or a wife, and had lived with the permanent feeling of being an object of ridicule and hence unable to declare his love for the girls he loved or to send them the verses he composed for them and then like a coward tore up. On account of that nose, that myopia of his, he had never held any woman save the whores of Bahia in his arms, known only love for sale, hasty, filthy encounters that he paid for twice over, the second time with purges and treatments with catheters that made him howl with pain. He, too, was a monster, maimed, disabled, abnormal. It was no accident that he had ended up where the cripples, the unfortunate, the abnormal, the long-suffering of this world had congregated. It was inevitable: he was one of them.

He wailed at the top of his lungs, curled up in a ball, clutching the Mother of Men with both his hands, stammering, bemoaning his wretched fate and his misfortunes, pouring out in a torrent, slavering and sobbing, his bitterness and his desperation, present and past, the disillusionments of his lost youth, his emotional and intellectual frustration, speaking to her with a sincerity he had never before been capable of, not even with himself, telling her how miserable and unhappy he felt because he had not shared a great love, not been the successful dramatist, the inspired poet that he would have liked to be, and because he knew now that he was about to die even more stupidly than he had lived. He heard himself say, between one panting breath and another: 'It isn't fair, it isn't fair, it isn't fair.' He realized that she was kissing him on the forehead, on the cheeks, on the eyelids as she whispered sweet, tender, incoherent words to him, as one does to newborn babies to enchant them and make them happy just by the sound of them . . . And in fact he felt great comfort, wondrous gratitude toward those magic words: 'My little one, my little son, little baby, little dove, little lamb . . .'

But they were abruptly brought back to the present, to violence, to the war. The earsplitting explosion that tore the roof away suddenly left them with the sky overhead, the beaming sun, clouds, the bright morning air. Splinters, bricks, broken roof tiles, twisted wire were flying in all directions, and the nearsighted journalist felt pebbles, clods of dirt, stones hit a thousand places on his body, face, hands. But neither he nor the woman nor the Lion of Natuba was knocked down as the building collapsed. They stood there clutching each other, clinging to each other, and he searched frantically through his pockets for his monocle painstakingly assembled from bits of glass, thinking that it had been reduced to shards again, that from now on he would not be able to count on even this scant aid. But there it was, intact, and still holding tight to the Superior of the Sacred Choir and the Lion of Natuba, he managed little by little to see, in distorted images, the havoc caused by the explosion. In addition to the roof, the front wall had also caved in, and except for the corner that they were in, the store was a mountain of rubble. Beyond the fallen wall he could vaguely make out piles of debris, smoke, silhouettes running.

And at that moment the place was suddenly filled with armed men, with armbands and blue headcloths; among them he could make out the massive bulk of Big João, naked to the waist. As the nearsighted journalist, his eye glued to the monocle, stood watching the men embrace Maria Quadrado, the Lion of Natuba, he trembled: they were going to take them away with them and he would be left all by himself in these ruins. He clung to the woman and the scribe, and past all sense of shame, all scruples lost, he began to whine to them not to leave him, to implore them, and the Mother of Men dragged him off by the hand after the two of them when the huge black ordered everyone out of there.

He found himself trotting along in a world turned topsy-turvy, a chaos of clouds of smoke, noise, mountains of debris. He had stopped weeping, all his senses focused now on the perilous task of skirting obstacles, of keeping from tripping, stumbling, falling, letting go of the woman. He had gone up Campo Grande dozens of times, heading for the square between the churches, and yet he recognized nothing: walls caved in, holes, stones, all manner of things scattered about everywhere, people scurrying in all directions, shooting, fleeing, screaming. Instead of cannon reports, he now heard rifle shots and children crying. He didn't know exactly when it was that he let go of the woman, but all of a sudden he realized that he was no longer clinging to her but to a quite different shape trotting along, the sound of its anxious panting breath mingling with his own. He was holding on to it by the thick locks of its abundant mane. The two of them were straggling, they were being left behind. He clutched his fistful of the Lion of Natuba's hair in an iron grip; if he let go of it, all would be lost. And as he ran, leapt, dodged, he heard himself begging him not to get too far ahead, to have pity on a poor soul who could not make his way along by himself.

He collided with something that he took to be a wall but turned out to be men's bodies. He felt himself being pushed back, turned away, when he heard the woman's voice asking to be let through. The wall opened, he caught a glimpse of barrels and sacks and men shooting and shouting to each other, and, with the Mother of Men on one side of him and the Lion of Natuba on the other, passed through a little door made of wooden pickets and entered a dark, closed space. Touching his face, the woman said to him: 'Stay here. Don't be afraid. Pray.' Straining his eyes, he managed to see her and the Lion of Natuba disappear through a second little door.

He sank to the floor. He was worn out, hungry, thirsty, sleepy, overcome by a desperate need to forget the whole nightmare. 'I'm in the Sanctuary,' he thought. 'The Counselor is here,' he thought. He was amazed at having ended up here, aware of how privileged he was: he was about to see and hear, from close at hand, the eye of the storm that had shaken all of Brazil, the most famous, the most hated man in the country. What good would it do him? Would he have the chance to tell people about it? He tried to overhear what they were saying there inside the Sanctuary, but the uproar outside kept him from catching a single word. The light filtering through the cane-stalk walls was a dazzling white and the heat stifling. The soldiers must be in Canudos, there must be fighting in the streets. He nonetheless felt a deep peace steal over him in this solitary, shadowy redoubt.

The picket door creaked and he glimpsed the dim silhouette of a woman with a kerchief on her head. She placed a bowl of food in his hands and a tin full of a liquid, which, when he took a sip of it, proved to be milk.

'Mother Maria Quadrado is praying for you,' he heard a voice say. 'Praised be Blessed Jesus the Counselor.'

'Praised be He,' he answered, continuing to chew and swallow. Every time he ate in Canudos his jaws ached, as though they had become stiff from disuse: it was an agreeable pain that his body rejoiced in. Once he had finished, he lay down on the floor, cradled his head in the crook of his arm, and fell asleep. Eating, sleeping: this was now the only happiness possible. The rifle shots were closer, then farther away again, then seemed to be coming from all around him, and there was the sound of hurrying footsteps. Colonel Moreira César's thin, ascetic, nervous face was there, just as he had seen it so many times as he rode alongside him, or at night when they camped, talking together after chow. He recognized his voice without a moment's hesitation, its peremptory, steely edge: the softening-up operation must be carried out before the final charge so as to save lives for the Republic; an abscess must be lanced immediately and without sentimentality, otherwise the infection would rot the entire organism. At the same time, he knew that the gunfire was growing heavier and heavier, the casualties, the cave-ins following one upon the other faster and faster, and he had the feeling that armed men were coming and going above him, trying their best not to trample him underfoot, bringing news of the war that he preferred to turn a deaf ear to because it was bad.

He was certain that he was no longer dreaming when he discovered that the bleating that he was hearing was coming from a little white lamb that was licking his hand. He stroked the creature's woolly head and it allowed him to do so without bolting in fear. The other sound was the voices of two people talking together alongside him. He raised to his eye his monocle of glass shards, which he had clutched tightly in his fist as he slept. In the dim light he recognized the vague silhouette of Father Joaquim and that of a barefoot woman dressed in a white tunic with a blue kerchief on her head. The curé of Cumbe was holding a rifle between his legs and was wearing a bandoleer of bullets around his neck. As well as he could make out, Father Joaquim had the look of a man who had been fighting: his spare locks were disheveled and matted with dirt, his cassock in tatters, one sandal was tied round his foot with a length of twine rather than a leather thong, and he was obviously completely exhausted. He was speaking of someone named Joaquinzinho.

'He went out with Antônio Vilanova to get food,' he heard him saying dejectedly. 'I heard from Abbot João that the whole group that was out in the trenches along the Vaza-Barris got back safely.' His voice choked up and he cleared his throat. 'The ones who survived the attack.'

'What about Joaquinzinho?' the woman said again.

It was Alexandrinha Correa, the woman people told so many stories about: that she knew how to find underground water sources, that she had been Father Joaquim's concubine. He was unable to make out her face. She and the curé were sitting on the floor. The inner door of the Sanctuary was open and there did not appear to be anyone inside.

'He didn't make it back,' the little priest said softly. 'Antônio did, and Honório, and many of the others who were at Vaza-Barris. But he didn't. Nobody could tell me what happened to him, nobody's seen him since.'

'I'd at least like to be able to bury him,' the woman said. 'Not just leave him lying there in the open, like an animal with no master.'

'He may not be dead,' the curé of Cumbe answered. 'If the Vilanova brothers and others got back, why shouldn't Joaquinzinho? Maybe he's on the towers now, or on the barricade at São Pedro, or with his brother at Fazenda Velha. The soldiers haven't been able to take the trenches there either.'

The nearsighted journalist suddenly felt overjoyed and wanted to ask about Jurema and the Dwarf, but he contained himself: he sensed that he ought not to intrude upon the couple's privacy at this intimate moment. The voices of the curé and the devout disciple were those of calm acceptance of fate, not at all dramatic. The little lamb was nibbling at his hand. He raised himself to a sitting position, but neither Father Joaquim nor the woman seemed to mind that he was there awake, listening.

'If Joaquinzinho is dead, it's better if Atanásio dies, too,' the woman said. 'So they can keep each other company in death.'

He suddenly had gooseflesh across the nape of his neck. Was it because of what the woman had said, or the pealing of the bells? He could hear them ringing, very close by, and heard Ave Marias chorused by countless voices. It was dusk, then. The battle had already gone on for almost an entire day. He listened. It was not over yet: mingled with the sound of prayers and bells were salvos of artillery fire. Some of the shells were bursting just above their heads. Death was more important to these people than life. They had lived in utter dereliction and their one ambition was to be given a decent burial. How to understand them? Perhaps, however, if a person were living the sort of life that he was at this moment, death would be his only hope of a reward, a 'fiesta,' as the Counselor always called it.

The curé of Cumbe was looking his way. 'It's sad that children must kill and die fighting,' he heard him murmur. 'Atanásio is fourteen, and Joaquinzinho isn't yet thirteen. They've been killing and risking being killed for a year now. Isn't that sad?'

'Yes, it is,' the nearsighted journalist stammered. 'Indeed it is. I fell asleep. How's the battle going, Father?'

'They've been stopped at São Pedro,' the parish priest of Cumbe answered. 'At the barricade that Antônio Vilanova erected this morning.'

'Do you mean here inside the city?' the nearsighted man asked.

'Just thirty paces from here.'

São Pedro. The street that cut through Canudos from the river to the cemetery, the one parallel to Campo Grande, one of the few that deserved to be called a street. Now it was a barricade and the soldiers were there. Just thirty paces away. A chill ran up his spine. The sound of prayers grew louder, softer, disappeared, mounted again, and it seemed to the nearsighted journalist that in the intervals between explosions he could hear the Counselor's hoarse voice or the tiny piping voice of the Little Blessed One there outside, and that the women, the wounded, the oldsters, the dying, the *jagunço* sharpshooters were all reciting the Ave Maria in chorus. What must the soldiers think of these prayers?

'It's also sad that a priest should be obliged to take rifle in hand,' Father Joaquim said, patting the weapon that he was holding across his knees, just as the *jagunços* did. 'I didn't know how to shoot. Father Martinez had never shot a rifle either, not even to go deer-hunting.'

Was this the same elderly little man the nearsighted journalist had seen whimpering and sniveling before Colonel Moreira César, half dead with panic?

'Father Martinez?' he asked.

He sensed Father Joaquim's sudden wariness. So there were other priests in Canudos with them. He imagined them loading their guns, aiming, shooting. But wasn't the Church on the side of the Republic? Hadn't the Counselor been excommunicated by the archbishop? Hadn't edicts condemning the mad, fanatical heretic of Canudos been read aloud in all the parishes? How, then, could there be curés killing for the Counselor?

'Do you hear them? Listen, listen: "Fanatics, Sebastianists! Cannibals! Englishmen! Murderers!" Who was it who came here to kill women and children, to slit people's throats? Who was it who forced youngsters of thirteen and fourteen to become combatants? You're here and you're still alive, isn't that true?'

He shook with terror from head to foot. Father Joaquim was going to hand him over to the *jagunços* to be made a victim of their vengeance, their hatred.

'Because the fact is you came with the Throat-Slitter, isn't that true?' the curé went on. 'And yet you've been given a roof over your head, food, hospitality. Would the soldiers do as much for one of Pedrão's or Pajeú's or Abbot João's men?'

In a choked voice, he stammered in answer: 'Yes, yes, you're right. I'm most grateful to you for having helped me so much, Father Joaquim. I swear it, I swear it.'

'They're being killed by the dozens, by the hundreds.' The curé of Cumbe pointed in the direction of the street. 'And what for? For believing in God, for living their lives in accordance with God's law. It's the Massacre of the Innocents, all over again.'

Was the priest about to burst into tears, to stamp his feet in rage, to roll about on the floor in despair? But then the near-sighted journalist saw that the priest, controlling himself with an effort, was beginning to calm down, standing there dejectedly listening to the shots, the prayers, the church bells. The journalist thought he heard bugle commands as well. Still not recovered from the scare that he had had, he timidly asked the priest if by chance he had seen Jurema and the Dwarf. The curé shook his head.

At that moment he heard a melodious baritone voice from close by say: 'They've been at São Pedro, helping to erect the barricade.'

The monocle of glass shards allowed him to make out, just barely, the Lion of Natuba alongside the little open door of the Sanctuary, either sitting or kneeling, but in any event hunched down inside his dirt-covered tunic, looking at him with his great gleaming eyes. Had he been there for some time or had he just come in? This strange being, half human and half animal, so disconcerted him that he was unable to thank him or utter a single word. He could hardly see him, for the light had grown dimmer, though a beam of waning light was coming in through the cracks between the pickets of the door and dying away in the unkempt mane of the scribe of Canudos.

'I wrote down the Counselor's every word,' he heard him say in his beautiful lilting voice. The words were addressed to him, an effort on the hunchback's part to be friendly. 'His thoughts, his evening counsels, his prayers, his prophecies, his dreams. For posterity. So as to add another Gospel to the Bible.'

'I see,' the nearsighted journalist murmured, at a loss for words.

'But there's no more paper or ink left in Belo Monte and my last quill pen broke. What he says can no longer be preserved for all eternity,' the Lion of Natuba went on, without bitterness, with that calm acceptance with which the journalist had seen the people of Canudos face the world, as though misfortunes, like rainstorms, twilights, the ebb and flow of the tide, were natural phenomena against which it would be stupid to rebel.

'The Lion of Natuba is an extremely intelligent person,' the curé of Cumbe murmured. 'What God took away from him in the way of legs, a back, shoulders, He made up for by way of the intelligence He gave him. Isn't that so, Lion?'

'Yes.' The scribe of Canudos nodded, his eyes never leaving the nearsighted journalist. And the latter was certain that this was true. 'I've read the Abbreviated Missal and the Marian Hours many times. And all the magazines and periodicals that people used to bring me in the old days. Over and over. Have you read a great deal too, sir?'

The nearsighted journalist felt so ill at ease that he would have liked to run from the room, even if it meant running right into the midst of the battle. 'I've read a few books,' he answered, feeling ashamed. And he thought: 'And I got nothing out of them.' That was something that he had discovered in these long months: culture, knowledge were lies, dead weight, blindfolds. All that reading – and it had been of no use whatsoever in helping him to escape, to free himself from this trap.

'I know what electricity is,' the Lion of Natuba said proudly. 'If you like, sir, I can teach you what it is. And in return, sir, you can teach me things I don't know. I know what the principle or the law of Archimedes is. How bodies are mummified. The distances between stars.'

But at that moment there was heavy gunfire from several directions at once, and the nearsighted journalist found himself thanking the battle that had suddenly silenced this creature whose voice, whose proximity, whose very existence caused him such profound malaise. Why was he so disconcerted by someone who simply wanted to talk, who so naïvely flaunted his talents, his virtues, merely to gain his warm fellow-feeling? 'Because I'm like him,' he thought. 'Because I'm part of the same chain of which he is the humblest link.'

The curé of Cumbe ran to the little door leading outside, threw it wide open, and a breath of twilight entered that revealed to the nearsighted journalist other of the Lion of Natuba's features: his dark skin, the fine-drawn lines of his face, the tuft of down on his chin, his steely eyes. But it was his posture that left him dumfounded: the face hunched over between two bony knees, the massive hump behind the head, like a big bundle tied to his back, and the extremities appended to limbs as long and spindly as spider legs. How could a human skeleton dislocate itself, fold itself around itself like that? What absurd contortions were built into that spinal column, those ribs, those bones?

Father Joaquim and those outside were shouting back and forth: there was an attack, people were needed at a certain place. He came back into the room and the journalist could dimly make out that he was picking up his rifle.

'They're attacking the barricades at São Cipriano and São Crispim,' he heard him stammer. 'Go to the Temple of the Blessed Jesus. You'll be safer there. Farewell, farewell, may Our Lady save us all.'

He ran out of the room and the nearsighted journalist saw Alexandrinha Correa take the lamb, which had begun to bleat in fright, in her arms. The devout disciple from the Sacred Choir asked the Lion of Natuba if he would come with her and in his harmonious voice he answered that he would stay in the Sanctuary. And what about him? What about him? Would he stay there with the monster? Would he tag along after the woman? But she had left now and deep shadow reigned once more in the little room with cane-stalk walls. The heat was stifling. The gunfire became heavier and heavier. He could see the soldiers in his mind's eye, penetrating the barricade of stones and sandbags, trampling the corpses underfoot, sweeping like a raging torrent down on the place where he was.

'I don't want to die,' he said slowly and distinctly, unable, he realized, to shed a single tear.

'If you like, sir, we'll make a pact,' the Lion of Natuba said in a calm voice. 'We made one with Mother Maria Quadrado. But she won't have time to get back here. Would you like us to make a pact?'

The nearsighted journalist was trembling so badly that he was unable to open his mouth. Below the heavy gunfire he could hear, like a peaceful, quietly flowing melody, the bells and the regular counterpoint of Ave Marias.

'So as not to die by the knife,' the Lion of Natuba explained. 'A knife plunged into a man's throat, slitting it the way you cut an animal's throat to bleed it to death, is a terrible insult to human dignity. It rends one's soul. Would you like us to make a pact, sir?'

He waited for a moment, and since there was no answer, he explained further: 'When we hear them at the door of the Sanctuary and it's certain that they're going to get inside, we'll kill each other. Each of us will hold the other's mouth and nose shut till our lungs burst. Or we can strangle each other with our hands or the laces of our sandals. Shall we make a pact?'

The fusillade drowned out the Lion of Natuba's voice. The nearsighted journalist's head was a dizzying vortex, and all the ideas that rose within him like sputtering sparks – contradictory, threatening, lugubrious – made his anxiety all the more acute. They sat there in silence, listening to the shots, the sound of running footsteps, the tremendous chaos. The light was dying fast and he could no longer see the scribe's features; all he could make out was the dim outline of his hulking, hunchbacked body. He would not make that pact with him, he would not be able to carry it out; the moment he heard the soldiers he would start shouting I'm a prisoner of the *jagunços*, help, save me, he would yell out Long live the Republic, Long live Marshal Floriano, he would fling himself on the quadrumane, he would overpower him and turn him over to the soldiers as proof that he wasn't a *jagunço*.

'I don't understand, I don't understand. What sort of creatures are you all anyway?' he heard himself say as he clutched his head in his hands. 'What are you doing here, why didn't all of you flee before they had you surrounded? What madness to wait in a rat trap like this for them to come kill you all!'

'There isn't anywhere to flee to,' the Lion of Natuba answered. 'That's what we kept doing before. That's why we came here. This was the place we fled to. There's nowhere else now – they've come to Belo Monte, too.'

The gunfire drowned out his voice. It was almost dark now, and the nearsighted journalist thought to himself that for him night would fall sooner than for the others. He would rather die than spend another night like the last one. He had a tremendous, painful, biological need to be near his two comrades.

In a fit of madness, he decided to go look for them, and as he stumbled to the door he shouted: 'I'm going to look for my friends. I want to die with my friends.'

As he pushed the little door open, fresh, cool air hit his face and he sensed – mere blurred shapes in the cloud of dust – the figures of the men defending the Sanctuary sprawled out on the parapet.

'Can I leave? Can I please leave?' he begged. 'I want to find my friends.'

'Come ahead,' a voice answered. 'There's no shooting just now.'

He took a few steps, leaning against the barricade, and almost immediately he stumbled over something soft. As he rose to his feet, he found himself in the arms of a thin, female form clutching him to her. From the warm odor of her, from the happiness that flooded over him, he knew who it was before he heard her voice. His terror turned to joy as he embraced this woman as desperately as she was embracing him. A pair of lips met his, clung to his, returned his kisses. 'I love you,' he stammered, 'I love you, I love you. I don't care now if I die.' And as he said again and again that he loved her, he asked her for news of the Dwarf.

'We've been looking for you all day long,' the Dwarf said, his arms encircling the journalist's legs. 'All day long. What a blessing that you're alive!'

'I don't care now if I die either,' Jurema's lips said beneath his.

'This is the house of the Pyrotechnist,' General Artur Oscar suddenly exclaims. The officials who are reporting on the number of dead and wounded in the attack that he was given orders to halt look at him in bewilderment. The general points to some half-finished skyrockets, made of reeds and pegs held together with pita fiber, scattered about the dwelling. 'He's the one who prepares their fireworks displays for them.'

Of the eight blocks – if the jumbled piles of rubble can be called 'blocks' – that the troops have taken in nearly twelve hours of fighting, this one-room hut, with a partition of wooden slats dividing it in two, is the only one that has been left standing, more or less. This is the reason why it has been chosen as general headquarters. The orderlies and officers surrounding the commandant of the expeditionary corps cannot understand why he is speaking of rockets just as the list of casualties after the hard day's battle is being read off to him. They do not know that fireworks are a secret weakness of General Oscar's, a powerful holdover from his childhood, and that in O Piauí he would seize on any sort of patriotic celebration as an excuse to order a fireworks display to be set off in the courtyard of the barracks. In the month and a half that he has been here, he has watched with envy, from the heights of A Favela, the cascades of lights in the sky above Canudos on certain nights when processions have been held. The man who prepares such displays is a master; he could earn himself a good living in any city in Brazil. Can the Pyrotechnist have died in today's battle? As the general ponders that question, he also pays close attention to the figures being read off by the colonels, majors, captains who enter and leave or remain in the tiny room already enveloped in darkness. An oil lamp is lit, and a detail of soldiers piles sandbags along the wall facing the enemy.

The general completes his calculations. 'It's worse than I had supposed, gentlemen,' he says to the fan of silhouettes. He has a tight feeling in his chest, and can sense how anxiously the officers are waiting. 'One thousand twenty-seven casualties! A third of our forces! Twenty-three officers dead, among them Colonel Carlos Telles and Colonel Serra Martins. Do you realize what that means?'

No one answers, but the general knows that all of them are perfectly aware that such a large number of casualties is tantamount to a defeat. He sees how frustrated, angry, astonished his subordinates are; the eyes of a number of them glisten with tears.

'Going on with the attack would have meant being completely wiped out. Do you understand that now?'

Because when, alarmed by the *jagunços'* resistance and his intuition that casualties among the patriots were already heavy – along with the tremendous shock to him of the death of Telles and of Serra Martins – General Oscar ordered the troops to confine themselves to defending the positions they had already taken, the order was greeted with indignation by many of these officers, and the general feared that some of them might even disobey it. His own adjutant, First Lieutenant Pinto Souza, of the Third Infantry Corps, protested: 'But victory is within our reach, sir!' It was not. A third of the troops *hors de combat*. An extremely high percentage, catastrophic, despite the eight blocks captured and the damage inflicted on the fanatics.

He puts the Pyrotechnist out of his mind and sets to work with his general staff. He dismisses the field officers, aides, or representatives of the assault corps, repeating the order to hold the positions already taken and not fall back a single step, and to strengthen the barricade, opposite the one that stopped them, which the troops had started to erect a few hours before when it became evident that the city was not going to fall. He decides that the Seventh Brigade, which has remained behind to protect the wounded on A Favela, will move forward to reinforce the 'black line,' the new front, already well established in the heart of the rebellious city. In the cone of light from the oil lamp, he bends over the map drawn by Captain Teotônio Coriolano, his staff cartographer, on the basis of reports that he has received and his own observations of the situation. A fifth of Canudos has been taken, a triangle which extends from the line of trench works at Fazenda Velha still in the hands of the *jagunços,* to the cemetery, which has been captured, thus allowing the patriot troops to occupy a position within less than eighty paces of the Church of Santo Antônio.

'The front is no more than fifteen hundred meters long at most,' Captain Guimarães says, making no attempt to conceal his disappointment. 'We're far from having them surrounded. We haven't occupied even a quarter of the circumference. They can come and go and receive supplies.'

'We can't extend the front until the reinforcements arrive,' Major Carrenho complains. 'Why are they leaving us stranded like this, sir?'

General Oscar shrugs. Ever since the ambush, on the day they arrived in Canudos, as he has seen the death toll among his men mount, he has kept sending urgent, justified pleas for more troops, and has even gone so far as to exaggerate the seriousness of the situation. Why don't his superiors send them?

'If there had been five thousand of us instead of three thousand, Canudos would be ours by now,' an officer says, thinking aloud.

The general forces them to change the subject by informing them that he is going to inspect the front and the new field hospital set up that morning along the ravines of the Vaza-Barris once the *jagunços* had been dislodged from there. Before leaving the Pyrotechnist's shack, he drinks a cup of coffee, listening to the bells and the Ave Marias of the fanatics, so close by he can't believe it.

Even at the age of fifty-three, he is a man of great energy, who rarely feels fatigue. He has followed the development of the attack in detail, watching through his field glasses since five this morning, when the corps began to leave A Favela, and he has marched with them, immediately behind the battalions of the vanguard, without halting to rest and without eating a single mouthful, contenting himself with a few sips from his canteen. Early in the afternoon, a stray bullet wounded a soldier who was marching directly alongside him. He leaves the shack. Night has fallen; there is not a star in the sky. The sound of the prayers is everywhere, like a magic spell, and drowns out the last bursts of rifle fire. He gives orders that no fires be lighted in the trench. Nonetheless, in the course of his slow tour of inspection via an itinerary full of twists and turns, escorted by four officers, at many points along the winding, labyrinthine barricade hastily thrown up by the soldiers, behind which they are lined up, their backs against the inner brick facing of the wall of debris, earth, stones, oil drums, and all manner of implements and objects, sleeping one against the other, some with enough high spirits still to be singing or poking their heads over the wall to insult the bandits – who must be crouching listening behind their own barricade, a mere five yards distant in some sections, ten in others, and in still others the two practically touching – General Oscar finds braziers around which knots of soldiers are making soup with scraps of meat, heating up chunks of jerky, or warming wounded men trembling with fever who are in such bad shape that they cannot be evacuated to the field hospital.

He exchanges a few words with the leaders of companies, of battalions. They are exhausted, and he discovers in them the same desolation, mingled with stupefaction, that he feels in the face of the incomprehensible things that have happened in this accursed war. As he congratulates a young second lieutenant for his heroic conduct during the attack, he repeats to himself something that he has told himself many times before: 'I curse the day I accepted this command.'

While he was in Queimadas, struggling with the devilish problems of lack of transport, of draft animals, of carts for the provisions, which were to keep him stuck there for three months of mortal boredom, General Oscar learned that before the army and the office of the President of the Republic had offered him command of the expedition three generals on active duty had refused to accept it. He now understands why he was offered what he believed in his naïveté to be a distinction, a command that would gloriously crown his career. As he shakes hands and exchanges impressions with officers and soldiers whose faces he is unable to see in the dark, he reflects on what an idiot he was to have believed that his superiors wanted to reward him by removing him from his post as commanding officer of the military district of O Piauí, where he had so peacefully put in his almost twenty years of service, so as to allow him, before retiring, to lead a glorious military campaign: crushing the monarchist-restorationist rebellion in the backlands of the state of Bahia. No, he had not been entrusted with this command in order to compensate him for having been passed over for promotion so many times and in order to recognize his merits at last – as he had told his wife when he announced the news to her – but in order to ensure, rather, that other high-ranking army officers would not get bogged down in a quagmire like this. Those three generals had been right, of course! Had he, a career officer, been prepared for this grotesque, absurd war, fought totally outside the rules and conventions of a real war?

At one end of the wall they are barbecuing a steer. General Oscar sits down to eat a few mouthfuls of grilled beef amid a group of officers. He chats with them about the bells of Canudos and those prayers that have just ended. The oddities of this war: those prayers, those processions, those pealing bells, those churches that the bandits defend so furiously. Once again he is overcome with uneasiness. It troubles him that those degenerate cannibals are, despite everything, Brazilians, that is to say, essentially the same as those attacking them. But what he – a devout believer who rigorously obeys the precepts of the Church and who suspects that one of the reasons he has not advanced more rapidly in his career is that he has always stubbornly refused to become a Freemason – finds most disturbing is the bandits' false claim that they are Catholics. Those evidences of faith – rosaries, processions, cries of 'Long live the Blessed Jesus' – disconcert him and pain him, despite the fact that at every Mass in the field Father Lizzardo inveighs against those impious wretches, accusing them of being apostates, heretics, and profaners of the faith. Even so, General Oscar cannot keep from feeling ill at ease in the face of this enemy that has turned this war into something so different from what he was expecting, into a sort of religious conflict. But the fact that he is disturbed does not mean that he has ceased to hate this abnormal, unpredictable adversary, who, moreover, has humiliated him by not falling to pieces at the very first encounter, as he was convinced would happen when he accepted this mission.

During the night he comes to hate this enemy even more when, after having inspected the barricade from one end to the other, he crosses the stretch of open terrain beyond on his way to the field hospital alongside the Vaza-Barris. At the halfway point are the Krupp 7.5s which have accompanied the attack, firing round after round of shells, without respite, at those towers from which the enemy causes so much damage to the troops. General Oscar chats for a moment with the artillerymen who, despite the lateness of the hour, are digging a trench with picks, reinforcing the cannon emplacement.

The visit to the field hospital, on the banks of the dry riverbed, stuns him; he must master himself so that the doctors, the medical aides, those who are dying will not notice. He is grateful that the visit is taking place in semidarkness, for the lanterns and campfires reveal only an insignificant part of the spectacle at his feet. The wounded are even more exposed to the elements than at A Favela, lying on the bare clay and gravel, still in the same groups in which they arrived, and the doctors explain to him that, as a crowning misfortune, all during the afternoon and part of the evening a strong wind has been blowing clouds of red dust into open wounds that they have no way of bandaging or disinfecting or suturing. On every hand he can hear screams, moans, weeping, delirious raving from fever. The stench is overpowering and Captain Coriolano, who is accompanying him, suddenly retches. He hears him burst into apologies. Every so often, the general stops to say a few affectionate words, to pat a wounded soldier on the back, to shake a hand. He congratulates them on their courage, thanks them in the name of the Republic for their sacrifice. But he remains silent when they halt before the bodies of Colonel Carlos Telles and Colonel Serra Martins, who are to be buried tomorrow. The former received a fatal bullet wound in the chest at the very beginning of the attack, as he was crossing the river; the second was killed in hand-to-hand combat as darkness was falling, leading his men in a charge against the *jagunços'* barricade. He is told that the colonel's dead body, pierced through with dagger, lance, and machete wounds, was found with the genitals, ears, and nose lopped off. In moments such as this, when he hears that a valiant, outstanding officer has been mutilated in this way, General Oscar tells himself that the policy of slitting the throats of all Sebastianists taken prisoner is a just one. The justification for this policy, as he sees it in the light of his conscience, is twofold: in the first place, these are bandits, not soldiers whom honor would bid them respect; and secondly, the lack of provisions leaves no alternative, since it would be more cruel to starve them out and absurd to deprive the patriots of rations in order to feed monsters capable of doing what they have done to this colonel.

As his tour of the field hospital is ending, he halts in front of a poor soldier whom two medical aides are holding down as they amputate one of his feet. The surgeon is squatting on his knees sawing, and the general hears him ask them to wipe the sweat out of his eyes. He must not be able to see much in any event, since the wind has come up again and is making the flames of the bonfire flicker. When the surgeon stands up, he recognizes Teotônio Leal Cavalcanti, the young man from São Paulo. They exchange greetings. As General Oscar starts back to his headquarters, the medical student's thin, tormented face accompanies him. A few days ago this young man, whom he did not know, presented himself before him, stood at attention, and said: 'I've killed my best friend and wish to be punished.' The general's adjutant, First Lieutenant Pinto Souza, was present at the interview, and on learning who the officer was whose suffering Teotônio, out of compassion, had ended by putting a bullet through his temple, the lieutenant had turned deathly pale. The scene made the general tremble with emotion. His voice breaking, Teotônio Leal Cavalcanti explained the state that First Lieutenant Pires Ferreira had been in – blind, his hands amputated, a broken man in body and spirit – the officer's pleas to be put out of his misery, and his own gnawing remorse at having done so. General Oscar has ordered him not to say one word about the matter and continue to perform his duties as though nothing had happened. Once the operations in the field are over, the general will decide his case.

Back at the Pyrotechnist's shack, he has already lain down in his hammock when Lieutenant Pinto Souza, who has just returned from A Favela, arrives with a message. The Seventh Brigade will be arriving at dawn to reinforce the 'black line.'

He sleeps for five hours, and the following morning he feels restored, brimming with energy as he drinks his coffee and eats a handful of the little cornmeal biscuits that are the treasure of his private rations. A strange silence reigns on the entire front. The battalions of the Seventh Brigade are about to arrive, and to cover their advance across the open terrain the general orders the gun crews of the Krupps to bombard the towers. Since the very first days, he has asked his superiors to send him, along with the reinforcements, those special steel-tipped 70 millimeter shells that were manufactured in the Rio Mint to pierce the deck plating of the rebels' boats during the September 6 uprising. Why do they pay no attention to this request? He has explained to the High Command that shrapnel and gas grenades are not sufficient to destroy those damned towers carved out of living rock. Why do they keep turning a deaf ear?

The day goes by with only sporadic gunfire, and General Oscar spends it supervising the disposition of the fresh troops of the Seventh Brigade along the 'black line.' During a meeting with his staff, it is decided that another attack is definitely out of the question until the reinforcements arrive. They will fight a holding action, while trying to advance gradually on the enemy's right flank – which at first glance would appear to be Canudos's weakest – in small-scale attacks, without exposing all the men at once. It is also decided that an expedition will be sent to Monte Santo, to escort those wounded in good enough condition to withstand the march.

At midday, as they are burying Colonels Silva Telles and Serra Martins, down by the river, in a single grave with two wooden crosses, a piece of bad news is brought to the general: Colonel Neri has just been wounded in the hip by a stray bullet as he was answering a call of nature at a crossarm in the 'black line.'

That night the general is awakened by heavy gunfire. The *jagunços* are attacking the two Krupp 7.5 cannons in the field and the Thirty-second Infantry Battalion is hastening to reinforce the artillerymen. The *jagunços* breached the 'black line' in the darkness, under the sentries' very noses. It is a hard-fought engagement for two hours, and casualties are high: there are seven dead and fifteen wounded, among them a second lieutenant. But the *jagunços* have fifty dead and seventeen taken prisoner. The general goes to see them.

It is dawn; the hills stand out against a bluish iridescence. The wind is so cold that General Oscar wraps a blanket around him as he strides across the open terrain. Fortunately, the Krupps are intact. But the violence of the fighting and the number of their comrades left dead and wounded have so incensed the artillerymen and the foot soldiers that General Oscar finds the prisoners half dead from the blows dealt them. They are very young, some of them just children, and among them are two women; all of them are skeleton-thin. General Oscar thus sees firsthand evidence of what all the prisoners confess: the great scarcity of food among the bandits. The men explain that it was the women and the youngsters who were doing the shooting, for the *jagunços'* mission was to try to destroy the cannons with picks, maces, crowbars, and hammers, or to clog them with sand. A good sign: this is the second time that they have tried, so the Krupp 7.5s are doing them a great deal of damage. Both the women and the youngsters are wearing blue headcloths and armbands. The officers present are revolted by this unimaginable barbarism: that the *jagunços* sent women and children out to fight strikes them as the height of human degradation, a mockery of the art and ethics of war. As he is leaving the scene, General Oscar hears the prisoners shouting 'Long live the Blessed Jesus' on learning that they are going to be put to death. Yes, the three generals who refused to come knew what they were doing; they had a premonition that waging a war against women and children who kill and who therefore must be killed, who die hailing the name of Jesus, is something that would not make any soldier happy. The general has a bitter taste in his mouth, as though he had been chewing tobacco.

That day passes uneventfully on the 'black line,' inside of which – the commanding officer of the expedition thinks to himself – it will be the usual routine till the reinforcements arrive: scattered gunfire from one or the other of the two dark, glowering barricades challenging each other, tourneys of insults flying back and forth above the walls without the objects of the insults ever seeing the insulters' faces, and the salvos of cannon fire against the churches and the Sanctuary, brief now because the shells are running out. The troops' food supplies are nearly gone; there are barely ten animals left to butcher in the pen erected behind A Favela, and they are down to the last few sacks of coffee and grain. The general orders the troops' rations reduced by half, though they are already meager.

But late that afternoon General Oscar receives a surprising piece of news: a family of *jagunços*, numbering fourteen people, voluntarily surrenders at the camp on A Favela. This is the first time since the beginning of the campaign that such a thing has happened. The news raises his spirits tremendously. Despair and privation must be undermining the cannibals' morale. He himself interrogates these *jagunços* at the camp on A Favela. The family consists of three decrepit elders, an adult couple, and rachitic children with swollen bellies. They are from Ipueiras and according to them – their teeth chatter with fear as they answer his questions – they have been in Canudos only a month and a half; they took refuge there not out of devotion to the

Counselor but out of panic on learning that a huge army was heading their way. They have made their escape from Canudos by leading the bandits to believe that they were going out to help dig trenches at the Cocorobó exit, which they in fact did do until evening, when, taking advantage of a moment when Pedrão wasn't watching, they slipped away. It has taken them a day to make their roundabout way to A Favela. They tell General Oscar everything they know about the situation in the bandits' lair and offer a somber picture of what is happening there, even worse than he had supposed – near-starvation, dead and wounded lying everywhere, widespread panic – and assure him that people would surrender if it weren't for *cangaceiros* like Big João, Abbot João, Pajeú, and Pedrão, who have sworn to kill every last relative of anyone who deserts. The general nonetheless takes what they tell him with a grain of salt: they are so obviously frightened nearly to death that they would come up with any sort of lie to gain his sympathy. He gives orders for them to be shut up in the cattle pen. The lives of all those who, following this family's example, voluntarily give themselves up are to be spared. His officers are as optimistic as he is: some of them predict that the enemy redoubt will collapse from within before the army reinforcements arrive.

But the following day the troops suffer a cruel reverse. A hundred and fifty head of cattle coming from Monte Santo fall into the hands of the *jagunços* in the most stupid way imaginable. Being overly cautious, in order to keep from falling into the trap of guides who have been conscripted into the army against their will in the *sertão* and who almost always prove to be on the side of the enemy when the troops are ambushed, the company of lancers herding the cattle along have relied solely on the maps drawn up by the army engineers. Luck has not been with them. Instead of taking the road via Rosário and As Umburanas, which leads to A Favela, they have veered off down the trail via O Cambaio and O Taboleirinho and suddenly landed up in the middle of the *jagunços* trenches. The lancers fight valiantly, keeping themselves from being wiped out, but they lose all the cattle, which the fanatics hasten to drive to Canudos with a heavy whip hand. From A Favela, General Oscar sees a surprising spectacle through his field glasses: the dust and the din raised by the little band of rustlers as they dash into Canudos amid the loud rejoicing of the degenerates. In an excess of fury that is not at all like him, he publicly dresses down the officers of the company that lost the cattle. This humiliating disaster will be a black mark on their service records! To punish the *jagunços* for the stroke of good luck that has brought them a hundred fifty head of cattle, the gunfire today is twice as heavy.

As the problem of provisions takes on critical proportions, General Oscar and his staff send out the gaucho lancers – who have never belied their fame as great cowboys – and the Twenty-seventh Infantry Battalion to get food 'wherever and however you can,' for hunger is both sapping the troops' strength and undermining their morale. The lancers return at nightfall with twenty head of cattle, and the general forbears to ask them where they got them; they are immediately butchered and the meat is distributed among the men at A Favela and in the 'black line.' The general and his adjutants order steps to be taken to improve communications between the two camps and the front. Safe routes are laid out with sentry posts all along them and the barricade is further reinforced. With his customary energy, the general also prepares to evacuate the wounded. Stretchers and crutches are made, the ambulance wagons are repaired, and a list of those who are to be evacuated is drawn up.

He sleeps that night in his hut on A Favela. The following morning, as he is taking his breakfast coffee and cornmeal biscuits, he realizes that it is raining. Dumfounded, he observes the miracle. It is a torrential rain, accompanied by a howling wind that drives the swirling downpour of muddy water this way and that. When he goes out with heartfelt rejoicing to get himself soaked to the skin, he sees that the entire camp is out splashing about in the rain and the mud, in wild excitement. It is the first rain in many months, a real blessing after these weeks of infernal heat and thirst. All the corps are storing the precious liquid in every container they can lay their hands on. He tries to see through his field glasses what is happening in Canudos, but there is a heavy fog and he is unable to make out even the towers. The downpour doesn't last long; a few minutes later a dust-filled wind is blowing once more. He has thought many times that, when this is all over, he will always have an indelible memory of these continuous, depressing winds that constrict one's temples. As he removes his boots so that his orderly can scrape the mud off them, he compares the dreariness of this landscape, without a bit of green, without a single flowering bush or shrub, with the luxuriant vegetation that surrounded him in O Piauí.

'Who would ever have thought that I'd miss my garden?' he confesses to Lieutenant Pinto Souza, who is drawing up the order of the day. 'I never understood my wife's passion for flowers. She would cut them back and water them all day long. It struck me as a form of sickness to be that fond of a garden. But now, in the face of this desolation, I understand.'

All the rest of the morning, as he hears reports from various subordinates and assigns them their duties, his mind is constantly on the blinding, suffocating dust. It is impossible to escape this torture even inside the barracks. 'When you don't eat dust with your barbecued meat, you eat your barbecued meat with dust. And always seasoned with flies,' he thinks.

A fusillade at dusk rouses him from his philosophical reverie. A band of *jagunços* – popping up out of the ground as though they had tunneled under the 'black line' – suddenly rushes a crossarm of the barricade, intending to cut it off. The attack takes the soldiers by surprise and they abandon their position, but an hour later the *jagunços* are driven out, with heavy losses. General Oscar and the officers conclude that the object of this attack was to protect the trenches at Fazenda Velha. All the officers therefore propose that they be occupied, by any possible means: this will hasten the surrender of this *jagunço* redoubt. General Oscar has three machine guns brought down from A Favela to the 'black line.'

That day the gaucho lancers return to camp with thirty head of cattle. The troops have a great feast, which puts everyone in a better humor. General Oscar inspects the two field hospitals, where final preparations are being made to evacuate the sick and wounded. In order to avoid long, heartrending farewell scenes, he has decided not to announce the names of those who will be making the journey till the very last moment, just as they are about to depart.

That afternoon, the artillerymen show him, in jubilation, four boxes full of shells for the Krupp 7.5s that a patrol has found along the road from As Umburanas. The projectiles are in perfect condition, and General Oscar authorizes what First Lieutenant Macedo Soares, the officer in charge of the cannons at A Favela, calls a 'fireworks display.' Sitting right next to the cannon, with his ears stopped up with cotton, like the servers of the pieces, the general witnesses the firing of sixty shells, all of them aimed at the heart of the traitors' resistance. Amid the great cloud of dust that the explosions raise, he anxiously observes the tall, massive towers that he knows are swarming with fanatics. Though they are chipped and full of gaping holes, they have not given way. How can the bell tower of the Church of Santo Antônio, which looks like a sieve and is leaning worse than the famous Tower of Pisa, still be standing? All during the bombardment, he eagerly hopes to see that tower reduced to ruins. God ought to grant him this favor, so as to help raise his spirits a bit. But the tower does not fall.

The next morning, he is up at dawn to see the wounded off. Sixty officers and four hundred eighty men are going back to Monte Santo, all those the doctors believe strong enough to survive the journey. Among them is the commander of the second column, General Savaget, whose wound in the abdomen has kept him out of action ever since his arrival at A Favela. General Oscar is happy to see him leave, for though their relations are cordial, he feels uncomfortable in the presence of this general without whose aid, he is certain, the first column would have been wiped out. The fact that the bandits were capable of luring him into this sort of abattoir through the use of extremely clever tactics has left General Oscar still convinced, despite the lack of any further proof, that the *jagunços* may have monarchist officers, or even English ones, advising them. This possibility is no longer mentioned, however, at staff meetings.

The farewell between the wounded who are leaving and those who are remaining behind is not a heartrending scene, with tears and protests, as he had feared, but a sober, solemn one. Those departing and those staying embrace each other in silence, exchange messages, and the ones who are weeping try to hide their tears. He had planned to give those leaving enough rations for four days, but the lack of supplies forces him to reduce this to one day's rations. The battalion of gaucho lancers, who will scour up food for the wounded on the journey, leaves with them. They are also escorted by the Thirty-third Infantry Battalion. As he sees them move slowly off in the early dawn light, miserable, half starved, their uniforms in tatters, many of them barefoot, he tells himself that when they arrive in Monte Santo – those who do not succumb along the way – they will be in an even worse state than they are now: perhaps his superiors will then understand how critical the situation is and send the reinforcements.

The departure of the expedition leaves behind an atmosphere of gloom and sadness among the men on A Favela and in the 'black line.' The morale of the troops has deteriorated because of the lack of food. The men are now eating the snakes and dogs they catch and are even toasting ants and swallowing them down to appease their hunger.

The war is now a matter of a few scattered shots from one side or the other of the two barricades. The combatants limit themselves to spying on each other from their respective positions; when they glimpse a profile, a head, an arm, there is a sudden burst of fire that lasts only a few seconds. Then silence sets in once again; it, too, brings on a numbing, hypnotic torpor, disturbed only by random shots from the towers and the Sanctuary, aimed at no precise target, but rather in the general direction of the dwelling in ruins occupied by the soldiers: the bullets pierce the thin walls of wooden pickets and mud and often wound or kill soldiers inside who are sleeping or dressing.

That evening, in the Pyrotechnist's shack, General Oscar plays cards with Lieutenant Pinto Souza, Colonel Neri (who is recovering from his wound), and two captains on his staff. They play on crates, by the light of an oil lamp. Suddenly they find themselves in the midst of a lively argument about Antônio Conselheiro and the bandits. One of the captains, who is from Rio, maintains that the explanation for Canudos is mixed blood, the mingling of Negro, Indian, and Portuguese stock that has slowly caused the race to degenerate to the point that it has now produced an inferior mentality, given to superstition and fanaticism. This view is vehemently countered by Colonel Neri. Haven't there been racial mixtures in other parts of Brazil which have produced no similar phenomena in those regions? Like Colonel Moreira César, whom he admires and practically idolizes, he is persuaded that Canudos is the work of the enemies of the Republic, the monarchists out to restore the Empire, the former rich slaveowners and the privileged elite who have incited these poor uneducated wretches to rebel and confused them by instilling in them a hatred of progress. 'The explanation of Canudos does not lie in race but in ignorance,' he declares.

General Oscar, who has followed this exchange with interest, is still perplexed and hesitates when they ask him his opinion. Yes, he finally says, ignorance allows aristocrats to turn these miserable wretches into fanatics and spur them on to attack what threatens the interests of the rich and powerful, for the Republic guarantees the equality of all men, thereby doing away with the privileges that are a right by birth under an aristocratic regime. But inwardly he is not at all convinced of what he is saying. When the others leave, he lies in his hammock thinking. What is the explanation of Canudos? Hereditary defects of people of mixed blood? Lack of education? A predisposition toward barbarism on the part of men who are accustomed to violence and who resist civilization out of atavism? Something to do with religion, with God? He finds none of these explanations satisfactory.

The next day, as he is shaving, without soap or a mirror, with a barber's razor that he himself sharpens on a whetstone, he hears galloping hoofbeats. He has given orders that all movements back and forth between A Favela and the 'black line' are to be made on foot, since men on horseback are too easy a target for the sharpshooters in the towers, and he therefore goes out to reprehend the disobedient riders. He hears cheers and hurrahs. The newcomers, three cavalrymen, cross the open terrain unharmed. The first lieutenant who dismounts at his side and clicks his heels identifies himself as the officer in charge of the platoon of advance scouts from General Girard's brigade of reinforcements, the vanguard of which will be arriving within the next two hours. The lieutenant adds that the four thousand five hundred soldiers and officers of General Girard's twelve battalions are impatient to place themselves at his command in order to annihilate the enemies of the Republic. At last, at long last, the nightmare of Canudos is about to end for him and for Brazil.

V

'Jurema?' the baron said in surprise. 'Jurema from Calumbi?'

'It happened during the terrible month of August,' the nearsighted journalist said, looking away. 'In July, the *jagunços* had stopped the soldiers, right there inside the city. But in August the Girard Brigade arrived. Five thousand more men, twelve more battalions, thousands of additional weapons, dozens of additional cannons. And food in abundance. What hope was there for the *jagunços* then?'

But the baron didn't hear him.

'Jurema?' he said again. He could see the visitor's glee, the delight he took in avoiding answering him. And he also noted that his joy, his happiness was due to the fact that he had mentioned her name, thereby attracting the baron's interest, so that now the baron would be the one who would oblige his visitor to speak of her. 'The wife of Rufino, the guide from Queimadas?'

The nearsighted journalist didn't answer him this time either. 'In August, moreover, the Minister of War, Marshal Carlos Machado Bittencourt, came in person from Rio to put an end to the campaign,' he went on, amused at the baron's impatience. 'We didn't know that in Canudos. That Marshal Bittencourt had installed himself in Monte Santo, organizing the transport, the provisioning, the hospitals. We didn't know that army volunteer doctors, volunteer medical aides, were pouring into Queimadas and Monte Santo. That it was the marshal himself who had sent the Girard Brigade. All that, in August. It was as though the heavens had opened to send a cataclysm down on Canudos.'

'And in the middle of this cataclysm you were happy,' the baron murmured, for those were the words his nearsighted visitor had used. 'Is that the Jurema you mean?'

'Yes.' The baron noted that his visitor was making no secret of his happiness now; his voice was filled with it, and it was making his words come pouring out. 'It's only right that you should remember her. Because she often remembers you and your wife. With admiration, with affection.'

So it was the same one, that slender, olive-skinned girl who had grown up in Calumbi, in Estela's service, whom the two of them had married to the honest, persevering worker that Rufino had been at that time. He couldn't get over it. That little half-tamed creature, that simple country girl who could only have changed for the worse since leaving Estela's service, had also played a role in the destiny of the man before him. Because the journalist's literal words, inconceivably enough, had been: 'But, in fact, it was when the world began to fall apart and the horror had reached its height that, incredible as it may seem, I began to be happy.' Once again the baron was overcome by the feeling that it was all unreal, a dream, a fiction, which always took possession of him at the very thought of Canudos. All these happenstances, coincidences, fortuitous encounters, made him feel as though he were on tenterhooks. Did the journalist know that Galileo Gall had raped Jurema? He didn't ask him, staggered as he was at the thought of the strange geography of chance, the secret order, the unfathomable law of the history of peoples and individuals that capriciously brought them together, separated them, made them enemies or allies. And he told himself that it was impossible for that poor little creature of the backlands of Bahia even to suspect that she had been the instrument of so many upheavals in the lives of such dissimilar people: Rufino, Galileo Gall, this scarecrow who was now smiling blissfully at the memory of her. The baron felt a desire to see Jurema again; perhaps it would do the baroness good to see this girl toward whom she had shown such affection in bygone days. He remembered that Sebastiana had felt a veiled resentment toward her for that very reason, and recalled how relieved she had been to see her go off to Queimadas with Rufino.

'To tell the truth, I didn't expect to hear you speak of love and happiness at this point,' the baron murmured, stirring restlessly in his chair. 'Certainly not with regard to Jurema.'

The journalist had begun talking about the war again. 'Isn't it curious that it should be called the Girard Brigade? Because, as I now learn, General Girard never set foot in Canudos. One more curious thing in this most curious of wars. August began with the appearance of those twelve fresh battalions. More new people still kept arriving in Canudos, in great haste, because they knew that now, with the new army on the way, the city was certain to be encircled. And that they would no longer be able to get in!' The baron heard him give one of his absurd, exotic, forced cackles, and heard him repeat: 'Not that they wouldn't be able to get out, mind you, but that they wouldn't be able to get in. That was their problem. They didn't care if they died, so long as they died inside Canudos.'

'And you . . . you were happy,' the baron said. Might this man not be even loonier than he had always seemed to him to be? Wasn't all this most probably just a bunch of tall tales?

'They saw them arriving, spreading out over the hills, occupying, one after the other, all the places by way of which they could slip in or out before. The cannons began to bombard them around the clock, from the north, the south, the east, the west.

But as they were too close and might kill their own men, they limited themselves to firing on the towers. Because they still hadn't fallen.'

'Jurema? Jurema?' the baron exclaimed. 'The little girl from Calumbi brought you happiness, made you a spiritual convert of the *jagunços*?'

Behind the thick lenses, like fish in an aquarium, the myopic eyes became agitated, blinked. It was late, the baron had been here for many hours now, he ought to get up out of his chair and go to Estela, he had not been away from her this long since the tragedy. But he continued to sit there waiting, itching with impatience.

'The explanation is that I had resigned myself,' the baron heard him say in a barely audible voice.

'To dying?' he asked, knowing that it was not death that his visitor was thinking about.

'To not loving, to not being loved by any woman,' he thought he heard him answer, for the words were spoken in an even less audible voice. 'To being ugly, to being shy, to never holding a woman in my arms unless I'd paid her money to do so.'

The baron sat there flabbergasted. The thought flashed through his mind that in this study of his, where so many secrets had come to light, so many plots been hatched, no one had ever made such an unexpected and surprising confession.

'That is something you are unable to understand,' the nearsighted journalist said, as though the statement were an accusation. 'Because you doubtless learned what love was at a very early age. Many women must have loved you, admired you, given themselves to you. You were doubtless able to choose your very beautiful wife from any number of other very beautiful women who were merely awaiting your consent to throw themselves in your arms. You are unable to understand what happens to those of us who are not handsome, charming, privileged, rich, as you were. You are unable to understand what it is to know that love and pleasure are not for you. That you are doomed to the company of whores.'

'Love, pleasure,' the baron thought, disconcerted: two disturbing words, two meteorites in the dark night of his life. It struck him as a sacrilege that those beautiful, forgotten words should appear on the lips of this laughable creature sitting all hunched over in his chair, his legs as skinny as a heron's twined one around the other. Wasn't it comical, grotesque, that a little mongrel bitch from the backlands should be the woman who had brought such a man as this, who despite everything was a cultivated man, to speak of love and pleasure? Did those words not call to mind luxury, refinement, sensibility, elegance, the rites and the ripe wisdom of an imagination nourished by wide reading, travels, education? Were they not words completely at odds with Jurema of Calumbi? He thought of the baroness and a wound opened in his breast. He made an effort to turn his thoughts back to what the journalist was saying.

In another of his abrupt transitions, he was talking once again of the war. 'The drinking water gave out,' he was saying, and as always he seemed to be reprimanding him. 'Every drop they drank in Canudos came from the source of supply at Fazenda Velha, a few wells along the Vaza-Barris. They had dug trenches there and defended them tooth and nail. But in the face of those five thousand fresh troops not even Pajeú could keep them from falling into the enemy's hands. So there was no more water.'

Pajeú? The baron shuddered. He saw before him that face with Indian features, that skin with a yellowish cast, the scar where the nose should have been, heard once more that voice calmly announcing to him that he had come to burn Calumbi down in the name of the Father. Pajeú – the individual who incarnated all the wickedness and all the stupidity of which Estela had been the victim.

'That's right, Pajeú,' the nearsighted visitor said. 'I detested him. And feared him more than I feared the soldiers' bullets. Because he was in love with Jurema and had only to lift his little finger to steal her from me and spirit her away.'

He laughed once more, a nervous, strident little laugh that ended in wheezes and sneezes. The baron's mind was elsewhere;

he, too, was busy hating that fanatical brigand. What had become of the perpetrator of that inexpiable crime? He was too beside himself to ask, afraid that he would hear that he was safe and sound. The journalist was repeating the word 'water.' It was an effort for the baron to turn his thoughts away from himself, to listen to what the man was saying. Yes, the waters of the Vaza-Barris. He knew what those wells were like; they lay alongside the riverbed, and the floodwaters that flowed into them supplied men, birds, goats, cows in the long months (and entire years sometimes) when the Vaza-Barris dried up. And what about Pajeú? What about Pajeú? Had he died in battle? Had he been captured? The question was on the tip of the baron's tongue and yet he did not ask it.

'One has to understand these things,' the journalist was now saying, wholeheartedly, vehemently, angrily. 'I was barely able to see them, naturally. But I was unable to understand them either.'

'Of whom are you speaking?' the baron asked. 'My mind was elsewhere; I've lost the thread.'

'Of the women and the youngsters,' the nearsighted journalist muttered. 'That's what they called them. The "youngsters." When the soldiers captured the water supply, they went out with the women at night to try to fill tin drums full of water so that the *jagunços* could go on fighting. Just the women and the children, nobody else. And they also tried to steal the soldiers' unspeakable garbage that meant food for them. Do you follow me?'

'Ought I to be surprised?' the baron said. 'To be amazed?'

'You ought to try to understand,' the nearsighted journalist murmured. 'Who gave those orders? The Counselor? Abbot João? Antônio Vilanova? Who was it who decided that only women and children would crawl to Fazenda Velha to steal water, knowing that soldiers were lying in wait for them at the wells so as to shoot them point-blank, knowing that out of every ten only one or two would get back alive? Who was it who decided that the combatants shouldn't risk that lesser suicide since their lot was to risk the superior form of suicide that dying fighting represented?' The baron saw the journalist's eyes seek his in anguish once again. 'I suspect that it was neither the Counselor nor the leaders. It was spontaneous, simultaneous, anonymous decisions. Otherwise, they would not have obeyed, they would not have gone to the slaughter with such conviction.'

'They were fanatics,' the baron said, aware of the scorn in his voice. 'Fanaticism impels people to act in that way. It is not always lofty, sublime motives that best explain heroism. There is also prejudice, narrow-mindedness, the most stupid ideas imaginable.'

The nearsighted journalist sat there staring at him; his forehead was dripping with sweat and he appeared to be searching for a cutting answer. The baron thought that he would venture some insolent remark. But he saw him merely nod his head, as though to avoid argument.

'That was great sport for the soldiers of course, a diversion in the midst of their boring life from day to day,' he said. 'Posting themselves at Fazenda Velha and waiting for the light of the moon to reveal the shadows creeping up to get water. We could hear the shots, the sound when a bullet pierced the tin drum, the container, the earthenware jug. In the morning the ground around the wells was strewn with the bodies of the dead and wounded. But, but . . .'

'But you didn't see any of this,' the baron broke in. His visitor's agitation vastly annoyed him.

'Jurema and the Dwarf saw them,' the nearsighted journalist answered. 'I heard them. I heard the women and the youngsters as they left for Fazenda Velha with their tin drums, canteens, pitchers, bottles, bidding their husbands or their parents farewell, exchanging blessings, promising each other that they would meet in heaven. And I heard what happened when they managed to get back alive. The tin drum, the bucket, the pitcher was not offered to dying oldsters, to babies frantic from thirst. No. It was taken straight to the trenches, so that those who could still hold a rifle could hold one for a few hours or minutes more.'

'And what about you?' the baron asked, scarcely able to contain his growing annoyance at this mixture of reverence and terror with which the nearsighted journalist spoke of the *jagunços.* 'Why is it you didn't die of thirst? You weren't a combatant, were you?'

'I wonder myself why I didn't,' the journalist answered. 'If there were any logic to this story, there are any number of times when I should have died in Canudos.'

'Love doesn't quench thirst,' the baron said, trying to wound his feelings.

'No, it doesn't quench it,' he agreed. 'But it gives one strength to endure it. Moreover, we had a little something to drink. What we could get by sucking or chewing. The blood of birds, even black vultures. And leaves, stems, roots, anything that had juice. And urine, of course.' His eyes sought the baron's and again the latter thought: 'As though to accuse me.'

'Didn't you know that? Even though a person doesn't drink any liquids, he continues to urinate. That was an important discovery, there in Canudos.'

'Tell me about Pajeú, if you will,' the baron said. 'What became of him?'

The nearsighted journalist suddenly slid down onto the floor. He had done so several times in the course of the conversation, and the baron wondered whether these changes of position were due to inner turmoil or to numbness in his limbs.

'Did I hear you say that he was in love with Jurema?' the baron pressed him. He suddenly had the absurd feeling that the former maidservant of Calumbi was the only woman in the *sertão,* a female under whose fateful spell all the men with any sort of connection to Canudos unconsciously fell sooner or later. 'Why didn't he carry her off with him?'

'Because of the war, perhaps,' the nearsighted journalist answered. 'He was one of the leaders. As the enemy began to close the ring, he had less time. And less inclination, I imagine.'

He burst into such painful laughter that the baron deduced that this time it would end in a fit not of sneezing but of weeping. But neither sneezes nor tears were forthcoming.

'As a result, I found myself wishing at times that the war would go on and even that the fighting would get worse so that it would keep Pajeú occupied.' He took a deep breath. 'Wishing that he'd get killed in the war or some other way.'

'What became of him?' the baron said insistently. The journalist paid no attention.

'But despite the war, he might very well have carried her off with him and taken her for his woman,' he said, lost in thought or in fantasy, his eyes fixed on the floor. 'Didn't other *jagunços* do that? Didn't I hear them, in the midst of all the shooting, day or night, mounting their women in hammocks, or pallets, or on the floors of their houses?'

The baron felt his face turn beet-red. He had never allowed certain subjects, which so often come up among men when they are alone together, to be discussed in his presence, not even when he was with his closest friends. If his visitor went any further, he would shut him up.

'So the war wasn't the explanation.' The journalist looked up at him, as though remembering that he was there. 'He'd become a saint, don't you see? That's how people in Canudos put it: he became a saint, the angel kissed him, the angel brushed him with its wings, the angel touched him.' He nodded his head several times. 'Perhaps that's it. He didn't want to take her by force. That's the other explanation. More farfetched, doubtless, but perhaps. So that everything would be done in accordance with God's will. According to the dictates of religion. Marrying her. I heard him ask her. Perhaps.'

'What became of him?' the baron repeated slowly, emphasizing each word.

The nearsighted journalist looked at him intently. And the baron noted how surprised he looked.

'He burned Calumbi down,' he explained slowly. 'He was the one who . . . Did he die? How did he die?'

'I suppose he's dead,' the nearsighted journalist said. 'Why wouldn't he be? Why wouldn't he and Abbot João and Big João – all of them – be dead?'

'You didn't die, and according to what you've told me, Vilanova didn't die either. Was he able to escape?'

'They didn't want to escape,' the journalist said sadly. 'They wanted to get in, to stay there, to die there. What happened to Vilanova was exceptional. He didn't want to leave either. They ordered him to.'

So he wasn't absolutely certain that Pajeú was dead. The baron imagined him, taking up his old life again, free again, at the head of a *cangaço* he'd gotten together again, with malefactors from all over, adding endless terrible misdeeds to his legend, in Ceará, in Pernambuco, in regions more distant still. He felt his head go round and round.

'Antônio Vilanova,' the Counselor murmurs, producing a sort of electrical discharge in the Sanctuary. 'He's spoken, he's spoken,' the Little Blessed One thinks, so awestruck he has gooseflesh all over. 'Praised be the Father, praised be the Blessed Jesus.' He steps toward the rush pallet at the same time as Maria Quadrado, the Lion of Natuba, Father Joaquim, and the women of the Sacred Choir; in the gloomy light of dusk, all eyes are riveted on the long, dark, motionless face with eyelids still tightly closed. It is not a hallucination; he has spoken.

The Little Blessed One sees that beloved mouth, grown so emaciated that the lips have disappeared, open to repeat: 'Antônio Vilanova.' They react, say 'Yes, yes, Father,' rush to the door of the Sanctuary to tell the Catholic Guard to go fetch Antônio Vilanova. Several men leave on the run, hurriedly making their way between the stones and sandbags of the parapet. At that moment, there is no shooting. The Little Blessed One goes back to the Counselor's bedside; he is again lying there silent, his bones protruding from the dark purple tunic whose folds betray here and there how frightfully thin he is. 'He is more spirit than flesh now,' the Little Blessed One thinks. The Superior of the Sacred Choir, encouraged at hearing the Counselor speak, comes toward him with a bowl containing a little milk. He hears her say softly, in a voice full of devotion and hope: 'Would you like a little something to drink, Father?' He has heard her ask the same question many times in these last days. But this time, unlike the others, when the Counselor lay there without answering, the skeleton-like head with long disheveled gray hair drooping down from it shakes from one side to the other: no. A wave of happiness mounts within the Little Blessed One. He is alive, he is going to live. Because in these recent days, even though Father Joaquim came to the Counselor's bedside every so often to take his pulse and listen to his heart to assure them that he was breathing, and even though that little trickle of water kept constantly flowing out of him, the Little Blessed One could not help thinking, as he saw him lying there, so silent and so still, that the Counselor's soul had gone up to heaven.

A hand tugs at him from the floor. He looks down and sees the Lion of Natuba's huge, anxious, bright eyes gazing up at him from amid a jungle of long, tangled locks. 'Is he going to live, Little Blessed One?' There is so much anguish in the voice of the scribe of Belo Monte that the Little Blessed One feels like crying.

'Yes, yes, Lion, he's going to live for us, he's going to live a long time still.'

But he knows that this is not true; something deep inside him tells him that these are the last days, perhaps the last hours, of the man who changed his life and those of all who are in the Sanctuary, of all who are giving their lives there outside, fighting and dying in the maze of caves and trenches that Belo Monte has now turned into. He knows this is the end. He has known it ever since he learned, simultaneously, that Fazenda Velha had fallen and that the Counselor had fainted dead away in the Sanctuary. The Little Blessed One knows how to decipher the symbols, to interpret the secret message of the coincidences, accidents, apparent happenstances that pass unnoticed by the others; he has powers of intuition that enable him to recognize instantly, beneath the innocent and the trivial, the deeply hidden presence of the beyond. On that day he had been in the Church of Santo Antônio, turned since the beginning of the war into a clinic, leading the sick, the wounded, the women in labor, the orphans there in the recitation of the Rosary, raising his voice so that this suffering, bleeding, purulent, half-dead humanity could hear his Ave Marias and Pater Nosters amid the din of the rifle volleys and the cannon salvos. And just then he had seen a 'youngster' and Alexandrinha Correa come running in at the same time, leaping over the bodies lying one atop the other.

The young boy spoke first. 'The dogs have entered Fazenda Velha, Little Blessed One. Abbot João says that a wall has to be erected on the corner of Mártires, because the atheists can now pass that way freely.'

And the 'youngster' had barely turned around to leave when the former water divineress, in a voice even more upset than the expression on her face, whispered another piece of news in his ear which he immediately sensed was far more serious still: 'The Counselor has been taken ill.'

His legs tremble, his mouth goes dry, his heart sinks, just as on that morning – how long ago now? Six, seven, ten days? He had to struggle to make his feet obey him and run after Alexandrinha Correa. When he arrived at the Sanctuary, the Counselor had been lifted up onto his pallet and had opened his eyes again and gazed reassuringly at the distraught women of the Choir and the Lion of Natuba. It had happened when he rose to his feet after praying for several hours, lying face down on the floor with his arms outstretched, as always. The women, the Lion of Natuba, Mother Maria Quadrado noted how difficult it was for him to get up, first putting one knee on the floor and helping himself with one hand and then the other, and how pale he turned from the effort or the pain of remaining on his feet. Then suddenly he sank to the floor once again, like a sack of bones. At that moment – was it six, seven, ten days ago? – the Little Blessed One had a revelation: the eleventh hour had come for the Counselor.

Why was he so selfish? How could he fail to rejoice that the Counselor would be going to his rest, would ascend to heaven to receive his reward for what he had done on this earth? Shouldn't he be singing hosannas? Of course he should be. But he is unable to; his soul is transfixed with grief. 'We'll be left orphans,' he thinks once again. At that moment, he is distracted by a little sound coming from the pallet, escaping from underneath the Counselor. It is a little sound that does not make the saint's body stir even slightly, but already Mother Maria Quadrado and the devout women hurriedly surround the pallet, raise his habit, clean him, humbly collect what – the Little Blessed One thinks to himself – is not excrement, since excrement is dirty and impure and nothing that comes from his body can be that. How could that little watery trickle that has flowed continually from that poor body – for six, seven, ten days – be dirty, impure? Has the Counselor eaten a single mouthful in these days that would make his system have any impurities to evacuate? 'It is his essence that is flowing out down there, it is part of his soul, something that he is leaving us.' He sensed this immediately, from the very first moment. There was something mysterious and sacred about that sudden, soft, prolonged breaking of wind, about those attacks that seemed never to end, always accompanied by the emission of that little trickle of water. He divined the secret meaning: 'They are gifts, not excrement.' He understood very clearly that the Father, or the Divine Holy Spirit, or the Blessed Jesus, or Our Lady, or the Counselor himself wanted to put them to the test. In a sudden happy inspiration, he came forward, stretched his hand out between the women, wet his fingers in the trickle and raised them to his mouth, intoning: 'Is this how you wish your slave to take Communion, Father? Is this not dew to me?' All the women of the Sacred Choir also took Communion, in the same way.

Why was the Father subjecting the saint to such agony? Why did He want him to spend his last moment defecating, defecating, even though what flowed from his body was manna? The Lion of Natuba, Mother Maria Quadrado, and the women of the Choir do not understand this. The Little Blessed One has tried to explain it and prepare them: 'The Father does not want him to fall into the hands of the dogs. If He takes him to Him, it is so that he will not be humiliated. But at the same time He does not want us to believe that He is freeing him from pain, from doing penance. That is why He is making him suffer, before giving him his recompense.' Father Joaquim has told him that he did well to prepare them; he, too, fears that the Counselor's death will upset them, will wrest impious protests from their lips, reactions that are harmful to their souls. The Dog is lying in wait and would not miss an opportunity to seize upon this prey.

He realizes that the shooting has begun again – a heavy, steady, circular fusillade – when the door of the Sanctuary is opened. Antônio Vilanova is standing there. With him are Abbot João, Pajeú, Big João, exhausted, sweaty, reeking of gunpowder, but with radiant faces: they have learned the news that he has spoken, that he is alive.

'Here is Antônio Vilanova, Father,' the Lion of Natuba says, rising up on his hind limbs toward the Counselor.

The Little Blessed One holds his breath. The men and women crowded into the room – they are so cramped for space that none of them can raise his or her arms without hitting a neighbor – are gazing in rapt suspense at that mouth without lips or teeth, that face that resembles a death mask. Is he going to speak, is he going to speak? Despite the noisy chatter of the guns outside, the Little Blessed One hears once again the unmistakable little trickling sound. Neither Maria Quadrado nor the women make a move to clean him. They all remain motionless, bending over the pallet, waiting.

The Superior of the Sacred Choir brings her mouth down next to the ear covered with grizzled locks of hair and repeats: 'Here is Antônio Vilanova, Father.'

The Counselor's eyelids flutter slightly and his mouth opens just a bit. The Little Blessed One realizes that he is trying to speak, that his weakness and his pain do not allow him to utter a single sound, and he begs the Father to grant the Counselor that grace, offering in return to suffer any torment himself, when he hears the beloved voice, so feeble now that every head in the room leans forward to listen: 'Are you there, Antônio? Can you hear me?'

The former trader falls to his knees, takes one of the Counselor's hands in his, and kisses it reverently. 'Yes, Father, yes, Father.' He is drenched with sweat, his face is puffy, he is panting for breath and trembling. The Little Blessed One feels envious of his friend. Why is Antônio the one who has been called, and not him? He reproaches himself for this thought and fears that the Counselor will make them all leave the room so as to speak to Antônio alone.

'Go out into the world to bear witness, Antônio, and do not cross inside the circle again. I shall stay here with the flock. You are to go out there beyond the circle. You are a man who is acquainted with the world. Go, teach those who have forgotten their lessons how to count. May the Divine guide you and the Father bless you.'

The ex-trader's face screws up, contorts into a grimace as he bursts into sobs. 'It is the Counselor's testament,' the Little Blessed One thinks. He is perfectly aware what a solemn, transcendent moment this is. What he is seeing and hearing will be recalled down through the years, the centuries, among thousands and thousands of men of every tongue, of every race, in every corner of the globe; it will be recalled by countless human beings not yet born. Antônio Vilanova's broken voice is begging the Counselor not to send him forth, as he desperately kisses the dark bony hands with the long fingernails. He should intervene, remind Antônio that at this moment he may not oppose a desire of the Counselor's. He draws closer, places one hand on his friend's shoulder; the affectionate pressure is enough to calm him. Vilanova looks at him with eyes brimming with tears, begging him for help, for some sort of explanation. The Counselor remains silent. Is he about to hear his voice once more? He hears, twice in a row, the soft little sound. He has often asked himself whether each time he hears it, the Counselor is experiencing writhing, stabbing, wrenching pains, terrible cramps, whether the Dog has its fangs in his belly. He now knows that it does. He has only to glimpse that very slight grimace on the emaciated face each time the saint quietly breaks wind to know that the sound is accompanied by flames and knives that are sheer martyrdom.

'Take your family with you, so that you won't be alone,' the Counselor whispers. 'And take the strangers who are friends of Father Joaquim's with you. Let each one gain salvation through his own effort. As you are doing, my son.'

Despite the hypnotic attention with which he is listening to the Counselor's words, the Little Blessed One catches a glimpse of the grimace contorting Pajeú's face: the scar appears to swell up and split open, and his mouth flies open to ask a question or perhaps to protest, beside himself at the prospect that the woman he wishes to marry will be leaving Belo Monte. In utter amazement, the Little Blessed One suddenly understands why the Counselor, in this supreme moment, has remembered the strangers whom Father Joaquim has taken under his wing. So as to save an apostle! So as to save Pajeú from the fall that this woman might mean for him! Or does he simply wish to test the *caboclo*? Or give him the opportunity to gain pardon for his sins through suffering? Pajeú's olive face is again a blank, serene, untroubled, respectful, as he stands looking down at the pallet with his leather hat in his hand.

The Little Blessed One is certain now that the saint's mouth will not open again. 'Only his other mouth is speaking,' he thinks. What is the message of that stomach that has been giving off wind and leaking water for six, seven, ten days now? It torments him to think that in that wind and that water there is a message addressed to him, which he might misinterpret, might not hear. He knows that nothing is accidental, that there is no such thing as sheer chance, that everything has a profound meaning, a root whose ramifications always lead to the Father, and that if one is holy enough he may glimpse the miraculous, secret order that God has instituted in the world.

The Counselor is mute once again, as though he had never spoken. Standing at one corner of the pallet, Father Joaquim moves his lips, praying in silence. Everyone's eyes glisten. No one has moved, even though all of them sense that the saint has spoken his last. The eleventh hour. The Little Blessed One has suspected that the end was at hand ever since the little white lamb was killed by a stray bullet as Alexandrinha Correa was holding it one evening, accompanying the Counselor back to the Sanctuary after the counsels. That was one of the last times that the Counselor had left the Sanctuary. 'His voice was no longer heard, he was already in the Garden of Olives.' Making a superhuman effort, he still left the Sanctuary every day to climb up the scaffolding, pray, and give counsels. But his voice was a mere whisper, barely understandable even to those who were at his side. The Little Blessed One himself, who remained inside the living wall of Catholic Guards, could catch only a few words now and again. When Mother Maria Quadrado asked the Counselor whether he wanted this little animal sanctified by his caresses to be buried in the Sanctuary, he answered no and directed that it be used to feed the Catholic Guard.

At that moment the Counselor's right hand moves, searching for something; his gnarled fingers rise and fall on the straw mattress, reach out, contract. What is he looking for, what is it he wants? The Little Blessed One sees his own distress mirrored in the eyes of Maria Quadrado, Big João, Pajeú, the women of the Sacred Choir.

'Lion, are you there?'

He feels a knife thrust in his breast. He would have given anything for the Counselor to have uttered his name, for his hand to have sought him out. The Lion of Natuba rises up and thrusts his huge shaggy head toward that hand to kiss it. But the hand does not give him time, for the moment it senses that that face is close it runs rapidly along it and the fingers sink deep into the thick tangled locks. What is happening is hidden from the Little Blessed One's eyes by a veil of tears. But he does not need to see: he knows that the Counselor is scratching, delousing, stroking with his last strength, as he has seen him do down through the many long years, the head of the Lion of Natuba.

The tremendous roar that shakes the Sanctuary forces him to close his eyes, to crouch down, to raise his hands to protect himself from what appears to be an avalanche of stones. Blind, he hears the uproar, the shouts, the running footsteps, wonders if he is dead and if it is his soul that is trembling. Finally he hears Abbot João: 'The bell tower of Santo Antônio has fallen.' He opens his eyes. The Sanctuary has filled with dust and everyone has changed places. He makes his way to the pallet, knowing what awaits him. Amid the cloud of dust he makes out the hand quietly resting on the head of the Lion of Natuba, who is still kneeling in the same position. And he sees Father Joaquim, his ear glued to the thin chest.

After a moment, the priest rises to his feet, his face pale and drawn. 'He has given his soul up to God,' he stammers, and for those present the phrase is more deafening than the din outside.

No one weeps and wails, no one falls to his knees. They all stand there as if turned to stone. They avoid each other's eyes, as though if they were to meet they would see all the filth in the other's soul, as though in this supreme moment all their most intimate dirty secrets were welling up through them. Dust is raining down from the ceiling, from the walls, and the Little Blessed One's ears, as though they were someone else's, continue to hear from outside, both close at hand and very far away, screams, moans, feet running, walls creaking and collapsing, and the shouts of joy with which the soldiers who have taken the trenches of what were once the streets of São Pedro and São Cipriano and the old cemetery are hailing the fall of the tower of the church that they have been bombarding for so long. And the Little Blessed One's mind, as though it were someone else's, pictures the dozens of Catholic Guards who have fallen along with the bell tower, and the dozens of sick, wounded, disabled, women in labor, newborn babies, centenarians who at this moment must be lying crushed to death, smashed to pieces, ground to bits beneath the adobe bricks, the stones, the beams, saved now, glorious bodies now, climbing up the golden stairs of martyrs to the Father's throne, or perhaps still dying in terrible pain amid smoking rubble. But in reality the Little Blessed One is neither hearing nor seeing nor thinking: there is nothing left of the world, he is no longer a creature of flesh and bone, he is a feather drifting helplessly in a whirlpool at the bottom of a precipice. As though through the eyes of another, he sees Father Joaquim remove the Counselor's hand from the mane of the Lion of Natuba and place it alongside the other, atop his body.

The Little Blessed One then begins to speak, in the solemn, deep voice in which he chants in the church and in processions. 'We shall bear him to the Temple that he ordered built and we shall keep a death watch over him for three days and three nights, in order that every man and woman may adore him. And we shall bear him in procession amid all the houses, through all the streets of Belo Monte in order that his body may for the last time purify the city of the wickedness of the Can. And we shall bury him beneath the main altar of the Temple of the Blessed Jesus and place on his tomb the wooden cross that he made with his own hands in the desert.'

He crosses himself devoutly and all the others do likewise, without taking their eyes off the pallet. The first sobs that the Little Blessed One hears are those of the Lion of Natuba; his entire little hunchbacked, asymmetrical body contorts as he weeps. The Little Blessed One kneels and the others follow suit; he can now hear others sobbing. But it is Father Joaquim's voice, praying in Latin, that takes possession of the Sanctuary, and for a fair time drowns out the sounds from outside. As he prays, with joined hands, slowly coming to, recovering his hearing, his sight, his body, the earthly life that he seemed to have lost, the Little Blessed One feels that boundless despair that he has not felt since, as a youngster, he heard Father Moraes tell him that he could not be a priest because he had been born a bastard child. 'Why are you abandoning us in these moments, Father?' 'What will we do without you, Father?' He remembers the wire that the Counselor placed around his waist, in Pombal, that he is still wearing, all rusted and twisted, become flesh of his flesh now, and he tells himself that it is a precious relic, as is everything else that the saint has touched, seen, or said during his stay on earth.

'We can't do it, Little Blessed One,' Abbot João declares.

The Street Commander is kneeling next to him; his eyes are bloodshot and his voice filled with emotion. But he says, with authority: 'We can't take him to the Temple of the Blessed Jesus or bury him the way you want to. We can't do that to people, Little Blessed One! Do you want to plunge a knife in their backs? Are you going to tell those who are fighting, even though they've no ammunition or food left, that the one they're fighting for has died? Are you capable of such an act of cruelty? Wouldn't that be worse than the Freemasons' evil deeds?'

'He's right, Little Blessed One,' Pajeú says. 'We can't tell them that he's died. Not now, not at this point. Everything would fall to pieces, it would be chaos, people would go crazy. We must keep it a secret if we want them to go on fighting.'

'That's not the only reason,' Big João says, and this is the voice that astonishes him most, for since when has this timid giant, whose every word must be dragged out of him by force, ever voluntarily opened his mouth to venture an opinion? 'Won't the dogs look for his remains with all the hatred in the world so as to desecrate them? Nobody must know where he is buried. Do you want the heretics to find his body, Little Blessed One?'

The Little Blessed One feels his teeth chatter, as though he were having an attack of fever. It is true, quite true; in his eagerness to render homage to his beloved master, to give him a wake and a burial worthy of his majesty, he has forgotten that the dogs are only a few steps away and that they would be bound to vent their fury on his remains like rapacious wolves. Yes, he understands now – it is as though the roof had opened and a blinding light, with the Divine in the center, had illuminated him – why the Father has taken their master to His bosom at this very moment, and what the obligation of the apostles is: to preserve his remains, to keep the demon from defiling them.

'You're right, you're right!' he exclaims vehemently, contritely. 'Forgive me; grief clouded my mind, or the Evil One perhaps. I know now; I understand now. We won't tell the others that he's dead. We'll hold his wake here, we'll bury him here. We'll dig his grave and nobody except us will know where. That is the Father's will.'

A moment before, he had felt resentment toward Abbot João,

Pajeú, and Big João for opposing the funeral ceremony. Now, however, he feels gratitude toward them for having helped him to decipher the message. Thin, frail, delicate, full of energy, impatient, he moves in and out among the women of the Choir and the apostles, pushing them, urging them to stop weeping, to overcome their paralysis that is a trap of the Devil, imploring them to get to their feet, to get moving, to bring picks, shovels to dig with. 'There's no time left, there's no time,' he says to frighten them.

And so he manages to communicate his sense of energy: they rise to their feet, dry their eyes, take courage, look at each other, nod, prod each other into moving. It is Abbot João, with that sense of practicality that never forsakes him, who makes up the white lie to tell the men on the parapets protecting the Sanctuary: they are going to dig a tunnel, of the sort found everywhere in Belo Monte these days to permit free passage between houses and trenches, in case the dogs block off the Sanctuary. Big João goes out and comes back with shovels. They immediately begin digging, next to the pallet, taking turns by fours, and on handing their shovels over to the next man, they kneel down to pray till it is their turn again. They go on in this way for hours, not noticing that darkness has fallen, that the Mother of Men has lighted an oil lamp, and that, outside, the shooting, the hate-filled shouts, and the cheers have begun again, stopped again, started yet again. Each time someone standing next to the pyramid of earth that has grown higher and higher as the hole has become deeper and deeper asks, the Little Blessed One's answer is: 'Deeper, deeper.'

When inspiration tells him that it is deep enough, all of them, beginning with himself, are exhausted, their hair and skin encrusted with dirt. The Little Blessed One has the sensation that the moments that follow are a dream, as he takes the head, Mother Maria Quadrado one of the legs, Pajeú the other, Big João one of the arms, Father Joaquim the other, and together they lift up the Counselor's body so that the women of the Sacred Choir may place beneath it the little straw mat that will be his shroud.

Once the body is in place, Maria Quadrado places on his chest the metal crucifix that was the sole object decorating the walls of the Sanctuary and the rosary with dark beads that he has never been without so long as any of them can remember. They lift up the remains, wrapped in the straw mat, once again, and hand them down to Abbot João and Pajeú, standing at the bottom of the grave. As Father Joaquim prays in Latin, they again work by turns, accompanying the shovelfuls of dirt with prayers. Amid his strange feeling that all of this is a dream, a sensation heightened by the dim light, the Little Blessed One sees that even the Lion of Natuba, hopping in and out between the legs of the others, is helping to fill the grave. As he works, he contains his grief. He tells himself that this humble vigil and this poor grave on which no inscription or cross will be placed is something that the poor and humble man the Counselor was in life would surely have asked for himself. But when it is all over and the Sanctuary is exactly as it has always been – except that the pallet is empty – the Little Blessed One bursts into tears. In the midst of his weeping, he hears the others weeping, too. Then after a while he gets hold of himself and in a subdued voice asks them all to swear, in the name of the salvation of their souls, that they will never reveal, even under the worst of tortures, whatever they might be, where the Counselor's body reposes. He has them repeat the oath, one by one.

She opened her eyes and continued to feel happy, as she had all that night, the day before, and the day before that, a succession of days that were all confused in her mind, till the evening when, after believing that he'd been buried beneath the rubble of the store, she found the nearsighted journalist at the door of the Sanctuary, threw herself into his arms, heard him say that he loved her, and told him that she loved him, too. It was true, or, at any rate, once she'd said it, it began to be true. And from that moment on, despite the war closing in around her and the hunger and thirst that killed more people than the enemy bullets, Jurema was happy. More than she could ever remember having been, more than when she was married to Rufino, more than in that comfortable childhood in the shadow of Baroness Estela, at Calumbi. She felt like throwing herself at the feet of the saint to thank him for what had happened to her life.

She heard shots close by – she had heard them in her sleep all night long – but she had not noticed any of the activity in the Menino Jesus, neither the running footsteps and cries nor the frantic hustle and bustle as people lined up stones and sacks of sand, dug trenches, and tore down roofs and walls to erect parapets such as had gone up everywhere in these last weeks as Canudos shrank in size in all directions, behind successive concentric barricades and trenches, and the soldiers captured houses, streets, corners one by one, and the ring of defenses came closer and closer to the churches and the Sanctuary. But none of this mattered: she was happy.

It was the Dwarf who discovered this abandoned house made of wooden palings, wedged in between other bigger dwellings, on Menino Jesus, the little street that joined Campo Grande, where there was now a triple barricade manned by *jagunços* under the command of Abbot João himself, and the zigzag street of Madre Igreja, which as the ring around Canudos tightened had now become the outer limit of the city to the north. The blacks of the Mocambo, which had been captured, and the few Cariris of Mirandela and Rodelas who had not been killed had fallen back to that sector. Indians and blacks now lived together side by side, in the trenches and behind the parapets of Madre Igreja, along with Pedrão's *jagunços*, who had gradually withdrawn there in turn after stopping the soldiers in Cocorobó, in Trabubu, and at the corrals and stables on the outskirts of Canudos. When Jurema, the Dwarf, and the nearsighted journalist came to stay at this little house, they found an old man sprawled out dead on top of his blunderbuss, in the shelter that had been dug in the only room in the dwelling. But they had also found a sack of manioc flour and a pot of honey, which they had husbanded like misers. They hardly ever went out, except to carry off corpses to some dry wells that Antônio Vilanova had turned into ossuaries, and to help erect barricades and dig trenches, something that took more of everyone's time than the fighting itself did. So many excavations had been made, both inside and outside the houses, that a person could very nearly go from any one place to another in what was left of Belo Monte – from house to house, from street to street – without ever coming up to the surface, like lizards and moles.

The Dwarf stirred at her back. She asked him if he was awake. He did not answer, and a moment later she heard him snoring. All three of them slept, one against the other, in the dugout shelter, so narrow they barely fit into it. They slept in it not only because bullets easily pierced the walls of wooden pickets and mud but also because at night the temperature went way down and their bodies, weakened by their forced fastings, shook with cold. Jurema looked closely at the face of the nearsighted journalist, who was curled up against her breast, fast asleep. His mouth was gaping open and a little thread of saliva, as thin and transparent as a spiderweb, was hanging from his lip. She brought her mouth down to his and very delicately, so as not to awaken him, sipped the little trickle. The nearsighted journalist's expression was calm now, an expression he never had when he was awake. 'He's not afraid now,' she thought. 'Poor thing, poor thing, if I could rid him of his fear, if I could do something so that he'd never be afraid again.' For he had confessed to her that even in the moments when he was happy with her, the fear was always there, like mire in his heart, tormenting him. Even though she now loved him as a woman loves a man, even though she had been his as a husband or a lover makes a woman his, in her mind Jurema went on taking care of him, spoiling him, playing with him, like a mother with her son.

One of the nearsighted journalist's legs stretched out and, after pressing down a little, slid between hers. Not moving, feeling her face flush, Jurema thought to herself that he was going to want to have her then and there, that in broad daylight, as he did in the dark of night, he was going to unbutton his trousers, raise her skirts up, get her ready for him to enter her, take his pleasure, and make sure that she took hers. A tremor of excitement ran through her from head to foot. She closed her eyes and lay there quietly, trying to hear the shots, to remember the war being fought just a few steps away, thinking about the Sardelinha sisters and Catarina and the other women who were devoting what little strength they had left to caring for the sick and wounded and newborn in the very last two Health Houses left standing, and of the little old men who carried the dead off to the ossuary all day long. In this way, she contrived to make that sensation, so new in her life, go away. She had lost all shame. She not only did things that were a sin: she thought about doing them, she wanted to do them. 'Am I mad?' she thought. 'Possessed?' Now that she was about to die, she committed, in body and in thought, sins that she had never committed before. Because, even though she had been with two men before, it was only now that she had discovered – in the arms of this being whom chance and the war (or the Dog?) had placed in her path – that the body, too, could be happy. She knew now that love was also an exaltation of the flesh, a conflagration of the senses, a vertigo that seemed to fulfill her. She snuggled up to this man sleeping alongside her, pressed her body as close to his as she could. At her back, the Dwarf stirred again. She could feel him, a tiny little thing, all hunched over, seeking her warmth.

Yes, she had lost all shame. If anyone had ever told her that one day she would sleep like this, squeezed in between two men, though one of them was admittedly a dwarf, she would have been horrified. If anyone had ever told her that a man to whom she was not married would lift up her skirts and take her in plain sight of the other one who lay there at her side, sleeping or pretending to be asleep, as they took their pleasure together and told each other, mouth pressed against mouth, that they loved each other, Jurema would have been scandalized and would have covered her ears with her hands. And yet, ever since that evening, this had happened every night, and instead of making her feel ashamed and frightening her, it seemed natural to her and made her happy. The first night, on seeing that they were embracing each other and kissing each other as though they were the only two people in the world, the Dwarf had asked them if they wanted him to leave. No, no, he was as necessary to both of them, as dearly loved as ever. And it was true.

The gunfire suddenly grew heavier, and for a few seconds it was as though the shots were landing inside the house, above their heads. Dirt and dust fell into the hole. Hunched over with her eyes closed, Jurema waited, waited for the direct hit, the explosion, the cave-in. But a moment later the shooting was farther in the distance. When she opened her eyes again, she found herself staring into blank watery eyes whose gaze seemed to glide past her. The poor thing had awakened and was half dead with fear again.

'I thought it was a nightmare,' the Dwarf said at her back. He had stood up and was peeking over the edge of the hole. Rising up on her knees, Jurema also looked out, as the nearsighted journalist continued to lie there. Many people were running down Menino Jesus toward Campo Grande.

'What's happening, what's happening?' she heard his voice say at her feet. 'What do you see?'

'Lots of *jagunços,*' the Dwarf said before she could answer. 'They're coming from Pedrão's sector.'

And just then the door opened and Jurema saw a bunch of men in the doorway. One of them was the very young *jagunço* she had met on the slopes of Cocorobó the day the soldiers arrived.

'Come on, come on,' he called to them in a loud voice that carried over all the shooting. 'Come and give a hand.'

Jurema and the Dwarf helped the nearsighted journalist out of the hole and guided him out into the street. All her life she had automatically done whatever anyone with authority or power told her to do, so that it took no effort on her part, in cases such as this, to rouse herself from her passivity and work side by side with people at any sort of task, without ever asking what they were doing or why. But with this man at whose side she was running along the twists and turns of Menino Jesus, that had changed. He was forever wanting to know what was happening, to the right and to the left, in front and behind, why people were saying and doing certain things, and she was the one who was obliged to find out in order to satisfy his curiosity, as consuming as his fear. The young *jagunço* from Cocorobó explained that the dogs had been attacking the trenches at the cemetery since dawn that morning. They had launched two attacks, and though they had not managed to occupy the trenches, they had taken the corner of Batista, and were thus in a position to advance on the Temple of the Blessed Jesus from behind. Abbot João had decided to erect a new barricade, between the trenches at the cemetery and the churches, in case Pajeú found himself obliged to fall back yet again. That was why they were collecting people, why the ones who had been in the trenches at Madre Igreja had come. The young *jagunço* ran on ahead of them. Jurema could hear the nearsighted journalist panting and could see him tripping over the stones and stumbling into the holes along Campo Grande and she was sure that at this moment he was thinking, as she was, of Pajeú. Yes, they would be meeting him face to face now. She felt the nearsighted journalist squeeze her hand, and squeezed his back.

She had not seen Pajeú again since the evening that she had discovered what happiness was. But she and the nearsighted journalist had talked a great deal about the *caboclo* with the slashed face whom both of them knew to be an even greater threat to their love than the soldiers. Ever since that evening, they had hidden out in refuges toward the north of Canudos, the section farthest away from Fazenda Velha, and the Dwarf would go out on forays to find out what was happening to Pajeú. The morning that the Dwarf came to report to them – they had taken shelter underneath a tin roof on Santo Elói, behind the Mocambo – that the army was attacking Fazenda Velha, Jurema had told the nearsighted journalist that the *caboclo* would defend his trenches to the death. But that same night they learned that Pajeú and the survivors from Fazenda Velha were in the trenches at the cemetery that were now about to fall. Thus, the hour when they would be forced to confront Pajeú had come. But even that thought could not take away the happiness that had come to be part of her body, like her skin and bones.

Happiness kept her – as nearsightedness and fear kept the man she was holding by the hand, as faith, fatalism, or habit kept those who were also running, limping, walking down to erect the barricade – from seeing what was all about her, from reflecting and drawing the conclusion that common sense, reason, or sheer instinct would have allowed her to draw from the spectacle: the little streets, which had once been stretches of dirt and gravel and were now seesaws riddled with shell holes, strewn with the debris of objects blown to bits by the bombs or torn apart by the *jagunços* to build parapets; the creatures lying about on the ground, who could scarcely be called men or women any more, since they had no features left on their faces, no light left in their eyes, no strength left in their muscles, yet through some perverse absurdity were still alive. Jurema saw them and did not realize that they were there, for they were scarcely distinguishable from the corpses that the old men had not yet had time to come get, the only difference between them being the number of flies swarming over them and the intensity of the stench they were giving off. She saw and yet did not see the vultures that were hovering above them and from time to time also being killed by the bullets, and the children with the blank faces of sleepwalkers poking about in the ruins or chewing on clods of dirt. They had run a long way, and when they finally stopped, she had to close her eyes and lean against the nearsighted journalist till the world stopped going round and round.

The journalist asked her where they were. It took Jurema some time to realize that the unrecognizable place was São João, a narrow lane between the jumble of little houses around the cemetery and the back of the Temple under construction. There were holes and rubble everywhere, and a crowd of people were frantically digging, filling sacks, drums, boxes, barrels, and casks with dirt and sand, and dragging beams, roof tiles, bricks, stones, and even carcasses of animals to the barrier that was going up there where before a picket fence had marked off the cemetery. The shooting had stopped, or else Jurema's ears had been so deafened that they could no longer distinguish it from the rest of the din. As she was telling the nearsighted journalist that Pajeú wasn't there, though both Antônio and Honório Vilanova were, a one-eyed man roared at them, asking what they were waiting for. The nearsighted journalist sat down on the ground and began scratching about. Jurema brought him an iron bar so he could do a better job of it. And then she plunged once again into the routine of filling gunnysacks, carrying them wherever she was told to, and taking a pickax to walls to get stones, bricks, roof tiles, and beams to reinforce the barrier, already several yards tall and wide. From time to time, she went to where the nearsighted journalist was piling up sand and gravel, to let him know that she was close at hand. She did not even notice that the shooting started again, died down, stopped, and then began yet again behind the stout barricade, nor that every so often groups of old men passed by, carrying wounded to the churches.

At one point a group of women, among whom she recognized Catarina, Abbot João's wife, came by and handed her some chicken bones with a little skin on them and a dipper full of water. She went to share this gift with the journalist and the Dwarf, but they, too, had been given the same rations. They ate and drank together, happy and yet disconcerted by this repast, knowing that the food supplies had long since given out and it was understood that the few remaining scraps were reserved for the men staying day and night in the trenches and the towers, their hands covered with powder burns and their fingers callused from shooting so much.

She had just gone back to work after this pause when she happened to look at the tower of the Temple of the Blessed Jesus and something caught her eye. Beneath the heads of the *jagunços* and the barrels of rifles and shotguns peeking out from the parapets on the rooftop and the scaffoldings, a little gnome-like figure, bigger than a child but smaller than an adult, had been left hanging suspended in an absurd posture on the little ladder that led up to the bell tower. She recognized him: it was the bell ringer, the little old man who acted as sexton, sacristan, and keeper of the keys of the churches, the one who, people said, scourged the Little Blessed One. He had continued to climb up to the bell tower just as night was falling every evening to ring the bells for the Ave Maria, after which, war or no war, all Belo Monte recited the Rosary. He had been killed the evening before, no doubt after ringing the bells, for Jurema was certain that she had heard them. A bullet must have hit him and his body been caught in the ladder, and no one had had time to get him down.

'He was from my village,' a woman who was working alongside Jurema said to her, pointing to the tower. 'Chorrochó. He was a carpenter there, when the angel's wings brushed him.'

She went back to her work, putting the bell ringer out of her mind, and forgetting about herself as well, she toiled away all afternoon, going every so often to where the journalist was. As the sun was setting she saw the Vilanova brothers running off toward the Sanctuary and heard that Pajeú, Big João, and Abbot João had also come by, running that way from different directions. Something was about to happen.

A little while later, she was leaning over talking to the nearsighted journalist when an invisible force compelled her to kneel, to fall silent, to lean against him. 'What's the matter, what's the matter?' he said, taking her by the shoulder and feeling her all over. And she heard him shout at her: 'Have you been wounded, are you wounded?' No bullet had struck her. It was just that all the strength had suddenly been drained from her body. She felt empty, without the energy to open her mouth or lift a finger, and though she saw leaning over her the face of the man who had taught her what happiness was, his liquid eyes opening wide and blinking, trying to see her better, and realized that he was frightened and knew that she ought to reassure him, she was unable to. Everything was far away, strange, make-believe, and the Dwarf was there, touching her, caressing her, rubbing her hands, her forehead, stroking her hair, and it even seemed to her that, like the nearsighted journalist, he was kissing her on the hands, the cheeks. She was not about to close her eyes, because if she did she would die, but there came a moment when she could no longer keep them open.

When she opened them again, she no longer felt so freezing cold. It was night; the sky was full of stars, there was a full moon, and she was sitting leaning against the nearsighted journalist's body – whose odor, thinness, heartbeat she recognized at once – and the Dwarf was there too, still rubbing her hands. In a daze, she noted how happy the two men were on seeing her awake once again, and felt herself being embraced and kissed by them so affectionately that tears came to her eyes. Was she wounded, ill? No, it had been exhaustion: she had worked so hard for such a long time. She was no longer in the same place as before. While she was lying in a faint, the gunfire had suddenly grown heavier and the *jagunços* had come running from the trenches in the cemetery; the Dwarf and the journalist had had to carry her to this street corner so that the men would not trample her underfoot. But the soldiers had not been able to get past the barricade erected along São João. The *jagunços* from the cemetery trenches who had escaped with their lives and many who had come from the churches had stopped them there. She heard the journalist telling her that he loved her, and at that very moment the world blew up. Dust filled her nose and eyes and she found herself knocked flat on the ground, for the journalist and the Dwarf had been thrown on top of her by the force of the shock wave. But she was not afraid; she huddled beneath the two bodies lying on top of her, struggling to utter the necessary sounds to find out if they were all right. Yes, just bruised from the chunks of stone, wood, and other debris that had rained down on them from the explosion. A confused, frantic, many-voiced, dissonant, incomprehensible outcry roiled the darkness. The nearsighted man and the Dwarf sat up, helped her to a sitting position, and the three of them stayed there where they were, hugging the only wall still standing on that corner. What had happened, what was happening?

Shadows were running in all directions, terrifying screams rent the air, but the strange thing to Jurema, who had drawn her legs up and was leaning her head on the nearsighted journalist's shoulder, was that along with the cries, the shrieks, the weeping and wailing, she could also hear loud bursts of laughter, cheers, songs, and now a single vibrant, martial song, being roared out by hundreds of voices.

'The Church of Santo Antônio,' the Dwarf said. 'They've hit it, they've brought it tumbling down.'

She looked, and in the dim moonlight, up above, where the smoke that had been hiding it was slowly being blown away by a breeze from the river, she saw the looming, imposing outlines of the Temple of the Blessed Jesus, but not those of the bell tower and roof of Santo Antônio. That was what the tremendous din had been. The screams and cries had come from those who had fallen with the church, from those crushed beneath its stones as it caved in, but not yet dead. With his arms about her, the nearsighted journalist kept shouting at the top of his lungs asking what was happening, what the laughing and singing were, and the Dwarf answered that it was the soldiers, beside themselves with joy. The soldiers! The soldiers shouting, singing! How could they be this close? The triumphant cheers were mingled in her ears with the moans, and sounded as though they were coming from even nearer at hand. On the other side of this barricade that she had helped to erect, a crowd of soldiers was milling about, singing, about to cross the space of just a few feet separating them from the three of them. 'Father, may the three of us die together,' she prayed.

But curiously enough, instead of fanning the flames of war, the fall of Santo Antônio appeared to bring a lull in the fighting. Still not moving from their corner, they heard the cries of pain and of victory gradually grow fainter, and then, after that, there came a calm such as had not reigned for many a night. There was not a single cannon or rifle report to be heard, only sounds of weeping and moaning here and there, as though the combatants had agreed on a truce so as to rest. It seemed to her at times that she fell asleep, and when she awoke she had no idea whether a second or an hour had gone by. Each time she was still in the same place, sheltered between the nearsighted journalist and the Dwarf.

At one of these times, she spied a *jagunço* from the Catholic Guard walking away from them. What had he wanted? Father Joaquim was asking for them. 'I told him you weren't able to move,' the nearsighted man murmured. A moment later the curé of Cumbe came trotting along in the dark. 'Why didn't you come?' she heard him say, in an odd tone of voice, and she thought: 'Pajeú.'

'Jurema is exhausted,' she heard the nearsighted journalist answer. 'She's fainted away several times.'

'She'll have to stay here, then,' Father Joaquim answered, in the same strange voice, not angry, but broken, disheartened, sad. 'You two come with me.'

'Stay here?' she heard the nearsighted journalist murmur, feeling him straighten up, his whole body tense.

'Be still,' the curé ordered. 'Weren't you the one who was so desperate to get away? Well, you're going to have your chance now. But not a word out of you. Come along, you two.'

Father Joaquim began to walk off. Jurema was the first one on her feet, gathering her strength together and thus putting an end to the journalist's stammering – 'Jurema can't . . . I . . . I . . .' – and demonstrating to him that indeed she could, that she was already on her feet, following along behind the curé's shadow. Seconds later, she was running, the nearsighted man holding her by one hand and the Dwarf by the other, amid the ruins and the dead and injured of the Church of Santo Antônio, still not able to believe what she had heard.

She realized that the curé was leading them to the Sanctuary, through a labyrinth of galleries and parapets with armed men. A door opened and by the light of a lamp she spied Pajeú. She doubtless uttered his name, thereby alerting the nearsighted journalist, for he immediately burst into sneezes that doubled him over. But it was not by order of the *caboclo* that Father

Joaquim had brought them here, for Pajeú was paying no attention to them at all. He was not even looking their way. They were in the women disciples' little room, the Counselor's antechamber, and through the cracks in the stake wall Jurema could see in the inner chamber the Sacred Choir and Mother Maria Quadrado kneeling and the profiles of the Little Blessed One and the Lion of Natuba. In the narrow confines of the antechamber, besides Pajeú, there were Antônio and Honório Vilanova and the Sardelinha sisters, and in the faces of all of them, as in Father Joaquim's voice, there was something unusual, irremediable, fateful, desperate, feral. As though they had not entered the room, as though they were not there, Pajeú went on talking to Antônio Vilanova: he would hear shots, disorder, confusion, but they were not to move yet. Not until the whistles sounded. Then yes: that was the moment to run, fly, slip away like vixens. The *caboclo* paused and Antônio Vilanova nodded gloomily. Pajeú spoke again: 'Don't stop running for any reason. Not to pick up anybody who falls, not to retrace your steps. Everything depends on that and on the Father. If you reach the river before the dogs notice, you'll get through. At least you have a chance to.'

'But you have no chance at all of getting out – neither you nor anyone else who goes with you to the dogs' camp,' Antônio Vilanova moaned. He was weeping. He grabbed the *caboclo* by the arms and begged him: 'I don't want to leave Belo Monte, much less if it means your sacrificing yourself. You're needed here more than I am. Pajeú! Pajeú!'

The *caboclo* slipped out of his grasp with a sort of annoyance. 'It has to be before it gets light,' he said curtly. 'After that, you won't be able to make it.'

He turned to Jurema, the nearsighted man, and the Dwarf, who were standing there petrified. 'You're to go too, because that's what the Counselor wishes,' he said, as though talking past the three of them to someone they couldn't see. 'First to Fazenda Velha, in Indian file, crouching down. And there where the youngsters tell you, you're to wait for the whistles to blow.

Then you're to dash through the camp and down to the river. You'll get through, if it be the Father's will.'

He fell silent and looked at the nearsighted man, standing with his arms around Jurema and trembling like a leaf. 'Sneeze now,' Pajeú said to him, in the same tone of voice. 'Not then. Not when you're waiting for the whistles to blow. If you sneeze then, they'll plunge a knife in your heart. It wouldn't be right if they captured everyone on account of your sneezes. Praised be Blessed Jesus the Counselor.'

When he hears them, Private Queluz is dreaming of Captain Oliveira's orderly, a pale young private whom he has been prowling around for some time and saw shitting this morning, crouched behind a little pile of rocks near the wells down by the Vaza-Barris. He has kept intact the image of those hairless legs and those white buttocks that he glimpsed, bared to the dawn air like an invitation. The image is so clear, steady, and vivid that Private Queluz's cock gets hard, swelling against his uniform and awakening him. His desire is so overpowering that even though he can hear voices nearby, and even though he is forced to recognize that they are the voices of traitors and not of patriots, his immediate reaction is not to grab his rifle but to raise his hands to his trousers fly to stroke his cock inflamed by the memory of the round buttocks of Captain Oliveira's orderly. Suddenly the thought is borne in upon him that he is alone, in open country, with the enemy close at hand, and instantly he is wide awake, every muscle tense, his heart in his mouth. What has happened to Leopoldinho? Have they killed Leopoldinho? They've killed him: he sees quite clearly now that the sentry didn't even have time to shout a warning or even realize that they were killing him. Leopoldinho is the soldier with whom he shares the guard in this empty stretch of land that separates A Favela from the Vaza-Barris, where the Fifth Infantry Regiment is encamped, the good buddy with whom he takes turns sleeping, thereby making the nights on guard duty more tolerable.

'Lots and lots of noise, so they'll think there are more of us,' their leader says. 'And above all, get them all confused, so they don't know whether they're coming or going, so they don't have the time or the inclination to look toward the river.'

'In other words, Pajeú, you mean really whoop it up,' another voice says.

'Pajeú!' Queluz thinks. Pajeú's there. Lying there in the middle of nowhere, surrounded by *jagunços* who will finish him off in short order if they discover him, on realizing that in the shadows, within reach of his hand, is one of the fiercest bandits in all Canudos, a choice prize, Queluz has an impulse which very nearly brings him bounding to his feet, to grab his rifle and blow the monster to bits. This would win him the admiration of one and all, of Colonel Medeiros, of General Oscar. They would give him the corporal's stripes he has coming to him. Because even though his length of service and his behavior under fire should have long since earned him a promotion, they keep turning him down for one on the stupid pretext that he's been caned too often for inducing recruits to commit with him what Father Lizzardo calls 'the abominable sin.' He turns his head, and in the light of the clear night he sees the silhouettes: twenty, thirty of them. How have they happened not to step on him? By what miracle have they failed to see him? Moving just his eyes, he tries to make out the famous scar on one of those faces that are a mere blur. It is Pajeú who is speaking, he is certain, reminding the others that they should set off dynamite sticks rather than shoot their rifles because that way they'll make a bigger racket, and warning all of them again that nobody is to blow his whistle before he does. He hears him bid them goodbye in a way that makes him laugh: Praised be Blessed Jesus the Counselor. The group breaks up into shadows that disappear in the direction of the regiment's camp.

He hesitates no longer. He scrambles to his feet, grabs his rifle, cocks it, aims it in the direction in which the *jagunços* are disappearing, and fires. But the trigger doesn't budge, though he squeezes it with all his might. He curses, spits, trembles with rage at the death of his buddy, and as he murmurs 'Leopoldinho, are you there?' he cocks his piece again and tries once more to fire a shot to alert the regiment. He is shaking the rifle to make it behave, to get across to it that it can't jam now, when he hears several explosions. Damn: they've gotten into the camp. It's his fault. They're setting off dynamite sticks to blow up his sleeping buddies. Damn: the sons of bitches, the fiends, they're butchering his buddies. And it's his fault.

Confused, infuriated, he doesn't know what to do. How have they managed to get this far without being discovered? Because – there's no doubt about it, since Pajeú is with them – these are *jagunços* who have come out of Canudos and made their way through the patriots' trenches so as to attack the camp from the rear. What in the world can have made Pajeú attack a camp of five hundred soldiers with just twenty or thirty men? All over the sector occupied by the Fifth Infantry Regiment there are people running this way and that, shots, a tremendous uproar. He is desperate. What is going to become of him? What explanation is he going to give when they ask him why he didn't give the alert, why he didn't shoot, shout, or do anything at all when they killed Leopoldinho? Who is there to deliver him from a new round of canings?

He grips the rifle hard, in a blind rage, and it goes off. The bullet brushes past his nose, giving him a red-hot whiff of gunpowder. It cheers him that his piece works, it restores his optimism, which, unlike others, he has never lost in all these months, not even when so many of the men were dying and they were all so hungry. Not knowing what he is going to do, he runs across the open stretch of ground in the direction of this bloody fiesta that the *jagunços* are having themselves, just as they said they would, and fires his four remaining bullets in the air, telling himself that the red-hot barrel of his rifle will be proof that he hasn't been sleeping, that he's been fighting. He trips and falls headlong. 'Leopoldinho?' he says. 'Leopoldinho?' He feels the ground in front of him, behind him, alongside him.

Yes, it's Leopoldinho. He touches him, shakes him. The fiends. He spits out the taste of vomit in his mouth, keeps himself from throwing up. They have sunk a knife in his neck, they have slit his throat the way they would a lamb's, his head dangles like a doll's when he lifts him up by the armpits. 'The fiends, the fiends,' he says, and without the thought distracting him from his grief and wrath at the death of his buddy, it occurs to him that going back to the camp with the dead body will convince Captain Oliveira that he wasn't asleep at his post when the bandits came, that he put up a fight. He advances slowly, stumbling along with Leopoldinho's body slung over his back, and hears, amid the shots and the fracas in the camp, the high-pitched, piercing screech of a strange bird, followed by others. The whistles. What are they up to? Why are the fanatical traitors entering the camp, setting off dynamite, and then beginning to blow whistles like mad? He staggers beneath the weight of Leopoldinho's body and wonders if it wouldn't be better to stop and rest.

As he approaches the huts he is struck by the chaos that reigns inside the camp: the soldiers, brutally awakened by the explosions, are shooting helter-skelter in all directions, disregarding the shouts and roars of the officers trying to impose order. At that moment, Leopoldinho shudders. Queluz is so stunned at this that he lets go of him and falls to the ground alongside him. No, he is not alive. What a stupid idiot he is! It was the impact of a bullet that shook the body like that. 'That's the second time tonight that you've saved my life, Leopoldinho,' he thinks. That knife thrust might have been meant for him, that bullet might have had his name on it. 'Thanks, Leopoldinho!' He lies there flat on the ground, thinking that it would be the last straw if he got shot by the soldiers of his own regiment, in a fury again, his mind going round and round again, not knowing whether to stay there where he is till the shooting dies down or whether to try at all costs to reach the huts.

He is still lying there, agonizing as to what he should do, when in the shadows on the mountainside that are beginning to dissolve into a shimmer of blue he spies two silhouettes running toward him. He is about to shout: 'Help! Come give me a hand!' when a sudden suspicion freezes the cry in his throat. He strains to see, till his eyes burn, whether or not they are wearing uniforms, but there is not enough light. He has unslung his rifle from his shoulder, grabbed a cartridge pouch from his knapsack, and is loading and cocking his gun by the time the men are almost upon him: none of them is a soldier. He fires point-blank at the one who offers the best target, and along with the report of his rifle, he hears the man's animal snort and the thud of his body as it hits the ground. And then his rifle jams again: his finger squeezes a trigger that refuses to budge even a fraction of an inch.

He curses and leaps aside as at the same time he raises his rifle in his two hands and lashes out at the other *jagunço,* who, after a second's hesitation, has flung himself on top of him. Queluz is good at fighting hand to hand, he has always shown up well in the tests of strength organized by Captain Oliveira. He feels the man's hot panting breath in his face and his head butting him as he concentrates on the most important thing, searching out his adversary's arms, his hands, knowing that the danger does not lie in these blows of his head that are like a battering ram but in the knife blade protruding like an extension of one of his hands. And, in fact, as his hands find and grip the man's wrists he hears his pants ripping and feels a sharp knife blade run down his thigh. As he, too, butts with his head, bites, and hurls insults, Queluz fights with all his strength to hold back, to push away, to twist this hand where the danger is. He has no idea how many seconds or minutes or hours it takes, but all of a sudden he realizes that the traitor is attacking him less fiercely, is losing heart, that the arm that he is clutching is beginning to go limp in his grip. 'You're fucked,' Queluz spits at him. 'You're already dead, traitor.' Yes, though he is still biting, kicking, butting, the *jagunço* is wearing out, giving up. Queluz feels his hands free at last. He leaps to his feet, grabs his rifle, raises it in the air, and is about to plunge the bayonet into the traitor's belly and fling himself on top of him when he sees – it is no longer dark but first light – the swollen face with a hideous scar all the way across it. With his rifle poised in the air, he thinks: 'Pajeú.' Blinking, panting for breath, his chest about to burst with excitement, he cries: 'Pajeú? Are you Pajeú?' He is not dead, his eyes are open, he is looking at him. 'Pajeú?' he shouts, beside himself with joy. 'Does this mean you're my prisoner, Pajeú?' Though he continues to look at him, the *jagunço* pays no attention to what he is saying. He is trying to raise his knife. 'Do you still want to fight?' Queluz says mockingly, stamping on his chest. No, he is paying no attention to him, as he tries to . . . 'Or maybe you want to kill yourself, Pajeú,' Queluz laughs, kicking the knife out of the limp hand. 'That's not up to you, traitor – it's up to us.'

Capturing Pajeú alive is an even more heroic deed than having killed him. Queluz contemplates the *caboclo*'s face: swollen, scratched, bitten. But he also has a bullet wound in the leg, for his trousers are completely blood-soaked. Queluz can't believe that he is lying there at his feet. He looks around for the other *jagunço*, and just as he spies him, sprawled on the ground clutching his belly, perhaps not dead yet, he notices several soldiers approaching. He gestures frantically to them: 'It's Pajeú! Pajeú! I've caught Pajeú!'

When, after having touched him, sniffed him, looked him over from head to foot, touched him again – and having given him a couple of kicks, but not many, since all of them agree that it's best to bring him in alive to Colonel Medeiros – the soldiers drag Pajeú to the camp, Queluz receives a welcome that is an apotheosis. The news that he has killed one of the bandits who have attacked them and has captured Pajeú soon makes the rounds, and everyone comes out to have a look at him, to congratulate him, to pat him on the back and embrace him. They box his ears affectionately, hand him canteens, and a lieutenant lights his cigarette. He mumbles that he feels sad about Leopoldinho, but he's really weeping with emotion at this moment of glory.

Colonel Medeiros wants to see him. As he walks to the command post, as if in a trance, Queluz does not remember the raging fury that Colonel Medeiros had been in the day before – a fury that took the form of punishments, threats, and reprimands that did not spare even the majors and captains – because of his frustration at the fact that the First Brigade had not participated in the attack at dawn, which everyone thought would be the final push that would enable the patriots to capture all the positions still occupied by the traitors. The rumor had even gone round that Colonel Medeiros had had a run-in with General Oscar because the latter had not allowed the First Brigade to charge, and that when he learned that Colonel Gouveia's Second Brigade had taken the fanatics' trenches in the cemetery, Colonel Medeiros had thrown his cup of coffee onto the ground and smashed it to bits. Rumor also had it that, at nightfall, when the General Staff halted the attack in view of the heavy casualties and the traitors' fierce resistance, Colonel Medeiros had drunk brandy, as though he were celebrating, as though there were anything to celebrate.

But, on entering Colonel Medeiros's hut, Queluz immediately remembers all that. The face of the commanding officer of the First Brigade is about to explode with rage. He is not waiting at the doorway to congratulate him, as Queluz imagined he would be. He is sitting on a folding camp stool, heaping abuse on someone. Who is it he's shouting at? At Pajeú. Peeking between the backs and profiles of the crowd of officers in the hut, Queluz spies the sallow face with the garnet-colored scar cutting all the way across it, lying on the ground at the colonel's feet. He is not dead; his eyes are half open, and Queluz, to whom no one is paying the slightest attention, who has no notion why they have brought him here and who feels like leaving, tells himself that the colonel's fit of temper is doubtless due to the distant, disdainful look in Pajeú's eyes as he gazes up at him. It is not that, however, but the attack on the camp: eighteen men have been killed.

'Eighteen! Eighteen!' Colonel Medeiros rages, clenching and unclenching his teeth as though champing at a bit. 'Thirty-some wounded! Those of us in the First Brigade spend the whole damned day up here scratching our balls while the Second Brigade fights, and then you come along with your band of degenerates and inflict more casualties on us than on them.'

'He's going to burst into tears,' Queluz thinks. In a panic, he imagines that the colonel is going to find out somehow that he went to sleep at his post and let the bandits get past him without giving the alarm. The commanding officer of the First Brigade leaps up from his camp stool and begins to kick and stamp his feet. The officers' backs and profiles block Queluz's view of what's happening on the ground. But seconds later he sees the *jagunço* again: the crimson scar has grown much larger, covering the bandit's entire face, a featureless, shapeless mass of dirt and mud. But his eyes are still open, and in them that indifference that is so strange and so offensive. A thread of bloody spittle trickles from his lips.

Queluz sees a saber in Colonel Medeiros's hands and he is certain that he is about to give Pajeú the *coup de grâce*. But he merely rests the tip of it on the *jagunço*'s neck. Total silence reigns in the hut, and Queluz finds himself in the grip of the same hieratic solemnity as the officers.

Finally Colonel Medeiros calms down. He sits back down on the camp stool and flings his saber on the cot. 'Killing you would be doing you a favor,' he mutters in bitter rage. 'You have betrayed your country, murdered your compatriots, sacked, plundered, committed every imaginable crime. There is no punishment terrible enough for what you have done.'

'He's laughing,' Queluz thinks to himself in amazement. Yes, the *caboclo* is laughing. His forehead and the little crest of flesh that is all that is left of his nose are puckered up, his lips are parted, and his little slits of eyes gleam as he utters a sound that is undoubtedly a laugh.

'Do you find what I'm saying amusing?' Colonel Medeiros says, slowly and deliberately. But the next moment his tone of voice changes, for Pajeú's face has turned rigid. 'Examine him, Doctor . . .'

Captain Bernardo da Ponte Sanhueza kneels down, puts his ear to the bandit's chest, observes his eyes, takes his pulse.

'He's dead, sir,' Queluz hears him say.

Colonel Medeiros's face blanches.

'His body's a sieve,' the doctor adds. 'It's a miracle that he's lasted this long with all that lead in him.'

'It's my turn now,' Queluz thinks. Colonel Medeiros's piercing little blue-green eyes are about to seek him out among the officers, find him, and he will hear the question he is so afraid of: 'Why didn't you give the alert?' He'll lie, he'll swear in the name of God and his mother that he did give it, that he fired warning shots and yelled out. But the seconds pass and Colonel Medeiros continues to sit there on the camp stool, contemplating the corpse of the bandit who died laughing at him.

'Here's Queluz, sir,' he hears Captain Oliveira say.

Now, now. The officers step aside to allow him to present himself before the commanding officer of the First Brigade. Colonel Medeiros looks at him, rises to his feet. Queluz sees – his heart is pounding in his chest – the colonel's face relax, notes that he is trying his best to smile at him. Queluz smiles back at him, gratefully.

'So you're the one who captured him?' the colonel asks.

'Yes, sir,' Queluz answers, standing at attention.

'Finish the job,' Medeiros says to him, holding his sword out to him with an energetic gesture. 'Put his eyes out and cut his tongue off. Then lop his head off and throw it over the barricade, so those bandits who are still alive will know what awaits them.'

VI

When the nearsighted journalist finally left, the Baron de Canabrava, who had accompanied him to the street, discovered that it was pitch-dark outside. On coming back into the house, he stood leaning against the massive front door with his eyes closed, trying to banish a seething mass of violent, confused images from his mind. A manservant came running with an oil lamp in his hand: would he like his dinner reheated? He answered no, and before sending the servant to bed he asked him whether Estela had eaten dinner. Yes, some time ago, and then she had retired to her room.

Instead of going upstairs to her bedroom, the baron returned to his study like a sleepwalker, listening to the echo of his footsteps. He could smell, he could see, floating like fluff in the stuffy air of the room, the words of that long conversation which, it now seemed to him, had been not so much a dialogue as two monologues running side by side without ever meeting. He would not see the nearsighted journalist again, he would not have another talk with him. He would not allow him to bring to life yet again that monstrous story whose unfolding had involved the destruction of his property, his political power, his wife. 'Only she matters,' he murmured to himself. Yes, he could have resigned himself to all the other losses. For the time he had left to live – ten, fifteen years? – he possessed the means to do so in the manner to which he was accustomed. It did not matter that this style of life would end with his death: he had, after all, no heirs whose fortunes he should be concerned about. And as for political power, in the final analysis he was happy to have rid himself of that heavy load on his shoulders. Politics had been a burden that he had taken upon himself because there was no one else to do so, because of the vast stupidity, irresponsibility, or corruption of others, not out of some heartfelt vocation: politics had always bored him, wearied him, impressed him as being an inane, depressing occupation, since it revealed human wretchedness more clearly than any other. Moreover, he harbored a secret resentment against politics, an absorbing occupation for which he had sacrificed the scientific leanings that he had felt ever since he was a youngster collecting butterflies and making herbariums. The tragedy to which he would never be able to resign himself was Estela. It had been Canudos, he thought, that stupid, incomprehensible story of blind, stubborn people, of diametrically opposed fanaticisms, that had been to blame for what had happened to Estela. He had severed his ties to the world and would not reestablish them. He would allow nothing, no one to remind him of this episode. 'I will have them give him work on the paper,' he thought. 'As a proofreader, a court reporter, some mediocre job that's tailor-made for a mediocrity like him. But I won't receive him or listen to him again. And if he writes that book about Canudos – though naturally he won't – I shall not read it.'

He went to the liquor cabinet and poured himself a glass of cognac. As he warmed the drink in the palm of his hand, sitting in the leather easy chair from which he had set the course of politics in the state of Bahia for a quarter of a century, the Baron de Canabrava listened to the harmonious symphony of the crickets in the garden, with a chorus of frogs joining in from time to time in dissonant counterpoint. What was making him so anxious? What was responsible for this feeling of impatience, this prickling sensation all over, as though he were forgetting something extremely urgent, as though in the next few seconds something decisive, something irrevocable were about to happen in his life? Canudos still?

He had not banished it from his mind: it was there again. But the image that had loomed up, vivid and threatening, before his eyes was not something that he had heard from the lips of his visitor. It had happened when neither that nearsighted man nor the little servant girl from Canudos who was now his woman, nor the Dwarf, nor any of the survivors of Canudos, was any longer about. It was old Colonel Murau who had told him about it, over a glass of port, the last time they had seen each other here in Salvador, something that Murau had heard in turn from the owner of the Formosa hacienda, one of the many burned to the ground by the *jagunços*. The owner had stayed on at the hacienda, despite everything, out of love for his land, or because he didn't know where else to go. And he had stayed on there all through the war, eking out a living thanks to the commercial deals he arranged with the soldiers. When he learned that the war was all over, that Canudos had fallen, he hurriedly made his way up there with a bunch of peons to lend a hand. When they sighted the hillsides of the former *jagunço* citadel, the army had gone. While still a fair distance away – Colonel Murau recounted, as the baron sat there listening – they had been dumfounded by a strange, indefinable, unfathomable sound, so loud it shook the air. And the air was filled, as well, with a terrible stench that turned their stomachs. But it was only when they made their way down the drab, stony slope of O Poço Trabubu and discovered at their feet what had ceased to be Canudos and become the sight that greeted their eyes, that they realized that the sound was that of the flapping wings and pecking beaks of thousands upon thousands of vultures, of that endless sea of grayish, blackish shapes covering everything, devouring everything, gorging themselves, finishing off, as they sated themselves, what neither dynamite nor bullets nor fires had been able to reduce to dust: those limbs, extremities, heads, vertebras, viscera, skin that the conflagration had spared or only half charred and that these rapacious creatures were now crushing to bits, tearing apart, swallowing, gulping down. 'Thousands upon thousands of vultures,' Colonel Murau had said. And also that, stricken with terror in the face of what seemed like a nightmare come true, the owner of the hacienda of Formosa and his peons, realizing that there was nobody left to bury, since the carrion birds were doing their work, had left the place on the run, covering their mouths and holding their noses. The intrusive, loathsome image had taken root in his mind and refused to go away. 'The end that Canudos deserved,' he had answered before forcing old Murau to change the subject.

Was this what was troubling him, making him anxious, setting his every nerve on edge? That swarm of countless carrion birds devouring the human rot that was all that was left of Canudos? 'Twenty-five years of dirty, sordid politics to save Bahia from imbeciles and helpless idiots faced with a responsibility that they were incapable of assuming, the end result of which was a feast of vultures,' he thought to himself. And at that moment, superimposed on the image of the hecatomb, there reappeared the tragicomic face, the laughingstock with the watery crossed eyes, the scarecrow frame, the overprominent chin, the absurdly drooping ears, speaking to him of love, of pleasure in a fervent voice: 'The greatest thing in all this world, Baron, the one and only thing whereby man can discover a measure of happiness, can learn what the word happiness means.' That was it. That was what was troubling him, upsetting him, causing him such anguish. He took a swallow of cognac, held the fiery liquid in his mouth for a moment, swallowed it, and felt its warmth trickle down his throat.

He rose to his feet: he had no idea as yet what he was going to do, what he wanted to do, but he was aware of a stirring deep within him, and it seemed to him that he had arrived at a crucial moment in which he was obliged to come to a decision that would have incalculable consequences. What was he going to do, what was it he wanted to do? He set the glass of cognac down on top of the liquor cabinet, and feeling his heart, his temples pounding, his blood coursing through the geography of his body, he crossed the study, the enormous living room, the vast entry hall – with not a soul around at this hour, and everything in shadow, though there was a faint glow from the street lamps outside – to the foot of the staircase. There was a single lamp lighting the way up the stairs. He hurried up, on tiptoe, so softly that even he was unable to hear his own footfalls. Once at the top, without hesitating, instead of heading for his own apartments, he made his way toward the room in which the baroness was sleeping, separated only by a screen from the alcove where Sebastiana had installed herself so as to be close at hand if Estela needed her in the night.

As his hand reached out toward the latch, the thought occurred to him that the door might be locked. He had never entered the room without knocking. No, the door was not barred. He entered, closed the door behind him, searched for the bolt, and slid it home. From the doorway he spied the yellow light of the night lamp – a candlewick floating in a little bowl of oil – whose dim light illuminated part of the baroness's bed, the blue counterpane, the canopy overhead, and the thin gauze curtains. Standing there in the doorway, without making the slightest sound, without his hands trembling, the baron slowly removed all his clothes. Once he was naked, he crossed the room on tiptoe to Sebastiana's little alcove.

He reached the edge of her bed without awakening her. There was a dim light in the room – the glow from the gas lamp out in the street, which took on a blue tinge as it filtered through the curtains – and the baron could make out the woman's sleeping form, lying on her side, the sheets rising and falling with her breathing, her head resting on a little round pillow. Her long loose black hair fanned out across the bed and over the side, touching the floor. The thought came to him that he had never seen Sebastiana standing up with her hair undone, that it must no doubt reach to her heels, and that at one time or another, before a mirror or before Estela, she must surely have played at enveloping herself in this long hair as though in a silken mantle, and the image began to arouse a dormant instinct in him. He raised his hands to his belly and felt his member: it was flaccid, but in its warmth, its complaisance, the swiftness and the feeling close to joy with which he unsheathed the glans from the prepuce, he sensed a profound life, yearning to be called forth, reawakened, poured out. The things he had been afraid of as he approached – what would the servant's reaction be? what would Estela's be if Sebastiana woke up screaming? – disappeared instantly and, as startling as a hallucination, the face of Galileo Gall flashed before his mind and he remembered the vow of chastity that the revolutionary had sworn to himself in order to concentrate his energies on things he believed to be of a higher order – action, science. 'I have been as stupid as he was,' he thought. Without ever having sworn to do so, he had kept a similar vow for a very long time, renouncing pleasure, happiness, in favor of that base occupation that had brought misfortune to the person he loved most dearly in this world.

Without thinking, automatically, he bent over and sat down on the edge of the bed, at the same time moving his two hands, one downward to pull back the sheets covering Sebastiana, and the other toward her mouth to stifle her cry. The woman shrank away, lay there rigid, and opened her eyes, and a wave of warmth, the intimate aura of Sebastiana's body reached his nostrils; he had never been this close to her before, and immediately he felt his member come to life, and it was as though he were also suddenly aware that his testicles existed, that they, too, were there, coming back to life between his legs. Sebastiana had been unable to cry out, to sit up: only to utter a muffled exclamation that brought the warm air of her breath against the palm of the hand that he was holding a fraction of an inch away from her mouth.

'Don't scream; it's best if you don't scream,' he murmured. He could hear that his voice was not firm, but what was making it tremble was not hesitation but desire. 'I beg you not to scream.'

With the hand that had pulled the sheets back, through her nightdress buttoned all the way up to the neck, he now fondled Sebastiana's breasts: they were large, well proportioned, extraordinarily firm for a woman who must be close to forty years old; he felt the nipples grow hard, shiver from the cold beneath his fingertips. He ran his fingers along the ridge of her nose, her lips, her eyebrows, with the most delicate touch of which he was capable, and finally sank them in the tangle of hair and gently wound her locks round them. Meanwhile, he tried to exorcise with a smile the tremendous fear he saw in the woman's stunned, incredulous gaze.

'I should have done this a long time ago, Sebastiana,' he said, brushing her cheeks with his lips. 'I should have done it the very first day I desired you. I would have been happier, Estela would have been happier, and perhaps you would have been, too.'

He brought his face down, his lips seeking the woman's, but struggling to break the hold of fear and surprise that had paralyzed her, she moved away, and as he read the plea in her eyes he heard her stammer: 'I beg you, in the name of what you love most, I implore you . . . The senhora, the senhora.'

'The senhora is there and I love her more than you,' he heard himself say, but had the sensation that it was someone else who was speaking, and still trying to think; he for his part was merely that body in heat, that member, completely roused now, that he felt bounding against his belly, erect and hard and wet. 'I'm also doing this for her, although you may not be able to understand that.'

Fondling her breasts, he had found the buttons of her nightdress and was popping them out of their little buttonholes, one after the other, as with his other hand he took Sebastiana by the nape of the neck and forced her to turn her head and offer him her lips. He could feel that they were ice-cold and tightly pressed together, and noted that the servant's teeth were chattering, that she was trembling all over, and that in the space of a few seconds she had become drenched with sweat.

'Open your mouth,' he ordered her, in a tone of voice that he had very seldom used in his life when speaking to servants, or to slaves when he had had them. 'If I must force you to be docile, I shall do so.'

He felt the servant – conditioned, doubtless by a habit, a fear, or an instinct of self-preservation that had come down to her from the depths of time, along with a centuries-old tradition that his tone of voice had succeeded in reminding her of – obey him, as at the same time her face, in the blue shadow of the alcove, contorted in a grimace in which fear was mingled now with infinite repulsion. But this did not matter to him as he forced his tongue inside her mouth, met hers violently, pushed it back and forth from one side to the other, explored her gums, her palate, tried his best to introduce a little of his saliva into her mouth and then suck it back and swallow it. Meanwhile, he had gone on ripping the buttons from her nightdress and trying to remove it. But though Sebastiana's spirit and her mouth had yielded to his will, her entire body continued to resist, despite her fear, or perhaps because an even greater fear than the one that had taught her to bow to the will of any person who had power over her made her defend what he was trying to take from her. Her body was still hunched over, rigid, and the baron, who had lain down in the bed and was trying to embrace her, felt himself stopped by Sebastiana's arms, held like a shield in front of her body. He heard her say something in a pleading, muffled whisper and he was sure that she had begun to cry. But he was concentrating his entire attention now on trying to remove her nightdress, which he was having difficulty pulling down past her shoulders. He had been able to put one arm around her waist and draw her to him, forcing her to press her body against his, as with his other hand he went on tugging the nightdress off. After a struggle – he could not have said how long it lasted – during which, as he pushed and pulled, his energy and his desire grew greater and greater by the moment, he finally managed to climb on top of Sebastiana. As he forced her legs, pressed as tightly together as though they were brazed, apart with one of his, he avidly kissed her neck, her shoulders, her bosom, and, lingeringly, her breasts. He felt himself about to ejaculate against her belly – an ample, warm, soft form against which his rod was rubbing – and closed his eyes and made a great effort to hold back. He managed to, and then slid all over Sebastiana's body, caressing her, sniffing her, kissing her haunches, her groin, her belly, the hairs of her pubis, afterward discovering them in his mouth, thick and curly. With his hands, his chin, he pressed down with all his strength, hearing her sobs, until he had made her part her thighs enough for his mouth to reach her vulva. As he was kissing it, sucking gently, burying his tongue in it, sucking its juices, overcome by an intoxication that, at long last, freed him of everything that was making him sad and bitter, of those images that were eating his life away, he felt the gentle pressure of fingers on his back. He turned his head and looked, knowing what he would see: Estela standing there looking at him.

'Estela, my love, my love,' he said tenderly, feeling his saliva and Sebastiana's juices running down his lips, still kneeling on the floor beside the bed, still holding the servant's legs apart with his elbows. 'I love you, more than anything else in the world. I am doing this because I have wanted to for a long time, and out of love for you. To be closer to you, my darling.'

He felt Sebastiana's body shaking convulsively and heard her sobbing desperately, her mouth and eyes hidden in her hands, and he saw the baroness, standing motionless at his side, observing him. She did not appear to be frightened, enraged, horrified – merely mildly intrigued. She was wearing a light nightdress, beneath which he could dimly make out in the half light the faint outlines of her body, which time had not contrived to deform – a still harmonious, shapely silhouette – and her fair hair, with none of the gray visible in the dim light, caught up in a hairnet with a few stray locks peeking out. As far as he could see, her forehead was not furrowed by that single deep wrinkle that was an unmistakable sign that she was greatly annoyed, the sole manifestation of her real feelings that Estela had never succeeded in controlling. She was not frowning; her lips, however, were slightly parted, emphasizing the interest, the curiosity, the calm surprise in her eyes. But what was new, however minute a sign it might appear to be, was this turning outward, this interest in something outside herself, for since that night in Calumbi the baron had never seen any other expression in the baroness's eyes save indifference, withdrawal, a retreat of the spirit. Her paleness was more pronounced now, perhaps because of the blue half shadow, perhaps because of what she was experiencing. The baron felt all choked up with emotion and about to burst into sobs. He could just make out Estela's bare white feet on the polished wood floor, and on impulse bent down to kiss them. The baroness did not move as he knelt there at her feet, covering her insteps, her toes, her toenails, her heels with kisses, pressing his lips to them with infinite love and reverence and stammering in a voice full of ardor that he loved them, and that they had always seemed extremely beautiful to him, worthy of intense worship for having given him, all during their life together, such unrequitable pleasure. On kissing them yet again and raising his lips to her frail ankles, he felt his wife move and immediately lifted his head, in time to see that the hand that had touched him on the back before was coming toward him once again, without haste or abruptness, with that naturalness, distinction, discretion with which Estela had always moved, spoken, conducted herself. He felt it alight on his hair and remain there, its touch soft and conciliatory, a contact for which he felt the most heartfelt gratitude because there was nothing hostile or reproving about it; on the contrary, it was loving, affectionate, tolerant. His desire, which had vanished completely, again made its appearance and the baron felt his penis become hard again. He took the hand that Estela had placed on his head, raised it to his lips, kissed it, and without letting go of it, turned back toward the bed where Sebastiana was still curled up in a ball with her face hidden, and stretching out his free hand he placed it on the pubis whose pronounced blackness was such a striking contrast to the matte duskiness of her skin.

'I always wanted to share her with you, my darling,' he stammered, his voice unsteady because of the contrary emotions he was experiencing: timidity, shame, devotion, and reborn desire. 'But I never dared, because I feared I would offend you, wound your feelings. I was wrong, isn't that so? Isn't it true that you would not have been offended or wounded? That you would have accepted it, looked upon it with pleasure? Isn't it true that it would have been another way of showing you how much I love you, Estela?'

His wife continued to observe him, not in anger, no longer in surprise, but with that calm gaze that had been characteristic of her for some months now. And he saw her turn after a moment to look at Sebastiana, who was still curled up sobbing, and saw that gaze, which until that moment had been neutral, grow interested, gently complaisant. Obeying this sign that he had received from the baroness, he let go of her hand. He saw Estela take two steps toward the head of the bed, sit down on the edge of it, stretch out her arms with that inimitable grace that he so admired in all her movements, and take Sebastiana's face between her two hands, with great care and precaution, as though she were afraid of breaking her. He did not want to see any more. His desire had returned with a sort of mad fury and the baron bent down toward Sebastiana's vulva once again, pressing his face between her legs so as to separate them, forcing her to stretch out, so as to be able to kiss it again, breathe it in, sip it. He remained in that position for a long time, his eyes closed, intoxicated, taking his pleasure, and when he felt that he could no longer contain his excitement he straightened up, got onto the bed, and crawled on top of Sebastiana. Separating her legs with his, fumbling about for her privates with an uncertain hand, he managed to penetrate her in a moment that added pain and rending to his pleasure. He heard her moan, and managed to see, in the tumultuous instant in which life seemed to explode between his legs, that the baroness was still holding Sebastiana's face between her two hands, gazing at her with pity and tenderness as she blew gently on her forehead to free a few little hairs stuck to her skin.

Hours later, when all that was over, the baron opened his eyes as though something or someone had awakened him. The dawn light was coming into the room, and he could hear birdsong and the murmur of the sea. He sat up in Sebastiana's bed, where he had slept by himself; he stood up, covering himself with the sheet that he picked up off the floor, and took a few steps toward the baroness's room. She and Sebastiana were sleeping, their bodies not touching, in the wide bed, and the baron stood there for a moment looking at them through the transparent mosquito netting, filled with an indefinable emotion. He felt tenderness, melancholy, gratitude, and a vague anxiety. He was walking toward the door to the hallway, where he had stripped off his clothes the evening before, when, on passing by the balcony, he was stopped short by the sight of the bay set aflame by the rising sun. It was something he had seen countless times and yet never grew tired of: Salvador at the hour when the sun is rising or setting. He went out onto the balcony and stood contemplating the majestic spectacle: the avid green of the island of Itaparica, the grace and the whiteness of the sailboats setting out to sea, the bright blue of the sky and the gray-green of the water, and closer by, at his feet, the broken, bright-red horizon of the roof tiles of houses in which he could picture in his mind the people waking up, the beginning of their day's routine. With bittersweet nostalgia he amused himself trying to identify, by the roofs of the Desterro and Nazareth districts, the family mansions of his former political cronies, those friends he didn't see any more these days: that of the Baron de Cotegipe, the Baron de Macaúba, the Viscount de São Lourenço, the Baron de São Francisco, the Marquis de Barbacena, the Baron de Maragogipe, the Count de Sergimirim, the Viscount de Oliveira. His sweeping gaze took in different points of the city: the rooftops of the seminary, and As Ladeiras, covered with greenery, the old Jesuit school, the hydraulic elevator, the customhouse, and he stood there for a time admiring the sun's bright reflections on the golden stones of the Church of Nossa Senhora da Conceição de Praia which had been brought, already dressed and carved, from Portugal by sailors grateful to the Virgin, and though he could not see it, he sensed what a multicolored anthill the fish market at the beach would be at this hour of the morning. But suddenly something attracted his attention and he stood there looking very intently, straining his eyes, leaning out over the balcony railing. After a moment, he hurried inside to the chest of drawers where he knew Estela kept the little pair of tortoiseshell opera glasses that she used at the theater.

He went back out onto the balcony and looked, with a growing feeling of puzzlement and uneasiness. Yes, the boats were there, midway between the island of Itaparica and the round Fort of São Marcelo, and, indeed, the people in the boats were not fishing but tossing flowers into the sea, scattering petals, blossoms, bouquets on the water, crossing themselves, and though he could not hear them – his heart was pounding – he was certain that those people were also praying and perhaps singing.

The Lion of Natuba hears that it is the first of October, the Little Blessed One's birthday, that the soldiers are attacking Canudos from three sides trying to breach the barricades on Madre Igreja, the one on São Pedro, and the one at the Temple of the Blessed Jesus, but it is the other thing that keeps ringing in his great shaggy head: that Pajeú's head, without eyes or a tongue or ears, has been for some hours balanced on the end of a stake planted in the dogs' trenches, out by Fazenda Velha. They've killed Pajeú. They've doubtless also killed all those who stole into the atheists' camp with him to help the Vilanovas and the strangers get out of Canudos, and they've doubtless also tortured and decapitated these latter. How much longer will it be before the same thing happens to him, to the Mother of Men, and to all the women of the Sacred Choir who have knelt to pray for the martyred Pajeú?

The shooting and the shouting outside deafen the Lion of Natuba as Abbot João pushes open the little door of the Sanctuary.

'Come out! Come out! Get out of there!' the Street Commander roars, gesturing with both hands for them to hurry. 'To the Temple of the Blessed Jesus! Run!'

He turns around and disappears in the cloud of dust that has entered the Sanctuary with him. The Lion of Natuba hasn't time to become frightened, to think, to imagine. Abbot João's words bring the women disciples to their feet, and some of them screaming, others crossing themselves, they rush to the door, pushing him, shoving him aside, pinning him against the wall. Where are his glove-sandals, those little rawhide soles without which he can hardly hunch along for any distance at all without injuring his palms? He feels all about in the darkened room without finding them, and aware that all the women have left, that even Mother Maria Quadrado has left, he trots hurriedly to the door. He doggedly focuses all his energy, his lively intelligence on the task of reaching the Temple of the Blessed Jesus as Abbot João has ordered, and as he lurches along through the maze of defenses surrounding the Sanctuary, bumping into things, getting all scratched and bruised, he notes that the men of the Catholic Guard are no longer there, not the ones who are still alive at any rate, because here and there, lying on top of, between, under the bags and boxes of sand are human beings whose feet, arms, heads his hands and feet keep tripping over. When he emerges from the labyrinth of barricades onto the esplanade and is about to venture across it, the instinct of self-preservation, which is more acute in him than in almost anyone else, which has taught him since he was a child to sense danger before anyone else, better than anyone else, and also to know instantly which danger to confront when faced with several at once, makes him stop short and crouch down amid a pile of barrels riddled with bullet holes through which the sand is pouring. He is never going to reach the Temple under construction: he will be swept off his feet, trampled on, crushed by the crowd frantically bolting in that direction, and – the huge, bright, piercing eyes of the scribe see at one glance – even if he manages to reach the door of the Temple he will never be able to make his way through that swarm of bodies shoving and pushing to get past the bottleneck that the door has become: the entrance to the only solid refuge, with stone walls, still standing in Belo Monte. Better to remain here, to await death here, than to go seek it in that crush that would be the end of his frail bones, that crush that is the thing he has feared most ever since he has been involved, willy-nilly, in the gregarious, collective, processional, ceremonial life of Canudos. He is thinking: 'I don't blame you for having abandoned me, Mother of Men. You have the right to fight for your life, to try to hold out for one day more, one hour more.' But there is a great ache in his heart: this moment would not be so hard, so bitter, if she, or any of the women of the Sacred Choir, were here.

Sitting hunched over amid barrels and sacks, peeking out first in one direction and then in another, he little by little gathers some idea of what is happening on the esplanade bounded by the churches and the Sanctuary. The barricade that was erected behind the cemetery barely two days ago, the one that protected the Church of Santo Antônio, has been taken and the dogs have entered, are entering the dwellings in Santa Inês, which is right next to the church. It is from Santa Inês that all the people who are trying to take refuge in the Temple have come: old men, old women, mothers with suckling babes in their arms, on their shoulders, cradled on their bosoms. But there are many people in the city who are still fighting. Opposite him, there are still continuous bursts of gunfire coming from the towers and scaffoldings of the Temple of the Blessed Jesus, and the Lion of Natuba can make out the sparks as the *jagunços* ignite the black-powder charges of their blunderbusses, can see the impacts of the balls that chip the stones, the roof tiles, the beams of everything around him. At the same time that he came to warn the disciples to run for their lives, Abbot João no doubt also came to take the men of the Catholic Guard protecting the Sanctuary off with him, and now all of them are doubtless fighting in Santa Inês, or erecting another barricade, tightening a little more that circle of which the Counselor so often – 'and so rightly' – used to speak. Where are the soldiers, from which direction will he see the soldiers coming? What hour of the day or evening is it? The clouds of dirt and smoke, thicker and thicker, irritate his throat and his eyes, make him cough, make it hard to breathe.

'And the Counselor? What about the Counselor?' he hears a voice say, almost in his ear. 'Is it true that he's gone to heaven, that the angels bore him away with them?'

The deeply wrinkled face of the old woman lying on the ground has only one tooth in its mouth and eyelids glued shut with a gummy discharge. She does not appear to be injured, simply utterly exhausted.

'Yes, he's gone to heaven,' the Lion of Natuba says, nodding his head, with the clear perception that this is the very best thing he can do for her at this moment. 'The angels bore him away.'

'Will they come to take my soul with them, too, Lion?' the old woman whispers.

The Lion nods again, several times. The little old woman smiles at him and then lies there immobile, her mouth gaping open. The shooting and the screaming coming from the direction of the fallen Church of Santo Antônio suddenly grow louder and the Lion of Natuba has the feeling that a hail of shots grazes his head and that many bullets embed themselves in the sandbags and barrels of the parapet behind which he has taken cover. He continues to lie there stretched out flat on the ground, his eyes closed, waiting.

When the din dies down a bit, he raises his head and spies the pile of rubble left when the bell tower of Santo Antônio collapsed two nights before. The soldiers are here. His chest burns: they are here, they are here, moving about among the stones, shooting at the Temple of the Blessed Jesus, riddling with bullets the multitude that is struggling in the doorway and that at this moment, after a few seconds' hesitation, on seeing them appear and finding itself being shot at, comes rushing out at them, hands outstretched, faces congested with wrath, indignation, the desire for vengeance. In seconds, the esplanade turns into a battlefield, with hand-to-hand fighting everywhere, and in the cloud of dust swirling all round the Lion of Natuba he sees pairs and groups grappling with each other, rolling over and over on the ground, he sees sabers, bayonets, knives, machetes, he hears bellows, insults, cries of 'Long live the Republic,' 'Down with the Republic,' 'Long live the Counselor, the Blessed Jesus, Marshal Floriano.' In the crowd, in addition to the oldsters and the women, there are now *jagunços*, men of the Catholic Guard who continue to pour onto the esplanade from one side. He thinks he recognizes Abbot João and, farther in the distance, the bronze-skinned figure of Big João, or perhaps Pedrão, advancing with a huge pistol in one hand and a machete in the other. The soldiers are also on the roof of the church that has caved in. They are there where the *jagunços* were, raking the esplanade with gunfire from the walls with their bell tower fallen in; he sees kepis, uniforms, leather cartridge belts up there. And he finally realizes what it is that one of them – suspended in empty air almost, up on the sheared-off roof above the façade of Santo Antônio – is doing. He is putting up a flag. They have raised the flag of the Republic over Belo Monte.

He is imagining what the Counselor would have felt, said, if he had seen that flag fluttering up there, already full of bullet holes from the round after round of shots that the *jagunços* immediately fire at it from the rooftops, towers, and scaffoldings of the Temple of the Blessed Jesus, when he spies the soldier who is aiming his rifle at him, who is shooting at him.

He does not crouch down, he does not run, he does not move, and the thought crosses his mind that he is one of those little birds that a snake hypnotizes in a tree before devouring it. The soldier is aiming at him and the Lion of Natuba knows by the jerk of the man's shoulder from the recoil of his rifle that he has fired the shot. Despite the blowing dust, the smoke, he sees the man's beady little eyes as he aims at him again, the gleam in them at the thought that he has him at his mercy, his savage joy at knowing that this time he will hit him. But someone roughly jerks him away from where he is and forces him to leap along, to run, his arm almost torn from its socket by the iron grip of the hand that is holding him up. It is Big João, naked to the waist, who shouts to him, pointing to Campo Grande: 'That way, that way, to Menino Jesus, Santo Elói, São Pedro. Those barricades are still standing. Clear out, go there.'

He lets go and disappears into the maze around the churches and the Sanctuary. Without the hand that was holding him up, the Lion of Natuba falls to the ground in a heap. But he lies there for only a few brief moments, getting back into place those bones that seem to have been dislocated in the mad dash. It is as though the yank given him by the leader of the Catholic Guard had started up a secret motor inside him, for the Lion of Natuba begins trotting along again amid the filth and debris of what was once Campo Grande, the only passage between dwellings wide enough and straight enough to merit the name of street and now, like the others, nothing but an open space strewn with shell holes, rubble, and corpses. He sees nothing of what he is leaving behind, what he is dodging around, hugging the ground, not feeling the cuts and bruises from the shards of glass and the stones, for he is entirely absorbed in the task of getting to where he has been told to go, the little alleyways of Menino Jesus, Santo Elói, and São Pedro Mártir, that slender snake that zigzags up to Madre Igreja. He will be safe there, he will stay alive, he will endure. But on turning the third corner of Campo Grande, along what was once Menino Jesus and is now a crowded tunnel, he hears bursts of rifle fire and sees reddish-yellow flames and gray spirals rising in the sky. He stops and squats down next to an overturned cart and a picket fence that is all that is left of a dwelling. He hesitates. Does it make sense to go on toward those flames, those bullets?

Isn't it better to go back the way he came? Up ahead, where Menino Jesus leads into Madre Igreja, he can make out silhouettes, knots of people walking back and forth slowly, unhurriedly. So that must be where the barricade is. It's best to make it up there, best to die where there are other people around.

But he is not as completely alone as he thinks he is, for as he goes up the steep incline of Menino Jesus, in little leaps, his name comes up out of the ground, shouted, cried out, to right and left: 'Lion! Lion! Come here! Take cover, Lion! Hide, Lion!' Where, where? He can see no one and goes on toward the top, climbing over piles of dirt, ruins, debris, and dead bodies, some of them with their guts spilling out or gobs of flesh torn away by the shrapnel, left lying there for many hours, perhaps days now, to judge by the terrible stench all round him, which, together with the smoke blowing into his face, suffocates him and makes his eyes water. And then, all of a sudden, the soldiers are there. Six of them, three with torches that they keep dipping into a can, no doubt full of kerosene, which another is carrying, for after dipping them into it they light them and hurl them at the dwellings, as the others fire point-blank at these same houses. He is less than ten paces away from them, rooted to the spot where he has first caught sight of them, looking at them in a daze, half blinded, when shooting breaks out all around him. He falls flat on the ground, though he does not close those great eyes of his, which watch in fascination as the soldiers, hit by the hail of bullets, collapse, writhe in agony, roar with pain, drop their rifles. Where, where have the shots come from? One of the atheists rolls toward him, clutching his face. He sees him go suddenly limp and motionless, with his tongue hanging out of his mouth.

Where have the shots come from, where are the *jagunços*? He remains on the alert, watching the fallen dogs intently, his eyes leaping from one to the other, expecting any one of the corpses to stand up and come finish him off.

But what he sees is something crawling swiftly out of a house and wriggling along the ground like a worm, and by the time he thinks to himself: 'A "youngster"!' there is not just one lad but three, the other two having come wriggling along the ground, too. The three of them paw and tug at the dead soldiers. They are not stripping them, as the Lion of Natuba thinks at first; they are removing their bullet pouches and their canteens. And one of the 'youngsters' lingers long enough to plunge a knife as long as his arm into the soldier closest to the Lion – one he had thought was dead, though evidently there was still a little bit of life in him – struggling with all his might to lift the heavy weapon.

'Lion, Lion!' It is another 'youngster,' signaling to him to follow him. The Lion of Natuba sees him disappear through a door standing ajar in one of the dwellings, as the other two make off in opposite directions, trailing their booty along after them. Only then does his little body, frozen in panic, finally obey him, and he is able to drag himself over to the door. Energetic hands just inside the doorway reach out for him. He feels himself lifted off his feet, passed to other hands, set down again, and hears a woman's voice say: 'Pass him the canteen.' They place it in his bleeding hands, and he raises it to his lips. He takes a long swallow, closing his eyes, deeply grateful, moved by the miracle of this liquid that he can feel extinguishing what seem like red-hot coals inside him.

As he answers questions from the six or seven armed persons who are in the open pit that has been dug inside the house – faces covered with soot, sweaty, some of them bandaged, unrecognizable – and tells them, panting for breath, what he has been able to see on the church square and on his way up here, he realizes that the pit opens downward onto a tunnel. A 'youngster' suddenly pops up between his legs, saying: 'More dogs setting fires, Salustiano.' Those who were listening to him go into action immediately, pushing the Lion aside, and at that moment he realizes that two of them are women. They, too, have rifles; they, too, aim them, with one eye closed, toward the street. Through the cracks between the stakes of the wall, like a recurrent image, the Lion of Natuba sees once again the silhouettes of soldiers in profile coming past with lighted torches that they are hurling inside the houses. 'Shoot!' a *jagunço* shouts, and the room fills with gunsmoke. The Lion hears the deafening report and hears other shots from close by. When the smoke clears away a little, two 'youngsters' leap out of the pit and crawl out into the street to gather up ammunition pouches and canteens.

'We let them get good and close before we shoot. That way they don't get away,' one of the *jagunços* says as he swabs out his rifle.

'They've set fire to your house, Salustiano,' a woman says.

'And Abbot João's,' the same man adds.

These are the houses opposite; they have caught fire together, and beneath the crackling of the flames the sound of people running back and forth, voices, shouts reach them, along with thick clouds of smoke that make them scarcely able to breathe.

'They're trying to fry us to death, Lion,' another of the *jagunços* in the pit says. 'All the Freemasons come into the city with torches.'

The smoke is so thick that the Lion of Natuba begins to cough, as at the same time that active, creative, efficient mind of his remembers something that the Counselor once said, which he wrote down and which, like everything else in the Sanctuary notebooks, is doubtless being reduced to ashes at this moment: 'There will be three fires. I shall extinguish the first three and the fourth I shall offer to the Blessed Jesus.' He says in a loud voice, gasping for breath: 'Is this the fourth fire, is this the last fire?' Someone asks timidly: 'What about the Counselor, Lion?' He has been waiting for that; ever since he entered this house he has known that someone would dare to ask him this question. He sees, amid the tongues of smoke, seven, eight solemn, hopeful faces.

'He went up . . .' The Lion of Natuba coughs. 'The angels bore him away.'

Another fit of coughing makes him close his eyes and double over. In the desperation that overcomes a person when he lacks for air, feeling his lungs expand, gasp, fail to receive what they need so badly, he thinks that this is really the end, that no doubt he will not go to heaven since even at this moment he is unable to believe that there is such a thing as heaven, and he hears, as if in a dream, the *jagunços* coughing, arguing, and finally deciding that they can't stay here because the fire is going to spread to this house. 'We're leaving, Lion,' he hears, and 'Keep your head down, Lion,' and unable to open his eyes, he holds out his hands and feels them grab hold of him, pull him, drag him along. How long does this blind journey last: gasping for air, bumping into walls, beams, people blocking his path, bouncing him back and forth and on through the narrow, curving tunnel through the dirt, with hands pulling him up inside a dwelling through a hole only to shove him back underground and drag him along again? Perhaps minutes, perhaps hours, but all the way along, his intelligence never ceases for a second to go over a thousand things once more, to call up a thousand images, concentrating, ordering his little body to hold out, to bear up at least to the end of the tunnel, and being amazed when his body obeys and does not fall to pieces as it seems to be about to do from one moment to the next.

Suddenly the hand that was holding him lets go and he falls down and down. His head is going to be smashed to bits, his heart is going to burst, the blood in his veins is going to come spilling out, his bruised little body is going to fly all to pieces. But none of that happens and little by little he calms down, quiets down, as he feels a less contaminated air bring him gradually back to life. He hears voices, shots, a vast hubbub. He rubs his eyes, wipes the dirt from his eyelids, and sees that he is in a house, not in the shaft of a tunnel but on the surface, surrounded by *jagunços*, by women sitting on the floor with children in their laps, and he recognizes the man who makes skyrockets and set pieces: Antônio the Pyrotechnist.

'Antônio, Antônio, what's happening in Canudos?' the Lion of Natuba says. But not a sound comes out of his mouth. There are no flames here, only a cloud of dust that makes everything a blur. The *jagunços* are not talking among themselves, they are swabbing out their rifles, reloading their shotguns, and taking turns watching outside. Why isn't he able to speak, why won't his voice come out?

He makes his way over to the Pyrotechnist on his elbows and

knees and clutches his legs. Antônio squats down beside him as he primes his gun. 'We've stopped them here. But they've gotten through at Madre Igreja, the cemetery, and Santa Inês. They're everywhere. Abbot João wants to erect a barrier at Menino Jesus and another at Santo Elói so they don't attack us from the rear,' he explains in a soft, completely untroubled voice.

The Lion of Natuba can readily picture in his mind this one last circle that Belo Monte has become, bounded by the little winding alleyways of São Pedro Mártir, Santo Elói, and Menino Jesus: not a tenth of what it once was.

'Do you mean to say they've taken the Temple of the Blessed Jesus?' he says, and this time his voice comes out.

'They brought it down while you were asleep,' the Pyrotechnist answers in the same calm voice, as though he were speaking of the weather. 'The tower collapsed and the roof caved in. The roar must have been heard as far as Trabubu, as Bendengó. But it didn't wake you up, Lion.'

'Is it true that the Counselor went up to heaven?' a woman interrupts him, neither her mouth nor her eyes moving as she speaks.

The Lion of Natuba does not answer: he is hearing, seeing the mountain of stones collapsing, the men with blue armbands and headcloths falling like a solid rain upon the multitude of sick, wounded, elderly, mothers in childbirth, newborn babies; he is seeing the women of the Sacred Choir crushed to death, Maria Quadrado reduced to a heap of flesh and broken bones.

'The Mother of Men has been looking for you everywhere, Lion,' someone says, as though reading his thoughts.

It is an emaciated 'youngster,' a mere string of bones with skin stretched tight over them, wearing a pair of trousers in rags, who has just come in the door. The *jagunços* unload the canteens and ammunition pouches he has brought in on his back.

The Lion of Natuba grabs him by one of his thin arms. 'Maria Quadrado? You've seen her?'

'She's in Santo Elói, at the barricade,' the 'youngster' answers. 'She's been asking everyone about you.'

'Take me to where she is,' the Lion of Natuba says in an anxious, pleading voice.

'The Little Blessed One went out to the dogs with a flag,' the 'youngster' says to the Pyrotechnist, suddenly remembering.

'Take me to where Maria Quadrado is, I beg you,' the Lion of Natuba cries, clinging to him and leaping up and down. Not knowing what to do, the lad looks toward the Pyrotechnist.

'Take him with you,' the latter says. 'Tell Abbot João that it's quiet here now. And come back as quickly as you can, because I need you.' He has been handing out canteens to people and hands the Lion the one he is keeping for himself. 'Have a swallow before you go.'

The Lion of Natuba drinks from it and murmurs: 'Praised be Blessed Jesus the Counselor.' He follows the boy out the door of the shack. Outside, he sees fires everywhere and men and women trying to put them out with bucketfuls of dirt. São Pedro Mártir has less rubble in it and the houses along it are full of people. Some of them call out to him and motion to him and several times they ask him if he saw the angels, if he was there when the Counselor went up to heaven. He does not answer, he does not stop. He has great difficulty making his way along, he hurts all over and can hardly bear to touch his hands to the ground. He shouts to the 'youngster' not to go so fast, that he can't keep up with him, and all at once – without crying out, without a word – the boy falls to the ground. The Lion of Natuba drags himself over to him but does not touch him, for where his eyes were there is now only blood, with something white in the middle of it, a bone perhaps, some other substance perhaps. Without trying to find out where the shot has come from, he begins to trot along more determinedly, thinking: 'Mother Maria Quadrado, I want to see you, I want to die with you.' As he goes on, he encounters more and more smoke and flames and then all at once he is certain that he will not be able to go any farther: São Pedro Mártir ends in a wall of crackling flames that completely blocks the street. He stops, panting for breath, feeling the heat of the fire in his face.

'Lion, Lion.'

He turns round. He sees the shadow of a woman, a ghost with protruding bones and wrinkled skin, whose gaze is as sad as her voice. 'You throw him into the fire, Lion,' she begs him. 'I can't, but you can. So they don't devour him, the way they're going to devour me.' The Lion of Natuba follows the dying woman's gaze, and sees, almost at her side, a corpse that is bright red in the light of the fire, and a feast going on: many rats, dozens perhaps, running back and forth over the face and belly of someone no longer identifiable as either man or woman, young or old. 'They're coming out from everywhere because of the fires, or because the Devil has won the war now,' the woman says, speaking so slowly that each word seems to be her last. 'Don't let them eat him. He's still an angel. Throw him on the fire, Little Lion. In the name of the Blessed Jesus.' The Lion of Natuba observes the feast: they have consumed the face and are hard at work on the belly, the thighs.

'Yes, Mother,' he says, approaching on his four paws. Rising up on his hind limbs, he reaches over and gathers up the little wrapped bundle that the woman is holding in her lap and clasps it to his chest. And standing on his hind paws, his back hunched, he pants eagerly: 'I'm taking him, I'm going with him. This fire has been awaiting me for twenty years now, Mother.'

As he walks toward the flames, the woman hears him chanting with his last remaining strength a prayer that she has never heard, in which there is repeated several times the name of a saint she does not recognize either: Almudia.

'A truce?' Antônio Vilanova said.

'That's what that means,' the Pyrotechnist answered. 'That's what a white cloth on a stick means. I didn't see him when he left, but many other people did. I saw it when he came back. He was still carrying that piece of white cloth.'

'And why did the Little Blessed One do that?' Honório Vilanova asked.

'He took pity on innocent people when he saw so many being

burned to death,' the Pyrotechnist answered. 'Children, old people, pregnant women. He went to ask the atheists to let them leave Belo Monte. He didn't consult Abbot João or Pedrão or Big João, who were all at Santo Elói and at São Pedro Mártir. He made his flag and set out by way of Madre Igreja. The atheists let him through. We thought they'd killed him and were going to give him back to us the way they did Pajeú: with no eyes, tongue, or ears. But he came back, carrying his white cloth. And we had already barricaded Santo Elói and Menino Jesus and Madre Igreja. And put out lots of fires. He came back in two or three hours and during that time the atheists didn't attack. That's what a truce is. Father Joaquim explained it.'

The Dwarf curled up next to Jurema. He was shivering from the cold. They were in a cave, where in the past goatherds used to spend the night, not far from the place where, before it burned down, the tiny village of Caçabu had stood, at a turnoff in the trail between Mirandela and Quijingue. They had been hiding out there for twelve days now. They made quick trips outside to bring back grass, roots, anything that could be chewed on, and water from a nearby spring. As the whole region round about was swarming with troops that were withdrawing, in small sections or in large battalions, toward Queimadas, they had decided to remain in hiding there for a while. The temperature went down very low at night, and since the Vilanovas did not allow a fire to be lit for fear that the light would attract a patrol, the Dwarf was dying of cold. Of the three of them, he was the one most sensitive to the cold because he was the smallest and the one who had grown thinnest. The nearsighted man and Jurema had him sleep between them, so as to warm him with their bodies. But, even so, the Dwarf dreaded seeing night fall, for, despite the warmth of his friends' bodies, his teeth chattered and he felt frozen to the bone. He was sitting between them, listening to the Pyrotechnist, and every other minute his pudgy little hands motioned to Jurema and the nearsighted man to move even closer to him.

'What happened to Father Joaquim?' he heard the nearsighted man ask. 'Was he, too . . .?'

'He wasn't burned to death and they didn't slit his throat,' Antônio the Pyrotechnist answered immediately in a reassuring tone of voice, as though he were happy to be able at last to tell them a piece of good news. 'He died of a bullet wound on the barricade at Santo Elói. He was standing right near me. He also helped people die pious deaths.' Serafim the carpenter remarked that perhaps the Father did not look favorably upon his dying on the barricade like that. He wasn't a *jagunço* but a priest, right? The Father might not look with favor on a man of the cloth dying with a rifle in his hand.

'The Counselor no doubt explained to Him why Father Joaquim had a rifle in his hand,' one of the Sardelinha sisters said. 'And the Father probably forgave him.'

'There's no doubt of that,' Antônio the Pyrotechnist said. 'The Father knows what He is about.'

Even though there was no fire and the mouth of the cave was hidden beneath bushes and cacti uprooted whole from the ground round about, the clear light of the night – the Dwarf imagined a yellow moon and myriads of bright stars looking down on the *sertão* in shocked surprise – filtered in to where they were sitting and he could see Antônio the Pyrotechnist's face in profile, his pug nose, his sharply chiseled forehead and chin. He was a *jagunço* the Dwarf remembered very well, because he had seen him preparing, back there in Canudos, those fireworks displays that lit up the sky with sparkling arabesques on the nights when there were processions. He remembered his hands covered with powder burns, the scars on his arms, and how, once the war began, he had devoted all his time and effort to making up the dynamite sticks that the *jagunços* hurled over the barricades at the soldiers. The Dwarf had been the first to recognize him when he had appeared at the entrance to the cave that afternoon, and had called out that it was the Pyrotechnist, so the Vilanova brothers, pistols in hand, wouldn't shoot.

'And why did the Little Blessed One come back?' Antônio Vilanova asked after a while. He was almost the only one who kept asking questions, the one who had quizzed Antônio the

Pyrotechnist all afternoon and evening, once they, too, had recognized him and embraced him. 'Had he taken leave of his senses?'

'I'm certain of that,' Antônio the Pyrotechnist said.

The Dwarf tried to picture the scene in his mind, the tiny pale-faced figure with the burning eyes returning to the little redoubt with his white flag, making his way amid the dead, the rubble, the wounded, the combatants, the burned-out dwellings, the rats which, according to the Pyrotechnist, had suddenly appeared everywhere to feast voraciously on the dead bodies.

'They have agreed,' the Little Blessed One said. 'You can surrender now.'

'We were to come out one by one, with no weapons, with our hands on our heads,' the Pyrotechnist explained, in the tone of voice of someone recounting the wildest story or of a drunk babbling nonsense. 'We would be considered prisoners and would not be killed.'

The Dwarf heard him heave a sigh. He heard one of the Vilanova brothers sigh too, and thought he heard one of the Sardelinha sisters weeping. It was odd: the Vilanova brothers' wives, the two of whom the Dwarf often confused, never burst into tears at the same time. One of them would begin to cry and then the other. But they had not shed a single tear until Antônio the Pyrotechnist had started answering Antônio Vilanova's questions that afternoon; all during the flight from Belo Monte and the days that they had been hiding out here, he had never seen them cry. He was trembling so badly that Jurema put her arm around his shoulders and rubbed him briskly up and down. Was he shivering from the cold here at Caçabu, or because he had fallen ill from hunger, or was it what the Pyrotechnist was recounting that was making him tremble like that?

'Little Blessed One, Little Blessed One, do you realize what you're saying?' Big João moaned. 'Do you realize what it is you're asking? Do you really want us to lay down our arms, to go out with our hands on our heads to surrender to the Freemasons? Is that what you want, Little Blessed One?'

'Not you,' the voice that always seemed to be praying answered. 'The innocent victims. The youngsters, the women about to give birth, the aged. May their lives be spared. You can't decide their fate for them. If you don't allow them to escape with their lives, it's as though you killed them. The fault will be yours, there will be innocent blood on your hands, Big João. It's a sin against heaven to let innocent people die. They aren't able to defend themselves, Big João.'

'He said that the Counselor spoke through his mouth,' Antônio the Pyrotechnist added. 'That he had inspired him, that he had ordered him to save them.'

'And Abbot João?' Antônio Vilanova asked.

'He wasn't there,' the Pyrotechnist explained. 'The Little Blessed One came back to Belo Monte by way of the barricade at Madre Igreja. And Abbot João was at Santo Elói. They told him the Little Blessed One had come back, but he couldn't get there right away. He was busy reinforcing that barricade, the weakest one. By the time he arrived, they had already begun to go off with the Little Blessed One. Women, children, the aged, the sick dragging themselves along.'

'And nobody stopped them?' Antônio Vilanova asked.

'Nobody dared,' the Pyrotechnist said. 'He was the Little Blessed One, the Little Blessed One. Not just anyone like you or me, but one who had been with the Counselor from the very beginning. He was the Little Blessed One. Would you have told him that he'd taken leave of his senses, that he didn't know what he was doing? Big João didn't dare to, nor I nor anyone else.'

'But Abbot João dared to,' Antônio Vilanova murmured.

'There's no doubt of that,' Antônio the Pyrotechnist said. 'Abbot João dared to.'

The Dwarf felt frozen to the bone and his forehead was burning hot. He could easily picture the scene: the tall, supple, sturdy figure of the former *cangaceiro* appearing there, his knife and machete tucked in his belt, his rifle slung over his shoulder, the bandoleers around his neck, so tired he was past feeling tired. There he was, seeing the unbelievable file of pregnant women, children, old people, invalids, all those people come back to life, walking toward the soldiers with their hands on their heads. He wasn't imagining it: he could see it, with the clearness and the color of one of the performances of the Gypsy's Circus, the ones back in the good old days, when it was a big, prosperous circus. He was seeing Abbot João: his stupefaction, his bewilderment, his anger.

'Stop! Stop!' he shouted, beside himself, looking all about, motioning to those who were surrendering, trying to make them come back. 'Have you gone out of your minds? Stop! Stop!'

'We explained to him,' the Pyrotechnist said. 'Big João, who was crying and felt responsible, explained to him. Pedrão came too, and Father Joaquim, and others. It took only a few words from them for Abbot João to understand exactly what was going on.'

'It's not that they're going to kill them,' he said, raising his voice, loading his rifle, trying to take aim at those who had already crossed the lines and were heading on. 'They're going to kill all of us. They're going to humiliate them, they're going to outrage their dignity like they did with Pajeú. We can't let that happen, precisely because they're innocent. We can't let the atheists slit their throats. We can't let them dishonor them!'

'He was already shooting,' Antônio the Pyrotechnist said. 'We were all shooting. Pedrão, Big João, Father Joaquim, me.' The Dwarf noted that his voice, steady until then, was beginning to quaver. 'Did we do the wrong thing? Did I do the wrong thing, Antônio Vilanova? Was it wrong of Abbot João to make us shoot?'

'You did the right thing,' Antônio Vilanova answered immediately. 'They died a merciful death. The heretics would have slit their throats, done what they did to Pajeú. I would have shot, too.'

'I don't know,' the Pyrotechnist said. 'I'm tormented by it. Does the Counselor approve? I'm going to be asking myself that question for the rest of my life, trying to decide whether, after having been with the Counselor for ten years, I'll be eternally damned for making a mistake at the last moment. Sometimes . . .'

He fell silent and the Dwarf realized that the Sardelinha sisters were crying – at the same time now – one of them with loud, indelicate sobs, the other softly, with little hiccups.

'Sometimes . . .?' Antônio Vilanova said.

'Sometimes I think that the Father, the Blessed Jesus, or Our Lady wrought the miracle of saving me from among the dead so that I may redeem myself for those shots,' Antônio the Pyrotechnist said. 'I don't know. Once again, I don't know anything. In Belo Monte everything seemed clear to me, day was day and night night. Until that moment, until we began firing on the innocent and on the Little Blessed One. Now everything's hard to decide again.'

He sighed and remained silent, listening, as the Dwarf and the others were, to the Sardelinha sisters weeping for those innocents whom the *jagunços* had sent to a merciful death.

'Because maybe the Father wanted them to go to heaven as martyrs,' the Pyrotechnist added.

'I'm sweating,' the Dwarf thought. Or was he bleeding? 'I'm dying,' he thought. Drops were running down his forehead, sliding down into his eyebrows and eyelashes, blinding his eyes. But even though he was sweating, the cold was freezing his insides. Every so often Jurema wiped his face.

'And what happened then?' he heard the nearsighted journalist ask. 'After Abbot João, after you and others . . .'

He fell silent and the Sardelinha sisters, who had stopped crying in their surprise at this intrusion, began weeping again.

'There wasn't any "after,"' Antônio the Pyrotechnist said. 'The atheists thought we were shooting at them. They were enraged at seeing us take this prey that they thought was theirs away from them.' He fell silent, then his voice echoed through the cave: '"Traitors," they shouted. We'd broken the truce and were going to pay for it. They came at us from all directions. Thousands of atheists. That was a piece of luck.'

'A piece of luck?' Antônio Vilanova said.

The Dwarf had understood. A piece of luck to have that torrent of uniforms advancing with rifles and torches to shoot at again, a piece of luck not to have to go on killing innocents to save them from dishonor. He understood, and in the midst of his fever and chills, he saw it. He saw how the exhausted *jagunços*, who had been sending people to merciful deaths, rubbed their blistered, burned hands in glee, happy to have before them once again a clear, definite, flagrant, unquestionable enemy. He could see that fury advancing, killing everything not yet killed, burning everything left to burn.

'But I'm sure he didn't weep even at that moment,' one of the Sardelinhas said, and the Dwarf could not tell whether it was Honório's wife or Antônio's. 'I can imagine Big João, Father Joaquim weeping because they had to do that to those innocents. But him? Did he weep?'

'I'm certain of that,' Antônio the Pyrotechnist said softly. 'Even though I didn't see him.'

'I never once saw Abbot João weep,' the same Sardelinha sister said.

'You never liked him,' Antônio Vilanova muttered bitterly, and the Dwarf knew then which of the two sisters was speaking: Antônia.

'Never,' she admitted, making no effort to hide her enmity. 'And even less now. Now that I know that he ended up not as Abbot João but as Satan João. The one who killed to be killing, robbed to be robbing, and took pleasure in making people suffer.'

There was a deep silence and the Dwarf could feel that the nearsighted man was frightened. He waited, every nerve tense.

'I don't ever want to hear you say that again,' Antônio Vilanova said slowly. 'You've been my wife for years, forever. We've gone through everything together. But if I ever hear you say that again, it's all over between us. And it will be the end of you, too.'

Trembling, sweating, counting the seconds, the Dwarf waited.

'I swear by the Blessed Jesus that I will never say that again,' Antônia Sardelinha stammered.

'I saw Abbot João weep once,' the Dwarf said then. His teeth were chattering and his words came out in spurts, well chewed. He spoke with his face pressed against Jurema's bosom. 'Don't you remember, didn't I tell you? When he heard the Terrible and Exemplary Story of Robert the Devil.'

'He was the son of a king and his mother's hair was already white when he was born,' Abbot João remembered. 'He was born through a miracle, if the work of the Devil can also be called a miracle. She had made a pact so as to give birth to Robert. Isn't that how it begins?'

'No,' the Dwarf said, with a certainty that came from having told this story all his life, one he had known for so long he couldn't remember where or when he had learned it, one he had taken about from village to village, told hundreds, thousands of times, making it longer, making it shorter, making it sadder or happier or more dramatic to fit the mood of his ever-changing audience. Not even Abbot João could tell him how it really began. His mother was old and barren and had to make a pact so as to give birth to Robert, yes. But he wasn't the son of a king. He was the son of a duke.

'Of the Duke of Normandy,' Abbot João agreed. 'Go ahead – tell it the way it really was.'

'He wept?' he heard a voice say as though from the next world, that voice he knew so well, always frightened, yet at the same time curious, prying, meddlesome. 'Listening to the story of Robert the Devil?'

Yes, he had wept. At one point or another, perhaps at the moment when he was committing his worst massacres, his worst iniquities, when, possessed, impelled, overpowered by the spirit of destruction, an invisible force that he was unable to resist, Robert plunged his knife into the bellies of pregnant women or slit the throats of newborn babes ('Which means that he was from the South, not the Northeast,' the Dwarf explained) and impaled peasants and set fire to huts where families were sleeping, he had noticed that the Street Commander's eyes were gleaming, his cheeks glistening, his chin trembling, his chest heaving. Disconcerted, terrified, the Dwarf fell silent – what mistake had he made, what had he left out? – and looked anxiously at Catarina, that little figure so thin that she seemed to occupy no space at all in the redoubt on Menino Jesus, where Abbot João had taken him. Catarina motioned to him to go on.

But Abbot João didn't let him. 'Was what he did his fault?' he said, transfixed. 'Was it his fault that he committed countless cruelties? Could he do otherwise? Wasn't he paying his mother's debt? From whom should the Father have sought retribution for those wicked deeds? From him or from the duchess?' His eyes were riveted on the Dwarf, in terrible anguish. 'Answer me, answer me.'

'I don't know, I don't know,' the Dwarf said, trembling. 'It's not in the story. It's not my fault, don't do anything to me, I'm only the one who's telling the story.'

'He's not going to do anything to you,' the woman who seemed to be a wraith said softly. 'Go on with the story, go on.'

He had gone on with the story, as Catarina dried Abbot João's eyes with the hem of her skirt, squatted at his feet and clasped his legs with her hands and leaned her head against his knees so as to make him feel that he wasn't alone. He had not wept again, or moved, or interrupted him till the end, which sometimes came with the death of Robert the Saint become a hermit, and sometimes with Robert placing on his head the crown that had become rightfully his on discovering that he was the son of Richard of Normandy, one of the Twelve Peers of France. He remembered that when he had finished the story that afternoon – or that night? – Abbot João had thanked him for telling it. But when, at what moment exactly had that been? Before the soldiers came, when life was peaceful and Belo Monte seemed the ideal place to live in? Or when life became death, hunger, holocaust, fear?

'When was it, Jurema?' he asked anxiously, not knowing why it was so urgent to situate it exactly in time. Then, turning to the nearsighted man: 'Was it at the beginning or the end of the performance?'

'What's the matter with him?' he heard one of the Sardelinha sisters say.

'Fever,' Jurema answered, putting her arms around him.

'When was it?' the Dwarf asked. 'When was it?'

'He's delirious,' he heard the nearsighted man say and felt him touch his forehead, stroke his hair and his back.

He heard him sneeze, twice, three times, as he always did when something surprised him, amused him, or frightened him. He could sneeze if he wanted to now. But he had not done so the night they had escaped, that night when one sneeze would have cost him his life. He imagined him at a circus performance in a village somewhere, sneezing twenty, fifty, a hundred times, as the Bearded Lady farted in the clown number, in every imaginable register and cadence, high, low, long, short, and it made him feel like laughing too, like the audience attending the performance. But he didn't have the strength.

'He's dropped off to sleep,' he heard Jurema say, cradling his head in her lap. 'He'll be all right tomorrow.'

He was not asleep. From the depths of that ambiguous reality of fire and ice, his body hunched over in the darkness of the cave, he went on listening to Antônio the Pyrotechnist's story, reproducing, seeing that end of the world that he had already anticipated, known, without any need to hear this man brought back to life from amid burning coals and corpses tell of it. And yet, despite how sick he felt, how badly he was shivering, how far away those who were speaking there beside him, in the dark of the night in the backlands of Bahia, in that world where there was no Canudos any more and no *jagunços*, where soon there would be no soldiers either, when those who had accomplished their mission left at last and the *sertão* returned to its eternal proud and miserable solitude, the Dwarf had been interested, impressed, and amazed to hear what Antônio the Pyrotechnist was relating.

'You might say that you've been restored to life,' he heard Honório say – the Vilanova who spoke so rarely that, when he did, it seemed to be his brother.

'Perhaps so,' the Pyrotechnist answered. 'But I wasn't dead. Not even wounded. I don't know. I don't know that, either. There was no blood on my body. Maybe a stone fell on my head. But I didn't hurt anywhere, either.'

'You fell into a faint,' Antônio Vilanova said. 'The way people did in Belo Monte. They thought you were dead and that saved you.'

'That saved me,' the Pyrotechnist repeated. 'But that wasn't all. Because when I came to and found myself in the midst of all those dead, I also saw that the atheists were finishing off with their bayonets those who had fallen, or shooting them if they moved. Lots of them went right by me, and not one of them bent over me to see if I was dead.'

'In other words, you spent an entire day playing dead,' Antônio Vilanova said.

'Hearing them pass by, killing off those who were still alive, knifing the prisoners to death, dynamiting the walls,' the Pyrotechnist said. 'But that wasn't the worst part. The worst part was the dogs, the rats, the black vultures. They were devouring the dead. I could hear them pawing, biting, pecking. Animals don't make mistakes. They know who's dead and who isn't. Vultures, rats don't devour people who are still alive. My fear was the dogs. That was the miracle: they, too, left me alone.'

'You were lucky,' Antônio Vilanova said. 'And what are you going to do now?'

'Go back to Mirandela,' the Pyrotechnist said. 'I was born there, I grew up there, I learned how to make skyrockets there. Maybe. I don't know. What about you?'

'We'll go far away from here,' the former storekeeper said. 'To Assaré, maybe. We came from there, we began this life there, fleeing from the plague, as we're doing now. From another plague. Maybe we'll end up where it all began. What else can we do?'

'Nothing, I'm certain of that,' Antônio the Pyrotechnist said.

Not even when they tell him to hasten to General Artur Oscar's command post if he wants to have a look at the Counselor's head before First Lieutenant Pinto Souza takes it to Bahia does Colonel Geraldo Macedo, commanding officer of the Bahia Police Volunteer Battalion, stop thinking about what has obsessed him ever since the end of the war: 'Has anyone seen him? Where is he?' But like all the brigade, regimental, and battalion commanders (officers of lesser rank are not accorded this privilege), he goes to have a look at the remains of the man who has been the death of so many people and yet, according to all witnesses, was never once seen to take up a rifle or a knife in his own hands. He doesn't see very much, however, because they have put the head in a sackful of lime inasmuch as it is very badly decomposed: just a few shocks of grayish hair. He merely puts in an appearance at General Oscar's hut for form's sake, unlike other officers, who stay on and on, congratulating each other on the end of the war and making plans for the future now that they will be going back to their home bases and their families. Colonel Macedo's eyes rest for a brief moment on the tangle of hair, then he leaves without a single comment and returns to the smoking heap of ruins and corpses.

He thinks no more about the Counselor or the exultant officers that he has left in the command post, officers whom, moreover, he has never considered to be his equals, and whose disdain for him he has reciprocated ever since he arrived on the slopes of Canudos with the battalion of Bahia police. He knows what his nickname is, what they call him behind his back: Bandit-Chaser. It doesn't bother him. He is proud of having spent thirty years of his life repeatedly cleaning out bands of *cangaceiros* from the backlands of Bahia, of having won all the gold braid he has and reached the rank of colonel – he, a humble *mestizo* born in Mulungo do Morro, a tiny village that none of these officers could even locate on the map – for having risked his neck hunting down the scum of the earth.

But it bothers his men. The Bahia police who four months ago agreed, out of personal loyalty to him, to come here to fight the Counselor – he had told them that the Governor of Bahia had asked him to take on this mission, that it was indispensable that Bahia state police should volunteer to go to Canudos so as to put an end to the perfidious talk going the rounds in the rest of the country to the effect that Bahians were soft toward, indifferent to, and even sympathetic secret allies of the *jagunços*, so as to demonstrate to the federal government and all of Brazil that Bahians were as ready as anyone else to make any and every sacrifice in the defense of the Republic – are naturally offended and hurt by the snubs and affronts that they have had to put up with ever since they joined the column. Unlike him, they are unable to contain themselves: they answer insults with insults, nicknames with nicknames, and in these four months they have been involved in countless incidents with the soldiers from other regiments. What exasperates them most is that the High Command also discriminates against them. In all the attacks, the Bahia Police Volunteer Battalion has been kept on the sidelines, in the rear guard, as though even the General Staff gave credence to the infamy that in their heart of hearts Bahians are restorationists, crypto-Conselheirists.

The stench is so overpowering that he is obliged to get out his handkerchief and cover his nose. Although many of the fires have burned out, the air is still full of soot, cinders, and ashes, and the colonel's eyes are irritated as he explores, searches about, kicks the bodies of the dead *jagunços* to separate them and have a look at their faces. The majority of them are charred or so disfigured by the flames that even if he came across him he would not be able to identify him. Moreover, even if his corpse is intact, how is he going to recognize it? After all, he has never seen him, and the descriptions he has had of him are not sufficiently detailed. What he is doing is stupid, of course. 'Of course,' he thinks. Though it is contrary to all reason, he can't help himself: it's that odd instinct that has served him so well in the past, that sudden flash of intuition that in the old days used to make him hurry his flying brigade along for two or three days on an inexplicable forced march to reach a village where, it would turn out, they surprised bandits that they had been searching for with no luck at all for weeks and months. It's the same now. Colonel Geraldo Macedo keeps poking about amid the stinking corpses, his one hand holding the handkerchief over his nose and mouth and the other chasing away the swarms of flies, kicking away the rats that climb up his legs, because, in the face of all logic, something tells him that when he comes across the face, the body, even the mere bones of Abbot João, he will know that they are his.

'Sir, sir!' It is his adjutant, Lieutenant Soares, running toward him with his face, too, covered with his handkerchief.

'Have the men found him?' Colonel Macedo says excitedly.

'Not yet, sir. General Oscar says you must get out of here because the demolition squad is about to begin work.'

'Demolition squad?' Colonel Macedo looks glumly about him. 'Is there anything left to demolish?'

'The general promised that not a single stone would be left standing,' Lieutenant Soares says. 'He's ordered the sappers to dynamite the walls that haven't fallen in yet.'

'What a waste of effort,' the colonel murmurs. His mouth is partway open beneath the handkerchief, and as always when he is deep in thought, he is licking at his gold tooth. He regretfully contemplates the vast expanse of rubble, stench, and carrion. Finally he shrugs. 'Well, we'll leave without ever knowing if he died or got away.'

Still holding his nose, he and his adjutant begin making their way back to the cantonment. Shortly thereafter, the dynamiting begins.

'Might I ask you a question, sir?' Lieutenant Soares twangs from beneath his handkerchief. Colonel Macedo nods his head. 'Why is Abbot João's corpse so important to you?'

'It's a story that goes back a long way,' the colonel growls. His voice sounds twangy, too. His dark little eyes take a quick glance all about. 'A story that I began, apparently. That's what people say, anyway. Because I killed Abbot João's father, some thirty years ago, at least. He was a *coiteiro* of Antônio Silvino's in Custódia. They say that Abbot João became a *cangaceiro* to avenge his father. And afterward, well . . .' He looks at his adjutant and suddenly feels old. 'How old are you?'

'Twenty-two, sir.'

'So you wouldn't know who Abbot João was,' Colonel Macedo growls.

'The military leader of Canudos, a heartless monster,' Lieutenant Soares says immediately.

'A heartless monster, all right,' Colonel Macedo agrees. 'The fiercest outlaw in all Bahia. The one that always got away from me. I hunted him for ten years. I very nearly got my hands on him several times, but he always slipped through my fingers. They said he'd made a pact. He was known as Satan in those days.'

'I understand now why you want to find him.' Lieutenant Soares smiles. 'To see with your own eyes that he didn't get away from you this time.'

'I don't really know why, to tell you the truth,' Colonel Macedo growls, shrugging his shoulders. 'Because it brings back the days of my youth, maybe. Chasing bandits was better than this tedium.'

There is a series of explosions and Colonel Macedo can see thousands of people on the slopes and brows of the hills, standing watching as the last walls of Canudos are blown sky high. It is not a spectacle that interests him and he does not even bother to watch; he continues on toward the cantonment of the Bahia Volunteer Battalion at the foot of A Favela, immediately behind the trenches along the Vaza-Barris.

'I don't mind telling you that there are certain things that would never enter a normal person's head, no matter how big it might be,' he says, spitting out the bad taste left in his mouth by his aborted exploration. 'First off, ordering a house count when there aren't any houses left, only ruins. And now, ordering stones and bricks dynamited. Do *you* understand why that commission under the command of Colonel Dantas Barreto was out counting the houses?'

They had spent all morning amid the stinking, smoking ruins

and determined that there were five thousand two hundred dwellings in Canudos.

'They had a terrible time. None of their figures came out right,' Lieutenant Soares scoffs. 'They calculated that there were at least five inhabitants per dwelling. In other words, some thirty thousand *jagunços*. But Colonel Dantas Barreto's commission was able to find only six hundred forty-seven corpses, no matter how hard they searched.'

'Because they only counted corpses that were intact,' Colonel Macedo growls. 'They overlooked the hunks of flesh, the scattered bones, which is what most of the people of Canudos ended up as. To every madman his own cherished mania.'

Back in the camp, a drama awaits Colonel Geraldo Macedo, one of the many that have marked the presence of the Bahia police at the siege of Canudos. The officers are trying to calm the men, ordering them to disperse and to stop talking among themselves about what has happened. They have posted guards all around the perimeter of the cantonment, fearing that the Bahia volunteers will rush out en masse to give those who have provoked them what is coming to them. By the smoldering anger in his men's eyes and the sinister expressions on their faces, Colonel Macedo realizes immediately that the incident has been an extremely grave one.

But before allowing anyone to offer an explanation, he gives his officers a dressing down: 'So then, my orders have not been obeyed! Instead of searching for the outlaw, you've let the men get into a fight! Didn't I give orders that there were to be no fights?'

But his orders have been obeyed to the letter. Patrols of Bahia police had been out scouring Canudos till the general had ordered them to withdraw so that the demolition squads could get to work. The incident had involved, in fact, one of these very patrols out searching for the corpse of Abbot João, three Bahians who had followed the barricade between the cemetery and the churches down to a depression that must at one time have been the bed of a little stream or an arm of the river and is one of the places where the prisoners who have been captured are being held, a few hundred people who are now almost exclusively women and children, since the men among them have had their throats slit by the squad led by Second Lieutenant Maranhão, who is said to have volunteered for his mission because several months ago the *jagunços* ambushed his company, leaving him with only eight men alive and unharmed out of the fifty under his command. The Bahia police came down there to ask the prisoners if they knew what had become of Abbot João, and one of the men recognized, among the group of prisoners, a woman from the village of Mirangaba who was a relative of his. On seeing him embrace a *jagunça*, Lieutenant Maranhão began hurling insults at him and saying, pointing a finger at him, that this was proof that the Bandit-Chaser's police, despite the republican uniforms they were wearing, were traitors at heart. And when the policeman tried to protest, the lieutenant, in a fit of rage, knocked him to the ground with one blow of his fist. He and his two buddies were then driven off by the gauchos in the lieutenant's squad, who kept yelling after them from a distance: '*Jagunços!*' They had returned to camp trembling with rage and stirred up their buddies, who for an hour now have been seething and champing at the bit to go avenge these insults. This was what awaited Colonel Geraldo Macedo: an incident, exactly like twenty or thirty others, that had come about for the same reason and involved almost word for word the same insults.

But this time, unlike all the others, when he has calmed his men down and at most presented a complaint to General Barbosa, the commanding officer of the first column, to which the Bahia Police Volunteer Battalion is attached, or to the Commander of the Expeditionary Forces, General Artur Oscar, if he regards the incident as an especially serious one, Geraldo Macedo feels a curious, symptomatic tingle, one of those intuitions to which he owes his life and his gold braid.

'That Maranhão isn't someone worthy of respect,' he comments, rapidly licking his gold tooth. 'Spending his nights slitting the throats of prisoners isn't really a job for a soldier but for a butcher, wouldn't you say?'

His officers remain silent, standing there looking at each other, and as he speaks and licks at his gold tooth, Colonel Macedo notes the surprise, the curiosity, the satisfaction on the faces of Captain Souza, Captain Jerônimo, Captain Tejada, and First Lieutenant Soares.

'I therefore am of the opinion that a gaucho butcher cannot take upon himself the privilege of mistreating my men, or of calling us traitors to the Republic,' he adds. 'He is duty-bound to show us respect, wouldn't you say?'

His officers stand there motionless. He knows that at this moment they have mixed feelings: joy at what his words hint at, and anxiety.

'Wait here for me. No one is to set foot outside this camp,' he says, starting to walk off. And as his subordinates speak up in protest and demand to accompany him, he stops them short: 'Stay here. That's an order. I intend to settle this matter by myself.'

He has no idea what he is going to do as he leaves the camp, followed, supported, by the eyes of his three hundred men, whose admiring gaze is like a warm pressure at his back; but he is going to do something, because he has felt a raging fury. He is not an angry man, nor was he one in his earlier years, at that age when all young men are angry; in fact, he had the reputation of only rarely losing his temper. His coolheadedness has saved his life many a time. But he is in a rage now, a tingling in his belly that is like the crackling of the burning fuse that precedes the explosion of a large charge of powder. Is he enraged because that throat-slitter called him Bandit-Chaser and the Bahian volunteers traitors to the Republic, because the man dared to lay hands on his police? That is the last straw. He walks along slowly, looking down at the cracked, stony ground, deaf to the explosions that are demolishing Canudos, blind to the shadows of the vultures tracing circles overhead, as meanwhile his hand, in an automatic gesture, as swift and efficient as in the good old days, since the years have left him with wrinkles and a bit stoop-shouldered but have not yet slowed his reflexes or made his fingers less agile, unholsters his revolver, breaks it open, checks that there are six cartridges in the six chambers of the cylinder, and places it back in its holster. The last straw. Because this entire experience, which was to be the greatest one in his life, the crowning reward of his perilous race toward respectability, has turned out instead to be a series of disillusionments and vexations. Instead of being recognized and treated with deference as the commanding officer of a battalion that is representing Bahia in this war, he has been discriminated against, humiliated, and offended, in his own person and in that of his men, and has not once been given the opportunity to show his worth. His one valiant deed thus far has been to demonstrate his patience. A campaign that has been a failure at least for him. He does not even notice the soldiers who cross his path and salute him.

When he arrives at the depression in the terrain where the prisoners are being held, he spies Second Lieutenant Maranhão, standing smoking as he watches him come toward him, surrounded by a group of soldiers dressed in the balloon pants worn by gaucho regiments. The lieutenant is not at all imposing physically and has a face that does not betray that murderous instinct to which he gives free rein in the darkness of the night; a short, slight man, with light skin, fair hair, a neatly clipped little mustache, and bright blue eyes that at first glance seem angelic. As Colonel Geraldo Macedo walks unhurriedly toward him, his face with the pronounced Indian features not betraying by the least muscle twitch or shadow of an expression what it is he intends to do – something that he himself does not know – he notes that there are eight gauchos around the lieutenant, that none of them is carrying a rifle – they have stacked them in two pyramids alongside a hut – but that all of them have knives tucked into their belts, as does Maranhão, who also has a bandoleer and a pistol. The colonel crosses the stretch of open ground where the horde of female specters have been herded together. Squatting, lying, sitting, leaning one against the other like the soldiers' rifles, the women prisoners watch him pass, the last flicker of life in them seemingly having taken refuge in their eyes. They have children in their arms, lying on their skirts, fastened to their backs, or stretched out on the ground alongside them. When the colonel is within a couple of yards of him, Lieutenant Maranhão tosses his cigarette away and comes to attention.

'Two things, Lieutenant,' Colonel Macedo says, standing so close to him that the breath of his words must strike the Southerner's face like warm puffs of breeze. 'First off: interrogate these women and find out where Abbot João died, or if he's not dead, what's become of him.'

'They have already been interrogated, sir,' Lieutenant Maranhão says in a docile tone of voice. 'By a lieutenant of your battalion. And after that by three of your men, who were so insolent I was obliged to reprimand them. I presume that you were informed. None of the prisoners knows anything about Abbot João.'

'Let's try again and see if we have any better luck,' Geraldo Macedo says in the same tone of voice as before: neutral, impersonal, restrained, without a trace of animosity. 'I want you personally to interrogate them.'

His little dark eyes, with crow's-feet in the corners, do not leave the young officer's surprised, mistrustful blue ones for a moment; they do not blink, nor do they move to the right or to the left. Colonel Macedo knows, because his ears or his intuition tells him so, that the eight soldiers on his left are standing there with every muscle tensed now, and that the lethargic gaze of all the women is upon him.

'I'll interrogate them, then,' the lieutenant says, after a moment's hesitation.

As the young officer, with a slowness that betrays how disconcerted he is by this order, unable to decide whether it has been given him because the colonel wants to try one last time to find out what has happened to the bandit, or whether he wants to make a show of his authority, makes his way through the sea of rags that parts, then closes again behind him as he passes asking about Abbot João, Geraldo Macedo does not look around even once at the gaucho soldiers. He deliberately keeps his back to them, and with his hands at his waist and his kepi tilted back, in a stance that is typical of him but also characteristic of any cowboy of the *sertão,* follows the lieutenant's progress among the women prisoners. In the distance, beyond the hills round about, explosions can still be heard. Not a single voice answers the lieutenant's questions; when he stops in front of a prisoner, stares her straight in the eye, and interrogates her, she merely shakes her head. Concentrating on what he has come there to do, his entire attention focused on the sounds coming from where the eight soldiers are standing, Colonel Macedo nonetheless has time to reflect that it is strange that such silence reigns among a crowd of women, that it is odd that not one of all those children is crying out of hunger or thirst or fear, and the thought occurs to him that many of those tiny skeletons must already be dead.

'As you can see, it's pointless,' Lieutenant Maranhão says, halting in front of him. 'None of them knows anything, just as I told you.'

'Too bad,' Colonel Macedo says in a thoughtful tone of voice. 'I'll leave here without ever finding out what happened to Abbot João.'

He stands there, his back still turned to the eight soldiers, staring into the lieutenant's blue eyes and white face, whose expression betrays his nervousness.

'In what other way may I be of service to you?' he finally mutters.

'You come from a long way away from here, isn't that so?' Colonel Macedo asks. 'I'm quite certain, then, that you don't know what the worst insult of all is in the eyes of people of the *sertão.*'

A very serious look comes over Second Lieutenant Maranhão's face, he frowns, and the colonel realizes that he can't wait any longer, for the young officer will end up pulling his pistol on him. With a lightning-quick, totally unexpected sweep of his open hand, he slaps that white face as hard as he can. The blow sends the lieutenant sprawling on the ground, and unable to rise to his feet, he remains there on all fours. Looking up at Colonel Macedo, who has taken one step so as to place himself directly alongside him, and now warns him: 'If you get up, you're dead. And also if you try to reach for your pistol.'

He looks him coldly in the eye, and even now his tone of voice has not changed in the slightest. He sees the hesitation in the lieutenant's reddened face there at his feet, and is certain now that the Southerner will not get to his feet or try to reach for his pistol. He has not drawn his own, moreover; he has merely raised his right hand to his waist and placed it just a fraction of an inch away from his cartridge belt. But in reality his mind is focused on what is happening behind his back, sensing what the eight soldiers are thinking, feeling, on seeing their leader in this predicament. But a few seconds later he is sure that they will not make a move either, that they, too, have lost the game.

'It's slapping a man in the face, the way I slapped yours,' he says, as he opens his trouser fly, swiftly flips out his penis, and watches the clear little stream of urine splash down on the seat of Lieutenant Maranhão's trousers. 'But pissing on him is an even worse one.'

As he tucks his penis back into his fly and buttons up, his ears still listening intently to what is going on behind him, he sees that the lieutenant has begun to tremble all over, like a man with tertian fever, that tears are welling up in his eyes, that he is all at sea, body and soul.

'It doesn't bother me a bit if I'm called Bandit-Chaser, because that's what I've been,' he finally says, seeing the lieutenant rise to his feet, weeping and trembling still, knowing how much he hates him and also knowing that he will not reach for his pistol now. 'But my men don't like being called traitors to the Republic, because it isn't true. They're as much republicans and patriots as anybody else.'

He licks his gold tooth, with a rapid flick of his tongue. 'You have three choices left to you now, Lieutenant,' he concludes. 'The first is to present a formal complaint to the General Staff, accusing me of abuse of authority. I might be demoted and even thrown out of the service. It wouldn't matter to me all that much, since as long as there are bandits I can always earn myself a living chasing them. The second is to come ask me for satisfaction, whereupon you and I will settle this matter man to man, taking off our officer's braid, with revolvers or knives or whatever other weapon you like. And the third is to try to kill me from behind. So then, what's your choice?'

He raises his hand to his kepi and gives a mock salute. This last quick glance tells him that his victim will opt for the first, or perhaps the second, but not the third choice, at least not right now. He walks off, not deigning to look at the eight gaucho soldiers, who still haven't moved a muscle.

As he is picking his way among the skeletons in rags on his way back to his camp, two thin grappling hooks take hold of his boot. It is an old woman with no hair, as tiny as a child, looking up at him through her gummy eyelashes. 'Do you want to know what happened to Abbot João?' her toothless mouth stammers.

'Yes, I do.' Colonel Macedo nods. 'Did you see him die?'

The little old woman shakes her head and clacks her tongue, as though sucking on something.

'He got away, then?'

The little old woman shakes her head again, encircled by the eyes of the women prisoners.

'Archangels took him up to heaven,' she says, clacking her tongue. 'I saw them.'

ff

Faber and Faber is one of the great independent publishing houses. We were established in 1929 by Geoffrey Faber with T. S. Eliot as one of our first editors. We are proud to publish award-winning fiction and non-fiction, as well as an unrivalled list of poets and playwrights. Among our list of writers we have five Booker Prize winners and twelve Nobel Laureates, and we continue to seek out the most exciting and innovative writers at work today.

Find out more about our authors and books
faber.co.uk

Read our blog for insight and opinion on books and the arts
thethoughtfox.co.uk

Follow news and conversation
twitter.com/faberbooks

Watch readings and interviews
youtube.com/faberandfaber

Connect with other readers
facebook.com/faberandfaber

Explore our archive
flickr.com/faberandfaber